全新！No.1
IELTS
雅思單字大全

全音檔下載導向頁面

https://www.booknews.com.tw/mp3/9789864543885.htm

掃描QR碼進入網頁後，按「全書音檔下載請按此」連結，可一次性下載音檔壓縮檔，或點選檔名線上播放。
全MP3一次下載為zip壓縮檔，部分智慧型手機需安裝解壓縮程式方可開啟，iOS系統請升級至iOS 13以上。
此為大型檔案，建議使用WIFI連線下載，以免占用流量，並請確認連線狀況，以利下載順暢。

☑ PREFACE

所有語言的基礎都在於單字

　　我認為所有語言的基礎都在於單字。如果不能確實掌握單字的意義與使用方法，那麼就算是大人，表達能力也比不上能夠正確使用單字的小孩。對於準備雅思測驗而言，提升單字知識與使用單字的能力，也扮演著提高英語能力並提升成績的決定性角色。沒有學好單字的人，就算花了再多時間與精力，學習也不會有效率。尤其因為雅思是針對想申請大學入學或移民的成人所進行的英語測驗，所以必須在聽、說、讀、寫四個部分的測驗中都表現出能夠適當使用成人詞彙的能力。一定要先認清這一點，準備才會有效果。

　　雖然需要準備雅思測驗的人很多，但市面上卻缺乏專門為雅思設計的單字書，使得有些人用多益或托福等其他測驗的單字書來準備考試。但是，雖然同樣是英語能力測驗，但每種測驗的目的都不同，題目型態與使用的單字也有很大的差別。如果不是使用專為雅思設計的單字書，而用其他測驗的單字做準備的話，效果就會大打折扣。即使為學習付出了努力，結果卻往往是浪費時間和精力。所以，為了滿足所有雅思考生的希望和要求，我們製作了這本對於準備雅思測驗而言最合適的專門單字書。

PERFECT IELTS VOCABULARY

　　這不是一本收集好單字、把單字放到書上就草草了事的書。在我們經營的雅思測驗討論區中，許多考生同心協力，花了超過三年的時間，決定哪些單字對於提升實際考試實力是有幫助的。經過不斷煩惱的繁複選字過程，以及許多考生的實際驗證，才得以完成這本真正為雅思測驗量身打造的單字書。

　　所有學習都不是兩三天的功夫就能完成，單字尤其如此。所以，就算要花很多時間，也請每天持續不中斷、扎實地學習單字。這樣的話，總有一天會發現自己已經具備穩健的單字實力，也一定能夠迎接獲得高分的美好時刻。

　　最後，我要衷心感謝在這本書誕生之前漫長的時間給予許多幫助的 Wisdom Garden 出版社編輯部，以及協助製作這本最好的雅思單字書的 IELTS School 工作人員，還有其中熱心學習的伙伴們。

張大錫

IELTS 雅思簡介

IELTS「雅思」國際英語測驗系統（The International English Language Testing System），是由劍橋大學英語考試院設計的英語能力測驗，評估受試者的聽、說、讀、寫溝通能力。IELTS 雅思測驗的成績，也是世界多國申請留學、移民、海外就業時需要的英語能力評估標準。

IELTS 雅思的考試內容

聽力	閱讀	寫作	口說
30 分鐘（播放題目）+ 10 分鐘（謄寫答案卡） 4 個部分，共 40 題	60 分鐘 3 篇文章，共 40 題	60 分鐘 2 篇文章 （150 字和 250 字）	11~14 分鐘 與考官面對面對話 形式

※IELTS 雅思測驗有「學術組」與「一般訓練組」兩種，兩者的閱讀、寫作測驗內容不同。一般訓練組以一般性、生活性的內容為主，學術組偏重於測試學術性文章的理解、分析與組織能力。

考試當天的注意事項

- 務必於上午 8:30 前抵達考場並完成報到手續，以免遭取消考試資格。
- 務必攜帶報名用的護照正本到場報到，並完成指紋掃描及數位照相程序。
- 僅限攜帶一枝鉛筆及一個橡皮擦進場應試，其他文具用品一概不得攜入。
- 手機、手錶、電子產品、藥品、私人物品皆不得攜入考場（可存放於現場置物間）。
- 報到後直接進入考場，請在報到前使用洗手間。筆試時間約三小時，沒有休息時間。
- 口試時間將於筆試結束後公布，請於口試時間 30 分鐘前抵達考場報到。

IELTS 雅思的計分方式

聽、說、讀、寫各項目皆採用 1-9 分的評分制，總分為四個項目的平均值。各項目成績及總成績皆以每 0.5 級分為級距呈現。各級分的意義如下：

9	8	7	6	5	4	3	2	1
專家級用者	優秀級用者	良好級用者	普通級用者	中等程度用者	有限度用者	極有限度用者	間歇用者	非英語用者

※ 雅思並沒有「及格」的標準，各機關要求的雅思成績也各有不同。但一般而言，英國碩士班大多要求總成績 6.5 分，學士班則是 5.5~6 分。

本書的格式說明

- 本書的拼字與用詞，以英國式為主，例如 realise、analyse、traveller、artefact… 等單字，皆與國內習慣的美國式不同。考試時用美式或英式英文作答皆可，選擇哪一種並不會影響分數，但要保持一致。
- 標點符號亦為英國式，一般的引號使用單引號「 ' ' 」而不是雙引號「 " " 」。而且，也不使用所謂的「serial comma」，例如「A, B and C」的「and」前面不會有逗號。（如果使用美式英文作答，也請採用美國的標點方式。）
- 雅思聽力測驗會出現英式、澳洲式、美式口音，甚至非母語人士（例如印度、日本）的口音。本書所提供的音檔，以國內考生較難聽懂的英式英語錄製。
- 為了表現英式發音的特徵，書中採用的音標為國際音標（IPA）。

☑ How to Use This Book

BASIC WORDS

即使一個單字也要正確了解！

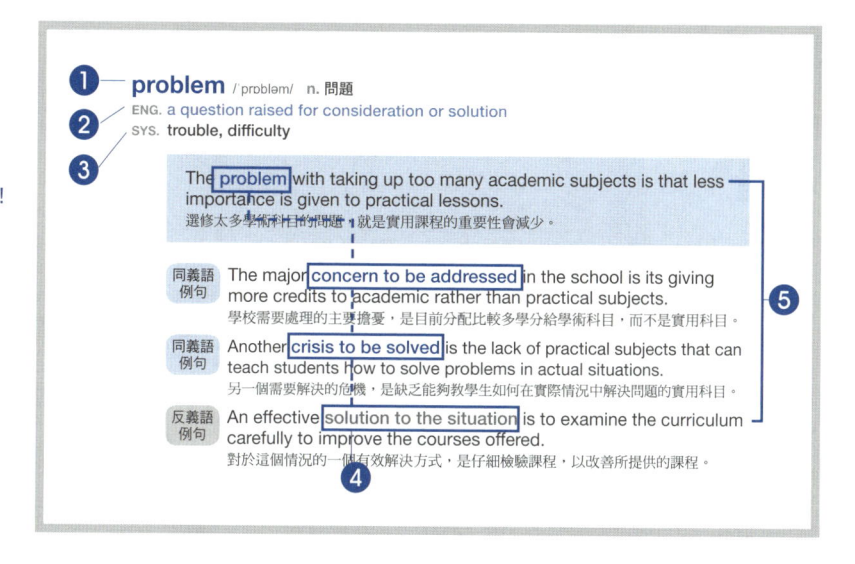

❶ **problem** / ˈprɒbləm/ n. 問題
❷ ENG. a question raised for consideration or solution
　　SYS. trouble, difficulty
❸ The problem with taking up too many academic subjects is that less importance is given to practical lessons.
　　選修太多學術科目的問題，就是實用課程的重要性會減少。

同義語例句　The major concern to be addressed in the school is its giving more credits to academic rather than practical subjects.
　　學校需要處理的主要擔憂，是目前分配比較多學分給學術科目，而不是實用科目。

同義語例句　Another crisis to be solved is the lack of practical subjects that can teach students how to solve problems in actual situations.
　　另一個需要解決的危機，是缺乏能夠教學生如何在實際情況中解決問題的實用科目。

反義語例句　An effective solution to the situation is to examine the curriculum carefully to improve the courses offered.
　　對於這個情況的一個有效解決方式，是仔細檢驗課程，以改善所提供的課程。

❹

❺

❶ 基礎單字

選擇題目中出現頻率最高的單字，不只提供中文意義，也提供英語解釋、同義詞、變化表達方式等等，讓讀者能夠擴充詞彙，並且正確理解及使用單字。

❷ 單字英語解釋

例如「safe」這個單字，在雅思閱讀測驗的文章中，就會以「free from danger」的形式來表達。以英語的敘述來理解單字意義，對於解答閱讀題目將有所助益。

❸ 同義詞

雅思評分標準中的「Lexical Resource」，是評鑑考生是否習得了各種多樣化的單字。所以，不能只是反覆使用普普通通的單字，還必須懂得使用多種單字加以變化。為了做到這一點，所以在單字之後補充了同義詞。

❹ 單字延伸

就像是用「free from danger」來表達「safe」的意思一樣，在這裡提供單字的同義與反義表達方式。為了幫助了解這些表達方式的用法，所以用例句的方式呈現。

❺ 語句內容變化延伸

不止是變換單字的表達形式，就連提供的例句，也經常以不同的表達方式重新敘述類似的內容，或者深入描寫、添加細節、概括簡述等等。反義語的例句，有時候會是和主要例句相反的內容。

✅ How to Use This Book

DAILY TOPIC
為各種主題做好準備！

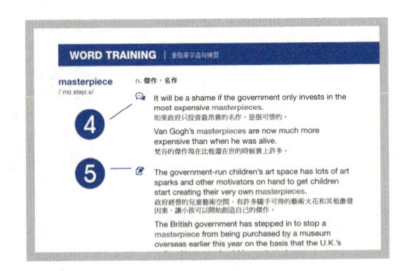

❶ Daily Topic
　　選擇出題頻率最高的主題，作為每週的學習內容，而每週又細分為不同的 Daily Topic，讓讀者能夠集中學習同一個主題的不同面向。

❷ 主題相關背景知識
　　了解關於不同主題的詳細知識，有助於進行雅思寫作、口說測驗時構思內容。

❸ 單字整理
　　整理主題文章裡中級程度以上的有用單字，和文章一起學習，就能自然擴充單字量，幫助提高得分。

❹ 口說範例
　　為了提高活用單字的能力，針對特定單字提供 15 個字左右的例句，作為口說內容的參考。

❺ 寫作範例
　　從單字延伸出敘述較為詳細的例句，作為寫作測驗時組織句子與內容的參考範例。

❻ 相關單字延伸

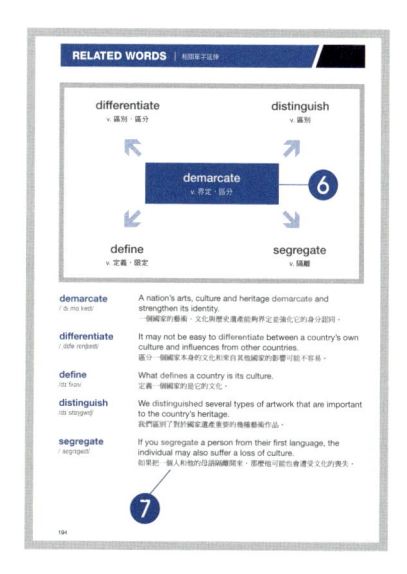

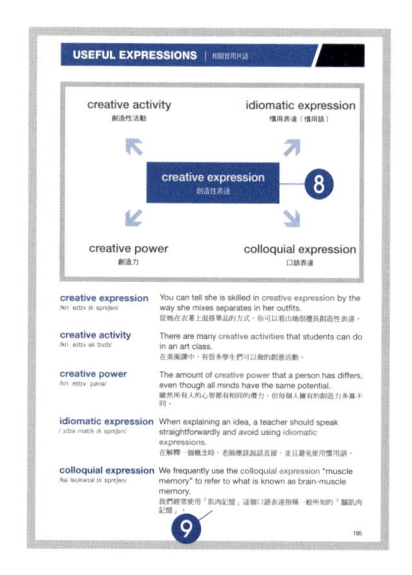

　　針對特定單字，延伸出相關或意義相同的單字，不但對於解答聽力、閱讀題目有幫助，也能夠避免在寫作、口說時重複使用相同的單字，提高詞彙能力方面的評價。

❼ 相關單字例句

　　每個延伸單字都附有例句，有助於了解同義詞、相關詞之間的些微差別，以及在句中的正確用法。

❽ 相關片語延伸

　　為了讓表達更加多樣化、具體化，提供由兩個單字組合而成的延伸片語。初學者可以在這個部分學習更多基礎單字，而中等程度以上的學習者則可以學到各種不同的片語和術語。

❾ 相關片語例句

　　每個延伸片語都附有例句，幫助讀者正確理解這些用語，並且活用在寫作、口說測驗中。

✅ CONTENTS

- 2　前言
- 5　如何使用本書

WEEK 1 TOPIC
ENVIRONMENT

- 12　MON　資源回收的重要性
- 20　TUE　溫室氣體排放
- 28　WED　全球暖化與災難
- 36　THU　保護動物免於絕種
- 44　FRI　噪音的負面影響
- 52　SAT　缺水
- 60　SUN　保護環境的法律

WEEK 2 TOPIC
EDUCATION

- 70　MON　教師的角色
- 78　TUE　在國外留學
- 86　WED　參加團隊比賽
- 94　THU　職業學校
- 102　FRI　給孩子大量的玩具
- 110　SAT　傳統與現代教育體系
- 118　SUN　處罰

WEEK 3 TOPIC
CULTURE

- 128　MON　我們為什麼該學習歷史
- 136　TUE　人們對於新聞的偏好
- 144　WED　挽救少數族群的語言免於滅絕
- 152　THU　不同文化間的衝突
- 160　FRI　穿著民族服裝
- 168　SAT　發展國際觀光
- 176　SUN　移民到其他國家

WEEK 4 TOPIC
ART

- 186　MON　政府對藝術的投資
- 194　TUE　把藝術放上網路
- 202　WED　讓孩子學習藝術的重要性
- 210　THU　成為有名的藝術家
- 218　FRI　年長與年輕世代的藝術鑑賞
- 226　SAT　藝術的商業價值
- 234　SUN　將建築作為一種藝術表達的形式

WEEK 5 TOPIC
TECHNOLOGY

- 244　MON　科技對社會的影響
- 252　TUE　科技對音樂產業的影響
- 260　WED　現代科學與舊科學
- 268　THU　複製技術的未來
- 276　FRI　工作中電腦的使用
- 284　SAT　網路銀行業務
- 292　SUN　電子設備中的有毒物質

WEEK 6 TOPIC
TRANSPORT

- 302　MON　塞車
- 310　TUE　公共運輸
- 318　WED　汽車的演進
- 326　THU　在城市騎自行車
- 334　FRI　如何減少車禍造成的傷亡
- 342　SAT　政府改善運輸系統的義務
- 350　SUN　想像未來的交通運輸

PERFECT IELTS VOCABULARY

WEEK 7 TOPIC
HEALTH

360	MON	兒童時期的肥胖
368	TUE	媒體對人們健康的影響
376	WED	身體活動量的性別差異
384	THU	不健康的飲食法
392	FRI	吃得健康
400	SAT	現代社會中的精神健康問題
408	SUN	讓每個人都能得到醫療保健服務

WEEK 8 TOPIC
MEDIA

418	MON	名人對年輕人的影響
426	TUE	西方電視節目對兒童的影響
434	WED	大眾傳播媒體的演變
442	THU	氣象預報
450	FRI	數位時代中的雜誌
458	SAT	看板廣告
466	SUN	酒類宣傳的負面影響

WEEK 9 TOPIC
LEISURE

476	MON	結伴旅行與獨自旅行
484	TUE	海外旅行對年輕人而言是寶貴的經驗
492	WED	團隊運動對兒童的好處
500	THU	極限運動
508	FRI	園藝活動
516	SAT	放鬆
524	SUN	在週末工作的優缺點

WEEK 10 TOPIC
SOCIAL LIFE

534	MON	從處罰犯罪到預防犯罪
542	TUE	用信用卡取代現金
550	WED	幸福與財富
558	THU	持續增加的老年人口比例
566	FRI	投資在年輕人身上的重要性
574	SAT	職場上的性別平等
582	SUN	大型零售業者與小型零售業者

WEEK 1
ENVIRONMENT

資源回收的重要性
溫室氣體排放
全球暖化與災難
保護動物免於絕種
噪音的負面影響
缺水
保護環境的法律

MON

IELTS **BASIC WORDS**

habitat /ˈhæbɪtæt/ n. 棲息地
ENG. the area or natural environment in which an organism normally lives
SYS. home, abode

> It is important to recycle paper to avoid cutting down trees, which are a habitat of many animals.
> 回收紙張以避免砍伐許多動物棲息的樹林，是很重要的。

同義語 例句 When humans recycle, they can prevent the destruction of animal home ground.
當人類資源回收時，就能避免對動物家園的破壞。

同義語 例句 Failing to recycle is indirectly destroying the natural home of thousands of creatures.
做不到資源回收，就是間接破壞成千上萬的動物的自然棲息地。

反義語 例句 Due to people's unwillingness to recycle, the forest is the most abused among all the places they visit.
由於人們不願意回收資源，在他們所到的地方之中，森林是被濫用最嚴重的。

whole /həʊl/ adj. 全部的
ENG. comprising the full quantity or amount
SYS. complete, total

> The whole nation is working on raising money to fund the orderly sorting of recyclable materials.
> 全國都在努力籌款，資助對可回收材料進行有條理的分類。

同義語 例句 The government provided the sum total of money that will finance the city's waste sorting and recycling.
政府提供了所需金錢的總額，資助城市的垃圾分類與回收。

同義語 例句 The entire amount of money allotted for waste collection was used very efficiently.
提撥到垃圾收取的全部金額被使用得非常有效率。

反義語 例句 Usually, recyclable waste in cities is sold in bulk rather than in pieces.
城市裡的可回收垃圾通常是大量而不是分件出售。

WEEK 1 TOPIC **ENVIRONMENT**

▶基礎單字擴充

strategy /ˈstrætɪdʒi/ n. 策略
ENG. an elaborate and systematic plan of action
SYS. policy, scheme

> The government must devise a sound **strategy** to encourage people to recycle.
> 政府必須設計一個適當的策略來鼓勵人們回收。

同義語例句 The **grand design** presented by the mayor aims to discipline people to recycle.
市長提出的宏觀設計，目標是訓練人們進行回收。

同義語例句 The city officials have designed a **scheme** to make sure everyone will strictly follow the proper recycling procedure.
市府官員設計了一項計畫，確保每個人都會嚴格遵守正確的資源回收程序。

反義語例句 The waste recycling day is a **spontaneous event** initiated by the residents.
垃圾回收日是由居民開始的自發性活動。

resistance /rɪˈzɪstəns/ n. 抗拒
ENG. the action of opposing something that you disapprove or disagree with
SYS. opposition, aversion

> The company owner's **resistance** to recycling gave him a disadvantage in the long run.
> 事業主對於資源回收的抗拒，最終對他造成了不利的結果。

同義語例句 The **lack of enthusiasm** of the workers to recycle is rooted from their boss' disregard for the environment.
員工對於資源回收缺乏熱衷，源自於老闆對環境的漠不關心。

同義語例句 The boss' **reluctance to accept** responsibilities of recycling discouraged investors in his business.
老闆不願意承擔資源回收的責任，使得事業的投資人感到失望。

反義語例句 The business owner's **total submission** to government laws on the environment earned him tax exemptions.
事業主對政府環境法令的完全配合，使他獲得了稅賦減免。

13

MON

TOPIC

The importance of recycling
資源回收的重要性

Most people know how important recycling is for the **preservation** of our natural environment. Recycling, or making new items from old ones, saves the Earth's natural resources, thereby helping the **environment**. For example, we know that paper comes from trees and many trees are being cut down just to produce paper. By recycling our newspapers, we can help lessen the **coppice** woodland **harvested.** Then again, the main problem with recycling programmes in most cities is the expenses incurred due to the growing population and increasing waste. Collection vehicles for recycling also add to the production of carbon dioxide. All drawbacks aside, we can help preserve the environment by recycling. In addition, by saving energy in **industrial** production through recycling, the greenhouse gas emissions from industrial plants are lessened and the use of fuels that **emit harmful** gases during production is also **minimised**. Finally, recycling **non-biodegradable** waste will contribute a lot to help reduce air pollution and greenhouse gases that **deplete** the ozone layer.

TRANS

　　大部分的人都知道資源回收對自然環境的保護有多重要。資源回收，或者說利用舊的東西製造新的東西，能夠節省地球的自然資源，所以對環境有幫助。舉例來說，我們知道紙張來自樹木，而許多樹被砍伐只是為了製造紙張。藉由回收報紙，我們能夠幫助減少矮樹林被採伐的情況。話說回來，大部分城市的回收計畫的主要問題，在於逐漸成長的人口和越來越多的垃圾衍生的費用。收取回收物品的車輛也增加了二氧化碳的產生。但撇開這些缺點不談，我們是可以藉由資源回收保護環境的。此外，藉著資源回收來減少工業生產所用的能源，工業廠房排放的溫室氣體會減少，而在生產過程中對於會散發有害氣體的燃料的使用也會被降到最低。最後一點，回收無法生物降解的垃圾，對於幫助減少空氣污染與破壞臭氧層的溫室氣體有很大的貢獻。

preservation
/ˌprɛzəˈveɪʃən/

n. 保護，保存
The most important task was the **preservation** of the wildlife around the lake.
最重要的工作是對於湖泊周遭野生動物的保護。

environment
/ɪnˈvaɪrənmənt/

n. 環境
We should protect the fish in their ocean **environment** from pollution caused by ships.
我們應該保護海洋環境中的魚類免於船隻造成的污染。

coppice
/ˈkɒpɪs/

n. 定期採伐的矮樹林
Walk from the water's edge to the small **coppice**.
從水邊步行到那座小小的矮林。

harvest
/ˈhɑːvɪst/

v. 收穫，收獲
The shellfish were **harvested** from the ocean using nets and traps.
甲殼類動物是用漁網和陷阱從海洋捕獲的。

industrial
/ɪnˈdʌstrɪəl/

adj. 工業的
China has made **industrial** progress in recent years.
中國近年來在工業上有所進步。

emit
/ɪˈmɪt/

v. 散發
The sun continued to **emit** light until late during August.
在八月的時候，太陽持續散發光芒到很晚的時候。

harmful
/ˈhɑːmfʊl/

adj. 有害的
The **harmful** effects of greenhouse gases in the atmosphere include climate change and global warming.
大氣中溫室氣體的負面影響包括氣候變遷與全球暖化。

minimise
/ˈmɪnɪmaɪz/

v. 最小化
To **minimise** the risk of injury while riding, the cyclist wore a helmet.
為了把騎車時受傷的風險降到最低，自行車手戴了安全帽。

non-biodegradable
/ˌnɒnbaɪəʊdɪˈgreɪdəbəl/

adj. 生物不可降解的
Plastic is **non-biodegradable**. In other words, it does not decompose over time.
塑膠是無法生物降解的。換句話說，它不會隨著時間經過而分解。

deplete
/dɪˈpliːt/

v. 損耗，耗盡
A day at home caring for triplets can really **deplete** your energy.
在家照顧三胞胎一天真的會耗盡你的精力。

WORD TRAINING | 重點單字造句練習

detergent
/dɪˈtɜːdʒənt/

n. 清潔劑

We should wash and recycle our detergent bottles after using them.
我們應該在用完清潔劑後清洗並回收瓶子。

Oil spill clean-up crews wash oil off of waterfowl using detergent in recycled bottles.
清除油料外洩的人員用裝在回收瓶裡的清潔劑洗去水鳥身上的油漬。

Teachers should ensure that their students understand the importance of recycling from a young age and demonstrate how to recycle glass, cardboard and detergents.
教師應該確保學生從小就了解資源回收的重要性，並示範如何回收玻璃、紙板和清潔劑。

Utilise the abrasive powers of recycled food remnants like ground peach pits, corn cobs and walnut shells to tackle household clean-up rather than using detergent.
利用磨碎的桃核、玉米芯、胡桃殼等回收食物殘餘物的磨擦力，代替清潔劑處理家庭清潔工作。

conservation
/ˌkɒnsəˈveɪʃən/

n. 節約，保護

The recycling of industrial non-hazardous wastes is the key to a successful resource conservation program.
非危險性工業廢棄物的回收，是資源節約計畫的成功關鍵。

The students learned the importance of conservation and now make a bigger effort to be eco-friendly.
學生學到了節約的重要性，現在會更努力對生態友善。

Many fashion designers today create couture garments from trash as an innovative way to show the importance of conservation and recycling.
今日有許多時尚設計師從垃圾中的材料製作時裝，以此作為一種表現節約與回收重要性的創新方式。

Recycling is one of the easiest ways for people to practise conservation at home in order to reduce our overabundant use of natural resources.
資源回收是人們在家實踐節約，以減少對自然資源的過度使用時最簡單的方法之一。

reusable
/riˈjuːzəbəl/

adj. 可再次使用的

💬 Many items around the home are reusable and should be recycled to prevent excess waste.
家裡有許多東西是可以再利用的，也應該回收以避免垃圾過多。

I found that a tin can is reusable by checking our city's recycling web page.
我看市府的回收網頁而發現罐頭是可以再利用的。

✏️ Plastic shopping bags are the best choice for those who cannot wash and dry their reusable bags regularly to prevent bacterial build-up.
對於無法定期清洗並晾乾可重複使用的袋子以防細菌滋生的人，塑膠購物袋是最佳選擇。

We are selling recycled aluminium bottles to promote reusable water bottles and to create awareness about the waste problems associated with disposable plastic water bottles.
我們正在販賣回收的鋁瓶，藉以宣傳可再次使用的水瓶，並且喚起（大眾）對於與拋棄式塑膠水瓶相關的垃圾問題的意識。

balance
/ˈbæləns/

n. v. 平衡

💬 To maintain a balance in the environment, I recycle most of my waste daily.
為了維持環境（生態）平衡，我每天回收自己大部分的垃圾。

When making compost, it is important to maintain a balance between carbon and nitrogen materials.
在做堆肥的時候，維持碳和氮化物的平衡很重要。

✏️ Biodiesel buses seem to balance social needs and environmental protection, but they are expensive to repair.
生質柴油公車似乎藉由提供公共運輸讓人使用，平衡了社會的需求與環境保護，但修理起來很貴。

The investors got together to present an eco-balance plan for a recycling plant that treats spent lead-acid batteries in order to offset the potential environmental impacts arising from its daily operations.
投資者聚在一起，提出了一個環境平衡計畫，就是建造回收用完的鉛蓄電池的工廠，以抵銷日常營運中對環境產生的潛在影響。

RELATED WORDS | 相關單字延伸

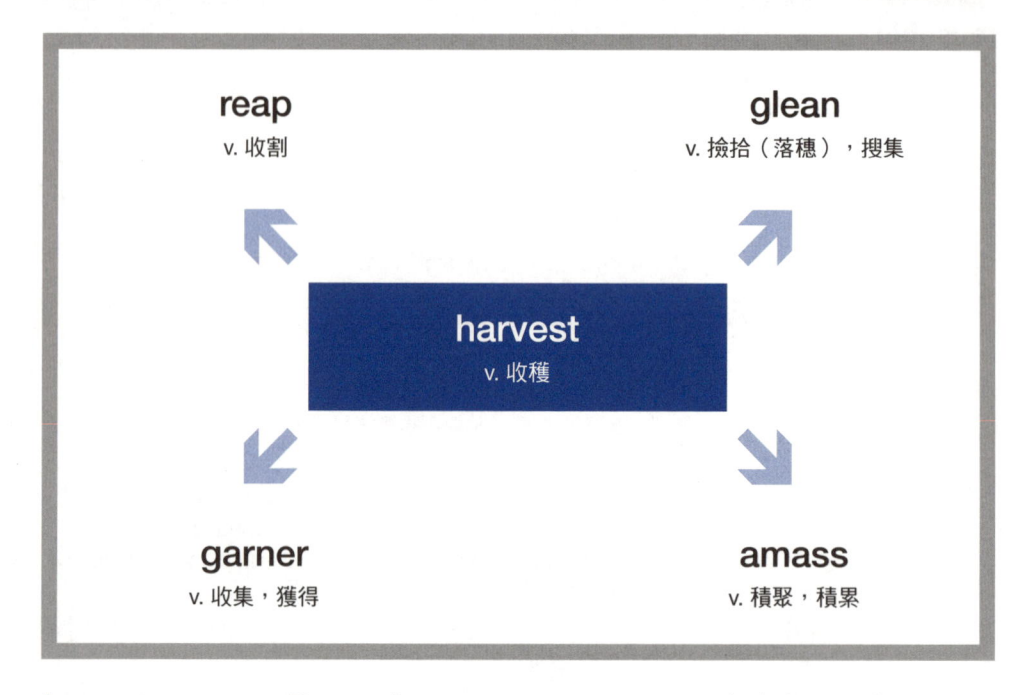

reap
v. 收割

glean
v. 撿拾（落穗），搜集

harvest
v. 收穫

garner
v. 收集，獲得

amass
v. 積聚，積累

harvest
/ˈhɑːvɪst/

By recycling our newspapers, we can help lessen the number of trees that are harvested.
藉由回收報紙，我們可以幫助減少砍伐的樹木數量。

reap
/riːp/

We can help lessen the number of trees reaped if we recycle paper.
如果我們回收紙張，就可以幫助減少砍伐的樹木數量。

garner
/ˈɡɑːnə/

We need to garner some wood for the camp fire.
我們需要收集一些營火用的木頭。

glean
/gliːn/

We can glean more from the data if we analyse it in more detail.
如果我們更詳細分析資料，就可以從中獲得更多。

amass
/əˈmas/

How many trees were saved because of the amassed recycled paper used?
有多少樹木因為回收紙的累積用量而免於砍伐？

USEFUL EXPRESSIONS | 相關實用片語

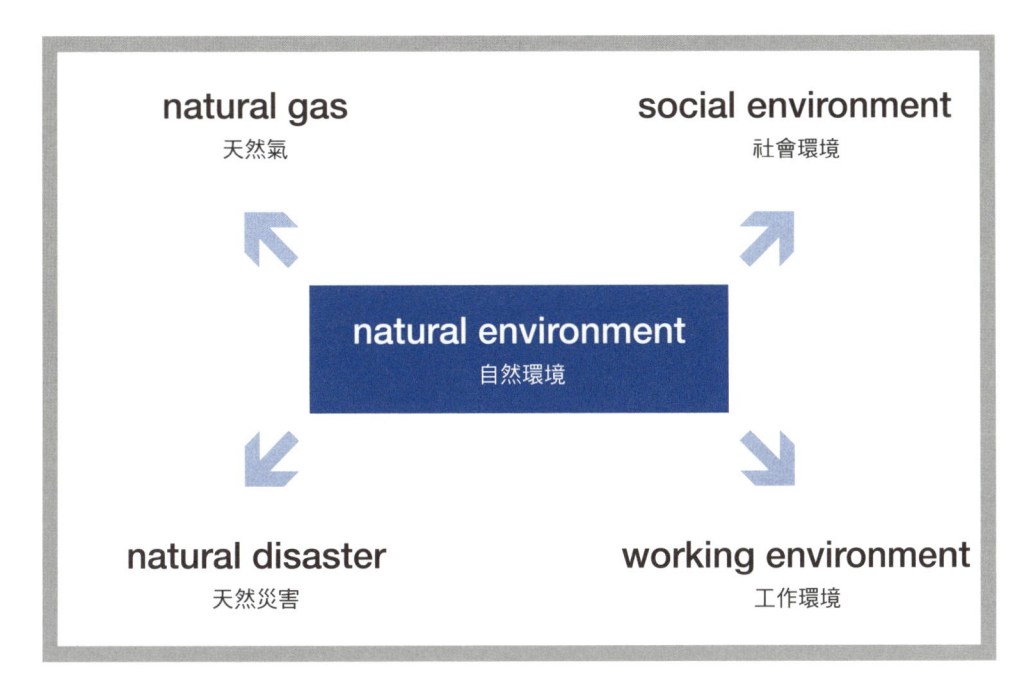

```
        natural gas              social environment
          天然氣                      社會環境
              ↖                  ↗
                 natural environment
                      自然環境
              ↙                  ↘
       natural disaster          working environment
          天然災害                    工作環境
```

natural environment
/ˈnatʃərəl ɪnˈvʌɪrənmənt/

The beauty of the natural environment shown on National Geographic Channel impresses many people.
國家地理頻道裡展現的自然之美，使許多人印象深刻。

natural gas
/ˈnatʃərəl gas/

Myanmar boasts many natural resources, including natural gas, timber, zinc, lead, petroleum and coal.
緬甸以擁有許多天然資源而自豪，其中包括天然氣、木材、鋅、鉛、石油和煤炭。

natural disaster
/ˈnatʃərəl dɪˈzɑːstə/

The NGO president encouraged member states to unite and respond to emergency needs during natural disasters.
那位非政府組織主席鼓勵成員國，在天然災害時團結並且回應緊急需求。

social environment
/ˈsəʊʃəl ɪnˈvʌɪrənmənt/

Citizens were surveyed about three main topics: cost of living, social environment and residential environment.
針對生活費、社會環境和居住環境這三個主題，對市民進行了意見調查。

working environment
/ˈwəːkɪŋ ɪnˈvʌɪrənmənt/

Employees unionised to establish a healthy working environment and minimum wage laws.
員工組成工會以建立健康的工作環境和最低工資法律。

TUE

IELTS **BASIC WORDS**

text /tɛkst/ n. 文字，正文，文本
ENG. a written passage consisting of graphs, characters, symbols or sentences; a book or other set of writings
SYS. publication, print

> The **text** written by the scientist was about greenhouse gas emissions.
> 這段由科學家撰寫的文字，是關於溫室氣體的排放。

同義語 例句　This **article to be printed** discusses the greenhouse gases emitted by human activities.
這篇即將刊出的文章，討論人類活動所排放的溫室氣體。

同義語 例句　His **written works** provide some insights regarding greenhouse gas emissions.
他的書面作品提供一些關於溫室氣體排放的洞見。

反義語 例句　The **absence of articles** in the newspaper about greenhouse gas emissions proves that people do not care much about them.
報紙上沒有刊登關於溫室氣體排放的文章，證明人們不太關心這個議題。

deadline /ˈdɛdlaɪn/ n. 期限
ENG. a narrow field of time that some sort of objective or task must be accomplished by
SYS. time limit, cut-off point

> The mayor gave them a **deadline** of one week to sort out the greenhouse gas emission problems in the city.
> 市長給了他們一星期的期限來解決城市中的溫室氣體排放問題。

同義語 例句　The mayor's **target date** to enforce the new greenhouse gas emission law is next Tuesday.
市長執行新的溫室氣體排放法規的目標日期是下星期二。

同義語 例句　The legislators agreed to draw up and pass a greenhouse gas emission law with a **finish date** of April 19.
立法委員同意在 4 月 19 日前制定並通過溫室氣體排放法規。

反義語 例句　People are disappointed that the **start date** of enforcing the new law is postponed.
對於新溫室氣體排放法律的執行開始日期被延後，人們感到失望。

WEEK 1 TOPIC **ENVIRONMENT**

▶基礎單字擴充

middle /ˈmɪdəl/ n. 中間 adj. 中間的
ENG. in-between; an area that is approximately central within some larger region
SYS. centre, midsection

> We were told to place all books about greenhouse gas emissions in the **middle** shelves.
> 我們被告知把所有關於溫室氣體排放的書籍放在中間書架。

同義語例句 The **central area** is allotted for current books like the one about greenhouse gas emissions.
中間區域是分配給像那本關於溫室氣體排放的書的當期書籍。

同義語例句 The space between the aisles becomes the **dividing portion** between books on greenhouse gas emissions and other books.
這兩排走道之間的空間，成為溫室氣體排放書籍與其他書籍的分隔部分。

反義語例句 The greenhouse gas emission law is the **ending point** of the protests about greenhouse gas emissions.
這項溫室氣體排放法律，是對溫室氣體排放的抗議的最終產物。

without /wɪðˈaʊt/ prep. 沒有⋯
ENG. lacking something
SYS. lacking, requiring

> Building a plant **without** thinking about greenhouse gas emissions is just irresponsible.
> 建造工廠而不考慮溫室氣體排放是不負責任的。

同義語例句 A city **short of** money cannot remedy the ill effects of greenhouse gas emissions.
欠缺經費的城市，無法彌補溫室氣體排放的不良影響。

同義語例句 Having a production facility **with the lack of** control on its greenhouse gas emissions is unethical.
擁有生產設施而不控制溫室氣體排放是不道德的。

反義語例句 A city **having enough budget** to come up with a solution to its greenhouse gas emissions is fortunate.
擁有足夠預算而能夠提出溫室氣體排放解決方案的城市是幸運的。

TUE

TOPIC | Greenhouse gas emissions
温室氣體排放

Greenhouse gases are necessary because they keep the planet's surface warmer than it otherwise would be. As the **concentrations** of these gases continue to increase in the **atmosphere**, however, the Earth's **temperature** is climbing above past levels. Studies show that the Earth's average surface temperature has increased by a couple of degrees in the last century. Most of the warming in recent **decades** is very likely the result of human activities. Other aspects of the **climate** are also changing, such as rainfall patterns, snow and ice cover, and sea level. If greenhouse gases continue to increase, climate models **predict** that the average temperature at the Earth's surface could increase to hazardous levels by the end of this century. Scientists are certain that human activities are changing the **composition** of the atmosphere, and that **escalating** the concentration of greenhouse gases will change the planet's climate. That being said, they are **irresolute** about by how much it will change and the exact effects it may **provoke.**

TRANS

溫室氣體是必需的，因為溫室氣體能使地球表面比沒有這些氣體的情況更溫暖。然而，隨著這些氣體的濃度在大氣中持續增加，地球的溫度也逐漸超越過去的水平。研究顯示，地球表面的平均溫度在上個世紀升高了幾度。近幾十年的暖化，大部分很可能是人類活動造成的結果。氣候的其他層面也正在改變，例如降雨模式、冰雪覆蓋範圍和海平面高度。如果溫室氣體持續增加，氣候模式預測，地球表面的平均溫度可能在本世紀末上升到危險的程度。科學家確信，人類活動正在改變大氣的結構，而進一步升高溫室氣體的濃度將會改變地球的氣候。話雖如此，科學家並不確定氣候會有多大的變化，以及可能引起的確切影響。

concentration
/ˌkɒnsənˈtreɪʃən/

n. 集中，濃度
There were high **concentrations** of gold particles in the rock we found.
在我們發現的岩石中，有高含量的黃金粒子。

atmosphere
/ˈatməsfɪə/

n. 大氣，大氣層
The rocket flew high up into the **atmosphere** before it fell to Earth again.
在降落回到地球之前，火箭被發射到大氣層的高處。

temperature
/ˈtɛmpərətʃə/

n. 溫度，氣溫
There is a great **temperature** difference between inside and outside.
裡面和外面的溫差很大。

decade
/ˈdɛkeɪd/

n. 十年
I saw my friend Joe yesterday for the first time in two **decades**.
昨天是我這二十年來第一次見到我的朋友 Joe。

climate
/ˈklʌɪmət/

n. 氣候
The **climate** in Antarctica is frigid year-round and sees little rainfall.
南極洲的氣候終年寒冷，而且降雨很少。

predict
/prɪˈdɪkt/

v. 預測
Can you **predict** what score you will get on the IELTS exam?
你能預測自己雅思測驗會拿幾分嗎？

composition
/ˌkɒmpəˈzɪʃən/

n. 組成，構成
The **composition** of dry air is 78% nitrogen and 21% oxygen by volume.
乾燥空氣的組成，以體積計算的話，有 78% 是氮氣，21% 是氧氣。

escalate
/ˈɛskəleɪt/

v. 逐步上升，使惡化
The number of trees being cut down yearly is **escalating**.
每年被砍伐樹木的數量正在增加。

irresolute
/ɪˈrɛzəluːt/

adj. 猶豫不決的
I stood **irresolute**, wondering if I should take the scary path or turn back.
我站著猶豫不決，不知道應該走那條可怕的小徑還是該折返。

provoke
/prəˈvəʊk/

v. 引起，激怒
I don't want to anger or **provoke** the dog into biting anyone.
我不想惹毛或是激怒那條狗咬任何人。

WORD TRAINING | 重點單字造句練習

fumes
/fjuːmz/

n.（難聞或有害的）煙霧，氣體

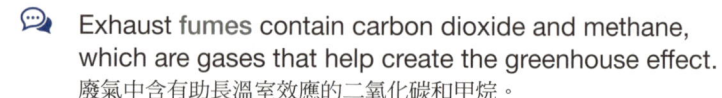

💬 Exhaust fumes contain carbon dioxide and methane, which are gases that help create the greenhouse effect.
廢氣中含有助長溫室效應的二氧化碳和甲烷。

Ozone at ground level is often made by vehicle fumes.
地面臭氧通常是車輛廢氣造成的。

✏️ Exhaust fumes come from the burning of fossil fuels in internal combustion engines, and they help create the greenhouse effect, which contributes to global warming.
廢氣是內燃機中化石燃料的燃燒產生的，而且會助長造成全球暖化的溫室效應。

The aim of this research is to get more detailed information about levels of car fumes as part of the next phase of the district council's monitoring programme.
這項研究的目的是獲得關於汽車廢氣排放量更詳細的資訊，也是區議會的監測計畫下個階段的其中一部分。

---

disposable
/dɪˈspəʊzəbəl/

adj. 可丟棄的，一次性使用的

💬 Restaurant owners should refrain from using disposable plastics and other non-biodegradable items.
餐廳老闆應該避免使用免洗塑膠餐具和其他不可生物降解的產品。

Some companies opt to eliminate the use of disposable products to decrease their waste production.
有些公司選擇減少使用拋棄式產品，以減少垃圾產生。

✏️ Parents should choose cloth diapers for their infants because it does not cause skin irritations or allergies, which usually come from the chemicals commonly found in disposable diapers.
父母應該為嬰兒選用布製尿布，因為不會造成肌膚起疹子或過敏，而這些症狀通常是拋棄式尿布中常見的化學物質造成的。

Disposable items like plastic bags take thousands of years to decay and pose serious environmental problems such as killing marine animals that mistake them for food.
塑膠袋之類的拋棄式產品，需要幾千年才能分解，也因為使海洋生物誤以為是食物而死亡，造成嚴重的環境問題。

口說範例 💬   寫作範例 ✍

drought
/draʊt/

n. 乾旱

💬 Our farmers need plenty of water to replenish the soil after a long drought.
長期乾旱後，我們的農民需要大量的水來滋潤土壤。

Drought prediction will only cause panic among the people in the region.
乾旱預測只會造成地區人民的恐慌。

✍ Extended drought is a serious problem since it gives rise to shortage in water and food supply, which then triggers poverty and social unrest in the region.
持續的乾旱是嚴重的問題，因為它造成水和食物供給的缺乏，進而引起乾旱地區的貧困和社會動盪。

The habitat damage brought by the severe drought should be addressed by the local government because it is already threatening our endangered species to extinction.
嚴重乾旱造成的棲息地破壞應該由地方政府解決，因為這已經對瀕危物種造成絕種的威脅。

menace
/ˈmɛnəs/

n. 威脅

💬 Cancer is a dreaded disease and considered as the number one menace to public health.
癌症是一種令人害怕的疾病，而且被認為是公眾健康的頭號威脅。

The menace of air pollution worldwide shouldn't be overlooked.
全球空氣污染的威脅不應該被忽視。

✍ The significant rise of sea surface temperature during the last century has revealed the menace of carbon dioxide and other greenhouse gases in the atmosphere.
上個世紀海平面溫度的顯著上升，顯示出大氣中二氧化碳和其他溫室氣體的威脅。

Scientists have become increasingly concerned about the menace of greenhouse gases released by submerged organic matter as it surfaces and decays in warm climates.
科學家越來越關注水中有機物在溫暖氣候下浮出水面並腐爛時所釋放出的溫室氣體的威脅。

RELATED WORDS | 相關單字延伸

structure
n. 結構

constitution
n. 構造

composition
n. 構成

make-up
n. 構成

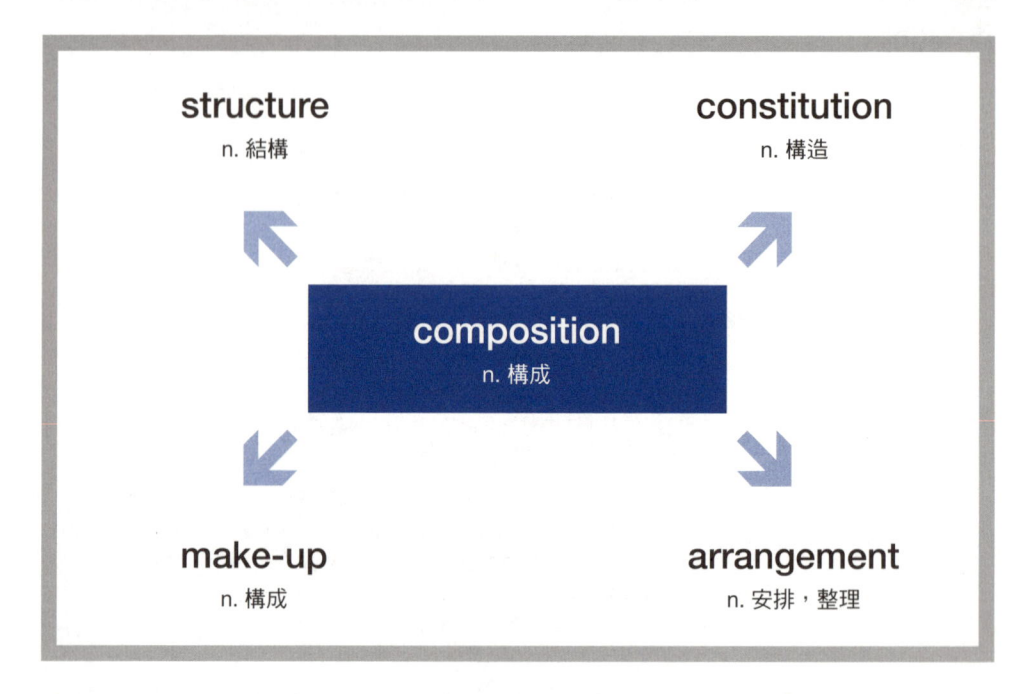

arrangement
n. 安排，整理

composition
/ˌkɒmpəˈzɪʃən/

Scientists are certain that human activities are changing the **composition** of the atmosphere.
科學家確信人類活動正在改變大氣的組成成分。

structure
/ˈstrʌktʃə/

Some wonder if the very **structure** of the ecosystem can withstand human activities.
有些人懷疑這個生態系統的根本結構能否承受人類的活動。

make-up
/ˈmeɪkʌp/

It took humans thousands of years to understand the **make-up** of the atmosphere.
了解大氣的組成成分，花了人類幾千年的時間。

constitution
/ˌkɒnstɪˈtjuːʃən/

The Earth's main atmospheric **constitution** is nitrogen, oxygen and argon gases.
地球的大氣主要組成是氮、氧和氬氣。

arrangement
/əˈreɪndʒmənt/

The **arrangement** of the solar panels was designed to maximise their exposure to sunlight.
太陽能板的配置是設計成能曝曬到最多陽光的形態。

USEFUL EXPRESSIONS | 相關實用片語

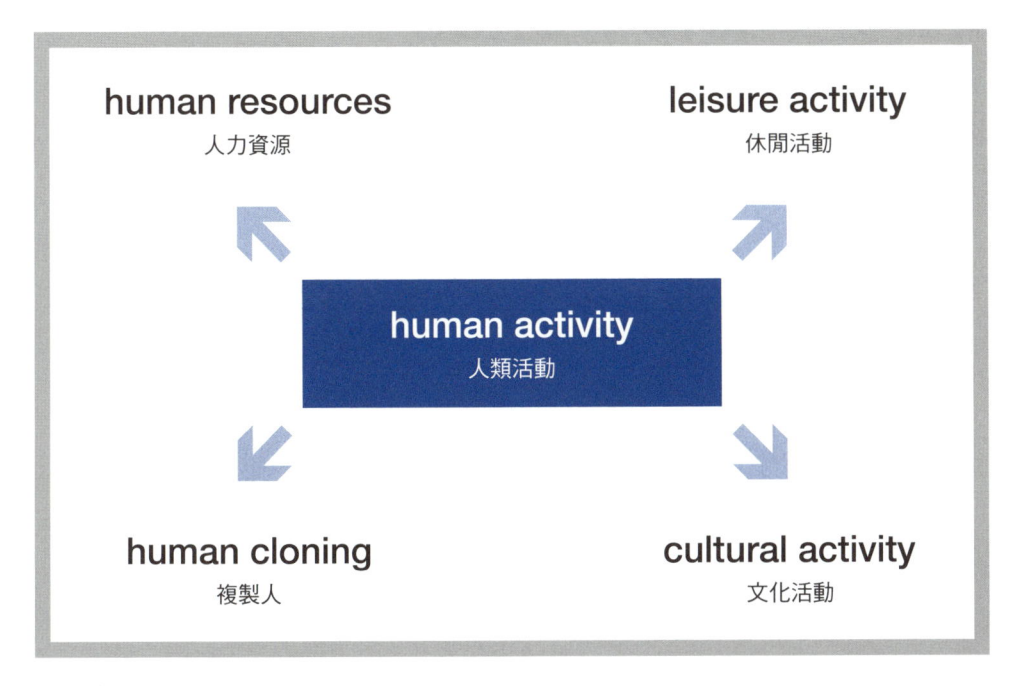

```
human resources          leisure activity
人力資源                  休閒活動

         human activity
         人類活動

human cloning            cultural activity
複製人                    文化活動
```

human activity
/ˈhjuːmən akˈtɪvɪti/
Short of such an upheaval, the societal and religious modes of human activity cannot catch up with the ceaseless momentum of science.
少了這種動盪的話，人類活動中的社會與宗教模式就無法跟上科學持續不斷的發展。

human resources
/ˈhjuːmən rɪˈsɔːsɪz/
Whether from cultural majorities or from multinational families, all children are considered the society's human resources.
不論是來自文化主流群體或跨國家庭，所有小孩都被認為是社會的人力資源。

human cloning
/ˈhjuːmən kləʊnɪŋ/
The UN has now banned all human cloning, despite England, Korea and China's dissent.
即使英國、韓國和中國有異議，但聯合國現在已經禁止所有複製人行為。

leisure activity
/ˈlɛʒə akˈtɪvɪti/
All elementary school students are now mandated to do leisure activities like art and music.
所有小學生現在都必須從事藝術、音樂之類的休閒活動。

cultural activity
/ˈkʌltʃərəl akˈtɪvɪti/
He is the officer in charge of all cultural activities in Sydney.
他是負責雪梨所有文化活動的官員。

WED

IELTS BASIC WORDS

produce /prəˈdjuːs/ v. 生產，產生
ENG. create, bring forth or yield
SYS. create, make

> The ecology team was able to **produce** a good result in their global warming awareness project.
> 生態學團隊能夠讓全球暖化意識（提升）計畫產生好的結果。

同義語例句 Their hard work and dedication in raising people's awareness about global warming **gave rise to** the endeavour's success.
他們為了提升人們對全球暖化的意識所付出的勤勞和投入，促成了這項努力的成功。

同義語例句 The ecology team worked their brains off to **bring forth** a project that can prevent global warming.
生態學團隊絞盡腦汁，要提出能夠防止全球暖化的計畫。

反義語例句 It is time to participate in projects that are aimed at **reducing** human practices that contribute to global warming.
是時候參與減少引起全球暖化的人類行為的計畫了。

excess /ˈɛksɛs/ adj. 過多的
ENG. being more than is usual
SYS. surplus, abundant

> **Excess** greenhouse gas emissions cause the Earth's temperature to rise.
> 過量的溫室氣體排放使得地球的氣溫上升。

同義語例句 The gauge indicated **an abundance of** greenhouse gases accumulated in the atmosphere causing global warming.
測量儀器顯示，有過多溫室氣體累積在大氣中，導致全球暖化。

同義語例句 The amount of carbon dioxide in the atmosphere is **beyond needed** to make the Earth comfortably warm.
大氣中的二氧化碳含量，超過了使地球溫暖舒適所需。

反義語例句 The city is **lacking provision** to purchase the equipment that helps determine the amount of greenhouse gases in the atmosphere.
對於購買幫助測量大氣中溫室氣體量的設備，這個城市的準備不足。

WEEK 1 TOPIC **ENVIRONMENT**

▶ 基礎單字擴充

confer /kənˈfɜː/   v. 商議，討論
ENG. to have discussions
SYS. consult, exchange views

> The city leaders **conferred** about how to minimise carbon dioxide emissions to prevent global warming.
> 城市領袖們商討如何減少二氧化碳排放以防止全球暖化。

同義語例句 The city leaders **talked over in detail** about the ways they could contribute to the prevention of global warming.
城市領袖們詳細討論了能夠幫助防止全球暖化的方法。

同義語例句 The employees were recommended to **speak with others** about their new ideas on how the company can help prevent global warming.
員工被建議和別人討論公司能怎樣幫助防止全球暖化的新想法。

反義語例句 Let us **not talk** about global warming if we are not ready to comply with the laws for preventing it.
如果我們還沒準備好遵守防止全球暖化的法律，那就不要討論全球暖化。

offer /ˈɒfə/   v. 提供
ENG. make available or accessible, provide or furnish
SYS. provide, put forward

> An incentive is **offered** to employees who would suggest how the company could contribute to the global warming prevention project.
> 對於建議公司對全球暖化預防計畫有所貢獻的方法的員工，會提供獎勵。

同義語例句 They will be **presented with** a plaque of appreciation for their dedicated service of advocating global warming prevention.
對於他們提倡防止全球暖化的奉獻，將會致贈獎牌以示感謝。

同義語例句 He was surprised an award was **given to** him to recognise his contributions in the global warming awareness campaign.
他獲得了表揚自己對全球暖化意識提升活動的貢獻的獎項，對此他感到很驚訝。

反義語例句 The company might **take back** the incentives given out to those who had failed to achieve the goals of the project.
對於沒有達成計畫目標的人，公司可能會收回發出的獎勵。

WED

01-3A

TOPIC: Global warming and disaster
全球暖化與災難

    The current **cycle** of global warming is **altering** our Earth's environment. While we **struggle** to decipher what causes it and how to stop it, the face of the Earth as we know it, from coasts and forests to snow-capped mountains, hangs in the balance. There are several greenhouse gases responsible for global warming, and humans emit them in a variety of ways. Most of them come from the **combustion** of fossil fuels in cars, factories and electricity production. Other contributors include methane released from landfills and agriculture and the loss of forests that would otherwise store carbon dioxide. Despite there being substantial evidence to prove that global warming exists, some cynics insist the phenomenon is nothing but a hoax. **Realistically**, if climate change is not **addressed** soon, we may well have passed the point that physical and biological systems can **adapt.** Worldwide **catastrophes** and **climactic** shifts will be **imminent** if we ignore this threat.

TRANS

    目前的全球暖化週期，正在改變地球的環境。雖然我們還很難解釋是什麼造成暖化，又該如何阻止暖化，但從海岸、森林到白雪覆蓋的山峰，我們熟悉的地球面貌已經岌岌可危。有若干溫室氣體與全球暖化相關，而人類以各種方式排放這些氣體。這些氣體大部分是汽車、工廠與電力生產中燃燒化石燃料造成的。其他因素則包括垃圾掩埋場與農業活動製造的甲烷，以及能夠儲存二氧化碳的森林減少。儘管有大量證據證明全球暖化現象存在，但有些憤世嫉俗者堅稱這個現象只不過是個騙局。現實上，如果不及早處理氣候變遷問題，我們可能會使情況超過物理與生態系統能夠調適的程度。如果我們忽視這個威脅，全球性的大災難和極大的變化將會逼近。

cycle
/ˈsaɪkəl/

n. 循環，週期

The **cycle** of seasons is due to the revolution of the Earth around the sun.
季節的循環是因為地球繞太陽公轉而產生的。

alter
/ˈɔːltɚ/

v. 改變，修改

I began **altering** the dress by raising the hem and ripping off the arms. 我從提高裙襬和裁掉袖子開始修改這件洋裝。

struggle
/ˈstrʌgəl/

v. 掙扎，奮鬥，做什麼的時候遇到困難

People in ancient times were always **struggling** for growth and survival.
遠古時代的人總是為了成長與生存而奮鬥。

combustion
/kəmˈbʌstʃən/

n. 燃燒

The **combustion** of fuels produces many kinds of greenhouse gases. 燃料的燃燒會產生多種溫室氣體。

realistically
/rɪəˈlɪstɪkli/

adv. 現實上，實際地

I need to know the rental fee so I can plan my finances **realistically**.
我需要知道租金，才能很實際地規畫財務。

address
/əˈdrɛs/

v. 對…說話，探討，處理

My classmate's behaviour was strictly **addressed** by the school principal.
我同學的行為受到校長嚴厲的處置。

adapt
/əˈdæpt/

v. 適應

I think I am too weak to **adapt** to living in a cold country.
我想我太過虛弱，無法適應居住在寒冷的國家。

catastrophe
/kəˈtæstrəfi/

n. 大災難

The 2011 earthquake in Japan was a major **catastrophe** due to the tsunami it caused.
2011 年在日本的那場地震，因為引發的海嘯而成為重大的災難。

climactic
/klaɪˈmæktɪk/

adj. 頂點的，高潮的

The story took a **climactic** turn when the heroine discovered her magic power.
這個故事在女主角發現自己的神奇力量時出現了高潮轉折。

imminent
/ˈɪmɪnənt/

adj. 逼近的

I knew the scary part of the movie was **imminent** when I heard the music.
我聽到那個音樂的時候，就知道電影恐怖的部分逼近了。

WORD TRAINING | 重點單字造句練習

renewable
/rɪˈnjuːəbəl/

adj. 可更新的，可再生的

💬 Wind power is one of the most convenient and safest sources of renewable energy.
風力是可再生能源中最便利與最安全的來源之一。

Renewable energy, such as solar and wind power, is increasingly seen as a cost-effective option.
可再生能源，像是太陽能與風力，越來越被視為有成本效益的選項。

✏️ Asia is embracing new technologies that will generate renewable energy from alternative sources to decrease the demand for fossil fuels, which are now gradually depleting.
亞洲正在接受從其他來源產生可再生能源的新技術，以減少對日漸耗竭的化石燃料的需求。

Since conventional power-grids cannot reach remote areas, people there are now being supplied by alternative and renewable energy from natural sources.
由於傳統電力網無法到達偏遠地區，所以現在那裡的人們從來自天然資源的替代性、可再生性能源獲得電力供給。

uninhabitable
/ˌʌnɪnˈhæbɪtəbəl/

adj. 無法居住的

💬 Global warming has caused our local wildlife sanctuary to dry up and become uninhabitable.
全球暖化已經造成本地野生動物保護區乾旱，變得無法居住。

Most of the area became uninhabitable after the forest fire.
大部分的地區在森林火災之後變得無法居住。

✏️ Our planet will soon become uninhabitable due to people who are constantly damaging and abusing the environment by exhausting all natural resources without exerting effort to replenish it.
因為那些持續破壞並濫用環境、耗盡天然資源又不努力彌補的人，我們的地球很快將變得不適合居住。

The air and noise pollution created by cars made the city uninhabitable to people and to the animals formerly residing in the area.
汽車製造的空氣與噪音污染使得城市不宜人居，也讓以前住在當地的動物無法生存。

ecosystems
/ˈiːkəʊsɪstəmz/

n. 生態系統

💬 It's reasonable to expect that ecosystems will change as plants and animals respond to global warming.
預期生態系統會隨著動植物對全球暖化產生反應而變化，是很合理的。

Most ecosystems are interconnected, so the chain reaction of warming effects could be immeasurable.
大部分的生態系統彼此互相連繫，所以暖化效應的連鎖反應可能是無法估量的。

✏️ Human beings are exposed to climate change through changing weather patterns and indirectly through changes in water, air and food quality, and changes in ecosystems, agriculture, industry and the economy.
人類從變化中的天氣型態感受到氣候變遷的影響，也從水質、空氣品質、食物品質、生態系統、農業、工業、經濟的變化間接地受到氣候變遷影響。

The ecosystems that are the most vulnerable to major biome shifts are the already hot regions around the equator, where the lush trees of rainforests may be replaced by savannas.
最容易發生重大生物族群變化的生態系統，是赤道附近原本已經很炎熱的地區，其中雨林繁茂的樹木可能會被莽原取代。

untreated
/ʌnˈtriːtɪd/

adj. 未處理的

💬 The dumping of untreated sewage into the sea and global warming are destroying the gulf's coral reefs.
在海洋中傾倒未經處理的污水，以及全球暖化，正在破壞海灣的珊瑚礁。

It is difficult to predict what global warming could cause if it is left unchecked or untreated. 全球暖化如果不受抑制或沒有獲得處理，會造成什麼影響，是很難預測的。

✏️ Dumping untreated wastes from pig production into waters has caused serious pollution.
把未經處理的豬隻生產廢棄物（糞便等）倒入水體，造成了嚴重的污染。

Doctors claim that more hot days due to global warming will increase the possibility of death in children and the elderly because heat stroke left untreated can be fatal.
醫師主張，全球暖化造成炎熱天數的增加，將提高孩童與老人的死亡機率，因為中暑沒有獲得治療可能會致命。

RELATED WORDS | 相關單字延伸

looming
adj. 隱約逼近的

impending
adj. 即將發生的，逼近的

imminent
adj. 逼近的

forthcoming
adj. 即將到來的

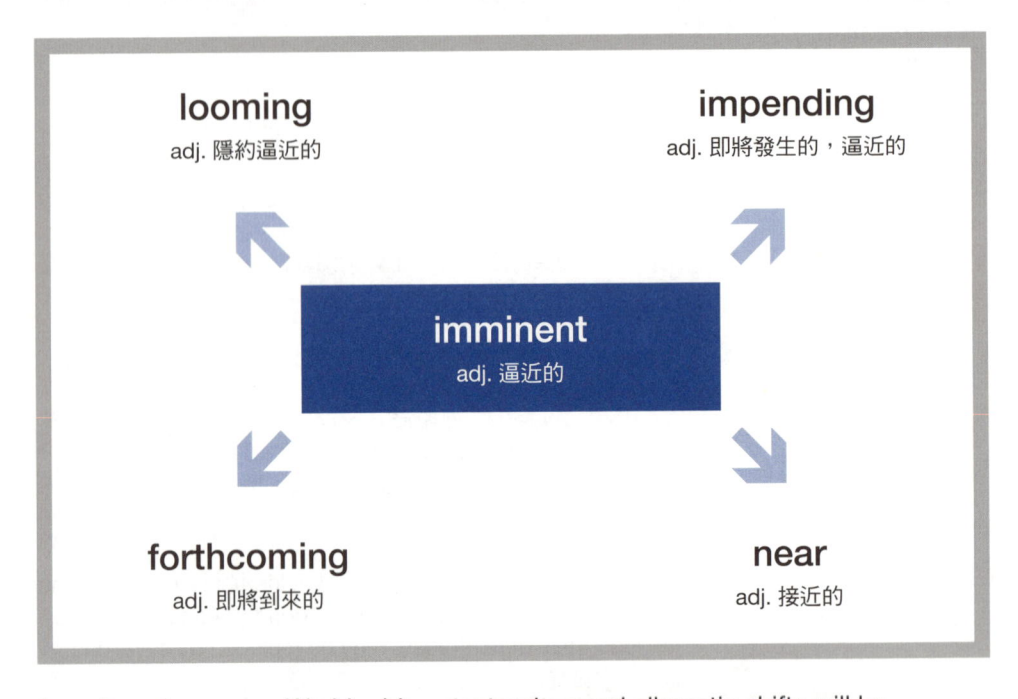

near
adj. 接近的

---

imminent
/ˈɪmɪnənt/

World-wide catastrophes and climactic shifts will be imminent if we ignore this threat.
如果我們忽視這個威脅，全球性的大災難和極大的變化將會逼近。

looming
/ˈluːmɪŋ/

Global warming is now looming thanks to our poor environmental decisions.
還真是多虧了我們糟糕的環境決策，全球暖化現在逐漸逼近了。

forthcoming
/fɔːθˈkʌmɪŋ/

The forthcoming heatwave might be a massive threat to the health of elderly people.
即將到來的熱浪，對老年人的健康可能是個巨大威脅。

impending
/ɪmˈpɛndɪŋ/

People are responding to the threat of the impending ice storm by stocking firewood.
人們正儲備柴火來應對逼近的冰風暴的威脅。

near
/nɪə/

People should plant trees near their homes to reduce greenhouse gases.
人們應該在住家附近種植樹木以減少溫室氣體。

USEFUL EXPRESSIONS | 相關實用片語

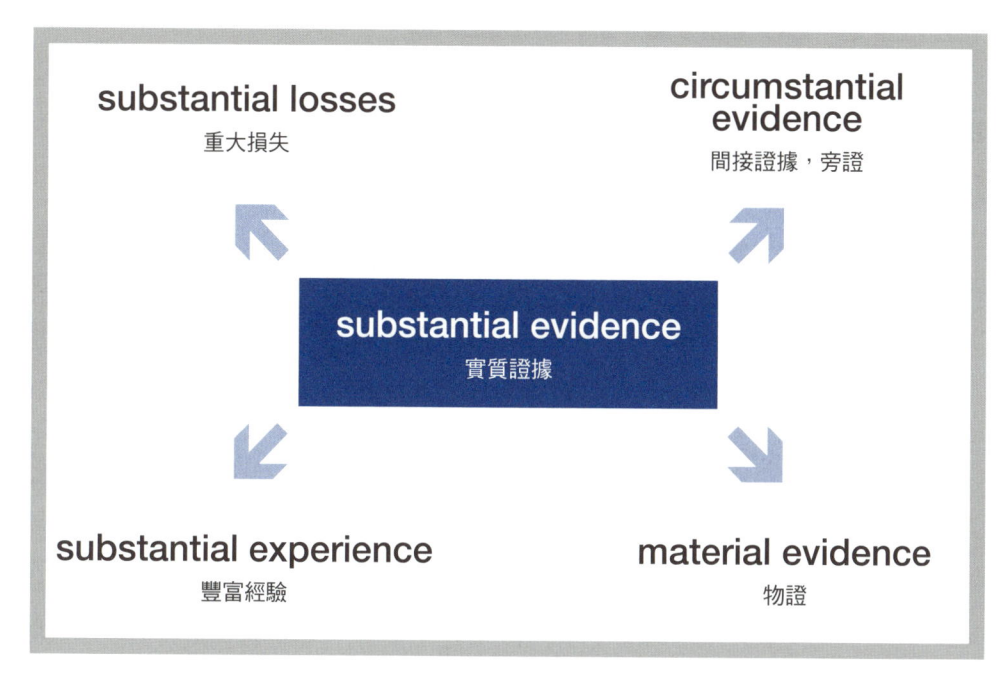

```
substantial losses          circumstantial evidence
重大損失                      間接證據，旁證
            ↖        ↗
         substantial evidence
              實質證據
            ↙        ↘
substantial experience      material evidence
豐富經驗                      物證
```

substantial evidence
/səbˈstænʃəl ˈɛvɪdəns/
The research scientists did not have enough substantial evidence to prove their theory.
研究的科學家沒有充足的實質證據來證明他們的理論。

substantial losses
/səbˈstænʃəl lɒsɪz/
Many investors have suffered substantial losses due to the financial crisis.
由於金融危機的關係，許多投資人遭遇到了重大的損失。

substantial experience
/səbˈstænʃəl ɪkˈspɪərɪəns/
Most employers will require all candidates to have substantial experience; however, many also demand a master's degree.
大部分的雇主會要求所有應徵者有豐富的經驗，但很多雇主也會要求具備碩士學位。

circumstantial evidence
/ˌsɜːkəmˈstænʃəl ˈɛvɪdəns/
The police force was unable to try and prosecute the accused because they only had circumstantial evidence.
警方無法起訴被告，因為他們只有間接證據。

material evidence
/məˈtɪərɪəl ˈɛvɪdəns/
The material evidence that the prosecution wants to show the court is in the plastic bag.
原告想要在法庭上出示的物證放在塑膠袋裡。

THU

IELTS **BASIC WORDS**

associate /əˈsəʊʃɪeɪt/ v. 把⋯和什麼聯想在一起
ENG. make a logical or causal connection
SYS. connect, relate

> If they can associate animal extinction with ecological imbalance, they will be convinced more easily to save endangered animals.
> 如果他們能把動物絕種和生態失衡聯想在一起,就會更容易被說服拯救瀕臨絕種的動物。

同義語 例句 I cannot quite establish the connection between fauna extinction and imbalance in flora.
我不太能把動物的滅絕和植物群的失衡聯想在一起。

同義語 例句 If we connect the pieces of information, we can conclude that animal extinction causes an imbalance in the whole ecosystem.
如果我們把這些片段資訊串聯起來,就可以做出動物滅絕導致整個生態系統失衡的結論。

反義語 例句 To avoid confusion, set apart your knowledge about Noah's ark of the Bible from the scientific concept of extinction.
為了避免混淆,要把你對聖經中諾亞方舟的認知和科學上的絕種概念區分開來。

rise /raɪz/ n. 上升,增加,興起
ENG. an increase in value to a higher point
SYS. ascent, climb

> There will be a rise of a new species whenever a species dies out.
> 每當有一個物種滅絕,就會有一個新物種興起。

同義語 例句 The quantity-of-species line shows an upward direction, indicating more species are becoming endangered.
物種數量的線圖顯示出上升的方向,表示有更多物種瀕臨絕種。

同義語 例句 The quantity-of-species line displayed an upward movement in the graph monitoring the count of endangered species.
在監測瀕危物種數量的圖表中,物種數量的折線顯示出上升的走勢。

反義語 例句 The sudden decline in the number of endangered species was due to the strong typhoon.
瀕危物種數量的突然下降,是因為強烈颱風來襲的關係。

WEEK 1 TOPIC **ENVIRONMENT**

▶基礎單字擴充

famous /ˈfeɪməs/ adj. 有名的
ENG. widely-known and esteemed; in the public eye
SYS. celebrated, famed

> The African elephants are a **famous** endangered species due to illegal ivory trading.
> 非洲象是因為非法象牙貿易而瀕臨絕種的著名動物。

同義語例句 Saving endangered species is **universally known** to be a responsibility of the WWF.
眾所周知，保護瀕危物種是世界自然基金會的任務。

同義語例句 WWF is **recognised by many** as the leader in protecting animals from dying out.
許多人認同世界自然基金會是保護動物免於絕種的先驅。

反義語例句 Some animal species are not **remarkable** enough to even be noticed as endangered.
有些動物物種不夠受人注目，甚至沒有被注意到瀕臨絕種。

pollution /pəˈluːʃən/ n. 污染
ENG. undesirable state of the natural environment being contaminated with harmful substances as a consequence of human activities
SYS. impurity, defilement

> Global **pollution** is one of the main causes why animals die out.
> 全球的污染是動物滅絕的主因之一。

同義語例句 The **unwanted substances** found in animal habitats cause them to get ill and die.
在動物棲息地發現的有害物質，使牠們生病、死亡。

同義語例句 The **contaminated matter** thrown into the animal's habitat kills them almost instantly.
丟棄到動物棲息地的受污染物質，會使動物幾乎立即死亡。

反義語例句 Animals' natural habitats must be kept free from pollution to avoid illnesses that may cause them to die out.
動物的自然棲息地必須保持無污染，以避免可能造成牠們滅絕的疾病發生。

TOPIC: Protect animals from dying out
保護動物免於絕種

Animal populations are disappearing at an alarming rate. Even in the face of threats like poaching, **habitat** loss and overuse of natural resources, we can still create a better future for wildlife every day. **Deforestation**, farming and development all result in **irreversible** changes like erosion, desertification and alteration of local climatic conditions. Such land use practices vastly alter or even **eliminate** wildlife habitat. In areas where rare **species** are present, habitat destruction can quickly force a species into **extinction.** Efforts for protecting these species will contribute to a **thriving**, healthy planet for people's health and well-being. Some say it is too expensive and time-consuming to protect animals from dying out when they serve no benefit to humans. This belief is **unfounded**. Plants and animals hold medicinal, agricultural, **ecological**, commercial and aesthetic value. **Endangered** species must be protected and saved so that future generations can experience their presence and value.

TRANS

動物族群正以驚人的速度消失中。即使面臨盜獵、棲息地喪失、過度使用自然資源等威脅，我們仍然能夠在每天的生活中為野生動物創造更好的未來。森林砍伐、農業和開發都會造成不可逆的變化，像是土壤侵蝕、沙漠化和當地氣候狀況的改變等等。這種土地利用行為會大幅改變甚至消滅野生動物的棲息地。在稀有物種所處的地區，棲息地的破壞會快速迫使物種滅絕。對這些動物的保護，將為人類的健康與福祉營造欣欣向榮且健康的地球。有些人說，如果動物對人類沒有利益的話，保護這些動物代價太高，也太浪費時間。這種想法是沒有根據的。動植物有醫藥、農業、生態、商業和美學的價值。瀕危物種必須受到保護，好讓未來的世代能夠感受到牠們的存在和價值。

habitat
/ˈhæbɪtæt/

n. 棲息地

Plant a garden in your backyard to create an animal **habitat**.
在你的後院種一座花園，創造動物的棲息地。

deforestation
/ˌdiːfɔːrɪˈsteɪʃən/

n. 森林砍伐

The Amazon rainforest has experienced terrible **deforestation** due to demand for farming land.
由於對耕地的需求，亞馬遜雨林受到了嚴重的森林砍伐。

irreversible
/ˌɪrɪˈvɜːsɪbəl/

adj. 不可逆的，不可挽回的

His decision to drop out of college was **irreversible** once his tuition was refunded.
一旦他的學費被退還，他從大學退學的決定就無法挽回了。

eliminate
/ɪˈlɪmɪneɪt/

v. 消除，消滅，淘汰

The judge decided to **eliminate** my sister from the competition because she was too young.
評審決定把我妹妹從比賽中淘汰，因為她太年輕。

species
/ˈspiːʃiːz/

n. 物種

Report any evidence of wildlife trafficking or sale of protected **species** you notice.
報告任何你注意到的非法交易野生動物或販賣受保護物種的證據。

extinction
/ɪkˈstɪŋkʃən/

n. 滅絕，絕種

Pollution is driving many species to **extinction**, including many types of fish on the Florida coastline.
污染正在使許多物種絕種，其中包括佛羅里達州海岸的許多種魚。

thriving
/ˈθraɪvɪŋ/

adj. 繁茂的，欣欣向榮的

Please take a look at how my herb garden is **thriving** in the kitchen window!
請透過廚房的窗戶，看看我的香草花園長得多茂盛！

unfounded
/ʌnˈfaʊndɪd/

adj. 沒有根據的

Accusing me of stealing a cookie is completely **unfounded** because I was sleeping.
指責我偷餅乾是完全沒有根據的，因為我剛才在睡覺。

ecological
/iːkəˈlɒdʒɪkəl/

adj. 生態（學）的

Killarney National Park in Ireland is of high **ecological** value because of its species diversity.
愛爾蘭的基拉尼國家公園因其物種多樣性而具有高度生態學價值。

endangered
/ɪnˈdeɪndʒəd/

adj. 瀕危的，瀕臨絕種的

The Australian government is now taking action to protect the **endangered** population of koalas.
澳洲政府正採取行動保護瀕危的無尾熊族群。

WORD TRAINING | 重點單字造句練習

contaminate
/kənˈtæmɪneɪt/

v. 污染

Waste can contaminate the habitats of plant and animal species, causing their extinction.
廢棄物會污染植物和動物物種的棲息地，導致其滅絕。

Oil spills contaminate waterways and threaten the extinction of fish species.
油料外洩會污染水道，並且造成魚類滅絕的威脅。

Scientists in the UK are reporting evidence that consumption of insects contaminated with a toxic metal may be a factor in the mysterious global decline of carnivorous plants.
英國科學家報告的證據顯示，攝取受到一種有毒金屬污染的昆蟲，可能是全球食肉植物神祕地減少的一項因素。

Pink dolphins, commonly found in the Amazon River of South America, are on the verge of extinction due to humans contaminating their natural habitat.
南美洲亞馬遜河常見的粉紅色淡水豚，由於人類污染牠們的自然棲息地而瀕臨絕種的危機。

reforestation
/ˌriːfɔːrɪˈsteɪʃən/

n. 再造林，林地復育

Scientists launched a long-term reforestation project to aid threatened Bornean rhino species.
科學家展開了長期的林地復育計畫，來幫助受到威脅的婆羅洲犀牛品種。

Please help us with the reforestation of endangered tree species in Brazil so that fewer animals will die.
請幫助我們進行巴西瀕危樹種的再造林，讓較少的動物死亡。

Some reforestation efforts focus on growing forests quickly because these woodlands are the key to many of the Earth's natural cycles, such as the carbon and water cycles.
有些林地復育工作著重於快速種植樹林，因為這些林地是地球許多自然循環的關鍵，例如碳與水的循環。

By using donor money to protect the habitat of the larger animals through reforestation programmes, the entire ecosystem can be protected from harm.
藉著使用捐助的資金，透過林地復育計畫保護大型動物的棲息地，整個生態系統都可以受到保護而免於傷害。

口說範例 寫作範例

diminish
/dɪˈmɪnɪʃ/

v. 減少

💬 The Seoul City Council faces a problem of rapidly diminishing waste disposal facilities.
首爾市議會面臨廢棄物處理設施迅速減少的問題。

The diminishing ozone layer allows more radiation from the sun to reach earth's surface.
逐漸變薄的臭氧層,使得更多來自太陽的幅射抵達地球表面。

✏️ The government should implement the use of alternative and renewable energy from natural sources like the sun to ease the demand for our diminishing energy source.
政府應該實行對天然來源的替代性及可再生能源的使用,像是陽光,以減輕對我們日漸減少的能源的需求。

Due to our gradually diminishing energy supply, scientists and environmentalists are now searching for ways to convert other natural and alternative resources to energy.
由於逐漸減少的能源供應量,科學家和環保人士現在正在尋找方法,將其他天然與替代性資源轉換為能量。

dump
/dʌmp/

v. 傾倒,丟棄

💬 The government should prohibit cruise ships from dumping their waste directly into the sea.
政府應該禁止遊艇把廢棄物直接倒進海裡。

People should stop dumping their old appliances near the beach.
人們應該停止將舊家電丟在海灘附近的行為。

✏️ The government should strictly implement laws that will prohibit people from dumping their waste directly into rivers and seas to prevent marine and coastal pollution.
政府應該嚴格執行禁止人們將廢棄物直接倒進河流與海洋的法律,以避免海洋與海岸污染。

People should learn how to reuse and recycle to decrease their waste production since we are already running out of landfills to dump our garbage.
人們應該學習如何再利用及回收,以減少廢棄物的產生,因為我們已經快要沒有垃圾掩埋地可以傾倒垃圾了。

RELATED WORDS | 相關單字延伸

eradicate
v. 根除，消滅

purge
v. 淨化，肅清

eliminate
v. 消除，消滅，淘汰

abolish
v. 廢除

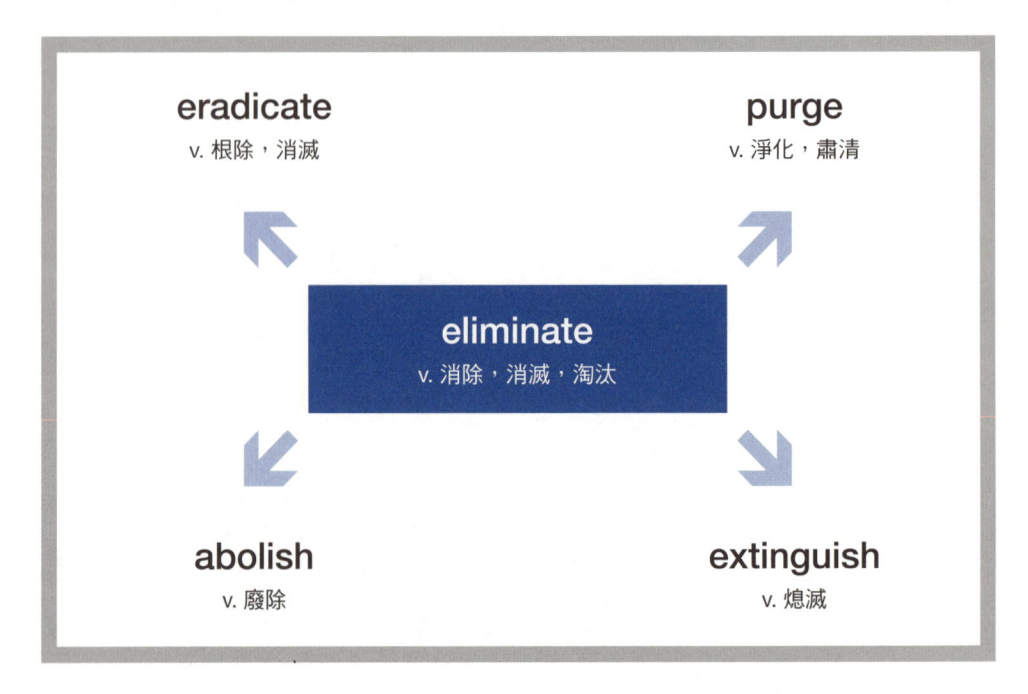

extinguish
v. 熄滅

eliminate
/ɪˈlɪmɪneɪt/

Land use practices vastly alter or even eliminate wildlife habitat.
土地利用行為會大幅改變甚至消滅野生動物的棲息地。

eradicate
/ɪˈrædɪkeɪt/

The wildlife was totally eradicated after fire swept the owl habitat.
火災席捲貓頭鷹的棲息地後，該地區的野生動物完全被滅絕了。

abolish
/əˈbɒlɪʃ/

The animal protectionists urge that the government abolish the laws which allow the euthanasia of stray dogs.
那些動物保護人士強烈要求政府廢除允許流浪狗安樂死的法律。

purge
/pɜːdʒ/

The alchemists' goal was to purge impurity to leave only perfection.
煉金術士的目標是清除不純的物質，只留下完美。

extinguish
/ɪkˈstɪŋgwɪʃ/

The campfire must be completely extinguished to prevent accidental wildfires.
營火應該要完全熄滅，以避免意外發生森林大火。

USEFUL EXPRESSIONS | 相關實用片語

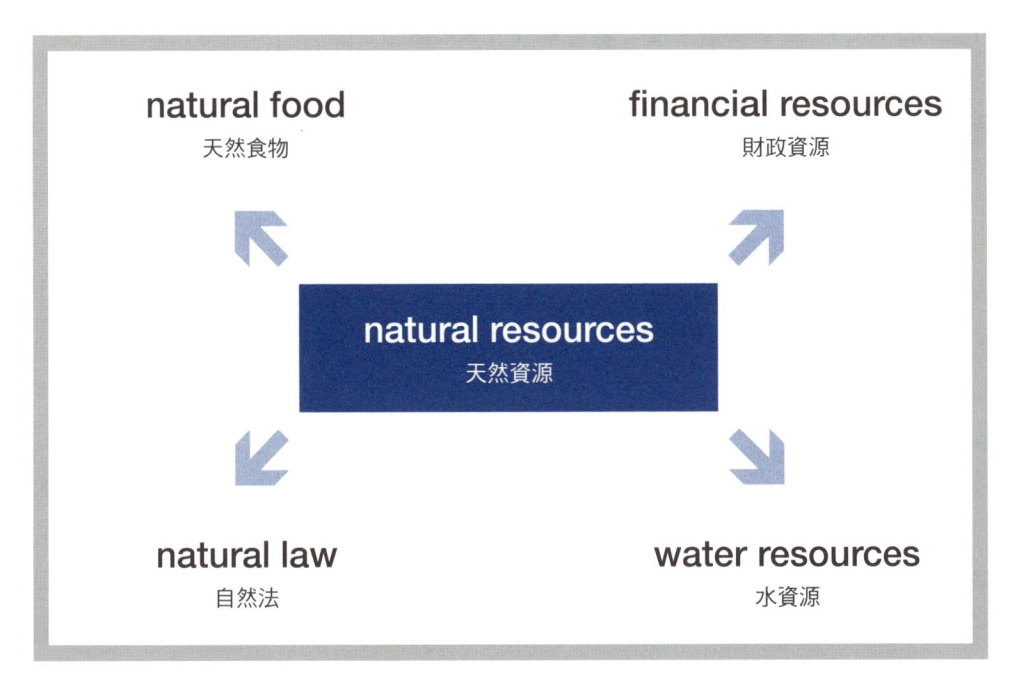

```
          natural food                    financial resources
          天然食物                            財政資源
                    ↖              ↗
                    ┌──────────────────┐
                    │ natural resources │
                    │      天然資源       │
                    └──────────────────┘
                    ↙              ↘
          natural law                     water resources
          自然法                             水資源
```

natural resources
/ˈnætʃərəl rɪˈsɔːsɪz/

Alaska is very rich in natural resources, and its oil accounts for a large proportion of U.S. stock.
阿拉斯加的天然資源非常豐富，而當地的石油佔美國石油存量很大的比例。

natural food
/ˈnætʃərəl fuːd/

Media campaigns today assure the public that natural foods improve one's overall health.
今日的媒體宣傳向大眾保證，天然食物能夠促進人的整體健康。

natural law
/ˈnætʃərəl lɔː/

All races are entitled to freedom under natural law.
在自然法之下，所有種族都有資格得到自由。

financial resources
/fʌɪˈnænʃəl rɪˈsɔːsɪz/

Companies should allocate more financial resources to their investments and their management training.
公司應該分配更多財政資源到投資和管理訓練方面。

water resources
/ˈwɔːtə rɪˈsɔːsɪz/

The land and water resources in the area have been protected under the same budget that protects raw materials.
該地區的土地和水資源，已經在保護原物料的同一筆預算中獲得了保障。

FRI

IELTS **BASIC WORDS**

trait /treɪt/ n. 特徵，特性
ENG. a distinguishing feature of a human's personal nature
SYS. feature, characteristic

> Their family members' unique trait of having a loud voice contributes to the noise problem in their home.
> 他們家庭成員說話大聲的特徵，造成了家裡的噪音問題。

- 同義語例句: An inherent attribute of Simon's family is their loud voice, which is noise pollution to a normal person's ear.
  Simon 的家庭與生俱來的一項特性是說話大聲，這對一般人的耳朵而言是噪音污染。

- 同義語例句: His genetically determined condition makes it difficult for him to cope with pollution.
  基因先天決定的問題，讓他很難應付污染。

- 反義語例句: His similarity with the others who have a strong dislike to noise pollution made him even more determined to stop it.
  因為和其他人同樣強烈厭惡噪音污染，所以他更加下定決心要杜絕噪音。

experiment /ɪkˈspɛrɪmənt/ n. 實驗
ENG. the act of conducting a controlled test or investigation
SYS. testing, research

> The experiment reveals new facts about the danger of noise pollution.
> 這個實驗揭露了關於噪音污染危險性的新事實。

- 同義語例句: This trial and error process enabled us to prove that noise pollution is indeed detrimental to our health.
  這個試行錯誤的過程，讓我們能證明噪音污染的確對健康有害。

- 同義語例句: The results of the investigation regarding noise pollution caused people to rethink what they listen to.
  關於噪音污染的調查結果，使得人們重新思考他們聽到的東西。

- 反義語例句: His haste to reach a baseless conclusion that noise pollution is always hazardous caused public disbelief.
  他急著推導出沒有根據的結論，說噪音污染總是有害，造成了大眾的不信任。

WEEK 1 TOPIC **ENVIRONMENT**

▶ 基礎單字擴充

identity /ʌɪˈdɛntɪti/ n. 個性，身分
ENG. individual characteristic by which a thing or person is recognised or known
SYS. individuality, distinction

> His **identity** as the most pro-active anti-noise pollution activist in the group is widely known.
> 他在團體中扮演最積極的反噪音污染激進人士的身分廣為人知。

同義語例句 His **distinct personality** encouraged his friends to participate in his protests against noise pollution.
他與眾不同的個性激勵了朋友們參與他的反噪音污染抗議。

同義語例句 The most **prominent trait** of the politician's character was perseverance, as shown in his persistent protests against noise pollution.
那位政治家最突出的個性特質是堅持不懈，這可以從他對噪音污染的持續抗議看出來。

反義語例句 The **common attribute** of our staff members is the attitude against noise pollution.　我們工作人員的共同特質是反噪音污染的態度。

statistics /stəˈtɪstɪks/ n. 統計
ENG. the mathematics of collecting and analysing data to draw conclusions and make predictions
SYS. sampling, data

> Our **Statistics** assignment requires us to measure the association between various indices of noise pollution.
> 我們的統計學作業要求我們計算多種噪音污染指標之間的相關程度。

同義語例句 The **collection and interpretation of data** on noise pollution is tedious and time-consuming work.
關於噪音污染的數據收集與解釋，是繁瑣又耗時的工作。

同義語例句 By **analysing the data**, we are able to mathematically derive different indices that determine the severity of noise pollution.
藉由分析數據，我們能夠以數學的方式推導出確定噪音污染嚴重性的多種不同指標。

反義語例句 Making **illogical deductions** is a silly thing to do especially when it comes to noise pollution measurements.
做出不合邏輯的推論是愚蠢的，尤其是涉及噪音污染測量的時候。

45

FRI

TOPIC: The negative effect of noise
噪音的負面影響

We know that **excessive** noise can be frustrating and harmful to our well-being, but we have become **desensitised** to high levels of noise and are **unconscious** of the negative effect it has on animals as well as ecological systems. For example, look at the effect that man-made noise is having on fish. The **clamour** of fishing crews and rumbling motors have led to the decrease of fish stocks in oceans and waterways. One possible reason for this is that fish cannot communicate to avoid **potential** predators while disturbed by the underwater noise pollution generated by the shipping industry. Experts have also **witnessed** fish attempting to avoid noisy areas, showing that noise affects their **distribution**. Ultimately, this affects reproduction and the availability of food sources. Of course, noise can directly affect human beings as well. The increasing complaints about noise pollution **indicate** that modern people have less **tolerance** to it, so it is not just the responsibility of **environmentalists** to fight noise pollution.

TRANS

我們知道過度的噪音可能會令人感到沮喪，而且對健康造成傷害，但我們對高度噪音已經麻木，也沒有意識到噪音對動物和生態系統的負面影響。舉例來說，我們可以看人為噪音對魚類產生的影響。漁船船員的喧鬧聲與隆隆作響的馬達，已經造成海洋與水道中的魚群減少。造成這個問題的一個可能理由，是受到航運業產生的水底噪音污染影響，使得魚類無法溝通並避免潛在的掠食者。專家也見證了魚類試圖避開吵雜區域的現象，這顯示噪音會影響牠們的分佈。結果，這影響了魚類的繁殖和我們食物來源的可得性。當然，噪音也會直接影響人類。越來越多對於噪音污染的投訴，顯示現代人比較不能容忍噪音污染，所以對抗噪音污染不止是環保人士的責任而已。

excessive
/ɪkˈsɛsɪv/

adj. 過度的

Excessive alcohol intake prior to driving is strictly prohibited to prevent road accidents.
為了避免交通事故,開車前飲酒過量是嚴格禁止的。

desensitise
/diːˈsɛnsɪtʌɪz/

v. 使麻木

I became **desensitised** to the smell of fish when I worked at the cannery.
我在罐頭工廠工作的時候,變得對魚腥味麻木了。

unconscious
/ʌnˈkɒnʃəs/

adj. 無意識的

When Mr. Lee swore, he was **unconscious** of the fact that he hurt Jane's feelings.
當 Lee 先生發誓的時候,他沒有意識到自己傷害了 Jane 的感情的事實。

clamour
/ˈklamə/

n. 吵鬧聲,喧囂聲

The crowd outside made such a **clamour** that I had to close the window.
外面的群眾很吵鬧,讓我不得不關上窗戶。

potential
/pəʊˈtɛnʃəl/

adj. 潛在的

The store owners should lower their selling prices to attract **potential** buyers.
店主應該降低售價來吸引潛在顧客。

witness
/ˈwɪtnəs/

v. 目擊,見證

My driving instructor said she has never **witnessed** a major car accident before.
我的駕駛教練說,她以前從來沒目擊過重大車禍。

distribution
/dɪstrɪˈbjuːʃən/

n. 分配

The **distribution** of canned foods to the poor fed many families. 對貧窮者分配罐頭食物,餵飽了許多家庭。

indicate
/ˈɪndɪkeɪt/

v. 表示

A reddish glow in the morning sky may **indicate** an approaching storm.
早晨天空的一抹紅光,可能表示暴風雨即將到來。

tolerance
/ˈtɒlərəns/

n. 容忍,耐受性

The easiest way to increase alcohol **tolerance** is to drink regularly.
增加酒量最簡單的方法是經常喝酒。

environmentalist
/ɪnˌvʌɪrənˈmɛntəlɪst/

n. 環保人士

Several **environmentalists** were arrested at the protest for blocking a logging truck.
幾位環保人士在抗議行動中因為阻擋載木車被逮捕。

WORD TRAINING | 重點單字造句練習

urbanisation
/ɜːbənaɪˈzeɪʃən/

n. 都市化

💬 Increasing urbanisation within the city has caused an alarming level of noise pollution.
城市裡逐漸增加的都市化，使得噪音污染達到驚人的程度。

Urbanisation has caused some animal migratory patterns to change due to increasing noise pollution.
由於增加的噪音污染，都市化造成了某些動物遷徙模式改變。

✎ Deer and other quiet animals are greatly affected by the urbanisation and subsequent noise pollution within their natural environment that rural to urban migration brings.
從農村到都市的遷徙所帶來的都市化和隨後對自然環境造成的噪音污染，讓鹿和其他安靜的動物受到很大的影響。

Environmental noise pollution will continue to increase in severity because of population growth, urbanisation and the associated growth in the use of increasingly powerful and highly mobile sources of noise.
因為人口成長、都市化，以及對更強力、極具流動性的噪音源的使用隨之成長，環境噪音污染的嚴重程度將持續增加。

observation
/ɒbzəˈveɪʃən/

n. 觀察

💬 According to my own observations, noise pollution within the city is on the rise.
根據我自己的觀察，城市裡的噪音污染正在成長。

City planners are making careful observations while constructing the building so that noise pollution is monitored. 都市計畫者在建設建築物的同時進行謹慎的觀察，讓噪音污染受到監控。

✎ According to the doctor's observation during the clinical research, there is a significant link between increase in blood pressure and consistent noise exposure among elderly patients. 根據醫師在臨床研究中的觀察，在老年患者中，血壓上升和持續曝露在噪音中有顯著的關聯。

In the study of the effects of noise pollution on threatened and endangered species, the observation methods were compared across groups in order to determine which method is more reliable.
在關於噪音污染對瀕危物種影響的研究中，對觀察方法進行了跨組別的比較，以確定哪種方法比較可靠。

口說範例 寫作範例

creature
/ˈkriːtʃə/

n. 生物，動物

💬 Many creatures, great or small, are threatened when noise pollution increases.
當噪音污染增加時，很多生物不論大小都會受到威脅。

Noise pollution on the surface can be deadly to most creatures living under water.
水面上的噪音污染，對於大部分生活在水底的動物可能是致命的。

✏️ Noise from the human world is disrupting life below the surface where almost every living creature depends on sound as a primary sense for mating, hunting and survival.
來自人類世界的噪音正在擾亂水面下的生活，因為水裡幾乎每種生物都依賴聲音作為交配、狩獵與生存的主要感官。

Marine creatures emit sounds to communicate, attract mates and express fear or distress, especially when predators are lurking in the vicinity.
海洋生物發出聲音來溝通、吸引配偶，以及表達恐懼或痛苦，尤其是掠食者潛伏在附近的時候。

---

interference
/ˌɪntəˈfɪərəns/

n. 干擾

💬 Loud noise leads to significant interference to people's work and concentration.
大聲的噪音會對人們的工作與專注力造成很大的干擾。

Noise not only induces hearing loss but also creates interferences to normal conversation.
噪音不僅會引起聽力損失，也會對正常的對話造成干擾。

✏️ A sound is considered a noise when it is already disrupting one's quality of life by bringing in interferences to normal activity like sleeping and conversation.
當一種聲音已經對睡眠、對話之類的正常活動造成干擾，破壞生活品質的時候，就被認為是噪音。

Noise causes interferences to people's daily activities because it's linked to certain medical conditions, like high blood pressure, anxiety disorder and insomnia.
噪音對人們的日常活動造成干擾，因為噪音和某些不適狀況有關，像是高血壓、焦慮症和失眠。

RELATED WORDS | 相關單字延伸

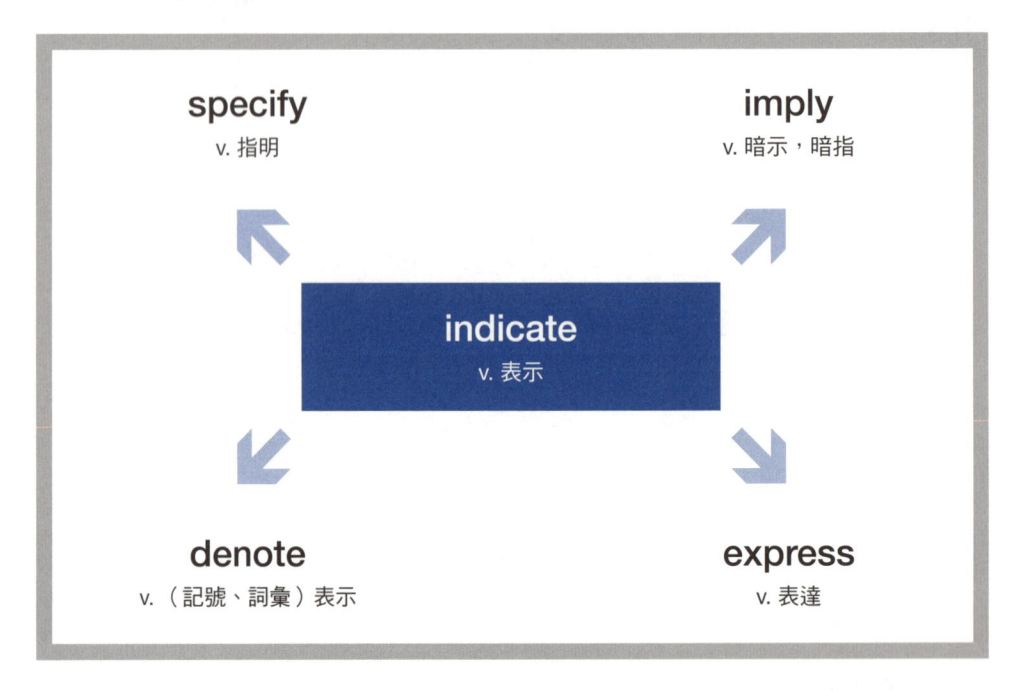

specify
v. 指明

imply
v. 暗示，暗指

indicate
v. 表示

denote
v.（記號、詞彙）表示

express
v. 表達

---

indicate
/ˈɪndɪkeɪt/

Increasing complaints may also indicate lower levels of tolerance to noise.
增加中的投訴可能表示對噪音的容忍程度變低。

specify
/ˈspɛsɪfʌɪ/

He couldn't specify the exact type of noise pollution that bothers him.
他無法指明困擾他的確切噪音污染種類。

denote
/dɪˈnəʊt/

The red mark denotes the source of noise pollution.
紅色的記號表示噪音污染的來源。

imply
/ɪmˈplʌɪ/

The real estate agent implied that noise pollution in the neighbourhood was troublesome.
房地產經紀人暗示這附近的噪音污染很令人煩惱。

express
/ɪkˈsprɛs/

The councillor expressed that noise pollution was a result of poor urban planning.
那位議員表示，噪音污染是糟糕的都市計畫造成的結果。

USEFUL EXPRESSIONS | 相關實用片語

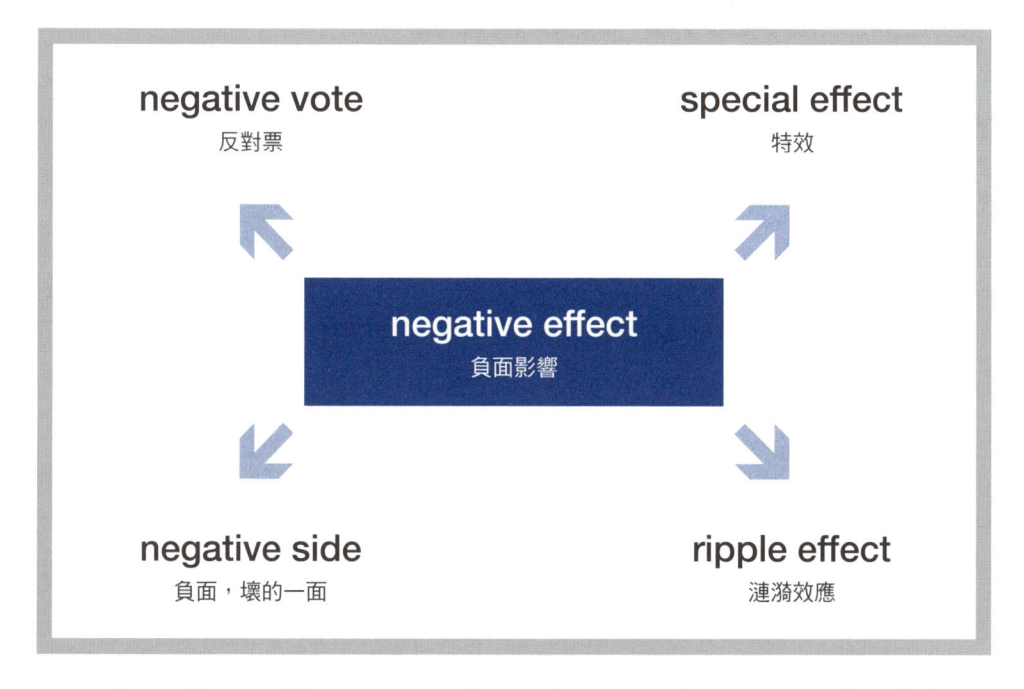

```
negative vote                    special effect
反對票                            特效

          negative effect
          負面影響

negative side                    ripple effect
負面，壞的一面                    漣漪效應
```

negative effect
/ˈnɛɡətɪv ɪˈfɛkt/

The negative effects of prolonged exposure to air pollution on the brain can lead to illness.
長期曝露於空氣污染，對腦部造成的負面影響，可能導致疾病。

negative vote
/ˈnɛɡətɪv voʊt/

When people approach the booth, they are prompted to cast either an affirmative or a negative vote.
當人接近圈票處，就會被提示要投贊成票還是反對票。

negative side
/ˈnɛɡətɪv sʌɪd/

He apologised for the comment that focused on the negative side of those who suffered during the period.
對於在那段期間受苦的人，做出聚焦於他們不好的一面的評論，他表示道歉。

special effect
/ˈspɛʃəl ɪˈfɛkt/

Film critics who watched the movie "Avatar" were impressed with its high level of special effects.
看過電影《阿凡達》的影評，對於片中高水準的特效印象深刻。

ripple effect
/ˈrɪpəl ɪˈfɛkt/

Twitter has stronger ripple effects for business than Facebook does because it connects strangers together.
對於商業而言，Twitter 的漣漪效應比 Facebook 強，因為它把陌生人串連在一起。

SAT

IELTS **BASIC WORDS**

reality /rɪˈalɪti/ n. 現實，真實
ENG. the quality of being real; that which exists objectively
SYS. fact, actuality

> The reality is that clean water today is scarce and that the situation will not improve in the coming years.
> 現實情況是，今日乾淨的水很稀少，而且這個情況在未來幾年都不會改善。

同義語例句 The **objective fact** of water shortage among countries today brings people together to work towards water conservation.
今日，各國水源短缺的客觀事實，使得人們共同努力節約用水。

同義語例句 In the **real world**, people waste water every day thinking that it is impossible for it to run out.
在現實世界裡，人們每天都浪費水，以為水是不可能用完的。

反義語例句 The belief that the world will never run out of clean water is an **absolute fallacy**.
認為這個世界的乾淨水源永遠不會用完，完全是個謬論。

predict /prɪˈdɪkt/ v. 預測
ENG. to state or claim that a particular event will occur in the future
SYS. guess, foretell

> It is tough to predict whether or not there will be enough clean water supply for the next ten years.
> 很難預測未來十年乾淨水源的供應是否充足。

同義語例句 The weatherman **anticipates** rain today to at least alleviate the water shortage.
氣象播報員預測今天的降雨至少能緩解缺水的問題。

同義語例句 If there is a chance to **tell something before it happens**, we will be able to save water before a drought is even declared.
如果有機會在事情發生前先預知的話，我們就可以在宣告乾旱之前節約用水。

反義語例句 If we **recall** what happened during the last water shortage, we will be reminded of how difficult it was.
如果我們回想上次缺水時發生的事，就會記得當時的處境有多困難。

WEEK 1 TOPIC **ENVIRONMENT**

▶基礎單字擴充

biology /baɪˈɒlədʒi/ n. 生物學
ENG. the science that studies living organisms
SYS. botany, organism

> My **Biology** teacher said that water shortage kills a lot of life forms.
> 我的生物老師說，缺水會造成許多生物死亡。

同義語例句 The **study of life** involves exploring how water supply affects the way organisms interact.
生命研究牽涉到探索水源供給如何影響生物互動的方式。

同義語例句 The **science of life processes** involves the effects of water shortage on animals.
關於生命過程的科學，涉及水的短缺對動物所造成的影響。

反義語例句 A **popular myth** is that some species can survive without water.
有些物種能在沒有水的情況下生存，是很多人的迷思。

explanation /ˌɛkspləˈneɪʃən/ n. 解釋
ENG. the act of explaining; making something comprehensible
SYS. reasoning, interpretation

> The simplest **explanation** for water shortage is nothing but water wastage.
> 對於缺水原因最簡單的解釋，就是浪費水。

同義語例句 His **description of the causes** of water shortage included various human acts of wasting water.
他對於缺水的起因說明，包括各種浪費水的人類行為。

同義語例句 The mayor's **detailed account** of the water shortage problem in the city helped the people realise the need for conservation.
市長對市內缺水問題的詳細說明，幫助人們了解到節約的需要（重要性）。

反義語例句 The mayor's **refusal to justify** his decision to conceal water shortage from the public disappointed them.
市長拒絕對隱瞞缺水問題的決定提出正當的理由，讓大眾感到失望。

SAT

TOPIC: Water shortage
缺水

The impacts of the global water and **sanitation** crisis are far-reaching. The effects of water shortage are not **confined** to the human world, but are seen throughout nature, disturbing the **lifecycles** of wildlife species. A prime cause of the global water shortage is the ever-increasing world population. As populations grow, industrial, agricultural and individual water demands **escalate**. In all honesty, water will probably become the most critical natural resource issue facing most parts of the world by the dawn of the next century. This tendency is also reflected in the observation that water will likely replace oil as a future cause of war between nations. Water shortages affect the environment, too. For example, **unsustainable withdrawals** through groundwater mining have major environmental **consequences**. They can desiccate the rivers and streams previously fed by the **groundwater** basins and **obliterate** the ecosystems that depended on them. In the last few years, global warming has received all of the press, but shortages of fresh water are **arguably** the greater environmental threat in many corners of the globe.

TRANS

全球水源與衛生的危機所造成的影響很深遠。缺水的影響不僅限於人類世界，也在整個自然界中出現，擾亂野生物種的生命週期。全球之所以缺水，主要是由於世界人口持續成長。隨著人口成長，工業、農業與個人的用水需求也大幅上升。說實在話，水可能在下個世紀初成為世界大部分地區所面臨最重要的自然資源問題。這個傾向也反映在一項觀察中，認為水可能取代石油，成為未來國家之間發動戰爭的原因。缺水也會影響環境。舉例來說，對地下水進行不可持續性的抽取，會對環境造成嚴重的後果。這樣可能會使先前由地下水盆地供應水源的河流與小溪乾涸，並且消滅賴以為生的生態系統。過去幾年，全球暖化已經受到所有報章雜誌關注，但乾淨水源的缺乏恐怕是地球許多角落中更嚴重的環境威脅。

sanitation
/ˌsænɪˈteɪʃən/

n. 衛生

A good community **sanitation** programme can reduce the incidents of communicable diseases, environmental illnesses and injuries.
良好的社區衛生計畫可以減少傳染性疾病、環境疾病和傷害的發生。

confine
/kənˈfaɪn/

v. 限制，局限

Many people become anxious on airplanes because they don't enjoy how **confined** they feel.
很多人在飛機上會變得焦慮，因為他們不喜歡被局限的感覺。

lifecycle
/ˈlaɪfˌsaɪkəl/

n. 生命週期，生活過程

The biology students studied the moth's **lifecycle** in detail.
生物系的學生詳細研究了蛾的生命週期。

escalate
/ˈɛskəleɪt/

v. 大幅增加，大幅上升

As wind speeds began to **escalate**, the man quickly ran to safety.
隨著風速開始加快，那名男子迅速跑到安全的地方。

unsustainable
/ˌʌnsəˈsteɪnəbəl/

adj. 無法持續的，不可持續性的

Oil is an **unsustainable** resource because it cannot form as fast as we use it.
石油是一種非持續性的資源，因為它形成的速度沒辦法和我們使用的速度一樣快。

withdrawal
/wɪðˈdrɔːəl/

n. 提取，提款

My banking fees were very expensive due to my many **withdrawals** from ATMs.
因為我的 ATM 提款次數很多，所以我的銀行手續費非常貴。

consequence
/ˈkɒnsɪkwəns/

n. 後果

There will be strict **consequences** for any child caught out of bed past 10:00 p.m.
任何小孩被逮到十點以後沒在床上的話，會有嚴厲的後果。

groundwater
/ˈgraʊndwɔːtə/

n. 地下水

Arsenic found in **groundwater** is brought about by the minerals dissolving from rocks and soil.
地下水中發現的砷，是岩石和土壤中的礦物質分解產生的。

obliterate
/əˈblɪtəreɪt/

v. 消滅（…的痕跡）

I had to **obliterate** the computer virus that was attacking my operating system.
我當時必須消滅攻擊我作業系統的電腦病毒。

arguably
/ˈɑːgjʊəbli/

adv. 可以說…

He is **arguably** the world's most famous Korean singer.
他可以說是全世界最有名的韓國歌手。

WORD TRAINING | 重點單字造句練習

fertile
/ˈfɜːtʌɪl/

adj. 肥沃的

💬 Uneven distribution of silt due to damming has caused a reduction in fertile land.
由於築壩使得淤泥分布不均，造成肥沃土壤減少。

Scientists expressed concern over the low water supply and the rapid decline of fertile soil.
科學家對於偏低的水源供應量和肥沃土地的快速減少表達了憂慮。

✍ Once-fertile farmland in India is now withered and cracked due to water shortages and the promotion of chemical agriculture.
由於缺水和化學農業的提倡，使得印度曾經肥沃的農地現在變得乾枯龜裂。

Nowhere is the water shortage more apparent than in the region of the River Nile, which was historically an area of fertile banks and access to an ample water supply.
沒有一個地方的缺水情況比尼羅河地區更明顯，而這裡曾經是歷史上有肥沃的河岸和豐沛水源的地區。

sewage
/ˈsuːɪdʒ/

n. 污水

💬 Waste and sewage discharged into the river made the water too toxic for human use.
排放到河流中的廢棄物和污水，使得河水毒性太強，無法讓人類使用。

The owner claims the problem is caused by a malfunctioning sewage treatment system.
業主聲稱問題是故障的污水處理系統造成的。

✍ The federal allocations are not enough to ensure a fully functioning water and sewage system.
要確保有完全發揮作用的供水與污水系統，光靠聯邦撥款是不夠的。

Severe pollution caused by factory discharges and sewage from fast-expanding cities has made one-third of the river unusable either for agricultural or industrial use.
快速擴張的城市中，工廠排放物和污水所造成的嚴重污染，已經使得這條河的三分之一無法供農業或工業使用。

greening
/ˈgriːnɪŋ/

n. 綠化，環保化

💬 **Greening** efforts have led to a reduction in water shortage issues in the area.
綠化的努力減少了該地區的缺水問題。

Many companies have taken up **greening** efforts in their office environments and are conserving more water at the workplace.
許多公司已經在辦公室環境進行綠化，並且在工作場所節省更多用水。

📝 A **greening** water law has been enacted to meet the growing water needs of human society as well as to maintain freshwater ecosystems and support environmental sustainability.
為了滿足人類社會持續成長的用水需求，以及維持淡水生態系統、支持環境永續，而頒布了水源綠化的法律。

If we focus only on the **greening** of fast food packaging but not addressing the water shortage problem, we will soon find ourselves in heaps of trouble.
如果我們只關注速食包裝的環保化，但不處理缺水的問題，我們很快就會陷入一堆麻煩。

smog
/smɒg/

n.（廢氣造成的）煙霧

💬 Air pollution combined with the afternoon's high temperature generates **smog**.
空氣污染加上下午的高溫，會產生煙霧。

The chemical gas expelled by cars brings **smog** and other pollutants in the air.
汽車排出的化學氣體，會把煙霧和其他污染物質帶進空氣中。

📝 **Smog** induces serious lung problems, which can be prevented by wearing face masks or by avoiding polluted areas when the temperature is at its peak in the afternoon.
煙霧會造成嚴重的肺部問題，這可以藉由戴口罩或者在下午氣溫最高時避開污染地區來預防。

The main component of **smog** is ground-level ozone, which is said to be harmful to human health and may induce lung problems like asthma and lung cancer.
煙霧的主要成分是地平面的臭氧，據說臭氧對人類的健康有害，而且可能誘發氣喘和肺癌等肺部問題。

RELATED WORDS | 相關單字延伸

heighten
v. 提高

soar
v. 升騰,暴漲

escalate
v. 大幅增加,大幅上升

accelerate
v. 加速

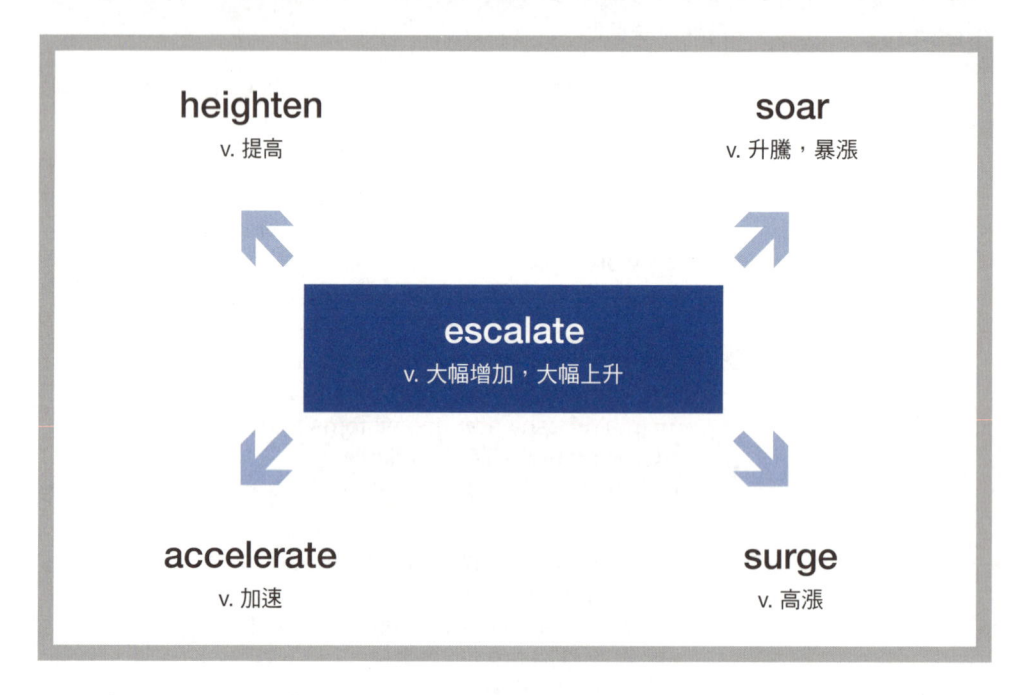

surge
v. 高漲

escalate
/ˈɛskəleɪt/

As populations grow, industrial, agricultural and individual water demands escalate.
隨著人口成長,工業、農業與個人的用水需求也大幅上升。

heighten
/ˈhʌɪtən/

The site was created in order to heighten global awareness of water conservation.
這個網站是為了提高全球對節約用水的意識而建立的。

accelerate
/əkˈsɛləreɪt/

When population growth accelerates, shortages in food and water worsen as well.
當人口成長加快,食物與水的短缺也會惡化。

soar
/sɔː/

Corn prices are soaring due to a severe drought in the U.S. and Canada.
由於美國和加拿大的嚴重乾旱,玉米價格飆漲。

surge
/səːdʒ/

Public demand for water surged in the industrial area.
在工業區,公眾的用水需求高漲。

USEFUL EXPRESSIONS | 相關實用片語

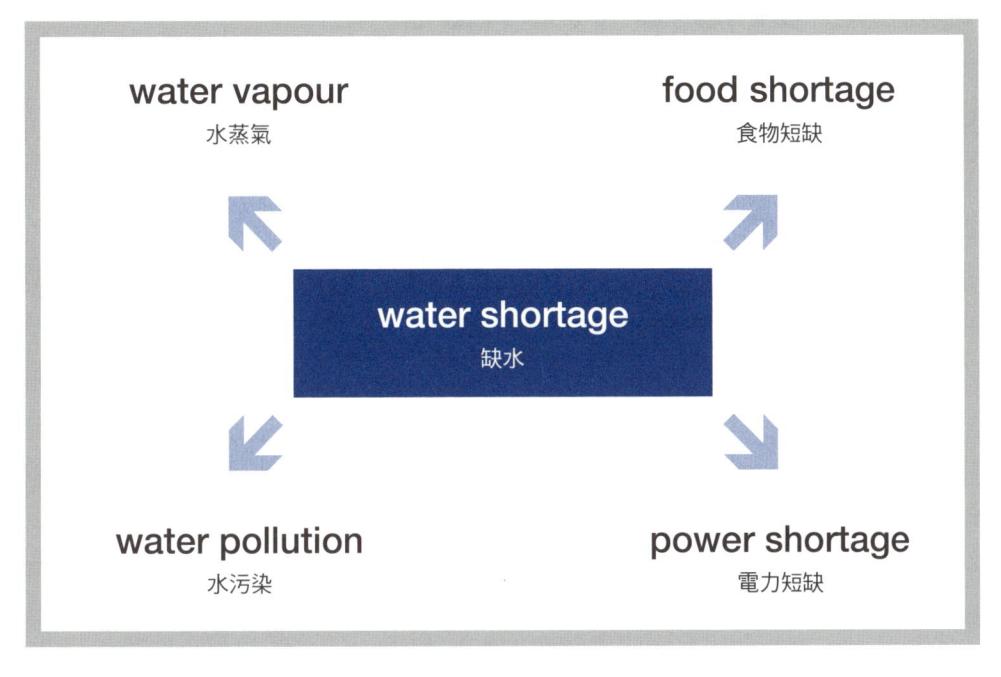

```
           water vapour                    food shortage
           水蒸氣                            食物短缺
                    ↖                   ↗
                        ┌─────────────┐
                        │water shortage│
                        │    缺水      │
                        └─────────────┘
                    ↙                   ↘
           water pollution                power shortage
           水污染                          電力短缺
```

water shortage
/ˈwɔːtə ˈʃɔːtɪdʒ/

It seems that billions of people will face water shortages if we maintain our current water consumption rate.
如果我們目前的耗水速度持續下去,數十億人看起來即將面臨缺水。

water vapour
/ˈwɔːtə ˈveɪpə/

The abundance of water vapour and sulphur in the sky might lead to sulphuric acid rain.
天空中豐富的水蒸氣和硫,可能導致硫酸雨。

water pollution
/ˈwɔːtə pəˈluːʃən/

Environmentalists suggest that most water pollution issues are a result of intense urbanisation along rivers.
環保人士暗示,大部分水污染問題是河流沿岸大幅都市化的結果。

food shortage
/fuːd ˈʃɔːtɪdʒ/

Since so many nations currently face food shortages, we should curtail the use of corn for fuel.
因為有這麼多國家正面臨食物短缺,所以我們應該減少將玉米作為燃料使用。

power shortage
/ˈpaʊə ˈʃɔːtɪdʒ/

Due to lack of coal that is responsible for the shutting down of power plants, the North is experiencing intermittent power shortages.
由於煤炭缺乏造成發電廠關閉,北部正遭遇到間歇性的電力短缺。

SUN

IELTS **BASIC WORDS**

growth /grəʊθ/ n. 成長
ENG. a progression from simpler to more complex forms; increase in size, number, value or strength
SYS. evolution, development

> The **growth** in the number of births of endangered species shows how well we protect the environment.
> 瀕危物種的出生數成長，顯示我們保護環境的成效有多好。

同義語 例句
The **process of development** of environmental protection laws must speed up, especially because certain animal species are at risk of extinction.
環保法規的發展過程必須加快，尤其是因為某些動物物種有滅絕的危機。

同義語 例句
The **gradual maturity** of the human race is indicated by their initiative and concern to protect their environment.
人類的逐漸成熟，顯現在保護環境的計畫與關注上。

反義語 例句
We must disrupt the **status quo** and reduce pollutants in the atmosphere.
我們必須打破現狀，並且減少大氣中的污染物。

payment /ˈpeɪmənt/ n. 支付，償還
ENG. a sum of money paid; compensation; the transfer of wealth from one party to another
SYS. wage, remuneration

> Our **payment** for being careless about our environment all these years are the calamities we suffer today.
> 我們這些年來輕忽環境所付出的代價，就是今日遭受的災難。

同義語 例句
The **money offered** will go a long way in helping the legislation of environmental protection.
這筆被提供的錢將可以持久協助環境保護立法。

同義語 例句
The **act of paying money** to get rid of environmental protection laws is considered bribery. 付錢擺脫環保法規的行為，被認為是賄賂。

反義語 例句
The illegal logger's **failure to pay** his fine as stated in the environmental protection law caused his imprisonment.
違法的伐木者沒有付出環保法規中規定的罰款，使他進了監獄。

WEEK 1 TOPIC **ENVIRONMENT**

▶基礎單字擴充

completion /kəmˈpliːʃn/　n. 完成
ENG. the act of completing or the state of being completed
SYS. attainment, accomplishment

> The **completion** of the environmental protection project called for an early celebration among the volunteers.
> 環保計畫的完成,讓志工準備提早慶祝。

同義語例句　The **act of finalizing** the environmental protection law expressed the president's willingness to step up in nature preservation.
定下環保法規的舉動,顯示出總統促進自然保護的意願。

同義語例句　The environmental protection project's **coming to fruition** delighted the environmentalist.
環境保護計畫的實現,讓那位環保人士感到高興。

反義語例句　The environmentalists' **failure to finish** the nature protection programme on time caused public disappointment.
環保人士無法準時完成自然保護計畫,造成了大眾的失望。

subject /ˈsʌbdʒɛkt/　n. 對象;主題
ENG. a person who is subjected to experimental or other observational procedures; someone who is an object of investigation
SYS. content, respondent

> The **subjects** interviewed about their opinion on the environmental protection law were left anonymous for the protection of their privacy.
> 為了保障隱私,被詢問對環保法規的意見的受訪者保持匿名。

同義語例句　The **person depicted** in the newspaper article was allegedly breaking the environmental protection law.
報紙報導中描寫的那個人,據說違反了環境保護法。

同義語例句　**The object of the study** was to find out if the endangered species is protected by the environmental protection law.
研究的目的是確認瀕危物種是否受到環境保護法的保護。

反義語例句　The endangered species was **not the only focus of study** in the latest research.　瀕危物種不是最近的研究裡唯一的重點。

TOPIC: Laws to protect the environment
保護環境的法律

Things are a lot better now for the environment than they were in decades past, almost exclusively thanks to the extensive **implementation** of a series of powerful environmental laws. There's no better way to get businesses to pollute less, to safely **dispose** of waste or to protect animal populations from their operations. There's simply no **market** incentive for businesses to do so; on the contrary, it's usually cheaper for businesses to choose not to operate in an environmentally conscious manner. This is why environmental laws should be upheld. Although environmental **regulations** have made some headway towards **decontaminating toxins** in the environment, monitoring air quality and protecting endangered species since they were introduced, there is still much room for improvement. As more **complex pollutants** threaten to **devastate** our ecosystem, it is likely that these laws will have to be vastly improved and **amended** in order to continue to provide protection to the environment and to public health.

TRANS

跟數十年前相比，現在的環境狀況已經改善許多，這幾乎都要歸功於一系列強力環保法規的廣泛實施。沒有更好的方法能讓企業減少污染、安全地處理廢棄物、保護動物族群不受它們的運作影響。完全沒有市場利益讓企業這麼做；相反的，選擇不以意識到環保的方式營運，對企業來說通常比較省錢。這就是環保法規應該受到維護的原因。雖然環保規定獲得採用後，已經在淨化環境毒素、監測空氣品質、保護瀕危物種方面取得了一些進展，但還有很多改進的空間。隨著更多複雜的污染物質產生破壞生態系統的威脅，很有可能必須大幅改善並修訂這些法律，以持續為環境與公眾健康提供保護。

implementation
/ˌɪmplɪmɛnˈteɪʃən/

n. 實行，實施

After the **implementation** of new rules, fewer players were injured.
在新規則實施後，比較少球員受傷了。

dispose
/dɪˈspoʊz/

v. 處置，處理

She must **dispose** of her old running shoes before I buy her new ones.　在我買新鞋給她之前，她必須先處理掉她的舊跑鞋。

market
/ˈmɑːkɪt/

n. 市場

More extensive **market** research was carried out to gauge consumer reactions.
為了衡量消費者的反應，進行了更廣泛的市場調查。

regulation
/ˌrɛɡjʊˈleɪʃən/

n. 規定

Courtroom **regulations** state that the room must be quiet during trials.
法庭規定表明，審判時法庭內必須保持安靜。

decontaminate
/ˌdiːkənˈtæmɪneɪt/

v. 消除…的污染，淨化

Disinfectants have been recommended for **decontaminating** hospital beds after use.
消毒劑被推薦用來消毒使用後的病床。

toxin
/ˈtɒksɪn/

n. 毒素

Toxins are secreted from the animal's saliva to help it stun its prey.　這種動物的唾液中分泌出毒素，幫助牠迷昏獵物。

complex
/ˈkɒmplɛks/

adj. 複雜的

The situation became more **complex** when an investigation was underway.　在調查進行途中，情況變得更複雜了。

pollutant
/pəˈljuːtənt/

n. 污染物

Not only do hybrid vehicles use less gas, they also emit fewer **pollutants**.
混合動力車不止用的油比較少，而且排出的污染物也比較少。

devastate
/ˈdɛvəsteɪt/

v. 毀壞，破壞

We don't have to **devastate** the planet to heat and cool our homes and workplaces.
我們不必（可以避免）為了讓家中和工作場所變得溫暖或涼爽而破壞地球。

amend
/əˈmɛnd/

v. 修訂，修改

In an effort to speed the process, the government will include **amended** documents.
為了加速進行的過程，政府將附上修訂過的文件。

WORD TRAINING | 重點單字造句練習

erosion
/ɪˈroʊʒən/

n. 侵蝕

💬 We have planted willow trees along the banks of the river to provide additional erosion protection.
我們在河的兩岸種植了柳樹，以提供額外的防止侵蝕保護。

The erosion of the mountainside tainted the once beautiful landscape, causing new building laws to be established.
山坡的侵蝕玷污了一度美麗的景色，促成了新建築法規的制定。

✏️ In order to protect the natural beauty of the seaside landscape, new building laws were introduced in an effort to reduce erosion as a result of ocean salt winds.
為了保護海濱景觀的自然美，採用了新的建築法規，以減少海邊帶有鹽分的風造成的侵蝕。

Erosion through deflation, the removal of loose materials, is being monitored by desert policy makers.
風的吹蝕，也就是帶走疏鬆物質的現象，所造成的侵蝕受到了沙漠政策制定者的監控。

biohazard
/ˈbʌɪoʊˌhæzəd/

n. 生物性危害

💬 In order to protect this city, we must enact laws which safeguard against biohazards.
為了保護這個城市，我們必須立法防範生物危害。

Clean-up companies have to comply with the biohazard clean-up procedures in medical facilities.
清潔公司在醫療機構中必須遵守生物性危害物質的清理程序。

✏️ Waste generated from veterinarian, agricultural and animal livestock management practices on a farm or ranch can be a biohazard and therefore must be regulated.
農場或牧場中因為獸醫、農業、牲畜管理行為而產生的廢棄物，可能造成生物性危害，所以必須受到管制。

Regulations on biohazard clean-up are set by several different departments that govern not only the public's health and safety but also protect the environment from contamination.
生物性危害物質清理的法律，是由幾個不同部門設立的，這些部門不止管轄大眾的健康與安全，也保護環境免於污染。

radioactive
/ˌreɪdɪəʊˈæktɪv/

adj. 放射性的

💬 We must develop standards for our protection from off-site releases of radioactive material in repositories.
我們必須制定標準,保護我們自己不受到釋放到儲藏廠外的放射性物質的危害。

The government has established a licensing system for the disposal of radioactive materials
政府已經建立放射性物質處理的核准許可制度。

✏️ We support the use of deep geologic repositories for the safe storage of radioactive waste, so we have set forth a proposal for new laws which would ensure this occurs.
我們支持使用地底深處的儲藏處所,安全存放放射性廢料,所以我們提出了能確保事情如此進行的新法律提案。

These laws limit releases of radioactive materials to the environment and notify future generations of the location and content of any disposal facilities.
這些法律限制放射性物質釋放到環境中的量,並且告知後代子孫所有處理設施的地點與內容物。

irreparable
/ɪˈrɛpərəbəl/

adj. 無法修復的,無法彌補的

💬 The government should fund researchers that may potentially save the area from irreparable damage.
政府應該資助可能把地區從無法彌補的損失中拯救出來的研究者。

Most human activities bring irreparable damage to the environment.
大部分的人類活動會對環境造成無法彌補的傷害。

✏️ The destructive storm left irreparable damage to the region, especially the little beach where big waves engulfed the whole area.
破壞性的風暴對這個地區留下無法彌補的損害,尤其是被巨浪完全吞沒的小海灘。

The dominance of fossil fuels have caused irreparable damage to the environment, people's health and communities around the world.
化石燃料的優勢地位對環境、人類健康與世界各地的社會造成了無法彌補的傷害。

RELATED WORDS | 相關單字延伸

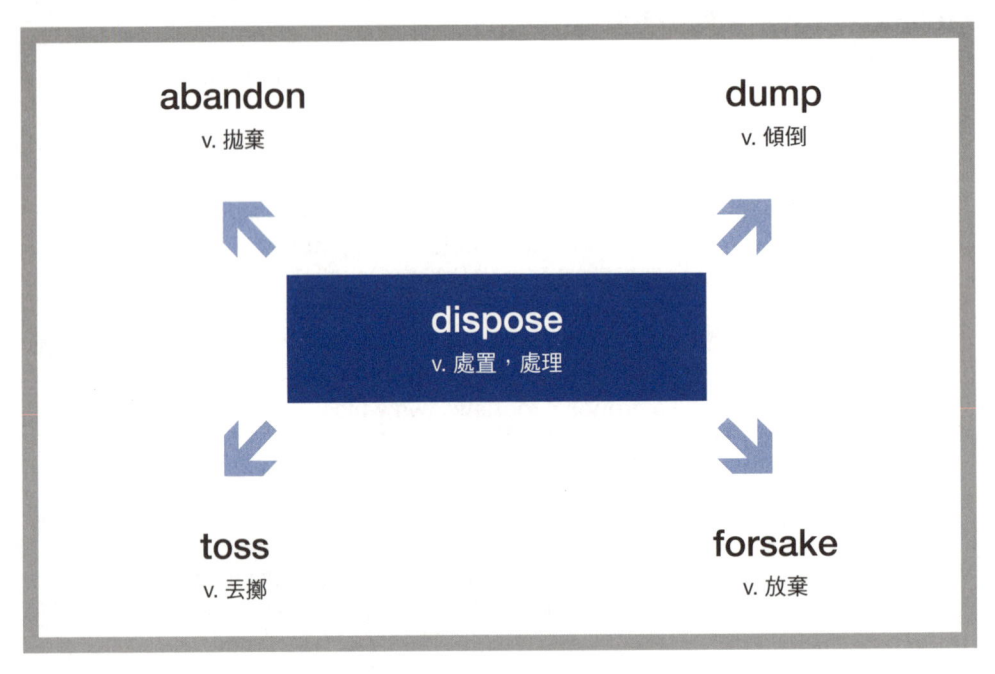

abandon
v. 拋棄

dump
v. 傾倒

dispose
v. 處置，處理

toss
v. 丟擲

forsake
v. 放棄

dispose
/dɪˈspoʊz/

Unfortunately, there's no good way to get businesses to pollute less or to safely dispose of waste.
遺憾的是，沒有好的方法能讓企業減少污染並且安全地處理廢棄物。

abandon
/əˈbændən/

The company must abandon its original waste removal policy and start recycling.
公司必須放棄原本的廢棄物清除政策，並且開始進行回收。

toss
/tɒs/

If we would toss our cans and bottles in the recycling bin, we would pollute less.
如果我們把瓶罐丟到回收筒，就可以減少污染。

dump
/dʌmp/

That manufacturer must dump its industrial waste properly to comply with environmental laws.
那家製造業者必須適當地傾倒工業廢棄物以遵守環保法規。

forsake
/fəˈseɪk/

My boss decided to forsake his principles and sell the offices.
我的老闆決定放棄他的原則，出售辦公室。

USEFUL EXPRESSIONS | 相關實用片語

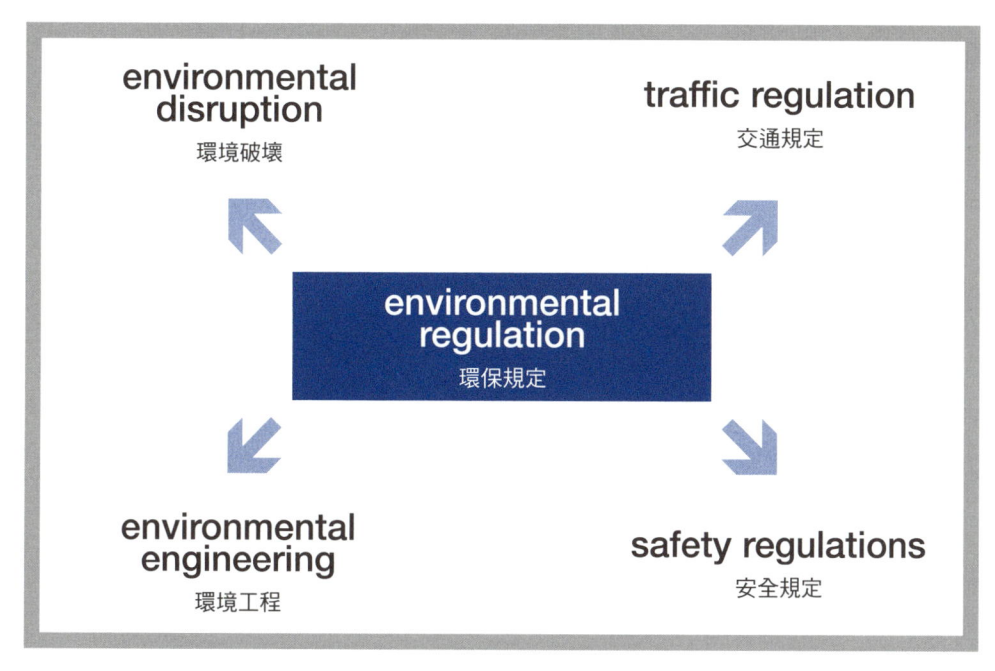

```
environmental disruption          traffic regulation
環境破壞                            交通規定
              ↖            ↗
              environmental regulation
              環保規定
              ↙            ↘
environmental engineering        safety regulations
環境工程                           安全規定
```

environmental regulation
/ɪnvʌɪrənˈmɛntəl rɛgjʊˈleɪʃən/

Carmakers now face environmental regulations worldwide, which can potentially affect sales overseas.
汽車製造商現在在世界各地都面對環保法規,這可能會影響到海外銷售額。

environmental disruption
/ɪnvʌɪrənˈmɛntəl dɪsˈrʌpʃn/

Though environmental disruption is inevitable, the policy to maximise economic strength will proceed as planned.
雖然環境破壞無法避免,但全力擴大經濟力量的政策將依計畫進行。

environmental engineering
/ɪnvʌɪrənˈmɛntəl ɛndʒɪˈnɪərɪŋ/

To get the job, applicants must show experience in environmental engineering or management.
要獲得錄用,應徵者必須展現在環境工程或管理方面的經驗。

traffic regulation
/ˈtrafɪk rɛgjʊˈleɪʃən/

It is every driver's responsibility to follow traffic regulations.
遵守交通規定是每位駕駛人的責任。

safety regulation
/ˈseɪfti rɛgjʊˈleɪʃən/

All work performed onsite must comply with the safety regulations created by the committee last week.
在現場進行的所有工作,都必須遵守委員會上週建立的安全規定。

WEEK 2
EDUCATION

教師的角色

在國外留學

參加團隊比賽

職業學校

給孩子大量的玩具

傳統與現代教育體系

處罰

MON

IELTS BASIC WORDS

aim /eɪm/ n. 目標
ENG. target; the goal intended to be attained
SYS. intent, purpose

> The teacher's **aim** is to prevent students from being left behind.
> 老師的目標是避免有學生落後。

同義語 例句 — The teacher's **objective** is to inform the students of the cause and effect of not finishing their studies.
老師的目標是告知學生沒有完成學習的原因和影響。

同義語 例句 — We hope that the **target result** of the education seminar will be realised.
我們希望教育研討會的目標結果能夠被實現。

反義語 例句 — The teacher's **lack of purpose** made it difficult to encourage students to finish their studies.
那位老師缺乏教學目的，結果就很難鼓勵學生完成學習。

continue /kənˈtɪnjuː/ v. 繼續
ENG. proceed; move ahead; travel onward in space and time
SYS. proceed, uphold

> The teacher asked her students to **continue** their hard work and dedication in searching for solutions to global problems.
> 這位老師要求學生繼續努力並且投入探尋解決全球問題的方法。

同義語 例句 — The teacher admired the students who **carry on** with their positivity and initiative in raising awareness on global problems.
這位老師很欣賞那些對於提高全球問題意識保持積極與主動的學生。

同義語 例句 — The teacher advised the students to **keep up** the good work in finding ways to solve global problems.
這位老師建議學生繼續保持在找尋全球問題解決方法時的良好表現。

反義語 例句 — The students **gave up** their research because they were not getting enough support from their teacher.
這些學生放棄了他們的研究，因為他們沒有獲得老師足夠的支持。

WEEK 2 TOPIC **EDUCATION**

▶基礎單字擴充

punishment /ˈpʌnɪʃmənt/ n. 處罰
ENG. the act of punishing; imposed penalty
SYS. retribution, sanction

> The teacher's **punishment** for misbehaving students was giving them extra work after school.
> 老師對不守規矩的學生的處罰，是給他們額外的課後作業。

同義語例句 The teacher's **rough treatment** towards her misbehaving students caused her suspension.
這位老師對不守規矩學生的粗暴對待，使得她被停職。

同義語例句 The teacher's **discipline** aims to scare most of the students to get them to behave in class.
這位老師的懲罰，目的在於讓大部分的學生感到恐懼，好讓他們在課堂上守規矩。

反義語例句 The students' **reward** for organizing their classroom without being told is getting longer breaks.
學生不須告知就自動整理教室的回報，是得到更長的下課時間。

positive /ˈpɒzɪtɪv/ adj. 正面的，積極的
ENG. constructive or optimistic
SYS. affirmative, constructive

> A **positive** comment from the teacher will leave in her student's heart forever.
> 老師的正面評語會永遠留在她學生的心中。

同義語例句 A teacher's compliments bring **favourable effects** in her students' lives as they grow up.
老師的稱讚會在成長過程中為學生的人生帶來有利的影響。

同義語例句 A teacher's mind and body must be in **good condition** to successfully mentor a student in a positive way.
老師的身心必須保持良好的狀態，才能用正面積極的方式成功地教導學生。

反義語例句 The teacher's **negative** disposition made her students dislike her.
這位老師負面的性情，使得她的學生不喜歡她。

71

MON

TOPIC: The role of a teacher
教師的角色

    Traditionally, teaching was a combination of information **dispensing**, **custodial** child care and sorting out **academically inclined** students from others. Teachers were told what, when and how to teach. They were required to educate every student in exactly the same way and were not held responsible when many failed to learn. Many teachers today, however, are encouraged to adapt and adopt new **practices** that acknowledge both the art and science of learning. They understand that the essence of education is a close relationship between a knowledgeable, caring adult and a secure, **motivated** child. They grasp that their most important role is to get to know each student as an individual in order to comprehend his or her unique needs, learning style, social and cultural background, interests and abilities. Their job is to **counsel** the little **scholars** as they grow and mature, helping them **integrate** their social, emotional and intellectual growth. Teachers have found they accomplish more if they adopt the role of educational guides, **facilitators** and co-learners.

TRANS

    傳統上，教學結合了資訊的提供、兒童監護，以及找出有學術傾向的學生。以前教師被告知應該教什麼、何時教、怎麼教。他們被要求用完全相同的方法教育每個學生，即使許多學生學習失敗時也不需要負責。然而，今日許多教師被鼓勵適應並採用認同學習的藝術與學習的科學的新方式。教師們明白教育的本質，就是有知識、有愛心的成人和安心、積極主動的孩童之間的親密關係。他們了解，自己最重要的角色是把每個學生當成獨立的個體來認識，以理解每個人的獨特需求、學習風格、社會文化背景、興趣和能力。教師的工作是在小小學者們成長與成熟的過程中給他們建議，以幫助他們整合社交、情緒與智力的發展。教師們發現，如果他們扮演教育指導者、促進者和共同學習者的角色，就能達到更多成果。

dispense
/dɪˈspɛns/
v. 配藥，分配
Pharmacists are not allowed to **dispense** certain medications without a doctor's prescription.
如果沒有醫師的處方箋，藥師就不可以配特定的藥物。

custodial
/kʌˈstəʊdɪəl/
adj. 監護的，看守的
There has been a role shift from grandparents as babysitters to **custodial** adults.
祖父母的角色已經從保姆轉變為有監護權的成人。

academically
/akəˈdɛmɪkli/
adv. 學術上，學業上
My son is doing well **academically**, but he struggles socially at school.
我兒子學業上表現很好，但在學校的社交方面很辛苦。

inclined
/ɪnˈklʌɪnd/
adv. 傾向於做什麼的
I noticed that young boys are often **inclined** to fight with each other.　我注意到年輕的男孩子經常有打架的傾向。

practice
/ˈpraktɪs/
n. 實踐，習慣
It is hard for people to put bad **practices** and ideas behind them to learn new techniques.
人很難放下不好的習慣和想法並學習新的技術。

motivated
/ˈməʊtɪveɪtɪd/
adj. 有做什麼的動機的
Mr. Kim was not **motivated** to clear his desk after he had been fired.　Kim 先生被開除後沒有動力清理他的桌面。

counsel
/ˈkaʊnsəl/
v. 建議，勸告
To **counsel** an employee for a performance issue, you need to be direct.
對員工提出關於工作表現的建議時，你的表達要很直接。

scholar
/ˈskɒlə/
n. 學者
Good students can become true **scholars** if they study diligently every day.
如果每天認真唸書的話，好學生就可以成為真正的學者。

integrate
/ˈɪntɪgreɪt/
v. 整合
I tried to **integrate** a French lesson into my History lesson on Napoleon.　我試著把法語課融入關於拿破崙的歷史課。

facilitator
/fəˈsɪlɪteɪtə/
n. 促進者，（研討會等等的）主持人
The **facilitator** of the presentation was just standing with his hands in his pockets!
這場簡報的主持人就只是雙手插口袋站著！

WORD TRAINING | 重點單字造句練習

instruction
/ɪnˈstrʌkʃən/

n. 教學，講授

The role of a teacher in literature-based instruction is a decision maker and mentor.
在以文獻為主的教學裡，教師的角色是決策者和指導者。

Many teachers abandoned lecture-based teaching in favour of instruction that challenges students to learn actively.
許多教師放棄了以講課為主的教法，而改用刺激學生主動學習的教學方式。

Teachers of vocational schools may provide instruction in literacy, numeracy, craftsmanship or vocational training, the arts, religion, civics, community roles and life skills.
職業學校的教師可以提供讀寫、計算、工藝或職業訓練、藝術、宗教、公民、社會角色與生活技能等方面的教學。

Montessori education centres on the preparation and organisation of learning materials to meet the needs and interests of the children rather than focusing on pedagogical instruction.
蒙特梭利教育著重於準備並組織學習材料，以符合兒童的需求及興趣，而不是把重點放在依循教學法的講授上。

coach
/kəʊtʃ/

n. 教練，指導者　v. 訓練，指導

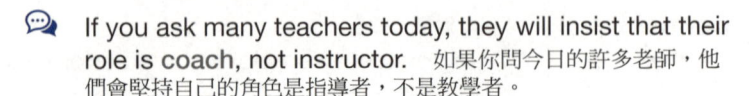

If you ask many teachers today, they will insist that their role is coach, not instructor.　如果你問今日的許多老師，他們會堅持自己的角色是指導者，不是教學者。

If teachers spent more time helping coach their students rather than berating them, the teacher's role would be stronger.　如果老師花更多時間幫助指導學生，而不是訓斥學生，教師的角色就會更有力。

A teacher-coach helps mentor new teachers by giving them ongoing guidance on areas of lesson planning, classroom management and classroom organisation.
教師指導員藉由提供課程規畫、班級經營與班級組織等領域持續的指導，來幫助指導新進的教師。

Just like a sports coach, a teacher must comfort and encourage his or her students when they are not doing well academically.　就像運動教練一樣，老師必須在學生課業表現不好時給予安慰並加以鼓勵。

74

severe
/sɪˈvɪə/

adj. 嚴重的，嚴格的

💬 The teacher implemented severe punishment for students who were not wearing their uniform properly.
老師對於沒有正確穿著制服的學生進行了嚴厲的懲罰。

Severe sanctions might turn children into angry and resentful adults.
嚴厲的懲罰可能會把孩子變成憤怒又怨恨的成人。

✍ Because of their specific learning needs, students with moderate to severe cognitive disabilities require special education and attention.
因為有特殊的學習需求，所以有中度到重度認知障礙的學生，需要特殊的教育和關注。

Education is very critical especially to those with severe disabilities because these children have distinctive needs and diverse styles when it comes to learning.
教育對於重度障礙者尤其重要，因為這些孩子在學習方面有獨特的需求和各自不同的學習風格。

didactic
/dɪˈdæktɪk/

adj. 說教的

💬 In England, didactic delivery of lectures amongst teachers is prevalent.
在英格蘭，說教式的講課方法在教師間很普遍。

The didactic approach is a fundamental problem that many educators resist to change.
說教的教育方式是許多教育者拒絕改變的一個根本問題。

✍ Didactic teachers are often referred to as lazy because they spend the least amount of time on lesson planning.
說教型的老師經常被稱為懶惰，因為他們花最少時間規畫課程。

We know that the teacher is a more didactic role, with the majority of interactions between the teacher and individual learners dominated by the former.
我們知道教師比較偏向說教式的角色，而教師與個別學習者之間的互動，大多由前者主導。

RELATED WORDS | 相關單字延伸

supply
v. 供應

administer
v. 管理

dispense
v. 分配

distribute
v. 分發，分配

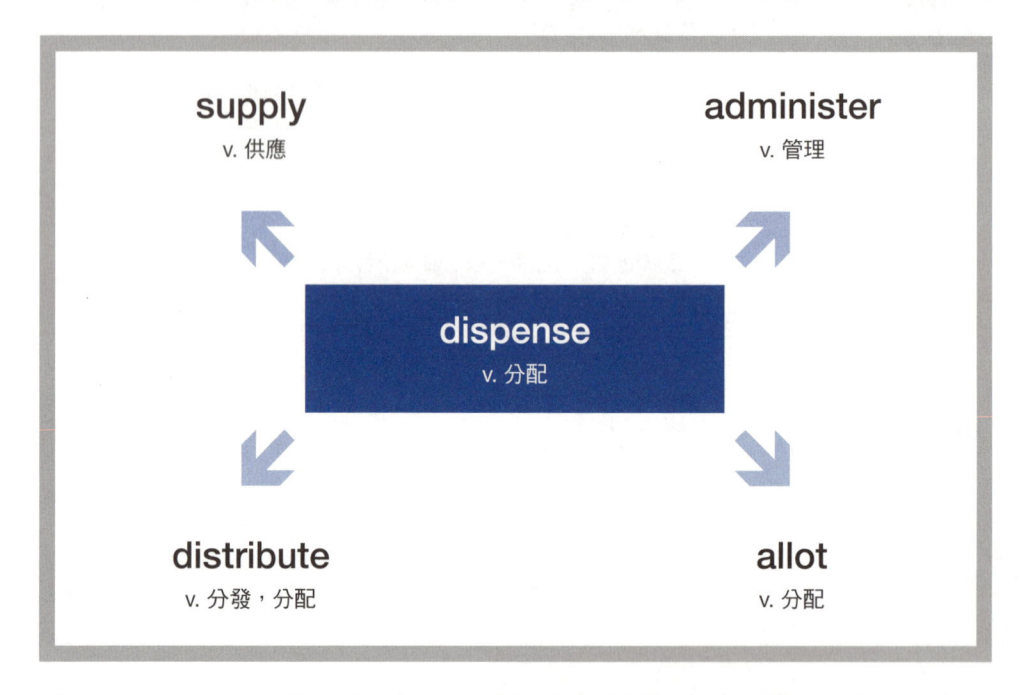

allot
v. 分配

dispense
/dɪˈspɛns/

Teaching is a combination of information-dispensing, custodial child care and sorting out academically inclined students from others.
教學結合了資訊的提供、兒童監護，以及找出有學術傾向的學生。

supply
/səˈplaɪ/

The preschool teacher was supplying all the students' parents with child care contacts.
幼稚園老師提供兒童保育機構的聯絡方式給所有學生的家長。

distribute
/dɪˈstrɪbjuːt/

As the teacher was distributing the test papers, the most academically proficient students smiled with confidence.
老師發下考卷時，課業能力最好的學生有自信地微笑。

administer
/ədˈmɪnɪstə/

The school secretary is in charge of administering child care in the event of an emergency.
學校祕書負責在緊急情形發生時管理兒童照顧。

allot
/əˈlɒt/

Rather than allotting homework to every child, the teacher gave it to one child only.
老師沒有分配作業給每個小孩，而是只給一個小孩作業。

USEFUL EXPRESSIONS | 相關實用片語

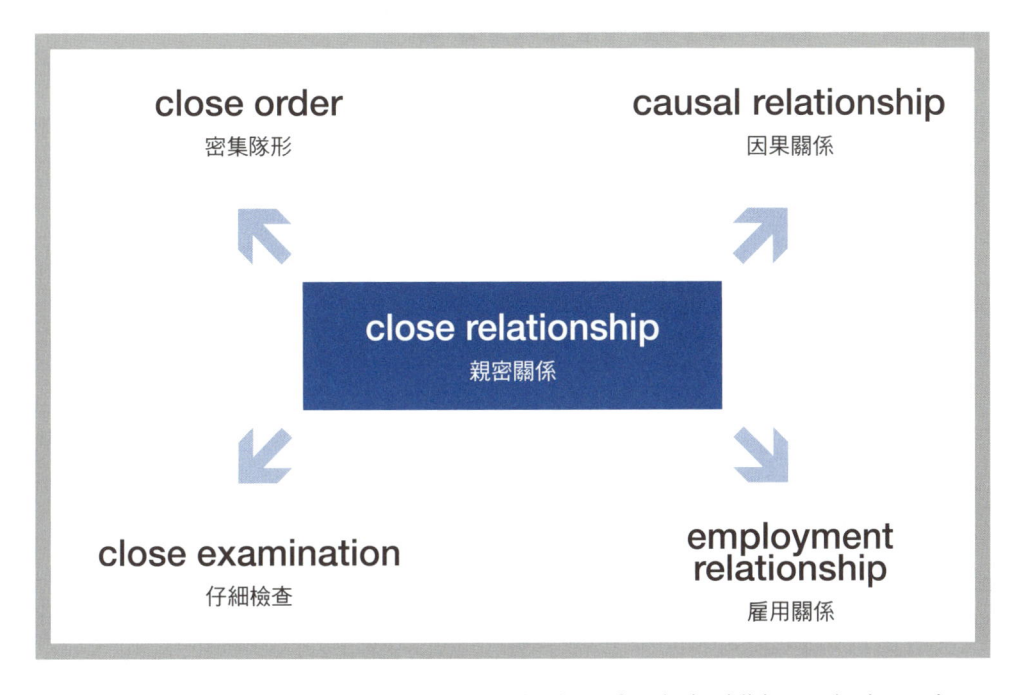

close order
密集隊形

causal relationship
因果關係

close relationship
親密關係

close examination
仔細檢查

employment relationship
雇用關係

---

close relationship
/kləʊs rɪˈleɪʃənʃɪp/
Every parent wants the best for their children, placing value on close relationships, hard work and gentleness.
每個家長都希望給孩子最好的，並且重視親密關係、付出努力與溫柔等方面。

close order
/kləʊs ˈɔːdə/
Army foot soldiers during the Middle Ages fought in close order with pikes and other heavy weapons.
中世紀的陸軍步兵排成密集隊形，手持長矛與其他重型武器戰鬥。

close examination
/kləʊs ɪɡˌzæmɪˈneɪʃən/
Police found nothing, though they performed a close examination of the institute.
雖然警方對那個機構進行了仔細的搜查，但還是什麼也沒有找到。

causal relationship
/ˈkɔːzəl rɪˈleɪʃənʃɪp/
The victim's suicide has a causal relationship with the psychological pressure he received during police interrogation.
受害者的自殺，和他在警方偵訊時受到的心理壓力有因果關係。

employment relationship
/ɪmˈplɔɪmənt rɪˈleɪʃənʃɪp/
Even third party contractors are in an employment relationship with the company.
即使是第三方的承包商，也和公司有雇用關係。

TUE

IELTS **BASIC WORDS**

learn /lɜːn/ v. 學習，認識到
ENG. gain knowledge or skills
SYS. study, acquire

> As foreign students, we should **learn** the importance of healthily adapting to our new environment.
> 身為外籍學生，我們應該學習用健康的方式適應新環境的重要性。

同義語例句 It is imperative to **bear in mind** that when in another country, we should do as the locals do.
身處另一個國家時，我們應該入境隨俗，這一點一定要謹記在心。

同義語例句 Foreign students **become informed** about different cultures as they experience living and studying in other countries.
外籍學生體驗其他國家的生活與學習時，就會知道關於不同文化的事。

反義語例句 Foreign students must keep paying attention to cultural differences, so that the differences do not **slip their mind**.
外籍學生必須持續注意文化差異，以免遺忘這些差異。

instruct /ɪnˈstrʌkt/ v. 指示，指導
ENG. give instructions or directions for some task
SYS. teach, educate

> The teacher will **instruct** foreign students how to register online.
> 老師會指導學生如何線上註冊。

同義語例句 Foreign students must wait for the leader to **give an order** before they start signing up for membership applications.
外籍學生必須等領導人下指示，再開始註冊進行會員申請。

同義語例句 The student assistants helped **familiarise** new foreign students **with the method** of enrolment.
學生輔導人員幫助新入學的外籍學生熟悉註冊的方法。

反義語例句 We can surely **learn from** foreign students why there is a need for some to study in other countries.
我們當然可以從外國學生身上了解為什麼有些人需要在其他國家就學。

WEEK 2 TOPIC **EDUCATION**

▶基礎單字擴充

prior /ˈprʌɪə/ adj. 先前的
ENG. anterior; earlier in time
SYS. former, previous

> There is a prior need for orientation before foreign students can come in for class.
> 外籍學生需要先接受新生訓練才能上課。

同義語例句 In the past years, there was a need for foreign students to take orientation courses before they were taken in.
在過去那些年,外籍學生在被接受之前需要上預備課程。

同義語例句 Foreign students are made to register earlier than the rest to give them time for orientation.
外籍學生被要求比其他人早註冊,讓他們有時間參加新生訓練。

反義語例句 The foreign students are allowed to join their classes right after they finish their orientation.
外籍學生被允許在完成新生訓練後馬上加入自己的班級。

willingness /ˈwɪlɪŋnəs/ n. 意願
ENG. compliance
SYS. eagerness, receptiveness

> His willingness to live alone in another country earned him a scholarship to study abroad.
> 他在其他國家獨自生活的意願,讓他獲得了海外留學獎學金。

同義語例句 His will to relocate made him a perfect candidate for the foreign exchange student programme.
他搬遷的意願,使他成為海外交換學生計畫完美的人選。

同義語例句 His readiness to comply with the requirements of the foreign exchange programme delighted the school administrators.
他準備好要遵守海外交換學生計畫的需求條件,讓學校的行政人員感到高興。

反義語例句 His lack of commitment towards studying abroad resulted in the cancellation of his exchange student scholarship.
他對於海外留學付出的奉獻不夠,造成他的交換學生獎學金被取消。

TUE

TOPIC: Studying in a foreign country
在國外留學

Studying **overseas** brings a range of benefits that one will enjoy long after completing studies. International study **enriches** academic experience through exposure to different teaching styles and environments, a diversity of students, and new places to live and travel. Not only does one experience other cultures, languages and education systems, but also becomes **habituated** to different ways of thinking. Such experience brings lasting benefits for personal growth, self-confidence, **independence** and one's **tolerance** of others. Thousands of students worldwide have studied overseas as part of their **tertiary** education. Many of these students are those who are **sensitive** to the importance of foreign academic credentials to potential employers. Employers, large or small, public or private, are **searching** for people who can contribute to their competitiveness in a globally connected world. And indeed, those who have studied overseas **possess** a great advantage in the workforce. The skills **acquired** through studying overseas are important building blocks for understanding business protocols in other cultures.

TRANS

海外留學會帶來許多好處，這些好處在完成留學很久以後都能夠享用。藉由接觸不同的教學風格與環境、各種各樣的學生，還有新的居住與旅遊環境，國際學習能讓學術經驗變得豐富。留學者不但能夠體驗其他文化、語言和教育體系，還能習慣不同的思考方式。這種經驗能為個人成長、自信、獨立以及對他人的容忍帶來長久的益處。全世界有成千上萬的學生已經在國外留學過，作為大專教育（第三階段教育）的一部分。這些學生中有許多是感受到海外學歷對潛在雇主的重要性的人。不論雇用的機構是大是小、是公家或私人，都在尋找能夠在全球互相連結的世界中對企業競爭力有所貢獻的人。的確，曾經在海外留學的人，在勞動力中擁有很大的優勢。透過海外留學而習得的技能，對於了解其他文化的商業交易規約而言是很重要的基礎。

overseas
/ˌəʊvəˈsiːz/

adv. 在海外，到海外
Would you prefer to go **overseas** by plane or by boat?
你比較喜歡搭飛機還是搭船到海外？

enrich
/ɪnˈrɪtʃ/

v. 使豐富
Your generous donation ensures food for the hungry and **enriches** your sponsor child's life.
您的慷慨捐贈能夠確保飢餓者有食物，也能豐富受資助孩童的生活。

habituated
/həˈbɪtʃʊeɪtɪd/

adj. 習慣了的
Some bears are becoming **habituated** to people and are moving closer to cities.
有些熊漸漸習慣人類，並且遷移到離城市比較近的地方。

independence
/ˌɪndɪˈpɛndəns/

n. 獨立
The project aims to teach women skills that will allow them to achieve financial **independence**.
這個計畫的目的是教婦女能夠達到經濟獨立的技能。

tolerance
/ˈtɒlərəns/

n. 容忍，寬容
The violence seemed so incompatible with Quebec's reputation for **tolerance** and openness.
這樁暴行似乎和魁北克寬容與開放的聲譽不相稱。

tertiary
/ˈtɜːʃəri/

adj. 第三的
In most countries, some form of secondary education is compulsory, but **tertiary** education is voluntary.
在大多數的國家，某種形式的第二階段教育（高中等級教育）是義務性的，但第三階段教育（大專等級教育）是自願性的。

possess
/pəˈzɛs/

v. 擁有
I **possess** both the knowledge and skills to change car tires on my own.
我有獨自更換汽車輪胎的知識和技能。

sensitive
/ˈsɛnsɪtɪv/

adj. 敏感的
Fragile ecosystems are highly **sensitive** to changes in temperature.
脆弱的生態系統對溫度的變化非常敏感。

search
/sɜːtʃ/

v. 搜查，尋找
Chuck **searched** the land, but did not find anyone there.
Chuck 搜索了那片土地，但沒有發現任何人。

acquire
/əˈkwaɪə/

v. 取得，習得（能力）
My sister wants the topaz ring that I **acquired** from my late aunt.
我妹妹想要我從過世的姑姑那邊得到的黃寶石戒指。

WORD TRAINING | 重點單字造句練習

clever
/ˈklɛvɚ/

adj. 聰明的

A clever student is usually one who can think critically.
一個聰明的學生通常是能夠批判性思考的人。

It was clever for the Education Board to add another year in primary school.
教育委員會把小學期間增加一年是明智的。

Some people who appear to be clever are not actually smart because they only know general knowledge which they gathered from quiz shows.
有些人看起來很聰明但其實不然，因為他們只知道看問答節目的時候得到的一般知識。

Nowadays, children are so clever that by the time they go to school, they already know about the lessons the teacher is about to teach them.
現在的小孩很聰明，甚至上學的時候已經知道老師要教的課了。

---

undergraduate
/ˌʌndɚˈgrædʒuət/

n. 尚未取得學位的大學生

Scholarships are offered to undergraduate and graduate students for short- and long-term study in Germany.
獎學金是提供給在德國短期或長期留學的大學生與研究生。

I earned my undergraduate degree while studying overseas in Vancouver.
我在溫哥華留學時，獲得了學士學位。

Opportunities are provided for U.S. undergraduate and graduate students to become more proficient in the cultures and languages of world regions critical to U.S. interests as they study abroad.
機會是提供給在海外留學的美國大學生與研究生，讓他們在國外留學時，更精通對美國利益關係重大的世界區域的文化及語言。

This programme seeks to lower the barriers for financially disadvantaged undergraduates to study abroad by offering scholarships.
這個計畫希望藉由提供獎學金，降低經濟弱勢的大學生到國外留學的門檻。

preparatory
/prɪˈparətəri/

adj. 預備的

💬 Travelling overseas is a great preparatory exercise for understanding new cultures.
到海外旅遊對於了解新的文化而言是很好的預備練習。

The one-year preparatory course is designed for foreign students who intend to study a second language. 這個為期一年的預備課程是為了想學習第二語言的外籍學生設計的。

✏️ Preparatory programmes let students gain the equivalency of a high school diploma, improve their language skills for studying abroad or help them gain access to postgraduate education.
預備課程讓學生獲得相當於高中文憑的學歷、提高海外留學時的語言技能，或者幫助他們獲得學士後教育。

Whether you study overseas or locally, our preparatory programmes help you acquire the skills, knowledge and confidence to continue your education and prepare you for the workplace. 不論你要在海外或國內就學，我們的預備課程都能幫助你獲得技能、知識與自信，讓你的教育能繼續下去，並且讓你對於職場有所準備。

introduction
/ˌɪntrəˈdʌkʃən/

n. 介紹，引進，採用，入門

💬 All of our overseas students will be given a brief introduction to the area.
我們所有的海外學生都會獲得對這個地區的簡單入門介紹。

Studying overseas will give students an introduction into a new language and culture.
海外留學將會帶領學生開始了解新的語言與文化。

✏️ Students who are interested in studying abroad can attend the two-day introduction to learn about what they need to prepare.
有興趣在國外留學的學生，可以參加為期兩天的介紹課程，了解需要準備些什麼。

Prior to the introduction of an International Faculty Exchange Programme, the University and its international partner shall enter into an agreement, which will set forth arrangements to facilitate the exchange.
在開始實施國際交換教授計畫之前，大學與國際伙伴應該先達成協議，協議內容將闡明安排事項以促進交換的進行。

RELATED WORDS | 相關單字延伸

augment
v. 擴大，加強

enhance
v. 提高

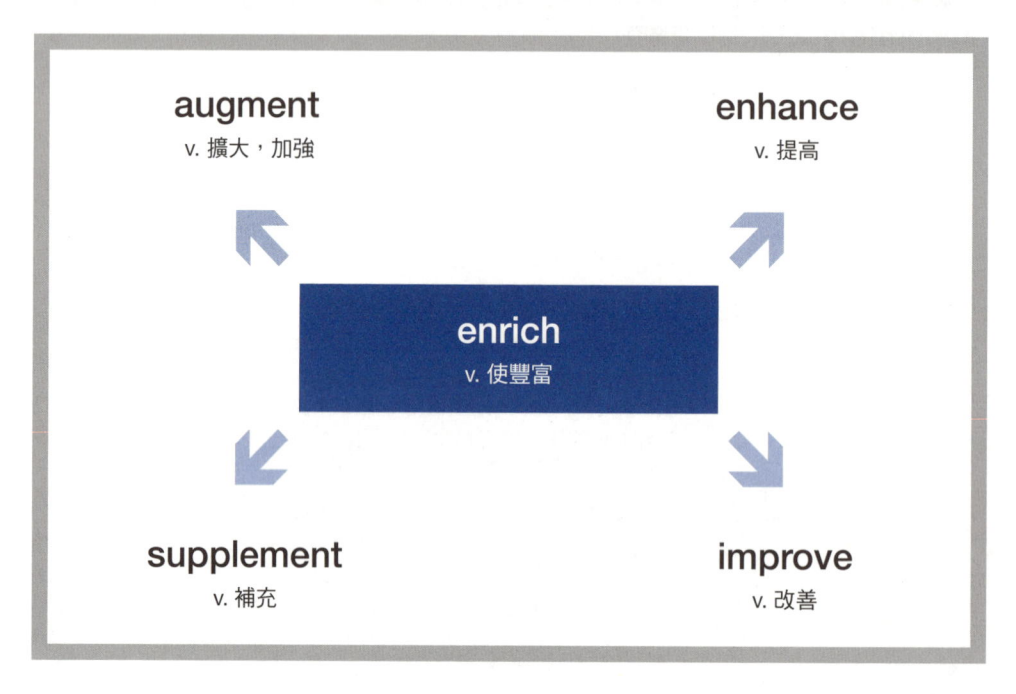

enrich
v. 使豐富

supplement
v. 補充

improve
v. 改善

enrich
/ɪnˈrɪtʃ/

International study enriches academic experience through exposure to different teaching styles and environments, a diversity of students, and new places to live and travel.
藉由接觸不同的教學風格與環境、各種各樣的學生，還有新的居住與旅遊環境，國際學習能讓學術經驗變得豐富。

augment
/ɔːɡˈmɛnt/

Many teachers augment their teaching styles to suit international students.
許多教師加強自己的教學風格，使教學適合國際學生。

supplement
/ˈsʌplɪmənt/

In order to supplement my education, I decided to travel and study internationally.
為了補充我自己的教育，我決定到國外旅遊並且學習。

enhance
/ɪnˈhɑːns/

Having a diversity of students in the classroom enhances the overall environment.
教室裡有各種各樣的學生，能提升整體的（學習）環境。

improve
/ɪmˈpruːv/

I chose to travel to a new country to improve my educational experience.
我選擇到新的國家旅遊，來改善我的教育經驗。

USEFUL EXPRESSIONS | 相關實用片語

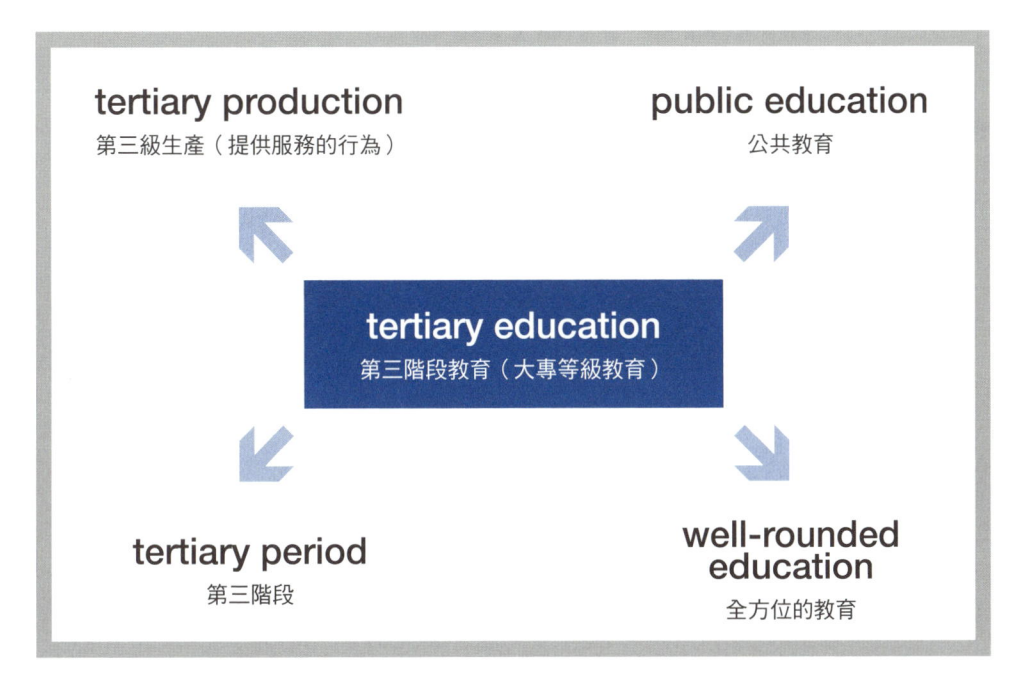

tertiary production
第三級生產（提供服務的行為）

public education
公共教育

tertiary education
第三階段教育（大專等級教育）

tertiary period
第三階段

well-rounded education
全方位的教育

---

tertiary education
/ˈtɚːʃəri ɛdjuˈkeɪʃən/

Many students in the country pursue a tertiary education at the institutions mentioned in the guide.
那個國家有很多學生在指南中提到的教育機構接受第三階段教育。

tertiary production
/ˈtɚːʃəri prəˈdʌkʃən/

In a soda factory, the fluid is mixed, carbonated, and the tertiary production involves transporting.
在汽水工廠中，液體被混合、加入二氧化碳，而第三級生產牽涉到運送。

tertiary period
/ˈtɚːʃəri ˈpɪərɪəd/

During the tertiary period of the experiment, the ants exposed to radiation became dominant.
在實驗的第三階段，接受到輻射線的螞蟻變得佔有優勢。

public education
/ˈpʌblɪk ɛdjuˈkeɪʃən/

After surveying 39 different countries, Germany came out in front as having the best public education system.
調查 39 個不同的國家之後，德國因為擁有最好的公共教育體系而勝出。

well-rounded education
/ˈwɛl ˈraʊndɪd ɛdjuˈkeɪʃən/

Part of getting a well-rounded education is taking classes in subjects outside one's declared major.
得到全方位教育的一部分，就是修習主修以外科目的課程。

WED

IELTS **BASIC WORDS**

significant /sɪgˈnɪfɪkənt/ adj. 重要的，顯著的
ENG. having or expressing a meaning
SYS. vital, substantial

> Each player of a basketball team has a **significant** role in every defence and offense.
> 籃球隊的每個球員，在每次攻防中都有重要的角色。

同義語例句 Even smaller basketball players **have a purpose** in the overall carrying out of game strategies.
即使是個子比較小的籃球員，在整體的比賽策略執行中也都有其作用。

同義語例句 The absence of even one basketball player **has major effect** on the entire game play of the team.
就算只有一名籃球員不在，也會對球隊的整體比賽有重大的影響。

反義語例句 Some players in a team are just **devoid of importance** that their non-participation is barely noticeable.
隊上某些球員就是缺乏重要性，就算沒參加也幾乎不會被注意到。

extinct /ɪkˈstɪŋkt/ adj. 絕種的
ENG. no longer in existence; lost or especially having died out leaving no living representatives
SYS. vanished, obsolete

> It is feared that because of the declining popularity of that sport, athletes with extraordinary abilities will soon be **extinct**.
> 人們擔心因為那種運動的流行程度下降，具有傑出能力的運動員很快會絕跡。

同義語例句 If extraordinary athletes **cease to exist**, sports fanatics would also decrease in number.
如果傑出的運動員不復存在，那麼運動迷的人數也會減少。

同義語例句 Extraordinary athletes like Michael Jordan are **dying out**.
像麥可喬丹一樣的傑出運動員越來越稀少。

反義語例句 Self-made super athletes are now **thriving and surviving** in the sports world.
自行訓練成為超級運動員的人，現在在體育界很興盛而且得以生存。

WEEK 2 TOPIC **EDUCATION**

▶基礎單字擴充

personal /ˈpəːsənəl/ adj. 個人的
ENG. concerning or affecting a particular person or his or her private life and personality
SYS. private, subjective

> My reason for preferring team sports to a solo sport is **personal**.
> 我偏好團體運動勝過個人運動，是出於個人因素。

同義語例句 The motivation to become a diligent team player **takes place within an individual**.
要成為勤勉的隊員，動機是出自於個人的內心。

同義語例句 An athlete's ideas to improve a team's game must not remain **confined to the person**, but shared with his team.
運動員提升團隊比賽的想法，不能限於個人，而應該和隊伍共享。

反義語例句 The athlete's anger towards the position given to him in the play is **not related to any person** in his team.
運動員對自己分配到的位置所感受到的憤怒，和隊上的任何人都無關。

value /ˈvaljuː/ n. 價值
ENG. beliefs of a person or social group on which they have an emotional investment
SYS. ideal, principle

> All players have significant **value** in the team and each plays a special role.
> 所有球員在隊上都有重要的價值，而且每個人都扮演特別的角色。

同義語例句 The unspoken **code of behaviour** when playing a team sport includes allowing performing teammates to be the star player.
團隊運動中不言自明的行為準則，包括讓表現好的隊友成為明星球員。

同義語例句 An athlete's perception of his own **worth** boosts his ego, helping him to perform better.
運動員對自我價值的認識，會強化他的自我，讓他表現得更好。

反義語例句 His **deviance from social norms** of playing fair pushed the coach to kick him out.
他偏離了公平比賽的社會準則，使得教練把他趕出去。

WED

TOPIC: Playing team games
參加團隊比賽

02-3A

Team sports provide children with many **opportunities**. First off, children can develop and strengthen their social skills while playing team sports. Successful participation in these sports requires children to learn how to **cooperate** with their **teammates**, how to follow directions and how to develop friendship. Participation in team sports can also teach children about being 'good sports', which **enables** them to develop the ability to show appreciation and respect for others for their accomplishments and to **empathise** with those who may not be as successful. One of the most important benefits of team sports is teaching children how to cope with **competition** in a healthy way. Other psychological benefits of team sport participation include learning how to solve problems, develop **patience** and **persistence**, and become self-disciplined. Unfortunately, budget restraints and increased **pressure** for academic achievement have forced many schools to eliminate physical education programmes. Since children who **participate** in regular physical activity have reduced risks of diabetes and obesity, we need to provide children with more opportunities to be physically active.

TRANS

團隊運動提供孩童許多機會。首先，孩子們能夠在進行團隊運動時培養並增強社交技能。要成功參與這些運動，孩童需要學習如何與隊友合作、如何遵守指示，以及如何培養友誼。參與團隊運動也能夠教導孩童要有「運動風度」，而有運動風度能夠讓他們培養對他人的成就表達欣賞與尊重的能力，並且同情可能不那麼成功的人。團隊運動最重要的好處之一，是教導孩童如何以健康的方式面對競爭。參與團隊運動在心理層面的其他好處還包括學習如何解決問題、培養耐心與毅力，以及變得自律。遺憾的是，預算限制和學業成就方面升高的壓力，迫使許多學校減少體育課程。由於參與定期體育活動的孩童罹患糖尿病和肥胖的風險會降低，所以我們需要提供孩童更多活動身體的機會。

opportunity
/ˌɒpəˈtjuːnɪti/

n. 機會

You have had several **opportunities** to apologise to me but have yet to do so.
你曾經有過幾次向我道歉的機會，但你還沒有道歉。

cooperate
/kəʊˈɒpəreɪt/

v. 合作

Students must **cooperate** with each other well for group presentations.
為了小組發表，學生必須彼此好好合作。

teammate
/ˈtiːmmeɪt/

n. 隊友

Rather than skating alone, Jenny practised with her **teammates** on Monday.
Jenny 星期一不是獨自溜冰，而是和她的隊友一起練習。

enable
/ɪˈneɪbəl/

v. 使⋯能夠

Money **enables** one to attain higher education abroad.
金錢能夠讓人有獲得海外高等教育的機會。

empathise
/ˈɛmpəθʌɪz/

v. 和⋯有同感，同情

He couldn't **empathise** with Sara's pain because he had never lost a pet before.
他無法對 Sara 的痛苦感同身受，因為他從來沒有失去過寵物。

competition
/ˌkɒmpɪˈtɪʃən/

n. 競爭

Mr. Kim had stiff **competition** at the hotdog-eating contest this year.
金先生今年在吃熱狗比賽中遭遇到激烈的競爭。

patience
/ˈpeɪʃəns/

n. 耐心

It is important to work hard with **patience** for success.
要獲得成功，帶著耐心努力工作是很重要的。

persistence
/pəˈsɪstəns/

n. 毅力

I know that with **persistence**, I will be able to stand up on the surfboard.
我知道只要有毅力，我就能在衝浪板上站起來。

pressure
/ˈprɛʃə/

n. 壓力 v. 施加壓力

I don't want to **pressure** you, but we must leave in five minutes.
我不想給你壓力，但我們必須在五分鐘內離開。

participate
/pɑːˈtɪsɪpeɪt/

v. 參加，參與

You can **participate** in this training programme to learn managerial skills.
你可以參加這個訓練計畫來學習管理技巧。

WORD TRAINING | 重點單字造句練習

cheat
/tʃiːt/

v. 作弊

Nobody likes a team player who cheats in order to win.
沒有人會喜歡為了獲勝而作弊的隊員。

I convinced the volleyball captain not to cheat and to play fairly.
我說服了排球隊長不要在比賽中作弊,要公平比賽。

For some players, losing isn't an option, so instead of trying harder and training longer, they cheat.
對某些選手而言,絕對不可以輸,所以他們不是更加努力、花更多時間訓練,而是作弊。

The coach cheated by falsifying his players' birth certificates so that a 12-year-old can be matched against and easily beat a 10-year-old.
那位教練作弊的方式是偽造選手的出生證明,讓 12 歲的選手可以被安排和 10 歲的選手對抗,並且輕易打敗對方。

upbringing
/ˈʌpbrɪŋɪŋ/

n. 養育,教養

My upbringing was very strict, and I didn't have much time to play sports.
我的家庭教育很嚴格,我也沒有很多時間參加體育活動。

The athlete rose above his tough upbringing and became an excellent player on his football team.
這位運動員克服了他艱難的成長過程,成為了足球隊裡優秀的隊員。

Parents should encourage their children to play sports because this type of upbringing inspires children to stay active for their whole lives.
父母應該鼓勵孩子運動,因為這種教養方式會激勵孩子一輩子保持活躍。

One way parents and community leaders can take an active role in improving the health of our children is to encourage participation in youth sports programmes throughout their upbringing.
在改善孩童健康方面,家長和社區領導者能夠扮演積極角色的方法之一,就是鼓勵孩子在成長過程中參與青少年運動計畫。

drill
/drɪl/

n. 訓練，操練

💬 I was late for football practice, so my coach made me do the drill alone.
我參加足球練習遲到了，所以教練要我自己做訓練。

The drill can also be modified so team players can perform jumpers or three-point shots.
訓練也可以做修改，讓隊員能夠練習跳投或三分球。

✏️ Drills are tedious and boring, but they are essential for improving players' skills.
訓練既冗長又無聊，但對於提升選手的技巧而言是不可或缺的。

Learning the fundamentals is essential to excelling in sports, and coaches often use drills to help players master those fundamentals.
要在運動中勝出，學習基礎是不可或缺的，而教練經常使用訓練來幫助選手精通這些基礎。

hone
/həʊn/

v. 磨練，精進

💬 If you want to hone your basketball skills, you should practise every night.
如果你想磨練你的籃球技巧，你應該每天晚上練習。

Volleyball is a great team sport to play, but many cannot hone their spiking skills.
排球是一項很棒的團隊運動，但是很多人無法精進自己的扣球技術。

✏️ She ran sprints at the track every evening in an attempt to hone her running skills, but in the end it was not enough for her to make the team.
她每天晚上都在跑道上短跑，試圖磨練自己的跑步技巧，但最終還是不足以讓她加入隊伍。

Your child might not be a good leader, but team sports can still hone his or her leadership skills for future use.
你的小孩或許不是好的領導者，但團隊運動仍然可以磨練他的領導技能，以備未來使用。

RELATED WORDS | 相關單字延伸

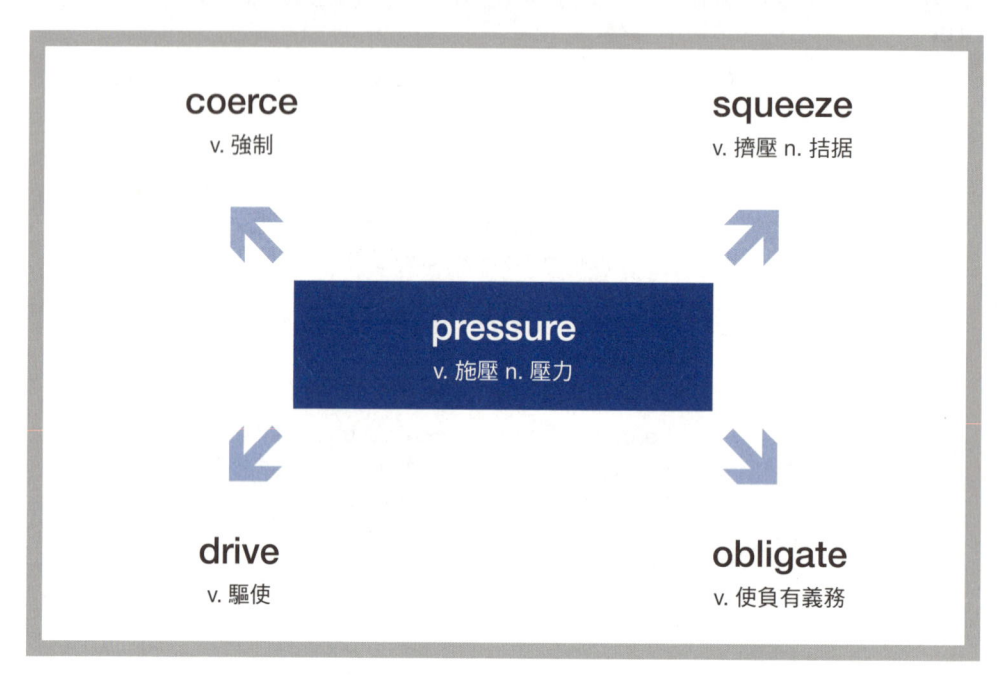

coerce
v. 強制

squeeze
v. 擠壓 n. 拮据

pressure
v. 施壓 n. 壓力

drive
v. 驅使

obligate
v. 使負有義務

pressure
/ˈprɛʃə/

Unfortunately, budget restraints and increased pressure for academic achievement have forced many schools to eliminate physical education programmes.
遺憾的是，預算限制和學業方面升高的壓力，迫使許多學校減少體育課程。

coerce
/kəʊˈɜːs/

The government will coerce schools to end their physical education programmes.
政府將強制學校結束體育課程。

drive
/drʌɪv/

The mischievous boy's classroom pranks such as "frog in the drawer" drive his teachers crazy.
這個淘氣男孩在教室的惡作劇，例如把青蛙放在抽屜裡，讓他的老師們抓狂。

squeeze
/skwiːz/

Schools everywhere have felt the squeeze in their budget and many have had to close.
各地的學校都感受到預算拮据，而許多學校不得不關閉。

obligate
/ˈɒblɪɡət/

Some students feel more obligated to pursue academic achievement than to participate in physical education.
有些學生覺得跟體育比起來，自己更有義務去追求學業成績。

USEFUL EXPRESSIONS | 相關實用片語

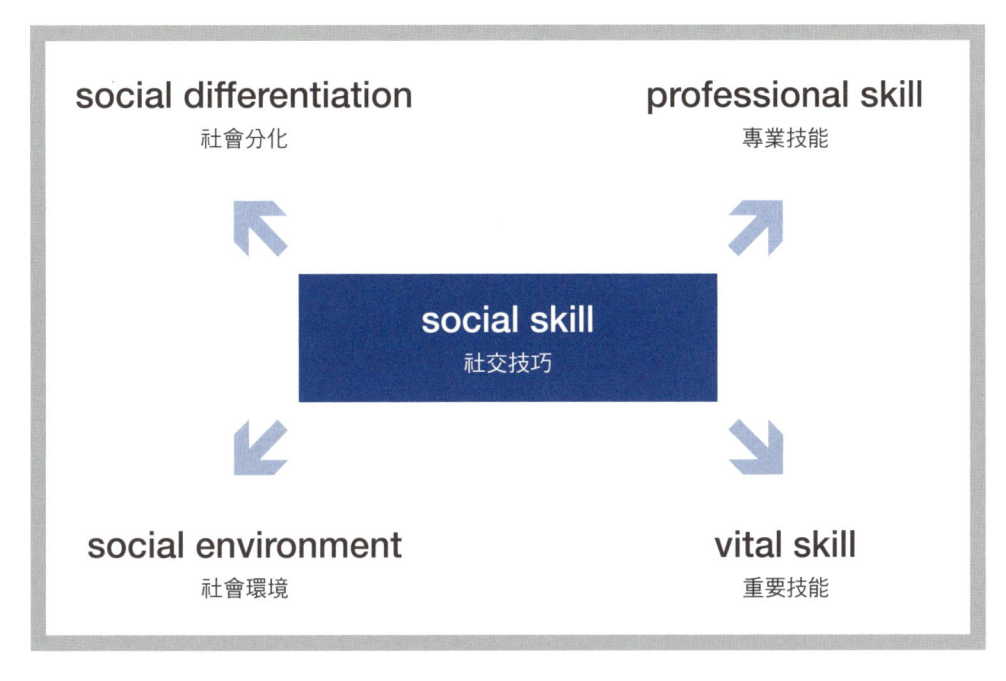

```
social differentiation          professional skill
社會分化                          專業技能
              ↖        ↗
          ┌─────────────────┐
          │  social skill   │
          │   社交技巧       │
          └─────────────────┘
              ↙        ↘
social environment               vital skill
社會環境                          重要技能
```

social skill
/ˈsoʃəl skɪl/

This class is of great interest to many because it focuses on the improvement of social skills.
很多人對這堂課相當有興趣，因為它著重於增進社交技巧。

social differentiation
/ˈsoʃəl ˌdɪfərɛnʃɪˈeʃən/

In the process of social differentiation, members of a society are assigned different roles and functions.
在社會分化的過程中，社會中的成員被分配不同的角色與功能。

social environment
/ˈsoʃəl ɪnˈvaɪrənmənt/

Being part of the same social environment means that many of our opinions are similar.
成為同一個社會環境的一部分，意味著我們有許多意見是類似的。

professional skill
/prəˈfɛʃənəl skɪl/

You must have good professional skills to be hired.
你必須擁有良好的專業技能才能獲得錄用。

vital skill
/ˈvaɪtəl skɪl/

The most vital skill one needs to succeed in life is being able to write well.
要在人生中成功，一個人需要的最重要的技能就是良好的寫作能力。

THU

IELTS **BASIC WORDS**

problem /ˈprɒbləm/ n. 問題
ENG. a question raised for consideration or solution
SYS. trouble, difficulty

> The **problem** with taking up too many academic subjects is that less importance is given to practical lessons.
> 選修太多學術科目的問題，就是實用課程的重要性會減少。

同義語例句 The major **concern to be addressed** in the school is its giving more credits to academic rather than practical subjects.
學校需要處理的主要擔憂，是目前分配比較多學分給學術科目，而不是實用科目。

同義語例句 Another **crisis to be solved** is the lack of practical subjects that can teach students how to solve problems in actual situations.
另一個需要解決的危機，是缺乏能夠教學生如何在實際情況中解決問題的實用科目。

反義語例句 An effective **solution to the situation** is to examine the curriculum carefully to improve the courses offered.
對於這個情況的一個有效解決方式，是仔細檢驗課程，以改善所提供的課程。

pessimistic /ˌpɛsɪˈmɪstɪk/ adj. 悲觀的
ENG. expecting the worst possible outcome
SYS. gloomy, distrustful

> Continuously verbalising **pessimistic** thoughts and ideas is not appropriate while learning.
> 學習時，一直在口頭上表達悲觀的想法和意見是不適當的。

同義語例句 The student took academic subjects **without** much **hope** of actually using what he learns in the real world.
這個學生選修學術科目時，對於在真實世界裡實際運用所學不抱太大希望。

同義語例句 Many university graduates nowadays **take a gloomy view** of their future. 現今許多大學畢業生對未來抱持著悲觀的看法。

反義語例句 Those who took up more practical subjects are expecting the **best results** of applying what they have learned.
選修了比較多的實用科目的人，對於應用自己所學的知識，期待著會有最好的結果。

WEEK 2 TOPIC **EDUCATION**

▶基礎單字擴充

belief /bɪˈliːf/ n. 信念
ENG. any cognitive content held as true
SYS. conviction, philosophy

> My belief is that practical subjects are more useful in our careers and daily life in general.
> 我的信念是,對於職業生涯和日常生活的整體而言,實用科目是比較有用的。

同義語例句 That there is a struggle among students in choosing academic or practical subjects is a fact that has been proven by studies.
學生會掙扎要選擇學術或實用科目,是已經獲得研究證明的事實。

同義語例句 His confidence in having learned practical subjects in depth encourages him to apply his knowledge in his job.
他有自信已經深入學習了實用科目,這份自信也鼓勵他把知識運用在工作中。

反義語例句 The objective opinion that academic subjects are more useful than practical subjects came as a shock to him.
認為學術科目比實用科目有用的反對意見,對他來說是個打擊。

recent /ˈriːsənt/ adj. 最近的
ENG. new; happening a short while ago
SYS. current, fresh

> His recent admission to the university slowly became a regret.
> 他最近進入了那間大學,讓他漸漸感到後悔。

同義語例句 Schools that are up-to-date with current trends are aware that they have to offer more practical subjects than academic ones.
跟得上目前趨勢的學校,知道必須提供比學術科目更多的實用科目。

同義語例句 The curriculum check just occurred in my department, ensuring that there are more practical subjects available than academic ones.
我的系上剛進行了課程審查,確保可選修的實用科目比學術科目多。

反義語例句 The times when curriculums were 90% comprised of academic subjects and only 10% practical subjects have long passed.
課程中 90% 是學術科目、只有 10% 是實用科目的時代早就過去了。

95

TOPIC | Trade schools
職業學校

After graduating from high school, young adults have many opportunities to further their education. While attending university may seem like an obvious step, trade schools also offer paths to future success. A school that can **certify** students to gain **employment** in numerous specific **fields** such as graphic design, culinary arts and massage therapy may make students more employable after graduation. These vocational schools offer practical skills that are trained in a hands-on **authentic** setting similar to the workplace. Employers may even prefer to **hire** individuals who come equipped with the specialised knowledge gained in trade schools over those with **scholastic** theories. While **pursuing** a bachelor's degree at university requires four years, **completing** a trade school may only take two. That being said, trade school graduates may have a hard time finding jobs outside of their specific fields, while multiple career avenues are **obtainable** for university graduates, which is why most students **resolve** to enrol in universities.

TRANS

高中畢業後，青少年有很多機會可以進一步接受教育。雖然上大學看起來可能是顯而易見的一步，但職業學校也提供通往未來成功的道路。能夠讓學生獲得證照，進而在諸如平面設計、烹飪、按摩療法等專門領域獲得工作的學校，可以使學生畢業後更適合受雇。這些職業學校藉由在類似實際職場的實務環境進行訓練，來提供實用的技能。雇主可能會比較想雇用在職業學校習得了專業知識的人，更勝於學習學術理論的人。在大學追求學士學位需要四年，但完成職業學校的學業可能只要兩年。話雖如此，職業學校的學生可能很難找到專業領域之外的工作，而大學畢業生卻有多種職業道路，這也是大部分學生決心要進入大學的理由。

certify
/ˈsɜːtɪfaɪ/

v. 頒發證書給⋯

A medical examiner has to be **certified** as a general practitioner first.
法醫必須先獲得一般開業證明。

employment
/ɪmˈplɔɪmənt/

n. 職業，工作

In order to gain **employment** in Canada, you must get a social insurance number.
要獲得加拿大的工作，你必須取得社會保險號碼。

field
/fiːld/

n. 領域

He chose medicine as his **field** of study to make his parents proud.
他選擇了醫學作為研究領域，好讓父母感到驕傲。

authentic
/ɔːˈθentɪk/

adj. 真正的，道地的

I was not convinced that his apology was truly **authentic** when I saw him smirk.
當我看到他竊笑的時候，我不相信他的道歉是真心的。

hire
/ˈhaɪə/

v. 雇用

The manager will **hire** the best candidate regardless of gender.
經理會雇用最好的人選，無關性別。

scholastic
/skəˈlæstɪk/

adj. 學校的，學術的

She embraced the **scholastic** tradition of her grandparents and entered medical school.
她繼承了祖父母的學術傳統，進入了醫學院。

pursue
/pəˈsjuː/

v. 追求

When **pursuing** a dream, you should believe that your goal is achievable.
在追求夢想的時候，你應該相信你的目標是可以達到的。

complete
/kəmˈpliːt/

v. 完成

After **completing** her seven-page essay, Jane continued studying English for three hours.
寫完七頁的論文後，Jane 繼續讀了三個小時的英文。

obtainable
/əbˈteɪnəbl/

adj. 能獲得的

Wealth and success in business are **obtainable** if you work hard enough.
如果你夠努力的話，你可以獲得商業上的財富與成功。

resolve
/rɪˈzɒlv/

v. 下決心

The parents **resolved** to enrol their kids in a private school.
這對父母決心讓他們的小孩進入私立學校。

WORD TRAINING | 重點單字造句練習

path
/pɑːθ/

n. 道路

💬 One's career path is usually dependent on their interest and educational background.
一個人的職業道路，通常取決於他們的興趣與教育背景。

Education, dedication and hard work are the path to success.
教育、奉獻與勤奮是通往成功的道路。

✏️ Education not only gives us theoretical knowledge but also leads us to the path of self-discovery that will assist us in achieving lasting success.
教育不僅給我們理論性的知識，也引導我們走上自我發現的道路，而這將有助於我們達到持久的成功。

Education plays the most fundamental part in the development of a country because it empowers individuals who will lead their country toward the path of success.
教育在國家發展中扮演最基本的角色，因為它能為即將帶領國家走上成功道路的人賦予力量。

career
/kəˈrɪə/

n. 職業

💬 A person's career choice should depend on his or her interest.
一個人的職業選擇應該取決於他的興趣。

It is best to continuously educate ourselves to advance our career.
我們最好持續接受教育以提升自己的事業。

✏️ Journalism is a career open to talented individuals who are willing to search for the truth at all costs and are eager to share them with others.
新聞這種職業，是開放給有才華、願意不惜一切代價找尋真相並渴望與他人分享的人。

College education is intended to provide students with the appropriate knowledge and skills which are essential for them to jump start and succeed in their chosen career.
大學教育的目的，在於為學生提供必要的適當知識與技能，讓他們在所選擇的職業中奪得先機並且成功。

口說範例 💬　寫作範例 ✍

undertake
/ˌʌndəˈteɪk/

v. 從事，進行

💬 It is very expensive to undertake academic research about certain medical topics.
進行某些醫學主題的研究是非常昂貴的。

Professors are responsible for guiding their students who are undertaking their research.
教授負責指導他們正在進行研究的學生。

✍ When one undertakes a task or job, it means that he or she is accepting the responsibility for it, so it's important to have a clear understanding of the instructions given.
當一個人進行一項任務或工作時，就表示他對這件事負責，所以清楚了解自己接受到的指示是很重要的。

The government officials should undertake collaborative projects with non-profit organisations to improve our education system, and thus allow our youth to attain a brighter future.
政府官員應該與非營利組織進行合作計畫，改善我們的教育體系，讓我們的年輕人擁有更光明的未來。

complicate
/ˈkɒmplɪkeɪt/

v. 使複雜

💬 Her solution for the math problem seemed to complicate it even more.
她對那道數學題目的解法似乎把它變得更複雜了。

The problem with my car was complicated by its faulty engine.
我車子的問題因為引擎故障變得更複雜了。

✍ The teacher should help the students improve their critical thinking and problem solving skills by complicating problems and questions that are usually easy to answer.
老師應該藉著把平常容易回答的問題複雜化，來幫助學生增進批判性思考與解決問題的能力。

Public archaeology is complicated, and I greatly appreciate those scholars who dedicate their time doing research on it.
公眾考古學很複雜，而我很感謝奉獻自己的時間研究它的學者。

RELATED WORDS ｜ 相關單字延伸

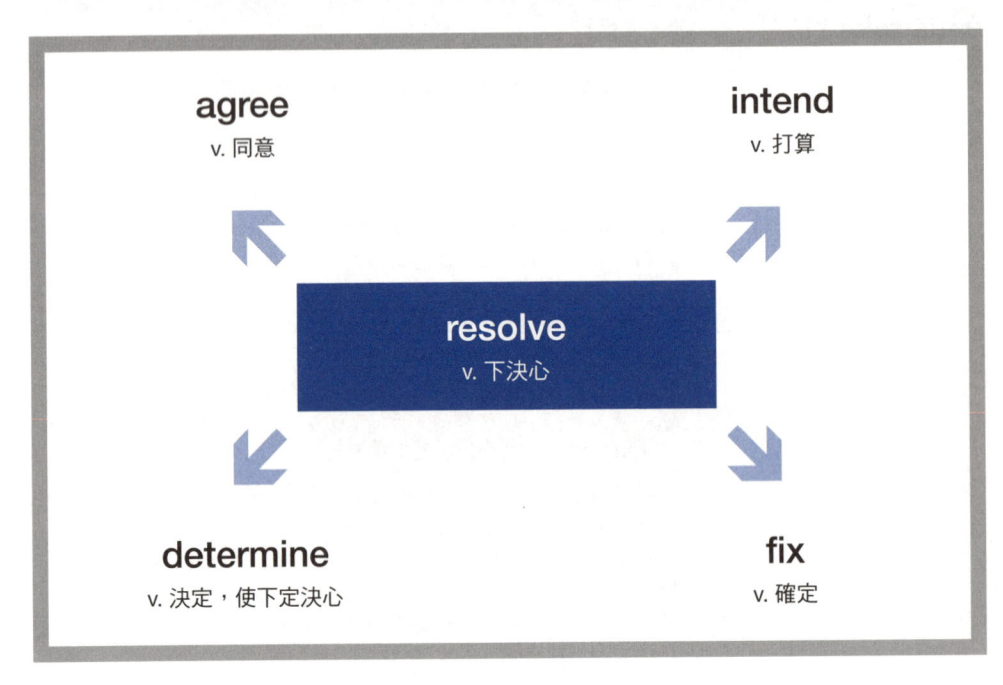

```
           agree                              intend
           v. 同意                             v. 打算

                          ┌─────────────┐
                          │   resolve   │
                          │   v. 下決心  │
                          └─────────────┘

          determine                            fix
    v. 決定，使下定決心                         v. 確定
```

resolve
/rɪˈzɒlv/
Most students **resolve** to enrol in universities.
大部分學生決心要進入大學。

agree
/əˈgriː/
Both his parents and teacher **agreed** to transfer him to a special school.
他的父母和老師都同意讓他轉學到特殊學校。

determine
/dɪˈtɜːmɪn/
She is **determined** to study hard and be the top student of her class.
她下定決心要努力用功，成為班上第一名的學生。

intend
/ɪnˈtɛnd/
I **intend** to go home early and prepare for tomorrow's math quiz.
我打算早點回家準備明天的數學小考。

fix
/fɪks/
The school administrators have not yet **fixed** the date for the final exams.
學校的行政人員還沒有確定期末考的日期。

USEFUL EXPRESSIONS | 相關實用片語

vocational guidance
職業輔導

alternative school
另類學校（體制外的學校）

vocational school
職業學校

vocational education
職業教育

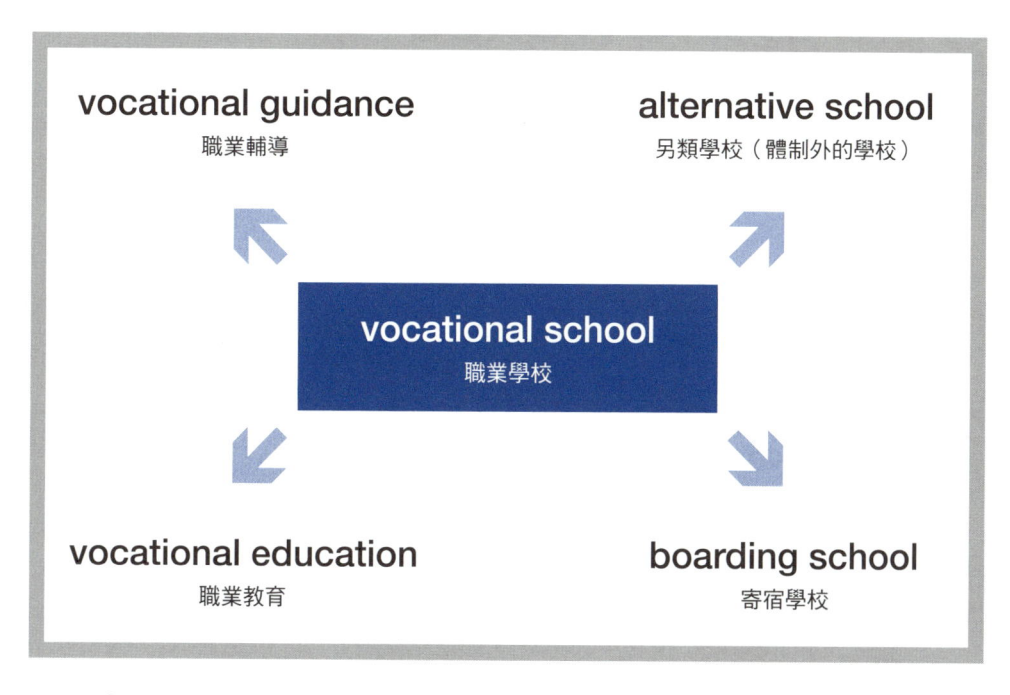

boarding school
寄宿學校

vocational school
/vəʊˈkeɪʃənəl skuːl/

Number of people enrolled in vocational schools last May exceeded that of the prior year by 4%.
去年五月進入職業學校的學生人數，超過前一年的人數達 4%。

vocational guidance
/vəʊˈkeɪʃənəl ˈɡʌɪdəns/

Many American students seek vocational guidance from their school counsellors before graduation.
許多美國學生在畢業前向學校裡的諮商輔導人員尋求職業輔導。

vocational education
/vəʊˈkeɪʃənəl ɛdjʊˈkeɪʃən/

Vocational education at a community college does not prepare one for higher education offered at a university.
社區大學的職業教育，無助於學生為接受大學高等教育做準備。

alternative school
/ɔːˈtəːnətɪv skuːl/

Some international students are being enrolled in alternative schools to help them adjust to a new educational setting.
許多國際學生會進入另類學校，幫助他們適應新的教育環境。

boarding school
/ˈbɔːdɪŋ skuːl/

A highly intelligent scholar named Arpeggio attended the most prestigious boarding school in town.
一位名叫 Arpeggio、非常聰明的學者，進入了城中最負盛名的寄宿學校。

FRI

IELTS **BASIC WORDS**

research /rɪˈsɜːtʃ/ n. 研究
ENG. systematic investigation to establish facts
SYS. experimentation, exploration

> His **research** was aimed to search for a toy that is both fun and educational.
> 他的研究目的是尋找既有趣又有教育性的玩具。

同義語例句 His **study** was geared towards finding an amusing toy that stimulates the mind.
他的研究是專門為了尋找能刺激心智的有趣玩具而設計的。

同義語例句 The **fact-finding** portion of his project led to the discovery of a fun and educational toy.
他的計畫裡調查事實的部分，帶領他發現有趣又有教育性的玩具。

反義語例句 His **jumping to conclusions** was caused by his haste to find the perfect solution.
他匆忙做出結論，是因為急著找到完美的解決方法而造成的。

area /ˈɛːrɪə/ n. 區域
ENG. a particular geographical region
SYS. land, region

> This **area** used to be where the children would play with their toys.
> 這個區域以前是小孩玩玩具的地方。

同義語例句 This **portion of land** was allotted as a play area for children.
這個地區被分配為小孩的遊戲區。

同義語例句 A **place** in this small town is designed specifically for children to play at.
這個小鎮的一塊地方特別設計成供兒童遊玩。

反義語例句 The **vacant lot** was where children gathered in the afternoons and played with their toys.
這塊空地曾經是孩子們在下午時聚集並且玩玩具的地方。

WEEK 2 TOPIC **EDUCATION**

▶ 基礎單字擴充

overstate /ˌəʊvəˈsteɪt/ v. 誇大
ENG. enlarge beyond bounds or truth
SYS. magnify, exaggerate

> Children tend to **overstate** things when telling stories about their toys.
> 孩子們在講關於他們玩具的故事時,通常會把事情誇大。

同義語例句 Some children **give misleading information** when asked about their toys.
有些孩子在被問到關於他們玩具的事情時,會說出讓人誤解的訊息。

同義語例句 Some kids **exaggerate** an incident, especially when it involves their toys.
有些孩子會把事件誇大,尤其是跟他們的玩具有關的時候。

反義語例句 Some kids **regard** their old toys **as less important** when they have a new one.
有些孩子在有新玩具的時候,會認為舊的比較不重要。

argument /ˈɑːgjʊmənt/ n. 爭論
ENG. a dispute where there is a strong disagreement
SYS. debate, discussion

> Children mostly get into an **argument** with other children over toys.
> 孩子們大多是和其他小孩爭論關於玩具的事。

同義語例句 The **difference of opinion** among kids on their toys sometimes leads to quarrels.
孩子們對於玩具的意見分歧,有時候會引起爭吵。

同義語例句 Some siblings have **irreconcilable differences** when it comes to their toys.
有些兄弟姐妹一講到他們的玩具,就會產生無法調解的意見不合。

反義語例句 Children **stop fighting** when each play with their own toys.
每個人都玩自己的玩具時,孩子們就會停止爭吵。

FRI

TOPIC: Giving a large number of toys to children
給孩子大量的玩具

Many children are being showered with toys these days. The truth is that toys are marvellous things because they teach children about the world and about themselves. Virtually all toys are educational to various degrees; however, the best toys engage the senses, **stimulate** creativity, spark **imagination**, **arouse** the **intellect** and promote social **interaction**. That said, it is important to ask if giving too many toys is **spoiling** our children. Toy accumulation seems to happen gradually and **inconspicuously**, but can sneak up on us. Reducing the amount of toys in our homes can have certain benefits. First, it can force our children to be more creative and **resourceful**, causing them to play outdoors more. Limiting the amount of **playthings** can also help increase a child's attention span, and perhaps most importantly, help **relinquish** the idea that material possessions can buy happiness. While toys can be excellent tools for learning and entertainment, we must uphold quality over quantity.

TRANS

如今許多孩子都有大量的玩具。事實上，玩具是很不可思議的東西，因為玩具可以教導孩子關於世界和他們自己的事。幾乎所有玩具都有程度或多或少的教育性。不過，最好的玩具能夠吸引感官、刺激創造力、引發想像力、激發智力，以及促進社交互動。話雖如此，問問給太多玩具是否會寵壞我們的孩子，是很重要的。玩具的累積似乎是逐漸而且不知不覺地發生，卻會悄悄接近並出現在我們的生活中。減少家中玩具的數量有一定的好處。首先，這樣可以促使我們的孩子更有創造力、更有機智，使他們更常在戶外玩耍。限制玩物的數量也有助於增進孩子的注意力廣度，而最重要的或許是能幫助他們放棄「物質的擁有可以買到幸福」的想法。雖然玩具可以是學習與娛樂的絕佳工具，我們還是必須重質不重量。

stimulate
/ˈstɪmjʊleɪt/
v. 刺激
The light show failed to **stimulate** my senses and left me feeling glum.
燈光秀沒能刺激我的感官，還讓我覺得憂鬱。

imagination
/ɪˌmædʒɪˈneɪʃən/
n. 想像力
My nephew has a wild **imagination** and often pretends to be a dinosaur.
我的侄子有豐富的想像力，而且經常假裝自己是恐龍。

arouse
/əˈraʊz/
v. 激發
The book was written to **arouse** readers' sense of nationalism.
寫這本書是為了喚起讀者的國家意識。

intellect
/ˈɪntəlɛkt/
n. 智力
She has a fine **intellect** with a straightforward attitude.
她兼具了聰明才智和直接的態度。

interaction
/ˌɪntərˈækʃən/
n. 互動
Her **interaction** with the board members was highly professional and appropriate at all times.
她和董事會成員的互動總是非常專業而且合宜。

spoil
/spɔɪl/
v. 寵壞
I don't believe that I am **spoiling** my children by paying for their education.
我不認為我幫小孩的教育付錢是在寵壞他們。

inconspicuously
/ˌɪnkənˈspɪkjuəsli/
adv. 不引人注意地
He tried to **inconspicuously** enter the movie theatre from the side to avoid paying.
他試著從旁邊偷偷進入戲院以避免付錢。

resourceful
/rɪˈsɔːsfʊl/
adj. 足智多謀的，機智的
When we get lost in the wilderness, it is important to be **resourceful** in order to survive.
我們在野外迷路時，隨機應變以求生存是很重要的。

plaything
/ˈpleɪθɪŋ/
n. 玩物
There was little money for toys, so home-made **playthings** sufficed. 當時沒有什麼錢可以買玩具，所以自製的玩物就夠了。

relinquish
/rɪˈlɪŋkwɪʃ/
v. 放棄
A person who wants to practise a monastic life should **relinquish** all earthly desires.
想要過修道生活的人，應該放棄所有世俗的欲望。

WORD TRAINING | 重點單字造句練習

suitable
/ˈsuːtəbəl/

adj. 適合的

💬 Toys suitable for children are the ones which are safe and age-appropriate.
適合孩童的玩具，應該是安全又適合其年齡的。

There are plenty of places in the city that are suitable for a picnic.
這座城市有很多適合野餐的地方。

✏️ It is very important to be prudent in choosing online references suitable for academic research because some websites contain outdated and unreliable information.
選擇適合學術研究的網路參考資料時，小心謹慎是非常重要的，因為有些網站包含過時而且不可靠的資訊。

Parents should learn how to choose sports that are suitable for their children's age and interest to promote lifelong fitness and prevent childhood obesity.
父母應該學習如何選擇適合孩子年齡與興趣的運動，以促進他們的終身健康並且預防兒童肥胖。

infant
/ˈɪnfənt/

n. 嬰兒，幼兒

💬 When parents give their infants a lot of toys, they will grow up spoiled. 當父母給他們的嬰兒很多玩具時，他們長大就會變成被寵壞的小孩。

There are many infant toys on the market that would make suitable gifts.
市面上有很多幼兒玩具可以當作合適的禮物。

✏️ When it comes to choosing appropriate toys for your infant or toddler, you are the best judge of your child's developmental stage.
在選擇適當的玩具給你的嬰兒或小孩的時候，你自己就是最能夠判斷小孩發展階段的人。

Handmaking infant toys allows you to control the quality of the toys, be certain of the toys' safety and save money while providing a variety of educational and enjoyable playthings for your kids.
手作幼兒玩具能夠讓你掌控玩具的品質、確定玩具的安全性，並且在為你的孩子們提供多種有教育性又好玩的玩具的同時又能省錢。

口說範例　寫作範例

condition
/kənˈdɪʃən/

n. 狀況

💬 Some families allow their children to play with many toys, even those in poor condition.
有些家庭讓他們的孩子玩許多玩具，就連貧窮的家庭也是。

His injured condition hindered him from excelling in his favourite sport, basketball.
他的傷勢讓他無法在最喜愛的籃球運動中有出色的表現。

✏️ Unlike other things, toys are not likely to be in pristine condition because they are played with, and the package is often discarded.
不像其他的東西，玩具不太可能保持嶄新的狀態，因為玩具是拿來玩的，而且包裝通常被丟棄。

I soon learned that my child was emotionally attached to every toy he owns, regardless of its condition or the other toys he had available to play with.
我很快就發現我的小孩對他擁有的每一個玩具都很眷戀，不管玩具的狀態如何，也不會因為有其他玩具可以玩而改變。

curiosity
/kjʊərɪˈɒsɪti/

n. 好奇心

💬 Children's curiosity will make them want to explore and discover everything around them.
孩子的好奇心會讓他們想要探索並且發現周遭的一切。

Children's books not only gratify a child's curiosity but also boost their imagination.
童書不僅滿足孩子的好奇心，還能激發他們的想像力。

✏️ The books that he read not only satisfied his insatiable curiosity but also led him towards the path of self-discovery and success.
他讀過的書不止滿足了他永無止境的好奇心，還引導他走向自我發現與成功的道路。

Curiosity is considered as the most fundamental part of children's capacity for learning because it is the driving force that leads them to exploration and discovery.
好奇心被認為是兒童學習能力中最基本的部分，因為它是引導孩子去探索並且發現的原動力。

RELATED WORDS | 相關單字延伸

provoke
v. 激起，激怒

awaken
v. 喚醒

arouse
v. 激發

stimulate
v. 刺激

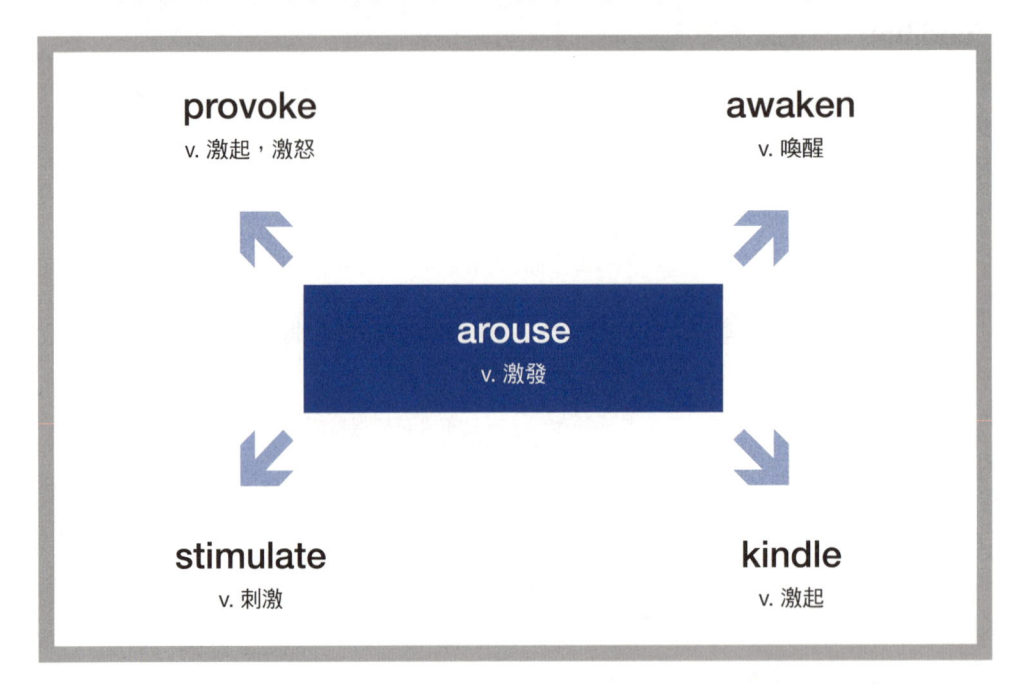

kindle
v. 激起

arouse
/əˈraʊz/

The best toys engage the senses, stimulate creativity, spark imagination, arouse the intellect and promote social interaction.
最好的玩具能夠吸引感官、刺激創造力、引發想像力、激發智力，以及促進社交互動。

provoke
/prəˈvoʊk/

The government's decision to implement 12-year compulsory education provoked anger among some parents.
政府實行十二年義務教育的決定，激怒了一些家長。

stimulate
/ˈstɪmjʊleɪt/

I find that Lego blocks stimulate the imagination of many children.
我發現樂高積木能刺激許多孩子的想像力。

awaken
/əˈweɪkən/

Video games have awakened my son's interest in interacting with other gamers socially.
電玩遊戲喚醒了我兒子對於和其他玩家進行社交互動的興趣。

kindle
/ˈkɪndəl/

It seems that Aidan's creativity has been kindled since he was given the art set.
自從 Aidan 得到繪畫用具組之後，他的創意似乎就被激發了。

USEFUL EXPRESSIONS | 相關實用片語

social control
社會控制

drug interaction
藥物相互作用

social interaction
社會互動

social pressure
社會壓力

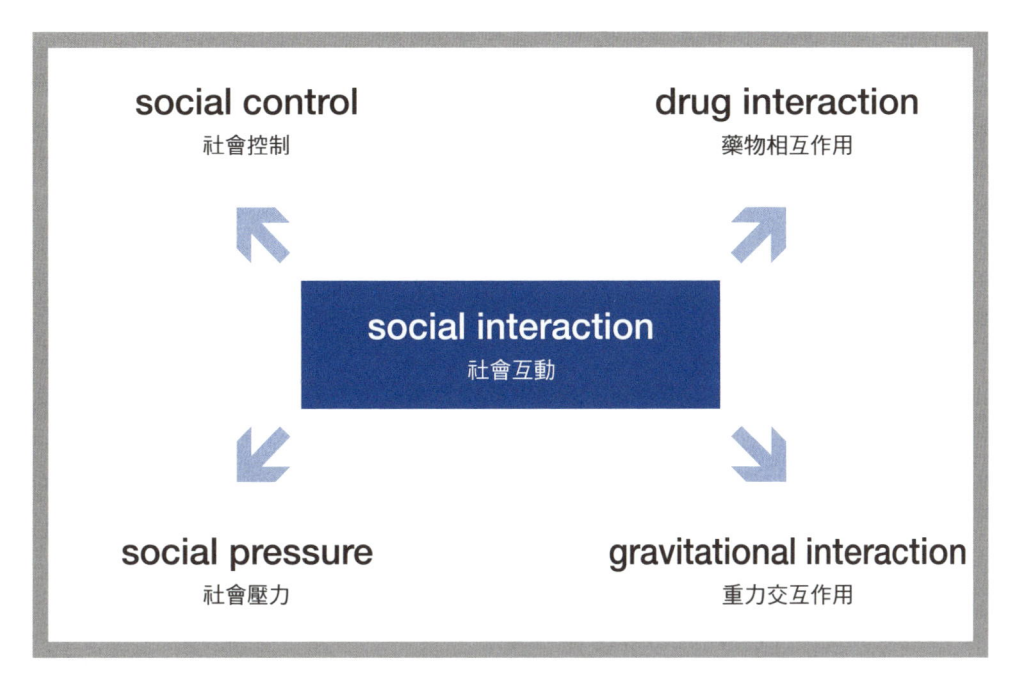

gravitational interaction
重力交互作用

social interaction
/ˈsəʊʃəl ɪntərˈækʃən/

A school environment provides children with social interaction, something that home-schooled children often lack.
學校可以為孩子提供社交互動,這往往是在家自學的小孩所缺乏的。

social control
/ˈsəʊʃəl kənˈtrəʊl/

When a government has a lack of social control, it risks corruption amongst the public.
政府缺乏社會控制力時,就會有大眾風氣腐敗的風險。

social pressure
/ˈsəʊʃəl ˈprɛʃə/

There is much social pressure on teens these days, urging them to improve their appearance through plastic surgery.
現今的青少年有許多社會壓力,讓他們覺得應該藉由整型改善自己的外貌。

drug interaction
/drʌg ɪntərˈækʃən/

The medication prescribed may have drug interaction risks, so please inform your physician of any discomfort.
處方上的藥物可能有藥物交互作用的風險,所以有任何不適時請通知你的醫師。

gravitational interaction
/ˌgrævɪˈteɪʃənəl ɪntərˈækʃən/

The gravitational interaction identified in Newton's theory of gravity offered many answers in Physics.
牛頓的引力理論中發現的重力交互作用,提供了許多物理學的答案。

SAT

IELTS **BASIC WORDS**

public /ˈpʌblɪk/ adj. 公共的
ENG. open to or concerning the people
SYS. society, population

> A sound education system should be freely available to the public.
> 一個健全的教育體系應該要能讓大眾自由利用。

同義語例句 Ideally, the government aims to make the education system open to all.
理想情況下，政府的目標是把教育體系對所有人開放。

同義語例句 Schools with an excellent education system should also offer some courses open to the community.
有優秀教育制度的學校，也應該提供一些對社區開放的課程。

反義語例句 It is sad that today's education system is only available to particular groups of people.
可悲的是，現今的教育體系只提供給特定的族群。

expectation /ɛkspɛkˈteɪʃən/ n. 期望
ENG. belief about the future
SYS. outlook, prospect

> It is our expectation that education will improve within ten years.
> 我們的期望是教育在十年內改善。

同義語例句 Our hope for tomorrow is that improvements in the education system will be evident.
我們對明天的希望是教育體系能夠有明顯的改善。

同義語例句 Our awareness of the forthcoming changes is essential for creating a better education system.
我們對於即將發生的改變的認知，對於創造更好的教育體系而言是不可或缺的。

反義語例句 All we have is dismay at the outcome of our efforts to revolutionise the education system.
我們有的就只是對改革教育體系的努力結果感到失望。

WEEK 2 TOPIC **EDUCATION**

▶基礎單字擴充

rubbish /ˈrʌbɪʃ/ n. 垃圾
ENG. worthless material that is to be disposed of
SYS. trash, garbage

> How do we improve the education system if all we teach children is **rubbish**?
> 如果我們教給孩子的東西都是垃圾，又該怎麼改善教育體系呢？

同義語例句 Some school **materials to be thrown away** are still taught in schools today.
有些應該丟掉的教材，到現在學校還在教。

同義語例句 The **unwanted materials** scrapped by the education board still linger in schools today.
那些被教育委員會棄之不用的材料，到現在還留在學校裡。

反義語例句 Lessons learned from lectures, rather than the education materials themselves, are **valuable treasures** for us.
對我們有貴重價值的東西，是在課堂上學到的事情，而不是教材本身。

devastate /ˈdɛvəsteɪt/ v. 破壞，摧毀
ENG. cause extensive destruction; ruin utterly
SYS. wreck, demolish

> The sudden change to the education system **devastated** teachers and students.
> 教育體系的突然改變，讓師生受到很大的打擊。

同義語例句 The students were **overwhelmed with** the new changes in the education system.
學生對於教育體系的新改變感到吃不消。

同義語例句 The teachers' dismay **ruined** the students' enthusiasm over the new education system.
老師的失望破壞了學生對新教育體系的熱情。

反義語例句 It is time to **build up** what the unhealthy education system has destroyed over the years.
是時候重建多年來被不健康的教育體系破壞的事物了。

111

SAT

TOPIC: Traditional and modern teaching methods
傳統與現代教學方法

With the **rapid** development of English language teaching in non-English-speaking countries, English teachers have become more aware that the exclusive use of either the **auditory** approach or grammar-translation method does not work. Teachers have also discovered that no single teaching method deals with everything concerning the context, form and content of the target language. However, these traditional methods of educating non-English speaking students are not necessarily **unworkable** alongside modern teaching methods. In fact, the idea that the two are **mutually** exclusive is **absurd**. What English language teachers need to do now is to **modernise**, not Westernise, English teaching. They need to combine the new with the old so as to adapt the communicative **approach** to traditional teaching structures. This means creating a **curriculum** that will **complement** existing methods and also **function** within the context of the culture where it is being taught.

TRANS

隨著英語教學在非英語系國家的快速發展，英語教師越來越意識到，單獨使用聽覺或文法與翻譯的教學方式是沒有效果的。教師們也發現，沒有一種單獨的教學方式能夠處理關於目標語言的脈絡、形式與內容的一切。不過，這些教導非英語系學生的傳統方式，不見得無法和現代的教學方式共同使用。事實上，認為這兩者互相排斥是荒謬的想法。英語教師現在需要做的，是把英語教學現代化而不是西化。他們需要結合新舊方法，讓溝通教學法能夠適合傳統的教學架構。這意味著創造出能夠補足現有方式，又能夠在進行教學的文化情境裡發揮作用的課程架構。

rapid
/ˈræpɪd/

adj. 快速的
The train ran along the track at such a **rapid** speed that I became frightened.
火車用很快的速度奔馳在軌道上，讓我感到害怕。

auditory
/ˈɔːdɪtəri/

adj. 聽覺的
The geese's raucous squawking was an **auditory** attack on the city.
鵝的吵啞叫聲對於城市是一種聽覺上的攻擊。

unworkable
/ʌnˈwɜːkəbəl/

adj. 行不通的，難以使用的
The metal was so stiff and impermeable that the artist deemed it completely **unworkable**.
這塊金屬很堅硬而且不滲透，所以藝術家認為它完全無法使用。

mutually
/ˈmjuːtʃʊəli/

adv. 互相
Environmental preservation and economic development should not be **mutually** exclusive.
環境保護與經濟發展不應該是互相排斥的。

absurd
/əbˈsɜːd/

adj. 荒謬的
It is **absurd** to think that a school can discipline its students with strict regulations.
認為學校可以用嚴格的規定管教好學生是荒謬的。

modernise
/ˈmɒdənʌɪz/

v. 現代化
The residents of this country have **modernised** their culture.
這個國家的居民已經將他們的文化現代化了。

approach
/əˈprəʊtʃ/

v. 接近 n. 方法
Be very careful as you **approach** the wasp nest or else you might be stung.
接近蜂巢時要非常小心，否則你可能會被螫。

curriculum
/kəˈrɪkjʊləm/

n. 學校的全部課程
The member in the parent advisory committee proposed a change in the science **curriculum**.
家長諮詢委員會的成員提出了修改科學課程項目的意見。

complement
/ˈkɒmplɪmənt/

v. 補充，補足
The illustrations in the children's book *The Little Prince* really **complement** the text.
童書《小王子》裡的插圖真的補足了文字的內容。

function
/ˈfʌŋkʃən/

n. 功能 v. 起作用
Use antibiotics with care if you have reduced kidney **function**.
如果你的腎功能已經衰退，要小心使用抗生素。

WORD TRAINING | 重點單字造句練習

literacy
/ˈlɪtərəsi/

n. 讀寫能力

The government should implement projects that will promote adult literacy.
政府應該實施提升成人識字率的計畫。

Some countries require their citizens to take a literacy test before voting.
有些國家要求他們的公民在投票前接受讀寫能力測試。

That the growth of literacy rate has been slower is due to the reformed education system that is focused more on being cost-effective rather than being effectively educative.
識字率的成長變得比較慢，是因為改革後的教育體系比較注重成本效益而不是教育效果。

Children's literacy in the present time is much better than 20 years ago because of the improved education system.
現今的兒童識字情況比起 20 年前好很多，是因為教育體系改進的關係。

intelligent
/ɪnˈtɛlɪdʒənt/

adj. 聰明的

Some extremely intelligent people are not able to understand simple things.
有些絕頂聰明的人無法理解簡單的事情。

Traditionally, chemistry was a subject that only very intelligent students could excel in.
傳統上，化學是只有非常聰明的學生才能表現突出的科目。

The intelligent students impressed their teacher when they all aced the National Assessment Examination, for which they had been preparing for the whole school year.
這些聰明的學生為了全國性的評量準備了一年，結果全都考了很好的成績，讓他們的老師印象深刻。

The teacher was too intelligent that her students could not catch up with her fast and complicated lectures, which resulted in poor class performance.
這位老師太聰明了，以致於學生跟不上她又快又複雜的講課，而這樣的講課也導致班級表現不佳。

cram
/kræm/

v. n. 硬塞，死記硬背

💬 Traditional schools often force students to cram for tests and assignments.
傳統學校經常強迫學生為了測驗和作業死記硬背。

I am thankful that modern education systems do not make students cram for tests.
我很感謝現代教育體系不會逼學生為了測驗死記硬背。

✍ Cram schools that prepare students for high school and university entrance examinations are established everywhere in response to the pressure created by our modern education system.
反應現代教育體系造成的壓力，到處都設立了讓學生準備高中和大學入學考試的補習班。

Cram schools are sometimes criticised, along with the modern countries in which they are prevalent, for not adequately honing their students' critical thinking and analytical skills.
補習班有時候會被批評為沒有充分磨練學生的批判性思考與分析能力，而補習班盛行的現代國家也連帶受到譴責。

qualification
/ˌkwɒlɪfɪˈkeɪʃən/

n. 資格

💬 I earned my teaching qualification while working at a traditional school ten years ago.
我十年前在一所傳統學校工作時獲得了教學資格。

Many students today take training courses to obtain professional qualifications.
今日有許多學生修習訓練課程以獲得專業資格。

✍ Based on the results of this meeting, a proposal was issued for the board to examine the effects that qualification policies can have upon the modern education system.
根據這次會議的結果提出了一項提案，要委員會檢視資格政策在現代教育體系中可能產生的影響。

The framework describes the main purposes and learning expectations for each qualification and the relationship between the qualifications.
這個架構描述每種資格的主要目的與學習期望，以及這些資格之間的關係。

RELATED WORDS | 相關單字延伸

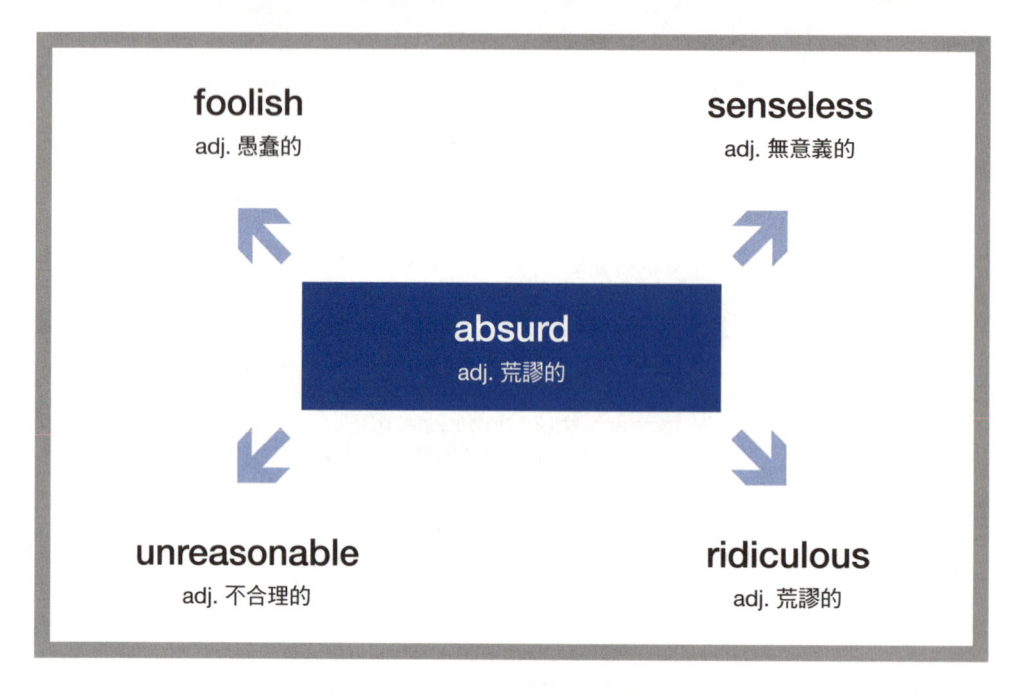

```
        foolish                    senseless
        adj. 愚蠢的                  adj. 無意義的

                    ┌─────────────┐
                    │   absurd    │
                    │  adj. 荒謬的  │
                    └─────────────┘

     unreasonable                  ridiculous
     adj. 不合理的                   adj. 荒謬的
```

absurd
/əbˈsɜːd/

In fact, the idea that the two are mutually exclusive is **absurd**.
事實上，認為這兩者互相排斥是荒謬的想法。

foolish
/ˈfuːlɪʃ/

The student kept asking **foolish** questions to interrupt the class discussion.
這個學生一直問愚蠢的問題打斷課堂討論。

unreasonable
/ʌnˈriːzənəbəl/

The teacher's punishment for the student's misbehaviour was utterly **unreasonable**.
這位老師對學生的品行不佳所做的處罰完全不合理。

senseless
/ˈsɛnsləs/

It is **senseless** to teach a student who is not willing to learn.
教導沒有意願學習的學生是沒意義的。

ridiculous
/rɪˈdɪkjʊləs/

It is **ridiculous** that some professors teach subjects that they have never learned before.
有些教授教自己以前沒學過的科目，這是很荒謬的。

USEFUL EXPRESSIONS | 相關實用片語

traditional practice
傳統習慣

production method
生產方式

traditional method
傳統方式

traditional technology
傳統技術

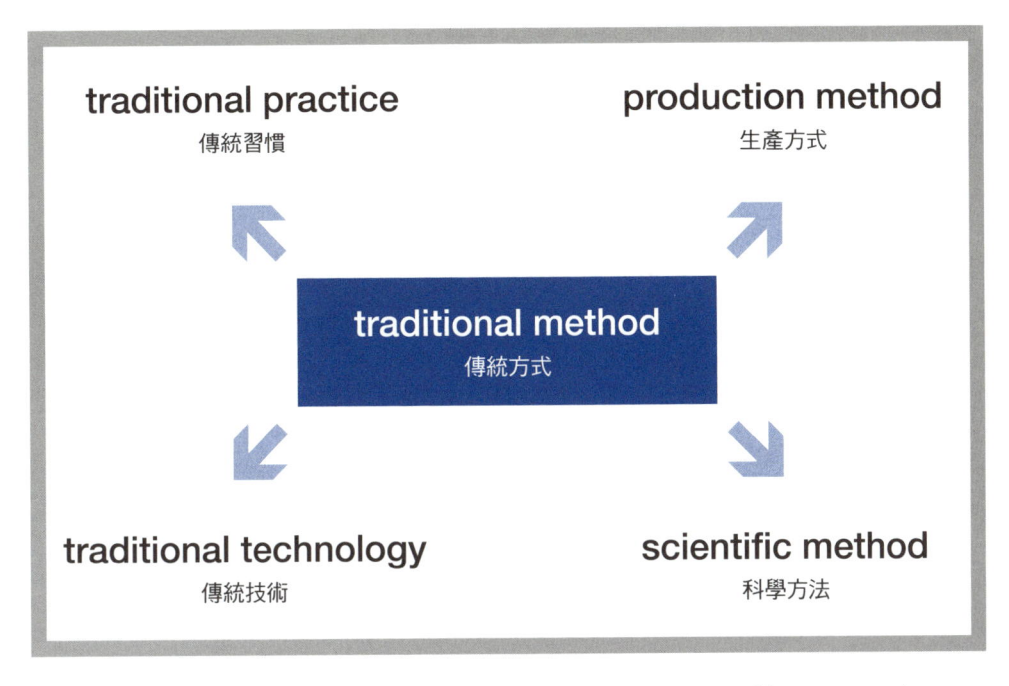

scientific method
科學方法

traditional method
/trəˈdɪʃənəl ˈmɛθəd/

During the monsoon season, many Korean people resort to traditional methods of keeping cool in high temperatures.
在季風時節,許多韓國人會尋求傳統方式,在高溫中保持涼爽。

traditional practice
/trəˈdɪʃənəl ˈpræktɪs/

Learning through rote memorisation is often criticised as a traditional practice in education that needs to be reformed.
藉由死背來學習,經常被批評為教育中需要改革的傳統習慣。

traditional technology
/trəˈdɪʃənəl tɛkˈnɒlədʒi/

Though technology has made modern farming much easier, many farmers still use traditional technology instead.
雖然科技已經讓現代農業容易許多,但很多農夫還是使用傳統技術。

production method
/prəˈdʌkʃən ˈmɛθəd/

The two main automakers in the world have superior production methods which have put them ahead of the competition.　世界上的兩大汽車製造商,擁有讓他們在競爭中領先的較佳生產方式。

scientific method
/ˌsʌɪənˈtɪfɪk ˈmɛθəd/

In all fields of science, the scientific method is the framework for investigating and answering questions.
在所有科學領域裡,科學方法都是調查與回答問題的準則。

SUN

IELTS **BASIC WORDS**

impact /ɪmˈpækt/ v. 影響
ENG. have an effect upon
SYS. affect, wallop

> Punishing children **impacts** their sense of compassion and forgiveness.
> 處罰孩童會影響他們的同情心與寬恕精神。

同義語例句 An adult's lack of compassion and forgiveness may **be the result of** punishment received in his childhood.
成人缺乏同情與寬恕，可能是小時候受到處罰的結果。

同義語例句 Physical punishment **has negative consequences on** a child's mental health.
體罰對於小孩的心理健康會造成負面的後果。

反義語例句 His advice seemed to **have no influence** on his son.
他的勸告似乎對他的兒子沒有產生影響。

response /rɪˈspɒns/ n. 回應
ENG. a statement made to address a question, request, criticism or accusation
SYS. reply, answer

> When asked about her punishment, her **response** was brief and sad.
> 被問到她受到的處罰時，她的回應簡短而且難過。

同義語例句 In her **reply**, she sadly talked about the punishment she suffered.
在她的回覆裡，她難過地談論自己受到的處罰。

同義語例句 Her **declaration** was that she was punished for her wrongdoings.
她陳述的聲明是，她因為自己做的壞事而受到了處罰。

反義語例句 Her **keeping mum** about her punishment stirred more rumours around town.
她對自己受到處罰保持沉默，引起城裡更多的傳聞。

118

WEEK 2 TOPIC **EDUCATION**

▶基礎單字擴充

cost /kɒst/ n. 費用，成本，代價
ENG. value measured by what must be given, done or undergone to obtain something
SYS. toll, price

> It seems that physical punishment is not worth the **cost** of what the children will lose.
> 以孩子所付出的代價而執行體罰，似乎並不值得。

同義語例句 Her **price to pay** for her crime is not enough for the victim to forgive and forget.
她為自己罪行付出的代價不足以讓受害者原諒並且遺忘。

同義語例句 The **damage** due to her illegal actions was beyond repair.
她非法行為造成的損害無法修復。

反義語例句 Using positive disciplining instead of physical punishment can bring numerous **benefits** to your child.
使用正面的管教方式而不是體罰，可以為你的小孩帶來許多好處。

similar /ˈsɪmɪlə/ adj. 相似的
ENG. having a resemblance
SYS. alike, resembling

> His punishment for theft was **similar** to that of the murderer.
> 他偷竊的處罰跟那個殺人犯的處罰差不多。

同義語例句 The punishment to the thief is **pretty much the same** as that to the murderer.
那個小偷的處罰跟那個殺人犯的差不多。

同義語例句 The sentence of the thief and that of the murderer are **closely comparable**.
小偷受到的判決跟殺人犯的很接近。

反義語例句 The punishment for stealing and the punishment for killing someone are **barely alike**.
偷東西和殺人的處罰非常不同。

119

TOPIC: Punishment
處罰

Young people today come to school with different values from past generations. Traditional approaches to **disciplining** students are no longer successful for many young people. The irony of punishment is that the more you use it to control your students' behaviour, the less real **influence** you have over them. This is because pressure **breeds resentment**. In addition, if students stop being **defiant** because they are being **forced** to behave, the teacher has failed. Students should **behave** because they want to—not because they have to in order to avoid punishment. This self-regulated behaviour does not always occur in reality, though. Although educators and psychologists persistently advocate encouragement rather than punishment for children's education, many teachers and parents often argue that punishment is more effective than encouragement to make a child study **diligently**. Rather than coercing good behaviour, however, I insist teachers aim at **propagating** responsibility rather than **obedience**.

今日來到學校的年輕人，價值觀和過去的世代不同。傳統的學生管教方式，對於許多年輕人而言不再管用了。諷刺的情況是，使用越多處罰來控制學生的行為，你對他們的實質影響力就越少。這是因為壓迫會滋生怨恨。而且，如果學生是因為被迫守規矩而不再反抗，老師就失敗了。學生守規矩應該要出於自願——而不是為了避免處罰而必須這麼做。不過，實際上這種自律的行為並不一定會發生。雖然教育學家與心理學家堅持提倡以鼓勵而非處罰來教育孩童，但許多老師與家長常常主張，要讓小孩勤奮學習，處罰比鼓勵更為有效。然而，我還是主張老師不應該強迫學生採取好的行為，應該以宣揚責任感而非服從精神為目標。

discipline
/ˈdɪsɪplɪn/

v. 訓練，管教

My father was the main adult **disciplining** us because my mother refused to do so.
因為我母親拒絕，所以我父親成了主要管教我們的大人。

influence
/ˈɪnfluəns/

n. 影響

I hope that that teenage boy does not have a bad **influence** on you. 我希望那個青少年男孩沒有對你造成不好的影響。

breed
/briːd/

v. 滋生

Ignorance **breeds** hatred, which is why I believe everyone should travel and see the world.
無知會滋生仇恨，所以我相信每個人都應該去旅行，看看這個世界。

resentment
/rɪˈzɛntmənt/

n. 怨恨

My older brother held a lot of **resentment** toward the high school bully.
我哥哥曾經十分怨恨高中的那個霸凌者。

defiant
/dɪˈfʌɪənt/

adj. 反抗的

The **defiant** soldier refused to take the prisoners to the other base camp.
反抗的士兵拒絕帶囚犯到另一個基地營。

force
/fɔːs/

v. 強迫

Parents should not **force** their children to read or write.
父母不應該強迫他們的孩子讀書或寫字。

behave
/bɪˈheɪv/

v. 行為舉止，守規矩

She began to **behave** strangely after dinner, so we assumed she was tired.
晚餐後她行為變得奇怪，所以我們假設她累了。

diligently
/ˈdɪlɪdʒəntli/

adv. 勤奮地

The elderly woman behind the counter knitted **diligently** as customers shopped.
櫃檯後面的老婦人在顧客購物時努力地編織著東西。

propagate
/ˈprɒpəɡeɪt/

v. 傳播

The Internet is an important tool that allows people to learn and **propagate** new knowledge.
網路是讓人學習並散播新知識的一項重要工具。

obedience
/əˈbiːdɪəns/

v. 服從，順從

I sent my dog Buddy to **obedience** training so he would stop chasing bicycles.
我送我的狗 Buddy 參加服從訓練，希望讓他停止追腳踏車。

WORD TRAINING | 重點單字造句練習

retake
/riˈteɪk/

v. 重新接受（考試），重拍（照片）

💬 As punishment for his rude facial expression, the student was not allowed to have his photo retaken.
為了處罰那個學生做出沒禮貌的表情，他不被允許重拍照片。

Students charged with cheating should not have the opportunity to retake the test.
被指控作弊的學生不應該有重考的機會。

✏️ One famous story tells how a professor forced his class of 600 to retake a mid-term exam after discovering that a third of the students had cheated.
有個著名的故事是說，一位教授在發現有三分之一的學生作弊之後，如何強迫這個有 600 名學生的班級重考期中考。

If you have too many traffic violations on record, you will be mandated to retake your driver's license examination.
如果你有太多交通違規紀錄，你必須重新接受駕照考試。

capacity
/kəˈpæsɪti/

n. 能力

💬 A child's mental capacity should not be limited to what she can learn in school.
孩子的心智能力不應該被侷限在學校裡能夠學到的內容。

Undoubtedly, children have the capacity to learn two languages at the same time.
無疑地，孩子有同時學習兩種語言的能力。

✏️ It is disappointing that a child with developmental delay has his mental capacity belittled by his own peers and teachers.
一個發展遲緩的孩子，心智能力被同儕和老師貶低，令人感到失望。

Slow learners still have the capacity to comprehend lessons, so teachers must never give them up, no matter how difficult it is.
遲緩的學習者仍然有理解課業的能力，所以不管有多困難，老師永遠不該放棄他們。

口說範例 寫作範例

pupil
/ˈpjuːpɪl/

n. 學生，小學生

💬 Discipline in school requires that the misbehaving pupils should be brought under control.
校規要求，行為不檢的學生應該加以控制。

A pupil should never feel that the punishment can clear her of all scores for her crime.
學生絕對不能認為處罰可以把犯罪的紀錄清除。

✎ Since studies show that a pupil's exam grade is the best criterion to assess a teacher's performance, schools are now thinking of basing their teacher's pay on the students' test scores.
因為研究顯示學生的測驗成績是評量教師表現的最佳標準，一些學校現在正在考慮以學生的測驗成績作為教師薪資的基準。

The pupil who interrupts the class, the one who destroys property and the one who is untruthful require different kinds of discipline.
打斷上課的學生、破壞財物的學生和不誠實的學生，各自需要不同的管教。

revise
/rɪˈvaɪz/

v. 修改，修訂，（英）複習

💬 Medical specialty societies have raised concerns about the penalty and are striving to revise the policy.
一些醫療專業協會對於處罰表達擔憂，並且正努力爭取修訂政策。

My daughter thinks that having to revise her math work is a form of punishment.
我女兒認為必須改正數學作業是一種懲罰。

✎ As punishment for taking three days off school, I had to revise my last essay and turn it in again for marks.
作為離校三天的處罰，我必須修改上一篇論說文並重新繳交以獲得分數。

I must revise the way I tabulate student marks in class because it is an unfair punishment for students to mark them on the curve or through other means.
我必須修改班上學生成績的製表方式，因為把學生標記在曲線上，或者用其他方式來標示，對他們都是一種不公平的處罰。

RELATED WORDS | 相關單字延伸

deference
n. 尊敬，敬重

conformity
n. 遵從

obedience
n. 服從

submission
n. 順從

compliance
n. 服從，遵守

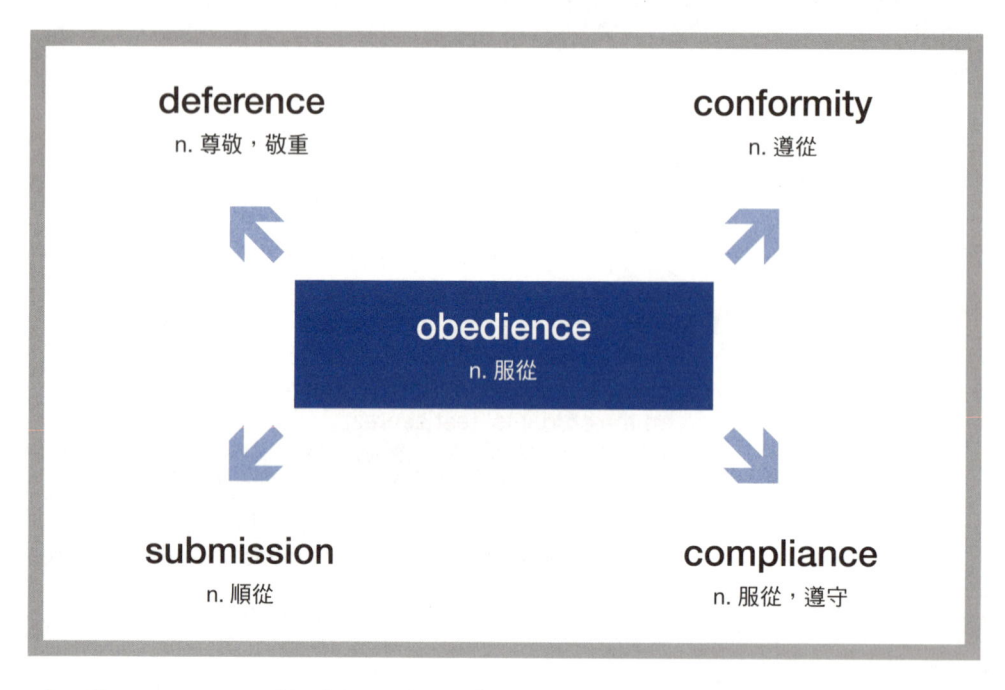

---

obedience
/əˈbiːdɪəns/

I insist teachers aim at promoting responsibility rather than obedience.
我主張老師應該以宣揚責任感而非服從精神為目標。

deference
/ˈdɛfərəns/

With great deference, the student deeply bowed to the teacher.
那位學生懷著深深的敬意，向那位老師深深一鞠躬。

submission
/səbˈmɪʃən/

The lady's total submission to her diet plan made it easy for her to lose her excess weight.
那位女士對於飲食計畫的完全服從，使得她很輕鬆地減去多餘體重。

conformity
/kənˈfɔːmɪti/

Teachers should not promote total conformity in schools because individuality is important.
教師在學校不應該提倡完全順從，因為個體性很重要。

compliance
/kəmˈplʌɪəns/

I will participate in the project not because I agree with its objective, but for mere compliance.
我會參加那項計畫，不是因為我認同它的目標，只是因為服從而已。

USEFUL EXPRESSIONS | 相關實用片語

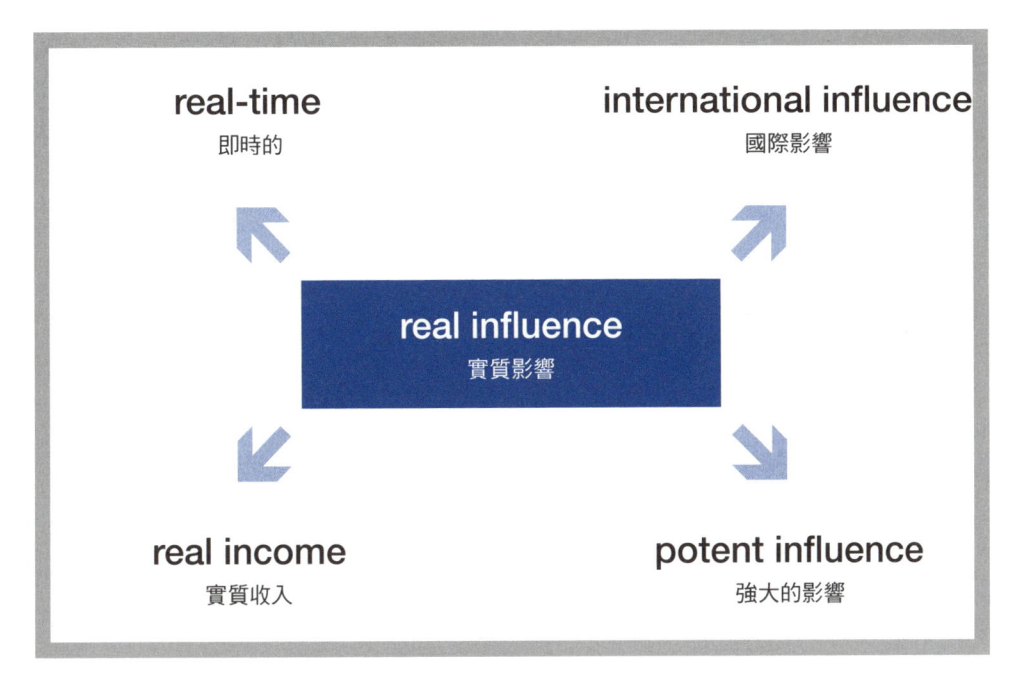

```
real-time              international influence
即時的                    國際影響

        real influence
         實質影響

real income            potent influence
實質收入                   強大的影響
```

real influence
/riːl ˈɪnfluəns/

Learning computer programming had a real influence on the career choices I've made.
學習電腦程式設計，對於我所做的職業選擇產生了實質的影響。

real-time
/ˈriːltaɪm/

The application allows real-time group texting besides standard message sending.
這個應用程式讓人在標準訊息傳送以外，還能即時群組傳訊。

real income
/riːl ˈɪnkʌm/

The people seeking wage increases most are those who have lost real income due to inflation.
最想要獲得加薪的人，是那些因為通貨膨脹而損失實質收入的人。

international influence
/ɪntəˈnæʃənəl ˈɪnfluəns/

The international influence of China's emerging economy is making Chinese a popular choice for language learners.
中國新興經濟體的國際影響力，使得中文成為受到語言學習者歡迎的選擇。

potent influence
/ˈpəʊtənt ˈɪnfluəns/

The most potent influence on youth today is arguably excessive violence in the media.
當今對青少年最強大的影響，可以說是媒體中過多的暴力。

WEEK 3
CULTURE

我們為什麼該學習歷史

人們對於新聞的偏好

挽救少數族群的語言免於滅絕

不同文化間的衝突

穿著民族服裝

發展國際觀光

移民到其他國家

MON

IELTS **BASIC WORDS**

wane /weɪn/   v. 變小，減少
ENG. decrease in extent or become weaker
SYS. disappear, decrease

> Students' interest in history is slowly **waning**.
> 學生對歷史的興趣正在慢慢減少。

同義語例句   The students' enthusiasm to learn history seems to **fade away** towards the end of the semester.
學生學習歷史的熱忱似乎會隨著學期末的接近而逐漸消失。

同義語例句   The students' excitement in their history class **becomes less visible** day by day.
學生對於歷史課的興奮感一天一天越來越不明顯。

反義語例句   The students' hunger for knowledge **intensifies**, especially when discussing history.
特別是在討論歷史的時候，學生對知識的渴望越發強烈。

reshape /riːˈʃeɪp/   v. 重塑
ENG. to form again or anew
SYS. remould, regulate

> It is time to **reshape** the methods of teaching history.
> 是時候重塑歷史教學的方式了。

同義語例句   We need to **give a new direction** to the way history is being taught.
我們需要給歷史教學一個新的方向。

同義語例句   We have to **transform** students' perception of history by teaching it better.
我們必須把歷史教得更好，來改變學生對歷史的觀感。

反義語例句   There is nothing wrong with how history is taught; let us **leave it as it is**.
歷史的教法沒有什麼錯；我們就讓它保持原狀吧。

WEEK 3 TOPIC CULTURE

▶基礎單字擴充

unique /juːˈniːk/ adj. 獨特的
ENG. being the only one of its kind
SYS. unequalled, unparalleled

> The professor had a **unique** way of teaching history with humour.
> 這位教授有他獨特的歷史幽默教學方式。

同義語例句 The teacher's **one of a kind** sense of humour kept students interested in her history class.
這位老師獨一無二的幽默感,讓學生對她的歷史課一直保持興趣。

同義語例句 The wit and humour in the history teacher's personality are **incomparable**.
這位歷史老師個性裡的機智和幽默是別人難以比擬的。

反義語例句 His methods of teaching are **like the rest**, boring and dull.
他的教學方式就跟其他人一樣,無聊而且沉悶。

entirely /ɪnˈtʌɪəli/ adv. 完全地
ENG. to a complete degree
SYS. wholly, altogether

> The professor's recollection of all his history lectures is **entirely** true and accurate.
> 這位教授對他所有歷史課的回憶完全真實並且正確。

同義語例句 The teacher remembers all major events in history, with **every detail included**.
這位老師記得歷史上的所有重大事件,包含每個細節。

同義語例句 The teacher can recite all remarkable events in history **without exception**.
這位老師能背誦出歷史上所有重要的事件,無一例外。

反義語例句 The teacher has mastery of history **only to a certain level**.
這位老師只精通歷史到某個程度。

MON

TOPIC
Why we should learn history
我們為什麼該學習歷史

Given all the demands that press in from living in the present and **anticipating** what is yet to come, why bother with learning history? With all the **desirable** and available branches of knowledge, why do educational programmes **urge** many students to study even more about ancient **civilisation** than they are required to? Any subject of study needs **justification**: its **advocates** must explain why it is worth the attention. Most widely accepted subjects—and history is certainly one of the **time-honoured** ones—**attract** some people who simply like the information and modes of thought involved. But those who are less **instinctively** drawn to the subject and more doubtful about why to bother need to know what the purpose is. In my opinion, history should be learned because it is essential to individuals and to society, and because history as a culture of knowledge **harbours** beauty.

TRANS

　　既然活在當下和預期未來的各種要求已經簇擁而來，何苦還要學習歷史呢？既然已經有各種大家想學而且可以學習的知識分支，為什麼教育計畫還是力勸許多學生學習超過必要範圍的古代文明知識呢？任何學習的科目都需要正當的理由：擁護者必須解釋為什麼一個科目值得注意。大部分廣為接受的科目——歷史當然是古老而受尊重的科目之一——都會吸引一些純粹喜歡當中的資訊與思考模式的人。但天性比較不受這個科目吸引、比較懷疑何苦要學的人，就需要知道學習的目的是什麼。在我看來，歷史是需要學習的，因為它對於個人和社會都是不可或缺的，也是因為歷史作為一種知識的文化蘊藏了美。

anticipate
/ænˈtɪsɪpeɪt/

v. 預期，期待

I have been **anticipating** my university graduation date for the past two weeks.
過去兩個禮拜，我一直在期待我大學畢業的日子。

desirable
/dɪˈzʌɪərəbəl/

adj. 想要的，值得要的

The most **desirable** breed of dog in Britain is the Labrador Retriever.
英國人最想要飼養的犬種是拉布拉多拾獵犬。

urge
/ˈəːdʒ/

v. 力勸，催促

The columnist strongly **urges** the implementation of a universal healthcare system.
那位專欄作家強力主張應該實施全民納保的保健體系。

civilisation
/ˌsɪvɪlʌɪˈzeɪʃən/

n. 文明

In Grade 4, many students learn about ancient Egyptian **civilisation** and study mummification.
在四年級時，很多學生學習古埃及文明並研究木乃伊製作。

justification
/dʒʌstɪfɪˈkeɪʃən/

n. 證明為正當，正當的理由

Being afraid of punishment is not a sufficient **justification** for withholding information from your mother.
害怕被處罰不足以成為你對母親知情不報的正當理由。

advocate
/ˈadvəkət/

n. 提倡者，擁護者

The **advocates** for homeless people hope the city will treat them equally as residents who have their own homes.
擁護遊民的人希望市府會像對有家的居民一樣公平對待他們。

time-honoured
/ˈtʌɪmˌɒnəd/

adj. 古老而受到尊重的，歷史悠久的

Lab mice, **time-honoured** experimental subjects, are often bred solely for science. 實驗室用的老鼠，是歷史悠久的實驗對象，通常只為了科學目的而飼養繁殖。

attract
/əˈtrakt/

v. 吸引

One effective method she used to **attract** men was batting her eyelashes.
她用來吸引男人的一個有效方法就是眨眼睛（拍動睫毛）。

instinctively
/ɪnˈstɪŋktɪvli/

adv. 本能地，直覺地

I **instinctively** knew where I would find the buried treasure.
我直覺地知道在哪裡會找到埋藏的寶藏。

harbour
/ˈhɑːbə/

v. 藏匿，藏有

If a man **harbours** a fugitive, he may get a fine or time in jail.
如果一個人窩藏逃犯，他可能會被罰款或坐牢。

WORD TRAINING | 重點單字造句練習

acculturation
/əkʌltʃəˈreɪʃən/

n. 文化涵化，文化適應

The study examined the influence of migration history and acculturation on the exam scores of Hispanic women.
這個研究檢視移民歷史和文化涵化對西班牙裔女性測驗成績的影響。

Acculturation can only be achieved by those who have a good understanding of the history and society of the area.
只有對地區的歷史與社會有良好了解的人，才能夠達成文化適應。

During the mid-twentieth century, studies of acculturation and historical cultural patterns replaced diffusion as the focus of anthropological research.
在二十世紀中期，對文化涵化與歷史文化模式的研究取代了文化傳播論，成為人類學研究的焦點。

Students who wish to gain a full understanding of another culture's history should first move to the chosen country and attempt to progress to a state of acculturation.
想要完全了解其他文化歷史的學生，應該先搬遷到選定的國家，然後試圖達到文化適應的狀態。

evidence
/ˈɛvɪdəns/

n. 證據

There is no evidence suggesting that students graduating with history degrees will face unemployment.
沒有證據顯示歷史系畢業的學生會面臨失業。

Evidence from a recent study indicates that History students are more knowledgeable than Math students.
最近研究的證據表明，歷史系的學生比數學系的學生更有知識。

We must study history because it offers an evidence base for the contemplation and analysis necessary for understanding how societies function.
我們必須學習歷史，因為對於了解社會如何運作時所需的思考與分析，歷史提供了一個證據基礎。

Students should study history because it offers evidence for the interaction between societies, providing international and comparative perspectives essential for responsible citizenship.
學生應該要學習歷史，因為它提供了社會之間交流的證據，因而提供了對於有責任感的公民身分而言必要的國際觀點與比較觀點。

indigenous
/ɪnˈdɪdʒɪnəs/

adj. 本土的，原住民的

💬 The indigenous people of Australia have a deeply entrenched connection with their history.
澳洲的原住民和他們的歷史有牢固的連結。

History and religion have an indigenous quality that makes them unique to each and every region.
歷史和宗教有一種本土的性質，讓它們在每個地區都是獨特的。

✏️ The political sovereignty of many indigenous nations in history marks substantive differences from that of other racial and ethnic groups in western civilisation.
歷史上許多原住民國家的政治主權，和西方文明中其他種族與族裔群體的主權有很大的不同。

Indigenous history is already a priority in Canadian elementary and secondary schools and already permeates humanities and social sciences classes in universities.
原住民歷史已經是加拿大小學與中學優先學習的內容，這也滲透到了大學的人文與社會課程裡。

descendant
/dɪˈsɛndənt/

n. 後裔

💬 When I learned about my family's history, I discovered that we were Mongol descendants.
在我了解自己的家族歷史時，我發現我們是蒙古後裔。

The descendants of their tribe usually wear their traditional clothes during festivals.
他們族群的後裔通常會在節慶時穿著傳統服裝。

✏️ The traditional dances and music from our ancestors should be passed on to our descendants to keep our culture alive.
我們祖先的傳統舞蹈與音樂應該流傳給後代，讓我們的文化存續下去。

The contributions of immigrants and the descendants of these immigrants from all over the world enabled the nation to become the most powerful of all.
來自世界各地的移民與其後代的貢獻，使這個國家成為所有國家中最強大的一個。

RELATED WORDS | 相關單字延伸

nurse
v. 照料，懷有（想法）

cherish
v. 珍惜，懷有（希望）

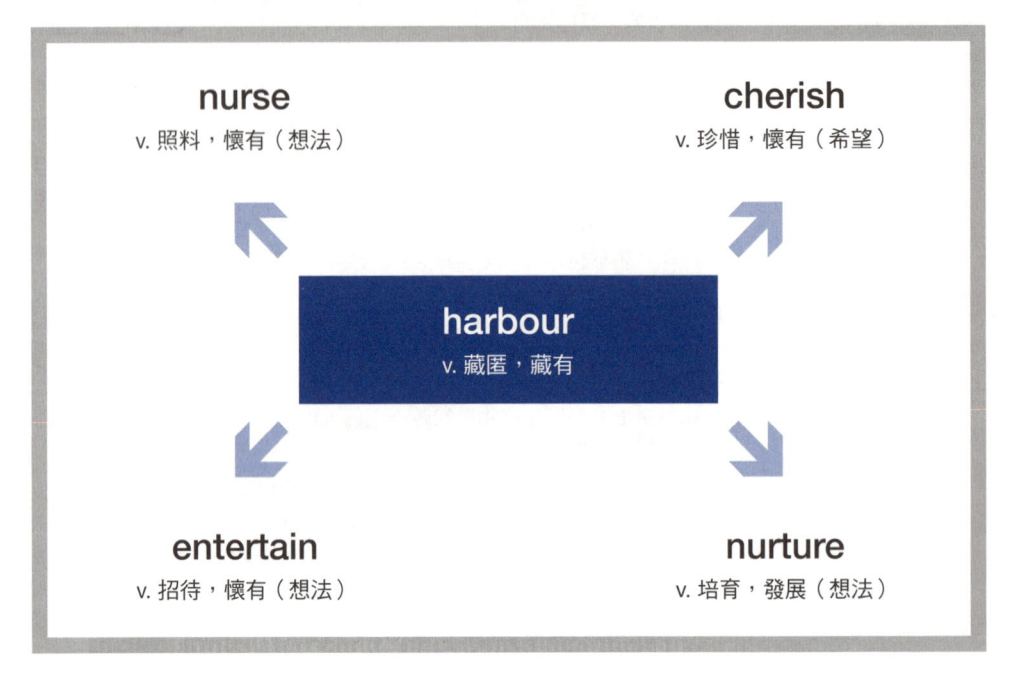

harbour
v. 藏匿，藏有

entertain
v. 招待，懷有（想法）

nurture
v. 培育，發展（想法）

harbour
/ˈhɑːbə/

History should be learned because it is essential to individuals and to the society, and because history as a culture of knowledge harbours beauty.
歷史應該被學習，因為它對於個人和社會都是不可或缺的，也是因為歷史作為一種知識的文化蘊藏了美。

nurse
/nɜːs/

One should not nurse feelings of defeat when faced with a setback.
面臨挫折的時候，不應該懷抱著失敗的情緒。

entertain
/ɛntəˈteɪn/

I have often entertained the thought that different perspectives of history should be studied.
我經常懷抱著不同歷史觀點都應該被研究的想法。

cherish
/ˈtʃɛrɪʃ/

Many societies cherish their unique histories, teaching the beauty of culture in history in schools.
許多社會珍惜自己獨有的歷史，並且在學校教授自身歷史文化之美。

nurture
/ˈnɜːtʃə/

When I was a high school student, I read a lot of historical novels and began to nurture the idea of studying history.
當我還是個高中學生的時候，我讀了許多歷史小說，並且開始發展出研究歷史的想法。

USEFUL EXPRESSIONS | 相關實用片語

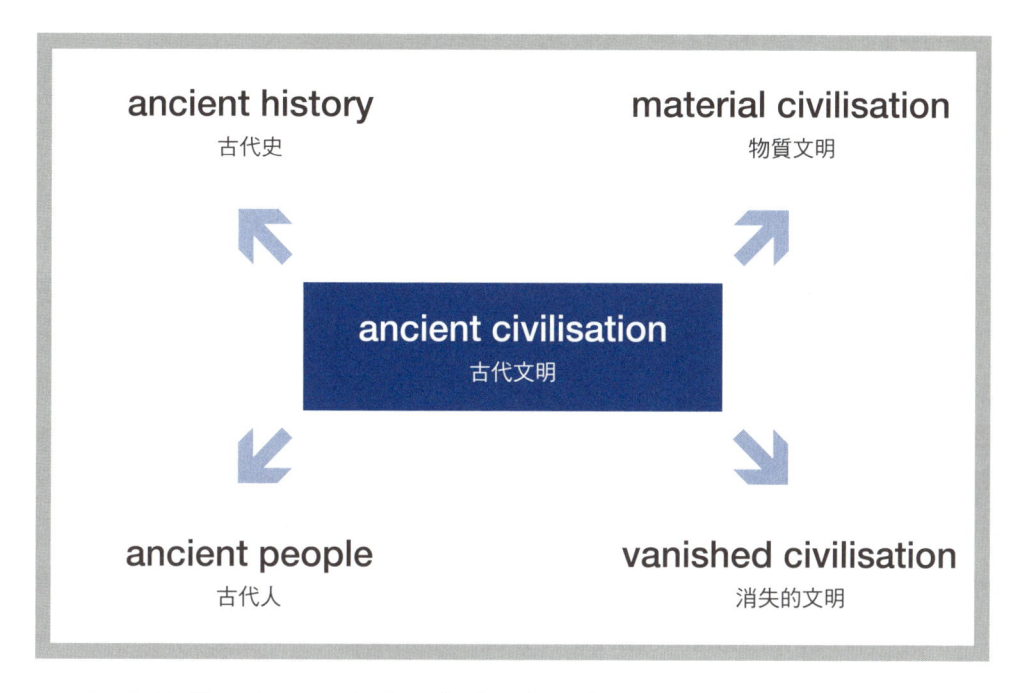

```
ancient history                    material civilisation
古代史                              物質文明

              ancient civilisation
                    古代文明

ancient people                     vanished civilisation
古代人                              消失的文明
```

ancient civilisation
/ˈeɪnʃənt ˌsɪvɪlaɪˈzeɪʃən/

Archaeologists have found traces of an ancient civilisation in the Bronze Age artefacts at Castlemartyr.
考古學家在卡斯爾馬特的青銅時代文物中找到了古代文明的痕跡。

ancient history
/ˈeɪnʃənt ˈhɪstəri/

He works for the Northeast Asia Project, researching the ancient history of Manchuria.
他參與「東北亞計畫」，研究滿洲地區的古代歷史。

ancient people
/ˈeɪnʃənt ˈpiːpəl/

Ancient people named the brightest stars 'Polaris' and 'Sirius' after the north and a dog, respectively.
古代人分別以北方和狗的稱呼，來為最亮的「Polaris（北極星）」和「Sirius（天狼星）」命名。

material civilisation
/məˈtɪəriəl ˌsɪvɪlaɪˈzeɪʃən/

American capitalism, entrepreneurship and material civilisation were advocated by The Newcomen Society of North America.
美國的資本主義、企業家精神和物質文明，是受到北美洲紐康門協會所提倡的。

vanished civilisation
/ˈvænɪʃt ˌsɪvɪlaɪˈzeɪʃən/

The Olmec are a vanished civilisation that existed from around 1400 BC in south-central Mexico.
奧爾梅克文明是西元前1400年左右曾經存在於墨西哥中南部的消失文明。

TUE

IELTS **BASIC WORDS**

reason /ˈriːzən/ n. 理由
ENG. basis or motive for an action
SYS. ground, rationality

> The **reason** for the global release of the news is to warn people of impending danger.
> 對全球發佈這個消息的理由，是要警告即將發生的危險。

同義語 例句 **On account of** public safety, public address system should be the main means of warning people of danger.
由於公眾安全的考量，公共場所廣播系統應該作為警告人們注意危險的主要方式。

同義語 例句 The **cause of action** was clearly to protect the public.
行動的原因顯然是為了保護大眾。

反義語 例句 As an **end result**, an international news report has been released to the public.
結果就是，一條國際新聞報導向大眾發布了。

factor /ˈfæktə/ n. 因素
ENG. anything that contributes to a result
SYS. component, element

> The main **factor** why the scandalous news was published was jealousy.
> 醜聞之所以被發佈的主要因素是嫉妒。

同義語 例句 The **element that affects the outcome** of the news exposure the most is showbiz rivalry.
影響新聞曝光結果的最大因素是娛樂圈的競爭。

同義語 例句 Insecurity of celebrities with each other is **part of** the rumours' **origin**.
名人對彼此的不安全感是傳聞的部分起因。

反義語 例句 Jealousy, rivalry and insecurity are **unrelated variables** in news exposés.
嫉妒、競爭與不安全感是和新聞曝光無關的變因。

136

WEEK 3 TOPIC **CULTURE**

▶基礎單字擴充

advance /ədˈvɑːns/　v. 前進，進展
ENG. move or bring forward
SYS. progress, proceed

> The international news about First World countries helps them **advance** even more.
> 關於第一世界國家的國際新聞，會幫助它們更進一步發展。

同義語例句 The impressive reports on leading nations challenge developing countries to just keep **pressing on**.
關於領先國家的那些令人印象深刻的報導，刺激開發中國家繼續加緊前進。

同義語例句 The news reports encouraged advancing countries to **go ahead** with their development plans.
那些新聞報導鼓勵發展中國家繼續進行開發計畫。

反義語例句 The news articles caused nations to **step back** and watch advanced countries pass them by.
那些新聞報導使得各國退縮，眼睜睜看著先進國家超越它們。

domain /dəʊˈmeɪn/　n. 領地，領域，範圍
ENG. territory over which rule or control is exercised
SYS. land, demesne

> The news displeased the president as it was discussing his **domain**.
> 這則新聞因為討論總統的權力範圍而使他不悅。

同義語例句 The leader did not appreciate the article about his **realm of control**.
領導人不喜歡那篇關於他的控制範圍的報導。

同義語例句 The president was not happy when his **scope of authority** was featured in a news item.
總統對於自己的權力範圍被一則新聞報導感到不高興。

反義語例句 The president's **powerlessness** is making headlines around the world.
總統的缺乏權勢上了全世界的頭條。

TOPIC: People's preferences for the news
人們對於新聞的偏好

Newspapers, **televised** newscasts and online news sources all make an effort to **publish** both international and national stories in their daily reports. Many people reading or watching these stories have their own **preferences**, however, oftentimes **opting** to watch only international briefs or national reports. The news companies are most of the time held **accountable** for being **impartial purveyors** of information, but despite this, the public can choose which type of story interests them the most. The danger of this freedom of choice is that it may lead to an **ignorant** public with a limited knowledge base. Criticism aside, it is nearly impossible for anyone to be completely **objective**, as everyone has their own biases and personal beliefs. All in all, reading or watching a breadth of reports on both international and local events is **advisable**, as it will create a more informed, well-rounded populace.

報紙、電視新聞報導和網路新聞來源，都努力在每天的報導中發布國際與國內新聞。不過，很多閱讀或觀看這些報導的人有自己的偏好，通常是選擇只看國際新聞摘要或國內報導。新聞公司通常被認為有責任成為公正的資訊提供者，但即使如此，大眾還是可以選擇哪種新聞報導最能引起他們的興趣。這種自由選擇的危險性，在於它可能造就一群知識來源有限的無知大眾。撇開這樣的批評不談，要任何人完全客觀都是幾乎不可能的，因為每個人都有自己的成見和個人信念。總之，廣泛閱讀或觀看關於國際與國內事件的報導是最好的，因為這樣可以創造一群更了解（社會）情況、見識更全面的民眾。

televised
/ˈtɛlɪvʌɪzd/

adj. 電視播出的
I remember how excited I was when the first programmes were **televised** in colour.
我記得電視節目最早以彩色播出時我有多興奮。

publish
/ˈpʌblɪʃ/

v. 出版，發布
J.K. Rowling decided not to **publish** any more of her famous Harry Potter books.
J.K. 羅琳決定不再為著名的哈利波特系列多出任何一本書。

preference
/ˈprɛfərəns/

n. 偏好
She asked me to write down my ice cream flavour **preferences** on the card.
她要求我在卡片上寫下我對冰淇淋口味的偏好。

opt
/ɒpt/

v. 選擇
Many Korean students are **opting** to attend universities in Australia.　許多韓國學生選擇到澳洲上大學。

accountable
/əˈkaʊntəbəl/

adj. 有責任的
You will be held **accountable** for your actions if you are caught shoplifting.
如果被抓到在店內行竊，你會被要求對自己的行為負責。

impartial
/ɪmˈpɑːʃəl/

adj. 不偏不倚的，公正的
When my two best friends were arguing, I chose to remain **impartial**.
當我最好的兩位朋友爭執時，我選擇保持中立。

purveyor
/pəˈveɪə/

n. 提供者，供應者
The most reputable **purveyors** have their licenses to sell concert tickets.
最有信譽的供應者有販售演唱會門票的執照。

ignorant
/ˈɪɡnərənt/

adj. 無知的
The first-year student was quite **ignorant** and often made uninformed remarks.
那個一年級的學生很無知，常常發表因為不了解情況而產生的言論。

objective
/əbˈdʒɛktɪv/

adj. 客觀的
John tried to remain **objective** as a police officer, but found it difficult at times.
身為警察，John努力保持客觀，但他發現有時候很困難。

advisable
/ədˈvʌɪzəbəl/

adj. 建議的，可取的，明智的
When on a boat, it is **advisable** that passengers wear a life vest.
在船上的時候，建議乘客穿著救生背心。

WORD TRAINING | 重點單字造句練習

enculturation
/ɪnˌkʌltʃəˈreɪʃən/

n. 文化適應

The media can be positively used for socialisation and enculturation among the young generations.
媒體可以正面地用於年輕世代的社會化與文化適應方面。

The media makes us products of our own enculturation unless we make a conscious effort to remain objective.
媒體使我們成為自己文化適應的產物,除非我們有意識地努力保持客觀。

The famous CEO featured in yesterday's newspaper suggested that foreign students learn well and ask for help to facilitate their enculturation process.
昨天報紙專題報導的知名執行長,建議外國學生好好學習並且尋求協助,以促進自身的文化適應過程。

Enculturation for international students is absolutely necessary, so there are many volunteers who help them understand the customs and traditions of the local culture.
國際學生的文化適應是絕對重要的,所以有許多義工幫助他們了解本地文化的習俗與傳統。

nationality
/ˌnæʃəˈnælɪti/

n. 國籍,民族

Discrimination based on nationality is illegal in some countries including the United States.
對於國籍的歧視,在包括美國的某些國家是違法的。

It is unlawful to pass someone over for a job or promotion because of his or her nationality.
因為某人的國籍而不考慮錄用他或讓他升職,是不合法的。

Despite the modern trend, marriages between two different nationalities are still prohibited in some cultures, which are strongly opposed by their younger generation.
儘管和現代的趨勢不同,不同國籍間的婚姻在某些文化中仍然是禁止的,而這些文化受到年輕世代的強烈反對。

It is essential to educate our youth about other nationalities by giving them books about world history to instil the importance of cross-culturalism.
給青少年關於世界歷史的書來灌輸他們跨文化主義的重要性,籍以教育他們關於其他民族的知識,是有必要的。

口說範例 💬   寫作範例 ✍️

race
/reɪs/

n. 種族

💬 Skin colour has long been used to classify people into races.
膚色長久以來一直被用來把人分類成（不同的）種族。

Sadly, race is often used as a basis for discrimination and oppression.
可悲的是，種族經常被當成歧視與壓迫的根據。

✍️ Happiness is our birthright regardless of race, sex or religion; thus, we are all entitled to find and pursue whatever makes us happy.
不論種族、性別或宗教，幸福都是我們與生俱來的權利。所以，我們都有權尋找並追求任何讓我們幸福（快樂）的事物。

It is important to educate our youth about different races and cultures to break down the barriers, namely prejudice and bigotry.
教育我們的年輕人關於不同種族與文化的知識以消除（種族間的）壁壘，也就是偏見與偏執，是很重要的。

culture-vulture
/ˈkʌltʃə ˈvʌltʃə/

n. 文化熱愛者，「文化禿鷹」

💬 The news broadcaster is quite a culture-vulture, travelling around and interviewing artists.
這位新聞主播是很熱愛文化的人，他跑遍各地採訪藝術家。

If you are deemed a culture-vulture, you may wish to investigate the social meaning of it.
如果你被認為是個文化熱愛者，你可能會想研究它的社會意義。

✍️ As I was reading the international news today, I was surprised to learn that our Prime Minister is considered a culture-vulture due to his policy on arts and culture.
我閱讀今天的國際新聞的時候，我很驚訝地得知我們的首相因為他的藝文政策而被認為是文化熱愛者。

Some culture-vultures today are into the music which most people consider noisy, and they are fans of body art involving excessive piercings and tattoos.
現今的某些文化熱愛者喜歡大部分的人認為很吵的音樂，而他們也是包括大量穿環與刺青的身體藝術的愛好者。

RELATED WORDS | 相關單字延伸

uninformed
adj. 不了解情況的，無知的

oblivious
adj. 不注意的，沒有察覺的

ignorant
adj. 無知的

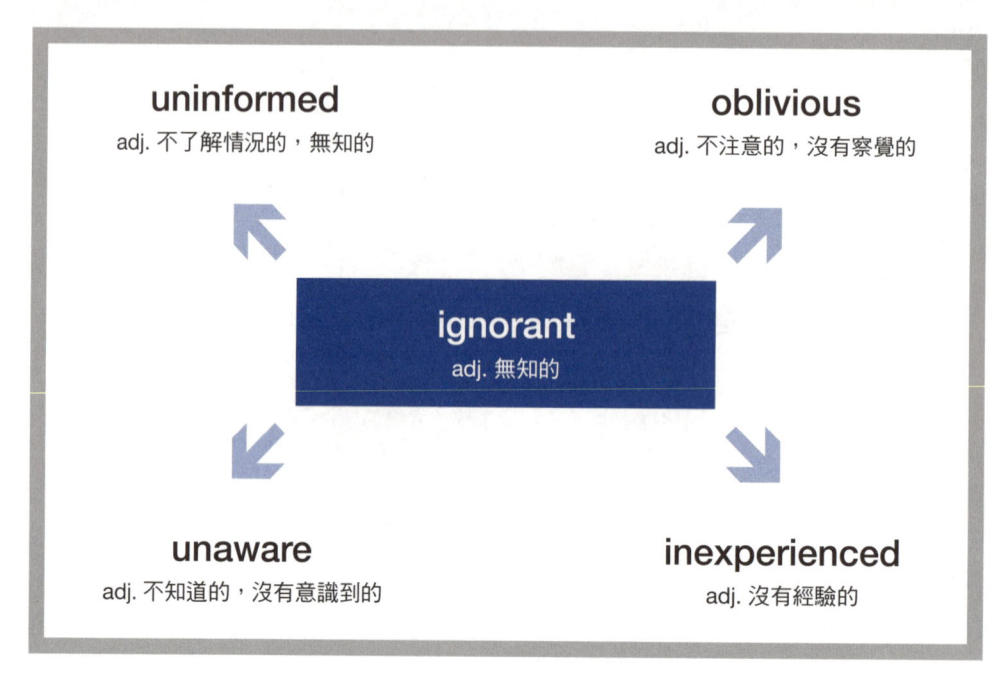

unaware
adj. 不知道的，沒有意識到的

inexperienced
adj. 沒有經驗的

ignorant
/ˈɪɡnərənt/

Freedom of choice means giving uneducated people the liberty to choose to remain ignorant.
選擇的自由意味著給未受教育的人選擇保持無知的自由。

uninformed
/ˌʌnɪnˈfɔːmd/

Prejudice is committed by people who are uninformed about the basics of society and culture.
偏見是不知道社會與文化的基本原則的人會犯的錯。

unaware
/ˌʌnəˈwɛː/

I was unaware of their country's beautiful traditions until I experienced it myself.
在我親身經歷之前，我都不知道他們國家美麗的傳統。

oblivious
/əˈblɪvɪəs/

He wore his shoes inside the temple, being completely oblivious to their culture.
他穿著鞋子進入寺廟，完全沒有注意到他們的文化。

inexperienced
/ˌɪnɪkˈspɪərɪənst/

Culture shock is often the problem encountered by inexperienced travellers.
文化衝擊通常是沒有經驗的旅行者會遇到的問題。

USEFUL EXPRESSIONS | 相關實用片語

personal rights 個人權利

popular belief 普遍的信念／看法

personal belief 個人信念

personal guidance 個人指導

folk belief 民間信仰

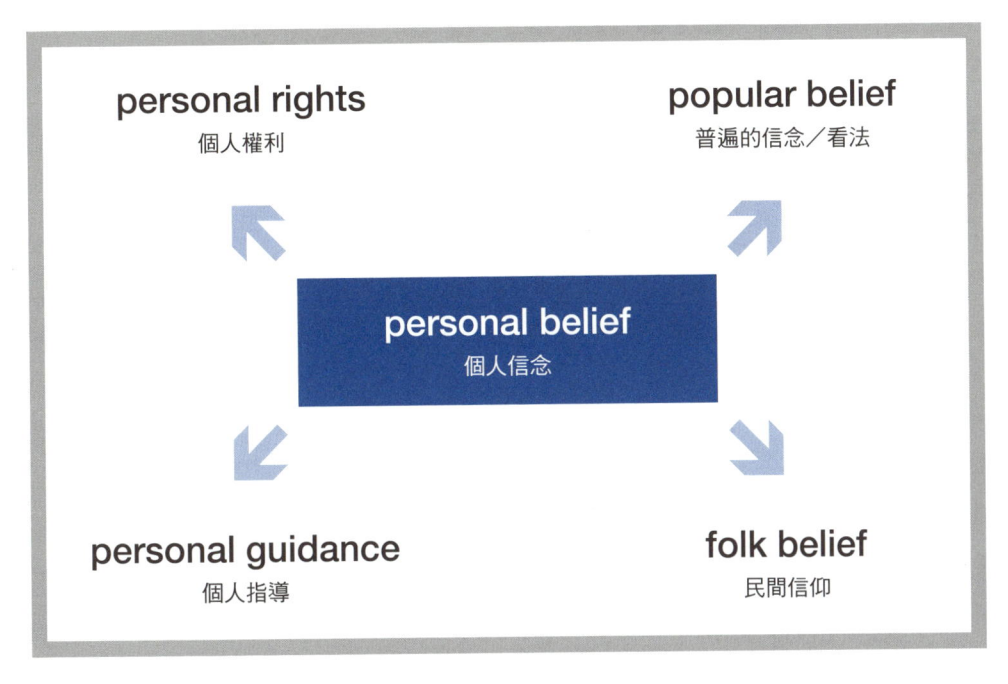

---

personal belief
/ˈpɚsənəl bɪˈliːf/

The laws that make serving in the military mandatory may be against some people's personal beliefs.
使軍中服役成為義務的法律，可能違背了某些人的個人信念。

personal rights
/ˈpɚsənəl rʌɪts/

The massive infringement on personal rights that resulted from Latin Conservatism was unpardonable.
拉丁保守主義所導致的大規模個人權利侵犯是不可原諒的。

personal guidance
/ˈpɚsənəl ˈɡʌɪdəns/

His staff worked hard because he treated them fairly, offering personal guidance and friendship.
他的員工努力工作，因為他公平對待員工，給予他們個人指導以及友誼。

popular belief
/ˈpɒpjʊlə bɪˈliːf/

Researchers have now dispelled the popular belief that all dinosaurs were cold-blooded and slow.
研究者現在已經消除了所有恐龍都是冷血並且行動緩慢的普遍看法。

folk belief
/fəʊk bɪˈliːf/

Ancient Taoist and bucolic folk beliefs are the roots of the traditional Chinese medicine used today.
古代道教與鄉間民俗信仰，是今日使用的傳統中醫學的根源。

WED

IELTS **BASIC WORDS**

search /sɜːtʃ/ v. 尋找
ENG. try to locate, discover or establish the existence of something
SYS. seek, explore

> He **searched** for native speakers in an attempt to save the language from dying out.
> 他尋找母語人士，試圖挽救那種語言免於滅絕。

同義語例句 He **looked for** locals who spoke the language to help save it.
他尋找說那種語言的當地人來幫忙挽救它。

同義語例句 The linguist **sought for** people who know the language to help keep it alive.
那位語言學家尋找知道那種語言的人來幫忙維持它的存活。

反義語例句 He did **not look for** anything that can prevent the language from dying out.
他沒有尋找任何可以防止那種語言滅絕的事物。

substitute /ˈsʌbstɪtjuːt/ v. 代替
ENG. put in the place of another
SYS. replace, interchange

> No language, not even English, can **substitute** for a native tongue.
> 沒有一種語言可以代替母語，就連英語也是一樣。

同義語例句 No majority language can **take the place of** any minority language.
沒有什麼主流語言可以成為任何少數族群語言的替代品。

同義語例句 It is not right to **give up** a mother tongue **in favour of** a universal language.
放棄母語而改用通用語言是不對的。

反義語例句 Families of native speakers must **use the same language** as often as possible.
母語人士的家庭應該盡量常用相同的語言。

WEEK 3 TOPIC **CULTURE**

▶ 基礎單字擴充

combine /kəmˈbʌɪn/ v. 結合
ENG. to bring to a state of unity
SYS. merge, compound

> The pidgin was formed by combining the grammars and words of their native language with those of English.
> 那個混雜語言是結合他們母語和英語的文法、詞彙而形成的。

同義語例句 They put together the elements of their native language and English to create an in-between language.
他們結合自己母語和英語的要素，創造出一種介於中間的語言。

同義語例句 Natives and foreigners should join forces in preserving languages by building corpora.
本地人和外國人應該藉著建立語料庫來合作保存它們。

反義語例句 We must discriminate local languages from English to emphasise and preserve their distinct uniqueness.
我們必須將當地語言與英語加以區別，以強調並保存當地語言特有的獨特性。

vacuum /ˈvakjuːm/ n. 真空
ENG. an empty area or space
SYS. vacancy, void

> It is impossible to preserve languages 100% unless we live in a vacuum.
> 要百分之百保存一個語言是不可能的，除非我們活在真空環境裡。

同義語例句 Avoiding linguistic influences completely is impossible unless the world around us is free of matter.
要完全避免語言影響是不可能的，除非我們周遭的世界完全沒有物質。

同義語例句 Our language stays uninfluenced only if the world around us is full of nothing.
只有在我們周遭的世界充滿空無的情況下，我們的語言才會不受影響。

反義語例句 Languages are inevitably influenced especially when multicultural people live in a packed space.
語言無可避免會受到影響，尤其是多種文化的人們居住在擁擠的空間的時候。

WED

TOPIC: Saving languages of few speakers from dying out

挽救少數族群的語言免於滅絕

In nearly every part of the world, there are languages on the verge of extinction. During the past several years, **linguists** have become increasingly concerned about ethno-linguistic groups which are either shifting from their original language to another that offers more opportunities, or whose **populace** is becoming so **reduced** that language preservation seems **futile**. Just as we in the developed world now have the affluence and ability to **preserve** threatened biological species, so too should we worry about language and culture extinction. Many believe we should accept changes in language use as **emblematic** of progress and therefore do nothing. Others say we should attempt some sort of language **salvage** or **revitalisation** programme. In the end, however, what keeps a **vernacular** alive is its social function, as the only people who can stop a language from **vanishing** are the speakers of that language.

TRANS

幾乎在世界的每個地方，都有語言瀕臨滅絕。在過去幾年，語言學家越來越擔憂民族語言族群逐漸從母語轉換到提供更多機會的另一種語言，或者人口減少了很多，使得語言保存似乎徒勞無功。就好像我們身處於已開發國家的人擁有富裕和能力來保存瀕危物種一樣，我們也應該擔心語言與文化的滅絕。很多人認為我們應該把語言使用情況的改變當成進步的象徵來接受，所以應該不要加以干涉。其他人則說我們應該試圖進行某種語言搶救或復興計畫。不過，使本地語言得以持續存活的因素，終究在於它的社會功能，因為能夠使一個語言免於消失的人，就只有那種語言的使用者而已。

linguist
/ˈlɪŋgwɪst/
n. 語言學家
We hired a **linguist** to analyse the younger generation's style of language.
我們雇用了語言學家來分析年輕一代的語言風格。

populace
/ˈpɒpjʊləs/
n. 大眾，民眾，人口
I don't see the candidate as a threat to the **populace**.
我不認為那位候選人對大眾是個威脅。

reduce
/rɪˈdjuːs/
v. 使減少
They have **reduced** the amount of sodium in my favourite brand of margarine.
他們把我最愛的人造奶油品牌的鈉含量減少了。

futile
/ˈfjuːtaɪl/
adj. 無用的，徒勞的
An effort to try to stop the criminal in the act would be **futile**.
試圖在犯罪現場阻止罪犯的努力將會是徒勞的。

preserve
/prɪˈzɜːv/
v. 保存
My aunt wanted to **preserve** the fruit we picked this summer by making jam.
我阿姨想用做果醬的方式來保存我們今年夏天採的水果。

emblematic
/ˌembləˈmatɪk/
adj. 象徵的
That family crest is **emblematic** of their Scottish lineage.
那個家族紋章象徵他們的蘇格蘭血統。

salvage
/ˈsalvɪdʒ/
n. 沉船救助，沉船打撈，搶救，挽救
The **salvage** operation not only saved the goods on the ship but also reduced damage to the environment.
打撈行動不但搶救了船上的物品，也減少了對環境的傷害。

revitalisation
/riːˌvaɪtəlaɪˈzeɪʃən/
n. 復興，振興
The company **revitalisation** project includes hiring fourteen new employees and changing the management structure.
公司振興計畫包括雇用十四名新員工以及改變經營架構。

vernacular
/vəˈnakjʊlə/
n. 本地語言，方言
I couldn't figure out what **vernacular** the woman was speaking in to her friend.
我搞不清楚那個女人跟她朋友說的方言是什麼。

vanish
/ˈvanɪʃ/
v. 消失
The Arctic ice is **vanishing** at a rapid pace due to global warming.
由於全球暖化，北極的冰層正快速消失中。

WORD TRAINING | 重點單字造句練習

maintenance
/ˈmeɪntənəns/

n. 維護，保持

💬 The project encourages language maintenance through the promotion of literacy in minority languages.
這個計畫藉著提升少數族群語言的讀寫能力來促進語言的維護。

Language maintenance project should be implemented for languages endangered by globalisation.
應該對全球化中瀕臨滅絕的語言進行語言維護計畫。

✍ International organisations, especially UNESCO, are devising ways to support the maintenance of languages which are vulnerable to extinction.
國際性的機構，尤其是聯合國教科文組織（UNESCO），正在設計方法來支持瀕臨滅絕語言的維護。

As a community loses its language, part of its culture is also lost, so the maintenance of minor languages is imperative to protect cultural diversity.
當一個社群失去了它的語言時，它的部分文化也失去了，所以小眾語言的維護對於保護文化多樣性是必要的。

belief
/bɪˈliːf/

n. 相信，信念

💬 Many people hold strong beliefs about saving languages from disappearing.
許多人對於保護語言免於消失有著強烈的信念。

If people hold strong anti-globalisation beliefs, they are also likely to support the preservation of threatened languages.
如果人們有強烈的反全球化信念，他們也很有可能支持瀕危語言的保護。

✍ Language reflects both the beliefs and the culture of a society, so when a culture dies out, its language usually goes with it.
語言同時反映社會的信念與文化，所以當一個文化滅絕，它的語言也通常會隨之而去。

Like in many indigenous cultures, the beliefs and practices about spirituality are passed verbally from one generation to the next by the stories and teachings of the elders.
就像在許多原住民文化裡一樣，關於靈性的信仰與習俗是以口語方式，藉由長者的故事與教導代代相傳的。

subculture
/ˈsʌbkʌltʃə/

n. 次文化

💬 Subcultures are believed to be brought about by the mixture of cultures in a country.
次文化被認為是國內多種文化的混合產生的。

Subcultures are usually propagated and invented through the use of media.
次文化通常是透過對媒體的使用來傳播並創造的。

✍️ Subcultures of music are a result of the society's evolution and the artists' constant reinvention of their art.
音樂的次文化是社會演進及藝人對自身藝術持續重新創造的結果。

Subculture is a precursor of a mainstream culture because as more people become inclined to these new ideas, the unconventional then becomes the new standard.
次文化是主流文化的先驅，因為當越來越多人傾向這些新的想法，原本的非常規就成為新的標準。

rooted
/ˈruːtɪd/

adj. 根植於⋯的，發源自⋯的

💬 Statistics show that the usage of Arabic-rooted words is on the decline.
統計顯示阿拉伯語源的單字使用率正在減少。

The immersion programme is rooted in Hawaiian-only pedagogy in an attempt to save the language.
這個沉浸式教學計畫根植於純夏威夷語的教學，試圖拯救這種語言。

✍️ English is rooted from many other languages such as French, German, Latin and Greek, making it irregular in many ways.
英文源自其他許多語言，例如法語、德語、拉丁語、希臘語等，使得它在許多方面不規則。

One Creole language, deeply rooted in English but with ties to West and Central African languages, is fading amongst the African American population living on the Sea Islands.
有一種深植於英語但和西非及中非語言有關聯的混合語，正在（美國東南部海岸）海群島地區的非裔美國人族群中逐漸消失。

RELATED WORDS | 相關單字延伸

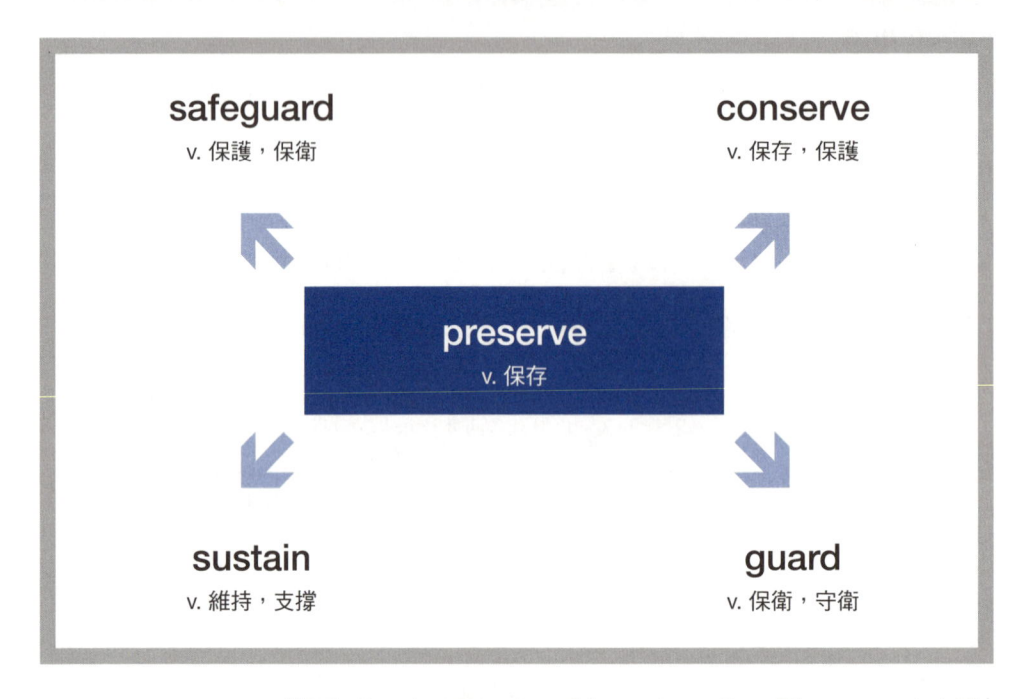

safeguard
v. 保護，保衛

conserve
v. 保存，保護

preserve
v. 保存

sustain
v. 維持，支撐

guard
v. 保衛，守衛

preserve
/prɪˈzɜːv/

We in the developed world now have the affluence and ability to preserve threatened biological species.
我們身處於已開發國家的人，現在擁有富裕和能力來保存瀕危物種。

safeguard
/ˈseɪfɡɑːd/

With our new wealth and knowledge, we should safeguard biological species facing extinction.
靠著新的財富與知識，我們應該保護面臨絕種的物種。

sustain
/səˈsteɪn/

In order to sustain the animal population, we must research more about invasive species.
為了維持動物族群，我們必須對入侵物種進行更多研究。

conserve
/kənˈsɜːv/

Developed nations should invest in conserving animal and plant populations facing extinction.
已開發國家應該投入資金來保護面臨絕種的動物與植物族群。

guard
/ɡɑːd/

What is the best way to guard biological species from losing their habitats due to industrial development?
要保護物種避免因工業開發失去棲息地，最好的方法是什麼？

USEFUL EXPRESSIONS | 相關實用片語

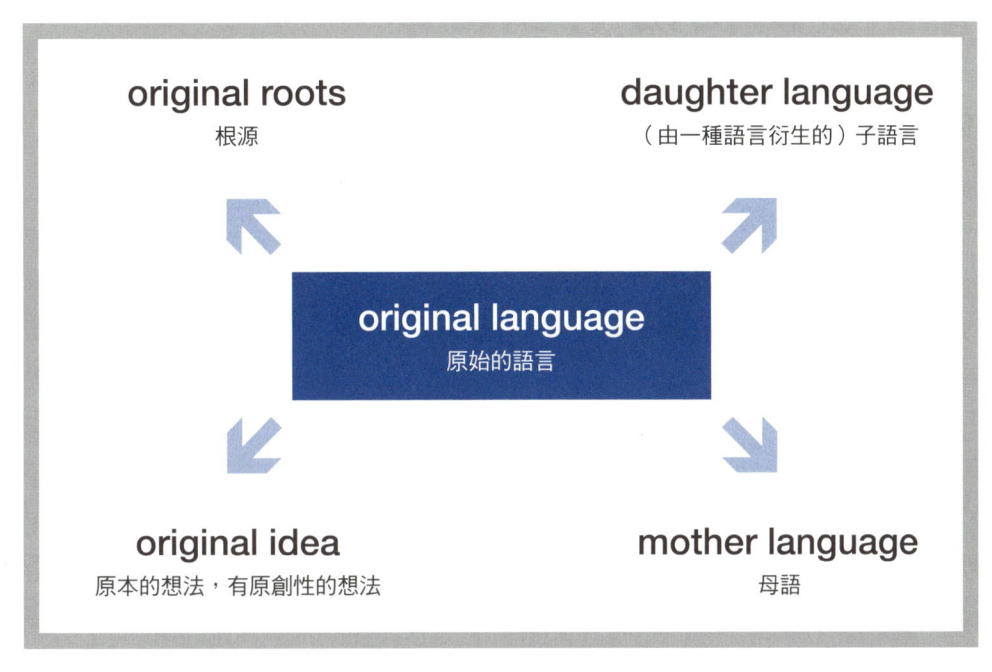

original roots
根源

daughter language
（由一種語言衍生的）子語言

original language
原始的語言

original idea
原本的想法，有原創性的想法

mother language
母語

---

original language
/əˈrɪdʒɪnəl ˈlæŋɡwɪdʒ/

The original language and meanings in the book were not translated correctly.
書裡的原始語言（遣詞用字）和意義沒有被正確翻譯。

original roots
/əˈrɪdʒɪnəl ruːts/

Many traditions with their original roots in the tropics continue in western English-speaking countries.
許多源自熱帶地區的傳統在西方英語國家延續著。

original idea
/əˈrɪdʒɪnəl ʌɪˈdɪə/

Coming up with a truly original idea for a restaurant can be difficult in this market.
為餐廳想出真正具有原創性的想法，在這個市場可能是很困難的。

daughter language
/ˈdɔːtə ˈlæŋɡwɪdʒ/

A daughter language is a language that has evolved from another tongue.
子語言是從另一種語言演變而來的語言。

mother language
/ˈmʌðə ˈlæŋɡwɪdʒ/

The government should promote multilingual education so that all mother languages can be represented.
政府應該促進多語言教育，好讓所有母語得以展現。

THU

IELTS BASIC WORDS

ground /graʊnd/ n. 根據，理由
ENG. a rational motive for belief or action
SYS. reason, foundation

> There are no grounds for conflicts between different cultures to end up in bloodshed.
> 沒有理由讓不同文化之間的衝突以流血收場。

同義語例句 The main reason why the conflict between the two cultures broke out was revealed.
這兩個文化之間的衝突爆發的主要原因被揭露了。

同義語例句 The leader gave the speech with an underlying intention to mend the conflict between the two cultures
那位領導人發表演說，其中隱含的目的是要修補兩個文化之間的衝突。

反義語例句 The two conflicting communities gave illogical arguments as to why they insist on continuing with the war.
關於為什麼要堅持繼續戰爭，這兩個互相衝突的社會提出了不合邏輯的論點。

pour /pɔː/ v. 傾瀉，湧出
ENG. to flow or cause to flow
SYS. spill, flow, drip

> Sentiments poured out from the opposing cultures regarding the war that just broke out.
> 關於剛爆發的戰爭，對立的文化中（產生的／累積的）情緒傾瀉而出。

同義語例句 It is time for our feelings to shift to a new place to avoid cultural wars.
是時候讓我們的情感轉移到新的地方來避免文化戰爭了。

同義語例句 We should unite in love to release the conflicts.
我們應該在愛中團結起來，把衝突釋放掉。

反義語例句 Anger generated from conflicts hinders love from flowing.
衝突所產生的憤怒，阻礙了愛的流動。

WEEK 3 TOPIC **CULTURE**

▶基礎單字擴充

mould /məuld/ v. 塑造
ENG. make something, usually for a specific function.
SYS. sculpt, make

> We should **mould** our nation to be accepting and open to different cultures.
> 我們應該把我們的國家塑造成能夠接受不同文化,並且對其保持開放。

同義語例句 It is good for the country to be **shaped into** one that accepts diverse cultures.
國家被塑造成能夠接受多元文化,是一件好事。

同義語例句 It is necessary to **form** an open and embracing culture.
塑造開放並且有包容力的文化是必要的。

反義語例句 If we **leave** our attitudes **unchanged**, our cultural conflicts will never be resolved.
如果我們讓自己的態度保持不變,那麼我們的文化衝突就永遠不會解決。

apply /əˈplaɪ/ v. 適用
ENG. be pertinent, relevant or applicable
SYS. appertain, relate

> The teachings of God also **apply** to the relation between countries.
> 神的教導也適用於國家之間的關係。

同義語例句 God cares for victims of cultural conflicts, and the same **goes for** their oppressors.
神會照看文化衝突的受害者,對於他們的壓迫者也是一樣(對他們也是成立的)。

同義語例句 The importance of maintaining peace **is relevant to** both the attacking and the attacked countries.
維持和平的重要性對於攻擊和被攻擊的國家都是有關係的(要緊的)。

反義語例句 A victim country's peace **means nothing** for the attacking country.
受害國家的和平對於攻擊的國家沒有意義。

153

THU

TOPIC | Conflicts between different cultures
不同文化間的衝突

Conflict is inherent to any kind of human interaction. Conflict **manifestation** in a **multicultural** environment is apparent when an array of diverse forces comes into play. It takes some skills to manage cultural **clash**. Before approaching the conflict, any person wishing to solve it should ask themselves how **acquainted** they really are with their multicultural environment and if they hold any **stereotypes** that may act as a form of **discrimination**. Anti-bias training can be beneficial to all people who want to understand how to **handle** conflict effectively in a **diverse** group. As conflict in a multicultural setting brings to mind differences between cultures, the key to conflict resolution is to connect people through their similarities. Differences break apart communications, resulting various **incongruent** messages instead of a universal one.

TRANS

衝突是任何人類互動中固有的本質。多元文化環境中的衝突顯現，在許多不同勢力產生作用的時候會很明顯。處理文化衝突需要一些技巧。在處理衝突之前，任何想要解決它的人都應該問自己實際上對自身的多文化環境有多熟悉，以及是否抱持著任何可能形成歧視的刻板印象。對抗偏見的訓練，對於所有想了解如何在多元團體中有效處理衝突的人都會是有益的。因為衝突在多元文化的情況下讓人想起文化間的差異，所以衝突解決的關鍵是用人們的相似處把他們連結起來。差異會破壞溝通，造成不一致的訊息，而不是普遍一致的訊息。

conflict
/ˈkɒnflɪkt/

n. 衝突

There was much **conflict** between the actor and the director on the movie set.
在電影片場，那位演員與導演之間有許多衝突。

manifestation
/ˌmænɪfɛˈsteɪʃən/

n. 跡象，顯現

Manifestations of the abuse she suffered were obvious when she tried dating again.
當她試圖再次約會時，曾經遭受過虐待的跡象表現得很明顯。

multicultural
/mʌltɪˈkʌltʃərəl/

adj. 多元文化的

Canada is a **multicultural** country where people of many ethnicities live and prosper.
加拿大是一個多元文化的國家，許多種族的民眾在那裡生活並且發展成功。

clash
/klæʃ/

v. 衝突

Don't wear yellow and purple together because they **clash** with each other.
不要把黃色和紫色穿在一起，因為它們相互衝突。

acquainted
/əˈkweɪntɪd/

adj. 熟悉的

He took her out on a date to get better **acquainted** with her.
為了要和她更加熟悉，他帶她出去約會。

stereotype
/ˈstɛrɪəʊtʌɪp/

n. 刻板印象

Young people often have the **stereotype** of being reckless and stupid.
年輕人通常背負著魯莽和愚笨的刻板印象。

discrimination
/dɪˌskrɪmɪˈneɪʃən/

n. 歧視

The disabled man felt not having wheelchair ramps at the entrance was **discrimination**.
那位殘障人士覺得入口處沒有輪椅坡道是一種歧視。

handle
/ˈhændəl/

v. 處理，應付

The nanny was able to **handle** caring for ten children at the same time.
這位保姆能夠應付同時照顧十個小孩。

diverse
/dʌɪˈvɜːs/

adj. 多樣的

Dad's talents are extremely **diverse**, as he plays the violin, sculpts and paints portraits.
爸爸的才能非常多樣，因為他拉小提琴、雕刻而且畫肖像。

incongruent
/ɪnˈkɒŋɡrʊənt/

adj. 不一致的

The new rules were **incongruent** with the requirements of the law.
新規定與法律的要求不一致。

WORD TRAINING | 重點單字造句練習

misconception
/mɪskənˈsɛpʃən/

n. 誤解

I'd like to clear up the common misconception that Korean society is based on money.
我想要消除認為韓國社會建立在金錢上的普遍誤解。

Some people have a misconception about different races and their cultures.
有些人對於不同種族和他們的文化有所誤解。

A man of science is usually not open to misconceptions about science and life in general.
科學人通常不接受對於科學與生命整體的誤解。

We encourage students to gain an understanding of cultural misconception and how the intricate relations between cultural practices, human action and material culture can cause conflict.
我們鼓勵學生了解文化上的誤解，以及文化慣例、人類行為、物質文化之間錯綜複雜的關係可能如何造成衝突。

prejudice
/ˈprɛdʒʊdɪs/

n. 偏見

It is wrong for a country to tolerate racial prejudice.
一個國家如果容忍種族偏見，那是錯誤的。

Respect and understanding are the only things that can eradicate prejudice.
尊重與了解是根除偏見唯一的方法。

In the past, lepers were treated as outcasts and faced with discrimination and prejudice from people due to the misconception about the disease.
在以前，由於對於痲瘋病的誤解，使得痲瘋病患者被當成受排斥的一群，並且面臨了人們的歧視與偏見。

Educating ourselves about other people's cultures and beliefs through frequent travelling will allow us to get rid of erroneous concepts, prejudice and bigotry.
透過頻繁的旅行，讓自己學習其他人的文化和信仰，可以讓我們擺脫錯誤的觀念、偏見與偏執。

ethnocentrism

/ˌɛθnəʊˈsɛntrɪzəm/

n. 民族優越感（民族中心主義）

💬 Ethnocentrism refers to judging other groups from our own culture's point of view, and it often causes conflict.
民族優越感指的是用我們自己的文化觀點去評價其他團體，而它經常造成衝突。

One of the most effective means for limiting intercultural conflict resulting from ethnocentrism is to watch our own reactions. 要減少因為民族優越感造成的文化間衝突，最有效的方式之一是留意我們自己的反應。

✏️ Ethnocentrism leads to misunderstanding as we often falsely distort what is meaningful and functional to other peoples through our own tinted glasses.
民族優越感會導致誤解，因為我們常常透過自己的有色眼鏡，錯誤地扭曲對其他民族而言有意義或有功用的事情。

There are extreme forms of ethnocentrism that pose serious social problems in the world community and are generally condemned, such as racism, colonialism and ethnic cleansing.
有些極端形式的民族優越感，造成國際社會上嚴重的社會問題，並且普遍受到譴責，像是種族主義、殖民主義、種族清洗等。

offence

/əˈfɛns/

n. 違法行為，冒犯

💬 An offence motivated by hate or prejudice is punishable by law.
由仇恨或偏見激發的犯法行為是可受法律懲罰的。

I took serious offence to his racist comments because they were hateful, ignorant and rude.
我對他的種族主義言論感到生氣，因為那懷有恨意、無知而且無禮。

✏️ Any person who commits an offence intentionally, such as the extensive destruction or appropriation of cultural property protected under the convention, should be prosecuted under the law.
任何故意犯法的人，例如對受公約保護的文化財產進行大規模破壞或私佔，都應該依法起訴。

It is an offence to import cultural property taken from occupied territory and then to sell, receive or re-export such property.
從被佔領的領土輸入文化財產並且出售、接受或再次輸出這類財產，是違法的行為。

RELATED WORDS | 相關單字延伸

manage
v. 管理，處理

administer
v. 管理，執行

handle
v. 處理

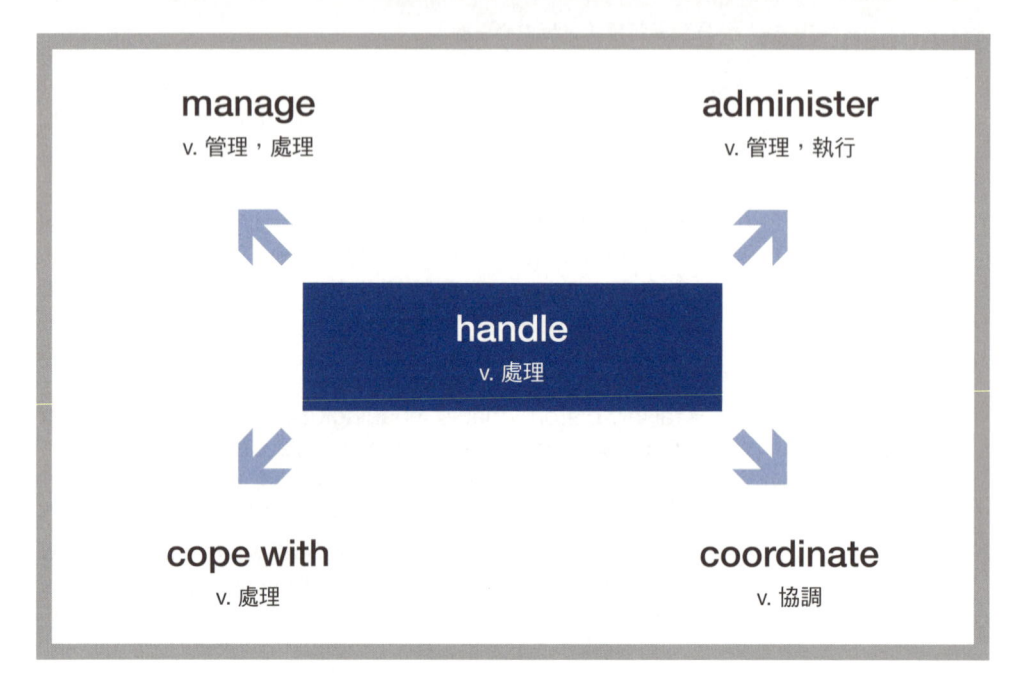

cope with
v. 處理

coordinate
v. 協調

handle
/ˈhændəl/

Anti-bias training can be beneficial to all people who want to understand how to handle conflict effectively in a diverse group.
對抗偏見的訓練，對於所有想了解如何在多元團體中有效處理衝突的人都會是有益的。

manage
/ˈmænɪdʒ/

In order to manage conflict fairly, people need to respect diversity within a group.
為了公平地處理衝突，人們需要尊重群體內的多樣性。

cope with
/kəʊp wɪð/

I can cope with high-stress situations thanks to my experience.
多虧有我的經驗，讓我能夠處理高度壓力的情況。

administer
/ədˈmɪnɪstə/

Make sure to administer diversity training to the group before they graduate.
記得要在那個團體畢業前對他們進行多元文化訓練。

coordinate
/kəʊˈɔːdɪneɪt/

The leader tried to coordinate the people, but their individual biases caused separation instead.
那位領導者試圖協調人們，但他們各自的偏見反而造成了分裂。

USEFUL EXPRESSIONS | 相關實用片語

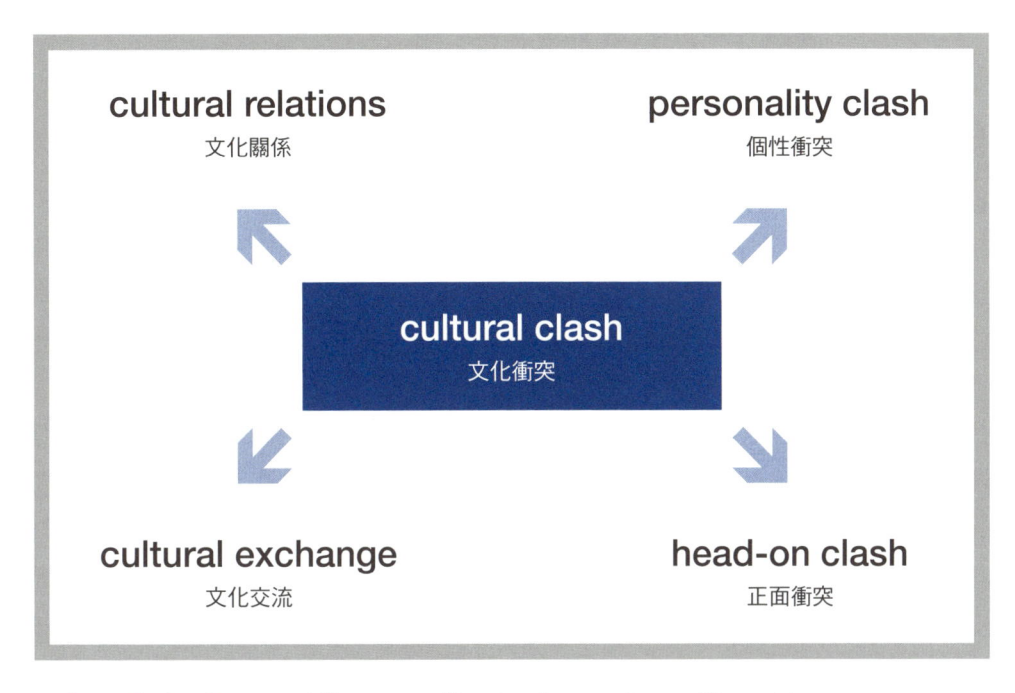

```
         cultural relations                personality clash
            文化關係                            個性衝突
                    ↖                    ↗
                        ┌─────────────┐
                        │cultural clash│
                        │   文化衝突    │
                        └─────────────┘
                    ↙                    ↘
         cultural exchange                 head-on clash
            文化交流                            正面衝突
```

cultural clash
/ˈkʌltʃərəl klæʃ/

When travelling to places where different languages are spoken, one may face a cultural clash.
當一個人旅行到說不同語言的地方時，他可能會面臨文化衝突。

cultural relations
/ˈkʌltʃərəl rɪˈleɪʃənz/

When studying the interaction between two countries, one should pay attention to their cultural relations.
研究兩個國家之間的相互影響時，應該要注意它們的文化關係。

cultural exchange
/ˈkʌltʃərəl ɪksˈtʃeɪndʒ/

The best plan is to develop a cultural exchange programme between Korean and New Zealand students.
最好的方案是發展韓國與紐西蘭學生之間的文化交流計畫。

personality clash
/pɜːsəˈnælɪti klæʃ/

The survey cited personality clashes as the chief reason of marriage dissolution in France.
這份調查指出，個性衝突是法國婚姻關係解除的主要理由。

head-on clash
/ˌhɛdˈɒn klæʃ/

If President Smith attempts to make Jones prime minister, a head-on clash may happen.
如果 Smith 總統要讓 Jones 當首相，一場正面衝突可能會發生。

FRI

IELTS **BASIC WORDS**

extreme /ɪkˈstriːm/ n. 極端 adj. 極端的
ENG. the furthest or highest degree of something
SYS. edge, limit

> Wearing a hanbok to work nowadays is an **extreme** manifestation of patriotism.
> 現在穿韓服上班是一種愛國主義的極端表現。

- 同義語 例句 — Being in a hanbok on an ordinary day is patriotism to the **ultimate degree**.
  在普通的日子穿著韓服是極度的愛國行為。

- 同義語 例句 — Requiring hanboks at work is an act of patriotism that is **beyond the limit**.
  要求工作時穿韓服是超過限度的愛國主義行為。

- 反義語 例句 — A **minimum** degree of respect is expected when we do not wear national clothes appropriately.
  當我們沒有適當穿著民族服裝時，只得到最小程度的尊重（幾乎得不到尊重）是可以預期的。

requirement /rɪˈkwaɪəmənt/ n. 要求，必要條件
ENG. anything indispensable
SYS. must, requisite

> Wearing national clothes periodically should be a **requirement** for cultural preservation.
> 定期穿著民族服裝應該是文化保護的一項必要條件。

- 同義語 例句 — Wearing national clothes is an **essential practice** to protect a dwindling culture.
  穿著民族服裝是保護逐漸式微的文化時不可或缺的行為。

- 同義語 例句 — Wearing traditional clothes is a **necessity** for a dying culture to survive.
  穿著傳統服裝是瀕臨消滅的文化要存活下去的必要行為。

- 反義語 例句 — Wearing national clothes is **something we can do without** in our daily life.　穿著民族服裝是我們在日常生活中不做也可以的事情。

WEEK 3 TOPIC **CULTURE**

▶基礎單字擴充

remove /rɪˈmuːv/ v. 去除
ENG. dispose of
SYS. extract, eliminate

> We must **remove** irrelevant influences from our national costumes.
> 我們必須去除我們民族服裝中不相關的影響。

同義語例句 It is ideal to **get rid of** influences of other cultures on our traditional clothing.
擺脫其他文化對我們傳統服裝的影響是理想的。

同義語例句 It is best to **chuck out** unrelated influences of pop culture on our national clothes.
最好把流行文化對我們民族服裝產生的無關影響給丟棄掉。

反義語例句 It is time to **bring back** the tradition of wearing our national clothes.
是時候把穿著我們民族服裝的傳統找回來了。

principle /ˈprɪnsɪpəl/ n. 原則
ENG. basic generalisation accepted as true
SYS. rule, concept

> It is a widely known **principle** that wearing national clothes helps preserve our culture.
> 穿著民族服裝有助於保存我們的文化,是廣為人知的原則。

同義語例句 The unwritten **body of rules** of cultural preservation includes wearing national costume.
關於文化保存的一系列不成文規定,包括穿著民族服裝。

同義語例句 It is a **law of nature** that people with the same skin unite.
膚色相同的人會團結在一起是自然法則。

反義語例句 That wearing the same national clothing will lead to the progress of a nation is a **myth**.
穿著相同的民族服裝能促成國家的進步是一項迷思。

161

FRI

TOPIC | Wearing national clothes
穿著民族服裝

As every person belongs to a culture and has the right to **disclose** it, personal **identity** may sometimes include wearing national or traditional clothes. Clothing, in terms of culture, reveals either historical **heredity**, religious beliefs or the specific culture a person belongs to. Those who follow **ethnic** traditions are **distinct** in a crowd given the specific clothing style they **sport**. Demonstrating a sense of belonging to a certain cultural community is the free right of every person. This freedom can be **likened** to that of freely declaring whom one is going to vote for. For instance, it is very easy to **distinguish** a traditional Indian woman from a traditional Muslim woman by the sari of an Indian woman and the hijab worn by a Muslim woman. Wearing traditional national **garments** brings people from the same culture together and shows their **unity**.

TRANS

因為每個人都屬於一個文化，而且有權力公開這一點，所以個人身分認同有時候可能包括穿著民族或傳統服裝。就文化而言，衣著揭示歷史繼承、宗教信仰或者一個人所屬的特定文化。那些遵循民族傳統的人，因為他們所誇示的服裝特定風格，所以在一群人之中是與眾不同的。展現對於某個文化群體的歸屬感，是每個人的自由權利。這種自由可以比擬為任意宣布要投票給誰的自由。舉例來說，藉由印度女性穿著的紗麗和穆斯林女性穿著的希賈布（頭巾），要區分傳統印度女性和穆斯林女性是很容易的。穿著傳統民族服裝能讓來自同一個文化的人們凝聚在一起，並且展現他們的團結。

disclose
/dɪsˈkloʊz/

v. 透露，公開

Unfortunately, I cannot **disclose** any information about our ongoing investigation.
很遺憾，我不能透露和進行中的調查相關的任何資訊。

identity
/ʌɪˈdɛntɪti/

n. 身分

The **identity** of the perpetrator was revealed to be a 32-year-old butcher.
罪犯的身分被揭露了，是一名32歲的屠夫。

heredity
/hɪˈrɛdɪti/

n. 遺傳

Her freckles and red hair come from **heredity**.
她的雀斑和紅髮來自遺傳。

ethnic
/ˈɛθnɪk/

adj. 種族的，民族的

Language is often one of the traits used to identify an **ethnic** group.
語言經常是用來認定民族族群的特徵之一。

distinct
/dɪˈstɪŋkt/

adj. 明顯不同的

She had one **distinct** patch of grey hair at the front of her head.
她的頭前面有一撮很明顯的白髮。

sport
/spɔːt/

v. 誇示，誇張地穿出來

If I must **sport** that awful shirt, at least give me a jacket to hide it!
如果我一定要穿出那件可怕的襯衫，那至少給我一件外套來遮它！

liken
/ˈlʌɪkən/

v. 把⋯比作

Her ability to argue was **likened** to that of a crown prosecution lawyer.
她和人爭論的能力被比喻為英國皇家檢控署的律師。

distinguish
/dɪˈstɪŋgwɪʃ/

v. 區別

It took me a while to **distinguish** the authentic bag from the counterfeit one.
我花了一點時間才分辨出真的包包和假貨的不同。

garment
/ˈɡɑːmənt/

n. 衣服

He took all of the **garments** that had been stained to the dry cleaners.
他把所有有污漬的衣服都送到乾洗店去。

unity
/ˈjuːnɪti/

n. 團結

In order to show **unity**, the softball team gave a loud cheer. 為了展現團結，壘球隊高聲歡呼。

WORD TRAINING | 重點單字造句練習

ceremony
/ˈsɛrɪməni/

n. 儀式，典禮

The pha sin is a wraparound that can be worn to a Thai ceremony.
pha sin 是一種可以穿到泰國儀式上的纏繞式衣物。

The national costumes of Indonesia can be seen at their traditional wedding ceremony.
印尼民族服裝可以在他們的傳統結婚典禮上看到。

The different kinds of traditional clothes worn by the attendees of the ceremony reflect the cultural diversity of the nation.
典禮參加者穿的不同種類的傳統服裝，反映這個國家的文化多元性。

The University no longer permits wearing any form of national dress by graduates at the graduation ceremony.
這所大學不再允許畢業生在畢業典禮上穿著任何形式的民族服裝。

custom
/ˈkʌstəm/

n. 習俗，慣例

The custom of people from Scotland is wearing a knee-length pleated kilt.
蘇格蘭人的習俗是穿著及膝的打摺蘇格蘭裙。

Their custom of offering animals to the gods was carried on to later generations.
他們將動物獻祭給神的習俗繼續流傳到後代。

They believe that dark-coloured clothing brings bad luck and should be avoided, while wearing brighter-coloured clothes, especially the colour red, is the custom.
他們相信深色衣服會帶來厄運而應該避免，穿亮色衣服則是傳統，尤其是紅色。

It is a custom in my family to purchase the traditional clothing of the countries that we visit while on vacation.
度假時在拜訪的國家購買傳統服飾，是我家的習慣。

口說範例   寫作範例

norm
/nɔːm/

n. 常態，標準，準則，規範

💬 People in urban Cambodia wear Western-style clothes; however, in less urban areas, traditional Cambodian clothing is the norm.
柬埔寨都會區的人穿著西式服裝，但在不那麼都市化的地區，穿著傳統柬埔寨服飾是常態。

Although languages vary in Nigeria, cultural and traditional norms are very similar.
雖然奈及利亞的語言各有不同，但文化與傳統的規範非常相似。

✏️ Appearance is one of the most obvious cultural norms. Within any given culture, there is a general consistency around clothes, makeup, jewellery, piercings and other embellishments.
外表是最明顯的文化規範。任何特定的文化，在服裝、化妝、珠寶、穿洞和其他裝飾方面都會有大體上的一致性。

Women who dress and act modestly are much more highly regarded in India than those who flout the cultural norm, and they are safer from sexual harassment.
比起無視文化規範的女性，穿著與舉止端莊的女性在印度更加受到尊重，也比較能安全避免性騷擾。

folkways
/ˈfəʊkweɪz/

n. 風俗，民俗

💬 Violating folkways with the way we dress does not usually have serious consequences, but it does command attention.
在穿著方面違反風俗，通常不會有嚴重的後果，但會引人注目。

The traveller failed to understand our folkways and did not remove his shoes before entering the house.
那個旅行者無法了解我們的風俗，在進入房屋前沒有脫掉鞋子。

✏️ Belching loudly after eating dinner at someone else's home breaks an American folkway, but wearing jeans and other informal attire to dinner does not.
在別人家裡吃晚餐後大聲打嗝違反美國風俗，但穿牛仔褲和其他非正式服裝去吃晚餐則否。

Folkways vary by culture, and can be seen as the British shake hands to greet or when the Japanese bow in apology.
民俗隨文化不同，這可以從英國人握手打招呼、日本人鞠躬道歉等方面看出來。

RELATED WORDS | 相關單字延伸

harmony
n. 和諧

unison
n. 一致,和諧

unity
n. 團結

accord
n. 一致

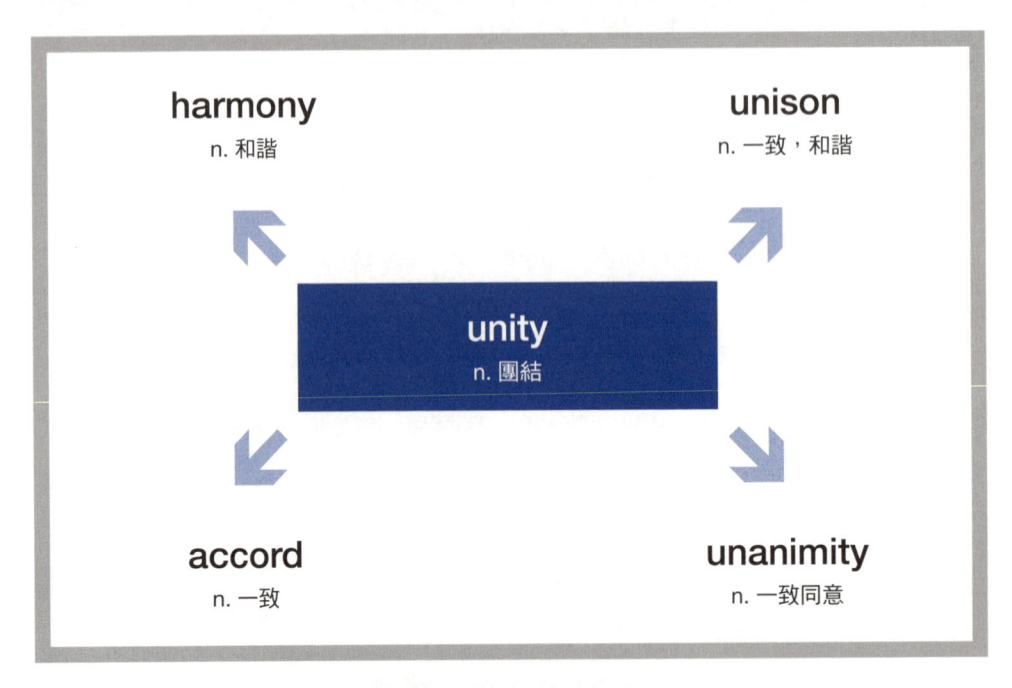

unanimity
n. 一致同意

unity
/ˈjuːnɪti/

Wearing traditional national garments brings people from the same culture together and shows their unity.
穿著傳統民族服裝能讓來自同一個文化的人們凝聚在一起,並且展現他們的團結。

harmony
/ˈhɑːməni/

I like seeing people wearing traditional garments because they look in harmony with one another.
我喜歡看到人們穿著傳統服裝,因為那樣他們看起來彼此和諧。

accord
/əˈkɔːd/

My jacket is in accord with many other national garments worn in Japan.
我的外套與日本穿著的許多其他民族服飾一致。

unison
/ˈjuːnɪsən/

The foreign bride wore hanbok to appear culturally in unison with the groom.
那位外國新娘穿韓服,以求和新郎在文化上看起來一致。

unanimity
/juːnəˈnɪmɪti/

People agree in unanimity that celebrating national unity is a positive thing.
人們一致同意慶祝國家團結是件正面的事。

USEFUL EXPRESSIONS | 相關實用片語

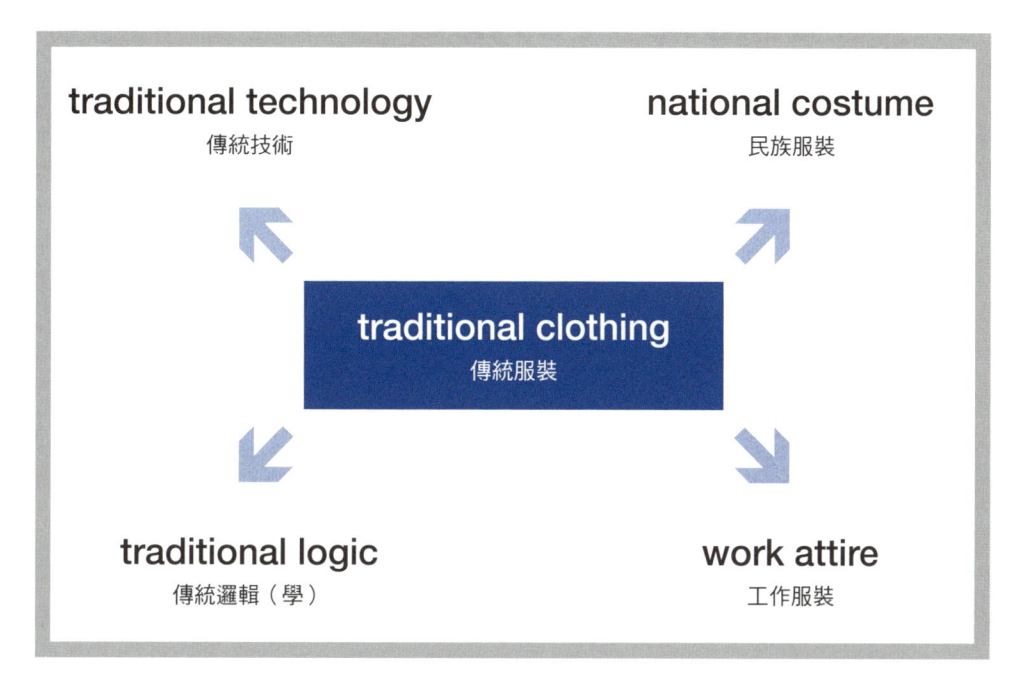

```
traditional technology          national costume
   傳統技術                          民族服裝
                ↖        ↗
              traditional clothing
                  傳統服裝
                ↙        ↘
   traditional logic              work attire
   傳統邏輯（學）                     工作服裝
```

traditional clothing
/trəˈdɪʃənəl ˈkloʊðɪŋ/

The villages in the interior are the only ones to retain their former lifestyle and wear traditional clothing daily.
這些內陸的村莊是現在僅存、仍然保留以往生活方式並且每天穿著傳統服裝的地方。

traditional technology
/trəˈdɪʃənəl tɛkˈnɒlədʒi/

The traditional technologies for retrieving coal are still in use today.
傳統的採炭技術，今日仍然在使用中。

traditional logic
/trəˈdɪʃənəl ˈlɒdʒɪk/

Traditional logic is based on Aristotle's ideas and is an obvious proposition that requires no proof.
傳統邏輯是以亞里斯多德的想法為基礎，這是不需要證明的明顯命題。

national costume
/ˈnaʃənəl ˈkɒstjuːm/

Those seeking for their Celtic identity have adopted the kilt, though this national costume was not historically worn by the Welsh.
尋求塞爾提克身分認同的人們採納了蘇格蘭裙，雖然威爾斯人在歷史上並不穿這種民族服裝。

work attire
/wɜːk əˈtʌɪə/

In their work attire, most female workers wear trousers rather than skirts.
在工作服裝方面，大部分的女性工作者穿褲子而不是裙子。

SAT
IELTS **BASIC WORDS**

patent /ˈpatənt/ n. 專利
ENG. a document granting an inventor sole rights to an invention
SYS. franchise, license

> The scientist had to travel abroad to obtain a **patent** for his latest invention.
> 這位科學家必須出國，以獲得他最新發明的專利。

同義語例句　The **franchise** of the restaurant is limited to only five countries, and that is why people travel from all over the world just to have a taste of its food.　這個餐廳的特許（加盟）經營權只限於五個國家，那就是為什麼人們從世界各地前往，只為了嚐一嚐。

同義語例句　The product's **production license** had to be obtained from another country, so its producers immediately took a trip to get it.
這個產品的生產特許權必須從另一個國家獲得，所以它的生產者立刻啟程去取得。

反義語例句　The businessman's **lack of license** to manufacture the product forced him to move his business to another country.
這位企業家因為缺少生產產品的許可證，迫使他把事業轉移到其他國家。

immediately /ɪˈmiːdiətli/ adv. 立即，馬上
ENG. without delay
SYS. now, instantly

> We must start the development of our nation **immediately** to attract more tourists.
> 我們必須立刻開始對國內的開發，以吸引更多觀光客。

同義語例句　Infrastructure must be developed **without delay** to call in foreign visitors to our country.
基礎建設必須立即開發，以吸引外國訪客到我們的國家。

同義語例句　Infrastructure development must commence **straight away** to avoid losing time in attracting tourists.
基礎建設開發必須現在馬上開始，以避免損失吸引觀光客的時間。

反義語例句　We must carefully and **not hurriedly** develop our country for better results.　我們必須謹慎、不要匆忙地開發我們的國家，以獲得更好的結果。

168

WEEK 3 TOPIC **CULTURE**

▶ 基礎單字擴充

invention /ɪnˈvɛnʃən/ n. 發明
ENG. the creation of something in the mind
SYS. design, conception

> The **invention** of railway systems helped promote international tourism.
> 鐵路系統的發明幫助促進了國際觀光。

同義語例句 The **emergence** of railways led to improvements in tourism.
鐵路的出現造就了觀光方面的改善。

同義語例句 After railway systems were **brought into existence**, international tourism started to develop quickly.
在鐵路系統出現之後,國際觀光開始快速發展。

反義語例句 The **abandoning** of railways threatens the development of tourism in rural areas.
鐵路的廢棄威脅到鄉村地區的觀光發展。

disdain /dɪsˈdeɪn/ n. 蔑視
ENG. lack of respect with intense dislike
SYS. contempt, despite

> The **disdain** for certain races is the main reason that international tourist arrivals are low.
> 對某些種族的蔑視是外國觀光客入境人數低迷的主要原因。

同義語例句 The **feeling of aversion** towards minority races stops tourists from travelling there.
對少數民族的厭惡感,阻止觀光客前往旅遊。

同義語例句 The fact that some still hold **contempt** for other races discourages people from travelling there.
有些人仍然輕視其他種族的事實,讓人們打消到那裡旅遊的念頭。

反義語例句 People's **high praise** for Caucasians makes it easy for the latter to travel the world.
人們對白種人的高度讚揚,讓白人在世界上旅遊時很輕鬆。

SAT

TOPIC: Developing international tourism
發展國際觀光

Tourism and culture are **inextricably** linked, and from an economic perspective becoming more important than ever. As many aspects of our lives become increasingly **globalised** and **homogenised**, it is the distinctive elements of culture that **define** us and attract others to us, thereby creating the domestic and international tourism industries. Unfortunately, the more tourists a destination receives, the more stress it often incurs. The construction of tourist resorts may result in deforestation and loss of biodiversity. An **influx** of tourism strains local communities by increasing competition for land and other natural resources and by introducing new cultural influences. While poorly managed tourism can destroy the way of life of local communities, responsible tourism with the involvement of local communities can be **beneficial** for **maintaining** the cultural practices that attract visitors. The most successful international tourism projects help to preserve local culture by **providing** an **alternative** source of **revenue** for communities.

TRANS

觀光與文化是緊密相連的，而且從經濟的角度來看也變得比以往更加重要。隨著我們生活中許多方面變得越來越全球化、同質化，文化中獨特的元素能夠定義我們，並且讓其他人被我們吸引，進而創造國內與國際的觀光產業。遺憾的是，當一個觀光地點接受越多遊客，就經常會產生越多壓力。度假村的建設可能導致森林砍伐及生物多樣性的損失。觀光活動的湧入會增加對土地與其他自然資源的競爭，並引進新的文化影響，而造成當地社區的緊張。雖然管理不當的觀光活動可能摧毀當地社區的生活方式，但負責任而且有當地社區參與的觀光活動，對於維持吸引遊客的文化習俗可能是有益的。最成功的國際觀光計畫可以為當地社區提供替代的收入來源，進而保存當地的文化。

inextricably
/ɪnɪkˈstrɪkəbli/

adv. 密不可分地

She is **inextricably** involved in the decision-making process.
她密切參與決策過程。

globalise
/ˈɡləʊbəlʌɪz/

v. 全球化

The Bangkok Charter identifies commitments required to address health issues in a **globalised** world.
曼谷憲章確認了在全球化的世界處理健康問題所需要的努力。

homogenise
/həˈmɒdʒənʌɪz/

v. 均質化，同質化

Beauty is starting to become **homogenised** across the globe, making most women go on diets.
美在全球各地開始趨於同化，使得大部分的女人都進行節食。

define
/dɪˈfʌɪn/

v. 定義，使明確

She failed to **define** where and when particular clients should be referred to.
她沒有清楚說明何時何地應該要提到特定客戶。

influx
/ˈɪnflʌks/

n. 湧入

There has been a steady **influx** of immigration from southern and eastern Europe.
來自東歐和南歐的移民持續湧入。

beneficial
/bɛnɪˈfɪʃəl/

adj. 有利的，有益的

I thought that learning how to knit might be **beneficial** to me in the future.
我想學習編織在未來可能對我有益。

maintain
/meɪnˈteɪn/

v. 維持，維護

While I was **maintaining** the garden, I noticed that deer had eaten the tulips.
當我在維護庭園時，我注意到鹿已經把鬱金香吃掉了。

provide
/prəˈvʌɪd/

v. 提供

The carer had grown tired of **providing** round-the-clock care for the elderly.
看護對於提供24小時老人照護已經感到疲憊。

alternative
/ɔːlˈtəːnətɪv/

adj. 替代的 **n.** 替代物

The **alternative** to getting angry would be staying calm and containing oneself.
發怒之外的替代方式，是保持冷靜並且控制自己。

revenue
/ˈrɛvənjuː/

n. 收入

Some say that oil **revenue** is funding the expansion of the war.
有人說石油的收入資助戰爭的擴大。

WORD TRAINING | 重點單字造句練習

alienation
/ˌeɪlɪəˈneɪʃən/

n. 疏離感，異化

💬 The most serious threat to tourism was the alienation of the majority of local people from the industry.
對觀光業最嚴重的威脅，是大部分當地人和觀光業之間的疏離感。

Globalisation's contribution to the alienation of individuals from their traditions may be the downside to it.
全球化造成個人與傳統的疏離，可能是它的缺點。

✍ Travelling is a kind of resistance to modernism, a failed attempt to subvert alienation which ultimately succeeds in confirming it.
旅行是一種對於現代主義的抗拒，一種想推翻疏離感，最後卻證明了疏離感的失敗嘗試。

Travelling for some is a search for an escape from the drudgery and alienation of everyday life in industrialised Western societies.
旅行對於某些人而言，是尋求從西方工業化社會日常生活裡單調沉悶的工作與疏離感中解脫。

cosmopolitan
/ˌkɑzməˈpɑlɪtən/

adj. 世界性的，國際性的

💬 My hometown has the cosmopolitan atmosphere of an international tourist destination.
我的家鄉有國際旅遊景點的世界性氛圍。

I want to live in a cosmopolitan city because my business depends on international tourism.
我想住在國際化的城市，因為我的事業仰賴國際觀光。

✍ The transportation system serves more than two million residents and thousands of travellers, and it is one of the many reasons for the city's cosmopolitan reputation.
這個交通運輸系統為超過兩百萬居民及數千名遊客提供服務，而它也是這個城市獲得世界性聲譽的許多原因之一。

Colombia's cosmopolitan capital city, Bogota, is a popular destination for both business and leisure travellers alike.
哥倫比亞的國際化首都波哥大，同時是商務與休閒旅客的熱門目的地。

resident
/ˈrɛzɪdənt/

n. 居民，（英）飯店住客

💬 Every resident of a city should act as an ambassador of it and promote tourism.
城市裡的每個居民都應該像城市大使一般促進觀光。

People often assume that a minority person is an international traveller and not a resident.
人們通常假設少數民族者是外國旅客而不是居民。

✏️ A non-resident traveller is an international traveller who is a resident of another country and enters through customs on a visit for a period of less than one year.
非居民旅客指的是身為其他國家居民的國外旅客，而且通過海關後拜訪期間不超過一年的人。

The growth of residents in local hotels could indicate that more holiday makers are staying in their own country to travel.　國內旅館的住客數成長，可能顯示有更多度假者留在自己的國家旅行。

centre of culture
/ˈsɛntə ɒv ˈkʌltʃə/

n. 文化中心地

💬 Modern centres of culture have the same cultural aspects as in much of the world.　現代的文化中心地區所擁有的文化面向，和世界上的許多地方相同。

Workers are contracted to build big tourist resorts in the city's centre of culture.
工人簽了合約，建設位於市內文化中心地區的大型度假村。

✏️ The regions we travelled to are considered centre of culture because such things as religion, organised social structures and the development of agriculture started and spread from these areas.
我們旅遊前往的地區被認為是文化的中心，因為諸如宗教、有組織的社會結構和農業的開發等等，都是從這些區域開始並且傳播的。

The New England centre of culture influenced southern and western margins of the Great Lakes westward to Oregon and Washington, reflecting New England's architecture and village patterns.
新英格蘭的文化中心地區影響了從五大湖南緣及西緣往西延伸到奧勒岡與華盛頓州的地區，反映出新英格蘭的建築與村莊形式。

RELATED WORDS | 相關單字延伸

harmonise
v. 使和諧，使協調

normalise
v. 標準化，正常化

homogenise
v. 均質化，同質化

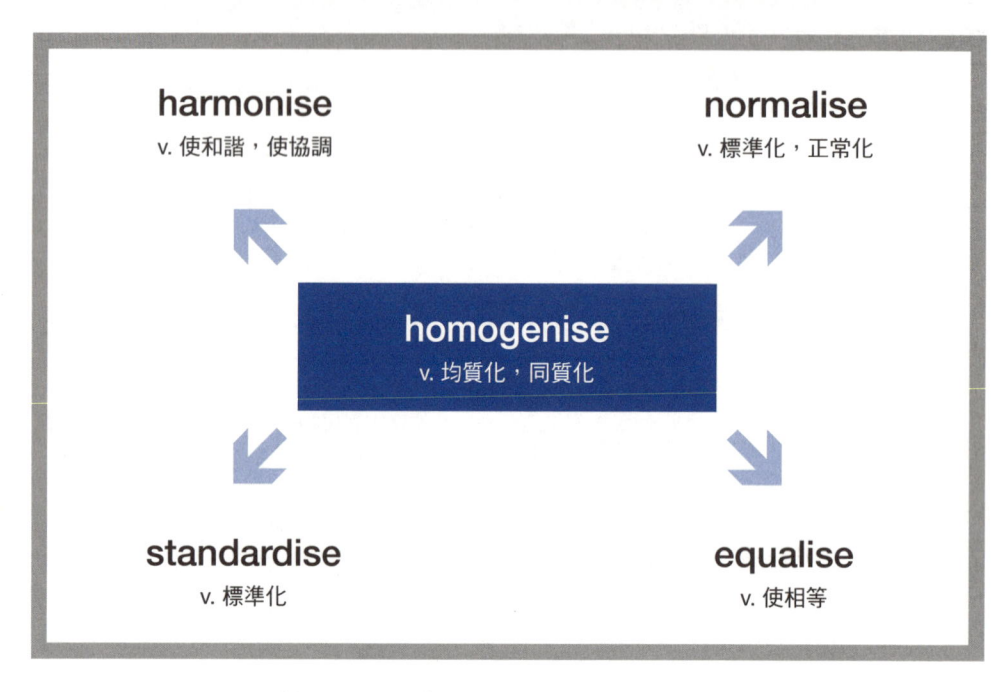

standardise
v. 標準化

equalise
v. 使相等

homogenise
/həˈmɒdʒənʌɪz/
Many aspects of our lives have become increasingly globalised and homogenised.
我們生活中許多方面變得越來越全球化、同質化。

harmonise
/ˈhɑːmənʌɪz/
In my life, I try to harmonise my family life with my dedication to global philanthropy.
在我的生活中，我努力協調我的家庭生活和對於全球慈善事業的奉獻。

standardise
/ˈstandədʌɪz/
In my opinion, globalisation will lead to a standardised, Western-style way of living worldwide.
就我來看，我認為全球化將會使全世界走向標準化的西方生活方式。

normalise
/ˈnɔːməlʌɪz/
If an individual's life is forcibly normalised by the government, it is an example of communism.
如果一個人的生活被政府強迫標準化，那就是一種共產主義的例子。

equalise
/ˈiːkwəlʌɪz/
Globalisation can be beneficial, but its tendency to equalise global cultures is worrisome.
全球化可以是有益的，但它使全球文化均一化的趨勢令人憂心。

USEFUL EXPRESSIONS | 相關實用片語

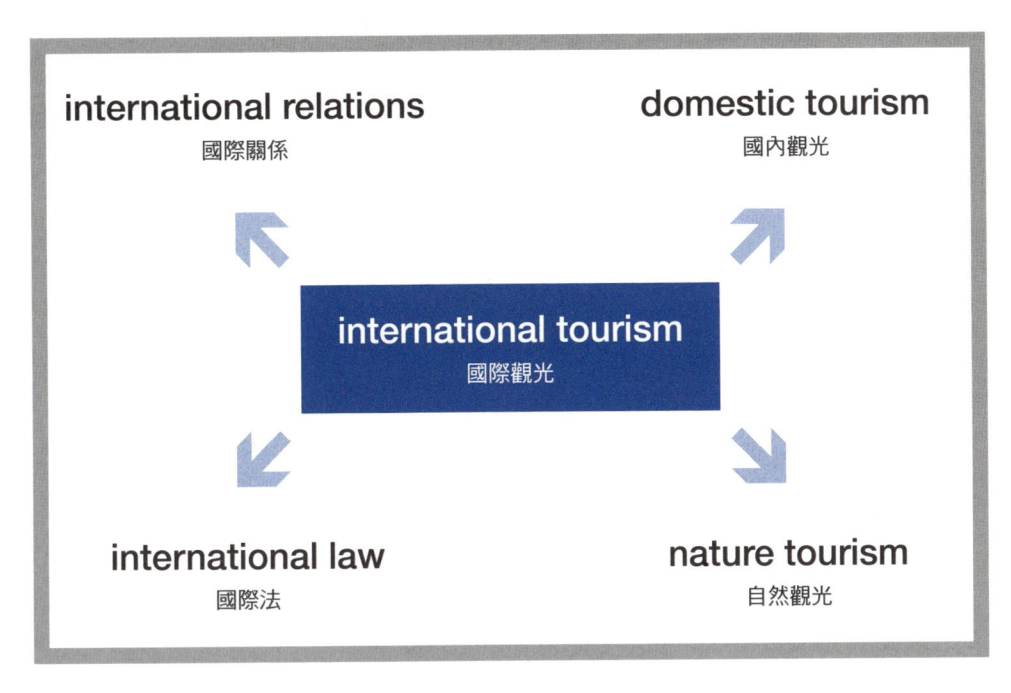

```
international relations          domestic tourism
國際關係                            國內觀光

              ↖              ↗

              international tourism
                     國際觀光

              ↙              ↘

international law                nature tourism
國際法                              自然觀光
```

international tourism
/ˌɪntəˈnæʃənəl ˈtʊərɪzəm/

There will be a continued growth in the field of international tourism according to global economists.
根據全球經濟學家的說法，國際觀光領域將會有持續性的成長。

international relations
/ˌɪntəˈnæʃənəl rɪˈleɪʃənz/

In an effort to confer about international relations, South Korean and Japanese leaders met yesterday.
為了商討國際關係，南韓和日本的領袖在昨天會面。

international law
/ˌɪntəˈnæʃənəl lɔː/

Most people agree that the Israeli bombings are a violation of international laws and deserve punishment.
大部分的人同意以色列的轟炸違反國際法，並且應該得到制裁。

domestic tourism
/dəˈmɛstɪk ˈtʊərɪzəm/

Through hosting regional events and having destinations showcased on TV, the government encouraged domestic tourism.
政府透過舉辦地區性活動以及在電視上展示旅遊景點來鼓勵國內觀光。

nature tourism
/ˈneɪtʃə ˈtʊərɪzəm/

The province is a mecca for nature tourism as it has a great variety of natural landscapes and animal species.
這個地區是自然觀光的聖地，因為它有種類多樣的自然景觀和動物物種。

SUN

IELTS **BASIC WORDS**

restrict /rɪˈstrɪkt/ v. 限制
ENG. place limits on
SYS. restrain, bound

> The government must restrict immigration policies to prevent illegal activities by aliens in our country.
> 政府必須限制移民政策，以避免外來者在我國從事非法活動。

同義語例句 It is necessary to draw a line when it comes to what we allow immigrants to do in our country.
說到我們允許移民在國內所做的事，劃清界線是必要的。

同義語例句 It is ideal to set boundaries when it comes to the activities of foreigners in our country.
說到外國人在國內的活動，我們最好設定界線。

反義語例句 Let us make immigration free from limits to encourage migrants to live in our country.
讓我們免除移民的限制，鼓勵移居者在我國生活。

array /əˈreɪ/ n. 排列，一系列
ENG. an orderly arrangement
SYS. matrix, arrangement

> There's such an array of good places to see in Switzerland that it's hard to decide where to go first.
> 在瑞士有許多好地方可以看，很難決定要先去哪裡。

同義語例句 It is an impressive line-up of significant people, who are intelligent enough to change their country.
這是個令人印象深刻的重要人士陣容，他們聰明得足以改變自己的國家。

同義語例句 The orderly arrangement of buildings is the result of urban planning.
建築物的整齊排列是都市計畫的結果。

反義語例句 The biggest flaw of a country open to immigration is its predisposition to a topsy-turvy governance.
一個開放移民的國家最大的缺點，是它的治理容易混亂的傾向。

WEEK 3 TOPIC **CULTURE**

▶基礎單字擴充

superiority /suːˌpɪərɪˈɒrɪti/ n. 優勢
ENG. quality of being at a competitive advantage
SYS. advantage, excellence

> The **superiority** of a country is usually the main reason why foreigners wish to immigrate.
> 一個國家的優勢通常是外國人希望移民入國的主要原因。

同義語例句 The possibility of becoming a **first class** citizen appeals to a lot of foreigners who wish to migrate.
成為高等公民的可能性,能吸引許多想要移居的外國人。

同義語例句 A **favourable position** in terms of financial stability is what migrants look for in migrating.
在財務穩定方面有利的位置,是移民者在移居時所追求的。

反義語例句 The **absence of advantage** in certain countries turns potential migrants off.
某些國家的缺乏優勢,使得可能的移民者失去興趣。

involve /ɪnˈvɒlv/ v. 包含,涉及,使參與
ENG. to include or contain as a necessary part; connect closely
SYS. affect, regard

> It is important to **involve** the whole family in deciding whether to migrate to another country.
> 在決定是否移民其他國家時,全家人的參與是很重要的。

同義語例句 The decision to migrate **calls for** the unanimous approval of all family members.
移民的決定需要所有家庭成員一致的同意。

同義語例句 All members of the migrating family should **engage as** decision makers in the whole process.
要移民的家庭中,所有成員都應該在整個過程中以決策者的身分參與。

反義語例句 Children should **distance themselves** from the matter of migration since they cannot think rationally yet.
孩子應該遠離移民的事宜,因為他們還不能理性思考。

TOPIC: Immigrating to other countries
移民到其他國家

Moving to a foreign country isn't easy, but it can be rewarding. **Pundits** from various **disciplines** have multiple reasons as to why people immigrate. When seen from an economic point of view, people often immigrate to gain financial stability and better future **prospects**. For example, if another country is offering higher wages and a **polished** lifestyle, it is appealing to become a permanent resident in that country. Many parents **strive** for their children to go abroad to **familiarise** themselves with foreign culture and language. The reality is that such parents try relentlessly to **endow** their children with enhanced career prospects and lifestyles. Changing **citizenship** to gain a new identity or gaining political rights and freedom is yet another reason why people **emigrate**. People often face great **consternation** concerning immigration, but the experience for many is very valuable.

遷移到外國並不容易，但可能是有益的。來自不同學科的專家，提出了人們之所以移民的多種理由。從經濟觀點來看，人們常常為了獲得經濟穩定和更好的未來展望而移民。例如，如果另一個國家提供更好的薪水和優雅的生活方式，那麼成為那個國家的永久居民就是有吸引力的。許多父母努力讓小孩出國熟悉外國文化和語言。事實是，這種父母永無休止地試圖給孩子更好的職業前景和生活方式。改變國籍以獲得新的身分或得到政治權利及自由，也是人們移居國外的理由。關於移民，人們通常會面對很大的驚慌，但這個經驗對很多人而言是非常寶貴的。

pundit
/ˈpʌndɪt/

n. 權威，專家
The flamboyant pair surprised some **pundits** by wearing traditional wedding attire.
這對浮華的伴侶穿著傳統的結婚服裝，讓一些專家感到意外。

discipline
/ˈdɪsɪplɪn/

n. 學科
Before you graduate, you must study a breadth of knowledge across all **disciplines**.
在畢業前，你必須學習遍及所有學科的廣泛知識。

prospect
/ˈprɒspɛkt/

n. 前景，展望
The **prospects** for economic growth are bleak.
經濟成長的前景沒有希望。

polished
/ˈpɒlɪʃt/

adj. 優雅的
He looked so **polished** in his suit that I compared him to James Bond.
他穿西裝看起來很優雅，使得我把他和詹姆士龐德相比。

strive
/strʌɪv/

v. 努力，奮鬥
She is **striving** to gain support from legislators.
她正努力獲得立法機關成員的支持。

familiarise
/fəˈmɪlɪərʌɪz/

v. 使熟悉
It took me some time to **familiarise** myself with their culture.
熟悉他們的文化花了我一些時間。

endow
/ɪnˈdaʊ/

v. 賦予，給予
Her great-aunt plans to **endow** each of her nieces and nephews with money.
她的姑婆／姨婆／舅婆計畫給她每個姪女、姪子一筆錢。

citizenship
/ˈsɪtɪzənˌʃɪp/

n. 公民權，國籍
When you want to apply for **citizenship**, you must take a test.
當你想要申請公民權時，你必須接受測驗。

emigrate
/ˈɛmɪɡreɪt/

v. 移民出國
The family decided to **emigrate** from China to the United States.
這家人決定從中國移民到美國。

consternation
/kɒnstəˈneɪʃən/

n. 驚愕，驚慌失措
The prince's affairs caused much **consternation** in the royal family.
王子的風流韻事造成了皇室裡很大的驚慌。

WORD TRAINING | 重點單字造句練習

diffusion
/dɪˈfjuːʒən/

n. 擴散，傳播

Immigration to the United States promotes the diffusion of many different religions.
往美國的移民，促進許多不同宗教的傳播。

An example of cultural diffusion is that there are now many sushi restaurants in the UK.
一個文化傳播的例子，是英國現在有很多壽司餐廳。

As long as there are monolingual speakers of languages of limited diffusion, there will be a need for expedients like short-term language courses.
只要有單一語言使用者使用傳播度有限的語言，就會有短期語言課程之類的權宜之計的需求。

The spreading of fashion trends is a classic case of hierarchical diffusion: newest trends are first seen in fashion shows and on celebrities, while department stores and local malls will receive the innovation later.
流行趨勢的傳播是（文化）層級擴散的經典例子：最新潮流會先在時尚秀和名人身上看到，而百貨公司和地方購物中心會晚一點接收到流行的創新。

rejection
/rɪˈdʒɛkʃən/

n. 拒絕，退回

Insufficient language test scores led to the rejection of his application.
語言測驗成績不足導致他的申請被拒絕。

Sometimes, after immigrating to a foreign country, a person can feel rejection from the new country.
有時候，在移民到外國之後，一個人會感覺到新國家的排斥。

The specific stamp symbolises that the passport holder has received a rejection for a UK visa.
這個特定的印章代表護照持有人曾經申請英國簽證被駁回。

A rejected immigration application cannot be re-submitted within 6 months after rejection.
被駁回的移民申請不能在駁回後六個月內重新提出。

region
/ˈriːdʒən/

n. 區域

💬 Each team is responsible for a specific region of the world.
每個團隊各自負責世界上的一個特定區域。

The amazing part of this region is its friendly people, who are very polite to immigrants.
這個區域令人驚奇的部分在於它友善的居民,他們對移民非常有禮。

✒ This particular region of China is known for its wonderful skyline, tall buildings and picturesque harbours.
在中國,這個特別的區域以美好的天際線、高聳的大樓和風景如畫的港口聞名。

This region has become a popular destination for world tourists as well as business travellers because of its cultural diversity.
因為這個地區的文化多樣性,所以它成為了全世界觀光客和商務旅行者喜愛的目的地。

racism
/ˈreɪsɪzəm/

n. 種族主義,種族歧視

💬 Despite a decline in hate crimes, racism is still a big problem in the United States.
雖然仇恨犯罪的件數下降,但種族歧視在美國仍然是很大的問題。

People who express blatant racism without shame is considered uneducated and should not be tolerated.
不知羞恥地公然表達種族歧視的人,被認為是沒教養而且不能容忍的。

✒ We should put an end to the endemic problem of racism by teaching the concept of cultural diversity to our youth.
我們應該教育青少年關於文化多樣性的概念,來終結地區性的種族歧視問題。

International organisations and the local governments of most countries are now implementing measures against racism to promote the equality of human beings.
國際組織和大部分國家的地方政府,現在正在實施對抗種族歧視的措施,以促進人類的平等。

RELATED WORDS | 相關單字延伸

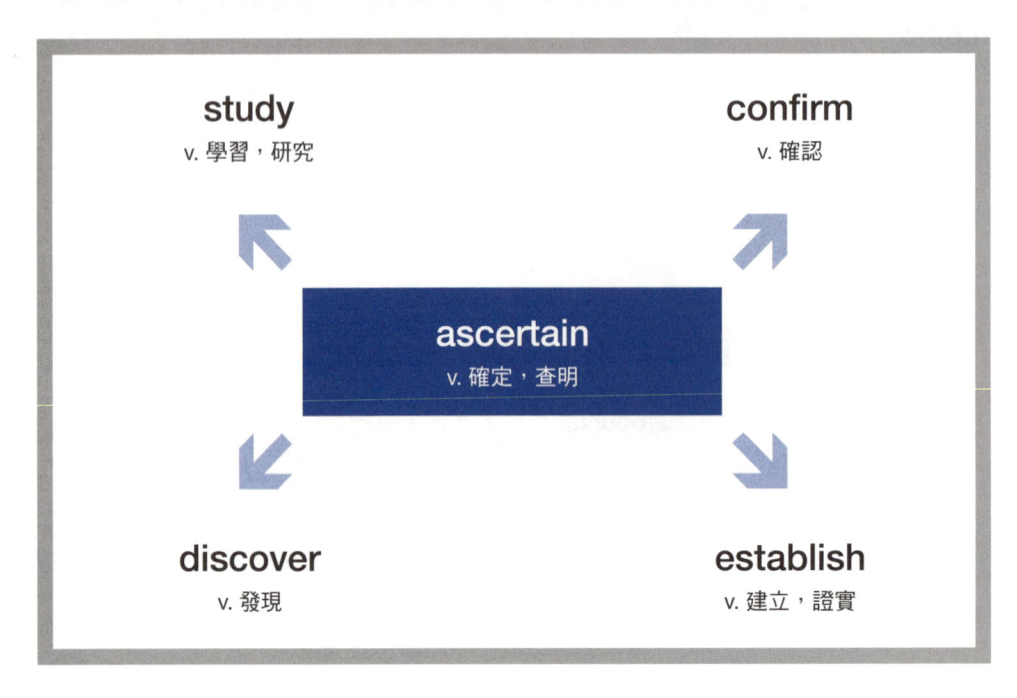

study
v. 學習，研究

confirm
v. 確認

ascertain
v. 確定，查明

discover
v. 發現

establish
v. 建立，證實

ascertain
/ˌæsəˈteɪn/
Researchers are trying to ascertain whether studying abroad can facilitate second-language acquisition.
研究者正試圖確定海外留學是否能夠促進第二語言的習得。

study
/ˈstʌdi/
Students find it difficult to study in a noisy and cluttered surrounding.
學生發現在吵鬧與雜亂的環境裡很難學習。

discover
/dɪˈskʌvə/
One can discover how important language really is when they travel abroad to new countries.
到新的國家旅行的時候，一個人會發現語言實際上有多重要。

confirm
/kənˈfɜːm/
Linguists have confirmed that people learn a new language faster if they visit a country where the language is commonly used.
語言學家已經確認，如果人們拜訪普遍使用一種語言的國家，就能把這個新的語言學得比較快。

establish
/ɪˈstæblɪʃ/
It has been established that the best way to learn about a culture is to learn its language.
學習一種文化最好的方法就是學習它的語言，這已經是獲得證實的事情。

USEFUL EXPRESSIONS | 相關實用片語

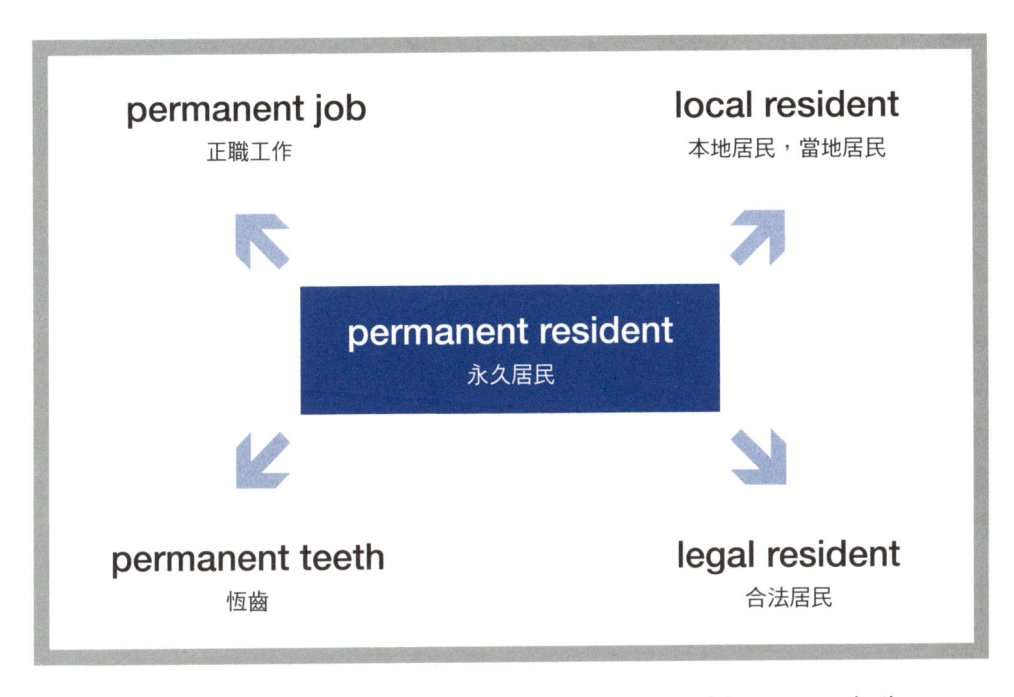

```
permanent job              local resident
正職工作                    本地居民，當地居民

            ↖         ↗
         permanent resident
              永久居民
            ↙         ↘

permanent teeth            legal resident
恆齒                        合法居民
```

permanent resident
/ˈpɜːmənənt ˈrɛzɪdənt/

He was granted permanent resident status in the United States after he married his American wife.
娶了美國的妻子之後，他獲得了美國的永久居民身分。

permanent job
/ˈpɜːmənənt dʒɒb/

Since the hiring freeze has been lifted, the company expects to hire for ten permanent jobs in September.
因為雇用凍結已經被取消，這家公司預計在九月為十個正職工作進行雇用。

permanent teeth
/ˈpɜːmənənt tiːθ/

Around the age of 6 is when children's permanent teeth grow.
六歲左右是兒童的恆齒生長的時候。

local resident
/ˈləʊkəl ˈrɛzɪdənt/

Several local residents are planning to express their opposition to City Council.
幾個當地居民計畫表達對市議會的反對意見。

legal resident
/ˈliːgəl ˈrɛzɪdənt/

Not many middle-class Iraqis are easily approved to become legal residents of Jordan.
沒有很多中產階級的伊拉克人能輕易獲准成為約旦的合法居民。

WEEK 4
ART

政府對藝術的投資

把藝術放上網路

讓孩子學習藝術的重要性

成為有名的藝術家

年長與年輕世代的藝術鑑賞

藝術的商業價值

將建築作為一種藝術表達的形式

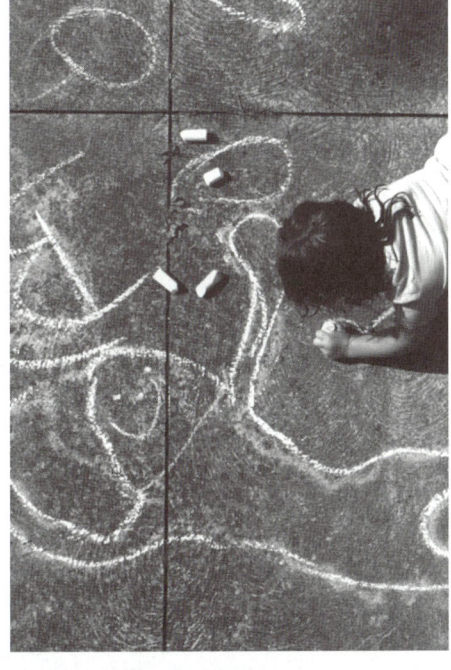

MON

IELTS BASIC WORDS

investigation /ɪnˌvɛstɪˈgeɪʃən/ **n. 調查**
ENG. an inquiry into unfamiliar or questionable activities
SYS. research, analysis

> The **investigation** revealed that the public is willing to contribute to the preservation of art.
> 調查顯示，大眾願意為藝術的保存做出貢獻。

- 同義語 例句: The public's **thirst for knowledge** encourages them to support scientific studies.
  大眾對知識的渴望，促使他們支持科學研究。
- 同義語 例句: The **quest for answers** convinced everyone to finance the scientific study.
  對答案的追求說服了每個人資助那個科學研究。
- 反義語 例句: The public's **denial of truth** threatens the progress of science for the next generations.
  大眾對真理的拒絕，威脅到為了後代的科學進展。

reproduce /ˌriːprəˈdjuːs/ **v. 重製，複製**
ENG. make a copy or equivalent of
SYS. replicate, recreate

> It is easy to **reproduce** artwork when artists are financed sufficiently.
> 當藝術家有足夠的資金援助時，要重製藝術作品很容易。

- 同義語 例句: Art is not difficult to **make again** if artists are not financially challenged.
  如果藝術家沒有財務困難，那麼要再重製藝術並不困難。
- 同義語 例句: The artists can **make more copies of** their works because they are financed to do so.
  那些藝術家可以把他們的作品製作更多份，因為他們獲得了資助來做這件事。
- 反義語 例句: The artist can **make only one copy** because of financial constraints.
  因為財務限制，那個藝術家只能製作一份作品。

WEEK 4 TOPIC **ART**

▶ 基礎單字擴充

successful /səkˈsɛsfʊl/ adj. 成功的
ENG. being marked by a favourable outcome
SYS. triumphant, victorious

> The government project supporting the arts was very **successful**.
> 支持藝術的政府計畫非常成功。

同義語例句 The art show's high number of visitors was considered a **goal accomplished** by the government.
這場藝術博覽會的高參觀人次，被認為是政府達成的一個目標。

同義語例句 Thanks to the government's financial support, the art awareness project is **thriving**.
多虧政府的財務支持，（提高）藝術意識計畫很成功。

反義語例句 Some art projects are **bound to fail** because they are insufficiently budgeted by the government.
有些藝術計畫注定會失敗，因為沒有獲得政府足夠的預算。

finance /fʌɪˈnans/ v. 提供資金給⋯
ENG. obtain or provide money for
SYS. support, subsidise

> The government promised to **finance** the art show.
> 政府承諾將資助藝術博覽會。

同義語例句 Government officials pledged to **pay for** the art show expenses.
政府官員保證將支付藝術博覽會的費用。

同義語例句 The government will **provide monetary backing** on all art shows launched by young artists.
政府將會為年輕藝術家發起的所有藝術博覽會提供金錢支援。

反義語例句 The government decided to **cut the budget** for arts and allot it for health care.
政府決定刪減藝術預算，並且分配到醫療保健方面。

187

MON

04-1A

TOPIC

The government's investment in art
政府對藝術的投資

Many countries would benefit greatly if they **announced** a **significant** injection of funding into their arts, culture and **heritage** sectors. It has been proven that major government **investment** into these sectors allows arts and culture to **flourish** and creates jobs and growth in the industries. A nation can be rich in every material sense, but if it fails to **nurture** creative expression, it is **impoverished** in immeasurable ways. A nation's arts, culture and heritage **demarcate** and strengthen its identity. Investments into the arts help express the unique national identity that a country has, which is precisely the reason why the government should fund these sectors, despite **naysayers** insisting it is a waste of tax dollars. In the end, the positive effect of governmental investment in creative industries should be acknowledged.

TRANS

許多國家如果能宣布挹注大筆資金到藝術、文化及歷史遺產部門，將會受益良多。事實證明，政府對這些部門的重大投資能使藝術與文化蓬勃發展，並且創造工作機會與產業的成長。一個國家可以在所有物質層面的意義上都是富裕的，但如果它無法培育創造性的表達，那麼它在無數的層面上都是貧窮的。一個國家的藝術、文化與歷史遺產能夠界定並強化它的身分認同。對藝術的投資有助於表現出國家所擁有的獨特國家認同，而這正是政府應該資助這些部門的理由，儘管反對者堅稱這是稅金的浪費。總而言之，政府的創意產業投資所造成的正面影響應該受到認可。

announce
/əˈnaʊns/

v. 宣布

People laughed when his name was **announced** incorrectly over the loudspeaker.
人們透過擴音器聽到他的名字被念錯之後大笑。

significant
/sɪɡˈnɪfɪkənt/

adj. 重大的，相當多的，相當大的

Our teacher pointed out one **significant** passage in our textbook. 我們的老師從課本裡指出了一個重要的段落。

heritage
/ˈhɛrɪtɪdʒ/

n. 遺產

The origin of her family's **heritage** dates back to the Feudal Era of Japan.
她家族的遺產起源可以追溯到日本的封建時代。

investment
/ɪnˈvɛstmənt/

n. 投資

I made a small **investment** in a company, and it is now worth millions.
我對一家公司做了一筆小投資，現在它已經價值數百萬。

flourish
/ˈflʌrɪʃ/

v. 茂盛，繁榮

I noticed her innate ability to **flourish** socially at the party.
我在派對上注意到她與生俱來、能夠在社交方面成功的能力。

nurture
/ˈnɚtʃɚ/

v. 培育，養育

Many single mothers are struggling to **nurture** their children independently.
很多單親媽媽很辛苦地獨立養育小孩。

impoverished
/ɪmˈpɒvərɪʃt/

adj. 貧窮的

These philanthropists go to **impoverished** countries and build clean water wells.
這些慈善家到貧窮國家建造乾淨的水井。

demarcate
/ˈdiːmɑːkeɪt/

v. 界定，區分

To **demarcate** your first thought from your second thought, use commas in the sentence.
要把第一個想法和第二個想法分開來，請在句子裡使用逗號。

naysayer
/ˈneɪˌseɪɚ/

n. 反對者

The **naysayers** in the crowd mocked the politician when he walked up to the podium.
群眾裡的反對者在那位政治家走上講台時加以嘲笑。

acknowledge
/əkˈnɒlɪdʒ/

v. 承認，認可

The politicians **acknowledged** the original culture of the American Indians.
那些的政界人士承認美國印第安人的原生文化。

WORD TRAINING | 重點單字造句練習

masterpiece
/ˈmɑːstəpiːs/

n. 傑作，名作

It will be a shame if the government only invests in the most expensive masterpieces.
如果政府只投資最昂貴的名作，是很可惜的。

Van Gogh's masterpieces are now much more expensive than when he was alive.
梵谷的傑作現在比他還在世的時候貴上許多。

The government-run children's art space has lots of art sparks and other motivators on hand to get children start creating their very own masterpieces.
政府經營的兒童藝術空間，有許多隨手可得的藝術火花和其他激發因素，讓小孩可以開始創造自己的傑作。

The British government has stepped in to stop a masterpiece from being purchased by a museum overseas earlier this year on the basis that the U.K.'s national treasure should be protected.
基於英國國寶應該受到保護的理由，英國政府在今年稍早的時候介入並阻止一件名作被海外的博物館收購。

artefact
/ˈɑːtɪfakt/

n. 文物

With the newest artefact added to the national gallery, the government has affirmed its arts patronage.
隨著最新的文物被納入國家藝廊，政府申明了對藝術的資助。

A fight between the U.S. government and Egypt ended when the government formally handed over the ancient artefact.
隨著美國政府正式交出了古文物，它和埃及之間的爭吵也結束了。

Museums, the government and other non-profit organisations will plan temporary exhibitions that involve bringing works of art and artefacts from abroad.
博物館、政府和其他非營利組織會籌畫引進國外藝術與文物的臨時展覽。

All their branches have extensive art, antique and artefact collections, which may provide cultural enlightenment to visitors.
他們所有分部都有廣泛的藝術、古董及文物收藏，這些收藏或許可以為訪客提供文化上的啟蒙。

genre
/ˈʒɒnrə/

n. 文藝作品的類型

💬 Certain art genres attract more attentions from collectors.
某些藝術類型吸引收藏家比較多的關注。

The municipal government decorates its public spaces with artwork of various genres.
市政府用多種類型的藝術作品來裝飾公共空間。

✏️ Public art is a new genre of art, which first appeared in Korea ten years ago, emphasising the site of an artwork and the collaborative working process with the residents of local communities and their local governments.
公共藝術是一種新類型的藝術，它在十年前首次出現在韓國，強調藝術作品的地點，以及和當地社區居民及地方政府的合作過程。

From massive national events like the opening and closing ceremonies of the Sydney Olympics, down to local municipal government-sponsored festivals, Australian performance art shows its difference from traditional genres.
上自雪梨奧運開幕及閉幕式之類的大型國家活動，下至地方市政府贊助的節慶活動，澳洲的表演藝術都展現出它與傳統類型的不同。

estimate
/ˈɛstɪmeɪt/

v. n. 估計，估價

💬 I would estimate that the government invests up to three million dollars annually in public art.
我估計政府每年投資公共藝術多達三百萬美元。

The most recent estimate of the newest painting purchased for the museum is two million dollars.
對於博物館收購的最新畫作，最近的估價是兩百萬美元。

✏️ According to the news, the governments of Finland, Sweden and Norway will finance the art project, which is estimated to cost $600 million.
根據新聞報導，芬蘭、瑞典、挪威的政府將會資助那個藝術計畫，計畫預估將花費六億美元。

The website offers a free online estimate and appraisal of artworks, provided the user has the artist's name, print number and a valid history of the work.
這個網站提供對藝術品的免費線上估價與評價，只要使用者有藝術家的名稱、作品版號以及該作品有根據的歷史即可。

RELATED WORDS | 相關單字延伸

differentiate
v. 區別，區分

distinguish
v. 區別

demarcate
v. 界定，區分

define
v. 定義，限定

segregate
v. 隔離

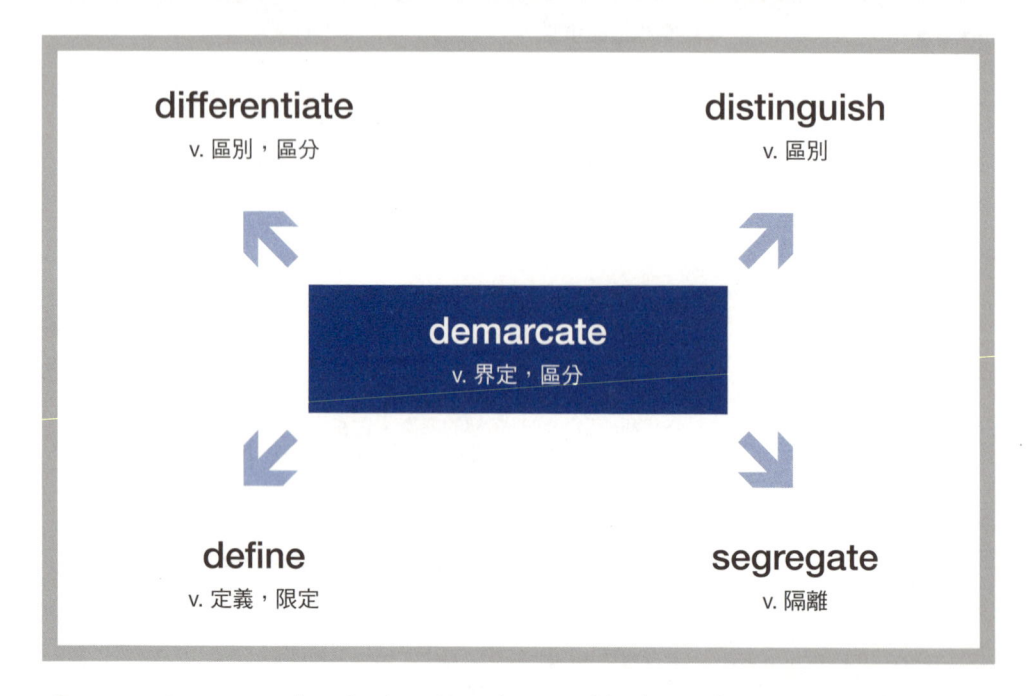

---

demarcate
/ˈdiːmɑːkeɪt/

A nation's arts, culture and heritage demarcate and strengthen its identity.
一個國家的藝術、文化與歷史遺產能夠界定並強化它的身分認同。

differentiate
/ˌdɪfəˈrɛnʃieɪt/

It may not be easy to differentiate between a country's own culture and influences from other countries.
區分一個國家本身的文化和來自其他國家的影響可能不容易。

define
/dɪˈfaɪn/

What defines a country is its culture.
定義一個國家的是它的文化。

distinguish
/dɪˈstɪŋgwɪʃ/

We distinguished several types of artwork that are important to the country's heritage.
我們區別了對於國家遺產重要的幾種藝術作品。

segregate
/ˈsɛgrɪgeɪt/

If you segregate a person from their first language, the individual may also suffer a loss of culture.
如果把一個人和他的母語隔離開來，那麼他可能也會遭受文化的喪失。

USEFUL EXPRESSIONS | 相關實用片語

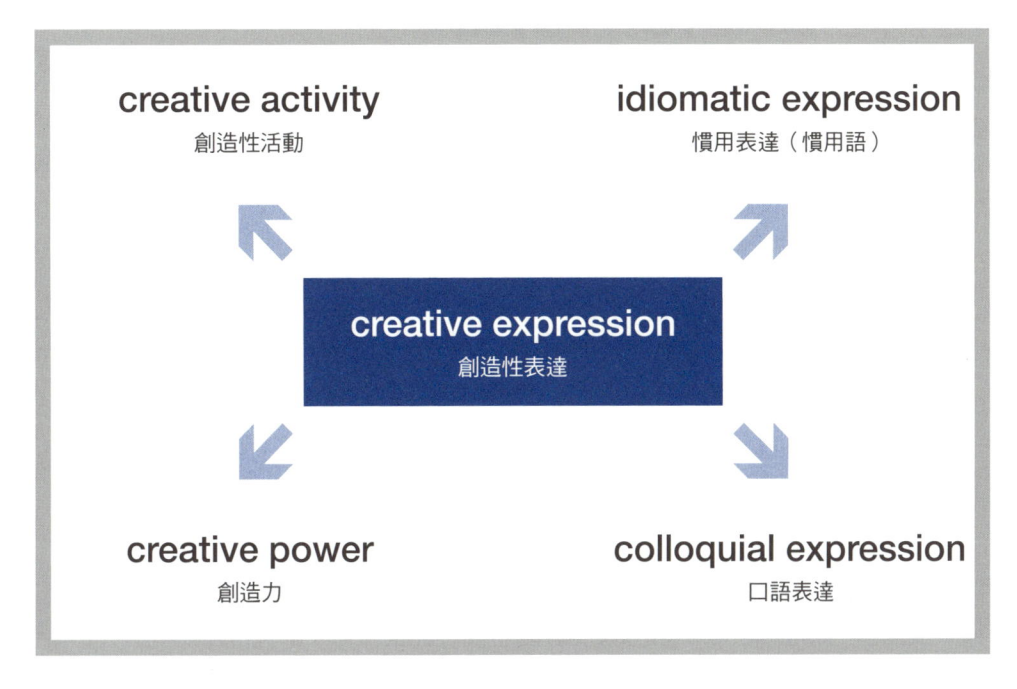

```
creative activity                    idiomatic expression
創造性活動                              慣用表達（慣用語）

              creative expression
                   創造性表達

creative power                       colloquial expression
創造力                                  口語表達
```

creative expression
/kriˈeɪtɪv ɪkˈsprɛʃən/

You can tell she is skilled in creative expression by the way she mixes separates in her outfits.
從她在衣著上混搭單品的方式，你可以看出她很擅長創造性表達。

creative activity
/kriˈeɪtɪv akˈtɪvɪti/

There are many creative activities that students can do in an art class.
在美術課中，有很多學生們可以做的創意活動。

creative power
/kriˈeɪtɪv ˈpaʊə/

The amount of creative power that a person has differs, even though all minds have the same potential.
雖然所有人的心智都有相同的潛力，但每個人擁有的創造力多寡不同。

idiomatic expression
/ˌɪdɪəˈmatɪk ɪkˈsprɛʃən/

When explaining an idea, a teacher should speak straightforwardly and avoid using idiomatic expressions.
在解釋一個概念時，老師應該說話直接，並且避免使用慣用語。

colloquial expression
/kəˈloʊkwɪəl ɪkˈsprɛʃən/

We frequently use the colloquial expression "muscle memory" to refer to what is known as brain-muscle memory.
我們經常使用「肌肉記憶」這個口語表達指稱一般所知的「腦肌肉記憶」。

TUE

IELTS BASIC WORDS

efficient /ɪˈfɪʃənt/ adj. 有效率的
ENG. being effective without wasting effort or expense; able to accomplish a purpose
SYS. effective, productive

> It is more efficient to create art with technological and innovative tools.
> 用科技的、創新的工具來創造藝術比較有效率。

同義語例句 An artistic tool should at least be able to bring about desired results, regardless of its brand or features.
不論品牌或特色是什麼,藝術工具至少都應該能夠帶來想要的結果。

同義語例句 Artistic tools in the market today are sufficiently capable of creating world-class art.
今日市面上的藝術工具足以創造世界級的藝術。

反義語例句 Most people complain that the artistic tools are useless.
大多數的人抱怨這些藝術工具沒有用。

calculate /ˈkælkjʊleɪt/ v. 計算,推測
ENG. determine mathematically or by reasoning
SYS. determine, estimate

> I cannot calculate how skilful or talented an artist is if he used a technological artistic tool.
> 如果藝術家使用科技的藝術工具,我就無法推測他多麼有技巧、多麼有才華。

同義語例句 It is difficult to judge the capability of an artist who uses innovative artistic tools.
要評斷使用創新藝術工具的藝術家的能力,是很困難的。

同義語例句 Some people cannot evaluate the artistic value of works done using new artistic tools.
有些人無法評價使用新藝術工具完成的作品的藝術價值。

反義語例句 It is difficult to account accurately for the artistry of someone who uses new artistic tools.
要正確說明使用新藝術工具的人的藝術才能,是很困難的。

WEEK 4 TOPIC **ART**

▶基礎單字擴充

train /treɪn/ v. 訓練
ENG. teach through practice; undergo instruction in preparation for something
SYS. guide, coach

> People who aim to be artists must also be **trained** to be familiar with technology to remain up-to-date.
> 以成為藝術家為目標的人，也必須接受訓練以熟悉科技，讓自己跟得上時代。

同義語例句 Artists must also **cultivate** their technology skills to keep up with the times.
藝術家也必須培養自己的科技能力來跟上時代。

同義語例句 Artists must **polish** their creative skills through both traditional and technological art.
藝術家必須透過傳統和科技藝術來精進自己的創意技巧。

反義語例句 Some older artists are **ignorant** of the art of the new millennium.
有些比較年長的藝術家對於新千禧年的藝術一無所知。

prepare /prɪˈpɛː/ v. 準備
ENG. make ready or suitable; equip in advance
SYS. ready, groom

> The best way to **prepare** for the arts of the future is to apply technology.
> 要為未來的藝術做準備，最好的方法就是應用科技。

同義語例句 Artists must **gear up** for the arts of tomorrow by learning to use new artistic tools.
藝術家必須藉由學習使用新的藝術工具，為明日的藝術做好準備。

同義語例句 A traditional artist must **be adapted to** advances in technology that may influence arts.
傳統的藝術家必須適應可能影響藝術的科技發展。

反義語例句 Some traditional artists that refuse to recognise technological art remain **unready** for the art of the future.
有些拒絕承認科技藝術的傳統藝術家，仍然沒有對未來的藝術做好準備。

195

TUE

TOPIC: Putting art on the Internet
把藝術放上網路

In the modern world, we are faced with the **dilemma** of whether or not to **rely** on new technology and give up traditional methods. This is especially obvious in the field of art. In the past, people had to **toil** to find an **outlet** for their **creativity**, costing time and money. Such **endeavours** that artists had to be **committed** to, however, are a lot easier today. With social media, free websites and eBay, the Internet **allows** aspiring artists to exhibit and sell their work online. The freedom of publishing and publicising one's own work without limits, however, may result in a poorer level of quality in general. In a perfect world, Twitter would probably nurture the modern day equivalent of Shakespeare, but the fact is those sparks of creativity are rare, and there are millions of talentless hacks who have equal access to the Internet, **clogging** the **bandwidth** with sub-par photography, writing and painting.

TRANS

在現代的世界，我們面對著是否要依賴新技術並且放棄傳統方法的兩難。這在藝術的領域尤其明顯。在過去，人們必須辛苦為自己的創造力尋找出路，既花時間也花金錢。不過，以前藝術家們必須投入的這種努力，在今日變得容易許多。有了社群媒體、免費網站和 eBay，網路讓有志成為藝術家的人能夠在線上展示並且販賣作品。但是，可以發表並宣傳作品而不受限的自由，可能會造成整體的品質水準下降。在完美的世界裡，Twitter 有可能培育出現代的莎士比亞，但事實上創造力的火花很少見，卻有數百萬同樣能上網但沒才華的三流作家，用低於一般水準的攝影、寫作和繪畫塞滿頻寬。

dilemma
/dɪˈlɛmə/

n. 困境，兩難

He is faced with the **dilemma** of whether to save his wife or her unborn child.
他面臨著要救她的妻子還是她未出生的小孩的兩難。

rely
/rɪˈlaɪ/

v. 依賴

When you **rely** on a friend to help you, your friendship will become stronger.
當你依賴朋友幫你，你們的友情就會變得比較堅固。

toil
/tɔɪl/

n. v. 辛苦

He pushed really hard, but his **toil** was in vain as the car was truly stuck.
他很用力推，但他的辛苦徒勞無功，車子真的卡住了。

outlet
/ˈaʊtlɛt/

n. 出口，出路

I often use karaoke as an **outlet** to sing out my frustrations and anger.
我經常用卡拉OK當成唱出挫折感與憤怒的出口。

creativity
/ˌkriːeɪˈtɪvɪti/

n. 創造力

The artist showed impressive **creativity** by using a pinecone in place of a brush.
這位藝術家用松果代替筆刷，展現出令人印象深刻的創造力。

committed
/kəˈmɪtɪd/

adj. 忠誠的，堅定的，投入的

I don't want to be **committed** to this job for the rest of my life.
我不想在剩下的人生中投入這份工作。

endeavour
/ɪnˈdɛvə/

n. 努力

I appreciate you for pursuing firefighting because it is a worthy **endeavour**.
我欣賞你有志從事消防業，因為這是一個值得付出的努力。

allow
/əˈlaʊ/

v. 允許，使能夠

If the weather **allows** it, we can go on a day hike in the forest.
如果天候狀況允許，我們可以白天的時候在森林健行。

clog
/klɒg/

v. 阻塞，塞滿

We noticed that a large ball of hair was **clogging** the drain in the sink.
我們注意到有一大團頭髮阻塞了水槽裡的排水管。

bandwidth
/ˈbændwɪtθ/

n. 頻寬

I have an incredibly large **bandwidth**, which makes web browsing very fast.
我有非常大的頻寬，讓網路瀏覽非常快速。

WORD TRAINING ｜ 重點單字造句練習

cyberart
/ˈsaɪbɑːrt/

n. 數位藝術，網路藝術

💬 Exposure to online cyberart can familiarise viewers with new technology.
接觸網路上的數位藝術，能讓觀看者熟悉新的科技。

Visual cyberart includes digital imagery created on the computer and its physical counterpart.
視覺的數位藝術包括在電腦上創作的影像，和它實體的成品。

✍ The exhibition, which is the first in Singapore's history, showcases cyberart works that exemplify and explore the interactions and productive tensions between art and technology.
這場新加坡史上第一次的展覽，展出的數位藝術作品示範並探索藝術與科技之間的交互作用與創作張力。

Computer graphics in some cyberart pieces are quite expressive in terms of space and structure, but relatively awkward capturing texture, atmosphere and emotion.
某些數位藝術作品的電腦繪圖，在空間與結構方面相當有表現力，但在捕捉質感、氣氛、情緒方面就相對笨拙。

respect
/rɪˈspɛkt/

n. v. 尊重，尊敬

💬 Though I respect the way the painting was constructed, I don't understand its use of technology.
雖然我尊敬這幅圖畫構成的方式，但我不懂它對於科技的使用。

We should have respect for artists who use technology in their work.
我們應該尊重在作品中使用科技的藝術家。

✍ I have respect for those who spend many hours creating computer fonts, which have earned more attention these years.
我尊敬那些花許多小時創造電腦字體的人，字體在這些年獲得了更多的注意。

Before using any clipart online, consider whether that image might be offensive or confusing to another culture as we don't want to lose the respect from international viewers.
在使用網路上的美工圖案之前，要先考慮圖像對於另一個文化是否有冒犯性或者令人困惑，因為我們不想要失去國外觀看者的尊敬。

gauge
/geɪdʒ/

v. 估量，判斷

💬 We should not gauge the value of a painting based on whether or not the artist was aided by technology.
我們不應該依據藝術家是否受到科技輔助來評斷一幅畫的價值。

He gauged that full integration of technology in the studio is only a matter of time.
他判斷將科技全面整合到工作室只是時間問題。

✏️ The video documenting the artworks of eight high-technology artists was shown in various public sites to gauge public awareness and acceptance of these works.
記錄八位高科技藝術家的作品的影片，在各種公共地點被播放，以判斷大眾對於這些作品的認知度與接受度。

In order to gauge the academic progress of the students, the dean of the school of art chose to bring the test back this year.
為了評估學生的學業進展，藝術學院的院長選擇在今年恢復測驗。

applaud
/əˈplɔːd/

v. 鼓掌，喝彩，稱讚

💬 They have been applauded for their art works and artistic efforts.
他們因為自己的藝術作品和藝術方面的努力而受到了讚賞。

The critic applauded the artist for his use of technology.
那位評論家讚賞那位藝術家對於科技的使用。

✏️ We applaud the art academy for offering the teen-only programme teaching filmmaking, motion graphics, special effects and professional photography with top-tier equipment and software.
我們讚賞那間藝術學院提供限青少年參加的學程，用頂級的設備與軟體教導電影製作、動畫、特效與專業攝影。

The university applauded the visual arts teachers, who help students move beyond superficial understanding to the deeper meanings expressed through images.
這所大學稱讚那些視覺藝術老師，他們幫助學生超越表面上的了解，而知道透過影像表現的更深層意義。

RELATED WORDS | 相關單字延伸

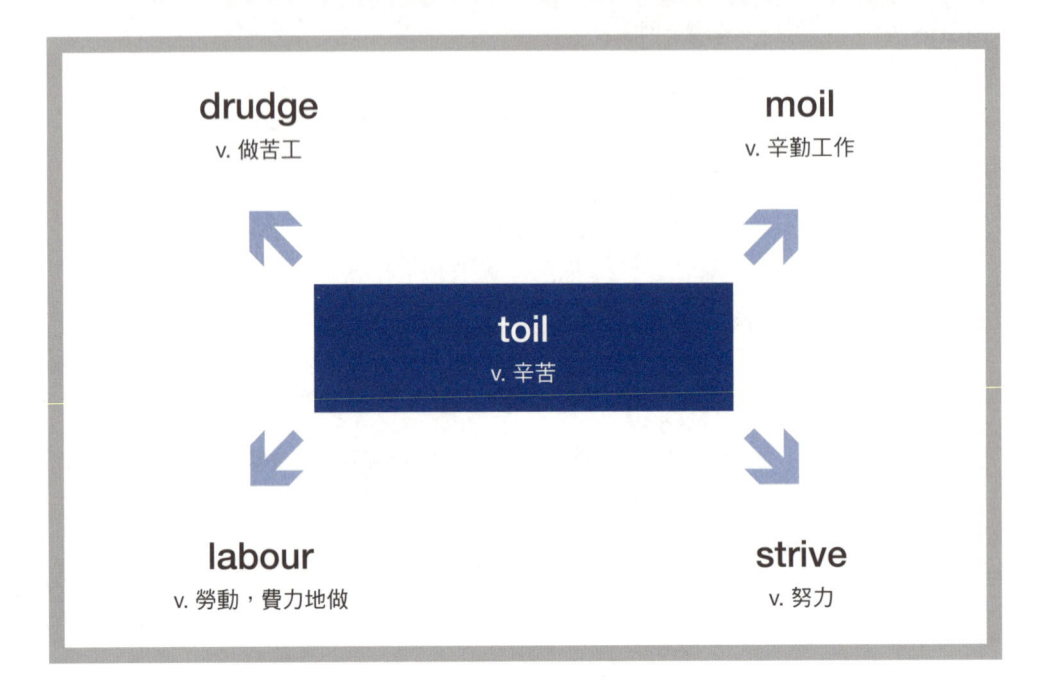

drudge
v. 做苦工

moil
v. 辛勤工作

toil
v. 辛苦

labour
v. 勞動，費力地做

strive
v. 努力

toil
/tɔɪl/

In the past, people had to toil to find an outlet for their creativity.
在過去，人們必須辛苦為自己的創造力尋找出路。

drudge
/drʌdʒ/

When people have to drudge through work, it is hard for them to come home and be creative.
當人們必須辛苦工作時，就很難在回家之後還有創造力。

labour
/ˈleɪbə/

Workers in farms and ranches labour all day long until they complete their tasks.
農田和牧場的工作者努力一整天，直到完成工作為止。

moil
/mɔɪl/

She moiled every day so that she could afford to take time off to pursue her creativity.
她每天辛勤工作，好讓自己有本錢休假，追求自己的創造力。

strive
/strʌɪv/

We strived for years to develop our children's creative talents.
我們努力了許多年來開發孩子的創意天分。

USEFUL EXPRESSIONS | 相關實用片語

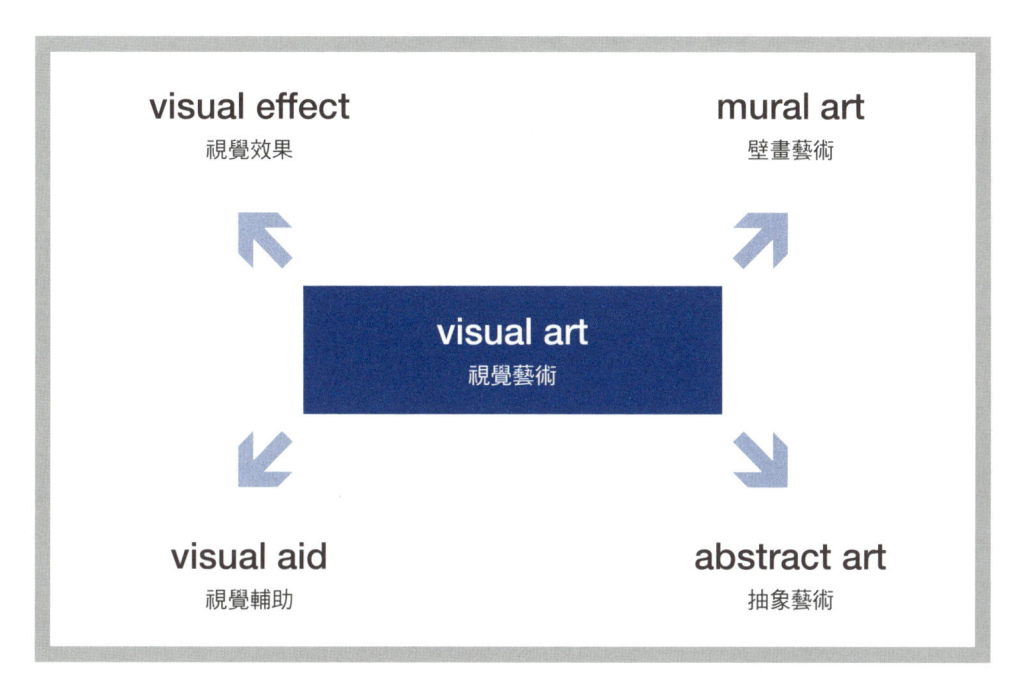

```
visual effect                    mural art
視覺效果                           壁畫藝術
           ↖              ↗
              visual art
              視覺藝術
           ↙              ↘
visual aid                       abstract art
視覺輔助                           抽象藝術
```

visual art
/ˈvɪʒuəl ɑːt/

Please see the gallery schedule for educational workshops on visual arts.
請看藝廊的時間表，查看關於視覺藝術的教育研習會的訊息。

visual effect
/ˈvɪʒuəl ɪˈfɛkt/

The fantastic visual effects in the 1999 movie *The Matrix* earned it a record-breaking number of awards.
1999 年的電影《駭客任務》中極佳的視覺效果，為它贏得了數量破紀錄的獎項。

visual aid
/ˈvɪʒuəl eɪd/

For high school students, the concept can be delivered with the use of visual aids or notes.
對於高中學生，這個概念可以藉由使用視覺輔助或筆記來傳達。

mural art
/ˈmjuərəl ɑːt/

Thousands of years ago, men began creating mural art in the form of animals and humans on cave walls.
幾千年前，人類開始在洞穴的牆上創造動物和人類樣式的壁畫。

abstract art
/ˈabstrakt ɑːt/

Before 1915, she was not a figurative artist but rather a pioneer of abstract art in America.
1915 年以前，她並不是具像藝術家，而是美國抽象藝術的先驅。

WED

IELTS **BASIC WORDS**

improve /ɪmˈpruːv/　v. 改善，增進
ENG. to raise to a more desirable condition
SYS. enhance, upgrade

> It is important for children to **improve** their writing skills as early as they can.
> 讓孩子們盡早提升自己的寫作能力是很重要的。

同義語 例句 Teachers strive to help students **make** their penmanship **better**.
老師們努力幫助學生，讓他們的手寫字跡變得更好。

同義語 例句 Knowing how to read **adds to** children's writing skills.
知道如何閱讀，能增進孩子的寫作技能。

反義語 例句 Children's writing and reading skills **worsened** after the widespread use of computers.
在電腦受到廣泛使用之後，孩子們的寫作與閱讀技巧變差了。

export /ɪkˈspɔːt/　v. 輸出，出口
ENG. sell or transfer abroad
SYS. trade, ship

> Some brilliant artworks are reproduced and **exported** for public enjoyment.
> 有些傑出藝術作品被複製並且出口供大眾欣賞。

同義語 例句 Some successful artworks are **sold overseas** for the world to see.
一些成功的藝術作品被販賣到海外，讓全世界看到。

同義語 例句 Some schools around the world **trade** their students' artworks to improve their interactions.
世界上有些學校交換學生們的藝術作品來促進彼此的交流。

反義語 例句 Some art pieces are **imported** to help teach our local students.
有些藝術作品是被進口用來幫助教育我們的本地學生。

WEEK 4 TOPIC **ART**

▶基礎單字擴充

output /ˈaʊtpʊt/ n. 產出物
ENG. what is produced in a given time period
SYS. production, turnout

> Children's **outputs** in art classes are displayed in the school lobby.
> 孩子們在藝術課做出來的作品，展示在學校大廳。

同義語例句 We can expect a **final product**, such as a painting, in all children's art classes.
在所有兒童的藝術課中，我們都可以期待一幅畫之類的最終成品產生。

同義語例句 The **things produced** by children at the end of each semester are always surprising.
孩子們在每學期結束時創造的東西總是讓人驚豔。

反義語例句 Learning ability is a **contributory factor** to making a masterpiece.
學習能力是創作出傑作的促成因素。

insignificant /ˌɪnsɪɡˈnɪfɪkənt/ adj. 不重要的，沒意義的
ENG. not worthy of notice
SYS. undistinguished, meaningless

> The physical appearance of an artwork is **insignificant** if there is no background story provided.
> 如果沒有提供背景故事，藝術作品的外觀就沒有意義。

同義語例句 This artwork's material is **irrelevant** to the artistic message it conveys.
這個藝術作品的材料對於它所傳達的藝術訊息而言並不相關。

同義語例句 An artwork **has no meaning** if the artist is not inspired.
如果藝術家沒有受到靈感啟發，藝術作品就沒有意義。

反義語例句 An artwork is **meaningful** if merely observing it changes the viewer.
如果只是觀看一件藝術品就能改變觀看者，它就是有意義的。

203

WED

04-3A

TOPIC | The importance for children to learn art
讓孩子學習藝術的重要性

There are many reasons why art should be a core of the curriculum for young children. Art is considered by some a **fundamental** need that **characterises** our existence and the human condition. Those who hold this view will **encourage** children to **appreciate** beauty and **aesthetics** within their surroundings. Indeed, art should be valued because it is an important means for self-expression; **spontaneity**, imagination and freedom from inhibition are desirable components for freedom of expression. Art is also valued as an emotional mode for communicating unconscious things that otherwise cannot be communicated. Art also **enhances** children's **cognitive** processes, involving children in problem solving, thinking and using symbol systems to record their thoughts, ideas and feelings. In many ways, art also **embodies** spiritual awareness.

TRANS

　　有許多理由應該使藝術成為年輕孩子們的課程核心。有些人認為藝術是一項基本的需求，它描繪出我們的存在和人類的狀態。抱持這個想法的人會鼓勵孩子們去欣賞自己週遭的美和美學。的確，藝術應該受到重視，因為它是自我表達的一種重要方式；自發性、想像力和免於抑制的自由，是表達自由的理想成分。藝術也因為作為一種情感模式，能夠傳達其他方法無法傳達的無意識事物而受到重視。藝術也增強孩子們的認知過程，使孩子們進行問題解決、思考，以及使用符號系統記錄他們的思想、概念和感受。在許多方面，藝術也體現了精神上的覺知。

fundamental
/fʌndəˈmɛntəl/

adj. 基本的
It is **fundamental** to know the alphabet before you can learn to read.
在能夠學習閱讀之前先知道字母是基本的。

characterise
/ˈkærəktərʌɪz/

v. 表示出⋯的特性
Which of the following descriptions best **characterises** abstract art?
下列哪個敘述最能表示抽象藝術的特性？

encourage
/ɪnˈkʌrɪdʒ/

v. 鼓勵
I **encourage** you to buy a Hyundai because it is very reliable.
我鼓勵你買現代汽車，因為它很可靠。

appreciate
/əˈpriːʃɪeɪt/

v. 欣賞，感謝，意識到
I have grown to **appreciate** her hard work and dedication to the project.
我漸漸可以領會她對於計畫的努力和奉獻。

aesthetics
/ɛsˈθɛtɪks/

n. 美學
Romantic artists showed their unique **aesthetics** in their attention to shapes and light.
浪漫派的藝術家在他們對於形狀與光的注意中展現獨特的美學。

spontaneity
/ˌspɒntəˈneɪɪti/

n. 自發性
She was fed up with his lack of **spontaneity**, so she ended their relationship.
她受夠了他缺乏自發性，所以結束了他們的關係。

inhibition
/ˌɪnhɪˈbɪʃən/

n. 抑制
I acted without **inhibition** and made foolish decisions.
我缺乏自制地行動，做出了愚笨的決定。

enhance
/ɪnˈhɑːns/

v. 提升，改善
I found that salting the meat first **enhances** its flavour as it cooks.
我發現先抹鹽在肉上面，可以在烹煮時提升它的風味。

cognitive
/ˈkɒgnɪtɪv/

adj. 認知的
Exercising can have **cognitive** benefits for children.
運動會對兒童有認知方面的助益。

embody
/ɪmˈbɒdi/

v. 體現，使具體化
Mother Theresa **embodied** all that is good about the human spirit.
德蕾莎修女體現人類精神的所有善良特質。

WORD TRAINING ｜ 重點單字造句練習

aptitude
/ˈæptɪtjuːd/

n. 傾向，天資，才能

💬 My son is already demonstrating a greater aptitude and ability for artistic expression.
我的兒子已經在藝術表達方面展現出比較多的天資和能力。

The school offers placement to children who show an aptitude for art and foreign languages.
這所學校提供名額給對於藝術和外語表現出天分的孩子。

📝 Artistic talent often shows itself at a very young age and, if nurtured, can become an important and rewarding aptitude in your child's adult life.
藝術天分通常在很小的年紀就展現出來，而如果受到培育的話，可能會成為你的孩子成年生活中重要而且有益的才能。

Some children are born with an aptitude for art, and nurturing art appreciation from a young age can be beneficial for them.
有些孩子天生就有藝術傾向，從小就培養藝術欣賞可能會對他們有益。

mastery
/ˈmɑːsteri/

n. 熟練，精通，精湛技藝

💬 Art is a learning experience that provides children with pleasure, challenge and a sense of mastery.
藝術是一種能提供孩子快樂、挑戰和熟練感的學習經驗。

It is important that children learn to have mastery of language skills.
讓孩子學習熟練語言技能是很重要的。

📝 Children who were introduced to clay during their toddler years have a better chance of achieving a certain level of mastery of the medium when they are older.
在學步期就接觸到黏土的兒童，長大的時候比較有機會對這種媒介達到一定程度的熟練度。

Art teachers should try their best to develop every student's unique skills and support them on the road to mastery.
藝術老師應該盡全力開發每位學生的獨特技能，並且在他們邁向精通的路程中支持他們。

competence
/ˈkɒmpɪtəns/

n. 能力

💬 Children can easily develop a higher degree of competence in the arts through early exposure.
透過早期接觸，孩子能輕易地在藝術方面發展出較高程度的能力。

Although literacy activities are crucial to pre-schoolers' development, art can also help to build emotional competence.
雖然讀寫能力方面的活動對於學齡前兒童的發展很重要，但藝術也有助於建立情感的能力。

✏️ While it is arguable whether art can improve children's cognitive competence and self-esteem, there are other important reasons for including art in the curriculum.
雖然藝術是否能提升孩子的認知能力和自尊還有疑義，但還有其他重要理由將藝術納入課程中。

Preschool teachers and parents can use art activities to encourage children's emotional competence skills, such as recognising, expressing and identifying specific feelings.
幼兒園的老師和家長可以用藝術活動激發兒童的情感能力技能，例如認出、表達並且辨識特定的情感。

adroitness
/əˈdrɔɪtnɪs/

n. 靈巧，機敏

💬 Encourage your children to express their opinions on works of art as a way to develop their artistic adroitness.
鼓勵你的孩子表達對於藝術作品的意見，作為發展他們藝術靈敏度的方法。

Using glue, scissors and watercolour can expand the adroitness of adolescents as they grow up.
使用膠水、剪刀和水彩可以讓青少年在成長時擴展靈巧性。

✏️ It is important to encourage the artistic adroitness in children because doing so strengthens their motor skills and improves their hand-eye coordination.
激發孩子的藝術靈敏度是很重要的，因為這麼做能強化他們的運動技能，並且促進他們的手眼協調。

This child shows a particular adroitness for the techniques associated with oil painting, proving the importance of teaching children art from a young age.
這個孩子在油畫相關的技巧方面展現出特別靈巧的能力，證明從小教導孩子藝術的重要性。

RELATED WORDS | 相關單字延伸

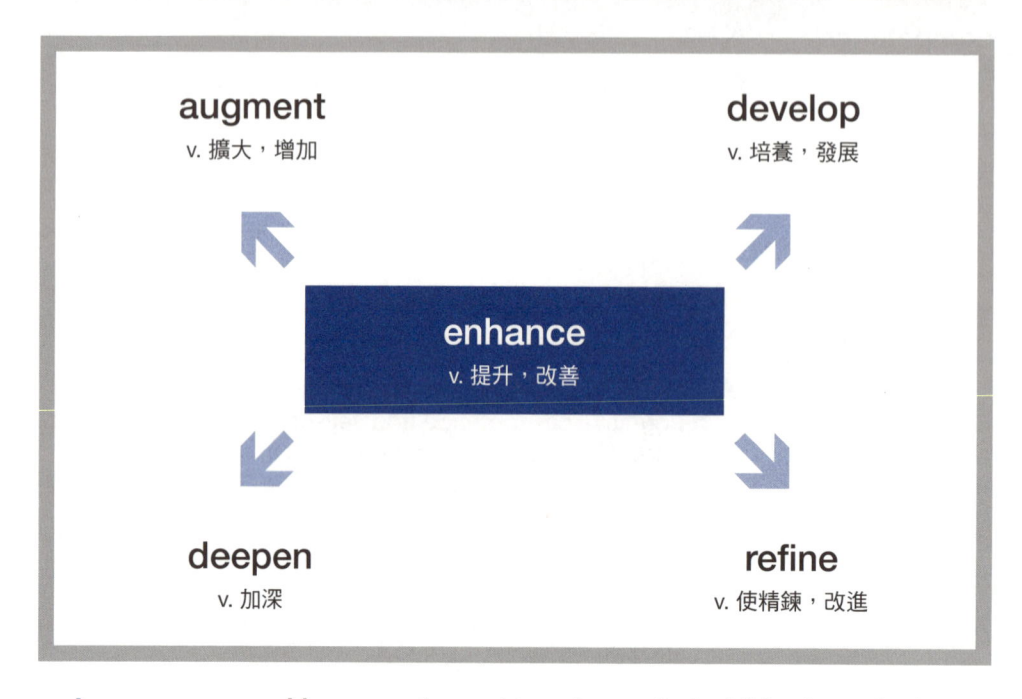

augment
v. 擴大，增加

develop
v. 培養，發展

enhance
v. 提升，改善

deepen
v. 加深

refine
v. 使精鍊，改進

---

enhance
/ɪnˈhɑːns/

Many parents want to enhance their children's aesthetic talents from a young age.
許多父母想要從小開始提高他們孩子的美學才能。

augment
/ɔːɡˈmɛnt/

She attempted to augment her child's development by enrolling him in art classes early on.
她試圖藉著為孩子早期報名藝術課程來增進他的發展。

deepen
/ˈdiːpən/

In the field of art, the best way to deepen your abilities is to pay attention to your feelings.
在藝術領域，加深能力最好的方法是注意你的感覺。

develop
/dɪˈvɛləp/

Surprisingly, the art course developed my problem-solving skills.
令人驚訝的是，藝術課培養了我的問題解決能力。

refine
/rɪˈfʌɪn/

My art professor said that painting my thoughts on canvas would refine my talent.
我的藝術教授說，把我的想法畫在畫布上，會精進我的才能。

USEFUL EXPRESSIONS | 相關實用片語

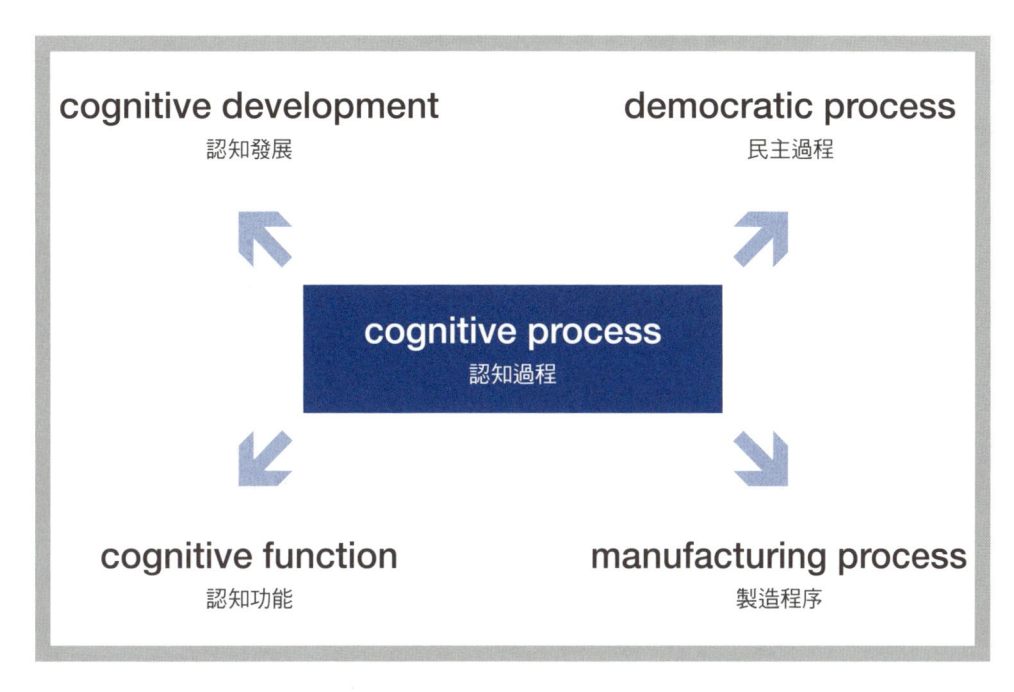

```
cognitive development              democratic process
     認知發展                            民主過程

                ↖         ↗
                 cognitive process
                     認知過程
                ↙         ↘

cognitive function             manufacturing process
    認知功能                         製造程序
```

cognitive process
/ˈkɑgnɪtɪv ˈproʊsɛs/

The cognitive process of focusing on one thing while trying to ignore others is called attention.
專注在一件事的同時又試圖忽略其他事情的認知過程稱為注意力。

cognitive development
/ˈkɑgnɪtɪv dɪˈvɛləpmənt/

In one recent study, a correlation was found between cognitive development and breastfeeding.
在最近的一項研究中,發現了認知發展與母乳哺育之間的相互關聯。

cognitive function
/ˈkɑgnɪtɪv ˈfʌŋkʃən/

Higher cognitive functions, such as memory and reasoning, presuppose the availability of knowledge and make use of it. 高層認知功能,例如記憶和推論,以知識的可得性為前提,並且會利用到知識。

democratic process
/dɛməˈkrætɪk ˈproʊsɛs/

Children can become aware of the democratic process through an election simulation.
孩子可以透過模擬選舉而了解民主過程。

manufacturing process
/mænjʊˈfæktʃərɪŋ ˈproʊsɛs/

According to the Ministry of Health, all viruses were eradicated during the manufacturing process of the drug. 根據衛生部的說法,所有的病毒在製藥過程中已經被完全消滅。

THU

IELTS **BASIC WORDS**

reaction /rɪˈakʃən/ n. 反應
ENG. a response to a stimulus
SYS. response, feedback

> The boy's reaction to the artist's advice was positive and delightful.
> 這個男孩對於藝術家給他的建議，反應是正面、愉快的。

同義語 例句
When the artist criticised the boy's work, his answer was to paint another piece.
當藝術家批評男孩的作品，他的回應是去畫另外一張圖。

同義語 例句
The general response of the critics about his work was that he needed more practice.
對於他的作品，評論家大致上的反應是他需要更多練習。

反義語 例句
His lack of response to the reviews disappointed the critics.
他對評論不作回應，讓評論家失望。

essential /ɪˈsɛnʃəl/ adj. 必要的
ENG. absolutely necessary
SYS. crucial, fundamental

> To become a great artist, it is essential to be open and resourceful.
> 要成為一個偉大的藝術家，開放與富有機智是必要的。

同義語 例句
Willingness to display vulnerability is vitally needed in being a good artist.
願意展現脆弱，對成為一個好藝術家是非常必要的。

同義語 例句
Being resourceful and open is of extreme importance to being a great artist.
富有機智與開放對於成為一個偉大的藝術家是非常重要的。

反義語 例句
Having money is not necessary in becoming a great artist.
有錢對於成為一個偉大藝術家並不是必要的。

WEEK 4 TOPIC **ART**

▶基礎單字擴充

engage /ɪnˈgeɪdʒ/ v. 從事，使從事
ENG. carry out or participate in an activity
SYS. pursue, participate

> A good artist must be able to engage in unfamiliar art forms and methods.
> 好的藝術家必須能夠涉足不熟悉的藝術形式和方法。

同義語例句 A good artist should be involved in unconventional methods to broaden his skills.
好的藝術家應該涉足非傳統的方式，以拓展他的技能。

同義語例句 A good artist must be willing to explore art forms he has not tried before.
好的藝術家必須願意探索自己以前沒嘗試過的藝術形式。

反義語例句 An artist becomes free from social limitations if he involves himself in freeform art.
如果藝術家讓自己進入自由形式的藝術，就不會受到社會限制的侷限。

prove /pruːv/ v. 證明
ENG. establish the validity of something
SYS. verify, determine

> An artist must prove his worth with the quality of his works.
> 一個藝術家必須憑藉他作品的品質來證明他的價值。

同義語例句 For an artist to be famous, his or her work must turn out to be marketable.
一個藝術家要成名，他的作品必須要是暢銷的。

同義語例句 An artwork must show evidence of the artist's technical and artistic abilities.
一件藝術作品必須展現出藝術家的技術與藝術能力的證據。

反義語例句 We ruled out the possibility that he copies other artists' work.
我們排除了他抄襲其他藝術家作品的可能性。

THU

04-4A

TOPIC | Becoming a famous artist
成為有名的藝術家

Artists are always wondering how to get more **exposure**. The most effective way of **marketing** paintings and gaining fame is online **promotion**. If you are pursuing an artistic career, focus on building your **reputation** to the point where galleries will deal with you – your online presence is a big part of this. There are many websites that will show your paintings, but very few viewers buy art online. Most galleries deal with local artists who approach them – they aren't searching online for **emerging** artists. While **boosting** your online exposure, try to take **critiques gracefully** and don't confuse them with personal criticism. Additionally, you should learn to accept compliments **benevolently**. As online exposure is not enough, you should join fine art societies and enter contests. Finally, find a reliable and reputable art agent to market your work and represent you in contract **negotiation**.

TRANS

藝術家們總是想知道要如何得到更多的曝光。行銷畫作與得到名氣最有效的方法是網路宣傳。如果你在追求以藝術作為職業的生涯，要專注於建立你的名聲，直到藝廊會和你交易的程度——你在網路上的呈現是其中很重要的一部分。有很多網站會展示你的畫作，但很少觀眾會在網路上買藝術作品。大部分的藝廊和主動接近他們的當地藝術家交易——他們不是上網搜尋剛出頭的藝術家。在提高你的網路曝光時，試著大方接受評論文章，而且不要把這些評論和針對個人的批評搞混。此外，你也應該學習善意地接受讚美。網路曝光不夠的時候，你應該加入美術協會，並且參加比賽。最後，找一個可靠、聲譽好的藝術經紀人來行銷你的作品，並且代表你進行合約協商。

exposure
/ɪkˈspəʊʒə/

n. 曝光

After the comedian appeared on the variety show, he gained more and more **exposure**.
當這位喜劇演員出現在那個綜藝節目之後，他得到了越來越多的曝光。

market
/ˈmɑːkɪt/

v. 行銷

The best way to begin **marketing** your soap is renting a Sunday bazaar table.
開始行銷你的肥皂最好的方式，是租一張週日市集的桌子。

promotion
/prəˈməʊʃn/

n. 宣傳

They are planning a **promotion** for the new laundry detergent.
他們正在為新的洗衣精計畫宣傳活動。

reputation
/ˌrɛpjʊˈteɪʃən/

n. 聲望

Her grooming company has a good **reputation** with the equestrians.
她的馬匹刷洗公司在馬術騎士間有良好的聲譽。

emerging
/ɪˈmɜːdʒɪŋ/

adj. 新興的

Elderly employees coming back from retirement is an **emerging** trend.
年長員工退休後重返崗位是一股新興的趨勢。

boost
/buːst/

v. 提高

He began by **boosting** my self-confidence, telling me how intelligent and pretty I am.
他先是提升我的自信，告訴我自己有多聰明、多漂亮。

critique
/krɪˈtiːk/

n. 評論文章

Her novel received several unfavourable **critiques** after its publication.
她的小說在出版後得到了幾篇負面評論。

gracefully
/ˈgreɪsfəli/

adv. 優雅地，得體地

The goalkeeper shook his opponent's hand **gracefully** after the loss.
那位守門員在輸球之後大方地與對手握手。

benevolently
/bɪˈnɛvələntli/

adv. 仁慈地，善意地

The child impressed everyone present when he **benevolently** donated his blanket.
當那孩子心地善良地捐贈出他的毛毯時，打動了現場的每一個人。

negotiation
/nɪˌgəʊʃɪˈeɪʃən/

n. 談判，協商

The contract **negotiation** came to a halt after the company restructuring. 合約談判在公司重組之後暫停了。

WORD TRAINING | 重點單字造句練習

prowess
/ˈpraʊɪs/

n. 高超的技藝

💬 He became a famous artist for his artistic prowess in impressionism.
他因為在印象派畫風中高超的藝術技藝，而成為了知名的藝術家。

Her prowess as an independent artist grew quickly after her first solo exhibition.
她身為獨立藝術家的技藝，在第一次個人展之後快速成長。

✍ Each time I read reviews on famous artists' works, their artistic prowess is not as eulogised as should be, despite their painstaking effort.
每次我閱讀關於知名藝術家作品的評論時，他們的高超藝術技藝並沒有得到應得的讚揚，即使他們已經很辛勤努力了。

The collection of abstract imagery shows the artist's painterly prowess, which is why he became famous early.
這一系列抽象圖像展現出這位藝術家的高超繪畫技藝，這也是他很早就成名的原因。

---

sculpture
/ˈskʌlptʃə/

n. 雕塑品

💬 Most of the items in the gift shop are ornaments, but there are also paintings and sculptures.
這間禮品店裡大部分的物品是裝飾品，但也有繪畫和雕塑品。

The famous artist is not only good at making sculptures, but also marketing them.
這位有名的藝術家不但擅長製作雕塑品，也很擅長行銷它們。

✍ I recall taking notes on various artists at school, and making flash cards of each painting and sculpture with all the known facts about them.
我想起自己在學校做關於各種藝術家的筆記，還有為每幅畫和雕塑品製作（記憶用的）閃卡，上面寫了所有關於作品的已知事實。

My art teacher thought it was ridiculous that I couldn't tell apart the sculpture of David by Michelangelo from Auguste Rodin's *The Thinker*.
我的藝術老師認為，我沒辦法區分米開朗基羅的大衛雕像和奧古斯特・羅丹的《沉思者》是很荒謬的。

口說範例　　寫作範例

artistry
/ˈɑːtɪstri/

n. 藝術才能，藝術技巧

💬 There are many artists who became famous for their artistry and are in high demand for their talents.
有很多藝術家因為他們的藝術才能而變得有名，也因為他們的天分而（讓他們的作品）有很高的需求。

I hope my artistry will someday make me famous.
我希望我的藝術才能有一天能讓我成名。

✍ To become famous, make informational handouts, show works that prove your artistry and try to get more exposure on social media.
想要變得有名，就製作資訊傳單、展示證明自己藝術才能的作品，並且試著在社群媒體獲得更多曝光。

Fortunately, independent artistry survived through the depths of lows, even though mainstream audience largely ignored it.
幸運的是，獨立藝術從低潮期存活下來了，即使主流觀眾大多忽略它。

admire
/ədˈmaɪə/

v. 欽佩，欣賞

💬 I have no desire to become a famous artist, but I do admire the drive of those who do.
我沒有成為有名藝術家的欲望，但我欣賞那些有這種欲望的人的幹勁。

It's hard to admire some artists who gained fame by exploiting others.
有些藉著利用別人而獲得名氣的藝術家，讓人很難欣賞。

✍ If you write a good review on an up-and-coming artist, people may admire you for your effort to support them.
如果你為剛嶄露頭角的藝術家寫一篇好的評論，人們可能會欣賞你支持他們的努力。

To become a famous artist, ask for comments from people who draw better than you do and make online friends with real artists whose work you admire.
要成為有名的藝術家，就請畫得比你好的人給你評論意見，並且和作品令你欣賞的真正的藝術家成為網路上的朋友。

215

RELATED WORDS | 相關單字延伸

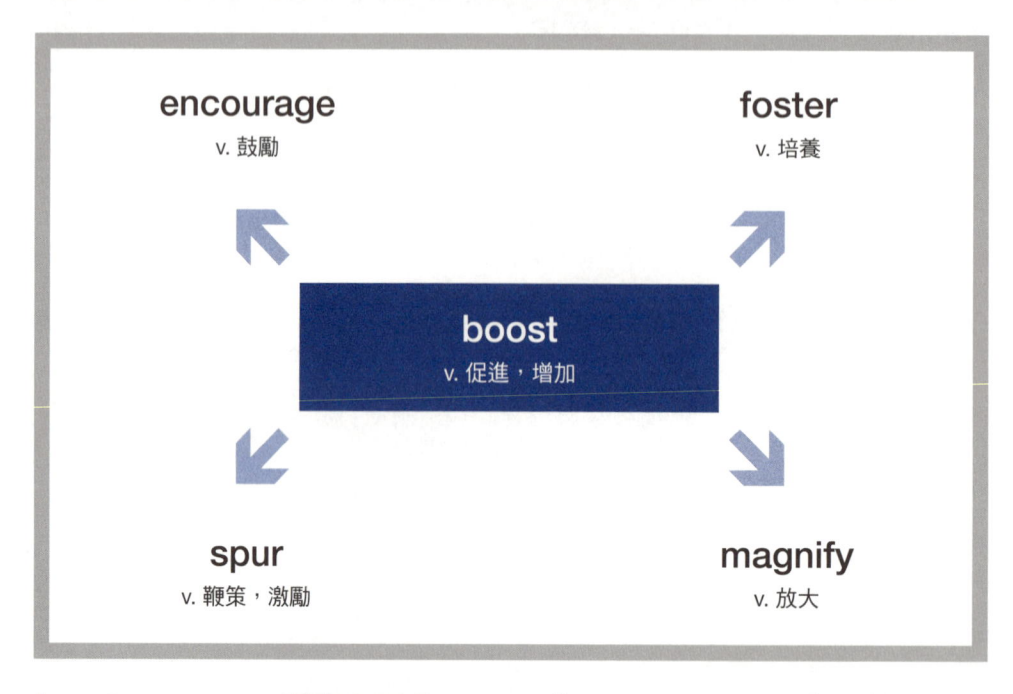

encourage
v. 鼓勵

foster
v. 培養

boost
v. 促進，增加

spur
v. 鞭策，激勵

magnify
v. 放大

boost
/buːst/

While boosting your online exposure, try to take critiques gracefully and don't confuse them with personal criticism.
在提高你的網路曝光時，試著大方接受評論文章，而且不要把這些評論和針對個人的批評搞混。

encourage
/ɪnˈkʌrɪdʒ/

I would encourage you to write your restaurant review online in a blog.
我會鼓勵你在部落格寫餐廳評論。

spur
/spɜː/

This website is great for inspiring people and spurring them on, but it isn't without criticism.
這個網站對於激勵人心以及鞭策人們前進非常好，但也不是沒有受到批評。

foster
/ˈfɒstə/

To foster a larger audience for your business, advertise on websites and blogs.
想為你的事業培養更大的觀眾群，那就在網站和部落格刊登廣告。

magnify
/ˈmagnɪfʌɪ/

I think you took the criticism from your online friend too personally and magnified your feelings.
我想你太把網路上朋友的批評當成是針對你個人的，也放大了你自己的感受。

USEFUL EXPRESSIONS | 相關實用片語

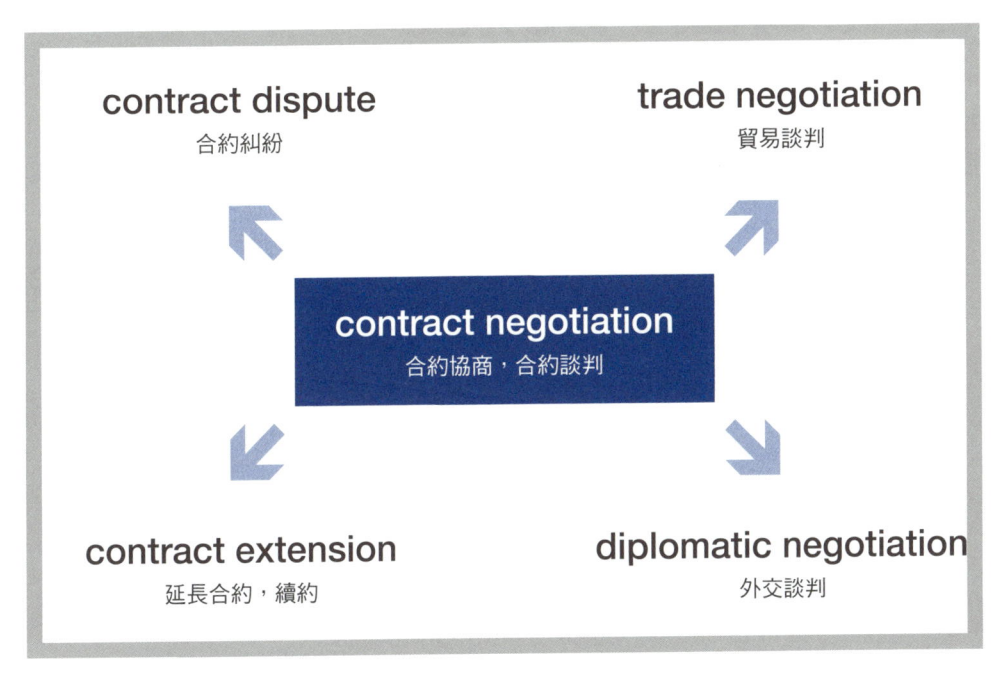

```
contract dispute              trade negotiation
合約糾紛                        貿易談判

           ↖         ↗
            contract negotiation
              合約協商，合約談判
           ↙         ↘

contract extension            diplomatic negotiation
延長合約，續約                   外交談判
```

contract negotiation
/ˈkɒntrakt nɪɡəʊʃɪˈeɪʃən/

After the contract negotiation, the employees have more paid holidays per year.
在合約協商之後，員工每年有更多的有薪假。

contract dispute
/ˈkɒntrakt ˈdɪspjuːt/

In order to avoid a contract dispute, the parties involved should meet and discuss the terms.
為了避免合約糾紛，相關各方應該會面討論條款。

contract extension
/ˈkɒntrakt ɪkˈstɛnʃən/

The English Premier League soccer team, Manchester United, have offered Park Ji-sung a contract extension.
英格蘭足球超級聯賽球隊曼聯已經提出與朴智星續約的邀請。

trade negotiation
/treɪd nɪɡəʊʃɪˈeɪʃən/

The original plans to complete free trade negotiations between the United States and Korea are unlikely.
完成美國和韓國之間自由貿易談判的原定計畫是不太可能的。

diplomatic negotiation
/dɪpləˈmatɪk nɪɡəʊʃɪˈeɪʃən/

Unfortunately, the diplomatic negotiations between the Soviets and the region failed to stop the war.
遺憾的是，蘇聯與那個區域之間的外交談判未能阻止戰爭。

FRI

IELTS BASIC WORDS

unmanageable /ˌʌnˈmænɪdʒəbəl/ adj. 難管理的，難處理的，難控制的
ENG. difficult to control, solve, or alleviate
SYS. difficult, uncontrollable

> The young artist's **unmanageable** temper might hinder the success of his exhibition.
> 那個年輕藝術家難控制的脾氣，可能會阻礙他展覽的成功。

同義語例句 Some new artists' artistic expression is getting **out of hand**.
有些新藝術家的藝術表達越來越失控。

同義語例句 The direction where the future of new artists is headed is **hard to control**.
新藝術家未來朝向的方向很難控制。

反義語例句 Under the guidance of the experienced curator, the young artist's dilemma can be **handled without trouble**.
在有經驗的策展人的引導下，這位年輕藝術家的困境可以毫無問題地處理。

abandon /əˈbændən/ v. 放棄
ENG. give up completely
SYS. forsake, ditch

> With the advent of the new era of technological art, some old artists have **abandoned** art altogether.
> 隨著科技藝術的新時代到來，有些老藝術家已經完全放棄了藝術。

同義語例句 Older artists **fell behind** a generation of artists that rely on technology to create art.
老一輩的藝術家落後了依靠科技創造藝術的新一代藝術家。

同義語例句 Older traditional artists **gave up** the idea of creating art with the aid of technology.
老一輩的傳統藝術家放棄了用科技輔助藝術創作的想法。

反義語例句 Some old artists **carry on** the same way of life as before.
有些老一輩的藝術家仍然繼續和以前一樣的生活方式。

WEEK 4 TOPIC **ART**

▶基礎單字擴充

provision /prəˈvɪʒən/ n. 供應
ENG. the activity of supplying or providing something
SYS. supplying, distribution

> The **provision** of new technology makes it easy for new artists to create masterpieces.
> 新科技的提供讓新銳藝術家容易創作出傑出作品。

同義語例句 The **stock of** new artistic tools enables young artists to make better artworks.
新藝術工具的資源讓年輕藝術家能做出更好的作品。

同義語例句 The **supplying** of new artistic tools equips new artists with unlimited creative possibilities.
新藝術工具的供應，讓新的藝術家具有無限的創造可能性。

反義語例句 The **lack** of technological knowledge of older artists limits the possibility of their artworks.
老一輩藝術家欠缺科技知識，限制了他們作品的可能性。

exercise /ˈɛksəsaɪz/ v. 運用
ENG. exert one's power or influence; put into service
SYS. practise, exert

> New artists must **exercise** their resourcefulness and not copy traditional artworks.
> 新藝術家必須運用他們的才智，不要複製傳統作品。

同義語例句 New artists must **apply** their creativity in making original art.
新藝術家必須運用他們的創造力，製作有原創性的藝術。

同義語例句 New artists should **make use of** new tools to transform traditional styles.
新藝術家應該運用新的工具來轉變傳統的風格。

反義語例句 It is time to **put** traditional art **to rest** and create modern art that keeps up with the times.
是時候放下傳統藝術，並且創造跟得上時代的現代藝術了。

TOPIC: Older and younger generations' arts appreciation

年長與年輕世代的藝術鑑賞

There is a very obvious **dichotomy** present in art appreciation according to a viewer's age. Speaking generally, it seems as though **contemporary** art is not appreciated by elderly people, whereas the younger generation often feels that **pastoral** landscape paintings are **passé**. Whenever the elderly refer to modern art, they usually mean the **abstract** paintings by artists like Jackson Pollock. They tend to criticise such artists and refuse to **discern** what their intention is. Some elderly people even **judge** all contemporary art as meaningless drips and splatters, **dismissing** the whole enterprise as nonsense. We often hear older people say that they have never been fond of any artwork that requires explanation. **Representational** art is only one genre that was dominant in the past, however, and in reality, contemporary art **comprises** a very broad spectrum of styles, approaches and subject matters.

TRANS

在藝術鑑賞方面，根據觀看者的年齡，有很明顯的二分情況。大致上來說，似乎當代藝術不受老年人青睞，而年輕一代經常覺得田園風景畫過時了。每當老年人提到現代藝術時，他們通常是指傑克遜‧波洛克之類藝術家的抽象畫。他們傾向於批評這類藝術家，並且拒絕辨別他們的創作意圖。有些年長者甚至斷定所有當代藝術都是無意義的滴墨與潑濺，完全不理會整個業界，覺得都是胡鬧。我們常聽到老年人說他們從來不喜歡任何需要解釋的藝術作品。不過，具象派藝術只是過去佔優勢的一種類型，而實際上，當代藝術涵蓋範圍廣泛的各種風格、方式與主題。

dichotomy
/daɪˈkɒtəmi/

n. 二分法，一分為二

The **dichotomy** between eastern and western cultures is apparent in their individual cuisines.
東方與西方文化的二分在它們各自的菜餚裡很明顯。

contemporary
/kənˈtɛmpəreri/

adj. 當代的

Some **contemporary** buildings are built with recycled materials, unlike architecture in the past.
有些當代建築以再生材料建造，和以前的建築不同。

pastoral
/ˈpɑːstərəl/

adj. 田園的

My lake cottage is peaceful and **pastoral** because it is far from the city.
我的湖邊小屋因為遠離城市，所以很寧靜並且有田園氣息。

passé
/ˈpaseɪ/

adj. 過時的

I think that hairstyle is **passé**—she needs a makeover!
我想那種髮型已經過時了──她需要改造一番！

abstract
/ˈabstrakt/

adj. 抽象的

The **abstract** painting shows the artist's feelings in her relationship.
這幅抽象畫展現出藝術家在她的情愛關係中的感受。

discern
/dɪˈsɜːn/

v. 分辨

I can't **discern** whether the room is small or simply cluttered.
我無法分辨這個房間是小或者只是凌亂。

judge
/dʒʌdʒ/

v. 判斷，斷定

If you **judge** people negatively by their ethnicity, you are a racist.
如果你因為別人的種族而對他們有負面的判斷，你就是個種族主義者。

dismiss
/dɪsˈmɪs/

v. 不考慮，不理會

Despite how hard I tried to ignore it, I couldn't **dismiss** the mole on her cheek.
不管我多努力嘗試忽略它，我還是無法不理會她臉頰上的痣。

representational
/ˌrɛprɪzɛnˈteɪʃənəl/

adj. 具象派的

One will not expect to see **representational** artworks in an abstract art show.
一個人不會預期在抽象藝術展裡看到具象派的作品。

comprise
/kəmˈpraɪz/

v. 包含

The library **comprises** of 500,000 books and manuscripts.
這間圖書館包含了 50 萬本書及原稿。

WORD TRAINING | 重點單字造句練習

portrait
/ˈpɔːtrət/

n. 肖像畫

💬 The portrait that I painted of my grandmother was appreciated by everyone in the nursing home.
我畫我奶奶的那張肖像，畫受到養老院每個人的讚賞。

Most children will be bored by old, dark portraits of obscure historical figures.
大部分的孩子會對老舊、暗沉的無名歷史人物肖像感到無聊。

✏️ Portraits of famous historical figures on the museum walls failed to interest the children.
博物館牆上的知名歷史人物肖像沒有引起孩子們的興趣。

Centuries-old portraits may take some time for a kid to appreciate, and therefore you may encounter resistance when going to a museum, but don't get discouraged.
有幾百年歷史的肖像，可能需要一些時間讓孩子懂得欣賞，所以去博物館的時候可能會遭到抗拒，但不要因此氣餒。

collage
/kəˈlɑːʒ/

n. 拼貼

💬 The younger generation has a much better appreciation for abstract art and collage than the elderly do.
年輕一代比起老一輩更懂得欣賞抽象藝術與拼貼創作。

The collage incorporates many different elements, and still looks well-balanced.
這幅拼貼包含許多不同的元素，而且仍然看起來很均衡。

✏️ He combined wax colours with newspaper collage to create the work, which was popular with both elder and young audiences alike.
他結合蠟彩和報紙拼貼，創造出這幅作品，而它受到了老年和年輕觀眾同樣的歡迎。

By combining collage and mixed media techniques, the young artist created a collection of critically acclaimed works.
藉著結合拼貼藝術與混合媒體技術，這位年輕藝術家創造出一系列受到評論讚賞的作品。

dexterity
/dɛkˈstɛrɪti/

n. （手的）靈巧

💬 The elderly often admire art showing great dexterity.
老一輩經常會對表現出極大靈巧度的藝術感到敬佩。

Art education develops a student's knowledge and dexterity through the learning process.
藝術教育在學習的過程中開發學生的知識和靈巧性。

✍ From dexterity and discipline to identity and distinctiveness, the shift in values of modern art is evident when we compare old and new reviews.
從靈巧性與訓練到個性與獨特性，現代藝術的價值觀轉變可以在我們比較新舊評論的時候顯現出來。

While I agree that drawing should not be merely a mastery of one's technique with manual dexterity, I also feel that beginning students would benefit from learning traditional technique.
雖然我同意繪畫不應該只是一個人對於手工靈巧的技術掌握，但我也覺得剛入門的學生會從學習傳統技巧中受益。

functional
/ˈfʌŋkʃənəl/

adj. 功能的，功能性的

💬 Artwork that is functional, like painted glassware or dishes, is often appreciated by older people.
功能性的藝術品，像是彩繪玻璃皿或餐盤，常常獲得老一輩的人欣賞。

There were some technical and functional differences between the two pieces.
這兩件作品有些技術性和功能性的差異。

✍ Art is functional in that it shows our differences, such as generational disparities, cultural variations and lifestyle discrepancies.
藝術是具有功能性的，因為它顯示出我們的差異，像是世代差異、文化差別和生活方式的不一致。

Although uninterested in purchasing artworks, the general public will buy consumer products designed by famous artists because they are functional.
雖然一般大眾對於購買藝術品沒有興趣，但他們會買知名藝術家設計的消費產品，因為它們是有功能的。

RELATED WORDS | 相關單字延伸

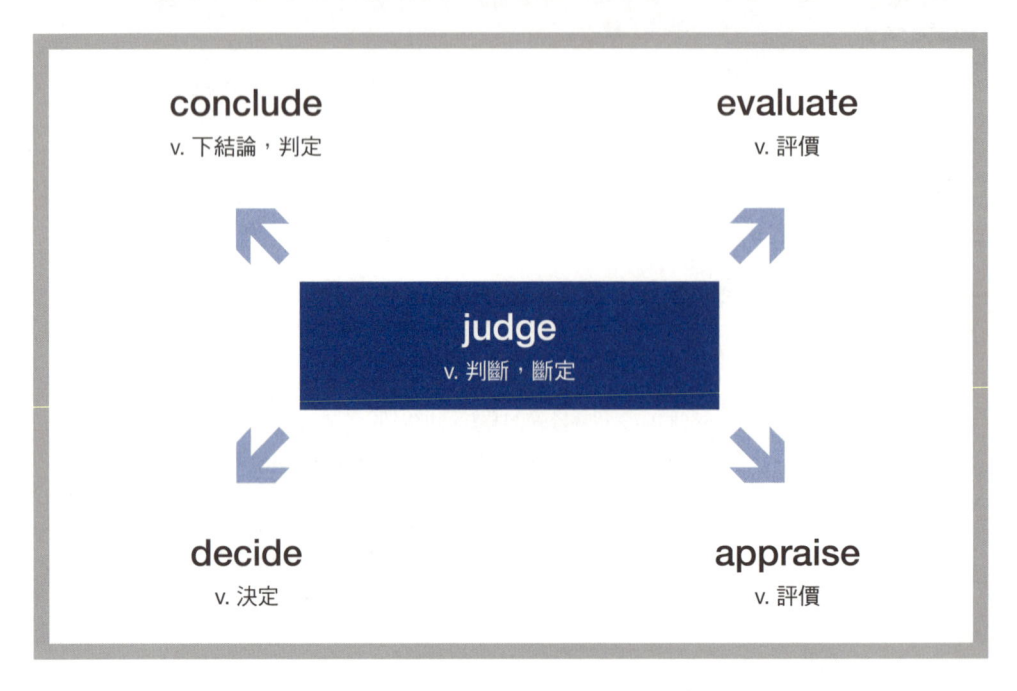

conclude
v. 下結論，判定

evaluate
v. 評價

judge
v. 判斷，斷定

decide
v. 決定

appraise
v. 評價

judge
/dʒʌdʒ/

Some elder people judge all contemporary art as meaningless drips and splatters, dismissing the whole enterprise as nonsense.
有些年長者斷定所有當代藝術都是無意義的滴墨與潑濺，完全不理會整個業界，覺得都是胡鬧。

conclude
/kənˈkluːd/

I will conclude that the artist has a unique style that speaks to everyone.
我的結論是，這位藝術家有一種能向每個人訴說的獨特風格。

decide
/dɪˈsaɪd/

I let my wife decide which piece of abstract art to hang in our living room.
我讓我的太太決定要把哪一件抽象藝術作品掛在我們的客廳。

evaluate
/ɪˈvæljueɪt/

It is difficult to grade and evaluate the children's paintings as most of them look like meaningless drips and splatters.
很難評分並評價這些孩子的畫作，因為大部分看起來像是無意義的滴墨與潑濺。

appraise
/əˈpreɪz/

In order to properly appraise the painting, the artist's signature had to be found.
為了正確評估這幅畫的價值，必須找出藝術家的簽名。

USEFUL EXPRESSIONS | 相關實用片語

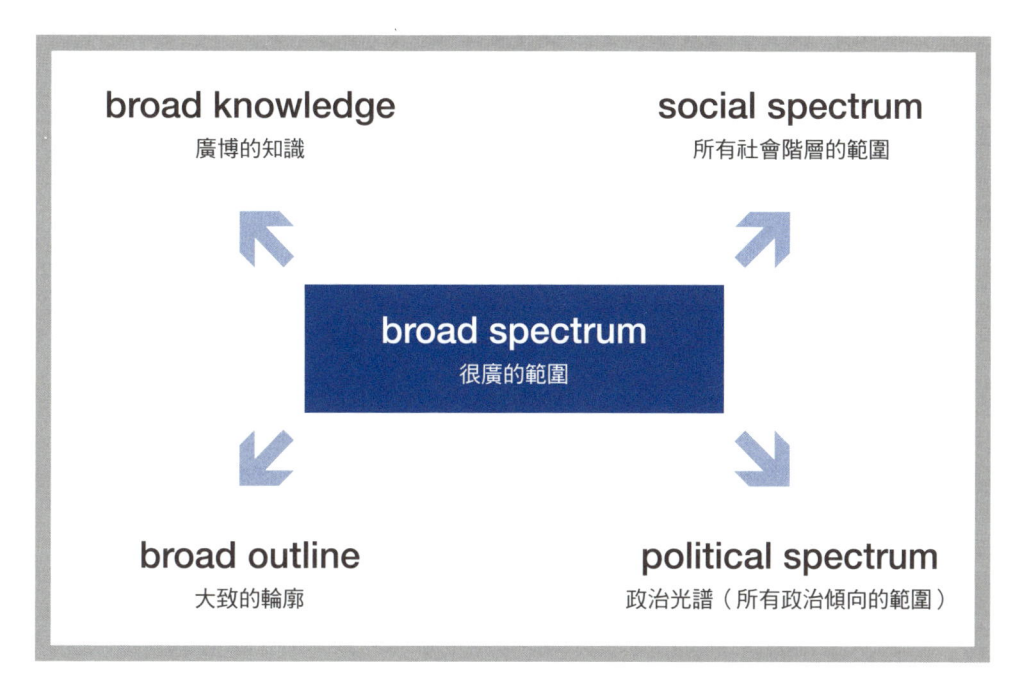

```
broad knowledge              social spectrum
廣博的知識                     所有社會階層的範圍

          ┌─────────────────────┐
          │   broad spectrum    │
          │     很廣的範圍       │
          └─────────────────────┘

broad outline                political spectrum
大致的輪廓                    政治光譜（所有政治傾向的範圍）
```

broad spectrum
/brɔːd ˈspɛktrəm/

There is a broad spectrum of people who use social media for different purposes.
為了各自不同的目的而使用社群媒體的人範圍很廣。

broad knowledge
/brɔːd ˈnɒlɪdʒ/

Having a broad knowledge of how agriculture affects the environment is beneficial for sustainability.
對農業如何影響環境具備廣博的知識，有益於永續發展。

broad outline
/brɔːd ˈaʊtlʌɪn/

Since President Clinton's endorsement, the broad outlines of the deal between Israel and Palestine had been apparent.
在柯林頓總統的背書之後，以色列與巴勒斯坦之間協議的大致輪廓就顯而易見了。

social spectrum
/ˈsəʊʃəl ˈspɛktrəm/

Our government should consider health across the social spectrum and encourage all citizens to lose weight.
我們的政府應該考慮各個社會階層的健康，並且鼓勵所有人民減重。

political spectrum
/pəˈlɪtɪkəl ˈspɛktrəm/

All people across the political spectrum are valued for their service to the community.
所有政治傾向的人都因為他們對社會的服務而受到重視。

SAT

IELTS BASIC WORDS

commute /kəˈmjuːt/ v. 通勤
ENG. travel regularly back and forth
SYS. journey, travel

> Some street artists **commute** to the same place to show their works.
> 有些街頭藝術家每天到同一個地方展示自己的作品。

同義語 例句 Street artists **trip** to crowded places to gather a bigger audience.
街頭藝術家旅行到人潮眾多的地方，聚集更多的觀眾。

同義語 例句 Street artists **travel between** big avenues and populated sidewalks to attract more viewers.
街頭藝人往返於大街及人潮密集的人行道，以吸引更多觀看的人。

反義語 例句 The artist who **stays put** in his small town remains unknown even among art enthusiasts.
停留在自己小鎮上的那位藝術家，仍然沒沒無聞，即使對於藝術熱愛者也是一樣。

income /ˈɪnkʌm/ n. 收入
ENG. the amount of money or its equivalent received during a period of time in exchange for labour or services
SYS. revenue, gains

> Great artists make substantial **income** selling their artwork in the market.
> 偉大的藝術家靠著在市場上銷售作品，獲得相當多的收入。

同義語 例句 Artists earn **financial gain** by auctioning their artworks to the public.
藝術家靠著向大眾拍賣作品賺取金錢收益。

同義語 例句 Artists expect a great **cash inflow** when their art style is popular and marketable.
藝術家期待當他們的藝術風格受歡迎而且銷路好時，會有大筆現金流入。

反義語 例句 The **money spent** on creating an artwork must not exceed its selling price.
花在創作藝術作品上的錢不可以超過它的售價。

226

advocate /ˈædvəkət/ v. 主張，擁護
ENG. speak, plead, or argue in favour of
SYS. support, recommend

> The authors **advocate** the policy of improving literacy in children.
> 那些作家擁護提升兒童讀寫能力的政策。

同義語例句 The authors **urge** people to seek education to improve their writing skills and literary awareness.
那些作家呼籲人們接受教育，以提升自身的寫作技巧與文學意識。

同義語例句 The authors **advise** people to learn about literature.
那些作家建議人們學習文學。

反義語例句 Some people **speak against** the freedom of expression in literature.
有些人抨擊文學中的表達自由。

valuable /ˈvæljʊbəl/ adj. 貴重的
ENG. having great material or monetary value for use or exchange; high in price or value
SYS. important, worthy

> These sculptures are very **valuable** because of the level of difficulty in creating them.
> 由於創作的難度，這些雕塑品非常有價值。

同義語例句 These sculptures are **of high importance** as they symbolise a past artistic era.
這些雕塑品很有重要性，因為它們象徵一個過去的藝術年代。

同義語例句 Preserving sculptures is **of great significance** because it is also a way of preserving history.
保存雕塑品具有相當大的重要性，因為它也是一種保存歷史的方式。

反義語例句 The effort of modernising the sculptures turned out to be **worthless**.
將那些雕塑品現代化的努力，結果證明是沒有價值的。

SAT

TOPIC: The commercial value of art
藝術的商業價值

The major **requirement** for collecting art is the desire for the object. One collector may be **seduced** by nineteenth-century landscape **etchings** while another finds **value** in late twentieth-century colour photography; the emotional connection felt creates personal values. Although personal values and preferences may vary greatly, the methods by which one **translates** an appreciation and passion for art into capital remain the same. A variety of factors must be considered in determining an artwork's **monetary** value, including condition, subject matter and rarity. That being said, the commercial value of art has always been and will always be **manipulated**. We see this when an expensive work is unquestionably **bestowed** aesthetic significance based on price alone. However, markets are as volatile as the **temperament** of the viewer, making the value of an artwork **perpetually** flexible.

TRANS

收集藝術的主要條件，是對於物品的欲望。一個收藏者可能深受十九世紀的風景蝕刻版畫吸引，而另一個人可能會在二十世紀晚期的彩色攝影裡發現價值；一個人感受到的情感連結，創造出個人的價值。雖然個人價值和偏好可能各有很大的不同，但將對藝術的欣賞與熱情轉換為資本的方法仍然是一樣的。在決定藝術品的金錢價值時，必須考量多種因素，包括作品的狀況、主題和稀有性。話雖如此，藝術的商業價值一直以來都受到操縱，往後也會一直這樣下去。我們可以在一件昂貴的作品只依據價格就被毫無疑問地賦予美學重要性時看出這種現象。不過，市場就像觀看者的情緒變化無常一樣波動不定，使得藝術作品的價值永遠都是有彈性的。

requirement
/rɪˈkwʌɪəmənt/

n. 必要條件

The university demands that some first-year courses be completed as a **requirement** for admission into the programme.
這間大學要求必須修畢某些一年級的課程，作為這個學程的參加條件。

seduce
/sɪˈdjuːs/

v. 引誘，誘惑

Try not to be **seduced** by dreams of being rich as you buy lottery tickets. 買樂透彩券時，試著不要被發財夢誘惑。

etching
/ˈɛtʃɪŋ/

n. 蝕刻，蝕刻版畫

The bronze sculpture found in the archaeological dig has strange **etchings** near its base.
在考古挖掘時發現的銅像，底座附近有奇怪的蝕刻。

value
/ˈvaljuː/

n. 價值

People put more **value** on material things rather than on things that really matter.
人們比較重視物質事物，而不是真正重要的事情。

translate
/transˈleɪt/

v. 轉換

Today's low inflation and steady growth in household income **translate** into more purchasing power.
現今的低通貨膨脹率與家庭收入穩定的成長，轉換成為更高的購買力。

monetary
/ˈmʌnɪtəri/

adj. 金錢的

He received gratitude but no **monetary** compensation for his services to the King.
對於他為國王所做的服務，他接受道謝，但沒有接受金錢報償。

manipulate
/məˈnɪpjʊleɪt/

v. 操縱

The salesman **manipulated** the elderly woman into buying a vacuum cleaner she didn't need.
銷售員巧妙地誘使老婦人買了她不需要的吸塵器。

bestow
/bɪˈstəʊ/

v. 授予，給予

They **bestowed** the diplomat with great respect as he entered the meeting room.
他們在外交官進入會議室時給予很大的尊重。

temperament
/ˈtɛmpərəmənt/

n. 性情，情緒變化無常

Bill has a happy **temperament** that immediately draws people to him.
Bill 具有開朗的性情，能馬上吸引別人接近他。

perpetually
/pəˈpɛtjʊəli/

adv. 永恆地，永久地

It rained **perpetually**, making me worried about the danger of flooding. 雨下個不停，讓我擔心洪水的危險性。

WORD TRAINING　｜　重點單字造句練習

evaluate
/ɪˈvæljʊeɪt/

v. 評價

In order to properly **evaluate** the commercial value of a painting, one must first establish provenance.
為了正確評價一幅畫的商業價值，必須先確定它的來歷。

The critic could not **evaluate** the artist's works fairly because she is his sister.
這位評論家無法公正地評價那位藝術家的作品，因為那是他的姐姐。

The commercial value of an artwork is the primary criterion most people will **evaluate** it, so a work may be deemed good simply because it is expensive.
一件藝術作品的商業價值，是大多數的人評價它的主要標準，所以一件作品可能只是因為很貴就被認為是好的。

The irrational exuberance of the contemporary art market is about the financial gain, not the fertility of art, and makes many people **evaluate** an artwork based on its commercial value.
當代藝術市場的非理性繁榮是為了獲得金錢，而不是為了讓藝術豐富，也使得很多人根據商業價值評價藝術作品。

content
/ˈkɒntɛnt/

n. 內容

The **content** of contemporary art reflects real-world issues.
當代藝術的內容反映真實世界的議題。

The **content** of an artwork determines its commercial value.
藝術作品的內容決定它的商業價值。

I believe that an artist's works should have substantial **content**, just like in literature and social sciences.
我認為藝術家的作品應該要有真實的內容，就像在文學和社會科學裡一樣。

The **content** and meaning of a particular artwork does not necessarily dictate its commercial value; the artist's fame does.
一件特定藝術品的內容和意義不必然決定其商業價值，藝術家的名氣才是決定的要素。

appraise
/əˈpreɪz/

v. 估價，評價

💬 All the artworks have been appraised by professionals before the auction.
在拍賣前，所有藝術品都經過專業人士估價。

The main criteria for appraising an artwork include condition, subject matter and rarity.
評估一件藝術作品價值的主要標準包括作品狀況、主題和稀有性。

📝 Collectors need to know how to appraise an artwork, especially when they purchase it as an investment rather than an ornament.
收藏家需要知道如何評估一件藝術作品的價值，尤其當他們是買來當成投資而不是當成裝飾的時候。

She did not purchase the unsold piece at the list price because its appraised value was lower.
她沒有按照定價買那幅沒賣出的作品，因為它的評估價值比定價低。

finesse
/fɪˈnɛs/

n. 精細的技巧，手腕

💬 The artwork's commercial value is astounding because the artist's finesse of touch is evident.
這件藝術作品的商業價值驚人，因為藝術家的精細筆觸顯而易見。

The finesse demonstrated by the artist in painting the water droplets increased the work's commercial value.
藝術家在畫那些水滴時展現的精細技巧，增加了作品的商業價值。

📝 Besides the artist's fame, meticulousness and finesse also add to the value of a painting.
除了藝術家的名氣以外，繪畫時的一絲不苟和精細的技巧也會增加一幅畫的價值。

The artist's finesse is evident in this painting, in which her fine touches, minute details and subtle atmosphere all come together.
這位藝術家的精細技巧可以在這幅畫裡看到，她精細的筆觸、細微的細節和微妙的氣氛都聚集在這幅畫裡了。

RELATED WORDS | 相關單字延伸

influence
v. 影響

mishandle
v. 不當地處理，不當地對待

manipulate
v. 操縱

control
v. 控制

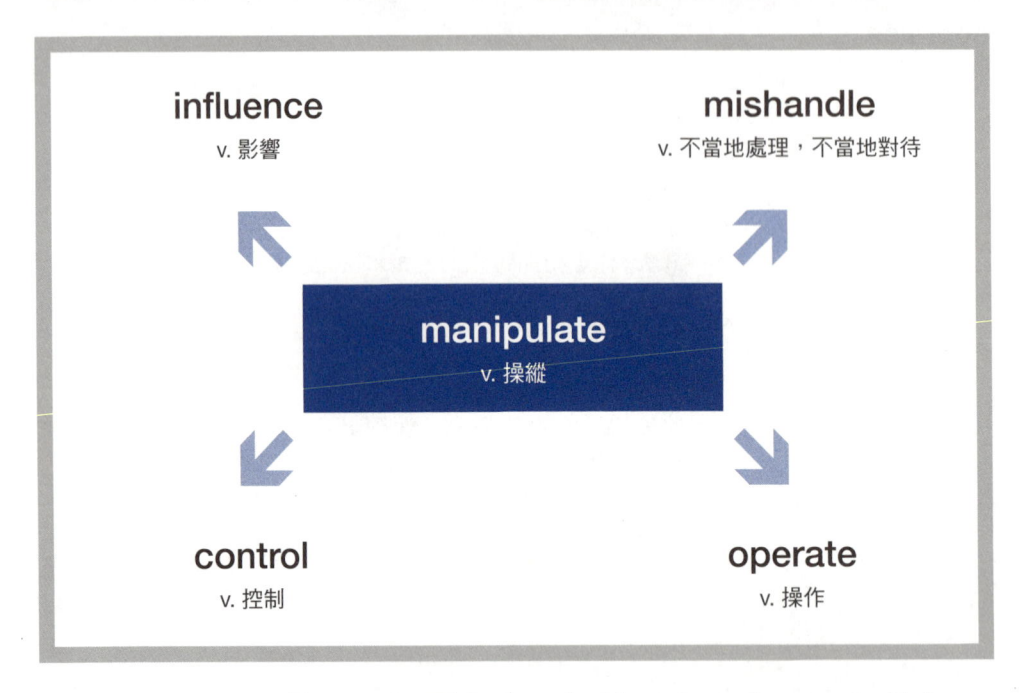

operate
v. 操作

manipulate
/məˈnɪpjʊleɪt/

The commercial value of art has always been and will always be manipulated.
藝術的商業價值一直以來都受到操縱，往後也會一直這樣下去。

influence
/ˈɪnfluəns/

Picasso greatly influenced 20th-century art, but he was not a commercial success at his time.
畢卡索對二十世紀的藝術影響很大，但他在自己的時代沒有獲得商業上的成功。

control
/kənˈtroʊl/

The commercial value of an artwork is controlled by global market trends, rather than the buyers themselves.
藝術品的價值受到全球市場趨勢控制，而不是買家自己。

mishandle
/mɪsˈhændəl/

The sculpture was damaged because of mishandling during transportation.
這件雕塑品因為運送過程中不當的搬運而受損了。

operate
/ˈɒpəreɪt/

The auction company is owned and operated by several artists who aim to improve every artist's financial situation.
這間拍賣公司由幾位藝術家擁有並經營，他們的目標是改善每個藝術家的經濟狀況。

USEFUL EXPRESSIONS | 相關實用片語

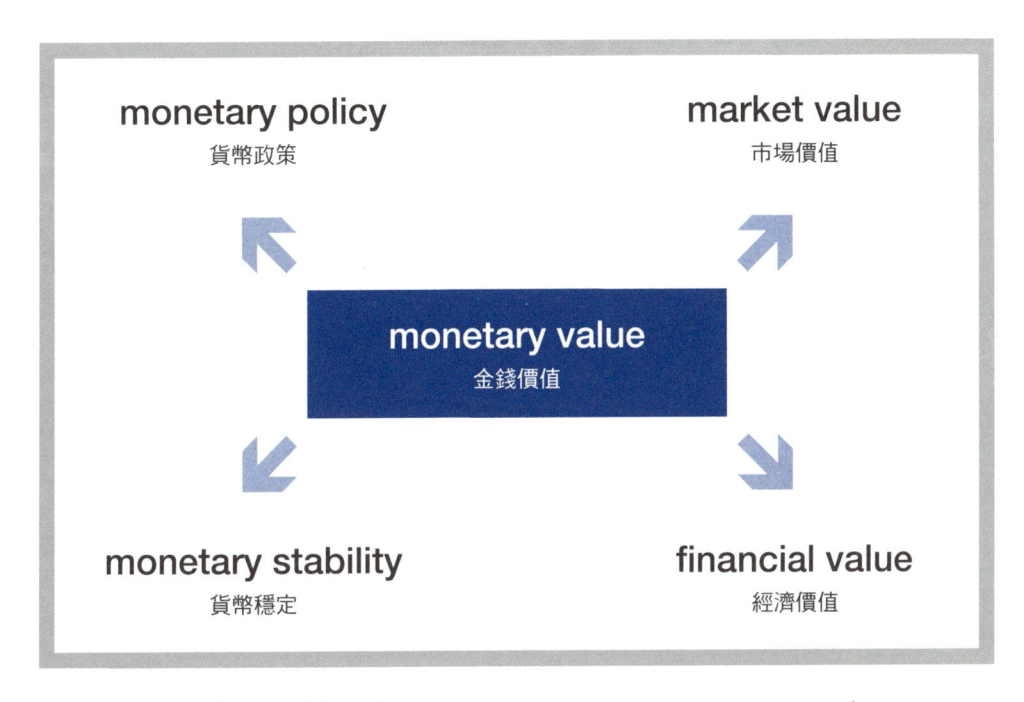

monetary policy
貨幣政策

market value
市場價值

monetary value
金錢價值

monetary stability
貨幣穩定

financial value
經濟價值

monetary value
/ˈmʌnɪtəri ˈvæljuː/

The gifts must represent a certain monetary value.
那些禮物必須呈現一定程度的金錢價值。

monetary policy
/ˈmʌnɪtəri ˈpɒlɪsi/

Third World countries execute their monetary policies very poorly, resulting in economic instability.
第三世界國家的貨幣政策執行得非常差，導致經濟不穩定。

monetary stability
/ˈmʌnɪtəri stəˈbɪlɪti/

Monetary stability must be achieved by developing the economy.
貨幣穩定必須藉由發展經濟達成。

market value
/ˈmɑːkɪt ˈvæljuː/

Samsung, Asia's largest electronics corporation by market value, has struck a sponsorship deal.
以市值來說是亞洲最大電子公司的三星，已經達成了一項贊助協議。

financial value
/fʌɪˈnænʃəl ˈvæljuː/

Some lifesaving treatments, including antibiotic medicine, have remarkable financial value.
一些救命的治療法，包括抗生藥劑，有顯著的經濟價值。

SUN

IELTS BASIC WORDS

examine /ɪgˈzamɪn/ v. 檢查，檢驗
ENG. to observe carefully or critically
SYS. study, analyse

> It is imperative to **examine** every wooden building to determine its historical value.
> 檢視每座木造建築以判定歷史價值是必要的。

同義語例句 Besides stability, an architect must also **check** a building's design and appearance.
除了穩定性以外，建築師也必須檢視一棟建築物的設計與外觀。

同義語例句 An architect must carefully **go over** the structure and appearance of a building before applying for a building permit.
在申請建築許可前，建築師必須仔細檢視一棟建築物的結構與外觀。

反義語例句 It is not enough to just **glance over** an architectural plan without considering the appearance.
只是稍微瀏覽一下建築計畫書而沒有考慮外觀是不夠的。

prefer /prɪˈfəː/ v. 偏好
ENG. to give priority or precedence
SYS. favour, select

> Some traditional architects **prefer** to consider a building's stability before designing its appearance.
> 有些傳統建築師偏好在設計外觀之前先考慮一棟建築物的穩定性。

同義語例句 Architects **like** it **better** if their buildings are sturdy during calamities rather than just looking pretty.
建築設計師比較喜歡他們的建築物在災難中很堅固，而不止是看起來漂亮。

同義語例句 The company **goes for** the traditional and sturdy building design, rather than the modern one.
這間公司選擇傳統而堅固的建築設計，而不是現代的設計。

反義語例句 He **likes** the modern design **the least** because it looks unstable.
他最不喜歡那個現代的設計，因為它看起來不穩定。

WEEK 4 TOPIC **ART**

▶基礎單字擴充

affect /əˈfɛkt/ v. 影響
ENG. to have an influence on or effect a change in
SYS. alter, influence

> The trends in visual arts **affect** the way modern architects design their buildings.
> 視覺藝術的趨勢影響現代建築師設計建築物的方式。

同義語例句 Will the physical appearance of a structure **bear upon** its stability in times of calamities?
結構的物理外觀在發生災難時是否會對穩定性產生影響?

同義語例句 Poor structural stability **impinges on** the safety of people in a building during an earthquake.
不佳的結構穩定度,在地震時會對建築物中人們的安全造成影響。

反義語例句 Physical appearance **has no impact** on the structural strength of a building.
物理外觀對建築物的結構強度沒有影響。

major /ˈmeɪdʒə/ adj. 主要的,重大的
ENG. greater than others in importance; great in scope or effect
SYS. great, significant

> Aesthetics is a **major** component in his architectural designs.
> 美學在他的建築設計中是主要的原素。

同義語例句 In fact, aesthetics **requires great attention** when designing a building.
事實上,在設計建築物的時候,美學需要受到很多的注意。

同義語例句 Aesthetics is **taken very seriously** when great architects design their buildings.
偉大的建築師設計建築物時,他們非常認真看待美學。

反義語例句 Aesthetics **falls secondary** to safety when it comes to architectural design.
在建築設計中,美學的優先度次於安全。

SUN

04-7A

TOPIC: Architecture as a form of artistic expression

將建築作為一種藝術表達的形式

Architecture can be said to be an **applied** art, and to some, it is the highest form of art. Truly **remarkable architecture** incorporates artistic elements. An architect, at his or her greatest, is a master artist whose tools are not chisels and brushes, but cranes, bulldozers, and scores of hands and minds. The greatest architectures that **chronicle** our history have sometimes even **outlasted** the civilisations that erected them and become **indispensable** to us. Before a building is recognised as a masterpiece, however, it is usually faced with rejection from the public. All too often, newly completed buildings are initially **reviled** for their **boldness**, and their **audacity** is not **cherished** until many generations later.

TRANS

建築可以說是一種應用藝術，而對於某些人而言，它是藝術的最高形式。真正非凡的建築會包含藝術的元素。建築師在表現得最好的時候，是一位藝術大師，他的工具不是鑿子和筆刷，而是起重機、推土機和許多人的手與腦。寫下我們歷史的偉大建築物，有時甚至存在得比建立它們的文明還要久，並且成為對我們而言不可或缺的東西。不過，在一棟建築物被認為是傑作之前，通常會面對大眾的抗拒。新落成的建築作品一開始常常因為它們的大膽而受到人們辱罵，而它們的大膽風格要到很多世代之後才會獲得珍惜。

applied /əˈplaɪd/
adj. 應用的
The government has supplied universities with funding in medicine, engineering and other **applied** disciplines.
政府已經提供大學在醫藥、工程與其他應用學科方面的資助。

remarkable /rɪˈmɑːkəbəl/
adj. 值得注意的，非凡的
It was truly **remarkable** that she lifted the man over her shoulder.
她把那個男人高舉過肩真是非常了不起。

architecture /ˈɑːkɪtɛktʃə/
n. 建築，建築物
The use of columns in the design of **architecture** is popular across many cultures.
圓柱在建築設計中的使用流行於許多文化。

chronicle /ˈkrɒnɪkəl/
n. 編年史，記述 v. 記述（歷史）
The movie **chronicles** the life of Queen Elizabeth.
這部電影記述伊莉莎白皇后的一生。

outlast /aʊtˈlɑːst/
v. 比…長久
The protester **outlasted** many people's initial predictions by not eating for an entire week.
抗議者一整個禮拜沒有進食，超過了許多人一開始的預測。

indispensable /ˌɪndɪˈspɛnsəbəl/
adj. 不可或缺的
Marc was an **indispensable** member of the police force, having been trained in conflict negotiation.
因為受過衝突談判的訓練，所以 Marc 是警方不可或缺的成員。

revile /rɪˈvaɪl/
v. 辱罵，謾罵
My neighbour's dog is the most **reviled** animal on the block due to his constant barking.
我鄰居的狗因為吠個不停，而成為街坊中最常被責罵的動物。

boldness /ˈbəʊldnəs/
n. 大膽，冒失
The host took no notice of the guest's **boldness** during dinner.
男主人沒有理會那位賓客在晚餐時的冒失行為。

cherish /ˈtʃɛrɪʃ/
v. 珍惜
She **cherishes** the photo album her late grandmother gave her.
她珍惜過世的奶奶給她的相簿。

audacity /ɔːˈdæsɪti/
n. 大膽，無畏
The skydiver showed great **audacity** as he jumped out of the plane.
那位高空跳傘者在他跳下飛機時展現出極大的膽識。

WORD TRAINING │ 重點單字造句練習

exposition
/ˌɛkspəˈzɪʃən/

n. 展覽會，博覽會

💬 Artists from across the state will participate in the exposition.
來自本州各地的藝術家會參加這場展覽。

The exposition features suppliers from around the world.
這場博覽會有來自全球各地的供應商。

✏️ Many architects went to the exposition to learn about how they can use the latest trends in their practice.
許多建築師參加那場博覽會，了解他們可以怎樣把最新趨勢運用在實務上。

The crystal tower in the centre of the venue represents the exposition's theme by incorporating Aztec motifs.
展場中央的水晶塔藉由採用阿茲提克的裝飾紋樣表現出博覽會的主題。

---

engraving
/ɪnˈgreɪvɪŋ/

n. 雕刻，雕版

💬 An English architectural illustrator founded the first studio for steel engraving in Germany.
一位英國的建築插畫家在德國創建立了第一家鋼鐵雕刻的工作室。

When an architect wants to impress the visitors of a building, he or she may add a detailed engraving to something.
當建築設計師想要讓拜訪建築物的人留下印象時，可能會為某個東西加上細膩的雕刻。

✏️ He is the author of various works on Ukrainian art, culture, architecture and traditional engraving and printing.
他是多種關於烏克蘭的藝術、文化、建築與傳統雕版印刷的著作的作者。

The entrance area features permanent engravings on a wide variety of materials, including stone, wood, glass, plastic, ceramics and metal.
入口區域有在多種材質上所做的永久雕刻，包括石材、木材、玻璃、塑膠、陶瓷和金屬。

ingenuity
/ˌɪndʒɪˈnjuːɪti/

n. 聰明才智，獨創性

💬 You can see the architectural ingenuity in these remarkable residential dwellings.
你可以在這些出色的住宅中看到建築的巧思。

I like to see how old buildings are restored with ingenuity and artistry.
我喜歡看老舊建築如何以創造力與藝術性獲得修復。

✍ The series of museums and libraries built over the past decade are now commonly described as the pride of the city because of the artistic ingenuity involved.
過去十年建設的一系列博物館和圖書館，因為其中的藝術巧思，現在被廣泛形容成是城市的驕傲。

Architectural ingenuity is greatly valued in this developing country because the government aims to create a modern image with spectacular buildings.
建築巧思在這個開發中國家很受重視，因為政府的目標是用壯觀的建築物創造現代的形象。

decoration
/ˌdɛkəˈreɪʃən/

n. 裝飾

💬 This feat of architecture is acclaimed as being splendid and complex, especially in decoration.
這項建築的壯舉被稱讚為既燦爛又複雜，尤其是在裝飾方面。

Well-placed stone decorations can add artistic value to a structure.
位置恰當的石頭裝飾可以為結構增添藝術價值。

✍ Baroque architecture features complex shapes and elaborate decoration on both the exterior and the interior.
巴洛克建築以建築物外部和內部的複雜形狀和精細裝飾為特色。

Islamic architecture is unique in its use of geometrical shapes such as polygons, stars and overlapping circles in its decorations.
伊斯蘭建築的獨特之處在於使用多邊形、星形和重疊的圓圈之類的幾何形狀作為裝飾。

RELATED WORDS | 相關單字延伸

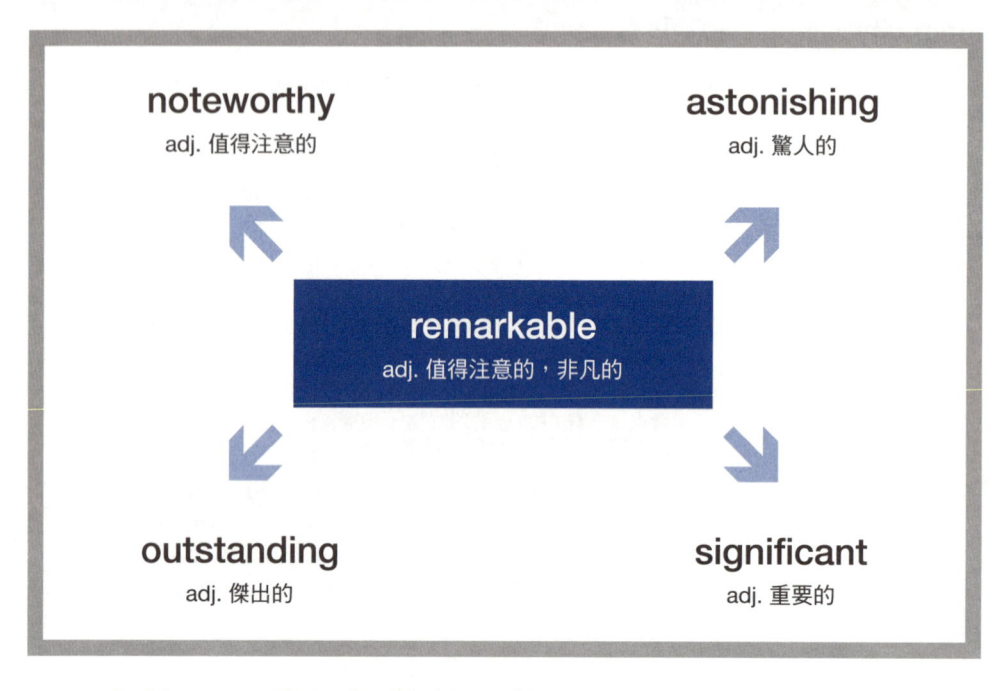

noteworthy
adj. 值得注意的

astonishing
adj. 驚人的

remarkable
adj. 值得注意的，非凡的

outstanding
adj. 傑出的

significant
adj. 重要的

remarkable
/rɪˈmɑːkəbəl/
Truly remarkable architecture incorporates artistic elements.
真正非凡的建築會包含藝術的元素。

noteworthy
/ˈnəʊtwɜːði/
The most noteworthy architecture of our time includes the Eiffel Tower and the Chrysler Building.
在我們的時代最值得注意的建築，包含艾菲爾鐵塔和克萊斯勒大廈。

outstanding
/aʊtˈstandɪŋ/
The architect is truly an artist because she is outstanding in creating original forms.
那位建築設計師確實是個藝術家，因為她創造出獨創外型的能力很傑出。

astonishing
/əˈstɒnɪʃɪŋ/
When I first saw the astonishing columns at the Roman Pantheon, I wondered how many people it takes to build such a spectacular building.
當我第一次看到羅馬神殿令人驚訝的圓柱時，我好奇需要多少人來建造這樣壯觀的建築。

significant
/sɪɡˈnɪfɪkənt/
Taj Mahal and Casa Mila are among the most significant architectures in the world because of their unique forms.
泰姬瑪哈陵和米拉之家因為獨特的外型而置身全世界最重要建築之列。

USEFUL EXPRESSIONS | 相關實用片語

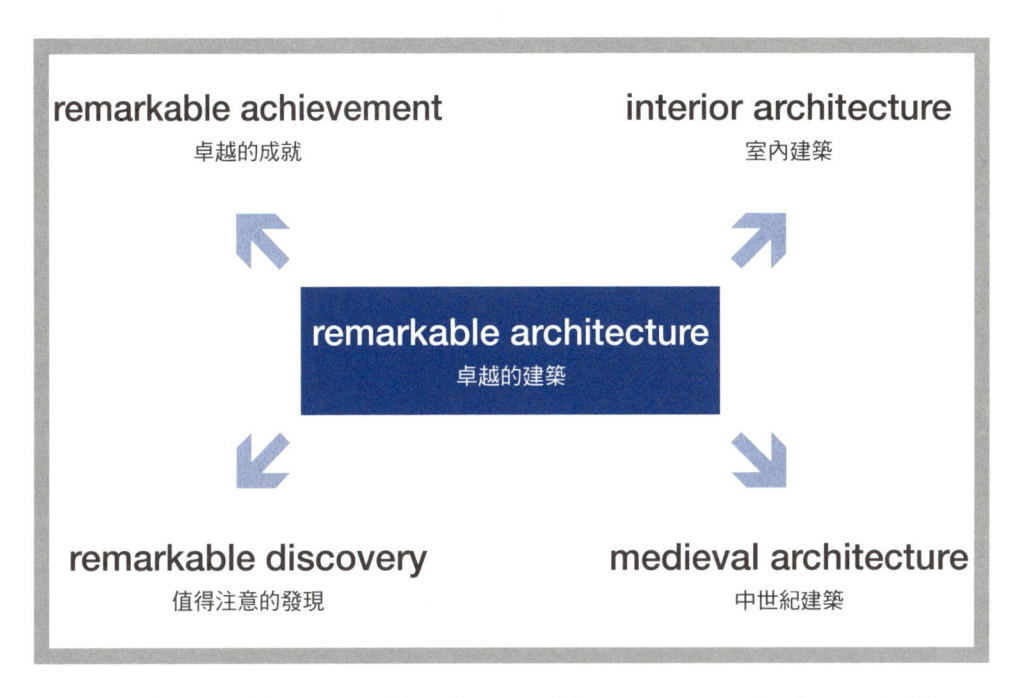

```
remarkable achievement          interior architecture
卓越的成就                        室內建築

            ↖        ↗
           remarkable architecture
                卓越的建築
            ↙        ↘

remarkable discovery            medieval architecture
值得注意的發現                     中世紀建築
```

remarkable architecture
/rɪˈmɑːkəbəl ˈɑːkɪtɛktʃə/
Egypt's pyramids are an example of remarkable architecture of the ancient times.
埃及金字塔是古代卓越建築的一個例子。

remarkable achievement
/rɪˈmɑːkəbəl əˈtʃiːvmənt/
Winning a swimming competition overseas is a remarkable achievement for the country.
在海外贏得游泳競賽，對國家而言是卓越的成就。

remarkable discovery
/rɪˈmɑːkəbəl dɪˈskʌvəri/
The most remarkable discovery that astronauts documented was the large cirrus clouds that formed on Mars.
太空人所記錄最驚人的發現是在火星上形成的巨大卷雲。

interior architecture
/ɪnˈtɪərɪə ˈɑːkɪtɛktʃə/
The Presbyterian Church has an interior architecture that reflects the older ways of decorating the pulpit.
這間長老教會教堂的室內建築，反映裝飾講道壇的舊式手法。

medieval architecture
/ˌmɛdɪˈiːvəl ˈɑːkɪtɛktʃə/
The most popular form of architecture in Medieval Europe is called medieval architecture.
中世紀歐洲最受歡迎的建築形式被稱為中世紀建築。

WEEK 5
TECHNOLOGY

科技對社會的影響

科技對音樂產業的影響

現代科學與舊科學

複製技術的未來

工作中電腦的使用

網路銀行業務

電子設備中的有毒物質

MON

IELTS **BASIC WORDS**

rate /reɪt/   n. 速度，比率
ENG. a magnitude or frequency relative to a time unit; measure of a part with respect to a whole; speed of progress or change
SYS. pace, speed

> With new inventions coming at an increasing rate, we can expect the next wave of technological revolution to come very soon.
> 隨著新發明出現的速度越來越快，我們可以預期下一波技術革命會很快到來。

同義語例句　Technology has sped the society's progress at a fairly fast pace.
科技以相當快的步調加速了社會的進步。

同義語例句　The proportion of people using high-technology devices is rather high in this country.
在這個國家裡，使用高科技設備的人的比率相當高。

反義語例句　The overall speed of technological growth is not as fast as desired.
科技成長的整體速度不如希望的那麼快速。

appear /əˈpɪə/   v. 出現，似乎
ENG. give a certain impression; come into sight or view
SYS. seem, look

> Technology appears as a helping hand to today's society.
> 科技以今日社會的幫手角色出現。

同義語例句　People today seem to be working less because of technology's assistance.
今日的人們似乎因為科技的協助而工作得比較少了。

同義語例句　As it turns out, we cannot live comfortably without the constant availability of technology.
從結果來看，沒有持續可得的科技，我們就無法過舒適的生活。

反義語例句　The fact that remains hidden is that we can live even without modern technology.
一直被隱藏的真相是，我們即使沒有現代科技也能生存。

WEEK 5 TOPIC **TECHNOLOGY**

▶基礎單字擴充

link /lɪŋk/ n. 連結，關聯
ENG. means of connection; something that joins or connects
SYS. relationship, tie

> There is a strong **link** between advanced technology and progressive society.
> 先進的科技與進步的社會之間有很強的關聯。

同義語例句 The **correlation** between technology and progress in society is very strong.
科技與社會進步之間的相關性很強。

同義語例句 Advanced technology is a major **connecting factor** in determining the society's progress.
先進的科技是一個決定社會進步的主要連結因素。

反義語例句 Technology seems to be an **irrelevant factor** for the country's economic growth last year.
科技對於這個國家去年的經濟成長似乎是不相關的因素。

pressure /ˈprɛʃə/ n. 壓力
ENG. force applied; a force that compels
SYS. difficulty, power

> Technology releases people from the **pressure** of performing laborious work.
> 科技將人們從進行費力工作的壓力中解放。

同義語例句 The expectation of achieving more is the **compelling force** that pushes people to innovate.
希望達成更多事情的期望，是促使人們創新的強制力量。

同義語例句 The responsibility of meeting deadlines is a **powerful force** pushing people to work longer.
趕上截止期限的責任，是促使人們工作得更久的強大力量。

反義語例句 The **absence of stress** at work may decrease the need for technology to accomplish tasks.
工作少了壓力，可能會減少用科技完成工作的需要。

245

MON

TOPIC: The effect of technology on society
科技對社會的影響

Technology allows us to share our life experiences with people around the globe **instantaneously**. We can choose to write our thoughts on Twitter, detail everything in a blog or combine the two. Information technology expands our **horizons**, but it also starts **interfering** with our lives. Some people, especially the **elite**, are prone to **exploit** technology to **insulate** themselves physically and mentally from their fellows. The **tendency** to refuse to engage with individual people and instead **objectify** them as if they were numbers on a computer screen generated by cold, impersonal **calculating logic** is concerning. Locked in an escapist world of digital culture, our society is growing dangerously close to denying our essential connection to others and to the natural world.

TRANS

科技讓我們能即時與全世界的人分享我們的生活經驗。我們可以選擇在推特寫下我們的想法、在部落格詳細描述一切，或者結合這兩者。資訊科技拓展我們的視野，但它也開始干擾我們的生活。有些人，尤其是菁英份子，容易利用科技將自己與同伴在身體上、精神上隔離開來。拒絕和個別的人交往，而將他們物化成像是電腦上冰冷、非人的運算邏輯所產生的數字的傾向，是令人擔憂的。鎖在數位文化逃避現實的世界，我們的社會正危險地接近拒絕與他人和自然世界間必要連結的地步。

instantaneously
/ˌɪnstənˈteɪnɪəsli/

adv. 瞬間地，即時地

My fingers were burned **instantaneously** when I tried to unscrew the hot light bulb.
當我試著要轉開燒燙的燈泡時，我的手指瞬間被燙傷了。

horizon
/həˈrʌɪzən/

n. 範圍，眼界，視野

My mom told me not to be afraid to broaden my **horizons** after high school.
媽媽告訴我，在高中畢業以後不要害怕去拓展自己的視野。

interfere
/ɪntəˈfɪə/

v. 干擾，干涉

The approaching storm was **interfering** with the radio transmission signal.
接近中的暴風雨干擾了廣播的傳送訊號。

elite
/eɪˈliːt/

n. 菁英

Mr. James was among the **elites** selected to sit at the head table. James 先生是被挑選出來坐在主桌的菁英之一。

exploit
/ɪkˈsplɔɪt/

v. 剝削，濫用，利用

The explorers **exploited** the indigenous population.
探險者剝削了原住民。

insulate
/ˈɪnsjʊleɪt/

v. 隔離

Using an ice box is a perfect way to **insulate** the beer from the sun's heat.
使用保冷箱是為啤酒隔絕太陽熱度的完美方法。

tendency
/ˈtɛndənsi/

n. 傾向

When I am nervous, I have a **tendency** to chew on my fingernails.
當我緊張的時候，我有咬指甲的傾向。

objectify
/ɒbˈdʒɛktɪfʌɪ/

v. 物化

I was offended by his comments which seemed to **objectify** all women as possessions.
我被他似乎將所有女人物化成財物的意見冒犯了。

calculating
/ˈkalkjʊleɪtɪŋ/

adj. 計算的，有算計的

The hypnotist had a **calculating** look on his face as he watched the crowd.
催眠師看著群眾時，臉上掛著算計的表情。

logic
/ˈlɒdʒɪk/

n. 邏輯

My dad said there's no **logic** in spending money on things you don't need.
我爸爸說把錢花在不需要的東西上是沒有邏輯（沒有道理）的。

WORD TRAINING | 重點單字造句練習

advancement
/ədˈvɑːnsmənt/

n. 進步，發展

💬 With the recent advancement in technology, you can now easily video-chat with anyone with a smartphone.
隨著最近科技的進步，你現在可以很容易地用智慧型手機和任何人進行視訊聊天。

Like most technological advancements, smartphones are evolving and becoming more and more powerful.
就像大部分的科技進步一樣，智慧型手機正在演進中，而且變得越來越強大。

✏️ Prior to the technological advancement of the Internet, news had to travel at a painstakingly slow speed by stagecoach and railway.
在網路的科技發展之前，新聞必須以費力的速度在驛馬車和鐵路上行進傳送。

An area of life that has experienced drastic technological advancement on a global scale is public transportation.
在全球規模經歷了極大技術進步的生活領域之一是大眾運輸。

replace
/rɪˈpleɪs/

v. 取代

💬 It is still impossible to replace all animal tests with non-animal alternatives.
目前還是不可能用非動物的方式取代所有動物實驗。

The traditional light bulbs have been replaced with energy-efficient LED lights.
那些傳統燈泡已經被換成能源效率高的 LED 燈了。

✏️ Thanks to modern technology, we can replace paper with electronic files and save forests from being chopped down.
多虧有現代科技，我們可以把紙換成電子檔案，並且保護森林免於砍伐。

Just like how traditional oil lamps have been replaced with electric lights, more and more people give up pens and papers in favour of computers when they "write" an article.
就像傳統油燈被電燈取代一樣，越來越多人在「寫」文章的時候放棄紙筆而改用電腦。

sedentary lifestyle
/ˈsɛdəntəri ˈlaɪfstaɪl/

n. 久坐的生活型態

💬 One contributor to the high rates of childhood obesity is the prevalence of technology that promotes sedentary lifestyles.
導致兒童肥胖率高的一個原因，是促成久坐生活型態的科技普及。

A sedentary lifestyle is not the sole reason that children suffer from obesity.
長時間久坐的生活型態，不是兒童有肥胖問題的唯一理由。

✍ Many recent studies on childhood obesity indicate that technology contributes to a sedentary lifestyle and weight gain in children.
最近許多關於兒童肥胖的研究指出，科技造成久坐的生活型態，以及兒童的體重增加。

My sister leads a sedentary lifestyle full of computer games, and now she has lower back pain for sitting too long.
我妹妹過著充滿電腦遊戲的久坐生活，結果她現在因為坐太久而有腰痛。

over-reliance
/ˌoʊvərɪˈlaɪəns/

n. 過度依賴

💬 Though many of us would hate to admit it, our over-reliance on technology has become somewhat pathetic.
雖然我們很多人不想承認，但我們對科技的過度依賴已經變得有點可悲。

Over-reliance on technology could negatively affect our capacity of independent thinking.
對於科技的過度依賴，可能會對我們獨立思考的能力造成負面影響。

✍ We are embracing technology and developing an over-reliance on it without fully understanding the long-term effect of this decision.
我們正在擁抱科技，並且發展出對科技的過度依賴，而沒有完全了解這個決定的長期影響。

During power outages, most people could not perform their usual daily tasks at work or at home because of their over-reliance on electrical appliances and equipment.
在停電的時候，大部分人不能進行平常在職場和在家裡的工作，因為他們對電器用品和設備過度依賴。

RELATED WORDS | 相關單字延伸

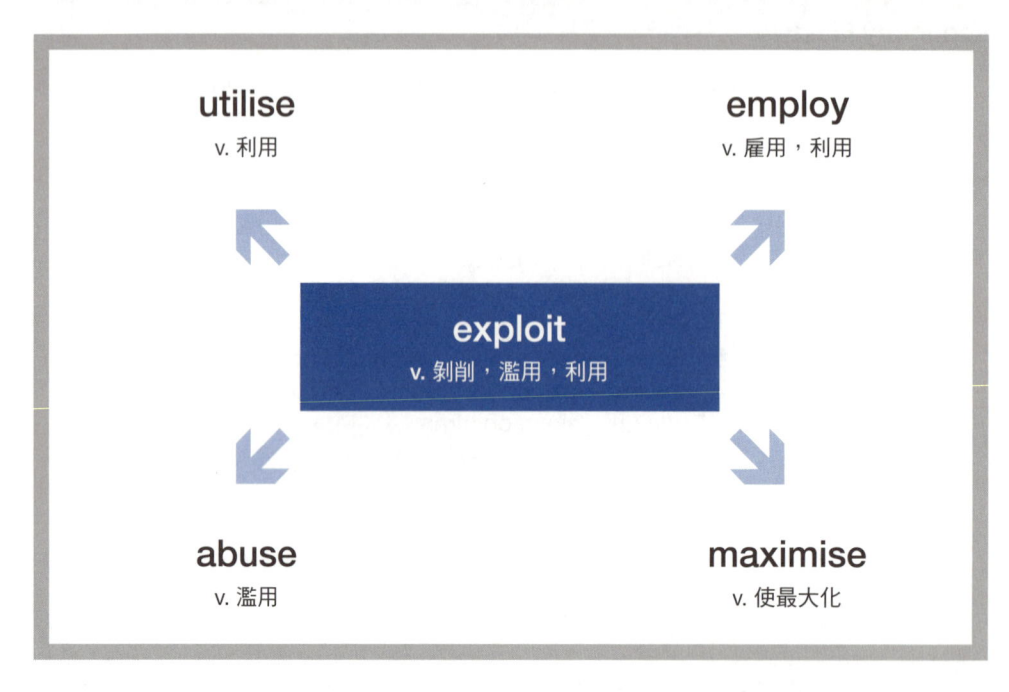

utilise
v. 利用

employ
v. 雇用，利用

exploit
v. 剝削，濫用，利用

abuse
v. 濫用

maximise
v. 使最大化

exploit
/ɪkˈsplɔɪt/

Some people are prone to exploit technology to insulate themselves physically and mentally from their fellows.
有些人容易利用科技將自己與同伴在身體上、精神上隔離開來。

utilise
/ˈjuːtɪlʌɪz/

It would be great if the rich would utilise their wealth to aid those in need.
如果有錢人用他們的財富來幫助有需要的人就太好了。

abuse
/əˈbjuːz/

I often see students abusing the computers at school, using them to play games rather than to do research.
我經常看到學生濫用學校的電腦，拿來玩遊戲而不是做研究。

employ
/ɪmˈplɔɪ/

We can facilitate our daily life by employing modern technology.
我們可以運用現代科技，讓我們每天的生活更容易。

maximise
/ˈmaksɪmʌɪz/

In order to maximise the benefits of using technology at work, all the employees must be properly trained.
為了將工作中使用科技的效益最大化，所有員工都必須經過適當訓練。

USEFUL EXPRESSIONS | 相關實用片語

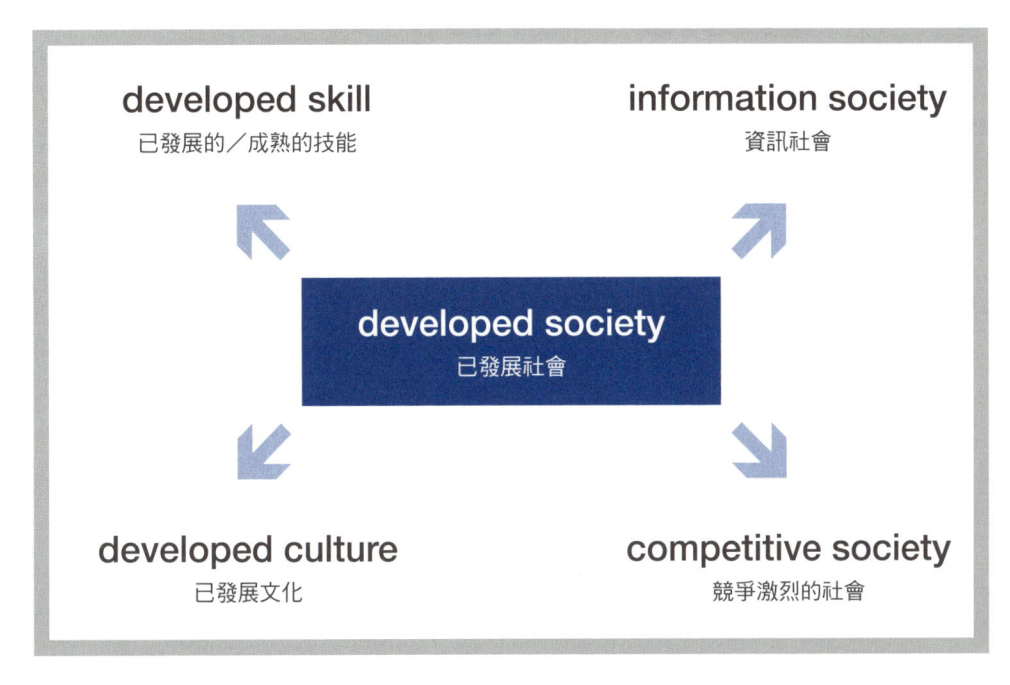

```
developed skill              information society
已發展的／成熟的技能              資訊社會
              ↖         ↗
              developed society
                 已發展社會
              ↙         ↘
developed culture            competitive society
已發展文化                     競爭激烈的社會
```

developed society
/dɪˈvɛləpt səˈsʌɪɪti/
Young people living in developed societies have a specific subculture which is unique to that age group.
生活在已發展社會的年輕人，有自己年齡層獨有的特定次文化。

developed skill
/dɪˈvɛləpt skɪl/
Many university graduates are required to have developed skills in word processing to gain employment.
許多大學畢業生必須有文書方面的成熟技能以獲得雇用。

developed culture
/dɪˈvɛləpt ˈkʌltʃə/
The developed culture and civilisation seen in the West shows the evolution of social consciousness.
西方社會可見的已發展文化與文明，展現出社會意識的演進。

information society
/ɪnfəˈmeɪʃən səˈsʌɪɪti/
Perhaps the most exciting part of living in an information society is the instantaneous availability of news.
或許生活在資訊社會最令人感到興奮的部分是新聞的立即可得性。

competitive society
/kəmˈpɛtɪtɪv səˈsʌɪɪti/
To gain success in the competitive society today, one must take many chances at work.
為了在當今競爭激烈的社會獲得成功，一個人必須在工作上冒許多險。

TUE

IELTS BASIC WORDS

expect /ɪkˈspɛkt/ v. 期待
ENG. to look forward to the probable occurrence or appearance of
SYS. ween, anticipate

> We can **expect** further development in technology as the processing speed of computers keeps improving.
> 隨著電腦的運算速度持續進步，我們可以預期科技會有進一步的發展。

同義語 例句　We **look forward to** even more technological advancements in various industries.
我們期待多種產業中更進一步的技術發展。

同義語 例句　We **rely on** technological advancements to bring economic growth.
我們依賴技術發展帶來經濟成長。

反義語 例句　We **are certain that** technological stagnation will not occur in the foreseeable future.
我們確信科技的停滯在可預見的未來不會發生。

daily /ˈdeɪli/ adj. 每天的 adv. 每天
ENG. occurring every day
SYS. regular, everyday

> In every industry, technology is needed **daily**.
> 在每個產業，科技都是每日必需的。

同義語 例句　All industries utilise technology **day after day**.
所有產業都是日復一日地利用科技。

同義語 例句　Technology is at work in every industry **without missing a day**.
每個產業都沒有一天不會用到科技。

反義語 例句　**Infrequent** use of technology will lead to lack of advancement in an industry.
不常使用科技，將導致產業缺乏進步。

WEEK 5 TOPIC **TECHNOLOGY**

▶ 基礎單字擴充

isolate /ˈaɪsəleɪt/ v. 使孤立，隔離
ENG. place or set apart from others
SYS. detach, exclude

> We cannot **isolate** technology from the overall success of today's industry.
> 我們不能將科技摒除於今日工業的整體成功之外。

同義語例句 It is impossible to **separate** technology from modern industry.
將科技和現代工業分開是不可能的。

同義語例句 If we **cut off** technology from the industry, industrial development will come to a halt.
如果我們把科技從工業中去除，工業發展就會停止。

反義語例句 Talent **joined together with** hard work is the formula for success.
天分和努力結合，是成功的公式。

additional /əˈdɪʃənəl/ adj. 額外的
ENG. further or supplementary
SYS. extra, more

> Technology is an **additional** element to assure an industry's success.
> 科技是保證產業成功的一個額外元素。

同義語例句 Besides workers' perseverance, a **further** factor leading to an industry's success is the utilisation of technology.
除了工作者的堅持不懈以外，讓產業成功更進一步的因素是對科技的利用。

同義語例句 **Not only** technology **but also** hard work and perseverance help an industry succeed.
除了科技以外，努力與堅持不懈也會幫助一個產業成功。

反義語例句 The company's success would be **limited** if it were not for the workers' perseverance.
要是沒有員工的堅持不懈，這間公司的成功就會很有限。

TOPIC: The impact of technology on the music industry

科技對音樂產業的影響

It is **obvious** that technology has changed our world **extraordinarily**. When it comes to the use of technology in the music industry, what was **inconceivable** a decade ago is now considered commonplace and a part of everyday life. For example, since its **launch**, iTunes music store has sold hundreds of millions of songs. The success of iTunes, however, isn't **lucrative** for record companies. Due to **piracy** and the growth of digital downloads, sales for physical CDs are declining rapidly. As physical CDs fade out, online music has become the new centre of attention. Artists have good reasons to pre-release or **exclusively** release their music on iTunes, as its tremendous growth has left music retailers **lagging** behind. Artists now make money from downloads on iTunes and through **royalties** from YouTube and radio stations playing their music. The change of business model shows how modern technology has **revolutionised** the music industry.

TRANS

很明顯，科技大大地改變了我們的世界。至於科技在音樂產業中的使用，在十年以前無法想像的，現在已經被認為司空見慣，而且是日常生活中的一部分。例如，自從 iTunes 音樂商店開始營業以後，它已經賣出數億首歌曲。然而，iTunes 的成功對於唱片公司而言卻無利可圖。由於盜版以及數位下載的成長，實體 CD 的銷售正迅速下跌。隨著實體 CD 淡出，網路音樂成為了新的注目焦點。藝人們有很好的理由在 iTunes 提前發行或獨家發行音樂，因為它極大的成長使音樂零售業者遠遠落後。藝人們現在靠著 iTunes 的下載，以及播放他們音樂的 YouTube 和廣播電台的權利金賺錢。商業模式的改變顯示現代科技如何為音樂產業帶來了變革。

obvious
/ˈɒbvɪəs/

adj. 明顯的
It is **obvious** that the children see the clown as a great entertainer.
顯然那些孩子把那個小丑當成很棒的表演者。

extraordinarily
/ɪkˈstrɔːdɪnɪrɪli/

adv. 非常，格外地
It will be an **extraordinarily** painful surgery to have.
這會是一個非常痛的手術。

inconceivable
/ˌɪnkənˈsiːvəbəl/

adj. 不能想像的
This kind of attitude toward religion would have been **inconceivable** a few years ago.
在幾年前，這種對於宗教的態度是無法想像的。

launch
/lɔːntʃ/

v. n. （船）使下水，發起，上市，發行
As I was about to **launch** my boat into the ocean, the trailer broke.
當我正準備要讓船進入海中的時候，拖船車壞了。

lucrative
/ˈluːkrətɪv/

adj. 賺錢的，有利可圖的
The investor thought that investing in the liquor company would be quite **lucrative**.
這個投資者認為投資這家酒品公司會很賺錢。

piracy
/ˈpʌɪrəsi/

n. 剽竊，盜版行為
Those caught downloading movies they didn't pay for will be charged with **piracy**.
被逮到沒有花錢購買而是下載電影的人，會被指控侵害版權。

exclusively
/ɪkˈskluːsɪvli/

adv. 獨佔地，排外地
The party is **exclusively** for those who are invited.
這場派對只限受邀者參加。

lag
/laɡ/

v. 落後
The fat dog was **lagging** behind the other dogs during the walk.
散步時，那條肥胖的狗落後在其他狗之後。

royalty
/ˈrɔɪəlti/

n. 版稅，權利金，礦區使用費
The gas company had to pay the landowners **royalties** before they drilled.
這家天然氣公司必須在開鑿之前付礦區使用費給地主。

revolutionise
/ˌrɛvəˈluːʃənʌɪz/

v. 使發生革命性的改變
The internet has **revolutionised** the way we communicate with one another.
網際網路徹底改變了我們彼此溝通的方式。

WORD TRAINING | 重點單字造句練習

reliability
/rɪˌlaɪəˈbɪlɪti/

n. 可靠性，可信度

When buying a new computer, reliability of the brand is a key point to consider.
買新電腦的時候，品牌的可靠性是要考慮的重點。

The latest consumer guide on car reliability helped me choose my new car.
關於汽車可靠性的最新消費者指南，幫助我選擇了我的新車。

A senior member of the technical staff warns that we should not release the new model before it has been thoroughly tested for its reliability.
一位資深的技術人員提醒，我們不應該在徹底測試可靠性之前發行新的機種。

We are an international company devoted to simplifying production process and improving product reliability for our clients.
我們是一家專注於為客戶簡化生產過程並改善產品可靠性的國際公司。

apparatus
/ˌæpəˈreɪtəs/

n. （一系列的）器材，設備，裝置

Advances in technology, methodology, apparatus and auxiliary equipment have facilitated chemical experiments.
技術、方法、器材和輔助設備的進步，使得化學實驗變得簡單。

A new portable, multi-purpose set of barbecue apparatus has been developed utilising state-of-the-art technology.
運用最先進技術，一款新的攜帶型、多功能烤肉用具組合被開發出來了。

While designing an experiment, the research team should decide what kind of apparatus is suitable for the purpose of research.
在設計實驗的時候，研究團隊應該決定什麼樣的裝置對於研究的目的是適合的。

Medical innovations can help prolong many lives, and some of the new methods work with existing medical apparatus.
醫療的創新可以幫助延長許多人的生命，而且有些新的方法可以用在現有的醫療設備上。

口說範例　寫作範例

invent
/ɪnˈvɛnt/

v. 發明

He tries to understand why and how people invent new technologies.
他試圖了解人們為什麼發明新的科技，又是怎麼發明的。

People invent new technologies to make their life easier.
人們發明新科技讓生活輕鬆一點。

I want to invent some new software to improve the information exchange between general staff and the management.
我想要開發新的軟體來改善一般員工和經營團隊之間的資訊交流。

Modern nations pour huge resources into education and scientific research, which form the bedrock of innovation and encourage people to invent new technologies.
現代國家投注龐大的資源到教育和科學研究方面，它們形成創新的基礎，並且鼓勵人們發明新科技。

commercialisation
/kəməːʃəlʌɪˈzeɪʃən/

n. 商業化，商品化

This forum is for professionals to discuss issues on technology commercialisation.
這個論壇是讓專業人士討論關於科技商業化的議題。

The developers need to understand the value of commercialisation strategies, both locally and globally.
開發者需要了解商業化策略在當地和在全球的價值。

Having done the necessary research and development, we are now ready to move forward and aim at the commercialisation of our new invention.
做了必要的研究和開發之後，我們現在準備好往前一步，以商業化我們的新發明為目標。

The commercialisation of computer technology will lead to the abandonment of certain ideals set in the developing stage.
電腦科技的商業化會導致開發階段設定的某些理想被捨棄。

RELATED WORDS | 相關單字延伸

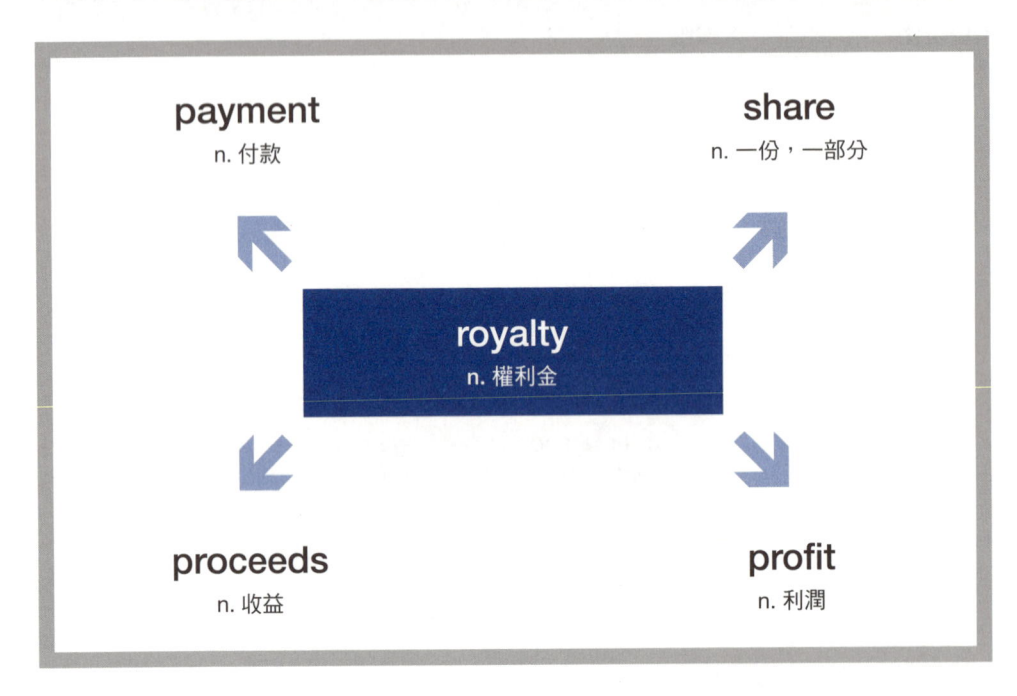

payment
n. 付款

share
n. 一份，一部分

royalty
n. 權利金

proceeds
n. 收益

profit
n. 利潤

royalty
/ˈrɔɪəlti/
Artists now make money from downloads on iTunes and through **royalties** from YouTube and radio stations playing their music.
藝人們現在靠著 iTunes 的下載，以及播放他們音樂的 YouTube 和廣播電台的權利金賺錢。

payment
/ˈpeɪmənt/
The musician receives monthly **payments** from radio stations after his single was released.
自從他的單曲發行之後，這位音樂人收到每個月來自廣播電台的付款。

proceeds
/ˈprəʊsiːdz/
Partial **proceeds** from every iTunes purchase this month will go toward the relief effort in Thailand.
這個月每筆 iTunes 購買的部分收益，將會用於泰國的救濟工作。

share
/ʃɛː/
Rather than spending his **share** of income frivolously, the drummer donated half to a struggling local radio station.
那位鼓手並沒有把他分到的收入隨便花掉，而是捐了一半給一家艱困的地方電台。

profit
/ˈprɒfɪt/
The band spends part of its **profits** on the efforts to fight illegal downloading.
這個樂團將部分獲利投入打擊非法下載的工作。

USEFUL EXPRESSIONS | 相關實用片語

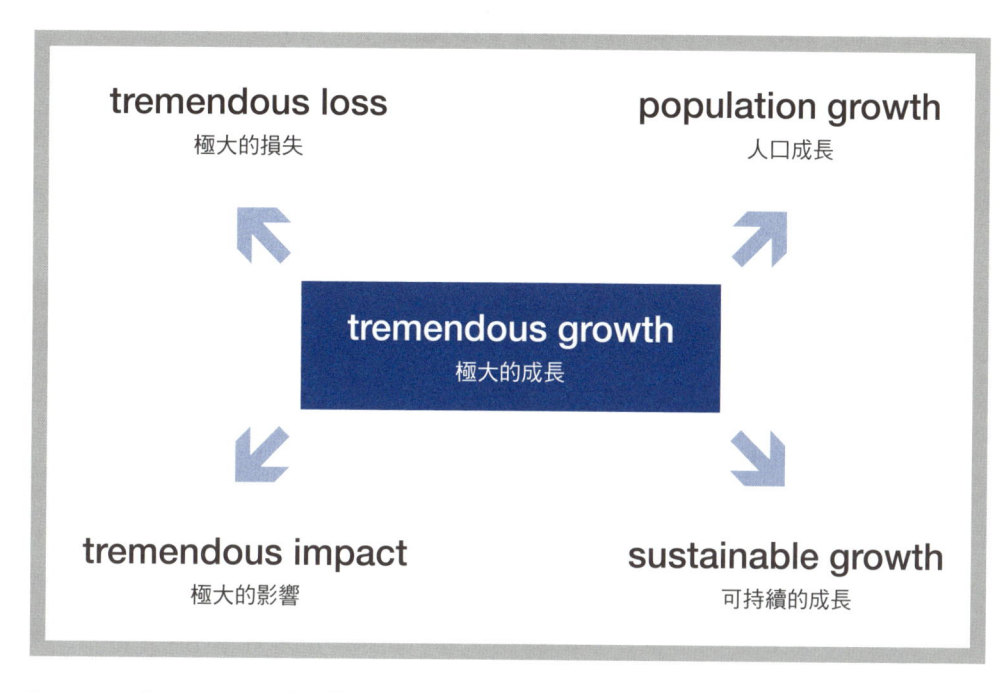

```
tremendous loss              population growth
極大的損失                      人口成長
              ↖     ↗
        ┌─────────────────┐
        │ tremendous growth│
        │    極大的成長     │
        └─────────────────┘
              ↙     ↘
tremendous impact            sustainable growth
極大的影響                      可持續的成長
```

tremendous growth
/trɪˈmɛndəs groʊθ/

There was tremendous growth in the trade between the EU and Korea in the past few years.
在過去幾年，歐盟與韓國之間的貿易有驚人的成長。

tremendous loss
/trɪˈmɛndəs lɒs/

Many factories suffered tremendous losses during the war.
許多工廠在戰爭期間遭受極大的損失。

tremendous impact
/trɪˈmɛndəs ˈɪmpækt/

Scientists warn that there will be a tremendous impact on wildlife if the ozone layer continues to be depleted.
科學家警告，如果臭氧層繼續被消耗，將會對野生動物產生巨大影響。

population growth
/ˌpɒpjuˈleɪʃən groʊθ/

Family planning constraints were imposed by the Chinese government to stop population growth.
中國政府強制執行了計畫生育的限制，以停止人口成長。

sustainable growth
/səˈsteɪnəbəl groʊθ/

The foundation has contributed to the current endeavours to promote sustainable growth and development.
這個基金會對於目前促進永續成長與發展的努力有所貢獻。

WED

IELTS **BASIC WORDS**

separate /ˈsɛpəreɪt/ v. 分隔，分開
ENG. act as a barrier between
SYS. divide, disunite

> There is no particular point in time when we can **separate** old science from modern science.
> 沒有一個特定的時間點可以讓我們將舊科學和現代科學區分開來。

同義語例句 The industrial era **stands between** the old and the modern scientific periods.
工業時代處於舊科學與現代科學時期之間。

同義語例句 It is impossible to **split up** the history of science into old and modern periods.
將科學的歷史劃分成舊時期與現代時期是不可能的。

反義語例句 The wisdoms from old science and modern science are **joined together** in the researcher's latest publication.
舊科學和現代科學的智慧，在那位研究者最新的著作裡被結合起來。

distinct /dɪˈstɪŋkt/ adj. 與其他不同的
ENG. distinguished as not being the same
SYS. distinguishable, different

> Old science is clearly **distinct** from modern science mainly by the nature of discoveries.
> 在發現的本質方面，舊科學清楚地有別於現代科學。

同義語例句 The old and modern sciences are **not alike** in terms of the discoveries during the periods.
就各自時期的發現而言，舊科學與現代科學並不相像。

同義語例句 There is a **clear-cut** difference between the old and modern scientific periods.
舊科學與新科學時期之間有明確的不同。

反義語例句 The old and modern sciences are very much **similar** in terms of scientists' drive for discovery.
就科學家尋求發現的動力而言，舊科學與現代科學是非常相似的。

WEEK 5 TOPIC **TECHNOLOGY**

▶基礎單字擴充

indicate /ˈɪndɪkeɪt/ v. 指出，顯示
ENG. to show the way to or direction of; be a signal for
SYS. signal, bespeak

> The development of modern science **indicates** a positive change in the present time.
> 現代科學的發展顯示出這個時代的一個正面改變。

同義語例句 The emergence of countless inventions **points to** the new age of science.
無數發明的出現，指向科學的新時代。

同義語例句 Recent inventions **symbolise** the period of new scientific discoveries.
近期的發明象徵新科學發現的時期。

反義語例句 Some irrelevant digressions **obscured** the meaning of his scientific discovery.
一些不相關的離題，讓人難以了解他的科學發現的意義。

confusion /kənˈfjuːʒən/ n. 混淆，困惑
ENG. mental state characterised by a lack of clear and orderly thought and behaviour
SYS. disarray, muddiness

> There seems to be some **confusion** between the old and modern sciences.
> 在舊科學與現代科學間似乎有一些混淆。

同義語例句 **Misunderstandings** of scientific discoveries are common in the past.
對於科學發現的誤解在過去很常見。

同義語例句 The **lack of certainty** in his argument makes his point of view unconvincing.
他的論述缺乏確定感，使得他的觀點不具說服力。

反義語例句 Scientists have **clear understanding** of modern scientific methods.
科學家對於現代科學方法有清楚的了解。

TOPIC: Modern science and old science
現代科學與舊科學

Astronomy is an **age-old** science, and its long history shows how traditional wisdom can evolve into modern knowledge. Ancient civilisations believed that the earth is the centre of the universe. In the **scheme** of Ptolemy, for example, the earth was surrounded by **successive** shells upon which the sun, moon and five planets **circumnavigated** the earth. This **geocentric** model of the universe had been accepted by many astronomers for 1700 years, until Copernicus and Galileo finally **substantiated** the idea that the earth and other planets **orbited** the sun. Today's astronomers usually credit the apparent **ignorance** of the ancients to the **lack** of modern instruments. Another example of how new evidence can challenge old theories is the origin of the moon. The geological evidence collected on the lunar surface suggests that, **contrary** to popular conception, the moon might be formed by the collision between early earth and another celestial body. Therefore, we can expect science to keep evolving as modern technology advances.

天文學是很悠久的科學，而它長久的歷史顯示傳統智慧能如何演變為現代知識。古代文明認為地球是宇宙的中心。例如在托勒密的系統裡，地球是被一些連續的外殼所圍繞，而太陽、月亮和五大行星就在那上面繞行地球。這個以地球為中心的宇宙模型受到許多天文學家接受長達 1700 年，直到哥白尼和伽利略終於證實了地球和其他行星繞行太陽的想法。今日的天文學家通常將古人的看似無知歸因於缺少現代儀器。新的證據如何挑戰舊理論的另一個例子，是月球的起源。在月球表面收集到的地質證據顯示，和一般的想法相反，月球可能是由早期的地球和另一個天體的撞擊形成的。所以，我們可以期待科學隨著現代科技的進步而持續演變。

age-old
/ˈeɪdʒəʊld/

adj. 古老的
The **age-old** tradition is preserved for its cultural significance.
這個古老的傳統因為它的文化意義而獲得保存。

scheme
/skiːm/

n. 計畫，體系
The civil engineer's **scheme** for the new bridge was approved by the city.
土木工程師的新橋樑計畫獲得市政府的批准。

successive
/səkˈsɛsɪv/

adj. 連續的
The geese waddled down to the lake in **successive** pairs, ready to feed.
鵝群一對接一對地搖搖擺擺走到湖邊準備吃食物。

circumnavigate
/səːkəmˈnavɪɡeɪt/

v. 環繞⋯航行
Spanish and Portuguese explorers **circumnavigated** the Earth many years ago.
西班牙與葡萄牙的探險者在許多年前航海環繞地球。

geocentric
/dʒiːəʊˈsɛntrɪk/

adj. 以地球為中心的
Most ancient models of the universe follow a **geocentric** pattern.
大部分的古代宇宙模型遵循以地球為中心的模式。

substantiate
/səbˈstanʃɪeɪt/

v. 證實
Newly discovered fossils **substantiated** the existence of the prehistoric creature.
新發現的化石證實了這種史前生物的存在。

orbit
/ˈɔːbɪt/

v.（天體等）沿軌道繞行
Neptune has fourteen recognised satellites **orbiting** it.
海王星有十四顆被認定的衛星繞行它。

ignorance
/ˈɪɡnərəns/

n. 無知
Ignorance led to the overhunting of elephants.
無知導致了對大象的過度獵捕。

lack
/lak/

n. v. 缺乏
I **lack** the imagination needed to believe that aliens have landed on Earth.
我缺乏相信外星人已經登陸地球所需的想像力。

contrary
/ˈkɒntrəri/

adj. 相反的
Contrary to popular belief, he is not interested in politics.
和普遍的想法相反，他其實對政治沒有興趣。

WORD TRAINING | 重點單字造句練習

machine learning
/məˈʃiːn ˈləːnɪŋ/
n. 機器學習

The self-driving car incorporates the latest machine learning techniques.
這台自動駕駛汽車含有最新的機器學習技術。

The application of machine learning to data mining enables the e-mail service to present more accurate ads.
將機器學習運用在資料挖掘，使得這個電子郵件服務能顯示更準確的廣告。

Some researchers claim that machine learning has been abused in the social site as its algorithm not only decides what kind of ads a user will see, but also filters out some messages from other people just because it assumes the user would not like them.
有些研究者主張機器學習在這個社交網站被濫用了，因為它的演算法不止決定使用者會看到什麼樣的廣告，還會濾除某些來自別人的訊息，就只是因為系統假定使用者可能不會喜歡。

One of the major ethical issues that will come up when applying machine learning techniques is whether the extensive analysis of personal correspondence is an invasion of privacy.
運用機器學習技術時會產生的主要道德議題之一是，對於個人通信內容的廣泛分析是不是一種對於隱私的侵犯。

automation
/ɔːtəˈmeɪʃən/
n. 自動化

I witnessed how automation improved the production rate of an aluminium smelter when I worked as an engineer there.　我在一家煉鋁廠擔任工程師的時候，見證到自動化如何提升了生產速率。

The assembly line can be considered one of the first forms of automation in the manufacturing industry.
組裝線可以被認為是製造業自動化最早的形式之一。

The history of automation in the manufacturing industry can be traced back to the early use of basic pneumatic and hydraulic systems.　自動化在製造業的歷史，可以追溯到早期對於基本氣動與液壓系統的使用。

The automobile industry is another example of automation, with robots taking over a lot of manual activities such as spot welding and spray painting.
汽車產業是另一個自動化的例子，其中機器人接替了許多手工活動，例如點焊與噴漆。

口說範例 寫作範例

artificial intelligence
/ˌɑːtɪˈfɪʃəl ɪnˈtelɪdʒəns/
n. 人工智慧

💬 In a broad sense, the quest for artificial intelligence is not new, and can be traced back to ancient times.
廣義來說，對於人工智慧的追求並不是新的想法，而且可以追溯到古代。

Some people say that modern technology has gone too far in attempting to replace humans with artificial intelligence.
有些人說現代科技試圖用人工智慧取代人類是做得太過火了。

✏️ Artificial intelligence has been utilised by some companies to assist decision making and prevent employees from taking action too hastily.
有些公司用人工智慧輔助決策，並且預防員工太匆促採取行動。

Robotic vacuum cleaners are among the most commercially successful inventions using artificial intelligence. They can actually map a room and decide the best route to go through every corner. 機器人吸塵器是運用人工智慧而在商業上最成功的發明之一。它們真的可以探勘一間房間的位置分布，並且決定行經每個角落的最佳路徑。

gadget
/ˈɡædʒɪt/
n. 小機械裝置，小玩意兒

💬 Many high-tech gadgets have non-replaceable batteries, fully sealed cases and incredibly complex components.
許多高科技的小玩意兒使用不可替換的電池、完全密封的外殼和非常複雜的組件。

For many teenagers, being unable to afford the latest gadgets means getting excluded from their peers.
對許多青少年來說，買不起最新的科技玩意兒就表示會被他們的同儕排擠。

✏️ As more and more new gadgets are manufactured every day, once popular products quickly fall prey to changes in fashion or get superseded by newer models.
隨著每天有越來越多的裝置被製造出來，曾經受歡迎的產品也很快地成為流行改變的犧牲品，或是被更新的機型取代。

Companies making high-tech gadgets are beginning to focus their attention on female consumers, who are now more sensitive to the new trends in technology.
製造高科技裝置的公司開始把注意力集中在女性消費者身上，她們現在對於科技的新趨勢更敏感了。

RELATED WORDS | 相關單字延伸

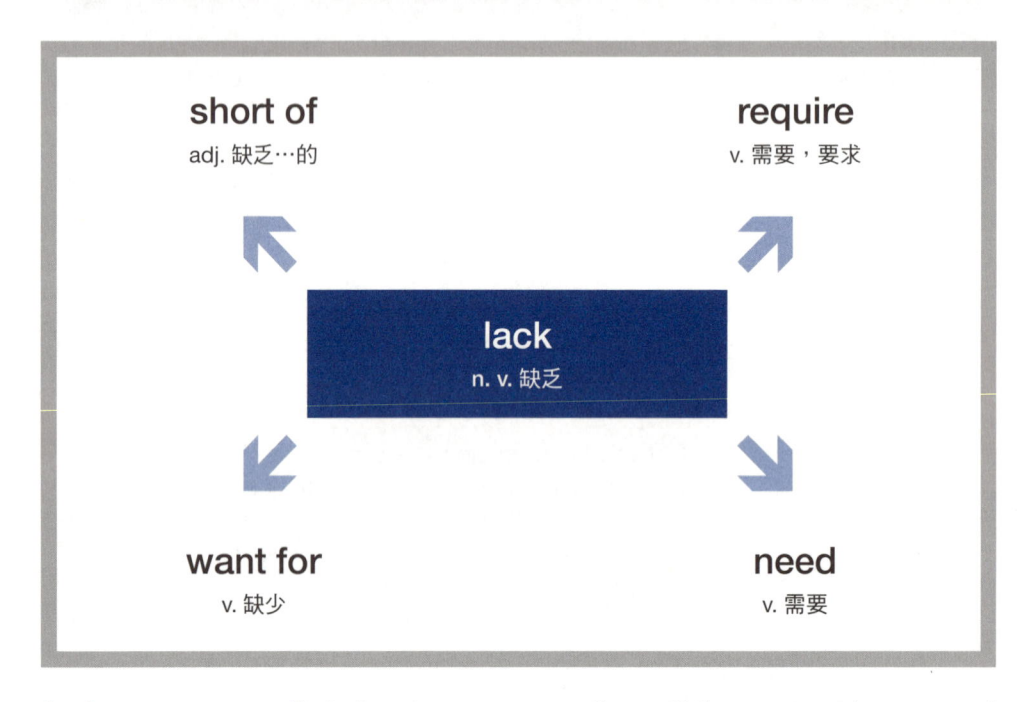

```
      short of                          require
      adj. 缺乏…的                        v. 需要，要求
           ↖                              ↗
                    ┌─────────────┐
                    │    lack     │
                    │  n. v. 缺乏  │
                    └─────────────┘
           ↙                              ↘
      want for                           need
      v. 缺少                            v. 需要
```

lack
/lak/

Today's astronomers usually credit the apparent ignorance of the ancients to the lack of modern instruments.
今日的天文學家通常將古人的看似無知歸因於缺少現代儀器。

short of
/ʃɔːt ɒv/

The astronomers are short of funding for their research programme.
那些天文學家缺少研究計畫所需的資金。

want for
/wɒnt fɔː/

In a modern society, most people will not want for food, water or shelter.
在現代社會，大部分的人不會缺少食物、水和住處。

require
/rɪˈkwʌɪə/

A large-scale telescope is required to see asteroids clearly.
要有大型的望遠鏡才能把小行星看清楚。

need
/niːd/

Since more qualified astronauts are needed, NASA should increase its funding to the programme.
因為需要更多有資格的太空人，NASA 應該要增加對計畫的資金投注。

USEFUL EXPRESSIONS | 相關實用片語

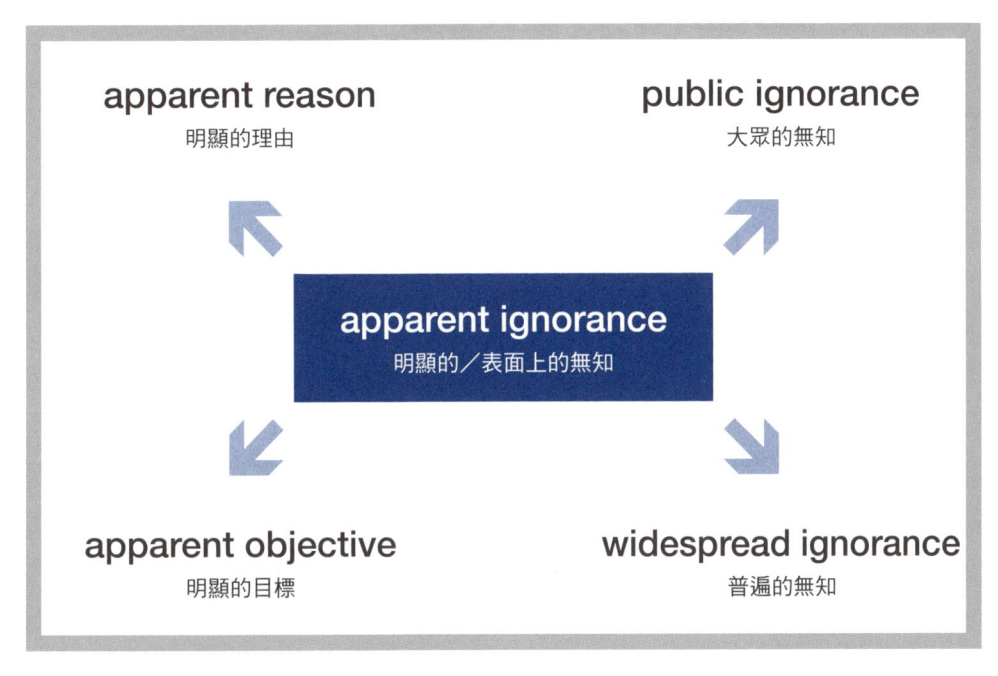

```
apparent reason              public ignorance
明顯的理由                      大眾的無知

          ↖        ↗
         apparent ignorance
         明顯的／表面上的無知
          ↙        ↘

apparent objective           widespread ignorance
明顯的目標                      普遍的無知
```

apparent ignorance
/əˈpærənt ˈɪɡnərəns/

With apparent ignorance, the president quoted from an inappropriate text in his speech.
總統很顯然無知地在演講中引用了一篇不恰當的文字裡的內容。

apparent reason
/əˈpærənt ˈriːzən/

The dancers stayed on stage for an apparent reason: they have another routine to perform.
舞者因為明顯的理由留在舞台上：他們還有另一套舞要表演。

apparent objective
/əˈpærənt əbˈdʒɛktɪv/

Their apparent objective is to contribute to human society through technology education.
他們明顯的目標是透過科技教育貢獻人類社會。

public ignorance
/ˈpʌblɪk ˈɪɡnərəns/

The campaign aims to deal with public ignorance about gender inequality.
這個活動的目標是處理大眾對於性別不平等的無知。

widespread ignorance
/ˈwʌɪdsprɛd ˈɪɡnərəns/

There is widespread ignorance about the negative consequences that globalisation may cause.
對於全球化可能造成的負面後果，大眾普遍一無所知。

THU

IELTS **BASIC WORDS**

creature /ˈkriːtʃə/ n. 生物，動物
ENG. a living being
SYS. individual, being

> Directly or indirectly, all **creatures** rely on plants to survive.
> 直接或間接地，所有動物都依靠植物存活。

同義語例句　All **living things** benefit directly or indirectly from plants.
所有動物都直接或間接受益於植物。

同義語例句　All **breathing beings** enjoy the benefits of plants in their lives.
所有會呼吸的動物，在生命中都享受到植物帶來的好處。

反義語例句　**Inanimate objects**, when used intelligently, can be tools for the advancement of technology.
如果有智慧地運用，無生命的物體就能成為科技進步的工具。

avoid /əˈvɔɪd/ v. 避免
ENG. stay clear from
SYS. prevent, refrain

> We must **avoid** relying too much on technology and learn to do things by ourselves.
> 我們必須避免過度依賴科技，並且學習靠自己做事情。

同義語例句　It is wise to **refrain from** technology once in a while to avoid stress.
偶爾忍住不用科技以避免壓力是明智的。

同義語例句　If there is an opportunity, it would be nice to **steer clear of** technology.
如果有機會的話，遠離科技是不錯的。

反義語例句　We must **face up to** the problem of over-dependence on technology.
我們必須面對過度依賴科技的問題。

WEEK 5 TOPIC **TECHNOLOGY**

▶基礎單字擴充

perceive /pəˈsiːv/ v. 察覺，意識到，把…看作
ENG. to become aware of directly through any of the senses, especially sight or hearing; to achieve understanding of
SYS. observe, notice

> Some people **perceive** technology as the necessary helping hand we need in the future.
> 有些人把科技看成我們未來必需的好幫手。

同義語例句 People **have a sense of** satisfaction over the thought that technology is our constant assistant.
對於科技是我們忠實的助手這個想法，人們感到滿足。

同義語例句 We can **realise** that technology is already indispensable as it is used in almost every aspect of our life.
我們可以了解到，科技已經是不可或缺的，因為它被使用在我們生活中幾乎每個方面。

反義語例句 Most people have **not noticed** that technology is making them lazy.
大部分的人沒有注意到科技正在讓自己變懶。

measure /ˈmɛʒə/ v. 測量，衡量
ENG. evaluate or estimate the nature, quality, ability, extent or significance of
SYS. assess, evaluate

> It is difficult to **measure** how important technology is to our life.
> 很難衡量科技對我們的生活有多重要。

同義語例句 There is no easy way to **size up** the significance of technology to our life.
沒有簡單的方法可以衡量科技對我們生活的重要性。

同義語例句 We must **weigh** the pros and cons of technology in our life.
我們必須衡量科技在我們生活中的利與弊。

反義語例句 We tend to **disregard** the value of technology in our life.
我們很容易忽略科技在我們生活中的價值。

TOPIC: The future of cloning
複製技術的未來

Cloning technology has **matured** so fast in recent years that it has drawn concern from the public. Many people **fear** that cloning technology will soon **replicate** human beings, causing a lot of religious, economic and social **tribulations**. In particular, most religious groups consider cloning humans as a **violation** of natural laws. Moreover, there are still many unsolved problems in cloning techniques. The biggest disadvantage of cloning may be the cloned animal's predisposition to disease due to lack of genetic **diversity**. That being said, cloning techniques could still be beneficial to humanity if used carefully. For example, the cloning of human organs could make organ **transplantation** available to more people in the future. There is a **chronic** shortage of suitable donor organs in the world, and many deserving patients perish while waiting for an available organ. We may even be able to **cure** cancer if cloning leads to a better understanding of cell **differentiation**. Despite the controversy around it, cloning technology has the potential to save thousands of lives.

TRANS

　　複製技術近年的迅速成熟，引起了大眾的擔憂。許多人害怕複製技術很快就會複製人類，並且造成許多宗教、經濟與社會的災難。尤其大部分的宗教團體認為複製人類是違反自然法則的行為。而且，複製科技中仍然有許多未解決的問題。複製的最大缺點，可能是被複製出來的動物因為缺乏基因多樣性而容易得病的傾向。話雖如此，如果謹慎使用的話，複製技術仍然可能對人類有益。例如，人類器官的複製可能讓更多人在未來有機會獲得器官移植。合適的捐贈器官，在全世界有長期缺乏的情況，而很多應該獲得移植的病患在等待捐贈器官的時候死去。如果複製技術讓我們對細胞分化有更好的了解，那麼我們甚至有可能治癒癌症。雖然有爭議，但複製技術有挽救成千上萬人生命的潛力。

mature
/məˈtʃʊə/

v. 成熟

Once the tree had **matured**, the family cut it down and decorated it for Christmas.
樹木一長成，這個家庭就把它砍下裝飾成聖誕樹。

fear
/fɪə/

v. 害怕

Swimmers in the ocean **fear** that sharks might come close while they are having a good time.
海裡游泳的人害怕鯊魚可能會在他們玩樂的時候接近。

replicate
/ˈrɛplɪkeɪt/

v. 複製

I tried to **replicate** the way that you drew the horse, but I failed.
我試著要複製你畫馬的畫法，但失敗了。

tribulation
/ˌtrɪbjʊˈleɪʃən/

n. 苦難

The arctic explorer faced many **tribulations** due to the frigid weather.
由於嚴寒的天氣，那位北極探險家受了許多苦。

diversity
/dʌɪˈvəːsɪti/

n. 多樣性

The **diversity** of animals in the region exceeded previous predictions, as seven new species were recently discovered.
該地區的動物多樣性超出之前的預測，因為最近發現了七個新物種。

violation
/vʌɪəˈleɪʃn/

n. 違反

The police officer fined the underage boy as he was in **violation** of the curfew.
警察對未成年的男孩罰款，因為他違反了宵禁。

transplantation
/ˌtrænsplɑːnˈteɪʃən/

n. 移植

As the scarcity of suitable organs for **transplantation** continues to grow, alternative sources have been suggested.
由於適合移植的器官越來越稀少，所以有人建議了替代的來源。

chronic
/ˈkrɒnɪk/

adj. 慢性的，長期的

The **chronic** neck pain that the nurse suffered made her unable to continue to work.
那位護士的慢性脖子疼痛使她無法繼續工作。

cure
/kjʊə/

v. 治癒

Scientists keep developing new medicine in an attempt to **cure** the fatal disease.
科學家持續開發新藥，試圖治療這種致命疾病。

differentiation
/ˌdɪfərɛnʃɪˈeɪʃn/

n. 區分，分化

The **differentiation** between the two conditions can be difficult.
那兩種疾病之間的區分有可能很困難。

WORD TRAINING ｜ 重點單字造句練習

breakthrough
/ˈbreɪkθruː/

n. 突破

We can see the breakthrough in the fields of virtual reality and augmented reality these years.
最近這些年,我們可以看到虛擬實境和擴增實境領域的突破。

The company is pursuing a breakthrough in battery design by using molten salts as an electrolyte.
藉由使用熔鹽作為電解質,這家公司正在尋求電池設計方面的突破。

The committee aims to identify the areas of technology development that could lead to a breakthrough in air and space transportation.
這個委員會的目標,是找出可能讓航空與太空運輸有所突破的科技發展領域。

The breakthrough in the development of light-emitting diodes (LEDs) ensures high brightness and low power consumption, enabling them to truly take the place of traditional light bulbs.
發光二極體(LED)發展的突破,確保高亮度和低耗能,使它們能真正取代傳統燈泡。

appliance
/əˈplaɪəns/

n. 器具,家電

Many college students keep small kitchen appliances in their dormitory room.
許多大學生的宿舍房間裡有廚房小家電。

I cannot imagine what life would be like without the electronic appliances we rely on daily.
我不能想像少了每天依賴的電器用品,生活會變成什麼樣子。

According to recent surveys, food preparation appliances have become very common, as most people own several such devices like coffee makers, toasters, etc.
根據最近的調查,準備食物的家電已經變得非常普遍,因為大部分的人都擁有幾台這類的設備,像是咖啡機、烤吐司機等等。

In the past decade, Internet connectivity extends beyond computers and phones to all kinds of digital products, including televisions, cameras and household appliances.
過去十年,(設備的)網路連線能力超越了電腦和電話的範圍,延伸到各種數位產品,包括電視、相機和家電。

gizmo
/ˈgɪzməʊ/

n. 小玩意兒

He has many high-tech gizmos in his office that I don't know how to use.
他辦公室裡有很多我不知道怎麼用的高科技小玩意兒。

We presented the latest news about a new gizmo that translates speech.
我們報告了關於能翻譯口語的新裝置的最新消息。

Many people use wearable gizmos not only to track their daily activity, but also to show them as a fashion statement.
許多人使用可穿戴的裝置，不止為了追蹤自己每天的活動，也為了當成一種時尚宣言來展示。

It seems that most gizmos and gadgets in the consumer electronics market have a very short life cycle, and today's iPhone might be tomorrow's Walkman.
大部分消費電子市場的小玩意兒似乎生命週期很短，而今天的 iPhone 有可能會是明天的 Walkman 隨身聽。

network
/ˈnɛtwɜːk/

n. 網路

I forgot the password of my router's wireless network.
我忘了我的路由器的無線網路密碼。

Alex is familiar with network management because he used to work in that business.
Alex 很熟悉網路管理，因為他以前在那個業界工作。

Building a system that can learn from experience is the general goal of neural-network technology, which is generally thought to be the next major advancement in the computing industry.
建立可以從經驗中學習的系統，是神經網路科技整體的目標，而這門科技被廣泛認為是運算產業的下一個重大進展。

Neural networks have a remarkable ability to derive meaning from complicated data and are used to detect patterns that are too complex to be noticed by humans or other computer techniques.
神經網路有優秀的能力，能從複雜的數據中推導出意義，並且被用來偵測太過複雜而無法被人類或其他電腦技術注意到的模式。

RELATED WORDS | 相關單字延伸

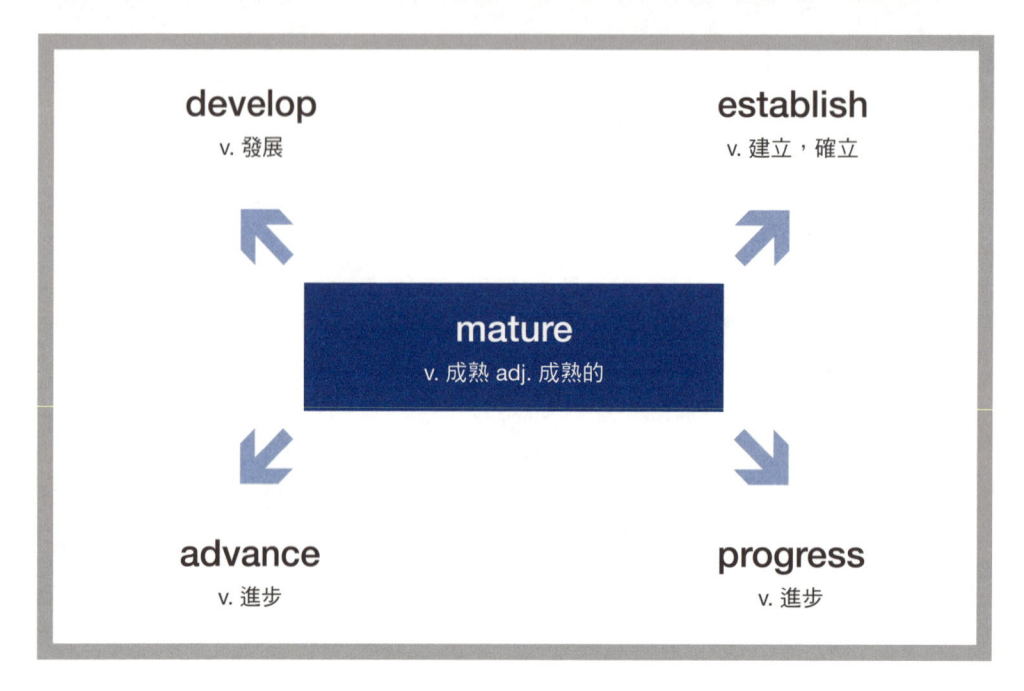

develop
v. 發展

establish
v. 建立，確立

mature
v. 成熟 adj. 成熟的

advance
v. 進步

progress
v. 進步

mature
/məˈtʃʊə/

Cloning technology has matured so fast in recent years that it has drawn concerns from the public.
複製技術近年的迅速成熟，引起了大眾的擔憂。

develop
/dɪˈvɛləp/

As cloning technology keeps developing, the public will probably benefit from it someday.
隨著複製技術持續發展，大眾有一天可能會從中受惠。

advance
/ədˈvɑːns/

With the advancing technology, we are now able to clone animals.
隨著科技進步，我們現在能夠複製動物。

establish
/ɪˈstæblɪʃ/

The city has established itself as a centre of technology development.
這個城市確立了自己身為科技發展中心的地位。

progress
/prəˈgrɛs/

Over the years, cloning technology has progressed and become an important issue.
多年以來，複製技術已經有所進展，並且成為了重要的議題。

USEFUL EXPRESSIONS | 相關實用片語

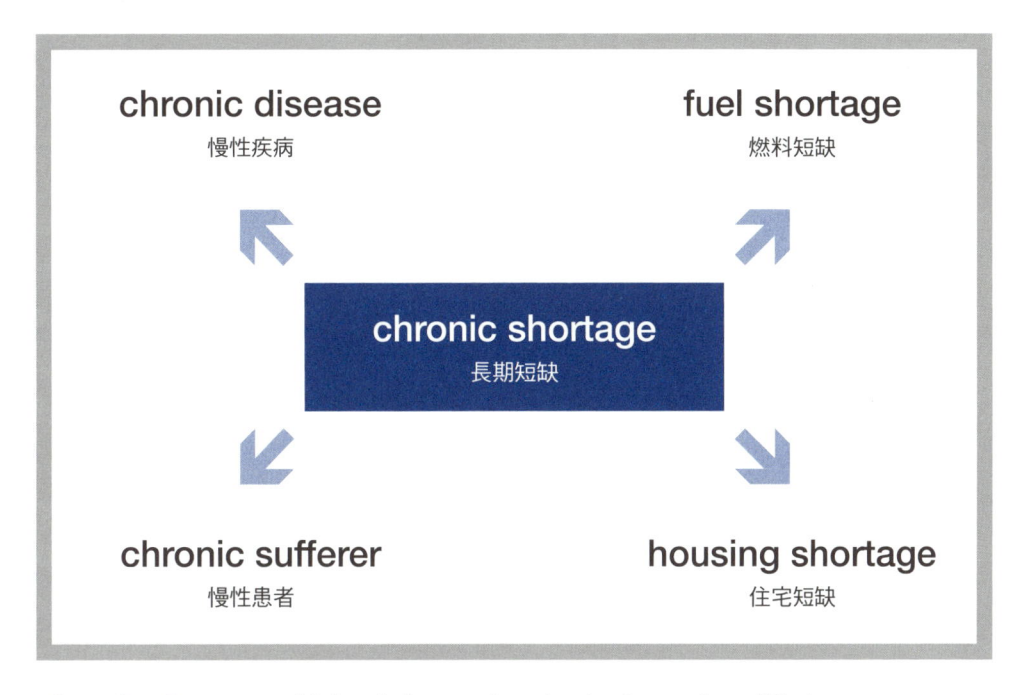

chronic disease
慢性疾病

fuel shortage
燃料短缺

chronic shortage
長期短缺

chronic sufferer
慢性患者

housing shortage
住宅短缺

chronic shortage
/ˈkrɒnɪk ˈʃɔːtɪdʒ/
Malaysia has a chronic shortage of qualified telecommunications employees despite its rapid development.
雖然發展快速，但馬來西亞長期缺乏符合資格的電信員工。

chronic disease
/ˈkrɒnɪk dɪˈziːz/
Chronic diseases in adults who were obese since their youth are rising.
從青少年時期就開始肥胖的成年人，他們的慢性疾病發生率正在增加。

chronic sufferer
/ˈkrɒnɪk ˈsʌfərə/
To participate in the study, one must be a chronic sufferer of neuralgia.
要參加這項研究，必須要是神經痛的慢性患者才行。

fuel shortage
/fjuːəl ˈʃɔːtɪdʒ/
The prolonged winter force northern populations to face food and fuel shortages for three months.
拖長的冬天迫使北方的居民面臨三個月的食物與燃料短缺。

housing shortage
/ˈhaʊzɪŋ ˈʃɔːtɪdʒ/
Housing shortages in America during the 1950s forced developers to build straight into mountainsides.
1950 年代，美國的住宅短缺迫使開發商直接將房屋蓋到山坡上。

FRI

IELTS **BASIC WORDS**

detection /dɪˈtɛkʃən/ n. 發現，發覺，偵測出來
ENG. the perception that something has occurred or some state exists
SYS. recognition, identification

> I run a scan on my PC once a month for the detection of viruses.
> 我每個月掃瞄一次電腦來偵測病毒。

同義語例句　It takes a long time tracking down computer viruses and getting rid of them.
追蹤到並且移除電腦病毒要花很長的時間。

同義語例句　Her job involves rooting out viruses from computers.
她的工作內容包括找到並根除電腦中的病毒。

反義語例句　His failure to notice the virus alert caused a major damage to his computer.
他沒有注意到電腦病毒的警告，因而造成電腦重大的損害。

refer v. /rɪˈfɜː/ 提到，參考
ENG. make reference or be relevant to; think of, regard or classify as
SYS. mention, represent

> The speaker referred to the use of computers in offices as a revolution.
> 那位演講者把辦公室中對電腦的使用稱為一個大變革。

同義語例句　When the time is ripe, I will bring up the issue of adopting new technologies again.
時機成熟的時候，我會再次提起採用新技術的議題。

同義語例句　In his discussion, the speaker will touch on the duties involved in his job.
在他的討論中，講者會簡單提到他的工作牽涉的職責。

反義語例句　The speaker said that most computer jobs today have nothing to do with actual programming.
講者說今日大部分的電腦工作和真正的程式設計無關。

WEEK 5 TOPIC **TECHNOLOGY**

▶基礎單字擴充

supply /səˈplʌɪ/ v. 供應
ENG. to make available for use
SYS. furnish, render

> The central office **supplies** the branch offices with the computers they need.
> 中央辦公室供應分支辦公室所需的電腦。

同義語例句 The employees are **provided with** all the technology equipment they need to facilitate daily tasks.
員工被提供了促進日常工作所需的所有科技設備。

同義語例句 The company **equipped** all departments with high-end computers.
公司為所有部門配備了高級的電腦。

反義語例句 The company might **take away** the laptop assigned to an employee if he or she abuses it.
如果員工濫用分配到的筆記型電腦，公司可能會把它收走。

relate /rɪˈleɪt/ v. 使有關聯
ENG. make a logical or causal connection
SYS. associate, colligate

> The workers' output is **related** to the efficiency of their computer equipment.
> 員工的產出和他們電腦設備的效率有關。

同義語例句 The productivity of workers **has something to do with** the efficiency of their computers.
員工的生產力和他們電腦的效率有點關係。

同義語例句 The relationship between equipment efficiency and workers' output **applies to** all industries.
設備效率與員工產出的關係，在所有產業都適用。

反義語例句 The workers' output, however, is **not connected with** how advanced or up-to-date their computers are.
然而，員工的產出與他們的電腦多先進或多現代無關。

277

FRI

TOPIC | The use of computers at work
工作中電腦的使用

As we keep moving forward in this information age, it is hard to **visualise conducting** business without computers. Each day, people around the world are **reliant** on computer technology to do tasks **efficiently** and economically. Computers are **routinely** used in word processing and other **applications** that require repetitive jobs to be **automated**. Furthermore, computers in the same company are often linked to one another through an internal network. This **networking** allows employees to quickly share the vast **array** of information they gather (particularly from the World Wide Web) with their **colleagues**. Connecting computers and other devices to a single internal network also enables administrators to monitor and control each device easily, and therefore improves the overall efficiency of a company.

TRANS

隨著我們在這個資訊時代持續前進，很難想像不用電腦進行業務的情況。每一天，世界各地的人們都依靠電腦科技，以求有效率而且經濟地進行工作。電腦一向被使用在文書處理方面，還有其他需要將反覆的工作自動化的應用方面。而且，同一家公司的電腦通常透過內部網路彼此連結。這樣的網路連結能使員工快速向同事分享收集到的大量資訊（尤其是從全球資訊網）。將電腦和其他設備連結到單一的內部網路，也能使管理員容易監控並控制每台設備，因而能夠促進公司的整體效率。

visualise
/ˈvɪʒjuəlʌɪz/

v. 視覺化，形象化，想像
She found it difficult to **visualise** her house when she tried to draw it.
當她要畫她的房子時，她發現很難想出它的樣子。

conduct
/kənˈdʌkt/

v. 進行
The scientists began **conducting** the experiment after it had been approved.
科學家們在實驗獲得批准之後開始進行。

reliant
/rɪˈlʌɪənt/

adj. 依賴的，依靠的
John is **reliant** on his mother to tidy up his room.
John 依賴他的母親把房間整理好。

efficiently
/ɪˈfɪʃəntli/

adv. 有效率地
Steve used the software program to edit his essay more **efficiently**.
Steve 使用這個軟體，讓他更有效率地編輯他的文章。

routinely
/ruːˈtiːnli/

adv. 例行地，慣常地
My mother **routinely** wakes up at 6:00 a.m. to feed our cat and make breakfast.
我的母親例行早上六點起床餵貓、做早餐。

application
/aplɪˈkeɪʃən/

n. 應用
There are several **applications** for this fitness machine, including rowing and weight training.
這個健身機器有幾種應用方式，包含划船運動與重量訓練。

automate
/ˈɔːtəmeɪt/

v. 自動化
Many workers were out of a job after most factories were **automated**.
大部分工廠自動化之後，許多工作者失業了。

networking
/ˈnɛtwəːkɪŋ/

n. 建立網路，建立人脈
Wireless **networking** eliminates the risk of tripping over network cables.
建置無線網路能消除被網路線絆倒的風險。

array
/əˈreɪ/

n. 一列，一系列，大量
There was an **array** of delicious desserts on the buffet table.
放自助餐點的桌上排列著許多美味的甜點。

colleague
/ˈkɒliːɡ/

n. 同事
Penny's **colleagues** at the department store recommended her to enter a local modelling competition.
Penny 在百貨公司的同事推薦她參加地方性的伸展台比賽。

WORD TRAINING | 重點單字造句練習

proficiency
/prəˈfɪʃənsi/

n. 熟練，精通

- Technological proficiency is becoming increasingly important in the workplace.
對於科技的熟練，在職場中變得越來越重要。

    Job security is tied to technological proficiency, even for a non-IT worker.
即使對於非資訊科技工作者而言，就業安全也和科技能力相關。

- He questions whether technological proficiency in the workplace is merely a set of skills or something bigger: a mode of creativity or a medium of thought or analysis.
他質疑科技能力在職場是否只是一套技能，或者是更大的東西：一種創造力的形式，或者想法或分析的媒介。

    Even if a company has professional IT workers, it may still expect other employees to have a certain level of technological proficiency.
即使一間公司有專業的資訊科技員工，可能也會期待其他員工有某種程度的科技能力。

mechanisation
/mɛkənʌɪˈzeɪʃən/

n. 機械化

- The mechanisation of office work began when typewriters and cash registers became popular.
辦公室工作的機械化，是從打字機和收銀機變得流行開始的。

    Mechanisation brought about division of labour in the office, which led to greater efficiency.
機械化造成了辦公室內的分工，而這使得效率變得更高。

- The mechanisation movement, which began in the Industrial Revolution, changed how people work by reducing manual labour with the introduction of new machinery.
從工業革命開始的機械化運動，藉由採用新的機械減少體力勞動，改變了人們工作的方式。

    Along with the process of mechanisation, workers who perform monotonous tasks requiring fewer skills, such as telephone switching, were gradually replaced by machines.　隨著機械化的過程，執行電話接線之類需要較少技能的單調工作的人，逐漸被機器取代。

redundancy
/rɪˈdʌndənsi/

n. 重複，多餘，解雇，失業

💬 The company president said it hopes to avoid compulsory redundancy.
公司總裁說，公司希望避免強制裁員。

Redundancy can be avoided by employing computers to minimise tasks in the first place.
一開始就用電腦將工作減到最少，可以避免因為人力過剩而裁員。

✏️ The hardware redundancy ensures that the failure of a single component does not cause the whole system to break down.
硬體的冗餘確保單一元件的故障不會造成整個系統停擺。

When he faced redundancy, the first thing he did was to learn about the technology that replaced him.
當他面臨裁員的時候，他所做的第一件事是去了解取代他的科技。

telecommunication
/ˌtɛlɪkəmjuːnɪˈkeɪʃən/

n. 電信

💬 Telecommunication plays an important role in modern offices, where fax and telephone have become necessary for daily work.
電信在現代辦公室中扮演重要角色，在辦公室中傳真和電話對於每天的工作已經是不可或缺的。

Qualified professionals are needed to build, test, install, maintain and upgrade our computers and telecommunications systems.
需要有資格的專業人士來建立、測試、安裝、維護並升級我們的電腦與電信系統。

✏️ When supervising the installation of telecommunications equipment in the workplace, value the opinions of your engineers and technicians.
在監督工作場所的電信設備安裝時，要重視你的工程師和技術人員的意見。

DS Company is a globally recognised manufacturer of telecommunications equipment, including telephones and fax machines.
DS 公司是全球知名的電信設備製造商，產品包括電話和傳真機。

RELATED WORDS | 相關單字延伸

mechanise
v. 使機械化

customise
v. 訂做，自訂

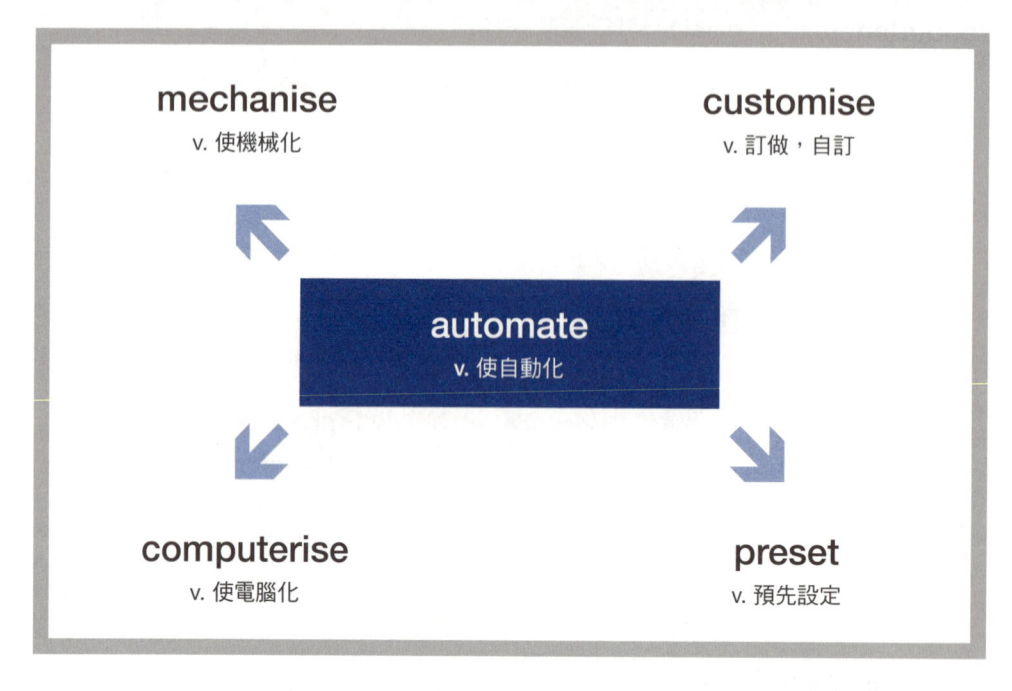

automate
v. 使自動化

computerise
v. 使電腦化

preset
v. 預先設定

automate
/ˈɔːtəmeɪt/

Computers are used for applications that require repetitive jobs that can be automated.
電腦被用於需要重複性工作而且可以被自動化的應用方面。

mechanise
/ˈmɛkənʌɪz/

Today, many jobs formerly carried out by men or animals have been mechanised.
今日，許多原先由人類或動物進行的工作已經被機械化了。

computerise
/kəmˈpjuːtərʌɪz/

The cannery has computerised its operations so that very few human labourers are needed.
這間罐頭廠已經將它的營運電腦化，這樣就只需要很少的勞動人力。

customise
/ˈkʌstəmʌɪz/

I customised the program to do my job, but the result wasn't satisfactory.
我自訂了程式（設定）來做我的工作，但結果不令人滿意。

preset
/priːˈsɛt/

I have preset my computer to remind me when it is break time.
我已經預先設定電腦在休息時間時提醒我。

USEFUL EXPRESSIONS | 相關實用片語

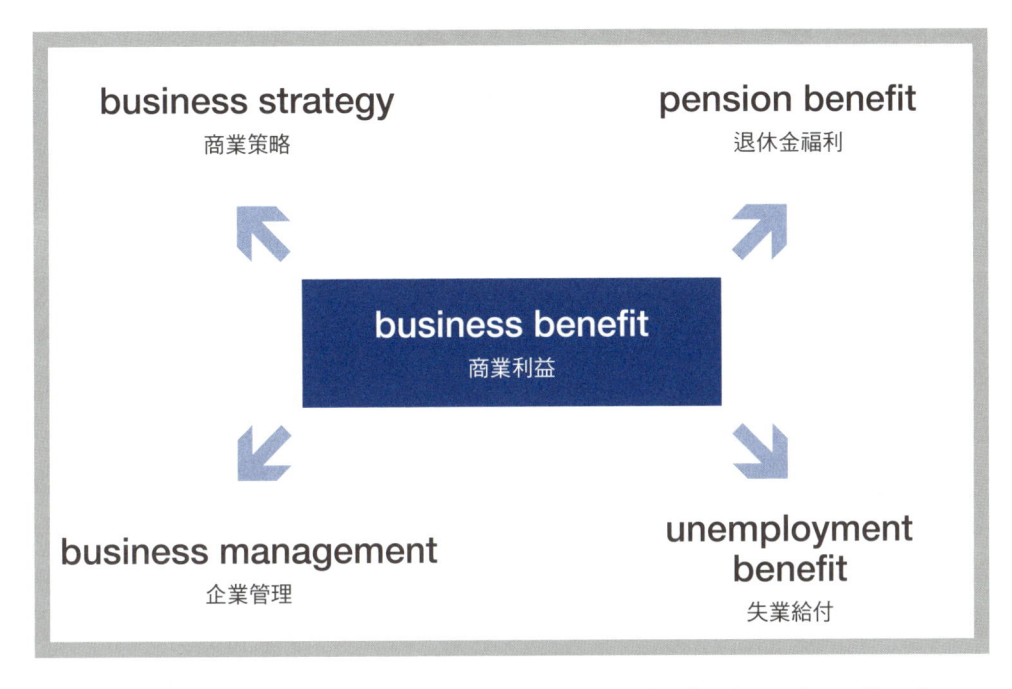

business strategy
商業策略

pension benefit
退休金福利

business benefit
商業利益

business management
企業管理

unemployment benefit
失業給付

business benefit
/ˈbɪznəs ˈbɛnɪfɪt/
It is difficult to measure the business benefits of corporate social responsibility.
企業社會責任的商業價值很難衡量。

business strategy
/ˈbɪznəs ˈstrætɪdʒi/
In order to increase price competitiveness, the company's business strategies will be reconfigured to improve productivity.
為了提升價格的競爭力，這家公司的經營策略將被重新設定以提高生產力。

business management
/ˈbɪznəs ˈmænɪdʒmənt/
Harvard University is known internationally for its business management courses.
哈佛大學因為它的企業管理課程而聞名國際。

pension benefit
/ˈpɛnʃən ˈbɛnɪfɪt/
She worried that her dismissal meant that her pension benefits would cease.
她擔心她被解雇意味著退休福利將會終止。

unemployment benefit
/ˌʌnɪmˈplɔɪmənt ˈbɛnɪfɪt/
In order to increase unemployment benefits and reduce interest rates, we must lobby the councillors.
為了增加失業救濟金以及降低利率，我們必須遊說議員。

SAT

IELTS **BASIC WORDS**

undermine /ˌʌndəˈmaɪn/ v. 逐漸損害
ENG. gradually lessen the effectiveness or power of
SYS. sabotage, weaken

> Prolonged use of computers can undermine children's health.
> 長時間使用電腦可能會逐漸損害孩子們的健康。

同義語 例句 Some people fear that the Internet may wipe out traditional media.
有些人害怕網路可能會完全消滅傳統媒體。

同義語 例句 An addiction to Internet surfing can damage a child's relationship with his or her parents.
對於上網的上癮，可能會傷害孩子和父母的關係。

反義語 例句 Internet overuse causes stress and frustration to build up.
過度使用網路會造成壓力和挫折感的累積。

demand /dɪˈmɑːnd/ n. 要求，需求
ENG. an urgent or peremptory request
SYS. request, order

> With the increasing demand for Internet access, the hotel chain started providing free Wi-Fi access in all its branches.
> 隨著對於網路連線的需求逐漸增加，這家連鎖飯店開始在所有分館提供免費 Wi-Fi 連線。

同義語 例句 A frequent request from our guests is for easier Internet access.
我們的房客經常提出的一個要求，是希望能更容易連線上網。

同義語 例句 Having Internet-related work experience is a requirement for many jobs these days.
最近，擁有網路相關的工作經驗是許多工作的必要條件。

反義語 例句 For many travellers, the availability of free Wi-Fi access is an important factor when choosing a hotel.
對許多旅行者而言，是否有免費 Wi-Fi 連線可用是選擇旅館時的重要因素。

WEEK 5 TOPIC **TECHNOLOGY**

▶基礎單字擴充

reduce /rɪˈdjuːs/ v. 減少
ENG. cut down on or make a reduction of
SYS. lessen, diminish

> We must reduce the time we spend on Internet surfing.
> 我們必須減少我們花在瀏覽網路的時間。

同義語例句 Experts advise people to cut down the number of hours they surf the Internet per day.
專家建議人們減少每天瀏覽網路的時數。

同義語例句 It would be better to cut back on Internet use.
大幅減少對於網路的使用會比較好。

反義語例句 The popularity of Internet surfing will further increase in the coming years.
網路瀏覽的普及在未來幾年會更加盛行。

criterion /kraɪˈtɪərɪən/ n. 標準，準則
ENG. a standard by which something can be judged or decided
SYS. standard, benchmark

> The main criterion for a good Internet search engine is the accuracy of search results.
> 一個好的網路搜尋引擎的主要標準，是搜尋結果的正確性。

同義語例句 A basis for judging a search engine is its efficiency.
一個評斷搜尋引擎的基準是它的效率。

同義語例句 A guiding principle for designing a website for children is to make it educational and visually attractive at the same time.
為兒童設計網站的一個指導原則是讓它既有教育性，又在視覺上有吸引力。

反義語例句 A non-scientific basis for website quality is popularity votes.
一個非科學的網站品質標準是人氣投票。

SAT

TOPIC | Online banking
網路銀行業務

Technological **advances** have opened up many new **possibilities** for Internet users, such as performing bank transactions online. Online banking has added an **innovative** dimension to customer convenience. Customers now have **unrestricted** access to their bank accounts at all times, and they never have to wait for banking hours to **execute** simple **transactions** or to **peruse** their transaction records. These services are commonly provided by banks that are **endeavouring** to make banking more convenient for their customers. Furthermore, as more and more banks offer online banking services, other banks must follow suit to stay competitive. Despite its advantages, however, the popularity of online banking also leads to some problems. For example, online banking has made in-person banking **superfluous**, causing many bank clerks to lose their jobs. There is also the risk of an online banking account being **hacked**.

TRANS

科技的進步為網路使用者開闢了許多新的可能性，例如在網路上進行銀行交易。網路銀行業務為顧客的便利增添了創新的層面。顧客現在隨時都能不受限制地使用他們的銀行帳戶，永遠不用等到銀行營業時間才能執行簡單的交易或者仔細閱覽交易紀錄。這些服務普遍由努力讓顧客執行業務更方便的銀行提供。而且，隨著越來越多銀行提供網路銀行服務，其他銀行也必須跟進以保持競爭力。雖然網路銀行業務有其好處，但它的普及也導致了一些問題。例如，網路銀行使得親身處理銀行業務變得不必要，造成許多銀行職員失去工作。網路銀行帳戶也會有被入侵的風險。

advance
/ədˈvɑːns/

n. 進步

Modern **advances** in medicine have contributed to the current ageing population trend.
現代在醫藥上的進步促成了目前的人口老化趨勢。

possibility
/ˌpɒsɪˈbɪlɪti/

n. 可能性

The new technology creates many **possibilities** for pharmaceutical research.
這項新科技為藥學研究創造許多可能性。

innovative
/ˈɪnəvətɪv/

adj. 創新的

We have seen some impressively **innovative** results in that cancer research.
我們在那項癌症研究中看到了一些令人印象深刻的創新成果。

unrestricted
/ˌʌnrɪˈstrɪktɪd/

adj. 無限制的

The management have **unrestricted** access to the archive.
經營團隊可以無限制使用檔案資料庫。

execute
/ˈɛksɪkjuːt/

v. 執行

Your plan sounds promising, but I am concerned about the difficulty of **executing** it.
你的計畫聽起來很有希望，但我擔心它執行起來的困難度。

transaction
/tranˈzakʃən/

n. 交易

For a limited time, there will be no **transaction** fee if you use our online banking service.
在限定期間內，如果你使用我們的網路銀行服務，將不會有交易手續費。

peruse
/pəˈruːz/

v. 仔細閱讀

Do you mind if I **peruse** the magazine while I wait for the doctor?
你介意我在等醫生時讀這本雜誌嗎？

endeavour
/ɪnˈdɛvə/

n. 努力

She is **endeavouring** to become a preschool teacher.
她正努力要成為一個幼教老師。

superfluous
/suːˈpəːfluəs/

adj. 多餘的，不必要的

Any extra food donations will be **superfluous** given the recent contributions.
考慮到最近的捐獻，任何更多的食物捐贈都是多餘的。

hack
/hak/

v.（駭客）入侵

My older brother had his computer **hacked** by someone in South America.
我哥哥的電腦遭到在南美洲的駭客入侵。

WORD TRAINING | 重點單字造句練習

comfort
/ˈkʌmfət/

n. 舒適

💬 The video-on-demand service enables us to watch a film in the comfort of our living room.
這個隨選視訊服務讓我們能在自家客廳舒適地看電影。

I'll get a lap desk so that I can work in comfort when using a notebook computer.
我會買一個膝上桌，讓我可以舒服地用筆記型電腦工作。

✏️ Since my job involves collecting information from the Internet all day, I need to get an ergonomically designed chair to maximise comfort.
因為我的工作要整天從網路上收集訊息，所以我需要買一張人體工學設計的椅子，讓我得到最大的舒適。

Many people prefer to surf the Internet in comfort and undisturbed, so many Internet cafés started to provide quiet and enclosed rooms for their customers.
很多人比較喜歡舒適而且不受打擾地上網，所以很多網咖開始提供安靜且封閉的房間給顧客。

imitate
/ˈɪmɪteɪt/

v. 模仿，仿效

💬 While surfing the Internet last night, I discovered some toys that require babies to imitate their parents' movements.
昨晚上網的時候，我發現了一些需要嬰兒模仿父母動作的玩具。

I imitated my brother when he was surfing the Internet and pretended I was clicking a mouse beside him.
我在我弟弟上網的時候模仿他，假裝我在他旁邊點滑鼠。

✏️ Parents should keep in mind that young children often imitate what they see and set a good example when watching TV and surfing the net.
父母應該記住年幼的孩子經常會模仿他們所看到的，並且在看電視、上網的時候建立好的榜樣。

The country's Internet censorship and restriction on freedom of speech have been so powerful that some other countries began imitating it.
這個國家的網路審查和對言論自由的限制相當有力，使得其他某些國家開始模仿它。

convenient
/kənˈviːnɪənt/

adj. 便利的

💬 Surfing the Internet is easy and convenient for people who have a smartphone.
對於有智慧型手機的人，上網很容易也很便利。

Having an unlimited data plan is convenient for those who want to surf the net anytime, anywhere.
擁有無限流量的（手機上網）方案，對於想要隨時隨地上網的人很便利。

✍ The Internet makes it convenient for everyone to gather information from around the world, and many people today cannot do their work without using search engines.
網路讓每個人能很方便地收集來自全世界的資訊，而今日許多人工作的時候不能不靠搜尋引擎。

This browser not only provides a fast and secure browsing experience but also features a convenient note-taking function, which allows you to scribble on a web page.
這個瀏覽器不但提供快速又安全的瀏覽經驗，而且還有便利的筆記功能，讓你能在網頁上塗寫。

unsociable
/ʌnˈsoʊʃəbəl/

adj. 不愛交際的，不利於交際的

💬 Staying up until morning surfing the net makes teenagers more unsociable.
熬夜上網到早上，使青少年變得更不愛交際。

Schools should limit each student's Internet access, especially for unsociable ones.
學校應該限制每位學生的網路使用，尤其是對於不愛交際的學生。

✍ If you find yourself always on the computer, you may have a computer addiction, which could make you more irritable and unsociable.
如果你發現自己總是在用電腦，你可能得了電腦成癮症，那可能會讓你變得更易怒、更不愛交際。

I often experience the unsociable side of smartphones in the elevator at work, as people would rather read their messages or surf the net rather than have conversations.
我在公司的電梯裡經常體驗到智慧型手機不利於社交的一面，因為人們寧願讀訊息或上網，卻不會交談。

RELATED WORDS | 相關單字延伸

examine
v. 檢查，檢視

inspect
v. 檢查，視察

peruse
v. 仔細閱讀

see
v. 看

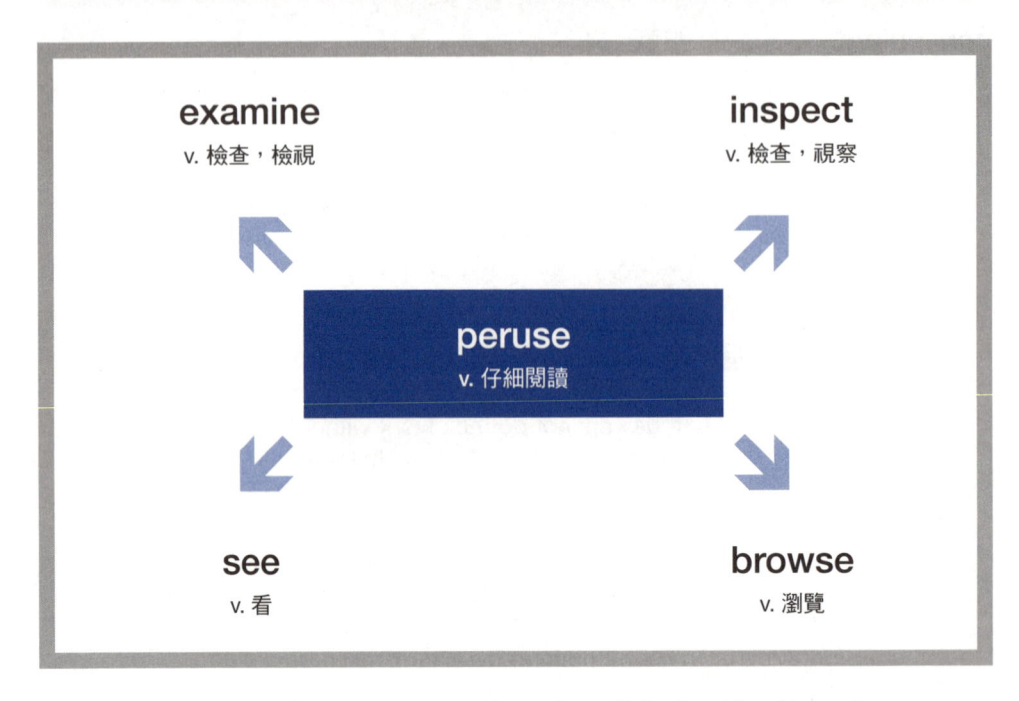

browse
v. 瀏覽

peruse
/pəˈruːz/

Customers never have to wait for banking hours to peruse their transaction records.
顧客永遠不用等到銀行營業時間才能仔細閱覽他們的交易紀錄。

examine
/ɪɡˈzamɪn/

I asked if I could examine the fine print on my mortgage documents at the bank today.
我今天在銀行詢問了我是否能夠檢查我抵押貸款文件上的合約細則。

see
/siː/

The customs officer needs to see a foreign traveller's passport to confirm his or her identity.
海關人員需要看外國旅客的護照以確認身分。

inspect
/ɪnˈspɛkt/

Sir, if you inspect the bank note carefully, you will see that it is counterfeit.
先生，如果你仔細檢查這張鈔票，就會發現是偽造的。

browse
/braʊz/

The customer browsed through the catalogue before making a purchase.
顧客在購買之前瀏覽了商品目錄。

USEFUL EXPRESSIONS | 相關實用片語

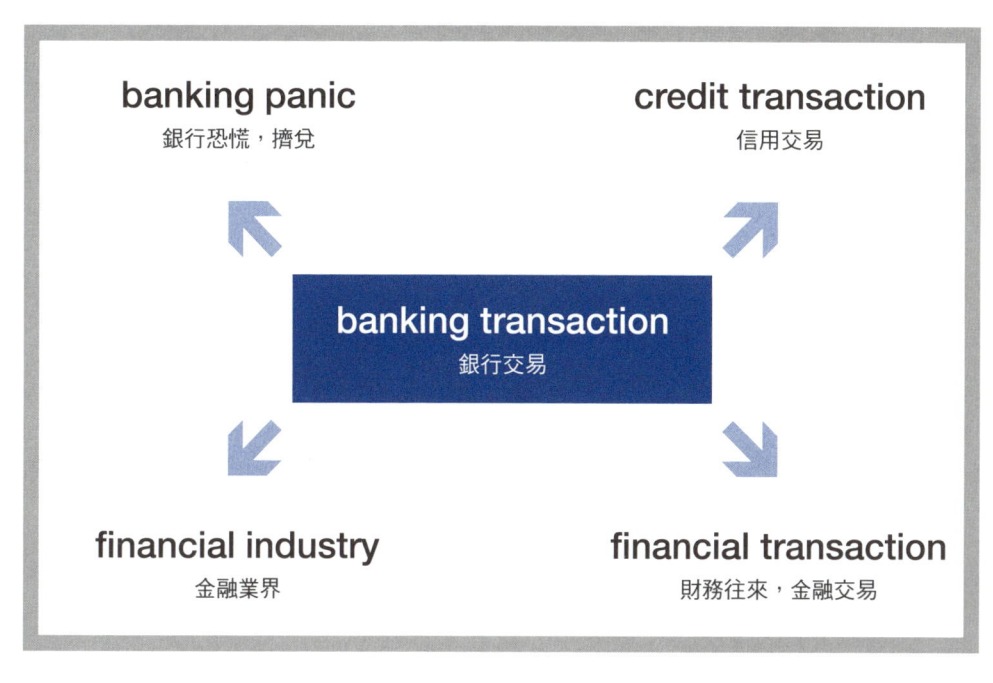

banking panic
銀行恐慌，擠兌

credit transaction
信用交易

banking transaction
銀行交易

financial industry
金融業界

financial transaction
財務往來，金融交易

banking transaction
/ˈbæŋkɪŋ trænˈzækʃən/

Making deposits and other banking transactions on unsecured sites can leak private information.
在不安全的網站辦理存款與其他銀行交易，可能會洩露隱私資訊。

banking panic
/ˈbæŋkɪŋ ˈpænɪk/

The Federal Reserve sold its assets to alleviate the banking panic felt by the public.
美國聯準會出售資產以減輕大眾銀行恐慌的情形。

financial industry
/fʌɪˈnænʃəl ˈɪndəstri/

In the financial industry, almost everyone knows the name Giannini because of his family's assets.
在金融業界，因為他的家族資產，所以幾乎每個人都知道 Giannini 的名字。

credit transaction
/ˈkrɛdɪt trænˈzækʃən/

In order to handle credit transactions, an employee must be trained in advance.
為了處理信用交易，員工必須事先受訓。

financial transaction
/fʌɪˈnænʃəl trænˈzækʃən/

We will scrutinise the financial transactions of any country engaged in producing weapons of mass destruction.
我們會仔細檢查任何從事大規模毀滅性武器生產的國家的金融交易。

SUN

IELTS BASIC WORDS

soar /sɔː/ v. 快速上升，高漲
ENG. go or move upward
SYS. rise, climb

> The demand for home appliances **soared** in recent years.
> 對於家電的需求，在最近這些年快速上升。

同義語例句 The amount of home technology inventions has **increased sharply**.
家庭科技發明的數量大幅增加了。

同義語例句 The demand for home technology equipment has **climbed** over the past decades.
在過去數十年，對於家庭科技設備的需求攀升了。

反義語例句 The demand for home technology equipment **took a dive** during the economic recession.
在經濟衰退期間，對於家庭科技設備的需求急速下降。

imitate /ˈɪmɪteɪt/ v. 模仿
ENG. to use or follow as a model
SYS. simulate, copy

> This robot **imitates** the way humans do actual housework.
> 這個機器人模仿人類實際做家事的方法。

同義語例句 These appliances **conform to** the safety standards set by the association.
這些家電符合那個協會設立的安全標準。

同義語例句 The action of the invention **mimics** the actual household chore it aims to do.
這個發明的動作模仿它要執行的實際家事作業。

反義語例句 The equipment did not work as I expected.
那個設備沒有像我預期中的那樣運作。

292

WEEK 5 TOPIC **TECHNOLOGY**

▶基礎單字擴充

consume /kənˈsjuːm/ v. 消耗,耗盡
ENG. spend extravagantly
SYS. squander, waste

> Without electronic equipment at home, housework would **consume** a lot of time.
> 家裡沒有電子設備,家事就會花費很多時間。

同義語例句 Some people feel that they **waste** their precious time doing housework manually.
有些人覺得他們浪費寶貴的時間親手做家事。

同義語例句 Some people do not want to **fritter away** their time working with their bare hands.
有些人不想要浪費時間徒手做事。

反義語例句 Home appliances enable us to **spend** time **wisely** by helping us out with housework.
家庭設備藉由幫助我們做家事,讓我們能聰明地利用時間。

approach /əˈprəʊtʃ/ v. 接近
ENG. move towards
SYS. reach, near

> We can feel a new era of technology is **approaching** as more and more smart devices emerge every year.
> 隨著每年有越來越多智慧裝置出現,我們可以感覺到新的科技時代正在接近。

同義語例句 As we **come near** the end of the year, it seems obvious that artificial intelligence will be the next big thing.
隨著我們接近年底,似乎很明顯地,人工智慧將會是未來的下一件大事。

同義語例句 As we **draw close** to the future, we become gradually dependent on technology to do the housework.
隨著我們接近未來,我們就逐漸依賴科技做家事。

反義語例句 Let us **move away from** the past when technology was viewed with scepticism.
讓我們遠離科技還被以懷疑的眼光看待的過去。

TOPIC: Toxics in electronic equipment
電子設備中的有毒物質

We all use computers, printers, cell phones and TVs, but we may not know that these electronics can be **deleterious** to our health. Mercury, lead and cadmium are just a few of the **hazardous** and toxic elements found in our electronics. With millions of **obsolete** personal computers lying in dumps worldwide, how do we prevent exposure to these harmful **contaminants**? The answer lies within how we **discard** our old electronics. Most cities offer electronics recycling services at designated locations, so citizens should take advantage of them. Most importantly, never **disassemble** electronics without proper training for there is a risk of exposure to the harmful elements **enclosed** within. As new **domestic** electronics continually **mushroom** in our lives, the negative effects on our health are **compounded**. Therefore, it is important to know the potential impact that these devices have upon our health.

TRANS

我們所有人都使用電腦、印表機、手機與電視，但我們可能不知道這些電子產品會毒害我們的健康。汞、鉛和鎘只是我們的電子產品中有害與有毒元素的其中幾種。全球有數以百萬計的廢棄個人電腦躺在垃圾堆裡，我們要怎麼預防自己曝露到這些有害的污染物質呢？答案就在於我們怎麼丟棄我們的老舊電子產品。大部分的城市提供指定地點的電子產品回收服務，所以市民應該利用這項服務。最重要的是，千萬不要在沒有適當訓練的情況下拆解電子產品，因為會有曝露到產品內部密封的有害物質的風險。隨著新的家庭電子產品持續大量出現在我們的生活中，對我們健康的負面影響也變得嚴重。所以，知道這些設備對我們健康可能的影響是很重要的。

deleterious
/ˌdɛlɪˈtɪərɪəs/

adj. 有害的
The **deleterious** effects of smoking include the risks of heart disease, stroke and lung cancer.
吸煙的有害影響包含心臟疾病、中風與肺癌的風險。

hazardous
/ˈhæzədəs/

adj. 危險的，有害的
The wet floor at the restaurant was **hazardous** for the guests and staff there.
那家餐廳的濕地板對於顧客和員工很危險。

obsolete
/ˈɒbsəliːt/

adj. 老舊的，過時的
New appliances with innovative functions and high energy-efficiency make old models **obsolete**.
有創新功能和高能源效率的新家電，讓舊的機種變得過時。

contaminant
/kənˈtæmɪnənt/

n. 污染物
The harmful **contaminants** found in the stream are killing the fish in it.
在溪流裡發現的污染物，正逐漸消滅溪中的魚。

discard
/dɪˈskɑːd/

v. 丟棄
You need to **discard** the electronics waste separately from the rest.　你需要把電子產品廢棄物和其他廢棄物分別丟棄。

disassemble
/ˌdɪsəˈsɛmbəl/

v. 拆解
The young boy decided to **disassemble** the radio to see how it worked.
那個小男孩決定拆解收音機，看看它是怎麼運作的。

enclose
/ɪnˈkləʊz/

v. 圍起，封入，隨信附上
You will find the key **enclosed** in this envelope, along with a considerable amount of cash.
你會找到信封裡附的鑰匙，還有一大筆現金。

mushroom
/ˈmʌʃruːm/

v. 迅速增長，迅速增加
The population began to **mushroom** in the post-war decade.
人口在戰後的十年開始急速增加。

domestic
/dəˈmɛstɪk/

adj. 家庭的，家事的，國內的
I am not a person who enjoys **domestic** duties, but I do them anyway.
我不是一個喜歡做家事的人，但我終究還是會做。

compound
/kəmˈpaʊnd/

v. 使…變得嚴重
When she lied to her father about where she was, she only **compounded** the situation.
當她沒跟她父親老實說自己去了哪裡的時候，她只是讓情況變得更嚴重。

WORD TRAINING | 重點單字造句練習

operating
/ˈɑpəreɪtɪŋ/

adj. 操作的，運作中的

💬 That electronic device is no longer in operating condition.
那個電子設備不在運作狀態中。

I couldn't find the operating switch at the back of the piece of equipment.
我找不到那件設備背後的操作開關。

✍ The heart of a mobile device is its operating system, which governs the activities of the hardware and offers a foundation for applications to function.
一件行動設備的核心是它的作業系統，作業系統會管理硬體的活動，並且提供應用程式運作的基礎。

The operating system can turn your laptop or PC into a home theatre system, with which you can fully enjoy watching movies and listening to music.
這個作業系統可以把你的筆記型電腦或個人電腦變成家庭劇院，藉以完全享受看電影和聽音樂的樂趣。

invention
/ɪnˈvɛnʃən/

n. 發明

💬 Besides the invention of new devices, we should also think about the recycling of old ones.
除了新設備的發明以外，我們也應該考慮到舊設備的回收。

Her father's invention was made while he was fiddling with his existing electronic devices at home.
她爸爸的發明，是他在家裡把玩自己現有的電子設備時發明出來的。

✍ In a time when enjoyment is everything, many electronics makers are now investing in the invention of state-of-the-art gaming devices.
在享樂就是一切的時代，許多電子產品製造商現在投資在最先進的遊戲設備的發明上。

What I like best about this invention is that besides using it as a normal cutting board, you can store chopped food in its built-in containers.
我最喜歡這個發明的地方，在於除了當成一般的砧板以外，還可以把剁碎的食物儲存在內建的容器裡。

diminish
/dɪˈmɪnɪʃ/

v. 減少，削弱

💬 There are times when the ease of using electronics at home diminishes the value of manual work.
有時候在家使用電子產品的便利會減低手工工作的價值。

When children realise they can spend time alone watching TV, the importance of their friends may be diminished.
當孩子發現自己可以花時間自己一個人看電視，他們朋友的重要性可能就會被減低。

📝 The Internet can diminish the development of children's reflective thinking and can dictate their perception of reality while dominating their home life.
網路可能會減弱孩子反省思考的發展，也有可能在主宰他們家庭生活的同時支配他們對現實的認知。

I don't mean that using the blender diminishes the nutrients, but I feel it might be a good learning experience to stir the sauce manually rather than to rely on technology.
我的意思不是用調理機會減少營養成分，但我覺得用手攪拌醬汁而不要依賴科技可能是很好的學習經驗。

facility
/fəˈsɪlɪti/

n. 設施

💬 A private home is not the best facility for experimenting with new and potentially dangerous technologies.
私人住宅不是拿來試驗新的、有潛在危險的科技最好的地方。

The research team is searching for a new facility to test the electronic devices.
研究團隊正在尋找新的設施來試驗那些電子設備。

📝 The investors will be building a house on the university campus to be used as a research facility for advanced energy-saving technologies in the home.
投資者們會在大學校園興建一棟房屋，作為研究居家先進節能技術的設施。

The research facility that we are building will help speed up the implementation of new technologies by allowing us to test and monitor them in a real house setting.
我們正在興建的研究設施，將能夠讓我們在實際的房屋場景中進行測試與監控，有助於加快新科技的實現。

RELATED WORDS | 相關單字延伸

surround
v. 圍繞

encapsulate
v. 將…裝入膠囊，將…封進內部

enclose
v. 圍起，封入，隨信附上

encircle
v. 環繞

wrap
v. 包裹

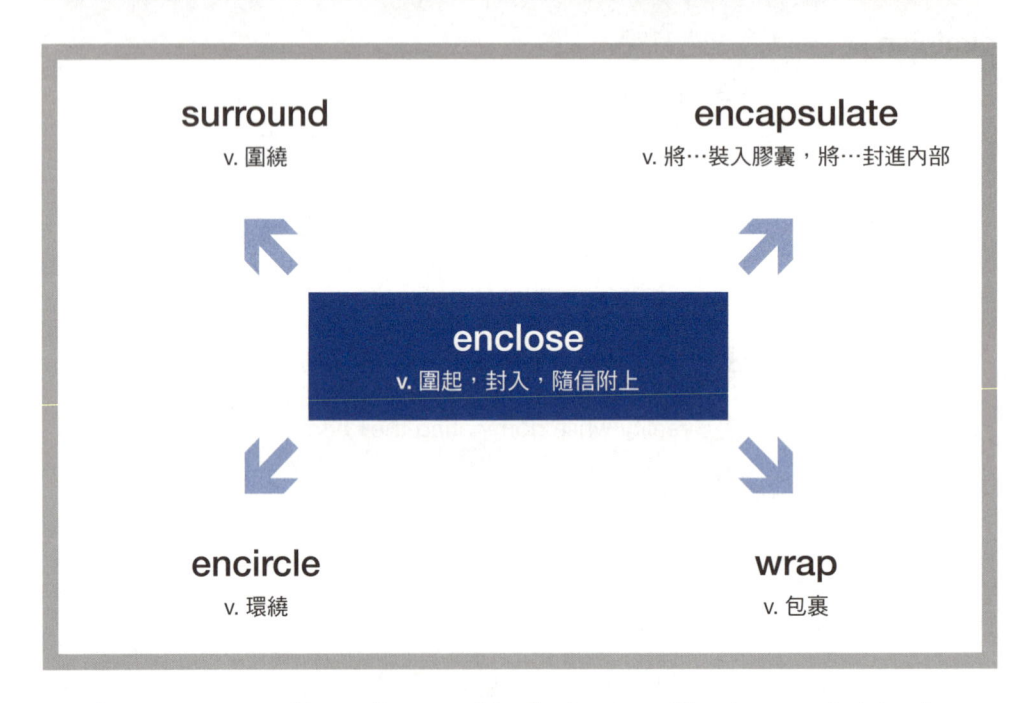

---

enclose
/ɪnˈkloʊz/

Never disassemble electronics without proper training for there is a risk of exposure to the harmful elements enclosed within.
千萬不要在沒有適當訓練的情況下拆解電子產品，因為會有曝露到產品內部密封的有害物質的風險。

surround
/səˈraʊnd/

The children today grow up surrounded by electronic devices.
今日的兒童在電子設備的環繞之下成長。

encircle
/ɪnˈsɜːkəl/

The industrial city is encircled by mountains.
那座工業城市被山所環繞。

encapsulate
/ɪnˈkæpsjʊleɪt/

There are many harmful elements encapsulated within electronics, including toxic heavy metals.
有許多有害元素被封裝在電子產品內，包含有毒的重金屬。

wrap
/ræp/

Wrap small and unused parts in a protective sleeve in case you need them someday.
把細小以及不用的零件用保護套包起來，以備哪一天需要時使用。

USEFUL EXPRESSIONS | 相關實用片語

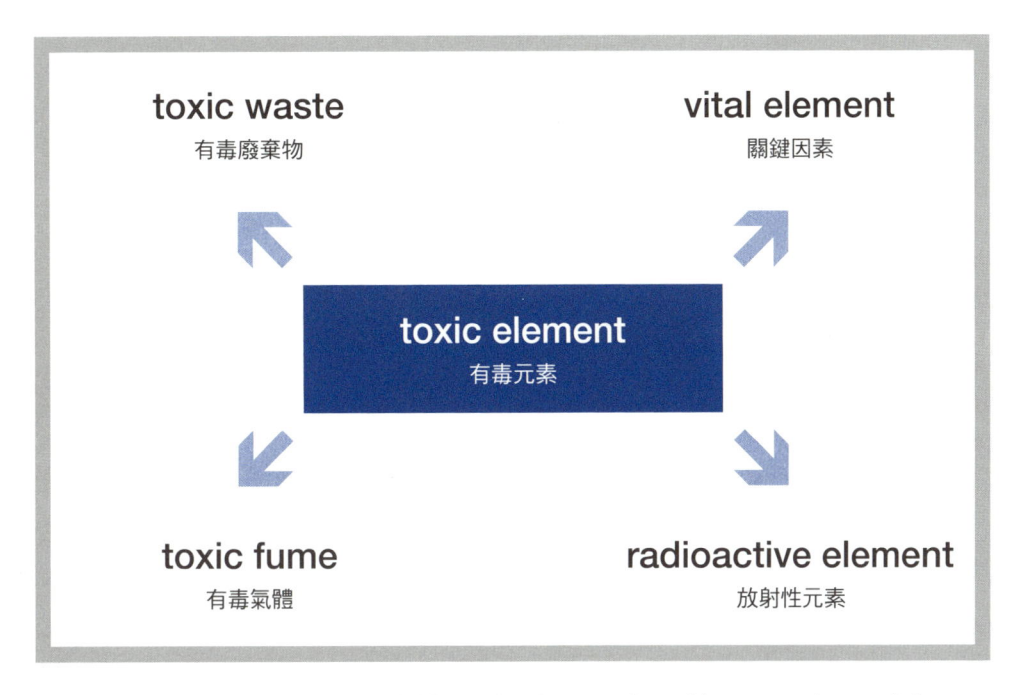

```
        toxic waste                    vital element
         有毒廢棄物                       關鍵因素
              ↖                          ↗
                    ┌─────────────────┐
                    │  toxic element  │
                    │     有毒元素     │
                    └─────────────────┘
              ↙                          ↘
         toxic fume                  radioactive element
         有毒氣體                       放射性元素
```

toxic element
/ˈtɒksɪk ˈɛlɪmənt/

The highly toxic element found in some glue and dyes are often accused of polluting the environment.
在某些膠水與染料中發現的這種高毒性元素經常被指控會污染環境。

toxic waste
/ˈtɒksɪk weɪst/

Finding a solution for the disposal of toxic waste proved to be quite difficult.
結果證明，要找到有毒廢棄物處理的解決方式是相當困難的。

toxic fume
/ˈtɒksɪk fjuːm/

When the chemical factory erupted in flames, clouds of toxic fumes escaped into the air.
當化學工廠起火爆炸時，有毒氣體的雲朵竄入空氣中。

vital element
/ˈvaɪtəl ˈɛlɪmənt/

The most vital element in creating a stable economic environment is building a sense of community.
建立穩定的經濟環境最關鍵的因素，在於建立共同體意識。

radioactive element
/ˌreɪdɪəʊˈæktɪv ˈɛlɪmənt/

Cancer has been known to result from exposure to radioactive elements.
癌症已被知道會因為暴露於放射性元素而導致。

WEEK 6
TRANSPORT

塞車

公共運輸

汽車的演進

在城市騎自行車

如何減少車禍造成的傷亡

政府改善運輸系統的義務

想像未來的交通運輸

MON

IELTS BASIC WORDS

valid /ˈvalɪd/ adj. 有效的，有根據的
ENG. well grounded in truth or logic, or having legal force
SYS. reasonable, substantial

> People usually use traffic jams as a **valid** excuse for being late for work.
> 人們通常會用塞車作為上班遲到的合理藉口。

同義語例句 Using traffic jams as an excuse for road accidents is **recognised as lawful** in some states.
用塞車當作道路事故發生的理由，在某些州被認為是符合法律的。

同義語例句 Being stuck in a traffic jam gave him a **bona fide** excuse for being late for work.
被塞車困住給了他上班遲到的正當理由。

反義語例句 Being stuck in a traffic jam is **not officially recognised** as an excuse for tardiness by the HR department.
被塞車困住不被人事部正式承認為遲到的理由。

retain /rɪˈteɪn/ v. 保留
ENG. hold back within; allow to remain in place
SYS. preserve, uphold

> When trapped in a traffic jam, we must **retain** our composure at all times.
> 受困於車陣的時候，我們必須隨時保持我們的冷靜。

同義語例句 In congested traffic, we should **hold back** unnecessary anger towards other travellers.
在擁擠的交通中，我們應該抑制對其他旅客不必要的憤怒。

同義語例句 We are expected to **hang on to** our patience to get through a traffic jam.
我們被期望能保持耐性以通過塞車車陣。

反義語例句 We must **let go** of our frustrations with traffic jams to avoid further stress.
我們必須釋放對於塞車的挫折感，以避免進一步的壓力。

WEEK 6 TOPIC **TRANSPORT**

▶基礎單字擴充

admit /ədˈmɪt/ v. 承認
ENG. declare to be true
SYS. confess, profess

> We must admit that traffic jams are mostly caused by violators of traffic rules.
> 我們必須承認塞車大多是違反交通規則的人造成的。

同義語例句 The traffic offenders must own up to their faults and change their ways.
違反交通規則的人必須承認他們的錯誤並改變他們的方式。

同義語例句 The traffic offenders must come clean and pay for their traffic offences to avoid repeating them.
違反交通規則的人必須誠實以告，並且為他們的交通違規付出代價，以避免重蹈覆轍。

反義語例句 Some traffic offenders deny the truth to avoid punishment.
有些違反交通規則的人否認事實以避免處罰。

gain /ɡeɪn/ v. 得到，增加
ENG. obtain; add in quantity
SYS. increase, obtain

> The authorities are trying to gain more understanding about the causes of traffic congestions.
> 當局正努力對於交通擁塞的起因得到更多了解。

同義語例句 Frustrations build up when we are caught in traffic jams during rush hour.
在尖峰時段受困塞車車陣時，我們的挫折感會逐漸增加。

同義語例句 Sometimes, female drivers get time to do their makeup while stuck in traffic.
有時女性駕駛人在塞車時會有時間化妝。

反義語例句 We should get rid of our quick temper to avoid stress during traffic jams.
我們應該擺脫我們的急躁脾氣，以避免塞車時的壓力。

303

MON

06-1A

TOPIC | Traffic jam
塞車

Faced with **maddening** amounts of traffic, most of us simply resort to leaning on the horn or **unleashing** a string of expletives. But as commute times increase and urban **infrastructure** gets increasingly **overburdened**, it may be time for some more avant-garde tactics. Around the world, cities have implemented extreme solutions to their congestion woes, from taxes to tolls to cable cars that soar above the vehicle-clogged streets. Before the 2012 Olympic Games, for example, London introduced a new transit corridor to transport sports fans via a cable-car network with the **intention** of **reducing** traffic during the events. To combat traffic **congestion** in the **metropolitan** areas, a number of European cities have even **commenced** reducing the supply of parking spots within their **core**. Whether these radical measures will solve traffic congestion in cities or not remains to be seen.

TRANS

面對令人發狂的交通量，我們大部分的人就只是憑著大聲按喇叭或狂瀉一連串咒罵來度過。但隨著通勤時間增長以及都市基礎建設越來越超過負荷，現在或許是使用更前衛的策略的時候了。在世界各地，一些城市已經實施了極端的解決方案來對付塞車問題，從徵稅、通行費到飛升在車輛堵塞的街道之上的纜車都有。例如在 2012 年的奧運會之前，倫敦引進了新的運輸走廊，利用纜車網路來輸送體育愛好者，目的是在賽事期間減少交通流量。為了打擊都會地區的交通擁塞，一些歐洲城市甚至開始減少城市核心地區的停車位供給。這些激進的措施是否將解決都市的交通擁塞問題，仍然有待觀察。

maddening
/ˈmadənɪŋ/

adj. 令人發狂的
Rick's ceaseless chatter was **maddening** to the people in the room.
Rick 的喋喋不休讓房間裡的人很抓狂。

unleash
/ʌnˈliːʃ/

v. 釋放，宣洩
After **unleashing** his anger on the little girl, he felt both relieved and embarrassed.
他對那個小女孩發洩完怒氣之後，覺得既放鬆又羞愧。

infrastructure
/ˈɪnfrəstrʌktʃə/

n. 基礎建設
The existing road **infrastructure** is no longer enough for the booming city.
現有的道路基礎設施對這個蓬勃發展的城市不再足夠了。

overburdened
/əʊvəˈbɜːdənd/

adj. 負擔過重的
Many students feel **overburdened** with homework days before the winter break.
很多學生在放寒假前幾天覺得自己的功課負擔過重。

intention
/ɪnˈtɛnʃən/

n. 意圖
He had no **intention** of travelling to Seoul with James.
他沒打算和 James 去首爾旅遊。

reduce
/rɪˈdjuːs/

v. 減少
I advised my aunt to **reduce** the size of her shoe collection.
我建議阿姨減少她鞋子的收藏量。

congestion
/kənˈdʒɛstʃən/

n. 擁擠，擁塞
You must have proper ventilation in a crowded room because **congestion** makes people sick.
在擁擠的房間內必須通風良好，因為擁擠會讓人感覺不舒服。

metropolitan
/mɛtrəˈpɒlɪtən/

adj. 大都市的
The parking officers were responsible for monitoring the entire **metropolitan** area.
這些停車監管員負責監管整個大都會地區。

commence
/kəˈmɛns/

v. 開始
Please do not enter the room after the meeting has already **commenced**.
請不要在會議已經開始以後進入房間。

core
/kɔː/

n. 核心
The company wants its other branches to concentrate on its **core** business.
這間公司要它的分公司專注於自己的核心業務。

WORD TRAINING | 重點單字造句練習

collide
/kəˈlaɪd/

v. 碰撞，衝突

- Be very careful not to collide with the car ahead of you in traffic jams.
  要非常小心不要在塞車時和前車碰撞。

- I saw a red car collide with a black one in the traffic jam.
  我看到一台紅色汽車和黑色汽車在塞車車陣中碰撞。

- A bus and a truck collided this morning on Main Street in front of a popular restaurant, creating a long traffic jam.
  一台公車和卡車今天早上在主街一間受歡迎的餐廳前面碰撞，造成很長的塞車車陣。

- Tailgating is a serious problem because this form of road rage can cause vehicles to collide with one another.
  緊跟前車是嚴重的問題，因為這種路上暴躁行為可能造成車輛彼此相撞。

departure
/dɪˈpɑːtʃə/

n. 離開，出發

- Rush hours are predictable because people's departure from work is usually between 4 and 5.　交通尖峰時段是可預測的，因為人們下班的時間通常在 4 點和 5 點之間。

- I missed the departure time of my flight because I was stuck in a traffic jam.
  我錯過了我的飛機出發的時間，因為我被塞在車陣中。

- By checking traffic information online, drivers can decide to join the traffic jam, postpone their departure for a while or make use of alternative routes.
  藉由上網查看交通資訊，駕駛人可以選擇加入塞車車陣、延後一下出發時間或是利用替代路線。

- Vehicular traffic toward the departure area of the airport got snarled to a snail's pace late Saturday afternoon after a motorist suffered from heat stroke while driving his van.
  前往機場出發區的車輛交通，在星期六下午因為一位駕駛者在開著自己的廂型車時中暑而堵塞到只有蝸牛的速度。

traffic
/ˈtræfɪk/

n. 交通

💬 When heavy **traffic** prohibits you from being punctual, you should call and explain why you will be tardy.
當擁擠的交通使你無法準時，你應該打電話並且解釋你為什麼會遲到。

Be careful when you're on the road driving your motorcycle and get stuck in a **traffic** jam.
當你在路上騎機車並且堵在車陣中時要小心。

✍ So heavy is the **traffic** congestion in Brazil's biggest city that residents must find ways of amusing themselves during the hours they spend in their cars.
在巴西最大的城市，塞車很嚴重，以致於居民待在車子裡的時候必須找方法娛樂自己。

Some consumers question whether or not electric cars will be able to survive **traffic** jams as a gasoline-powered car can.
有些消費者質疑電動車是否能像汽油動力車一樣撐過塞車。

shuttle
/ˈʃʌtəl/

n. 接駁工具

💬 Rather than being caught in a traffic jam, it is better to take the courtesy **shuttle**.
與其被困在車陣中，還不如搭乘免費接駁車。

Shuttle minibuses are the most suitable for a region where there are huge influxes of tourists.
接駁小巴士對於有大量遊客湧入的地區來說是最適合的。

✍ Every casino in town operates **shuttle** buses from the ferry terminal to pick up prospective gamblers so they won't have to waste time in traffic jams.
在城中的每間賭場都有接駁巴士從渡輪碼頭處接可能的賭客，讓他們不用浪費時間在車陣中。

Inhabitants waste hours every day sitting in traffic, as we did today travelling on the **shuttle** bus to the conference centre, but everyone is used to it.
居民每天浪費幾個小時坐在車上，就好像我們今天搭接駁公車去會議中心一樣，但是大家都已經習慣了。

RELATED WORDS | 相關單字延伸

pressurise
v. 給⋯加壓，逼迫

encumber
v. 妨礙，阻塞

overburden
v. 使負擔過重

impose
v. 強加（負擔）

compel
v. 強迫

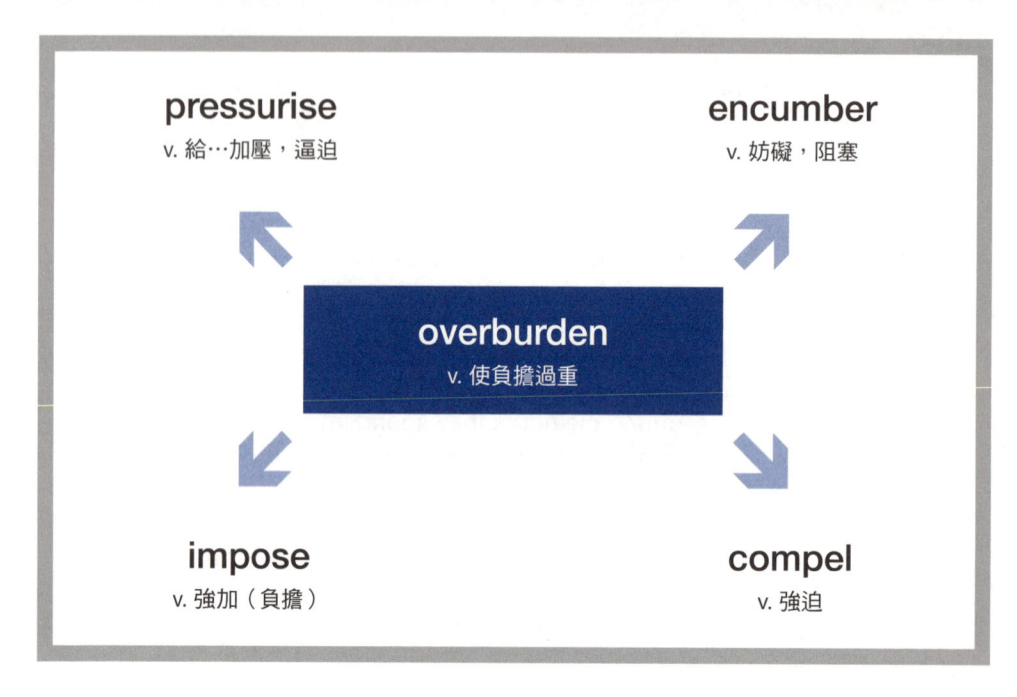

---

overburden
/ˌəʊvəˈbɜːdən/

As commute times grow and urban infrastructure gets increasingly overburdened, it is time for change.
隨著通勤時間增長以及都市基礎建設越來越超過負荷，現在是改變的時候了。

pressurise
/ˈprɛʃərʌɪz/

The residents pressurised the government to take action to reduce traffic congestion.
居民逼迫政府採取行動減少塞車。

impose
/ɪmˈpəʊz/

Nothing will ever change if we continue to impose commuting fees on poor students.
如果我們繼續將通勤費的負擔加在窮學生身上的話，什麼都不會改變。

encumber
/ɪnˈkʌmbə/

The roadways in our city are so encumbered with traffic that commute times are on the rise.
我們城市的道路交通很塞，所以通勤時間正在增加中。

compel
/kəmˈpɛl/

Adverse circumstances compelled him to close his transportation business.
不利的情況迫使他結束他的運輸事業。

USEFUL EXPRESSIONS | 相關實用片語

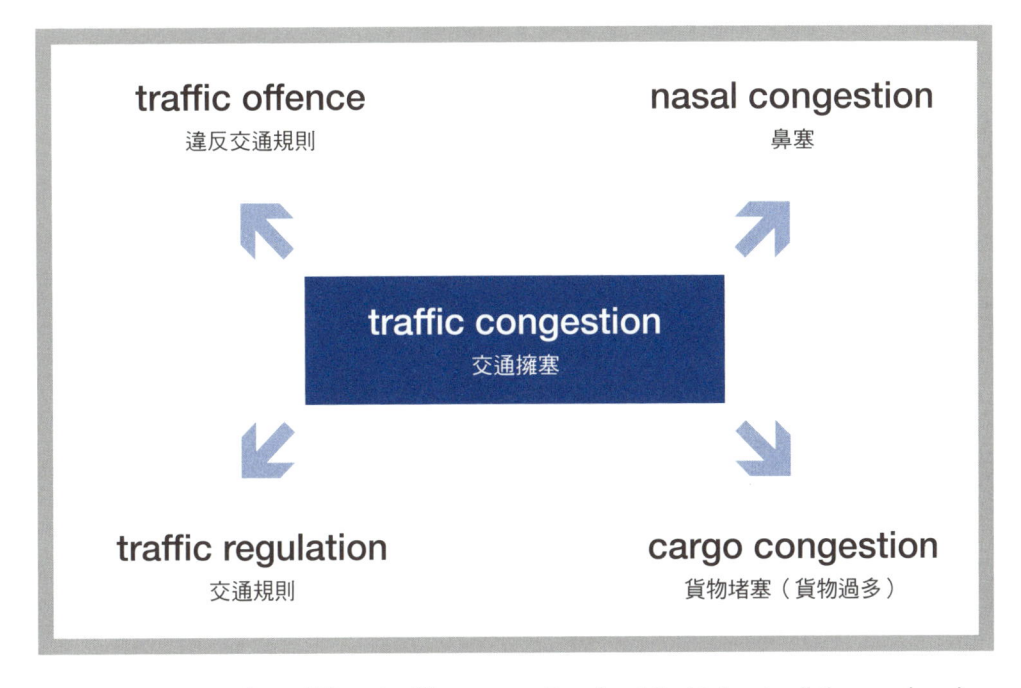

traffic offence
違反交通規則

nasal congestion
鼻塞

traffic congestion
交通擁塞

traffic regulation
交通規則

cargo congestion
貨物堵塞（貨物過多）

traffic congestion
/ˈtræfɪk kənˈdʒɛstʃən/
When traffic congestion is at its highest, all the roadworks should be temporarily suspended.
當交通擁塞達到最高峰時，所有道路工程都應該暫時停止。

traffic offence
/ˈtræfɪk əˈfɛns/
Driving through a red light is a common traffic offence.
開車闖紅燈是常見的違反交通規則行為。

traffic regulation
/ˈtræfɪk rɛgjʊˈleɪʃən/
In order to reduce pedestrian deaths, traffic regulations in this city have been made stricter.
為了降低行人死亡的發生，這個城市的交通規則被定得更嚴格了。

nasal congestion
/ˈneɪzəl kənˈdʒɛstʃən/
People suffering from chronic nasal congestion often claim they lack the sense of smell.
患有慢性鼻塞的人經常自稱缺乏嗅覺。

cargo congestion
/ˈkɑːɡəʊ kənˈdʒɛstʃən/
On the dock, workers have blamed cargo congestion on the staff walkout and subsequent strike.
在碼頭上，工人們將貨物堵塞怪罪於員工聯合罷工和隨後的罷工抗議活動。

TUE

IELTS **BASIC WORDS**

collapse /kəˈlaps/ v. 崩潰，倒塌
ENG. abruptly fall down or fail
SYS. crash, prostrate

> The train **collapsed** when a bolt in the railway loosened.
> 鐵軌有一根螺栓鬆開，造成列車倒了下來。

同義語 例句 The new train **broke down** because it was overloaded with passengers.
新列車因為乘客超載而故障了。

同義語 例句 The railway company **crumbled** after 50 years of service.
那間鐵路公司在服務 50 年之後瓦解了。

反義語 例句 The government plans to **build** another railway system to stimulate development.
政府計畫建設另一個鐵路系統來刺激發展。

absorb /əbˈzɔːb/ v. 吸收，承受
ENG. take up mentally; take in; cause to become one with
SYS. assimilate, acquire

> It is difficult to **absorb** the fact that we will have to pay more tax to sustain public transport.
> 我們將必須付更多稅來維持公共運輸的事實，讓人很難接受。

同義語 例句 He seemed unable to **take in** what his teacher said in class.
他好像不能理解老師在課堂上講的話。

同義語 例句 It is frustrating to know that public transport is not improved despite the increasing taxes that **suck up** taxpayers' money.
知道即使逐漸增加的稅金吸走納稅人的錢，公共運輸還是沒有改善，讓人感到洩氣。

反義語 例句 It is time to **give off** our frustrations to the government in the Public Transport Conference.
是時候在大眾運輸會議上發洩我們對於政府的失望了。

WEEK 6 TOPIC **TRANSPORT**

▶基礎單字擴充

original /əˈrɪdʒɪnəl/ adj. 起初的，原始的
ENG. preceding all others in time; first
SYS. fresh, initial

> The **original** plan was to build a railway to connect the city with the harbour.
> 原來的計畫是建設一條鐵路把這座城市和港口連接起來。

同義語例句　When travelling with an infant on public transport, ample space is of **primary** importance.
用公共運輸和嬰兒一起旅行的時候，充足的空間是最重要的。

同義語例句　The train that has a restaurant and toilet on board is the **first of its kind**.
那款車上有餐廳與廁所的列車是首開先河。

反義語例句　**Second-hand** cars are not ideal for long road trips.
二手車對於長途開車旅行不理想。

purify /ˈpjʊərɪfʌɪ/ v. 淨化
ENG. remove impurities; become clean
SYS. filter, refine

> The train's air-conditioning system **purifies** the air in the cabins.
> 這輛列車的空調系統會淨化車廂裡的空氣。

同義語例句　The positive pressure in the room **makes** the air **free from contamination**.
這個房間裡的正壓讓空氣不受污染。

同義語例句　The air-conditioning system **filters** the air from outside the train.
空調系統會過濾來自列車外的空氣。

反義語例句　The air pollution **stained** the interior of the train.
空氣污染讓列車內部沾染了顏色。

311

TOPIC: Public transport
公共運輸

Public transport is **essential** for transporting a large number of people, and it can also be used to transport **commodities**. It is a sector of the economy that **satisfies** the needs of the population and is often the backbone of a city. The means of public transport include rail, aquatic, automobile and air transport. Each of the modes of transport has **identifiable** characteristics in terms of strengths and weaknesses. For example, the advantages of rail include high **frequency** of traffic, relatively low rates and swift **conveyance** of goods over long distances. The disadvantages, on the other hand, include limited number of carriers, large **capital** investments in industrial and technology base and high energy intensity of transport. At the other extreme, taxis have the advantages that rail transport lacks, **including** door to door convenience and flexibility, but they fail in their dependence on weather and road conditions. Whatever the means of transportation taken, we are **dependent** on its **efficiency**.

公共運輸對於運送許多的人來說是必要的，而它也可以用來運送大宗物資。它是滿足居民需求的經濟部門，也通常是城市的支柱。公共運輸的方式包括軌道、水路、汽車與航空運輸。每種運輸方式以優缺點而言各有顯而易見的特色。例如，軌道運輸的優點包括高交通頻率，相對低的費用和長距離快速運送貨品的能力。另一方面，缺點包括有限的運輸業者、工業與技術基礎的大額投資，以及運輸的能量密集度高。在另一個極端，計程車有軌道運輸缺少的優點，包括戶到戶的便利性和靈活性，但輸在對於天氣和路況的依賴。不論採用哪種運輸方式，我們都依賴它的效率。

essential
/ɪˈsɛnʃəl/

adj. 必要的

It is **essential** to wear gloves while investigating a crime scene to prevent contaminating the evidence.
在勘察犯罪現場時戴手套以避免污染證據是必要的。

commodity
/kəˈmɒdɪti/

n. 商品，大宗物資

Animals are sometimes treated like **commodities** traded on the international market.
動物有時被當成國際市場上交易的商品來對待。

satisfy
/ˈsatɪsfʌɪ/

v. 滿足

She said that taking just one sip of hot chocolate **satisfies** her sweet tooth.
她說啜飲一口熱巧克力就能滿足她對甜食的欲望。

identifiable
/ʌɪdɛntɪˈfʌɪəbəl/

adj. 可識別的

The hydrogen sulphide leak was **identifiable** by the smell of rotten eggs in the air.
硫化氫外洩可以從空氣中的臭雞蛋味辨識出來。

frequency
/ˈfriːkwənsi/

n. 頻率

The harder you try, the greater will be the **frequency** of success. 你越努力嘗試，成功的頻率就會越高。

conveyance
/kənˈveɪəns/

n. 運送，運輸

Uphill **conveyance** from the skiing resorts is provided by a snowcat with cosy seating.
從滑雪度假村到山上的運輸，是由備有舒適座位的雪地履帶車提供的。

capital
/ˈkapɪtəl/

n. 資本

Traditional credit risk models are inadequate because they underestimate the required equity **capital**.
傳統的信用風險模型並不充分，因為它們低估必需的權益資本。

include
/ɪnˈkluːd/

v. 包含

The challenges he faces **include** learning difficulties like dyslexia and ADHD.
他面對的挑戰包含閱讀障礙及注意力不足過動症之類的學習困難。

dependent
/dɪˈpɛndənt/

adj. 依靠的，依賴的

Whether you will be allowed to go to the party tonight is **dependent** on how well you do your chores.
你會不會被允許參加今晚的舞會，取決於你的家事做得多好。

efficiency
/ɪˈfɪʃənsi/

n. 效率

A new pair of scissors has a higher **efficiency** than an old, rusty pair. 新的剪刀比舊的、生鏽的效率要高。

WORD TRAINING | 重點單字造句練習

terminus
/ˈtɜːmɪnəs/

n. 終點站，總站

A bus terminus is a designated place where buses start their scheduled routes.
巴士總站是巴士開始定時路線的指定地點。

In the UK, a public bus terminus is often located near a roundabout.
在英國，公共巴士總站經常位於圓環附近。

While it may be of prime importance to the passenger, the location of a terminus may be decided for reasons other than the public's convenience.
雖然地點對於乘客而言可能是最重要的，但總站的地點有可能是因為公眾的便利以外的理由而決定的。

Before exiting the shuttle bus at the central terminus, the passengers were thanked by the driver for their use of public transportation and encouraged to use it again.
在中央總站從接駁巴士下車之前，駕駛員感謝乘客使用公共運輸，並且鼓勵他們再次使用。

---

block
/blɒk/

v. 阻擋，堵塞

I cannot see the car because the trees are blocking my view.
我看不見那台車，因為樹木擋住了我的視野。

The products were not delivered because the landslide blocked all vehicles going to the city.
那些產品沒有送達，因為山崩阻擋了所有前往那個城市的車輛。

The disaster that happened last week is so severe that roads are still blocked and the families living in the affected areas are still without shelter and electricity.
上週發生的災害很嚴重，以致於道路仍然受阻，而且住在受影響地區的家庭仍然沒有避難的地方和電力。

The traffic congestion was caused by the protesting farmers who blocked the road with large trucks.
塞車是因為抗議的農夫用大卡車把路擋住而造成的。

public transport
/ˈpʌblɪk ˈtrænspɔːt/

n. 公共運輸

💬 A lack of public transport will result in more traffic congestion and pollution.
公共運輸的缺乏會造成更多交通堵塞和污染。

Advocates of public transport claim that investing in it will reduce the public's transport costs.
公共運輸的擁護者宣稱投資在這方面將會減少大眾的交通成本。

✍ Some supporters of public transport believe that the use of government funds in this sector will ultimately save taxpayers' money in many ways.
有些公共運輸的支持者認為，將政府資金使用在這個部門，最終將能夠在許多方面為納稅人省錢。

Although there is a continuing debate around the true efficiency of public transport, it is generally regarded as significantly more energy-efficient than private transport.
雖然對於公共運輸真正效率的討論還是持續中，但一般而言公共運輸被認為比私人運輸的能源效率高出許多。

proscription
/prəʊˈskrɪpʃən/

n. 禁止

💬 Public transit workers are now confronting the city's proscription against public-employee strikes.
公共運輸員工現在面臨城市當局對於公務員罷工的禁止。

Some users of public transport are calling for the proscription against carrying animals on city buses.
一些公共運輸的利用者要求禁止攜帶寵物搭市公車。

✍ The city government's proscription against drunk driving aims to promote responsible driving and decrease alcohol-related accidents.
市政府對酒駕的禁止，目的在於促進負責駕駛，以及減少飲酒造成的事故。

Fare inspectors on public transport work under the statutory proscription outlawing riders evading fares, and they can issue tickets to those who disobey.
公共運輸的票務員是在規定逃票者犯法的禁令之下工作的，而且他們可以對不服從的人開罰單。

RELATED WORDS　|　相關單字延伸

proficiency
n. 精通，熟練

effectiveness
n. 有效性

efficiency
n. 效率

competence
n. 能力，技能

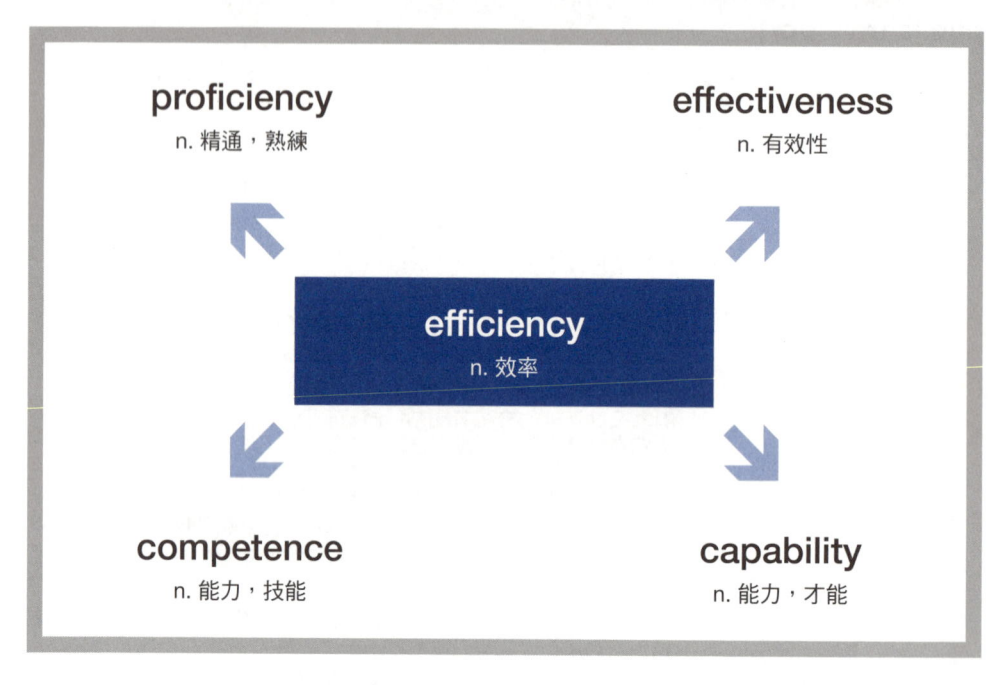

capability
n. 能力，才能

efficiency
/ɪˈfɪʃənsi/

Whatever the means of transportation taken, we are dependent on its efficiency.
不論採用哪種運輸方式，我們都依賴它的效率。

proficiency
/prəˈfɪʃənsi/

Those who want to be a bus driver must take the driving test to prove their driving proficiency.
想要成為公車司機的人，必須接受駕駛測驗，證明他們的駕駛能力。

competence
/ˈkɒmpɪtəns/

I trust the taxi driver's competence in navigating the city streets.
我相信這位計程車司機導航城市街道的能力。

effectiveness
/ɪˈfɛktɪvnəs/

The effectiveness of a road sign for drivers is related to its size and colour.
交通標誌對駕駛人的效用與它的大小和顏色有關。

capability
/ˌkeɪpəˈbɪlɪti/

The car is a perfect choice because of its capability, comfort and eco-friendly system.
這台車是一個完美的選擇，因為它的性能、舒適度以及環保的系統。

USEFUL EXPRESSIONS | 相關實用片語

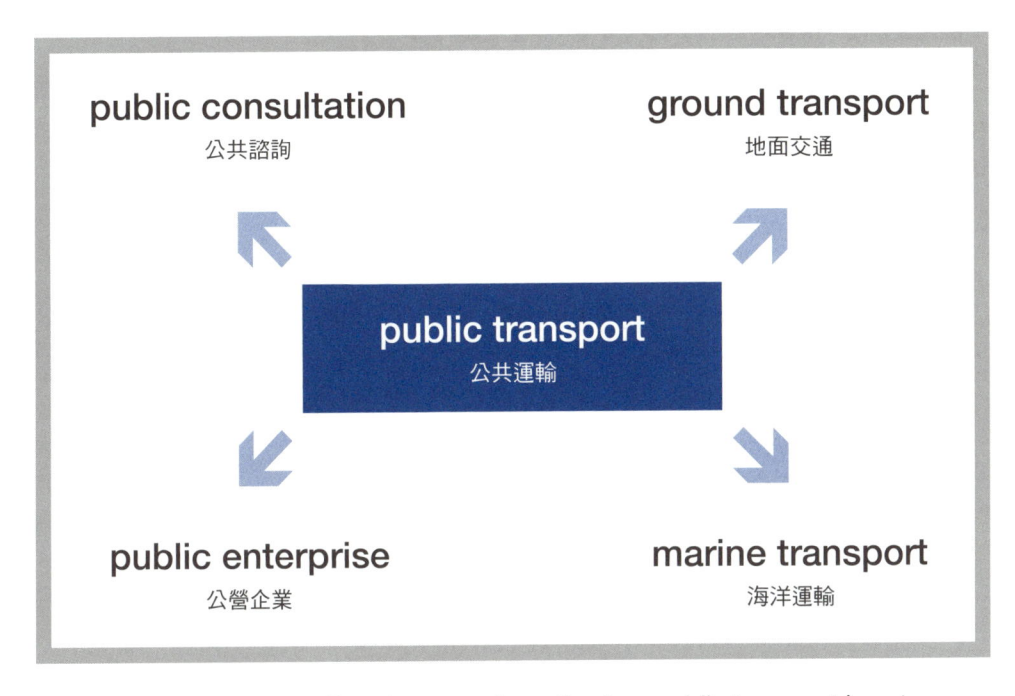

```
public consultation          ground transport
公共諮詢                       地面交通

            public transport
               公共運輸

public enterprise            marine transport
公營企業                       海洋運輸
```

public transport
/ˈpʌblɪk trænˈspɔːt/
People generally walk when public transport is not available or when the distance is short.
人們通常在沒有公共運輸可用或者距離短的時候走路。

public consultation
/ˈpʌblɪk ˌkɒnsəlˈteɪʃən/
A public consultation was held at the community centre to discuss health and environmental issues.
在社區中心舉辦了一場公共諮詢，討論健康與環境議題。

public enterprise
/ˈpʌblɪk ˈentəpraɪz/
The government keeps promoting privatisation of public enterprises in these years.
這些年來，政府持續推動公營企業的私有化。

ground transport
/ɡraʊnd trænˈspɔːt/
The total cost, including hotel, airfare and ground transport, is $400 per person.
包括旅館、機票費用與地面交通的總費用是每人 400 美元。

marine transport
/məˈriːn trænˈspɔːt/
The Maritime Provinces offer excellent marine transport services.
加拿大的海洋省份提供優秀的海運服務。

WED

IELTS **BASIC WORDS**

several /ˈsɛvərəl/ adj. 幾個的
ENG. being of a number more than two or three but not many
SYS. some, various

> There are several advantages of the old forms of transport over the new ones.
> 舊式的交通工具有幾個比新交通工具好的優點。

同義語 例句 — **A few** benefits of the rail transport include affordability and practicality.
鐵路運輸的幾個優點包括費用經濟性和實用性。

同義語 例句 — The train fares 5 years ago and today differ only by **a small amount**.
五年前的列車票價與今天的票價只相差一點點。

反義語 例句 — **A large number of** people can be moved at one time on trains.
火車可以一次移動很多的人。

conclusion /kənˈkluːʒən/ n. 結論，結束
ENG. the closing or last part; end or finish
SYS. end, termination

> At the conclusion of his journey, he returned to the main station.
> 在旅程的最後，他回到了總站。

同義語 例句 — The train's **last stop** is at the border of this city.
這台列車的最後一站是在這個城市的邊界。

同義語 例句 — At the **end** of his three-day train journey, he saw his family.
在他三天火車旅行的最後，他見到了他的家人。

反義語 例句 — The **starting point** of the railway is at the terminus near the city hall.
鐵路的起始點在市政府附近的總站。

WEEK 6 TOPIC **TRANSPORT**

▶ 基礎單字擴充

proportion /prəˈpɔːʃən/ n. 比例
ENG. the relation between things
SYS. ratio, balance

> The **proportion** of commuters taking the train is lower than before.
> 搭火車通勤的人，比例比以前低。

同義語例句 The **percentage** of people who commute to work by train has increased over time.
搭火車通勤上班的人，百分比隨著時間增加了。

同義語例句 The **ratio** of people who commute by train and those by car is different from what the researchers expected.
搭火車通勤和開車通勤的人數比率，和研究者預期的不同。

反義語例句 The **imbalance** between urban and rural areas became more obvious after the construction of the railway.
城鄉地區之間的不均衡，在鐵路建設之後變得更明顯。

shift /ʃɪft/ n. 轉移，轉變
ENG. a qualitative change
SYS. transformation, transmutation

> In the past decade, the **shift** in the way commuters get to work is obvious.
> 在過去十年，通勤族上班方式的轉變很明顯。

同義語例句 As automobiles became more and more affordable, many commuters made a **switch** from taking trains to driving their own cars.
隨著汽車變得越來越便宜，許多通勤者從搭火車變成開自己的車。

同義語例句 There was a **change in position** between the first and second most popular modes of transport.
第一和第二普遍的交通方式，它們的名次對調了。

反義語例句 The development of rail transport in my city remains at **status quo**.
我的城市的鐵路交通發展維持在現狀。

WED

06-3A

TOPIC: The evolution of cars
汽車的演進

    Transport has developed over the years with **astonishing** innovations. All forms of transport, including air, marine, rail and road transport, are **critical** to economic growth, as they **unite** communities and **contribute** to the **flow** of people and goods. As countries experience population growth and **modernisation**, availability of transport has become increasingly important. Cars, for example, are among the most popular forms of transport today because they are readily available anytime for their owners. Before cars became so popular, however, they have changed a lot over time. Since the first car was **fabricated** in 1885, a number of improvements have been **accomplished**. In fact, vintage automobiles look prehistoric compared with today's **streamlined**, genteel models. The first car only had three wheels, and it lacked much of the equipment we take for granted today. Riding in a car that doesn't have brakes or indicators today would cause **bedlam** on the roads! Fortunately, cars today are much safer and more reliable than they were before. One can only dream of how the design of cars will be transformed in the future.

TRANS

    交通在這些年來逐漸發展，其中也有驚人的創新。所有交通的形式，包括航空、海上、鐵路與道路交通，對經濟成長都至關重要，因為它們把社區彼此連結起來，並且促進人與商品的流動。隨著各國經歷人口成長與現代化，交通的可得性也變得越來越重要。例如汽車，是今日最普遍的交通形式之一，因為它們對於車主而言是隨時可得（可利用）的。不過，在汽車變得這麼流行之前，它們隨著時間改變了很多。自從第一輛汽車在1885年被製造出來以後，已經完成了許多改進。事實上，和今日流線形、優雅的款式相比，舊式汽車看起來就像史前產物一樣。第一輛汽車只有三個輪子，也缺少很多我們今日習以為常的設備。現在如果開沒有煞車或方向燈的車的話，會造成路上大亂！還好，今日的汽車比以前的來得安全也可靠許多。我們只能夢想汽車的設計在未來會被改變成什麼樣子。

astonishing
/əˈstɒnɪʃɪŋ/

adj. 驚人的
There were an **astonishing** number of people inside the tiny house during the hailstorm.
發生雹暴時有驚人的人數在那個小房子裡。

modernisation
/mɒdənʌɪˈzeɪʃən/

n. 現代化
Malaysia saw a boom in the economy after its extensive **modernisation** of the school system.
馬來西亞在學校系統大規模現代化之後，經濟開始繁榮。

critical
/ˈkrɪtɪkəl/

adj. 關鍵的
The decision he's going to make will be a **critical** one.
他即將做出的決定很關鍵。

unite
/juːˈnʌɪt/

v. 聯合
When a person **unites** with someone else in marriage, it's beautiful.
當一個人在婚姻上與另一個人連結，是一件很美的事。

contribute
/kənˈtrɪbjuːt/

v. 捐獻，貢獻
She **contributed** to the school musical by painting the stage backdrops for the scenes.
她藉著畫舞台背景而對學校音樂劇有所貢獻。

flow
/fləʊ/

n. 流動
The project will help decrease the **flow** of people from rural areas to the cities.
這個計畫將有助於減少從鄉村地區到城市的人口流動。

fabricate
/ˈfabrɪkeɪt/

v. 製造
My job is to find flaws in the wood after the table has been **fabricated**.
我的工作是在桌子被製造以後找出木頭裡的瑕疵。

accomplish
/əˈkʌmplɪʃ/

v. 完成，達到
The barista **accomplished** the difficult task of selling expensive coffee.
咖啡師達成了銷售昂貴咖啡的困難任務。

streamlined
/ˈstriːmlʌɪnd/

adj. 流線形的
Fish are **streamlined** in order to move through the water with minimum resistance.
魚是流線形的，以便在水中以最小阻力移動。

bedlam
/ˈbɛdləm/

n. 混亂喧鬧的場面
The Miami Dolphins' loss caused absolute **bedlam** on the streets.　邁阿密海豚隊輸球，造成街頭徹底的騷亂。

WORD TRAINING | 重點單字造句練習

avenue
/ˈavənjuː/

n. 大街，大道

💬 In the past, the avenue that my house was built on was wide enough for city traffic.
在過去，我房子所在的那條大街對於城市的交通是夠寬的。

Drivers used to be able to park on the avenue, but that is outlawed today.
駕駛人以前可以在街上停車，但現在被法律禁止了。

✏️ The government is responsible for managing traffic on roads and avenues and repairing any road in poor condition.
政府負責管理道路的交通，以及修理狀態不佳的道路。

Road transport is just as important today as it ever was in the past, yet most of the area's avenues were constructed before the Second World War.
今日道路交通和往昔一樣重要，但這個區域大部分的道路是在第二次世界大戰以前建造的。

canalisation
/kanəlʌɪˈzeɪʃən/

n. 運河開鑿，將河流改造為運河

💬 Canalisation ensures sufficient depth of water for the navigation of freight ships.
運河開鑿確保有足夠的水深讓貨運船航行。

The river became more usable after the canalisation of the lower portion of it.
河流在下游部分改造為運河之後，變得更加實用。

✏️ Modern canalisation has rendered many small rivers navigable and created a good depth for vessels in large rivers.
現代的運河開鑿使得許多小河變得可以航行，也在大河裡為航隻創造很好的深度。

It is not clear whether the canalisation project of the river, initially started over 25 years ago, is compatible with the need of modern ships.
這條河在超過 25 年之前開始的運河改造計畫，是否能符合現代船隻的需要並不清楚。

channel
/ˈtʃænəl/

n. 海峽，航道

Tourists have marvelled at the view on both sides of the channel.
遊客對航道兩側的景色感到驚奇。

The English Channel ferry has transported hundreds of vehicles and thousands of passengers.
這艘英吉利海峽渡輪已經運送了數百輛車和數千名乘客。

This channel is now used for the tourists to take one-hour boat ride around three main canals.
這條航道現在用來讓遊客進行一小時內環遊三條主要運河的乘船航行。

The workers needed a walkway between the cliffs for the transport of materials and the inspection and maintenance of the channel.
那些工作者需要一條峭壁之間的走道，作為材料運輸與航道的檢查與維護之用。

boatload
/ˈboʊtloʊd/

n. 船的載貨量，很大的量

He imported wine by the boatload, employing small cargo ships to do the work.
他進口酒的量很大，是雇用小型貨船來進行進口工作。

Digital cameras record a boatload of information every time you take a picture.
數位相機在你每次拍照時都會記錄許多資訊。

In the past, the British government used to send boatloads of convicts to its colonies, but such practice is no more an option today.
在過去，英國政府將一艘一艘的罪犯送到殖民地，但這種做法現在已經不是一種選擇了（不能再做了）。

Indonesian authorities did not answer why they left a boatload of asylum seekers unassisted before their ship sank last week.
印尼當局沒有回答為什麼他們上週讓一艘載滿尋求庇護者的船沉沒，而沒有予以救助。

RELATED WORDS | 相關單字延伸

bestow
v. 授予，贈與

impart
v. 傳授，透露

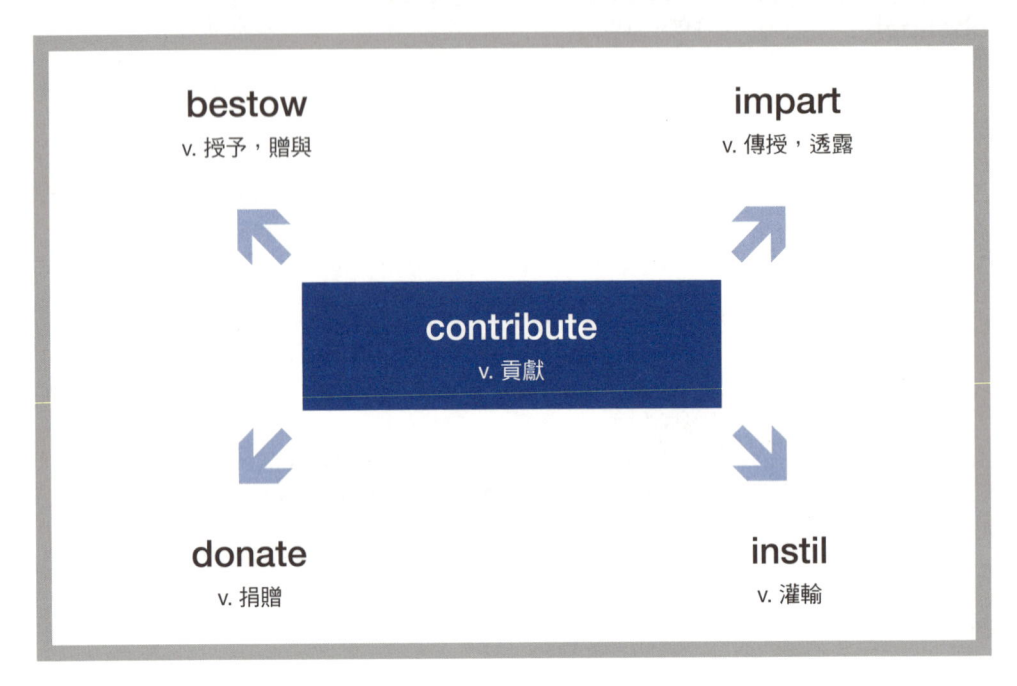

contribute
v. 貢獻

donate
v. 捐贈

instil
v. 灌輸

contribute
/kənˈtrɪbjuːt/

All forms of transport are critical to economic growth, as they unite communities and contribute to the flow of people and goods.
所有交通的形式對經濟成長都至關重要，因為它們把社區彼此連結起來，並且促進人與商品的流動。

bestow
/bɪˈstəʊ/

In order to increase traffic safety, the city bestowed street lights to the residents on First Avenue.
為了提升交通安全，市政府為第一大道的居民設置了路燈。

donate
/dəʊˈneɪt/

I hope the traffic safety board will donate $1,000 to the Drinking and Driving Counterattack campaign.
我希望交通安全委員會會捐贈一千美元給「反擊酒駕」活動。

impart
/ɪmˈpɑːt/

If the engineers had imparted the information to the council earlier, our pedestrian bridge would have been built already.
如果工程師早點把訊息告訴議會，我們的行人天橋應該早就蓋好了。

instil
/ɪnˈstɪl/

We instilled in our children from a young age the importance of being safe around railway tracks.
我們從小就灌輸孩子在鐵軌附近保持安全的重要性。

USEFUL EXPRESSIONS | 相關實用片語

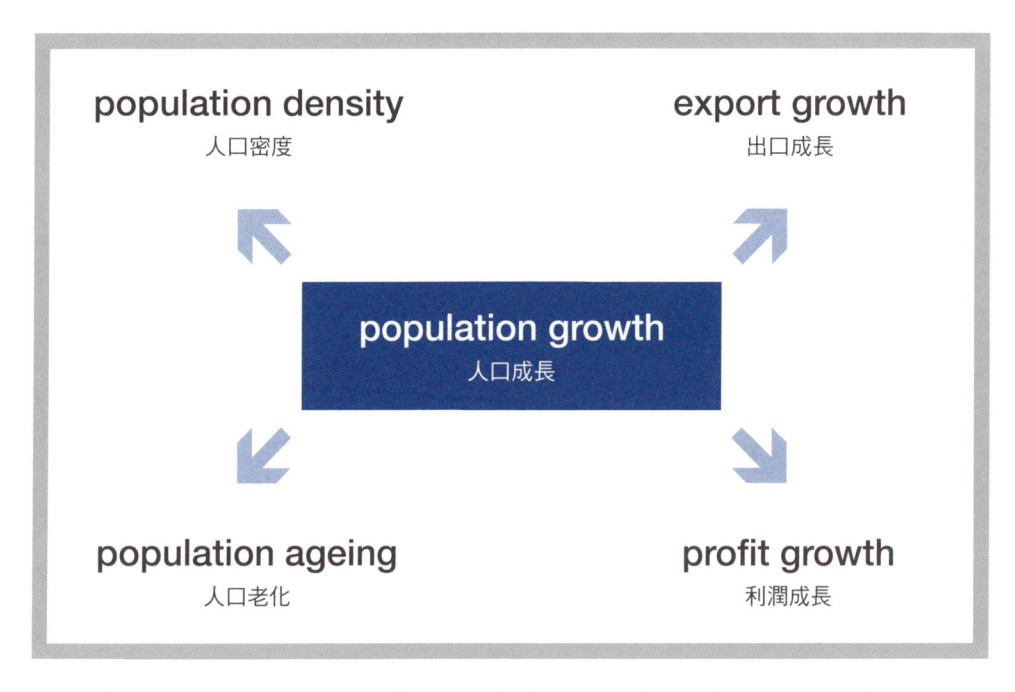

```
population density          export growth
   人口密度                    出口成長
              ↖        ↗
              population growth
                 人口成長
              ↙        ↘
population ageing           profit growth
   人口老化                    利潤成長
```

population growth
/ˌpɒpjuˈleɪʃən ˈɡrəʊθ/
In our city, population growth has been soaring thanks to city development and immigration.
在我們的城市，人口因為都市發展與移民而大幅成長。

population density
/ˌpɒpjuˈleɪʃən ˈdɛnsɪti/
The population density of Korea has led to the emergence of compact apartments resembling matchboxes.
韓國的人口密度導致像是火柴盒一樣的小公寓套房出現。

population ageing
/ˌpɒpjuˈleɪʃən ˈeɪdʒɪŋ/
We can see the negative effects of population ageing when examining the economic burden of retirees on societies.
我們可以在檢視退休者對社會的經濟負擔時看到人口老化的負面影響。

export growth
/ˈɛkspɔːt ɡrəʊθ/
The Korean manufacturer is predicting a better month to come as domestic demand and export growth are improving.
這家韓國製造商預測下個月會有好轉，因為國內需求和出口的成長都在改善。

profit growth
/ˈprɒfɪt ɡrəʊθ/
It may be easier to focus on the expansion of sales rather than on profit growth.
專注於銷售的擴張而不是利潤的成長，可能比較容易。

THU

IELTS **BASIC WORDS**

survey /ˈsɚˌveɪ/ n. 調查
ENG. a detailed critical inspection
SYS. study, scrutiny

> A **survey** revealed that people riding bikes are more productive at work.
> 一項調查顯示,騎自行車的人在工作上比較有生產力。

同義語 例句
A **close examination** of bike riding showed that it is advantageous.
一項對騎自行車的仔細調查,顯示它是有益的。

同義語 例句
The group's **observation** of bike riders made people aware that bike riding is beneficial.
這個團體對於自行車騎士的觀察,讓人們發現騎自行車是有益的。

反義語 例句
His **assumption** is that many people ride bikes because they do not know how to drive.
他的假設是,許多人騎自行車是因為不懂得怎麼開車。

attempt /əˈtɛmpt/ n. 企圖,嘗試
ENG. earnest or conscientious activity intended to do or accomplish something
SYS. venture, undertaking

> The freshman's **attempt** to ride his bike to school saved him some money.
> 那位大學一年級生騎自行車上學的嘗試,為他省了一些錢。

同義語 例句
His **experiment** of cycling to school to cut fuel costs was successful.
他騎自行車上學省油錢的實驗成功了。

同義語 例句
The boy's best **try** to avoid being late is riding his bike to school.
那個男孩為了避免遲到的最好的嘗試,是騎自行車上學。

反義語 例句
His **lack of effort** to learn to ride the bike will become a future disadvantage.
他沒有付出努力學騎自行車,會成為他未來的不利條件。

WEEK 6 TOPIC **TRANSPORT**

▶基礎單字擴充

include /ɪnˈkluːd/ v. 包含
ENG. have as a part
SYS. contain, involve

> The government should **include** bike lanes when constructing roads.
> 政府建設道路時應該包含自行車道。

同義語例句 The government must also **take into account** bike riders when legislating traffic laws.
政府立定交通法規時，也必須考慮到自行車騎士。

同義語例句 Traffic laws must also **consist of** rules that apply to bike riders.
交通法規也必須包含適用於自行車騎士的規則。

反義語例句 The city's biggest mistake was **omitting** bicycle facilities from its projects.
這個城市最大的錯誤就是從計畫中刪掉了自行車用的設施。

stage [steɪdʒ] v. 使上演，發動（運動等）
ENG. plan, organise and carry out something
SYS. arrange, organise

> The cyclists **staged** a protest when the police charged a rider with jaywalking.
> 當警察控告一位騎士亂穿越馬路時，自行車騎士們發起了抗議活動。

同義語例句 The Cyclists Association **put together** a rally to show their disagreement with the new laws.
自行車騎士協會安排了一場群眾集會來表示他們對於新法規的不同意。

同義語例句 The Bike Group **arranged** a meeting with the authorities about the new road rules.
自行車團體安排了一場與當局討論新道路規則的會議。

反義語例句 The government **prevented** the grand protest of cyclists nationwide from happening.
政府阻止了全國自行車騎士大抗議的發生。

327

THU

TOPIC: Riding bicycles in the city
在城市騎自行車

Those who are **trapped** into driving a car to work every day often have to face a particular **misery** called gridlock. When cars are bumper to bumper, gasoline, time and patience are **squandered**. Commuters **idle** in heavy, blocked traffic while their wages are **transformed** into greenhouse gases and other pollutants. Faced with such problems caused by traffic congestion, many wish they had an **economical**, more environmentally friendly and much healthier way to get to work. Therefore, some people **opt** to ride their bikes to work instead. These bike commuters **hustle** past thousands of **immobilised** cars while travelling to work, getting healthy exercise and improving their **stamina** every day on their commute. By cycling to work, you can save your money and save our planet at the same time.

TRANS

那些每天不得不開車上班的人，經常必須面臨叫做交通大堵塞的苦難。當車輛前車貼後車的時候，汽油、時間和耐性都被揮霍了。通勤族在繁忙而堵塞的交通中無所事事，而他們的薪水變成了溫室氣體和其他污染物。面對這些因交通堵塞而造成的問題，許多人希望他們有經濟、更環保而且健康得多的上班方式。所以，有些人選擇改為騎自行車上班。這些自行車通勤族在上班時快速越過數千輛動彈不得的汽車，每天通勤路上都做到健康的運動並且促進他們的活力。藉由騎自行車上班，你可以同時省下自己的金錢，並且拯救我們的星球。

trap
/træp/

v. 使受困

Many people are still **trapped** under the walls that collapsed during the earthquake.
許多人仍然受困於地震時倒塌的牆下。

misery
/ˈmɪzəri/

n. 苦難

Debt problems can occur at any time and cause **misery**.
債務問題隨時都可能發生並造成痛苦。

squander
/ˈskwɒndə/

v. 浪費，揮霍

The teenager **squandered** his weekly allowance away at the mall.　這個年輕人在購物中心揮霍了他當週的零用錢。

idle
/ˈʌɪdəl/

v. 無所事事　adj. 無所事事的，懶惰的

It is important to get daily physical activity because being **idle** makes us unhealthy.
每天做身體的活動很重要，因為怠惰會讓我們不健康。

transform
/transˈfɔːm/

v. 轉變

The lizard **transformed** the colour of its skin in order to match its environment.
這隻蜥蜴改變了牠皮膚的顏色以配合環境。

economical
/iːkəˈnɒmɪkəl/

adj. 節約的，經濟的

Regular servicing often proves more **economical** than repairing following a breakdown.
定期保養往往證明會比故障後再維修更經濟。

opt
/ɒpt/

v. 選擇

If you had **opted** to open the door to your left, you would have won a car.
如果你剛才選擇開你左邊的門，你就會贏得一輛車。

hustle
/ˈhʌsəl/

v. 硬推，急速行進

You'll have to **hustle** if you hope to get to the train on time.
如果你想準時趕上列車，就要加快腳步。

immobilised
/ɪˈməʊbɪlʌɪzd/

adj. 被固定的，不能動的

Her neck was **immobilised** by the neck brace the paramedics put on her.
她的脖子被急救人員用護頸固定。

stamina
/ˈstamɪnə/

n. 耐力，精力

Running every day can improve your **stamina**.
每天跑步可以增進你的耐力。

WORD TRAINING | 重點單字造句練習

lane
/leɪn/

n. 巷子，車道

💬 I will follow traffic rules from now on to avoid a bus lane violation.
我從現在起會遵守交通規則，避免違規進入公車道。

Traffic is inevitable even if we have plenty of lanes for different vehicles.
交通（流量）是不可避免的，即使我們有足夠的車道給不同車輛。

✏️ The government will be promoting the usage of bikes, which means it will be reducing parts of the road to give way to new bike lanes.
政府將會推動自行車的使用，意思是政府將會縮減道路的一部分，讓新的自行車道使用。

In addition to its obvious health benefits and economical advantage, riding a bike has become more convenient because of the city's additional bike lanes.
除了明顯的健康效益與省錢優點以外，騎自行車也因為這個城市增加額外的自行車道而變得更加便利。

---

path
/pɑːθ/

n. 小徑，路線

💬 An important bicycle path is missing on the map.
地圖上遺漏了一條重要的自行車小徑。

The best way to get to town is to cycle along the valley path.
去城裡最好的方法是沿著山谷的路徑騎自行車。

✏️ Since the big bumps and holes on that path are dangerous for cyclists, the government has built a cycle track as an alternative.
因為那條小徑的大隆起和坑洞對於自行車騎士很危險，所以政府建設了一條自行車專用道作為替代。

In order to accommodate changing demands and to encourage an active lifestyle, the city paved a new path for cyclists.
為了適應改變中的需求，並且鼓勵多運動的生活型態，市政府為自行車騎士鋪設了一條新的路徑。

口說範例 寫作範例

fare
/fɛː/

n. 票價

💬 To avoid paying a fare for public transport, try cycling to work.
為了避免支付公共運輸的票價，試試看騎腳踏車上班。

The city is planning to raise bus fares despite the decline in public transport use.
即使公共運輸的使用率下降，市政府還是計畫要調漲公車票價。

📝 Instead of paying public transport fares, you can cycle to work for free and be eco-friendly at the same time.
你可以不用付公共運輸票價，而是免費騎自行車上班，同時還能保護環境。

Cycling commuters can not only keep in good shape but also save money because they don't have to pay for fuel or bus fares.
自行車通勤族不僅能保持健康，還能省錢，因為他們不必付汽油或公車票價的錢。

carry
/ˈkari/

n. 運送，輸送

💬 It is dangerous for such a small school bus to carry so many students.
讓這麼小的校車搭載這麼多學生很危險。

The Underground carries more than three million passengers every day.
倫敦地下鐵每天運送超過三百萬名乘客。

📝 They claim that the spaceship is very sophisticated and that it can carry six people while staying in the lunar orbit.
他們宣稱這艘太空船非常精密，而且可以在停留在月球軌道的同時搭載六個人。

Our space technology already went farther than imagined, and in fact, before 1960, no one predicted that rockets would actually be able to carry humans into space.
我們的太空科技已經超越了想像，事實上，在 1960 年之前，沒有人預測到火箭將可以真的搭載人類進入太空。

RELATED WORDS | 相關單字延伸

ineffective
adj. 沒有效果的

unused
adj. 沒有使用的

idle
adj. 無所事事的，懶惰的

stagnant
adj. 停滯的

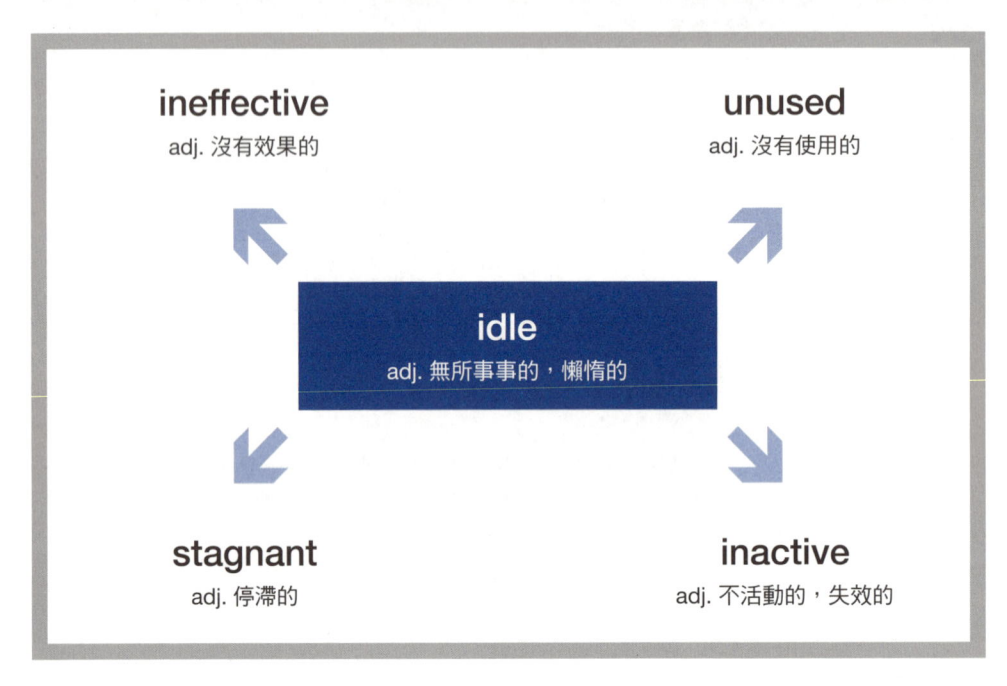

inactive
adj. 不活動的，失效的

---

idle
/ˈʌɪdəl/

Commuters idle in heavy, blocked traffic while their wages are transformed into greenhouse gases and other pollutants.
通勤族在繁忙而堵塞的交通中無所事事，而他們的薪水變成了溫室氣體及其他污染物。

ineffective
/ˌɪnɪˈfɛktɪv/

Single-lane roadways prove ineffective in our city during rush hour.
結果證明，單線道路在本市的尖峰時間是沒有效果的。

stagnant
/ˈstagnənt/

It seems as though traffic on Main Street is stagnant between 3:30 and 7:00pm on weekdays.
主街的交通似乎在平日下午 3:30 到 7:00 之間是停滯的。

unused
/ʌnˈjuːzd/

The high-occupancy vehicle lanes on that highway are largely unused when traffic is slow.
那條高速公路的高乘載車道，在交通緩慢的時候大部分沒有被使用。

inactive
/ɪnˈaktɪv/

When the power goes out and traffic lights are inactive, many accidents occur.
當停電而紅綠燈失效時，許多事故會發生。

USEFUL EXPRESSIONS | 相關實用片語

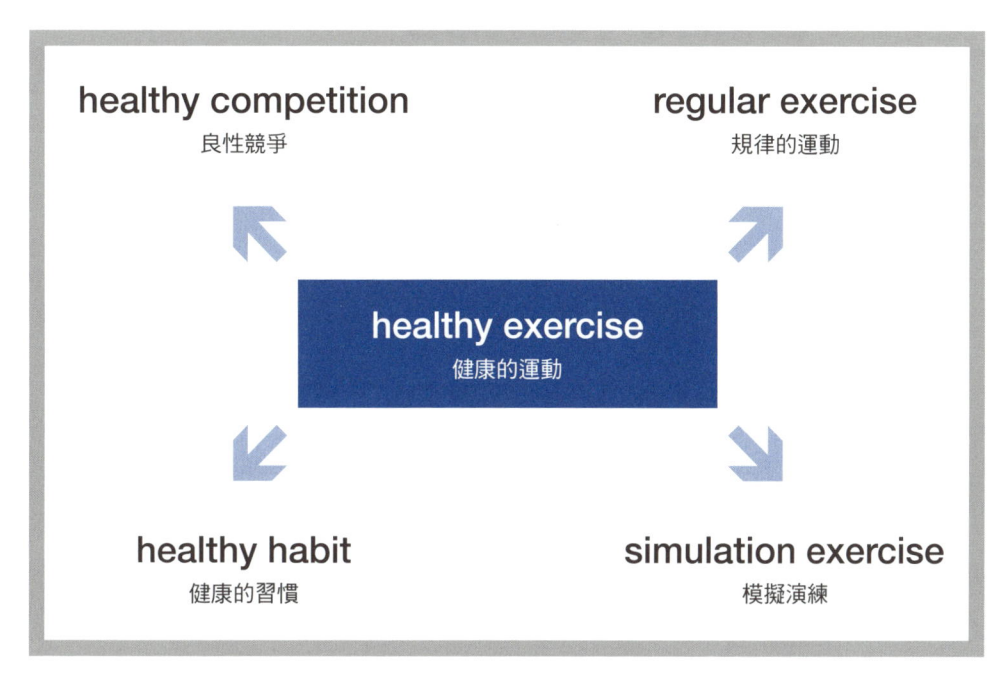

```
        healthy competition              regular exercise
           良性競爭                          規律的運動
                ↖                        ↗
                     healthy exercise
                        健康的運動
                ↙                        ↘
          healthy habit                simulation exercise
           健康的習慣                         模擬演練
```

healthy exercise
/ˈhɛlθi ˈɛksəsaɪz/

It is necessary to get healthy exercise besides limiting calorie intake to achieve weight loss.
要能減肥，除了限制熱量攝取以外，也必須做健康的運動。

healthy competition
/ˈhɛlθi kɒmpɪˈtɪʃən/

Some say that healthy competition among private schools will widen students' choices.
有些人說私立學校之間的良性競爭可以拓展學生的選擇。

healthy habit
/ˈhɛlθi ˈhæbɪt/

When you have a problem that you've long neglected, an effective solution is to develop healthy habits to deal with it.
當你有一個被你長期忽略的問題時，一個有效的解決辦法就是培養健康的習慣來處理它。

regular exercise
/ˈrɛgjʊlə ˈɛksəsaɪz/

Those suffering from pneumonia can benefit from regular exercise and a balanced diet.
罹患肺炎的人，可以從規律的運動與均衡的飲食中受益。

simulation exercise
/sɪmjuːˈleɪʃən ˈɛksəsaɪz/

Worrying about a possible pandemic, the mayor has advised to organise simulation exercises in hospitals.
因為擔心疾病可能會大流行，所以市長建議在醫院安排模擬演練。

FRI

IELTS BASIC WORDS

vanish /ˈvænɪʃ/ v. 消失
ENG. to disappear quickly from sight
SYS. exit, dwindle

> The drunk driver **vanished** right after the big accident.
> 那名酒醉駕駛在重大事故後馬上消失不見。

同義語例句 The victim's possessions **were lost** in the car crash.
受害者的財物在車禍中不見了。

同義語例句 As the smoke **faded away**, the crash scene became more visible to the passers-by.
當煙霧散去，路過的人就比較能看見車禍現場。

反義語例句 After the car crash, a number of paramedics quickly **showed up** to help.
在車禍之後，一些急救人員迅速現身幫忙。

deteriorate /dɪˈtɪərɪəreɪt/ v. 惡化，退化，變壞
ENG. to diminish or impair in quality
SYS. degenerate, worsen

> Because of the accidental blow to his head, his memory is **deteriorating**.
> 因為他的頭部遭受的意外撞擊，他的記憶力正在惡化。

同義語例句 After the car crash, his mental cognition **became worse** as the days went by.
在車禍之後，他的心智認知能力隨著日子過去而變差。

同義語例句 His rehabilitation stopped when his car crashed, and everything **went downhill** from there.
當他的車子撞毀，他的復健就停了下來，而一切從此之後就每況愈下。

反義語例句 His injuries from the car crash are expected to **get better** in a few weeks.
他在車禍中受的傷預期在幾個星期之後將會好轉。

WEEK 6 TOPIC **TRANSPORT**

▶基礎單字擴充

confidence /ˈkɒnfɪdəns/ n. 信心
ENG. the feeling that one can rely on someone or something
SYS. trust, belief

> He has the **confidence** that air bags can save his life during a crash.
> 他有信心安全氣囊可以在車禍時拯救他的生命。

同義語例句 He put his **full trust** in the airbags when he lost his brakes.
煞車失靈的時候，他把所有信任都寄託於安全氣囊。

同義語例句 He was in a **state of assurance** when the airbags went off during his crash.
當安全氣囊在車禍中彈出來時，他處在很有信心的狀態。

反義語例句 His **lack of faith** in his car made him purchase a new one to avoid accidents.
他對自己車子缺乏信心，使得他買了一台新車以避免車禍。

practice /ˈpræktɪs/ n. 練習
ENG. systematic training by multiple repetitions
SYS. rehearsal, exercise

> It takes **practice** to become a good driver and avoid accidents.
> 要成為好的駕駛並且避免事故，需要練習。

同義語例句 **Repeated exercise** of defensive driving will help avoid road accidents.
反覆練習防禦性駕駛，有助於避免道路交通事故。

同義語例句 **What leads to good** driving **skills** is nothing but actual driving.
能夠養成良好的駕駛技巧的，就只有實際駕駛而已。

反義語例句 His **first attempt** at driving resulted in a crash with another vehicle.
他第一次嘗試駕駛，造成了和其他車輛的車禍。

FRI

TOPIC: How to reduce road casualties
如何減少車禍造成的傷亡

Car crash-related deaths and injuries are largely **preventable**. To reduce road casualties, we should seek improvements in several **domains** including vehicle safety, roadway safety and road user behaviour. First, **manufacturers** must be required by law to **engineer** cars that meet a minimum safety standard, and car owners should not **neglect** any repairs needed. As to roadway safety, motorists may blame roadway design for accidents, but usually it is not the cause. In fact, it is poor road maintenance that contributes to a large number of **collisions**, so cities should **adopt** standards to ensure that signage is maintained, construction sites are well marked and roads are salted in poor conditions. Lastly, behaviour can be improved by **protective** policies including seatbelt and child safety seat legislation. The proper use of occupant **restraints** remains the most cost-effective method available to **curtail** death, injuries and economic loss resulting from motor vehicle collisions.

TRANS

車禍造成的死亡與傷害大部分是可以預防的。為了減少車禍傷亡，我們應該追求幾個領域的改善，包括車輛安全、道路安全與用路人的行為。首先，製造商必須被法律要求，設計符合最低安全標準的汽車，而車主不應該疏忽任何必要的修理。至於道路安全，駕駛人可能會把事故歸咎於道路的設計，但它通常不是造成事故的原因。事實上，是糟糕的道路保養造成許多衝突事故，所以城市應該採用標準，確保交通標誌受到維護、工地有清楚標示，而且路況不好時灑鹽（防止結凍）。最後，行為可以藉由包括安全帶與兒童安全座椅立法等保護性政策得到改善。正確使用安全帶（乘客約束裝置）仍然是減少汽車衝撞造成的死傷與經濟損失最有成本效益的方法。

preventable /prɪˈvɛntəbəl/
adj. 可預防的
Forest fires are **preventable** provided that people employ common sense when using flammable materials.
只要大家在使用易燃材料時運用常識，那麼森林火災是可以預防的。

domain /dəʊˈmeɪn/
n. 領域
He oversees many **domains** within the company, including payroll and training of new employees.
他監督公司內許多領域，包括發薪與新進員工的訓練。

manufacturer /ˌmænjʊˈfæktʃərə/
n. 製造商
Toy **manufacturers** in China were sued for using lead-based paint on the figurines.
中國的玩具製造商被控告在小塑像上使用含鉛塗料。

engineer /ˌɛndʒɪˈnɪə/
n. 工程師　v. 設計製造
Weak protection laws enabled domestic producers to reverse-**engineer** and imitate foreign technologies.　沒有影響力的保護法規，使得國內的生產者能夠進行逆向工程，並且模仿國外的科技。

neglect /nɪˈglɛkt/
v. 忽略
If you **neglect** washing under your fingernails daily, you could get infected.　如果你忽略每天洗你的指甲，你可能會被感染。

collision /kəˈlɪʒən/
n. 碰撞
You can avoid **collisions** during a baseball game by shouting when you plan to catch a ball.
你可以藉由在打算接球時叫喊來避免棒球比賽中的碰撞。

adopt /əˈdɒpt/
v. 採用
I plan to **adopt** a new method because I have lost faith in the one I am using now.
我決定採用新的方法，因為我對自己現在使用的方法已經失去了信心。

protective /prəˈtɛktɪv/
adj. 保護的
Many people cover their cell phone screens with a **protective**, removable plastic sheet.
有很多人用保護性的、可移除的塑膠膜覆蓋他們的手機螢幕。

restraint /rɪˈstreɪnt/
n. 限制，束縛
Never use those types of **restraints** when arresting non-violent suspects.
當逮捕非暴力嫌疑犯時，絕對不要使用那些類型的束縛用具。

curtail /kəˈteɪl/
v. 縮短，縮減
I managed to sharply **curtail** the conversation with my bellhop.　我設法快速縮短與旅館行李員的談話。

WORD TRAINING | 重點單字造句練習

interstate
/ˌɪntəˈsteɪt/

n.（美國）州際公路　adj. 州際的

💬 Two teenagers died in a fatal car accident on the interstate.
兩名青少年在州際公路的一場致命車禍中死亡。

On Friday, a car caught fire after a forceful collision with a truck on the interstate.
星期五，一台車在州際公路與卡車強烈撞擊後著火。

✏️ The interstate highway network is generally safe and does not see too many car accidents thanks to policing efforts and highly visible signage.
因為警察巡邏的努力和可見度高的交通標誌的關係，州際公路網通常很安全，而且沒有太多車禍。

When a car accident happens within the city, there are usually fewer fatalities given the lower speed compared to that on an interstate.
當車禍發生在市內，死傷通常比較少，因為車速比州際公路上低。

cargo
/ˈkɑːɡəʊ/

n. 貨物

💬 A truck carrying live chickens as cargo was involved in a car accident on our street yesterday.
昨天一台載著活雞的卡車捲入了我們街上的一場車禍。

He has been injured in a truck accident caused by unsecured cargo.
他曾經在一場因為貨物沒有固定好而造成的卡車車禍中受傷。

✏️ Any experienced driver will tell you that it's vital to take extra caution around trucks with heavy cargo on the road.
任何有經驗的駕駛都會告訴你，在路上接近載著很重的貨物的卡車時，格外小心是很重要的。

Most people who buy pickup trucks are interested in the ability to haul cargo easily, but many owners fail to practise driving before heading out onto accident-prone roads.
大多數買貨卡車的人，是對於能夠輕易運送貨物的能力有興趣，但許多車主並沒有在前往事故好發路段前練習駕駛。

relocation
/riːləʊˈkeɪʃən/

n. 搬遷

💬 On the day of relocation, the truck driver was distracted and caused a collision.
在搬遷的日子，卡車司機分心並且造成了衝撞事故。

The relocation company promises to cover all transport costs, including those in the event of an accident.
搬遷公司承諾支付所有運送費用，包括發生車禍時的費用。

✍ The authorities are worried that the relocation of a cow herd will cause more deaths on the road.
相關當局擔心牛群的遷移會造成路上更多人死亡。

Relocation is a common reason why people use car transport services, and hiring a certified driver minimises the risk of damages caused by an accident.
搬遷是人們使用汽車運輸服務的常見理由，而且雇用合格的駕駛人可以把車禍造成損失的風險降到最低。

span
/spæn/

n. 跨度，期間　v. 跨越

💬 The wreckage from the car accident seemed to span from one side of the road to the other.
車禍的殘骸似乎遍及路的兩側（從一側跨到另一側）。

He has encountered tough times in the span of his NFL career, including a car crash.
他在美國橄欖球聯盟生涯期間遭遇到了一些困難的時期，而這段生涯中包括了一場車禍。

✍ Three eastbound lanes of the bridge are open now following a three-car crash that closed the span for more than an hour.
在造成橋樑東向三線道路封閉超過一小時的三車碰撞事故之後，現在這個範圍的車道開放了。

When you are overly tired, your attention span decreases and reaction times are delayed, which might lead to serious driving consequences, with the worst being susceptibility to accidents.
當你過於疲勞時，你的注意力範圍會減少、反應時間會被延遲，這可能造成嚴重的駕駛後果，最糟的是可能容易發生車禍。

RELATED WORDS | 相關單字延伸

seatbelt
n. 安全帶

band
n. 帶子

restraint
n. 限制，束縛

constraint
n. 限制，抑制

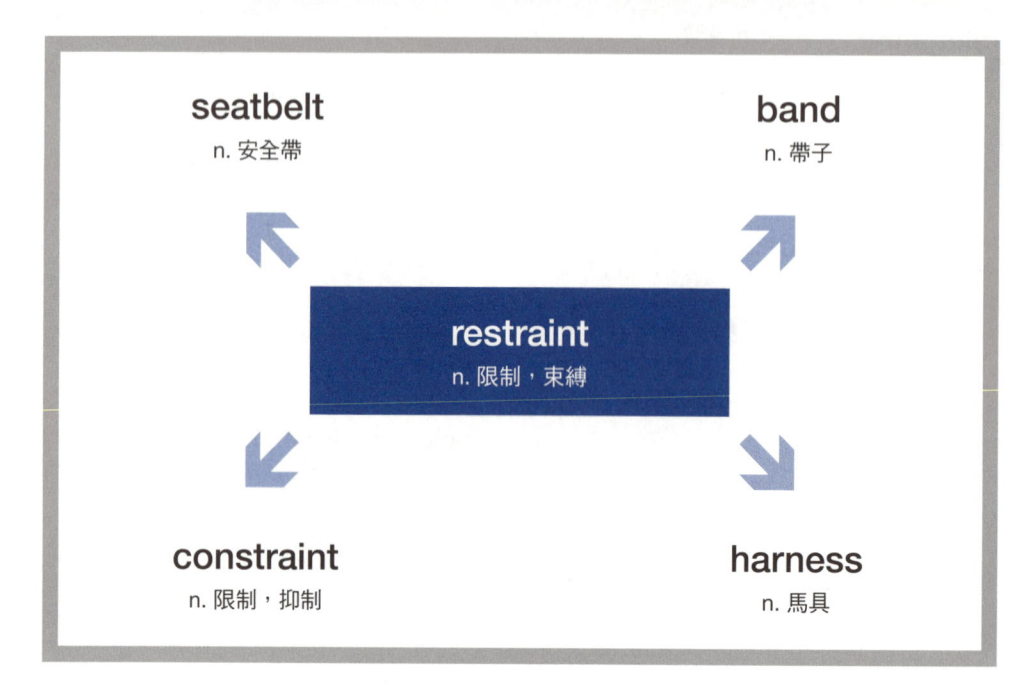

harness
n. 馬具

restraint
/rɪˈstreɪnt/

The proper use of occupant **restraints** remains the most effective method to reduce motor vehicle collision injuries.
正確使用安全帶（乘客約束裝置）仍然是減少汽車衝撞造成的傷害最有效的方法。

seatbelt
/ˈsiːtbɛlt/

If she had been wearing her **seatbelt** when the accident occurred, she would have been unharmed.
要是事故發生時她繫著安全帶，就不會受傷了。

constraint
/kənˈstreɪnt/

There are no **constraints** on the choice of subject for the essay.
文章的主題選擇並沒有限制。

band
/band/

Could you please tighten the **band** around your lap in case of an accident?
可以請您綁緊大腿周圍的帶子以防事故發生嗎？

harness
/ˈhɑːnəs/

I placed my horse in the **harness** to prevent injuries.
我把我的馬用馬具拴住，以避免受傷。

USEFUL EXPRESSIONS | 相關實用片語

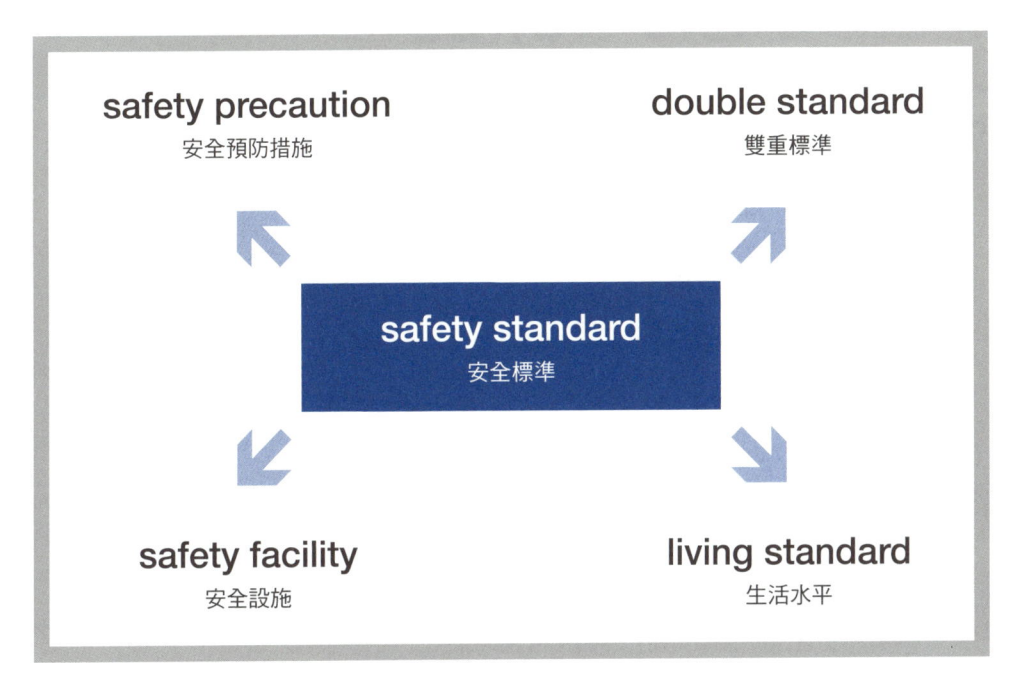

safety precaution
安全預防措施

double standard
雙重標準

safety standard
安全標準

safety facility
安全設施

living standard
生活水平

safety standard
/ˈseɪfti ˈstændəd/
Observing safety standards is top priority for the technicians.
遵守安全標準,對技術人員來說是首要之務。

safety precaution
/ˈseɪfti prɪˈkɔːʃən/
Mountain ski slopes in the area were constructed recklessly without proper safety precautions.
那個地區的山坡滑雪道建設得很草率,沒有做適當的安全預防措施。

safety facility
/ˈseɪfti fəˈsɪlɪti/
The airport, opened in 1969, was equipped with full safety facilities ahead of its time.
這座機場在 1969 年開設,備有領先時代的完整安全設施。

double standard
/ˈdʌbəl ˈstændəd/
Many fans of Martha Stewart became upset about the media's double standards toward her.
Martha Stewart 的許多影迷對於媒體對她的雙重標準感到生氣。

living standard
/ˈlɪvɪŋ ˈstændəd/
Low living standards and high unemployment rates are forcing many people to look for jobs abroad.
低生活水平與高失業率正迫使許多人尋找國外的工作。

SAT

IELTS BASIC WORDS

dangerous /ˈdeɪndʒərəs/ adj. 危險的
ENG. involving or causing danger or risk
SYS. perilous, harmful

> It will be **dangerous** if the city's transport system remains unimproved.
> 如果本市的運輸系統仍舊不改善，會很危險。

同義語例句 The worsening conditions of the city's transport system could be **life-threatening**.
本市運輸系統惡化中的狀況可能會危及生命。

同義語例句 The city's transport system **lacks security**, causing worry among passengers.　本市的運輸系統缺乏安全性，造成乘客們的擔憂。

反義語例句 With the government's improvement of the transport system, a journey free from **harm** is assured.
因為政府對於運輸系統的改善，確保了在旅程中不會遭受傷害。

contribute /kənˈtrɪbjuːt/ v. 貢獻，出力
ENG. help to cause or bring about
SYS. give, donate

> The public must also **contribute** to the improvement of the transport system by making suggestions.
> 大眾也必須藉由提供建議，對運輸系統的改善出一份力。

同義語例句 It is important for people to **chip in** their ideas for the public transport's improvement.
人們提出改善公共運輸的想法是很重要的。

同義語例句 People must **share** their ideas for the advancement of public transport.
人們必須分享他們的想法，以利公共運輸的進步。

反義語例句 The control over public transport must remain in the possession of the government.
對公共運輸的控制權，必須保持為政府所有。

WEEK 6 TOPIC **TRANSPORT**

▶基礎單字擴充

transport /trænˈspɔːt/ v. 運輸，運送
ENG. move something or somebody around
SYS. transfer, deliver

> A new system must be added to **transport** not only people but also cargo.
> 必須加入新的系統，以便不止是運送人群，也運送貨物。

同義語例句 People can now **send** their cargo **to** other places with the new transport system.
人們現在可以用新的運輸系統將他們的貨物寄送到其他地方。

同義語例句 It is now possible for people to have their cargo **delivered** to other cities with ease.
人們現在能夠輕易地讓他們的貨物被送到其他城市。

反義語例句 People have no choice but to **leave behind** large cargo when travelling. 人們別無選擇，只能在旅行時將大型貨物留下。

fact /fakt/ n. 事實
ENG. knowledge or information based on real occurrences
SYS. truth, actuality

> The **fact** is that it is the government's duty to improve our transport system.
> 事實是，改善我們的運輸系統是政府的義務。

同義語例句 The **truth** is that it is up to the government to improve the transport system.
事實是，改善運輸系統是政府的責任。

同義語例句 The **reality of the situation** is that it is the government's responsibility to improve the transport system.
真實的情況是，改善運輸系統是政府的責任。

反義語例句 I heard a **rumour** that taxpayers will be shouldering the development cost of the new transport system.
我聽到傳言說納稅人將要負擔新運輸系統的開發成本。

SAT

TOPIC: The government's duty to improve the transport system
政府改善運輸系統的義務

Every major city needs a **reliable** public transport system. As taxpayers' money has been spent on public transport such as bus and tram, they should expect the government to provide satisfactory services that cater to most people's need. With the recent increase in **fuel** prices, many people would be willing to use public transport **assuming** that improvements were made. At a time when we need to **drastically** improve public transport to provide increased **mobility** and reduce environmental consequences, increasing efficiency is particularly important. Programmes for increasing public transport efficiency usually run on a **continuum** ranging from making **incremental improvements** to individual public transit **routes** to coordinating multiple routes and improving them across the board. One more improvement the government can also make is to introduce hybrid electric buses, which are cleaner and more energy-efficient than the ones which solely run on **diesel**.

TRANS

每個主要城市都需要可靠的公共運輸系統。因為納稅人的錢被用在諸如公車、輕軌電車之類的公共運輸工具上，他們應該期望政府提供符合大部分人的需要、令人滿意的服務。隨著最近燃料價格上漲，假如有所改善的話，大部分的人應該會願意使用公共運輸。在我們需要大幅改善公共運輸以提供更高的機動性並減少環境影響的時刻，提升效率尤其重要。提升公共交通效率的計畫，通常介於對個別公共運輸路線逐漸進行改善，以及結合許多路線並且全面改善的兩種做法之間。還有一個政府可以進行的改善，是採用油電混合公車，它們比單純靠柴油運作的公車來得乾淨而且更有能源效率。

reliable
/rɪˈlaɪəbəl/

adj. 可靠的

Gossip magazines and tabloids are not very **reliable** sources of information.
八卦雜誌與小報不是非常可靠的消息來源。

fuel
/fjuːəl/

n. 燃料

It is the job of the department to maintain and check the engine's **fuel** efficiency.
維護與檢查引擎的燃料效率是這個部門的工作。

assuming
/əˈsjuːmɪŋ/

conj. 假設⋯

She will take you out for ice cream **assuming** you are not lactose intolerant.
假如你沒有乳糖不耐症的話，她會帶你出去吃冰淇淋。

drastically
/ˈdræstɪkli/

adv. 大幅地

The final sentence for the criminal was announced today, with a **drastically** reduced penalty.
對罪犯的最後判決今天宣布了，處罰被大幅減少。

mobility
/məʊˈbɪləti/

n. 移動性，機動性

A motorised wheelchair is an excellent investment for the elderly with **mobility** issues.
電動輪椅對有行動問題的老人家是一項很棒的投資。

continuum
/kənˈtɪnjʊəm/

n. 連續

An alternative solution can lie somewhere on the **continuum** between the two extremes.
替代的解決方案可能位於兩個極端之間的某個地方。

incremental
/ˌɪŋkrɪˈmɛntəl/

adj. 遞增的

The company has suspended its **incremental** pay progression policy. 這家公司中止了它的薪資漸增政策。

improvement
/ɪmˈpruːvmənt/

n. 改善，改進

Thanks to the government's efforts, the **improvements** of the public transport system are now evident.
多虧有政府的努力，公共運輸系統的改善現在顯而易見。

route
/ruːt/

n. 路線

Always check the **route** number of the bus to know where it goes. 永遠要查看公車路線號碼以得知公車會去的地方。

diesel
/ˈdiːzəl/

n. 柴油

People are slowly replacing traditional **diesel** in favour of biodiesel. 人們正慢慢地將傳統柴油替換為生質柴油。

WORD TRAINING | 重點單字造句練習

bill of lading
/bɪl əv ˈleɪdɪŋ/

n.（海運等的）提單（證明貨物由承運人接管或裝船的單據）

A truck driver must give the bill of lading to his or her employer, who then reports it to the government.
卡車司機必須把提單交給雇主，而雇主隨後會向政府報告。

Discrepancies in bills of lading should be dealt with by the companies involved, not the government.
提單內容的不一致，應該由牽涉的公司處理，而不是由政府處理。

Shipping management software can facilitate the management of bills of ladings, enhance your customer service and reduce overall freight costs.
運輸管理軟體可以使提單的管理變得容易、提升顧客服務，並且減少整體的貨運成本。

Bills of ladings issued by the shipper provide the basic document for road freight, and inspecting them allows the government to improve the overall transport system.
由運送業者發出的提單，提供道路貨運的基本文件，而檢視這些單據能讓政府改善整體運輸系統。

electricity
/ˌɪlɛkˈtrɪsɪti/

n. 電力

When it comes to making transportation more environmentally friendly, vehicles powered by electricity play a central role.
說到讓交通變得更環保，由電力驅動的車輛扮演了核心的角色。

Using vehicles powered by electricity could significantly reduce a commuter's transport costs.
使用由電力驅動的車輛有可能大幅降低通勤者的交通費用。

Despite today's increased use of renewable resources to generate electricity, many people still question whether electric cars are really much more eco-friendly than those running on petrol.
雖然現今已經更常使用再生資源產生電力，但許多人還是質疑電力車是否真的比石油驅動的車來得環保許多。

Vehicles powered by electricity have higher energy efficiency than those running on petrol, but some people feel turned off by their lack of speed.
電力驅動的車比石油驅動的車具有更高的能源效率，但有些人對它們缺乏速度感到倒胃口。

charge
/tʃɑːdʒ/

n. 收費，費用　v. 收費

💬 How much does the government charge taxpayers every year to sustain the country's transport systems?
政府每年向納稅人收多少錢來維持國家的交通系統？

The government could impose a charge on property owners near a new or improved transport hub.
政府可以向位於新的或改善過的交通樞紐附近的地主徵收費用。

✏️ Due to the rising costs of fuel and government taxation, distributors are now taking measures to increase their minimum charge for freight shipping.
由於燃料費用與政府課稅增加，經銷商正在採取措施，增加貨運的最低收費。

Improved fee collection system can increase the efficiency of collecting individual motorists' charges for using the highway.
改善過的收費系統，可以增加向個別駕駛人收取高速公路使用費的效率。

carrier
/ˈkærɪə/

n. 運輸公司

💬 At the initiative of a national carrier and freight forwarder, a non-government and non-profit organisation was established.
由於一間全國性貨運公司暨貨運代理公司的發起，一個非政府、非營利組織成立了。

The government aims to enhance the service quality in road carrier and freight forwarder industries.
政府的目標是提升道路貨運與貨運代理業界的服務品質。

✏️ As a logistics manager, I am committed to working with suppliers, forward warehouse operators, distributors and the carrier to improve the speed of delivery.
身為物流經理，我致力於和供應商、代理倉儲營運商、經銷商以及貨運公司合作，以提升運送速度。

The Federal Government must actively pursue agreements to improve U.S. carriers' access to international markets.　聯邦政府必須積極爭取協議，增進美國的運輸公司進入國際市場的能力。

RELATED WORDS | 相關單字延伸

dependable
adj. 可靠的

responsible
adj. 負責的

reliable
adj. 可靠的

trustworthy
adj. 值得信賴的

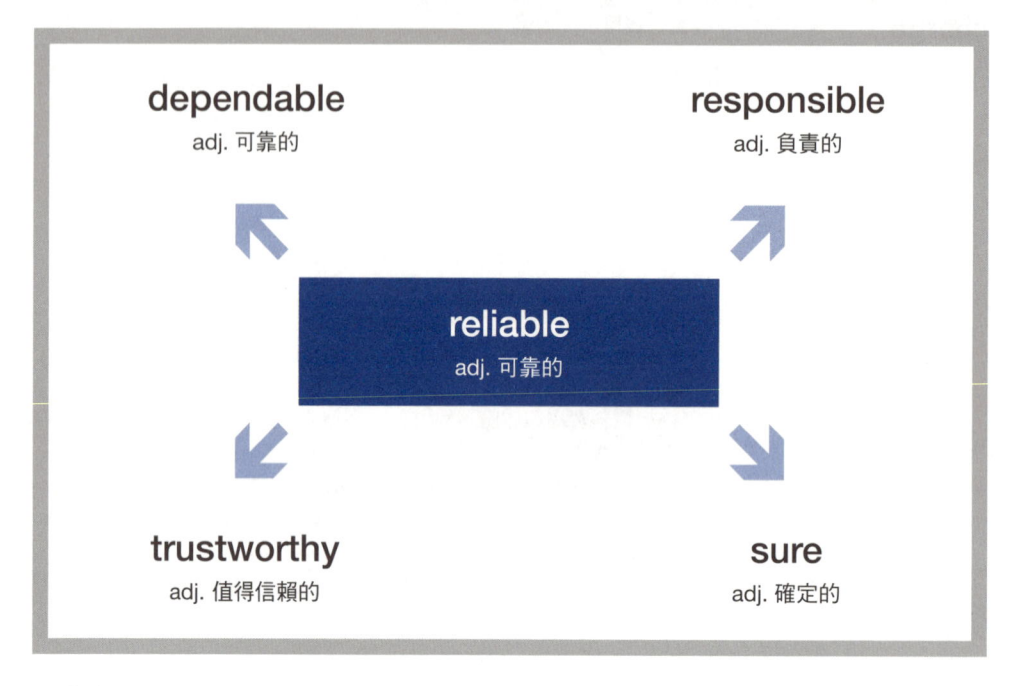

sure
adj. 確定的

reliable
/rɪˈlaɪəbəl/

Trains and subways are very reliable, especially during rush hour.
火車與地鐵非常可靠,尤其是在尖峰時段。

dependable
/dɪˈpɛndəbəl/

Riding bicycles is not dependable, especially when you are running late or dressed formally.
騎自行車是不可靠的,尤其是當你快要遲到或是穿著正式服裝時。

trustworthy
/ˈtrʌstwɜːði/

A reckless bus driver is never trustworthy when it comes to your safety as a commuter.
說到你身為通勤者的安全,一個開車魯莽的公車駕駛絕對是不值得信任的。

responsible
/rɪˈspɒnsɪbəl/

Drivers should be very responsible, especially when driving a public utility vehicle.
駕駛員應該要非常有責任感,特別是在駕駛公用交通車輛時。

sure
/ʃɔː/

I am not sure at what time exactly I will arrive because of the heavy traffic.
因為交通繁忙,所以我不確定我到達的準確時間。

USEFUL EXPRESSIONS | 相關實用片語

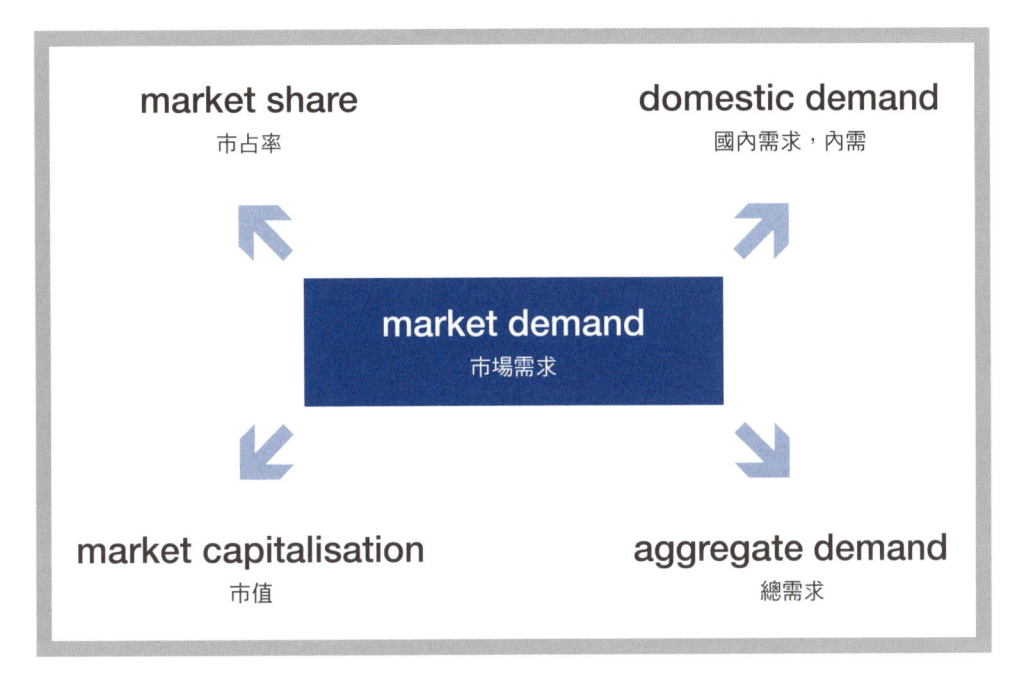

market share
市占率

domestic demand
國內需求，內需

market demand
市場需求

market capitalisation
市值

aggregate demand
總需求

---

market demand
/ˈmɑːkɪt dɪˈmɑːnd/

In Korea, the market demand for import automobiles has risen despite the slowing economy.
在韓國，儘管經濟趨緩，但對於進口汽車的市場需求上升了。

market share
/ˈmɑːkɪt ʃɛː/

In terms of overall market share, Apple's music player falls behind those of local manufacturers.
就整體市占率而言，蘋果的音樂播放器落後本地製造商的產品。

market capitalisation
/ˈmɑːkɪt ˌkapɪtəlʌɪˈzeɪʃən/

The movie theatre operator has a market capitalisation of an estimated 577.2 billion won.
這家經營電影院的公司有估計 5772 億韓元的市值。

domestic demand
/dəˈmɛstɪk dɪˈmɑːnd/

Japan's domestic demand, according to the IMF, is strengthening thanks to corporate investments and a strong labour market.
根據 IMF（國際貨幣基金組織）的說法，由於企業投資以及強大的勞動力市場，日本的內需正在增強。

aggregate demand
/ˈagrɪgət dɪˈmɑːnd/

The aggregate demand for goods must not be larger than the total amount of resources.
對商品的總需求絕對不能大於資源的總量。

SUN

IELTS **BASIC WORDS**

compare /kəmˈpɛr/ v. 比較
ENG. to consider or describe as similar
SYS. equate, liken

> We can **compare** the past and present to get an idea of the future transport system.
> 我們可以比較以前與現在，以獲得對於未來運輸系統的想法。

同義語 例句 — **Setting** the past **against** the present transport system is an unfair comparison.
把過去和現在的運輸系統相比，是不公平的比較。

同義語 例句 — If we **match** the past **with** today's transport system, we may be restricting its possibilities in the future.
如果我們把過去和今日的運輸系統相比，我們可能是在限制它未來的可能性。

反義語 例句 — It is illogical to **take** the past and present transport systems **separately**.
分別看待過去和現在的運輸系統是不合邏輯的。

encourage /ɪnˈkʌrɪdʒ/ v. 鼓勵
ENG. inspire with confidence; give hope or courage to
SYS. cheer, reassure

> People are **encouraged** to be creative to invent new means of transport in the future.
> 人們被鼓勵要有創意，並且在未來發明新的交通運輸方式。

同義語 例句 — Teachers **stimulate** their students to think of a possible transport system for the future.
老師們激勵學生想出未來可能的運輸系統。

同義語 例句 — Scientists are **urged on** to innovate and improve existing transport systems.
科學家們被鼓勵創新，並且改善現有的運輸系統。

反義語 例句 — The government is **deprived of** hope for the invention of an innovative transport system.
政府對於發明創新的運輸系統不抱希望。

350

WEEK 6 TOPIC **TRANSPORT**

▶ 基礎單字擴充

endure /ɪnˈdjʊə/ v. 忍受
ENG. to carry on through, despite hardships
SYS. tolerate, accept

> We must **endure** the drawbacks of our current transport systems until future innovations emerge.
> 我們必須忍受現有運輸系統的缺點，直到未來的創新出現。

同義語例句 We should **put up with** the disadvantages we suffer today in some outdated transport systems.
我們應該容忍今日在某些過時的運輸系統中遭遇到的缺點。

同義語例句 We should learn to **live with** the fact that transport systems have their disadvantages.
我們應該學會接受運輸系統有自己的缺點。

反義語例句 Some **refuse to suffer** commuting via outdated transport systems, so they buy their own cars.
有些人拒絕忍受用過時的運輸系統通勤的痛苦，所以他們購買自己的車。

integrate /ˈɪntɪɡreɪt/ v. 整合
ENG. to make into a whole by bringing all parts together
SYS. incorporate, amalgamate

> It is ideal to **integrate** recent technology into old transport systems to improve them.
> 將最近的科技整合到舊的運輸系統以求改善，是很理想的做法。

同義語例句 Developers try to **combine** the safety features of old transport systems and today's innovations.
開發者們努力將舊運輸系統的安全特色和今日的創新結合。

同義語例句 It would be easier if we **join together** in coming up with new means of transport.
如果我們一起構想新的交通方式，就會比較容易。

反義語例句 Let us **break down** our current transportation systems into components and analyse how to improve them.
讓我們將現在的運輸系統的構成要素分解出來，並且分析如何改善。

351

SUN

TOPIC | Imagining the transport of the future
想像未來的交通運輸

In the future, mass **transit** will be low cost, personalised and more environmentally friendly. Also, fuel-efficient, zero emission vehicles will use high technology to assist drivers in a wide variety of ways. Vehicles will **converse** with each other, with the road and with traffic signals. They will also use vision **enhancement** devices to **navigate** through bad weather and warn drivers of a possible collision with a **pedestrian** or animal. If you are getting drowsy or **straying** from your lane, they will let you know. The ultimate goal of future vehicles is driverless cars. In the future, we will relax during swift, smooth commutes free from **aggressive** lane changes, defensive brake-tapping and road rage as our vehicles **chauffeur** by themselves. Many **foresee** high **occupancy** vehicle lanes filled with fast-moving robotic cars carrying commuters reading e-mails and working on their laptops.

TRANS　在未來，大眾運輸將會是低費用、個人化而且更環保的。而且，有能源效率、零排放的車輛將會使用高科技，以各種方式協助駕駛者。車輛將會和彼此、和道路以及交通號誌溝通。它們也會使用視覺強化設備在惡劣天氣中行駛，並且警告駕駛人可能撞上行人或動物。如果你變得昏昏欲睡或者偏離車道，它們會讓你知道。未來車輛的終極目標是無人駕駛汽車。在未來，我們將會在迅速、順暢的通勤路途中放鬆，沒有激烈的變換車道、防禦性的踩剎車和道路上的暴躁駕駛行為，而我們的車輛會自行駕駛。許多人預測高承載車輛車道將充滿快速行動的機器人車輛，裡面載著閱讀電子郵件以及用筆記型電腦工作的通勤者。

transit
/ˈtransɪt/

n. 運輸

Nowadays, the Australian government is rapidly developing a public **transit** system.
現在，澳洲政府正快速發展公共運輸系統。

converse
/kənˈvəːs/

v. 交談

You can **converse** with the store manager to know more about the product.
你可以和店經理交談，以得知更多關於產品的訊息。

enhancement
/ɪnˈhɑːnsmənt/

n. 提高，提升，改善

Clean Water Projects have led to the **enhancement** of millions of people's quality of life.
乾淨用水計畫已經提升了數百萬人的生活品質。

navigate
/ˈnavɪɡeɪt/

v. 航行，導航，駕駛

If you cannot **navigate** a canal without hitting the side, you shouldn't be the captain.
如果你無法在運河航行而不撞到旁邊，你就不應該當船長。

pedestrian
/pɪˈdɛstrɪən/

n. 行人

The **pedestrian** crossed the road quickly to avoid being hit by oncoming traffic.　行人快速穿越馬路以避免被來車撞上。

stray
/streɪ/

v. 偏離

The boy scouts refrained from **straying** off the trail because they were afraid of bears.
童子軍避免離開路徑，因為他們害怕熊。

aggressive
/əˈɡrɛsɪv/

adj. 侵略性的，積極強硬的

The photographer was **aggressive** when trying to snap a shot of the singer.
那位攝影者試圖拍下歌手的照片時很有侵犯性。

chauffeur
/ˈʃəʊfə/

v. 當汽車司機

My mom will **chauffeur** us on weekends as long as we promise to train hard.
只要我們保證努力接受訓練，我媽媽就會開車載我們。

foresee
/fɔːˈsiː/

v. 預見

The professor could **foresee** what was going to happen to me after graduation.
那位教授當時能夠預見我畢業後會發生什麼事。

occupancy
/ˈɒkjəpənsi/

n. 佔用，汽車承載人數

The taxi did not pick up our party because of the car's maximum **occupancy** of four persons only.
那輛計程車沒有載我們這群人，因為車子的最大承載人數只有四個人。

WORD TRAINING | 重點單字造句練習

transference
/ˈtrænsfərəns/

n. 轉移，（財產的）轉讓

💬 To make a smooth transference of vehicles, the bus company and the government seek to reach an agreement.
為了順利轉讓車輛，公車公司和政府試圖達成協議。

A proper transference of government-owned vehicles should be made before they are transported overseas.
在政府擁有的車輛運往海外之前，應該進行適當的轉讓程序。

✍ After the transference of vehicles was complete, the government official thought about the future of public transport system.
在車輛的轉讓完成後，那位政府官員思考大眾運輸系統的未來。

In order to tackle corruption, the government should issue a decree to regulate the transference of property.
為了對付貪污，政府應該發出政令來管制財產的轉讓。

vehicle
/ˈviːɪkəl/

n. 車輛

💬 We should develop more energy-efficient vehicles to improve our environment.
我們應該開發更有能源效率的車輛來改善環境。

The plan to have all vehicles tested for emissions annually was abandoned.
讓所有車輛每年接受排氣測試的計畫被捨棄了。

✍ Only if we can power the vehicle by means other than petrol can we say that it is innovative and environmentally friendly.
只有在我們能以石油以外的方式驅動這台車輛的情況下，我們才能說它是創新又環保的。

The conglomerate, which develops new types of vehicles and transport systems, is interested in financing the city's project of constructing underground railways.
那個開發新型車輛和運輸系統的企業集團，有興趣為這個城市建造地下鐵路的計畫出資。

口說範例 💬　　寫作範例 ✍

airfield
/ˈɛfiːld/

n.（機場）飛機起降、維護的場地

💬 In the future, the city is planning to build a new airfield to accommodate international imports.
這個城市預計在未來建設新的飛行場地，以應對國際的進口。

The airfield is regularly maintained to ensure the airport's ranking in the world remains the same.
飛行場地定期維護，以確保機場在全世界的排名保持相同。

✍ The ground lease stipulates that authorities must update the airfield-use plan at least every ten years and meet prescribed requirements.
地面租約規定，當局必須至少每十年更新飛行場地的使用計畫，並且符合規定的要求。

The airport facility and airfield runways opened this year are testaments to the government's commitment to facilitating air transport.
今年開幕的機場設施與機場跑道，證明了政府致力於讓空中運輸更加便利。

freight
/freɪt/

n. 貨物，貨運

💬 In the future, there may be new and better ways to deliver freight than by ship.
在未來可能會有比船運更新更好的方式來運送貨物。

The world's freight companies may merge in the future to create larger multinational enterprises.
世界的貨運公司在未來可能會合併，創造出更大的跨國企業。

✍ The fast growth of rail freight prompts railway companies to plan capacity expansions while they improve their anti-collision systems at the same time.
鐵路貨物的快速成長，促使鐵路公司在改善防撞系統的同時，也計畫列車容量的擴充。

To reduce the impact of transportation on the environment, we can work on reducing fuel consumption in the freight industry, improving engine efficiency and finding cleaner fuel sources.
要減少交通運輸對環境的影響，我們可以著手於減少貨運業的燃料消耗、改善引擎效率，以及尋找更乾淨的燃料來源。

RELATED WORDS | 相關單字延伸

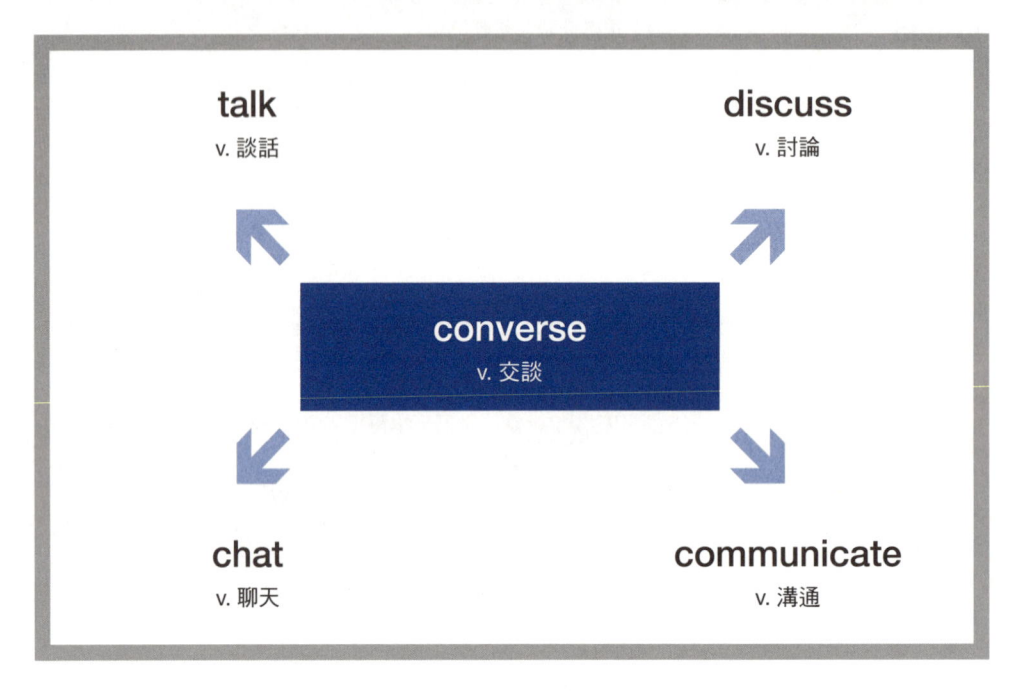

talk
v. 談話

discuss
v. 討論

converse
v. 交談

chat
v. 聊天

communicate
v. 溝通

converse
/kənˈvɜːs/
Vehicles will converse with each other, with the road and with traffic signals in the future.
車輛未來將會和彼此、和道路以及交通號誌溝通。

talk
/tɔːk/
I often talk to my friends using a Bluetooth headset as I drive.
我經常在開車時用藍牙耳機麥克風和我的朋友交談。

chat
/tʃat/
My mother and I will chat over coffee on Sunday afternoon after church service.
我和我媽在星期天上教會之後的下午會喝咖啡聊天。

discuss
/dɪˈskʌs/
I want to discuss the future of communications technology with you.
我想和你討論未來的通訊科技。

communicate
/kəˈmjuːnɪkeɪt/
I wish my vehicle could communicate with traffic signals and change red lights to green ones.
我希望我的車子可以和交通號誌溝通，並且把紅燈變成綠燈。

USEFUL EXPRESSIONS | 相關實用片語

ultimate cause 根本原因

common goal 共同目標

ultimate goal 終極目標

ultimate solution 終極解決方案

sales goal 銷售（營業額）目標

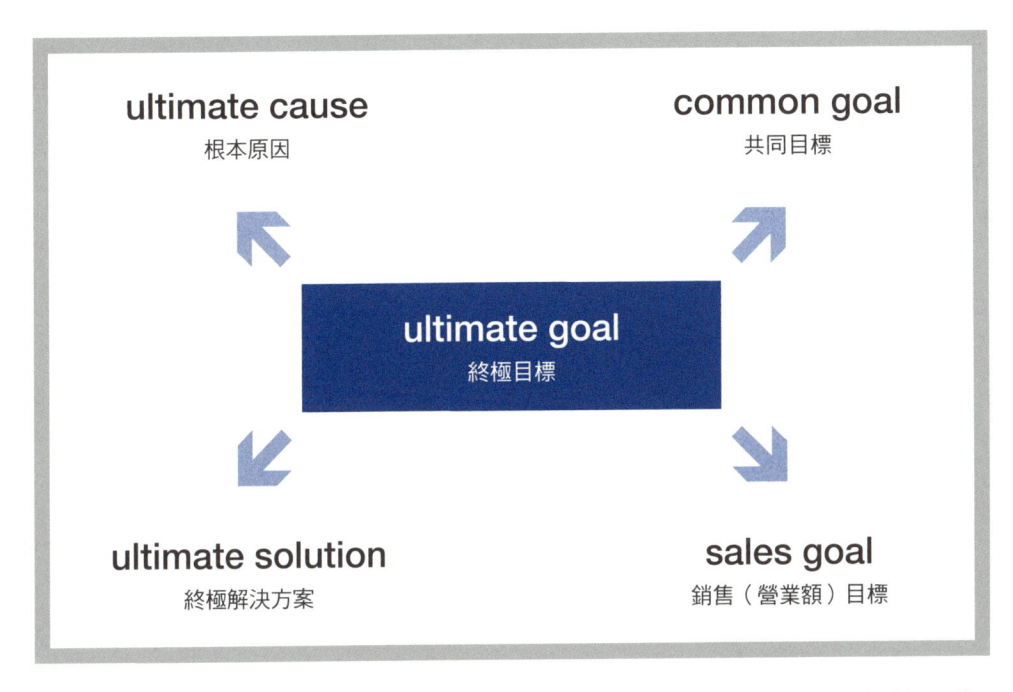

---

ultimate goal
/ˈʌltɪmət ɡəʊl/

My **ultimate goal** is to finish the Ironman Triathlon in Hawaii.
我的最終目標是完成夏威夷的鐵人三項比賽。

ultimate cause
/ˈʌltɪmət kɔːz/

The **ultimate cause** of grief for him was that he failed the university entrance exam.
他悲傷的根本原因是大學入學測驗不合格。

ultimate solution
/ˈʌltɪmət səˈluːʃən/

The **ultimate solution** against human rights infringements online is not the Internet real-name system.
對於網路上侵犯人權行為的終極解決方案，並不是網路實名制度。

common goal
/ˈkɒmən ɡəʊl/

All members of the team should work toward a **common goal** to be successful.
隊上所有成員應該朝著共同的目標努力，以獲得成功。

sales goal
/seɪlz ɡəʊl/

This quarter's **sales goal** is $1.2 million according to the latest budget.
依照最新的預算，這一季的銷售目標是 120 萬美元。

WEEK 7
HEALTH

兒童時期的肥胖
媒體對人們健康的影響
身體活動量的性別差異
不健康的飲食法
吃得健康
現代社會中的精神健康問題
讓每個人都能得到醫療保健服務

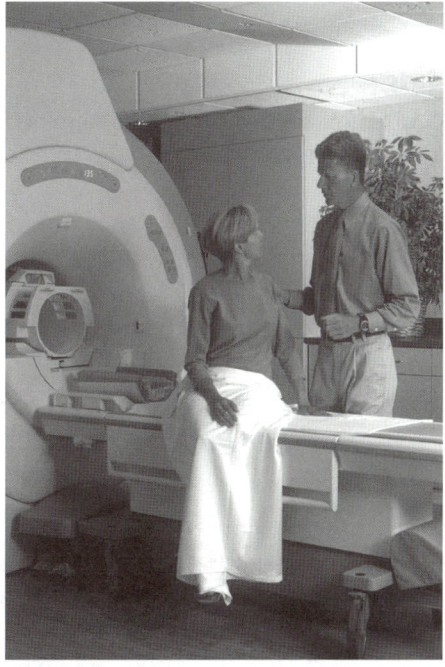

MON

IELTS **BASIC WORDS**

proceed /prəˈsiːd/ v. 繼續進行，接著進行
ENG. to go forward or onward
SYS. continue, progress

> It is tough to **proceed** with the advocacy of exercise among obese children.
> 要繼續推廣肥胖兒童做運動很困難。

同義語例句　Obese children will find it difficult to **carry on** with strenuous activities.
肥胖兒童會覺得很難持續做費力的運動。

同義語例句　Obese children need to work harder to **keep up** their exercise routine.
肥胖兒童需要更努力保持自己的日常例行運動。

反義語例句　Overweight children need to **refrain from** sedentary lifestyles.
過重的孩子需要擺脫久坐的生活型態。

advise /ədˈvaɪz/ v. 建議
ENG. give advice to; inform of something
SYS. counsel, recommend

> Parents are **advised** to watch their children's eating habits for the latter to avoid obesity.
> 建議父母觀察孩子的吃飯情況，讓後者（孩子）避免肥胖。

同義語例句　Children are given letters to **apprise** their parents about obesity.
孩子們拿到了告知父母關於肥胖的信件。

同義語例句　Flyers were sent to parents to **give** them **notice** on childhood obesity.
傳單發給了父母，通知他們關於兒童時期肥胖的訊息。

反義語例句　The incorrect weight loss tips **misled** many dieters into thinking that they can keep overeating and lose weight at the same time.
那些不正確的減重訣竅誤導了許多節食者，讓他們相信他們可以在過度飲食的同時還能減重。

WEEK 7 TOPIC **HEALTH**

▶基礎單字擴充

cultivate /ˈkʌltɪveɪt/ v. 栽培，培育，培養
ENG. foster the growth of; teach or refine to be discriminative in taste or judgment
SYS. develop, foster

> We must **cultivate** a sense of food awareness among school cafeteria managers to appropriately serve the students.
> 我們必須培養校內餐廳管理人員對於食物的意識，以供應學生適當的餐點。

同義語 例句 School cafeterias should **refine** their recipes to make their food suitable for both obese and non-obese children.
校內餐廳應該改進他們的烹飪方式，讓他們的食物同時適合肥胖孩童與其他兒童。

同義語 例句 School administrations should **improve** their kitchen equipment to cater to children with weight problems.
學校管理單位應該改善廚房設備，以適應有體重問題的兒童的需求。

反義語 例句 The government should not **neglect** school cafeterias when it tries to tackle childhood obesity problems.
在試圖處理兒童肥胖問題時，政府不應該忽視校內餐廳。

waste /weɪst/ v. 浪費
ENG. use inefficiently or inappropriately; spend thoughtlessly; get rid of
SYS. dissipate, misuse

> Eating food without enough nutrients is **wasting** money.
> 吃沒有足夠營養成分的食物是在浪費錢。

同義語 例句 Obese children should learn to **throw away** their unhealthy food.
肥胖兒童應該學習丟掉他們不健康的食物。

同義語 例句 Processed foods should be **excluded** from children's meals.
加工食物應該從兒童的三餐中去除。

反義語 例句 Eating too much and not exercising cause fat to **build up**.
吃太多又不運動會造成脂肪增長。

MON

TOPIC
Childhood obesity
兒童時期的肥胖

Most **overweight** and **obesity** problems in childhood emerge when a child eats too much and does not exercise enough. When energy **ingested** is more than energy burned off through physical activity, weight gain happens. On the other hand, a **minute** number of childhood obesity cases are related to uncommon **genetic** diseases. Since bad eating habits are the major cause of childhood obesity, it is important that children **maintain** a healthy and balanced diet. Preschools and day nurseries play an important role in teaching a child good eating habits and how to live an active **lifestyle**. Also, schools should encourage students and their families to gain **nourishment** by eating **wholesome** fruits and vegetables at every meal. By being **active** and keeping healthy habits, children can avoid getting obese and become healthier in their adulthood.

TRANS

大部分童年時期超重與肥胖的問題，是在小孩吃太多又運動不夠的時候發生的。當攝取的熱量多於透過身體活動燃燒的熱量時，體重增加就會發生。另一方面，有少數的兒童期肥胖案例與罕見遺傳疾病有關。由於不良的飲食習慣是兒童肥胖的主要原因，所以兒童維持健康與均衡的飲食是很重要的。幼兒園和日間托育中心在教導兒童好的飲食習慣以及如何保持活動的生活型態方面，扮演重要的角色。另外，學校也應該鼓勵學生和他們的家庭藉由每餐食用健康的蔬果來獲得營養。藉由多運動和保持健康的習慣，兒童可以避免肥胖，並且在成人時期變得比較健康。

overweight
/ˈəʊvəweɪt/
n. 過重　v. 過重的
She instigated divorce proceedings just because her husband became **overweight** after they married.
她只因為丈夫婚後變得過重就發起離婚程序。

obesity
/əʊˈbiːsɪti/
n. 肥胖
It's difficult for people who have never struggled with **obesity** to empathise with the obese.
從來沒為了肥胖奮鬥過的人，很難對肥胖的人感同身受。

ingest
/ɪnˈdʒɛst/
v. 攝取
The product would only be expected to be harmful if orally **ingested** in large amounts.
這種產品只有在大量口服攝取的時候會被認為是有害的。

minute
/mʌɪˈnjuːt/
adj. 微小的
The **minute** army was in danger of being defeated by the larger, more powerful brigade.
這支小小的軍隊有被更大、更強力的軍旅打敗的危險。

genetic
/dʒəˈnɛtɪk/
adj. 基因的，遺傳的
Some people incorrectly assume that premature birth is mostly **genetic** and runs in the family.
有些人錯誤地認定早產大多是遺傳性的，而且會遍及家族中。

maintain
/meɪnˈteɪn/
v. 維持
Eating small, frequent meals every day may help one **maintain** a normal weight.
每天少量多餐可能有助於維持正常體重。

lifestyle
/ˈlʌɪfstʌɪl/
n. 生活型態
For modern people, religion is no more a necessity in their life, but a **lifestyle** choice.
對現代人而言，宗教不再是生活中的必需，而是一種生活型態的選擇。

wholesome
/ˈhəʊlsəm/
adj. 對健康有益的
The technology was created to provide **wholesome** and safe drinking water at a reasonable cost.
這種技術是為了以合理的費用提供健康、安全的飲水而創造的。

nourishment
/ˈnʌrɪʃmənt/
n. 營養的食物；滋養，養育
Sensing that it needed to find **nourishment**, the kid goat searched for its mother.
因為感覺到自己需要（母親的）滋養，所以小羊尋找牠的母親。

active
/ˈaktɪv/
adj. 活動的
Children should have at least one hour of **active** play daily to keep themselves healthy.
孩子們應該每天至少花一小時進行活動性的遊戲來保持健康。

WORD TRAINING | 重點單字造句練習

appetite
/ˈæpɪtaɪt/

n. 食慾

💬 Some experts theorise that obese children have inherited their large appetite from their parents.
有些專家的理論是，肥胖兒童遺傳了他們父母的大胃口。

Once obese children gain an appetite for unhealthy foods, it is difficult to train them otherwise.
一旦肥胖兒童對不健康的食物產生食慾，就很難訓練他們不去吃。

✏️ Obese children are often those who eat whatever is within their reach and are unable to control their appetite. 肥胖的兒童通常是那些會吃身邊任何東西而且無法控制食慾的孩子。

Despite many studies done, it is still an enigma to doctors as to how some people develop such a large appetite and consequently become morbidly obese.
雖然有過許多研究，但對於某些人如何培養出這麼大的胃口並且導致病態肥胖，對醫師而言仍然是個謎。

fitness
/ˈfɪtnəs/

n. （身體的）健康，健身

💬 The general fitness of children in this country is poor, which is quite concerning.
這個國家的兒童整體健康情況不佳，令人相當擔憂。

It can be humiliating for an obese child to have his or her fitness tested at school.
對肥胖兒童來說，在學校接受體能測試可能是件羞辱的事。

✏️ To combat childhood obesity, many schools and communities have implemented fitness programmes aimed at getting children off the couch and into sports.
為了打擊兒童時期的肥胖，許多學校與社區已經實施健身計畫，目標是讓孩子離開沙發去做運動。

One of the ways we can help obese children regain fitness is to promote healthy diet at home.
我們能幫助肥胖兒童重獲健康的其中一個方法，就是宣導在家中的健康飲食。

well-being
/wɛlˈbiːɪŋ/

n. 健康與幸福感

💬 It is important to monitor both the physical and psychological well-being of children.
同時監控兒童的身體與心理健康是很重要的。

There are five main food groups that all children need to eat every day to maintain their well-being.
有五大類食物是所有孩童都要每天吃以維持健康的。

✍ People with obesity can improve their well-being through a high-fibre, low-fat diet, which will lower their blood cholesterol levels and keep them feeling fuller for longer between meals.　肥胖的人可以藉由高纖維、低脂肪的飲食來促進健康，這種飲食會降低他們血液中的膽固醇濃度，並且讓他們在兩餐之間有更久的飽足感。

Prebiotics are substances which induce the growth of beneficial microorganisms in the gastrointestinal tract and therefore contribute to people's well-being.
益生原是促進腸胃道中有益微生物成長的成分，也因此對人們的健康有貢獻。

unbalanced
/ʌnˈbalənst/
adj. 不平衡的，不均衡的

💬 Children that eat an unbalanced diet often run the risk of developing obesity.
吃不均衡飲食的兒童常常有發展成肥胖的風險。

Consuming junk foods frequently and having an unbalanced diet are the major factors causing obesity in children.
常吃垃圾食物和飲食不均衡是造成兒童肥胖的主要因素。

✍ An unbalanced diet might cause psychological problems such as anxiety, depression and emotional eating, which could then lead to obesity.
不均衡的飲食可能造成心理問題，如焦慮、沮喪和情緒性的飲食，而情緒性的飲食又可能導致肥胖。

Childhood obesity, which often results from an unbalanced diet, can cause problems such as heart disease, back problems, joint problems and poor circulation.
兒童期肥胖通常是不均衡的飲食造成的，可能會引起諸如心臟疾病、背部問題、關節問題以及循環不良等等的毛病。

RELATED WORDS | 相關單字延伸

sustenance
n. 食物，營養

food
n. 食物

nourishment
n. 營養的食物

diet
n. 飲食

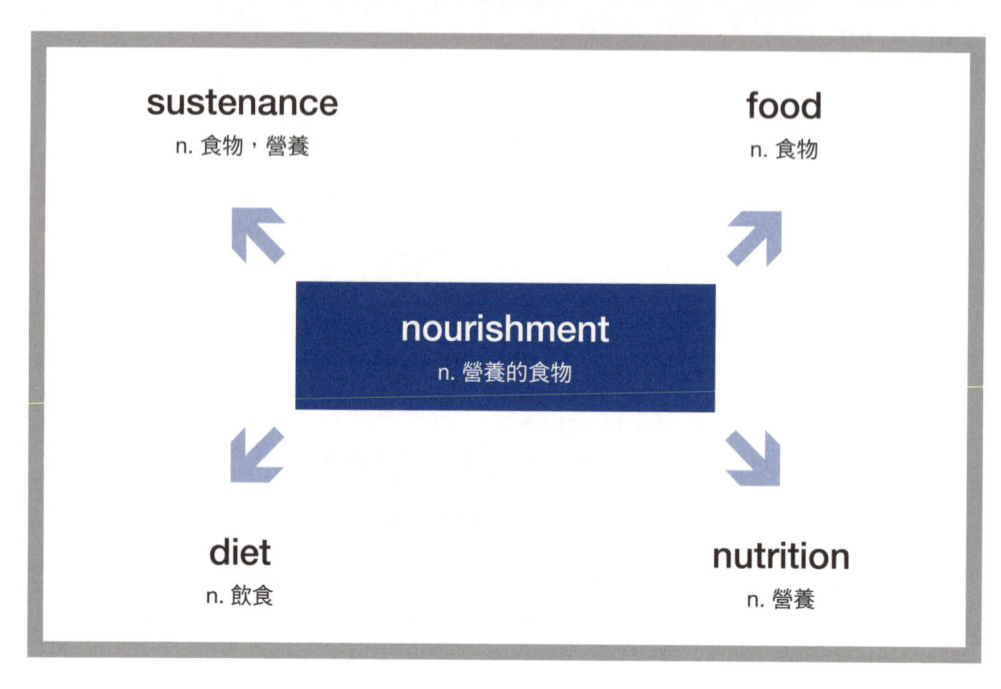

nutrition
n. 營養

nourishment
/ˈnʌrɪʃmənt/

Schools should encourage students and their families to gain **nourishment** by eating wholesome fruits and vegetables at every meal.
學校應該鼓勵學生和他們的家庭藉由每餐食用健康的蔬果來獲得營養。

sustenance
/ˈsʌstənəns/

It is important that students get enough **sustenance** during their school day.
讓學生在他們上課的一天中得到足夠的營養食物是很重要的。

diet
/ˈdaɪət/

Educators should teach children about proper **diet** so that these children can let their families know how to eat healthily.
教育人員應該教導孩子們適當的飲食，讓這些孩子能告訴家人如何吃得健康。

food
/fuːd/

I wish that every school-aged child had enough **food** each day to be healthy.
我希望每個學齡兒童每天都吃足夠的食物來保持健康。

nutrition
/njuˈtrɪʃən/

Nutrition classes should be taught in every elementary school so that everyone grows up healthy.
每所小學都應該教營養課，讓每個人長大後都是健康的。

USEFUL EXPRESSIONS | 相關實用片語

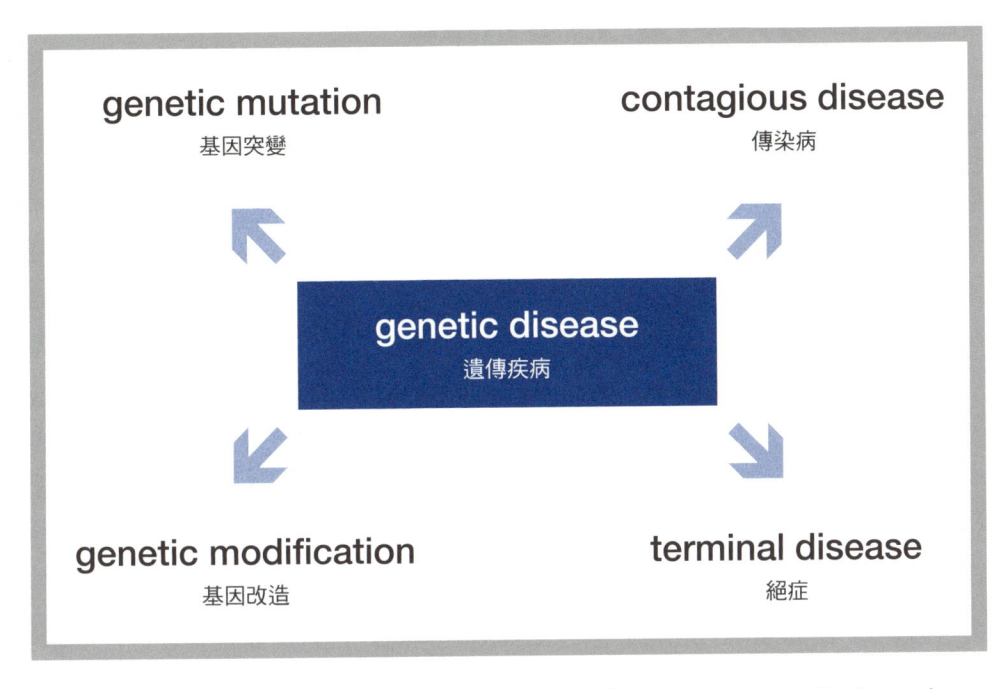

```
       genetic mutation              contagious disease
         基因突變                          傳染病
              ↖                      ↗

                   ┌──────────────────────┐
                   │   genetic disease    │
                   │      遺傳疾病          │
                   └──────────────────────┘

              ↙                      ↘
       genetic modification          terminal disease
         基因改造                         絕症
```

genetic disease
/dʒəˈnɛtɪk dɪˈziːz/

Animal and human studies have revealed that certain genetic diseases can now be addressed.
對於動物與人類的研究顯示，某些遺傳疾病現在是可以處理的。

genetic mutation
/dʒəˈnɛtɪk mjuːˈteɪʃən/

Genetic mutations can result from new and untested chemicals used in household products.
基因突變有可能因為家用品中使用的新的、未經測試的化學物質而造成。

genetic modification
/dʒəˈnɛtɪk ˌmɒdɪfɪˈkeɪʃən/

Despite the criticism, I think the genetic modification of crops might be beneficial.
儘管受到批評，但我認為作物的基因改造可能是有益的。

contagious disease
/kənˈteɪdʒəs dɪˈziːz/

Prevention and treatment of cholera, a highly contagious disease, are actually quite simple.
霍亂這種傳染性極強的疾病，預防和治療的方法其實很簡單。

terminal disease
/ˈtɜːmɪnəl dɪˈziːz/

When she began to lose her memory, she saw a doctor who diagnosed her with a terminal disease.
當她開始失去記憶，她去看了醫生，而醫生診斷她得了不治之症。

TUE

IELTS **BASIC WORDS**

exchange /ɪksˈtʃeɪndʒ/ v. 交換
ENG. give to and receive from one another
SYS. trade, swap

> We can exchange weight loss tips and stories with our friends.
> 我們可以和朋友交換減重的訣竅和故事。

同義語 例句 It is easier for people who have healthy friends to switch to a healthier lifestyle.
有健康的朋友的人，要轉換到更健康的生活型態比較容易。

同義語 例句 Obesity can be reversed by changing one's bad eating habits with the help of friends.
肥胖可以藉著朋友幫助改變不好的飲食習慣來逆轉。

反義語 例句 To lose weight, overweight people should refrain from keeping problems to themselves because their friends are there to listen.
想要減重，過重的人不應該隱藏自己的問題，因為他們的朋友會傾聽他們。

ruin /ˈruːɪn/ v. 毀壞，毀掉
ENG. to destroy completely
SYS. devastate, wreck

> Sudden weight loss can ruin one's appetite and sense of taste.
> 突然的減重可能會搞壞一個人的食慾和味覺。

同義語 例句 Drastic weight loss can slow down a person's metabolism.
激烈的減重可能會讓一個人的新陳代謝變慢。

同義語 例句 Improper exercise plans can mess up a person's body functions and cause injury.
不適當的運動計畫可能搞壞一個人的身體功能，並且造成受傷。

反義語 例句 Following a proper exercise plan will help build up your health and stamina.
遵守適當的運動計畫將有助於增強你的健康和耐力。

WEEK 7 TOPIC **HEALTH**

▶基礎單字擴充

sign /saɪn/ n. 跡象
ENG. an indication of the presence or occurrence of something else
SYS. indication, hint

> One **sign** of a slimming pill being effective is speedy weight loss.
> 減肥藥有效的一個跡象是迅速的減重。

同義語例句　If you find yourself getting sick from taking slimming pills, that should be a **cue** to stop taking them.
如果你發現自己吃減肥藥變得不舒服，那應該暗示著你要停止服用。

同義語例句　A **perceptible indication** of successful weight loss is being able to put on skinny jeans more easily.
成功減重的一個可以感受到的跡象，是能夠更容易穿上緊身牛仔褲。

反義語例句　The popularity of slimming pills gives people a **false impression** that one can lose weight without exercise.
減肥藥的流行給人們一種錯誤的印象，覺得不用運動也能減重。

distance /ˈdɪstəns/ n. 距離
ENG. extent of space between two objects
SYS. interval, span

> The **distance** of the marathon is about 26 miles.
> 馬拉松的距離大約是 26 英里。

同義語例句　The total **length** of the marathon course is about 26 miles.
馬拉松路線的總長度大約是 26 英里。

同義語例句　The columns of the architecture are placed at regular **intervals**.
那座建築的柱子以固定的間隔安置。

反義語例句　The two runners were **neck to neck** throughout the race.
那兩位跑者在比賽全程始終不相上下。

TUE

TOPIC | The media's influence on people's health
媒體對人們健康的影響

There is general agreement that **advertisements** in the media indeed shape public **notions** of health. However, there is a good deal of **disagreement** as to whether the advertisements' influence is positive or negative. For example, advertisements for weight-loss programmes and diet-related food and drink may promote health awareness among the audience. On the other hand, the media also **perpetuates** poor diet decisions through fast food commercials. What is even more **alarming** is the issue of body image. Young **adolescents** are led to believe that the media portrayal of the ideal body is how their bodies should look, causing girls to adopt fad diets that may lead to serious eating **disorders** and making boys **susceptible** to the use of steroids. School health educators and other teachers must **incorporate** media literacy into health education to **ameliorate** these problems and help students combat the mixed health messages found in the media.

TRANS

一般人普遍同意媒體中的廣告的確會形塑大眾對於健康的觀念。然而，對於廣告的影響是正面還是負面的，人們的意見很不一致。例如，減重課程和減肥相關食品、飲料的廣告，可能會提升觀眾的健康意識。另一方面，媒體也透過速食廣告，讓糟糕的飲食選擇一直延續下去。更令人擔憂的是身體意象的議題。少年族群受到誘導，相信媒體對於理想身體的描繪就是他們的身體應該看起來的樣子，使得女孩們採用可能導致嚴重飲食失調的流行飲食法，而男孩們很可能會使用類固醇。學校的健康教育工作者和其他老師必須將媒體素養（辨識媒體影響的能力）融入健康教育，以求改善這些問題，並且幫助學生對抗媒體中混雜不一的健康訊息。

advertisement
/əd'vɜːtɪzmənt/

n. 廣告

The president's re-election campaign placed emphasis on **advertisements** in newspapers.
總統競選連任的宣傳活動著重於報紙廣告。

notion
/'nəʊʃən/

n. 觀念，想法

People have mistaken **notions** about what successful business people should say and do.
人們對於成功商業人士應該說什麼、做什麼有錯誤的觀念。

disagreement
/dɪsə'griːmənt/

n. 意見不一致，爭論

Disagreement can sometimes lead to advancement.
意見不一致有時候會促成進步。

perpetuate
/pə'pɛtʃʊeɪt/

v. 使永久存在

Inappropriate social policies can **perpetuate** the cycle of poverty.
不適當的社會政策可能會使貧窮的循環延續下去。

alarming
/ə'lɑːmɪŋ/

adj. 令人擔憂的

It is **alarming** that banned additives are found in foods sold in the UK.
被禁止的添加物在英國販賣的食物中被發現，令人感到擔憂。

adolescent
/adə'lɛsənt/

n. 青少年

Elderly people often remark that **adolescents** these days have no respect for the authorities.
老一輩的人時常說現在的青少年對政府當局沒有敬意。

disorder
/dɪs'ɔːdə/

n. 失調

Children that have autism often suffer from mental **disorders** as well.
有自閉症的孩子通常也受精神問題的困擾。

susceptible
/sə'sɛptɪbəl/

adj. 易受影響的

Those plants are **susceptible** to frost in harsh winters, causing them to rarely flower in summer.
那些植物容易在嚴寒的冬天遭受霜害，使得它們夏天很少開花。

incorporate
/ɪn'kɔːpəreɪt/

v. 納入，包含

I tried to **incorporate** the colour blue in the painting and create a bright atmosphere at the same time.
我試著將藍色融入畫中，同時創造明亮的氣氛。

ameliorate
/ə'miːlɪəreɪt/

v. 改善

This strategy can also **ameliorate** hacking problems.
這個策略也可以改善駭客入侵的問題。

WORD TRAINING | 重點單字造句練習

injurious
/ɪnˈdʒʊərɪəs/

adj. 造成傷害的，有害的

💬 One should learn to break habits that are injurious to one's health.
一個人應該改掉有害自身健康的習慣。

It's important to control stress because it may be injurious to one's health.
控制壓力是很重要的，因為壓力可能會傷害一個人的健康。

✏️ Smoking cigarettes, drinking alcohol, sleeping all day and eating fatty foods are bad habits that should be avoided because they are injurious to one's health.
抽煙、喝酒、整天睡覺、吃高脂肪食物都是應該避免的壞習慣，因為它們會傷害一個人的健康。

Habitual alcohol drinking is injurious to one's health because it may cause medical conditions such as heart attack, diabetes and cancer.
習慣性飲酒對一個人的健康有害，因為它可能會造成某些病症，例如心臟病、糖尿病、癌症等。

depression
/dɪˈprɛʃən/

n. 沮喪，憂鬱症

💬 Teens reporting higher media exposure have significantly greater odds of developing depression.
報告自身的媒體曝露時間較高的青少年，有顯著較高的機率產生憂鬱症。

Comparatively little research has examined the relationship between violence in the media and depression.
檢視媒體中的暴力與憂鬱症關係的研究相對較少。

✏️ The time spent engaging with electronic media may replace time that would otherwise be spent on social, intellectual or athletic activities that may prevent depression. 花在接觸電子媒體的時間，可能會取代原本可以花在社交、智力或體育等等可以預防憂鬱症的活動的時間。

Recent research has established that body dissatisfaction caused by media exposure is a major risk factor for low self-esteem, depression and eating disorders such as bulimia.
最近的研究證實，接觸媒體所造成的對身體的不滿，是低自尊、憂鬱症、暴食症之類的飲食失調的主要危險因子。

sickly
/ˈsɪkli/

adj. 多病的，不健康的　adv. 病態地

💬 The girl reading the beauty magazines looked quite sickly and ate nothing for lunch.
在看美容雜誌的女孩子看起來很不健康，而且沒吃午餐。

It is unfortunate that many young girls believe that being sickly thin is beautiful.
遺憾的是，許多年輕女孩相信病態的瘦是美的。

✒️ Being quite sickly and close to death, the anorexic celebrity apologised to the audience for not being a positive role model for young people.
非常不健康而且逼近死亡的厭食症名人向觀眾道歉，因為自己沒有做年輕人的正面榜樣。

The new fad diet is completely unhealthy according to my mother, who has tried zero-meat, zero-sugar diet and became so sickly pale and therefore had to abandon it.
根據我母親的說法，新的流行飲食法完全不健康，而她自己曾經嘗試過無肉、無糖飲食，結果變得病態地蒼白，因而必須放棄。

restore
/rɪˈstɔː/

v. 使恢復

💬 After one recovers from an illness, it is important to get enough sleep to restore health.
在從疾病中復原之後，睡眠充足以恢復健康是很重要的。

Vitamin pills may help restore one's youthful glow.
維生素可能可以幫助恢復一個人的年輕光采。

✒️ The electronic retinal implants that have been successful in restoring the sight of the blind in clinical trials are now available in some western countries.
在臨床試驗中成功恢復盲人視力的電子視網膜植入，現在在某些西方國家可以使用到了。

Yoga is an ancient practice that is known to contribute to one's health because it not only helps maintain good posture but also helps restore one's inner balance.
瑜伽是一種已知對健康有貢獻的古老實踐，因為它不僅幫助維持好的姿勢，也有助於恢復一個人的內在平衡。

RELATED WORDS | 相關單字延伸

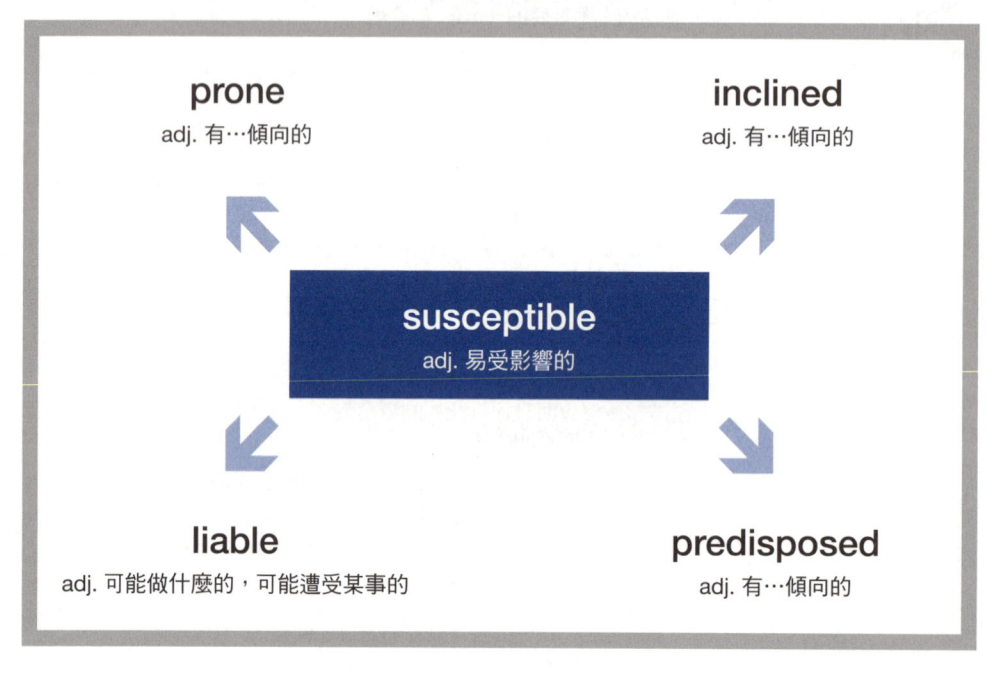

prone
adj. 有…傾向的

inclined
adj. 有…傾向的

susceptible
adj. 易受影響的

liable
adj. 可能做什麼的，可能遭受某事的

predisposed
adj. 有…傾向的

---

susceptible
/səˈsɛptɪbəl/

Women are more susceptible to heart disease than men.
女性比男性更容易罹患心臟疾病。

prone
/prəʊn/

If you are prone to motion sickness, avoid reading books when travelling, especially in cars or on trains.
如果你很容易暈車，旅途中避免看書，尤其是在汽車或者火車上時。

liable
/ˈlʌɪəbəl/

Many people are liable to try fad diets because of the celebrity weight loss stories they see on TV.
很多人很容易因為看了電視上名人的減重故事就去嘗試流行的飲食法。

inclined
/ɪnˈklʌɪnd/

I am more inclined to go on a diet than I am to try steroids to transform my body.
比起嘗試用類固醇來改造我的體型，我更傾向於控制飲食。

predisposed
/ˌpriːdɪˈspəʊzd/

The media is predisposed to showing commercials for diet pills because drug companies fund them.
媒體偏好播放減肥藥的廣告，是因為藥廠會給他們資金。

USEFUL EXPRESSIONS | 相關實用片語

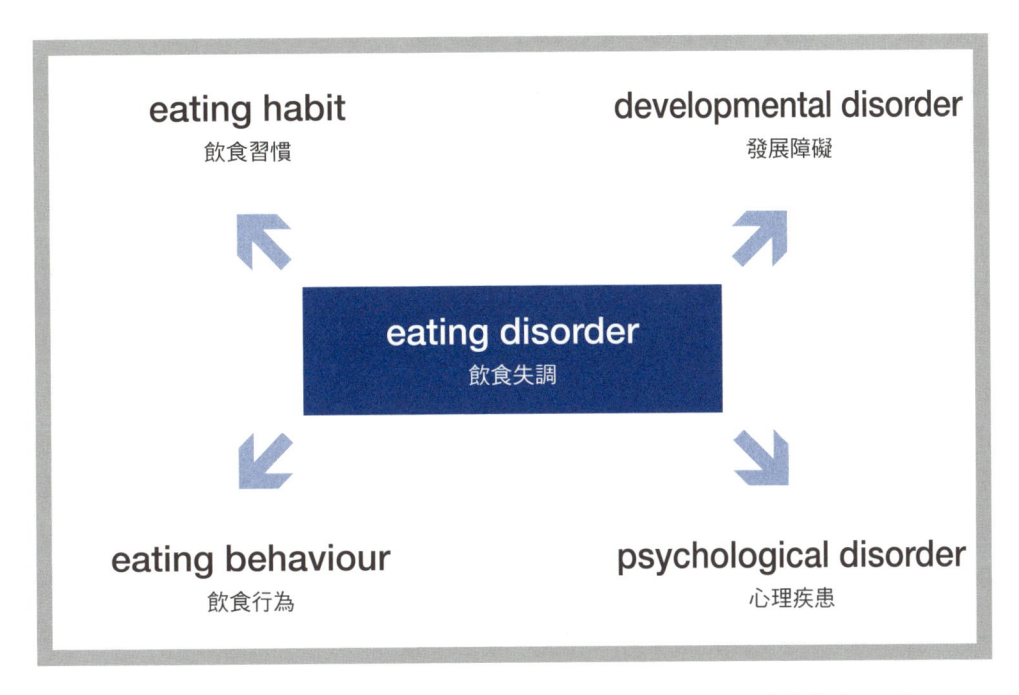

```
        eating habit                    developmental disorder
         飲食習慣                              發展障礙

                    ┌─────────────────────┐
                    │   eating disorder   │
                    │      飲食失調        │
                    └─────────────────────┘

       eating behaviour                 psychological disorder
         飲食行為                              心理疾患
```

eating disorder
/ˈiːtɪŋ dɪsˈɔːdə/

The media keeps covering the celebrity's eating disorders every day because everyone is talking about her.
媒體持續每天報導那位名人的飲食失調問題，因為每個人都在討論她。

eating habit
/ˈiːtɪŋ ˈhæbɪt/

According to the news report, there is a definite relationship between IQ and eating habits.
根據新聞報導，智商與飲食習慣有絕對的關係。

eating behaviour
/ˈiːtɪŋ bɪˈheɪvjə/

This manual will teach you the ways to control your poor eating behaviour.
這本手冊會教你控制自己不良飲食行為的方法。

developmental disorder
/dɪˌvɛləpˈmɛntəl dɪsˈɔːdə/

Autism is defined as being a special developmental disorder.
自閉症被定義為一種特殊的發展障礙。

psychological disorder
/ˌsaɪkəˈlɒdʒɪkəl dɪsˈɔːdə/

Whether drug dependence is a deeply rooted psychological disorder is up for debate.
藥物依賴是不是一種根深蒂固的心理疾患還有待討論。

WED

IELTS BASIC WORDS

discard /dɪˈskɑːd/ v. 丟棄，拋棄
ENG. to throw away
SYS. reject, drop

> It is time to **discard** unhealthful foods in our fridge and fill it with healthful ones.
> 現在是把我們冰箱裡不健康的食物丟掉，並且裝進健康食物的時候了。

同義語例句 To kick-start a healthy lifestyle, **toss out** foods that tempt you to go back to bad eating habits.
要發動健康的生活型態，就把引誘你回到不好的飲食習慣的食物丟掉。

同義語例句 **Throw away** processed food products to avoid eating them.
把加工食品丟掉以避免去吃它們。

反義語例句 Not holding on to preserved food can make a person healthier.
不要緊緊抓住加工食物，可以使一個人更健康。

confine /kənˈfaɪn/ v. 限制
ENG. place limits on
SYS. limit, restrain

> In the cities, most busy people's food choices are **confined** to a small set of fast foods which are economical yet unhealthy.
> 在都市，大部分忙碌的人的食物選擇侷限於一小群經濟但不健康的速食。

同義語例句 People are sometimes **tied down** by unhealthy foods just because they are way cheaper.
人們有時候受到不健康食物的束縛，就只是因為它們便宜得多。

同義語例句 An addiction to greasy foods **holds** us **back** from healthy lifestyles.
對油膩食物成癮，會阻礙我們活出健康的生活型態。

反義語例句 While eating healthier food may **set** us **free** from life-threatening diseases, doing so will cost us a lot more.
雖然吃比較健康的食物可能讓我們免於威脅生命的疾病，但這麼做也會多花我們很多錢。

WEEK 7 TOPIC **HEALTH**

▶基礎單字擴充

root /ruːt/ n. 根本，根源
ENG. the basic cause, source, or origin of something
SYS. source, origin

> The **root** of all weight-related diseases is improper eating habits.
> 所有與體重有關的疾病，根源都是不當的飲食習慣。

同義語例句 The **main cause** of diseases is unhealthy food intake.
造成疾病的主要原因是不健康的食物攝取。

同義語例句 The **main reason** why he became overweight is that he ate too much, but not exercising further aggravated the problem.
他變得過重的主要原因是吃了太多東西，但不運動更加重了這個問題。

反義語例句 The **result** of his binge eating is uncontrollable weight gain.
他暴食行為的結果，是無法控制的體重增加。

live /lɪv/ v. 活，活著
ENG. to remain alive
SYS. exist, survive

> If you wish to **live** on for a long time, change your unhealthy lifestyle now.
> 如果你想要活得長久的話，現在就改變你不健康的生活型態。

同義語例句 Most people want to maintain healthy lifestyles and **stay alive** longer.
大部分的人都想要維持健康的生活型態，並且活得久一點。

同義語例句 It is never too late to give up an unhealthy lifestyle to **keep yourself alive** longer.
拋棄不健康的生活讓自己活得更久，永遠不嫌晚。

反義語例句 We should not let our hopes of becoming healthier just **die out**.
我們不應該讓自己變得更健康的希望消逝。

WED

TOPIC: Gender differences in physical activity levels
身體活動量的性別差異

One can **theorise** that women are less active than men simply by considering the **gender** difference in activity levels among school children. Girls have a **propensity** to join smaller groups and engage in verbal activities, like conversation and **socialising**. On the other hand, most boys play in larger groups, which lend themselves to more physically active activities like football. It is a **concern** that girls' activity levels are **inferior** to boys, and lower activity levels could be contributing to obesity and **unwholesome** lifestyles. The different ways girls and boys behave on the playground suggest that the **provision** of playtime activities at school is necessary for girls to take part in more **vigorously** active play. If girls do increasingly less physical activity, they may face **adverse** health consequences later in life, such as heart disease, diabetes and mental health problems.

TRANS

僅僅考慮學童身體活動量的性別差異，就可以推論女人沒有男人那麼常活動。女孩傾向於參加小團體，以及參與語言活動，像是會話與社交。另一方面，大部分的男孩會在大的團體裡玩，這讓他們更適合足球之類運動身體的活動。女孩的活動量低於男孩，是令人擔憂的，而較低的活動量可能造成肥胖和不健康的生活型態。男孩和女孩在遊戲場行為方式的不同，暗示著在學校提供遊戲時間的活動是必要的，好讓女孩可以參與活動量更旺盛的遊戲。如果女孩的身體活動越來越少，他們在未來的人生中可能會面臨不利的健康狀況，例如心臟病、糖尿病以及精神健康問題。

theorise
/ˈθɪərʌɪz/

v. 創立理論，理論化
Many people **theorise** that I am a troublemaker given my arm tattoos.
很多人因為我手臂上的刺青而推斷我是個麻煩製造者。

gender
/ˈdʒɛndə/

n. 性別
The doctor looked at the mother and revealed the **gender** of her baby.
醫師看著母親，並且告訴她嬰兒的性別。

propensity
/prəˈpɛnsɪti/

n. 傾向
On hot days, he has a **propensity** for walking around barefoot.
在炎熱的日子，他傾向於打赤腳到處走。

socialising
/ˈsəʊʃəlʌɪzɪŋ/

n. 社交
He makes up his failure at **socialising** by being an accomplished pianist.
他藉由當個有造詣的鋼琴家，彌補自己在社交上的失敗。

concern
/kənˈsəːn/

n. 關心的事，擔心
Tuberculosis is the main **concern** of the epidemiological study.
肺結核是這個流行病學研究的主要關注點。

inferior
/ɪnˈfɪərɪə/

adj. 較低的，較差的
Nobody should try to make another person feel **inferior** for any reason.
沒有人應該因為任何原因而試圖讓另一個人感到低下。

unwholesome
/ʌnˈhəʊlsəm/

adj. 不健康的
Unwholesome foods may lead to certain medical conditions that may be dangerous to children.
不健康的食物可能導致某些可能對孩童有危險性的症狀。

provision
/prəˈvɪʒən/

n. 提供，供應
The fee also includes the **provision** of lighting for the band.
費用也包含為樂團提供燈光設備。

vigorously
/ˈvɪɡərəsli/

adv. 強而有力地，精神旺盛地
Doing exercise **vigorously** at least three days a week will help maintain a normal blood circulation.
每週至少三天做高活動量的運動，將有助於維持正常的血液循環。

adverse
/ˈadvəːs/

adj. 不利的，有害的
The family moved to the countryside because of the **adverse** conditions they faced.
因為面對不利的情況，這個家庭搬到了鄉下。

WORD TRAINING | 重點單字造句練習

physical fitness
/ˈfɪzɪkəl ˈfɪtnəs/

n. 體適能

💬 He wants not only to maintain physical fitness but also to look like his favourite sports star.
他不止想要維持體適能,還想要看起來像他最愛的運動明星一樣。

Both men and women should maintain their physical fitness if they want to live a good life.
想要過好的生活,不管男人或女人都應該保持自己的體適能。

✏️ Research has proved that men get better results than women do when it comes to achieving target physical fitness levels.　研究證明,在達成體適能目標這方面,男人會得到比女人更好的結果。

Since the bodies of people who have more muscle burn more calories, men tend to lose weight faster than women with the same workouts and level of physical fitness.　因為肌肉比較多的人,他們的身體會燃燒比較多的卡路里,所以在做相同的運動以及體適能程度相同情況下,男人通常減重的速度比女人快。

flexibility
/ˌflɛksɪˈbɪlɪti/

n. 彈性,柔軟度

💬 Men should work on increasing their flexibility because they are generally less flexible than women.
男人應該努力增加自己的身體柔軟度,因為他們一般而言沒有女人那麼柔軟。

The risk of injury decreases as flexibility increases.
受傷的風險隨著柔軟度的增加而減少。

✏️ Women are known to be more flexible than men, and they should try to use their superior flexibility in exercises such as yoga and Pilates.
大家知道女人比男人柔軟,而她們應該試著在瑜伽、皮拉提斯之類的運動中運用自己較佳的柔軟度。

In addition to improving flexibility, stretching may actually boost the rate at which muscles recover after workouts and races, and this applies to women as well as men.
除了增進柔軟度以外,伸展運動實際上也能加快肌肉在運動與賽跑後恢復的速度,而這不止適用於男人,也適用於女人。

anxiety
/æŋˈzʌɪəti/

n. 焦慮

💬 In truth, anxiety is a natural emotion for all humans, regardless of age or gender. 事實上，焦慮對所有人來說都是一種自然的情緒，不分年齡或性別。

While anxiety affects women in greater numbers than men, it's by no means a strictly female problem.
雖然受焦慮影響的女人比男人多，但它絕不是專屬於女性的問題。

✏️ Women are more likely to be victims of physical or mental abuse, a known risk factor for anxiety and other stress-related disorders.
女人比較容易成為身體或精神虐待的受害者，而這是焦慮和其他與壓力相關的失調症狀的已知危險因子。

Instead of seeking professional help, men tend to self-medicate their anxiety by using alcohol or street drugs.
男人傾向於不尋求專業協助，而是自己使用酒精或毒品來「治療」焦慮。

strength
/strɛŋθ/

n. 力量

💬 Most people who do strength training develop stronger and slightly larger muscles.
大部分做肌力訓練的人，會練出比較強壯而且稍微變大的肌肉。

Even though women can develop a fair amount of strength through training, men generally remain stronger. 即使女人可以透過訓練培養出相當程度的力量，但男人大致上還是比較強壯。

✏️ Since a man will have more muscle mass than a woman of the same weight, men generally have better strength than women. 因為男人會比體重相同的女人有更多的肌肉組織，所以男人一般而言力量比女人強。

Compared to women, men have higher levels of testosterone, which is the hormone that aids muscle growth, so they benefit more than women from strength training regimes and will end up gaining more muscle mass. 和女人相比，男人體內的睪固酮含量比較高，這是能幫助肌肉成長的荷爾蒙，所以男人在肌力訓練中獲得的效益比女人大，最終也會長出比較多的肌肉。

RELATED WORDS | 相關單字延伸

worry
n. 擔心

unease
n. 不安

concern
n. 關心的事，擔心

distress
n. 痛苦，苦惱

apprehension
n. 憂慮

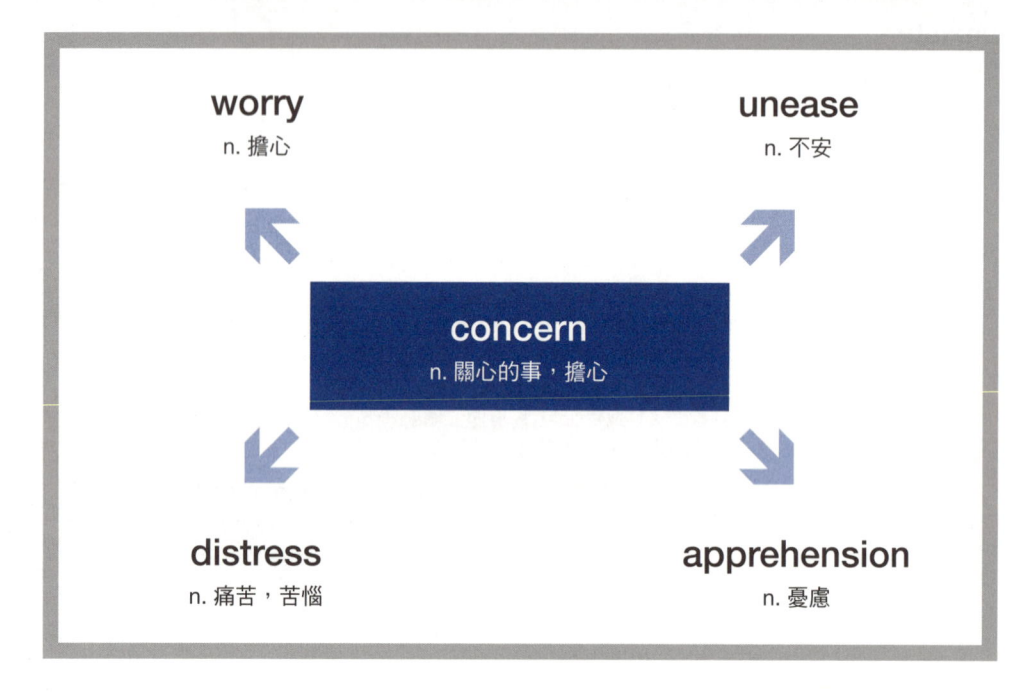

---

concern
/kənˈsəːn/

Aspirin intake is part of the physician's concern.
阿斯匹靈的攝取是那位醫師關注的其中一件事。

worry
/ˈwʌri/

I have no worry about minor headache because it usually resolves on its own.
我不擔心輕微的頭痛，因為它通常會自己好。

distress
/dɪˈstrɛs/

An excessive amount of distress may be considered pathologic.
過多的心理痛苦可能會被認為是病態的。

unease
/ʌnˈiːz/

Feeling of unease is one of the classic symptoms of anxiety disorder.
不安的感覺是焦慮症的一種典型症狀。

apprehension
/æprɪˈhɛnʃən/

There is widespread apprehension about the future among today's teenagers.
今日的青少年普遍對未來感到憂慮。

USEFUL EXPRESSIONS | 相關實用片語

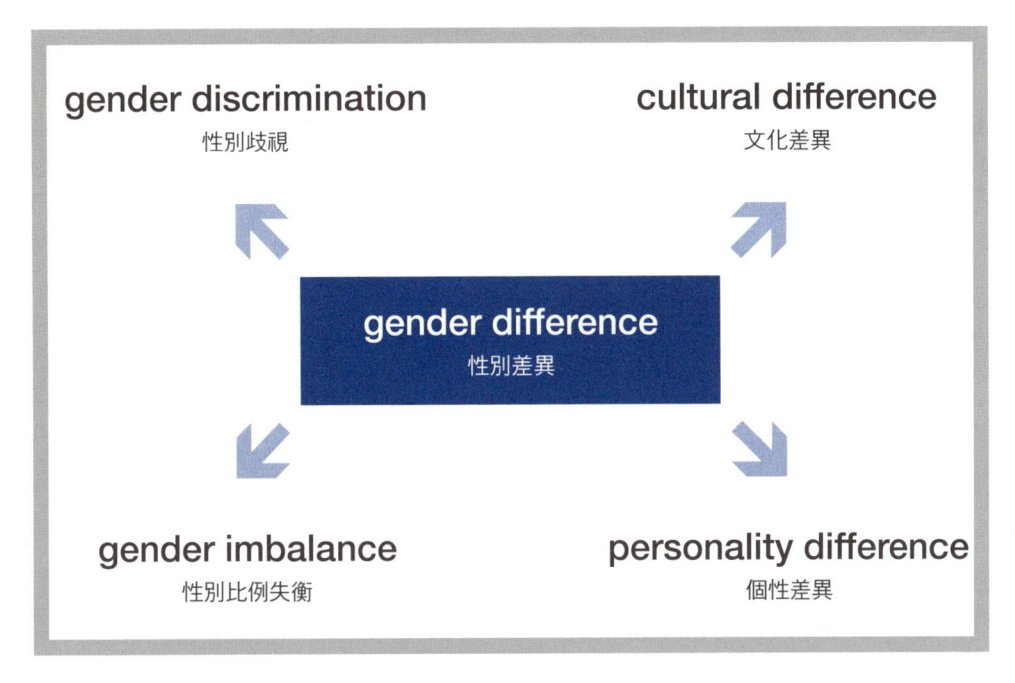

```
gender discrimination          cultural difference
性別歧視                         文化差異

            gender difference
               性別差異

gender imbalance              personality difference
性別比例失衡                      個性差異
```

gender difference
/ˈdʒɛndə ˈdɪfərəns/

All people have the same human rights regardless of economic, ethnic or gender differences.
不論經濟、種族或性別的差異，所有人都有相同的人權。

gender discrimination
/ˈdʒɛndə dɪˌskrɪmɪˈneɪʃən/

The state should not interfere with disagreements in the workplace, even if there is overt gender discrimination.
國家不應該干涉職場裡的爭執，即使是有明顯的性別歧視。

gender imbalance
/ˈdʒɛndə ɪmˈbæləns/

All experts agree that gender imbalances may have serious social implications.
所有專家都同意，性別比例失衡可能會在社會上造成嚴重的後果。

cultural difference
/ˈkʌltʃərəl ˈdɪfərəns/

Even though our country does not restrict interracial marriages, people are often divided by cultural differences.
即使我們的國家並不限制跨種族的婚姻，人們還是經常被文化差異分隔。

personality difference
/ˌpɜːsəˈnælɪti ˈdɪfərəns/

The personality differences among my colleagues do not seem to cause many problems.
我同事之間的個性差異似乎沒有造成太多問題。

THU

IELTS **BASIC WORDS**

boundary /ˈbaʊndəri/ n. 邊界，界限
ENG. line or plane; the limit or extent of something
SYS. bounds, borderline

> Only a professional can determine the **boundary** between an unhealthy eating habit and addiction.
> 只有專業人士能夠判定不健康的飲食習慣與上癮的邊界。

同義語 例句 There is a fine **dividing line** between unhealthy habits and addiction.
在不健康的習慣與上癮之間有一條細微的分界線。

同義語 例句 If you go beyond the **cut-off point** between an unhealthy habit and addiction, you may put your health at risk.
如果你越過了不健康的習慣與上癮之間的分界點，你可能會讓你的健康受到危害。

反義語 例句 If we have an **excess** of certain unhealthy behaviour, we had better ask for help to avoid addiction.
如果我們某種不健康的行為過多，那麼最好尋求協助，以避免上癮。

possibility /ˌpɒsɪˈbɪlɪti/ n. 可能性
ENG. capability of existing or happening or being true
SYS. feasibility, potentiality

> There is a great **possibility** that an unhealthy eater will not reach age 50.
> 飲食不健康的人有很大的可能性不會活到 50 歲。

同義語 例句 The **chance** of a person with unhealthy eating habits reaching age 50 is low.
飲食習慣不健康的人活到 50 歲的可能性很低。

同義語 例句 The **likelihood** of dying before age 50 increases when one has unhealthy eating habits.
當一個人有不健康飲食習慣時，50 歲之前死亡的可能性會增加。

反義語 例句 Without doubt, exercise and healthy diet will lead to a longer life.
無疑地，運動和健康的飲食會讓壽命變長。

WEEK 7 TOPIC **HEALTH**

▶基礎單字擴充

share /ʃɛr/ v. 分享
ENG. have in common; use jointly; give out as one's portion
SYS. apportion, distribute

> We should share accurate health information with others.
> 我們應該和他人分享正確的健康資訊。

同義語例句 The website distributes information about the latest findings in medical research.
這個網站散布關於醫學研究最新發現的資訊。

同義語例句 Make it a habit to divide up the responsibility of preparing meals between you and your partner.
要習慣和你的伴侶分攤做飯的責任。

反義語例句 We should keep information from questionable sources to ourselves and avoid spreading it.
我們應該保留來源可疑的資訊不讓別人知道,並且避免傳播。

allocate /ˈæləkeɪt/ v. 分配
ENG. distribute according to a plan; set apart for a special purpose
SYS. assign, designate

> We must allocate ample time for healthy activities such as exercise.
> 我們必須分配足夠的時間給運動之類的健康活動。

同義語例句 If we set aside time for sports and exercise, we will have a healthier body.
如果我們留出時間給體育和運動,我們就會有更健康的身體。

同義語例句 We should get rid of unhealthy habits and reserve some time for physical activities.
我們應該甩開不健康的習慣,並且預留一些做身體活動的時間。

反義語例句 Not making time for physical activities will make it difficult for us to have a healthy body.
不留出時間做身體活動,會讓我們很難擁有健康的身體。

THU

TOPIC | Unhealthy diets
不健康的飲食法

Diets can help people who are **rotund** to start a healthier lifestyle and get back on track with their fitness. Dieting could be dangerous, however, when the diet promises **dramatic** weight loss in a short **interval**. This type of dieting carries **acute** health consequences. When people lose weight fast by **starving** themselves, undesirable side effects are **inevitable**. The body is not designed to be **malnourished** and function well at the same time. In starvation mode, the **metabolism** is upset, and the body loses muscle tissue as well as fat. A healthy diet is well-balanced and includes proteins, minerals and vitamins that come from vegetables, fruit, meat, **dairy** products and whole grains. Any diet that does not call for **sacrifice** or patience is not worth the trouble or the money to try.

TRANS

飲食法可以幫助圓胖的人開始比較健康的生活型態，並且回到健康的正軌。然而，當飲食法保證可以在短期之內達到戲劇化的減重時，飲食減肥就有可能是危險的。這種飲食減肥方式會造成急劇的健康後果。當人靠著讓自己挨餓以快速減重時，討厭的副作用是無可避免的。身體不是設計成可以同時營養不良又運作良好的。在飢餓狀態中，新陳代謝會混亂，而身體除了減去脂肪也會失去肌肉。健康的飲食是均衡的，而且包含來自蔬菜、水果、肉、乳製品和全穀的蛋白質、礦物質和維生素。任何不要求犧牲或耐心的飲食法，都不值得花工夫或金錢嘗試。

rotund
/rəʊˈtʌnd/

adj. 圓胖的

I was tapped on the shoulder by a **rotund** gentleman who asked what I was doing.
我被一個圓胖的紳士拍肩問我在做什麼。

dramatic
/drəˈmatɪk/

adj. 戲劇性的

The **dramatic** ending to the novel surprised everyone who read it.
這部小說戲劇性的結尾讓所有讀過它的人都很驚訝。

interval
/ˈɪntəvəl/

n. 間隔

Please jump over two hurdles in every thirty-second **interval**.
請在每 30 秒的時間內跳過兩個跨欄。

acute
/əˈkjuːt/

adj. 急劇的，急性的，嚴重的

An overdose of acetaminophen can lead to **acute** liver failure.
過量使用乙醯氨酚可能導致急性肺衰竭。

starve
/stɑːv/

v. 挨餓，使挨餓

The commercial on TV showed children **starving** in Africa and asked for donations.
這支電視廣告播放兒童在非洲挨餓的畫面，並且要求捐款。

inevitable
/ɪnˈɛvɪtəbəl/

adj. 不可避免的

Given her height, it was **inevitable** that she would bump her head on the door frame.
考慮到她的身高，她的頭會撞上門框是無可避免的。

malnourished
/malˈnʌrɪʃt/

adj. 營養不良的

More than 800 million people are chronically **malnourished**.
有超過 8 億人慢性營養不良。

metabolism
/mɪˈtabəlɪzəm/

n. 新陳代謝

I have a high **metabolism**, so I can eat anything I want without gaining weight.
我的新陳代謝率高，所以我可以吃任何想吃的東西而不變胖。

dairy
/ˈdɛːri/

adj. 乳品的

Milk and other **dairy** products may help strengthen our bones and teeth.
牛奶和其他乳製品可能有助於強化我們的骨骼與牙齒。

sacrifice
/ˈsakrɪfʌɪs/

n. 犧牲　**v.** 犧牲

I absolutely refuse to **sacrifice** my weekend plans to babysit my little sister.
我絕對拒絕犧牲我的週末計畫去看顧我的妹妹。

WORD TRAINING | 重點單字造句練習

hunger
/ˈhʌŋɚ/

n. 飢餓

💬 In order to change our bad eating habits, we must relearn what hunger feels like.
為了改變我們不良的飲食習慣，我們必須重新學習饑餓是什麼感覺。

Unhealthy people tend to eat fast food to satisfy their hunger.
不健康的人傾向於吃速食來滿足他們的飢餓。

✏️ If people don't switch to healthy snacks to appease their hunger, they will eventually have health problems.
如果人們不改用健康的零食來緩解他們的飢餓，最後就會有健康的問題。

To lose weight, you should know the difference between physical hunger and emotional hunger.
想要減重，你就應該知道身體的飢餓和情緒上的飢餓之間的不同。

poorly
/ˈpɔːli/

adv. 糟糕地

💬 Watching too much television, eating poorly and other harmful habits can develop early in childhood.
看太多電視、飲食很糟糕和其他有害的習慣，可能在兒童時期早期開始養成。

Bad eating habits can cause children to perform poorly at school.
不良的飲食習慣有可能造成孩子在學校表現不好。

✏️ According to research, those with low incomes and less education are more likely to smoke, consume excessive alcohol and eat poorly.
根據研究，低收入、低教育的人比較有可能抽菸、飲酒過量以及吃得差。

Before heading to a staff party or other functions where food will be served, eat a little at home in case that the food is poorly prepared or not to your taste.
在前往員工派對或其他供應食物的聚會時，先在家吃一點東西，以防食物做得不好或者不合你胃口。

prevent
/prɪˈvɛnt/

v. 避免

💬 Exercise is the best way to improve blood circulation and prevent heart diseases.
運動是改善血液循環以及避免心臟疾病最好的方法。

Keeping your hands clean is the best way to prevent the spread of infection.
保持雙手乾淨是避免感染傳播最好的方法。

✎ You can prevent skin diseases by maintaining a proper and balanced diet, getting enough sunlight and observing proper hygiene.
你可以藉由維持適當且均衡的飲食、曝曬充足的陽光以及保持衛生來避免皮膚疾病。

Gingivitis can be prevented by brushing three times a day, flossing every night and maintaining a diet with adequate amount of vitamin C to help improve the integrity of the gums.
牙齦發炎可以藉由一天刷牙三次、每晚使用牙線，以及維持有足量維生素 C 的飲食以幫助促進牙齦健全來預防。

cool-down
/ˈkuːldaʊn/

n. 緩和運動　v.（cool down）使平靜下來

💬 Missing the cool-down should not become a habit, especially when some stretching is necessary.
不做緩和運動不應該成為一種習慣，尤其當伸展運動是必需的時候。

After exercising strenuously, people should cool down their muscles.
費力做完運動後，人們應該要讓他們的肌肉緩和下來。

✎ Letting your heart rate slowly come down after a workout is a must, but skipping a cool-down isn't a big deal.
讓你的心跳速率在運動後慢慢降下來是必要的，但省略不做緩和運動沒有什麼關係。

Try to finish your workout with a few minutes of light exercise to cool down, such as stretching from head to toe.
試著在運動結束的時候做幾分鐘的輕度運動作為緩和，例如從頭到腳做伸展。

RELATED WORDS | 相關單字延伸

unavoidable
adj. 不可避免的

inescapable
adj. 無法逃避的

inevitable
adj. 不可避免的

certain
adj. 確定的

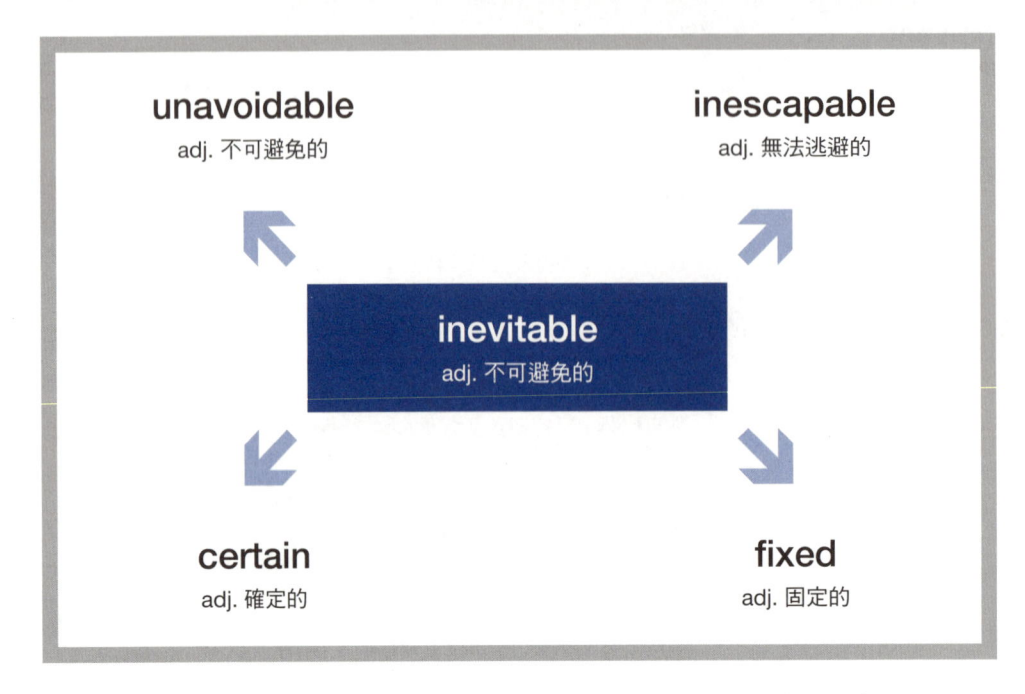

fixed
adj. 固定的

inevitable
/ɪnˈɛvɪtəbəl/

When people lose weight fast by starving themselves, undesirable side effects are inevitable.
當人靠著讓自己挨餓以快速減肥時，討厭的副作用是無可避免的。

unavoidable
/ˌʌnəˈvɔɪdəbəl/

Side effects are unavoidable when people lose weight by starving themselves.
當人們靠著讓自己挨餓來減重時，副作用是無可避免的。

certain
/ˈsɜːtən/

I know for certain that James will lose a lot of his muscle mass if he keeps starving himself.
我很確定如果 James 繼續讓自己挨餓的話，他會失去很多肌肉。

inescapable
/ˌɪnɪˈskeɪpəbəl/

It is an inescapable truth that you have to eat less and exercise more to lose weight.
無法逃避的事實是，你必須靠著少吃多動來減重。

fixed
/fɪkst/

One should have a fixed time for exercise to lose weight effectively.
一個人應該要有固定的時間運動以有效減重。

USEFUL EXPRESSIONS | 相關實用片語

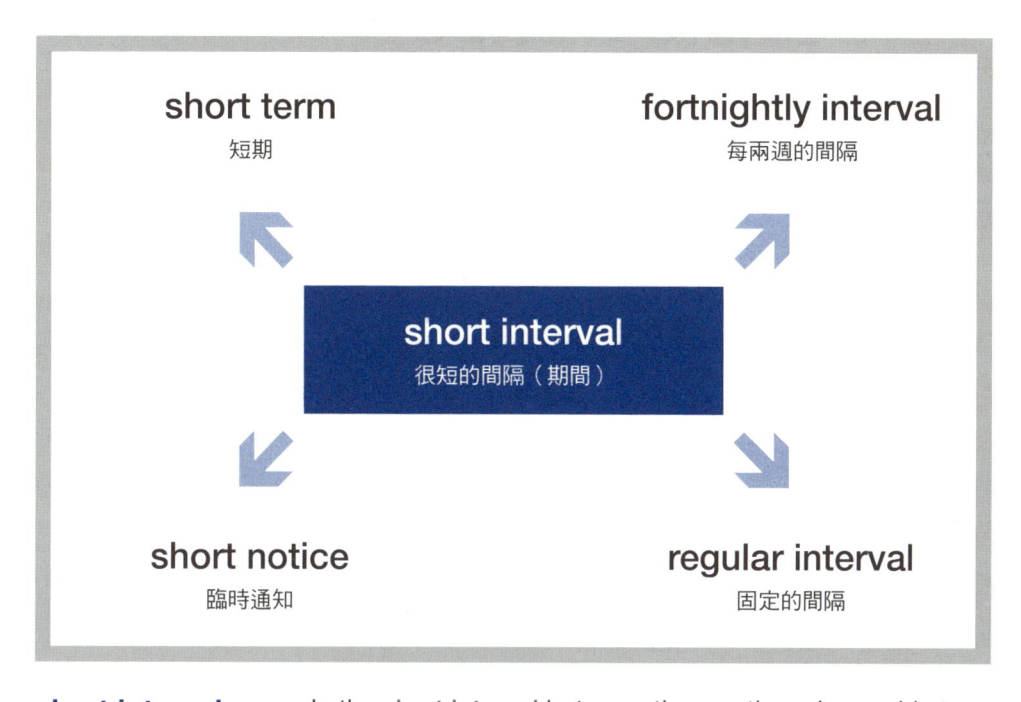

```
          short term                    fortnightly interval
             短期                         每兩週的間隔
                ↖                      ↗
                      short interval
                      很短的間隔（期間）
                ↙                      ↘
          short notice                  regular interval
            臨時通知                       固定的間隔
```

short interval
/ʃɔːt ˈɪntəvəl/

In the short interval between the meetings, I was able to call my children and check up on them.
在會議之間很短的時間，我能夠打電話給我的小孩查知他們的情況。

short term
/ʃɔːt tɜːm/

Nicotine causes a short-term increase in heart rate and blood pressure.
尼古丁會造成短期心跳加速與血壓增高。

short notice
/ʃɔːt ˈnəʊtɪs/

Dr. Fisher cancelled all of his appointments at the office for tomorrow on a short notice.
Fisher 博士臨時取消了明天在辦公室的所有會面。

fortnightly interval
/ˈfɔːtnʌɪtli ˈɪntəvəl/

The treatment should be administered at fortnightly intervals to prevent the risk of overdose.
治療應該每兩週一次加以管理，以防止藥劑過量的風險。

regular interval
/ˈrɛgjʊlə ˈɪntəvəl/

Subjects that are exposed to noise at regular intervals perform as well as those who work without interruption.
以固定時間間隔曝露在噪音中的受測者，和在沒有干擾的情形下工作的人表現一樣好。

FRI

IELTS **BASIC WORDS**

conventional /kənˈvɛnʃənəl/ adj. 慣常的，傳統的
ENG. based on or in accordance with general agreement, use or practice
SYS. formal, established

> Having three meals daily is the **conventional** eating routine in many cultures.
> 每天吃三餐是許多文化中慣常的飲食時間規畫。

同義語 例句   Having three meals every day is **in accord with the convention**.
每天吃三餐是符合傳統習慣的。

同義語 例句   Our habit of eating breakfast, lunch and dinner every day is **derived from tradition**.
我們每天吃早餐、午餐、晚餐的習慣是從傳統而來的。

反義語 例句   Some types of diets nowadays **do not conform to standards** and sometimes even challenge them.
今日某些類型的飲食法並不符合標準，有時甚至會挑戰標準。

raise /reɪz/ v. 增加，提高
ENG. to increase the level or amount
SYS. elevate, lift

> Let us **raise** our awareness of which foods are healthy and which we should avoid.
> 讓我們提高對於哪些食物健康、哪些食物應該避免的意識。

同義語 例句   Most diets recommend **increasing** vegetable and fruit intake.
大部分的飲食法建議增加蔬果的攝取。

同義語 例句   We should not only eat healthily but also **get more** physical activity.
我們不止應該吃得健康，也應該做更多身體活動。

反義語 例句   Knowing which foods are healthy to eat **reduces** the chances of having weight-related diseases.
知道吃哪些食物是健康的，會減少得到體重相關疾病的機率。

WEEK 7 TOPIC **HEALTH**

▶基礎單字擴充

massive /ˈmæsɪv/ adj. 巨大的，大量的，大規模的
ENG. imposing in size, bulk, solidity, scale, scope, degree or power
SYS. great, huge

> Consuming unhealthy foods excessively can have **massive** effects on our health.
> 過度食用不健康的食物，會對我們的健康產生巨大的影響。

同義語 例句 Consuming **an enormous amount of** food will lead to obesity.
吃很大量的食物會導致肥胖。

同義語 例句 Eating **a large amount of** salty food will damage kidneys and cause bloating.
吃大量鹹食會傷害腎臟並引起腹脹。

反義語 例句 Eating **a slight amount of** salt will help in regulating body fluids.
吃少量的鹽有助於調節體液。

accomplish /əˈkʌmplɪʃ/ v. 完成，達到
ENG. to succeed in doing
SYS. fulfil, execute

> One way to **accomplish** health goals is devising exercise and meal plans.
> 達成健康目標的一個方法，是制定運動與飲食計畫。

同義語 例句 In order to achieve a healthy weight, we need to **carry out** a proper plan for exercise and diet.
為了達到健康的體重，我們需要實行適當的運動與飲食計畫。

同義語 例句 Eating healthily and exercising will **contribute to** successful weight loss.
吃得健康以及運動會促進成功減重。

反義語 例句 To maintain a healthy weight, we should not **give up** good habits such as exercising and eating healthily.
為了維持健康的體重，我們不應該放棄運動與吃得健康之類的好習慣。

393

FRI

TOPIC | Eating healthily
吃得健康

Food **nourishes** our bodies and gives us the energy to maintain body functions, so it is **vital** that everyone takes in enough nutrients by eating **quality** food. One should **consume** the types and amounts of food recommended by nutritionists to meet the needs for vitamins, minerals and other nutrients. Eating a **nutritious** and balanced diet is one of the best **precautions** against illnesses and promotes good health. In particular, a healthy diet will reduce your risk of obesity, type-two **diabetes**, heart diseases, certain types of cancer and osteoporosis. Besides disease prevention, a healthy diet will also contribute to your vitality. Many people find their stamina and strength improved after they adopt good eating habits. That being said, a certain amount of exercise is still necessary for one to be truly energetic. It is recommended that adults **accumulate** at least 2 hours of **moderate** exercise to **vigorous** physical activity each week.

TRANS

食物能滋養我們的身體，並且提供我們維持身體機能的能量，所以每個人都吃優質的食物來攝取足夠的營養素是很重要的。一個人應該吃營養學家所建議的食物種類與份量，以滿足維生素、礦物質與其他營養素的需要。吃有營養而且均衡的飲食，是預防疾病最好的方法之一，也可以促進健康。尤其，健康的飲食會減少你肥胖、得到第二型糖尿病、心臟疾病、某些種類的癌症和骨質疏鬆症的風險。除了預防疾病，健康的飲食也會對你的活力有所貢獻。有很多人在採取好的飲食習慣之後，發現自己的耐力與力量有所改善。話雖如此，要讓一個人真的有活力，一定程度的運動還是必要的。建議成人每週累積至少 2 小時的中度至強度身體運動。

nourish
/ˈnʌrɪʃ/

v. 滋養

Shea butter and palm oil can intensely **nourish** and rehydrate the skin.
乳油木果脂和棕櫚油可以強力滋潤肌膚並且補充水分。

vital
/ˈvaɪtəl/

adj. 極為重要的，必不可少的

This vendor is absolutely **vital** to the success of the Sunday afternoon flea market.
這個販賣業者對於星期天下午的跳蚤市場是否能夠成功非常重要。

quality
/ˈkwɒlɪti/

n. 品質

He expected only the meat of finest **quality** when going to the butcher shop.
當他前往肉鋪時，他只期待買到品質最好的肉。

consume
/kənˈsjuːm/

v. 消耗，吃掉

After the snake finished **consuming** the mouse, it slithered away slowly.
蛇把老鼠吃掉之後，就慢慢蛇行離開。

nutritious
/njuˈtrɪʃəs/

adj. 有營養的

You should check the label on the cereal box to make sure it's **nutritious** enough.
你應該查看穀片盒子上的標示，確定它夠營養。

precaution
/prɪˈkɔːʃən/

n. 預防措施

With a few sensible **precautions**, people with epilepsy can swim.
只要有一些明智的預防措施，患有癲癇病的人就能游泳。

diabetes
/ˌdaɪəˈbiːtiːz/

n. 糖尿病

Her father, who was quite old and overweight, suffered from **diabetes**. 她年老又過重的父親為糖尿病所苦。

accumulate
/əˈkjuːmjʊleɪt/

v. 累積

I don't want my old armoire in the storeroom because it will **accumulate** dust.
我不希望把我的雕飾衣櫃放在儲藏室裡，因為它會累積灰塵。

moderate
/ˈmɒdərət/

adj. 中等的，適度的，溫和的

Moderate exercise can help strengthen muscles and improve blood circulation.
溫和的運動可以幫助強化肌肉及改善血液循環。

vigorous
/ˈvɪɡərəs/

adj. 精力充沛的，激烈的

Doing **vigorous** exercise about three times a week is very healthy. 一個星期大概做三次激烈的運動是非常健康的。

WORD TRAINING ｜ 重點單字造句練習

nutrient
/ˈnjuːtrɪənt/

n. 營養素

💬 Most foods contain the nutrients you need for your body to stay healthy.
大部分的食物含有讓你的身體保持健康所需的營養素。

Human beings need a variety of nutrients to maintain their body functions and live a healthy life.
人類需要多種營養素來維持身體機能，並且活出健康的人生。

✏️ These foods have been chosen for the athlete's diet because they are rich sources of nutrients which ensure his best performance.
這些食物被選為那位運動員的飲食內容，因為它們是能確保他最佳表現的營養素的豐富來源。

Including sufficient nutrients in your diet can help you prevent osteoporosis and eye diseases and lower your risk of developing hypertension as well as some cancers.
在你的飲食中包含充足的營養素，可以幫助你預防骨質疏鬆症和眼睛疾病，並且降低你產生高血壓和某些癌症的風險。

ill
/ɪl/

adj. 生病的

💬 If you don't feed your children healthy food, they may become ill.
如果你不餵小孩健康的食物，他們可能會生病。

You may be surprised to know that even healthy foods can make you ill.
你可能會驚訝就連健康的食物也可能使你生病。

✏️ Children who always have foods around them tend to eat too much and suffer ill health as a result.
身邊總是有食物的小孩，傾向於吃得太多，結果變得不健康。

Vegetables and fruits can reduce your chance of becoming ill since they contain antioxidants, which help improve your immune system.
蔬菜水果可以減少你生病的機率，因為它們含有抗氧化成分，可以幫助改善你的免疫系統。

heal
/hi:l/

v. 痊癒，治癒

💬 Collagen is one of the major proteins responsible for faster healing of wounds.
膠原蛋白是負責讓傷口更快癒合的主要蛋白質之一。

Depending on the injury's extent, a bone fracture can heal in about three to twelve weeks.
根據傷勢狀況，骨折可以在大約三週到十二週之後痊癒。

✏️ Hippocrates, the father of medicine, once stated that the natural healing force within each of us is the greatest force in getting well.
醫學之父希波克拉底曾經說過，我們體內的自然療癒力是獲得健康的最大力量。

Aloe vera is a plant which is rich in Vitamin E and is known to help heal sunburned skin.
蘆薈是一種富含維生素 E 的植物，並且以能夠幫助治療曬傷的皮膚而為人所知。

hygiene
/ˈhʌɪdʒiːn/

n. 衛生

💬 Children should be taught about oral hygiene in primary school.
孩童應該在小學時被教導口腔衛生。

It is important for mothers to observe proper hygiene, especially when feeding their infants.
母親遵守良好的衛生是很重要的，尤其是在餵她們的嬰兒時。

✏️ School children should be taught about the importance of personal hygiene to prevent the spread of diseases.
學童應該被教導個人衛生的重要性，以預防疾病的傳播。

Food handlers should be trained to observe hygiene procedures while preparing food so as to prevent the spread of viruses and bacteria that may cause food-borne diseases.
處理食物的人應該被訓練在準備食物時遵守衛生程序，以避免可能造成食源性疾病的病毒及細菌的傳播。

RELATED WORDS │ 相關單字延伸

wholesome
adj. 有益健康的

nutritive
adj. 與營養有關的，有營養的

nutritious
adj. 營養的

beneficial
adj. 有益的

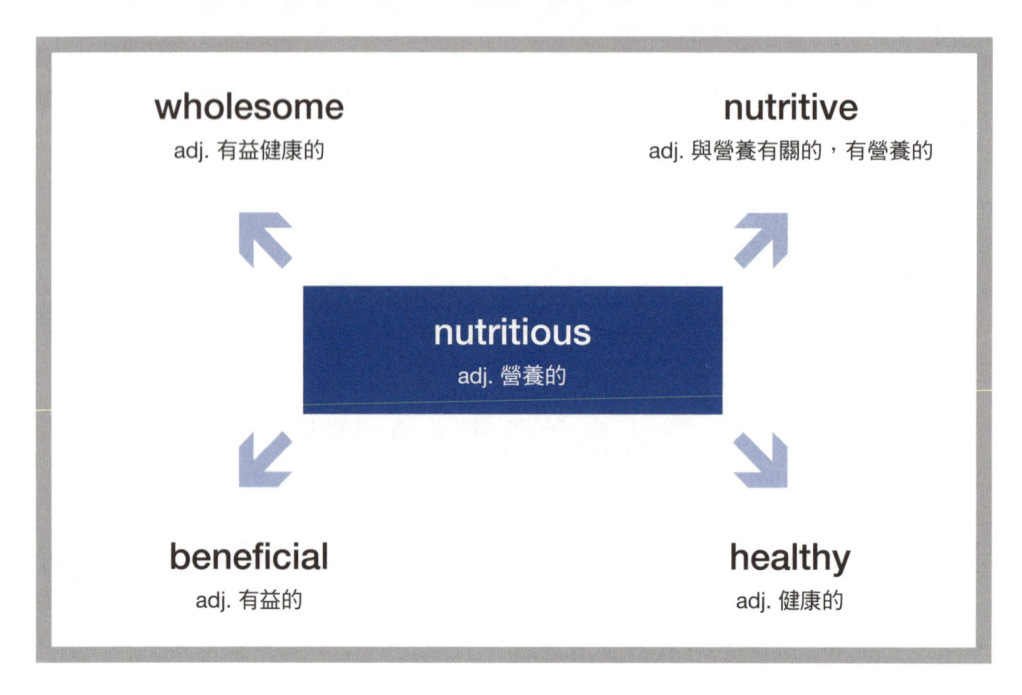

healthy
adj. 健康的

nutritious
/njuˈtrɪʃəs/

Eating a nutritious and balanced diet is one of the best ways to protect and promote good health.
吃營養而且均衡的飲食是保護與促進良好健康的最佳方式之一。

wholesome
/ˈhoʊlsəm/

Stock your pantry shelves with wholesome foods that contribute to your health.
要在你的食品儲藏架上存放對你的健康有益的健康食物。

beneficial
/bɛnɪˈfɪʃəl/

Vitamins A, C and E are beneficial to the skin.
維生素 A、C、E 對皮膚有益。

nutritive
/ˈnjuːtrɪtɪv/

It is important to eat foods which are high in nutritive values to stay healthy.
吃營養價值高的食物來保持健康很重要。

healthy
/ˈhɛlθi/

Healthy foods can help you live an energetic life and prevent diseases.
健康的食物可以幫助你活出有活力的人生並預防疾病。

USEFUL EXPRESSIONS | 相關實用片語

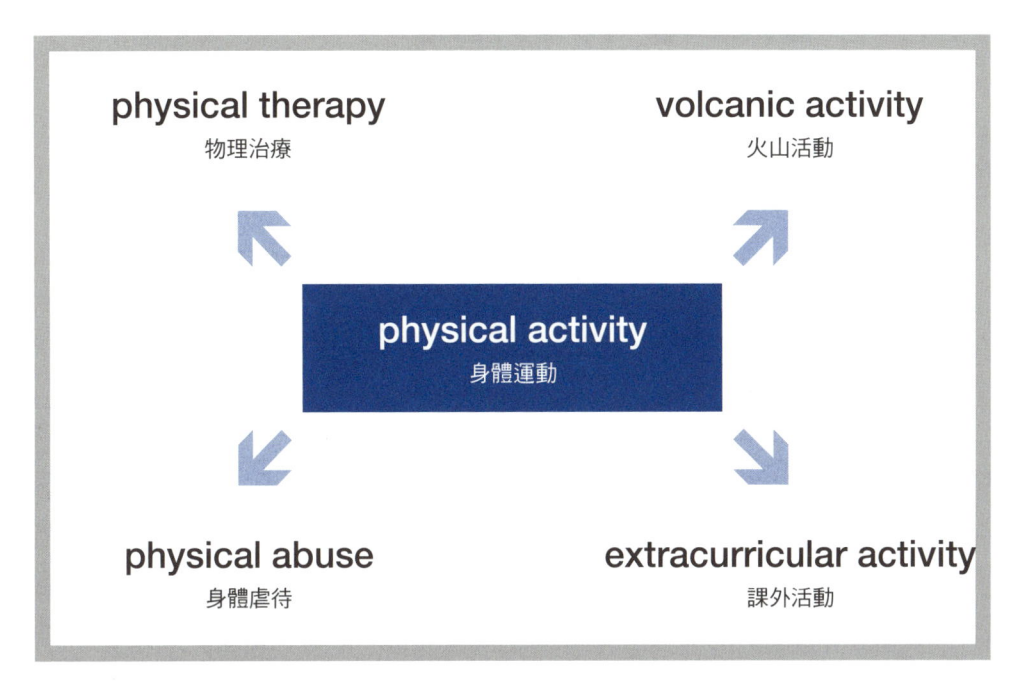

```
physical therapy        volcanic activity
物理治療                    火山活動
          ↖         ↗
         physical activity
            身體運動
          ↙         ↘
physical abuse         extracurricular activity
身體虐待                    課外活動
```

physical activity
/ˈfɪzɪkəl akˈtɪvɪti/

The doctor ordered her to rehabilitate through walking and other low-impact physical activities.
醫生要她用散步和其他低衝擊的身體運動來做復健。

physical therapy
/ˈfɪzɪkəl ˈθɛrəpi/

The only thing that might mend her bended back, according to the doctor, is physical therapy.
根據醫生所說，唯一可能改善她的駝背的，是物理治療。

physical abuse
/ˈfɪzɪkəl əˈbjuːz/

The psychiatrist is quite worried about the psychological trauma that the physical abuse has caused the victim.
精神科醫師很擔心身體虐待對被害者造成的心理創傷。

volcanic activity
/vɒlˈkanɪk akˈtɪvɪti/

Mercury has seen quite a lot of volcanic activity over the years, according to scientists.
根據科學家所說，水星多年來有非常大量的火山活動。

extracurricular activity
/ɛkstrəkəˈrɪkjʊlə akˈtɪvɪti/

Studies have shown that students involved in extracurricular activities do better at school.
研究顯示，從事課外活動的學生在學校表現得比較好。

SAT

IELTS **BASIC WORDS**

resemble /rɪˈzɛmbəl/ v. 像，類似
ENG. to exhibit similarity or likeness to
SYS. duplicate, mirror

> If people's eating pattern now **resembled** that in the past, we would all be healthier.
> 要是人們現在的飲食模式和以前一樣，我們就都會比較健康了。

同義語 例句 What is now considered healthy does not **come close** to what was considered healthy back then.
現在被認為健康的東西，和過去被認為健康的東西並不接近。

同義語 例句 Let us **be like** our ancestors, who only ate natural food at proper meal times.
讓我們像我們的祖先一樣，在合適的用餐時間吃天然的食物。

反義語 例句 Models in the past **look different** from those who are considered beautiful in this age.
過去的模特兒和這個時代被認為美麗的模特兒看起來不一樣。

deliver /dɪˈlɪvə/ v. 遞送，發表
ENG. to carry something to a destination
SYS. convey, present

> People look forward to modern research results **delivering** mind-boggling answers to health questions.
> 人們期待對於健康問題提出驚人答案的現代研究結果。

同義語 例句 Modern studies **provide** more accurate answers to health questions.
現代研究提供對於健康問題更精確的答案。

同義語 例句 Health research nowadays **gives out** more answers.
現代的健康研究給出更多答案。

反義語 例句 Even with modern technology, studies still fail to provide answers to the simplest health questions.
即使有了現代科技，研究仍然無法提供最簡單的健康問題的答案。

WEEK 7 TOPIC **HEALTH**

▶ 基礎單字擴充

own /oʊn/ adj. 自己的
ENG. belonging to one's self
SYS. personal, exclusive

> People now have their **own** beliefs that are different from those in the past.
> 人們現在有自己和過去不同的想法。

同義語例句 The ideas **belonging to** young people today are often considered ridiculous by old people.
屬於今天年輕人的想法，經常被老年人認為是荒謬的。

同義語例句 People in the present day have their **individual** thoughts about what is healthy for them.
現代的人對於什麼是對自己健康的，有各自的想法。

反義語例句 Adopting the lifestyle of older generations is like living **someone else's** life.
採用過去世代的生活型態，就好像在過別人的生活一樣。

exceed /ɪkˈsiːd/ v. 超過
ENG. be greater in scope or size
SYS. transcend, surpass

> A medical breakthrough usually **exceeds** the general public's imagination.
> 醫學上的突破通常會超越一般大眾的想像。

同義語例句 Medical studies that **go beyond** expectations are considered innovative.
超越期待的醫學研究被認為是創新的。

同義語例句 Breakthroughs in medicine will surely **stand out** in the medical industry.
醫藥的突破當然會在醫學產業脫穎而出。

反義語例句 Cures that **fall short** of expectations should be improved or replaced by better ones.
達不到期待的療法應該予以改善，或者以更好的療法代替。

401

TOPIC: Mental health problems in modern society

現代社會中的精神健康問題

Public **awareness** of mental health is now **heightened**, and many people have noticed the growing number of **diagnosed** mental illnesses that have **emerged** and their impact on society. Medical experts say that anxiety and depression are the most common psychological **ailments** in recent years. There are many reasons for the rise in **incidence** of mental illness, but one of the biggest contributing factors seen is stress caused by overwork. Our society's fixation on material **wealth** and status is **exacting** its price on us, driving us to work longer and harder, to the **detriment** of our own well-being. The global recession and some employers' unspoken expectation that we work overtime are also contributing to the problem. In our increasingly busy lives, it is worth stepping back and realising that our most valuable possession is our health and that physical and mental health are **interwoven**.

TRANS

現在，大眾對於精神健康的意識提高了，而許多人也注意到精神疾病發生並且被診斷出來的件數越來越多，以及這對於社會的影響。醫學專家說，焦慮和憂鬱是近幾年最常見的心理疾病。精神疾病發生率的上升有許多理由，但我們看到的最大因素之一，是過勞造成的壓力。我們的社會對於物質財富與地位的執著，正向我們索取代價，驅使我們工作得更久、更努力，而損害了我們自己的健康與幸福。全球性的經濟衰退，以及某些雇主沒有說出口但想要我們加班的期望，也是造成問題的原因。在我們日益繁忙的生活裡，我們值得往後退一步，並且了解我們最寶貴的財產是自己的健康，還有身體與精神健康是相互交織的。

awareness
/əˈwɛːnəs/

n. 意識

She gives speeches in elementary schools to raise children's **awareness** of burn injuries.
她在小學發表演說,以提升兒童對於燙傷的認知。

heighten
/ˈhʌɪtən/

v. 提升

The number of fatalities greatly **heightened** public concern about road safety.
死亡的人數大大地升高了大眾對於道路安全的擔憂。

diagnose
/ˈdʌɪəgnəʊz/

v. 診斷

Before the doctor **diagnosed** the boy, he asked his family members to enter.
在醫生為男孩診斷之前,他要求他的家人進入診療室。

emerge
/ɪˈməːdʒ/

v. 浮現,出現

As she **emerged** from the lake, the moonlight shone on her face and neck. 當她浮出湖面,月光閃耀在她的臉和脖子上。

ailment
/ˈeɪlmənt/

n. 疾病

She believed that she had many **ailments**, but in reality, she wasn't sick at all.
她過去相信自己有許多疾病,但事實上她根本就沒有生病。

incidence
/ˈɪnsɪdəns/

n. 發生,發生率

New Zealand now has the highest **incidence** of skin cancer in the world. 紐西蘭現在有全世界最高的皮膚癌發生率。

wealth
/wɛlθ/

n. 財富

One should always maintain and improve his or her own health because it is real **wealth**.
人永遠都要維持並改善自己的健康,因為那是真正的財富。

exact
/ɪɡˈzakt/

v. 索求,施加(報復)

After hearing the not-guilty verdict in court, the victim's father decided to **exact** revenge on the defendant.
聽到法庭上的無罪判決之後,受害者的父親決定要報復被告。

detriment
/ˈdɛtrɪmənt/

n. 損害

You can enjoy eating meat without **detriment** to your health by paying attention to how much you eat.
藉由注意自己吃了多少,你可以享用肉類而不會損害自己的健康。

interweave
/ɪntəˈwiːv/

v. 交織

The facts and the lies were so expertly **interwoven** that the argument sounded convincing.
事實和謊言交織得如此巧妙,使得論點聽起來很有說服力。

WORD TRAINING | 重點單字造句練習

wellness n. 健康
/ˈwɛlnəs/

💬 You can make time for wellness now, or you can make time for sickness later.
你可以現在為健康留出時間,或者在以後為疾病花時間。

Some junk food companies of the past have switched sides and started making food products that improve our wellness.
有些過去的垃圾食物公司轉換了陣營,開始製造增進我們健康的食品。

✏️ The yoga phenomenon has grown dramatically over the past decade, with thousands of people today embarking on this ancient exercise that promotes health and wellness of the mind and body.
瑜伽現象在過去十年戲劇性地成長,今日有成千上萬的人開始進行這項能夠促進心靈與身體健康的運動。

Many consumers today spend a significant amount of money on healthier foods, exercise equipment and supplements, becoming a major target group for the health and wellness industry.
今日許多消費者花費大量的金錢在比較健康的食物、運動器材和補充食品上,成為健康產業的主要目標族群。

---

regularly
/ˈrɛɡjələli/

adv. 規律地,定期地

💬 Exercising regularly, eating healthy foods and getting enough sleep are the key to health.
規律運動、吃健康的食物和睡眠充足,是健康的關鍵。

If your growth plates have already closed, exercising regularly won't help increase your height anymore.
如果你的生長板已經關閉,那麼規律運動也不會再幫助你長高了。

✏️ Exercising regularly can make one live longer because it can enhance blood circulation, improve one's mood and brain function, and most of all, it can help burn excess calories.
規律運動可以讓人活得更久,因為這樣能夠促進血液循環、改善情緒與大腦功能,而且最重要的是有助於燃燒過多的熱量。

Exercising regularly reduces the amount of stress hormones in the body and improves cognitive function, and therefore is very beneficial for teenagers during their stressful and busy school years.
規律運動會減少體內的壓力荷爾蒙並且改善認知功能,所以在青少年壓力大而忙碌的學校時期非常有益。

sanitary
/ˈsænɪtəri/

adj. 衛生上的，衛生的

💬 There should be sufficient sanitary conveniences in every workplace.
每個工作場所都應該要有充足的衛生便利設施（廁所）。

We are one of the UK's leading manufacturers of bathroom sanitary ware and pride ourselves on our products' high quality.　我們是英國浴廁衛生用具（馬桶等）的領導製造商之一，並且以我們產品的高品質自豪。

✏️ Most people would expect hotels and motels to meet the highest sanitary standards, but to tell the truth, quite a few accommodation establishments are shockingly filthy and unsafe.
許多人會期望飯店和汽車旅館符合最高的衛生標準，但說實話，有相當多住宿設施驚人地骯髒而且不安全。

The general aim of modern public health and sanitary policies is to ensure that the health of all members of a community is protected and improved.
現代公共健康與衛生政策大致上的目標，是確保社會所有成員的健康受到保護及改善。

coordination
/kəʊˌɔːdɪˈneɪʃən/

n. 協調

💬 Today's research shows the symptoms of autism may include difficulties with coordination and motor skills.
今日的研究顯示，自閉症的症狀可能包含協調與運動能力的困難。

After learning to play soccer, my coordination is much better than it was in the past.
學習踢足球以後，我的協調性比過去好多了。

✏️ Fine motor skills and hand-eye coordination improve during the crawling period, so babies should be encouraged to develop the ability of picking up very small things, such as cereal, with dexterity.
精確運動技巧與手眼協調在爬行時期會變好，所以嬰兒應該被鼓勵培養靈巧地撿起細小物品如穀片的能力。

In the past, children who were late in the development of coordination skills received little attention because many believed they would grow out of it, but today we know the importance of therapy for them.　在過去，協調能力發展比較晚的小孩得到的關注很少，因為很多人相信他們長大就會有所改善，但今天我們知道治療對他們的重要性。

RELATED WORDS | 相關單字延伸

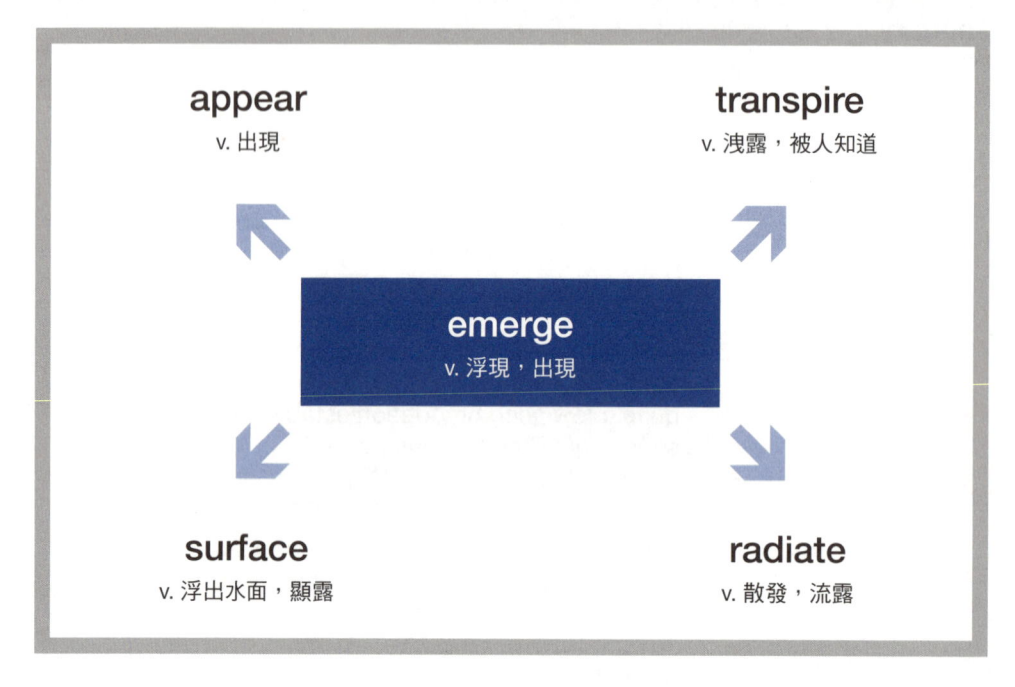

appear
v. 出現

transpire
v. 洩露，被人知道

emerge
v. 浮現，出現

surface
v. 浮出水面，顯露

radiate
v. 散發，流露

emerge
/ɪˈmɜːdʒ/

Many people have noticed the growing number of diagnosed mental illnesses that have emerged and their impact on the society.
許多人注意到精神疾病發生並且被診斷出來的件數越來越多，以及這對於社會的影響。

appear
/əˈpɪə/

Her mental illness seemed to appear out of nowhere.
她的精神疾病似乎不知從何而來（沒有理由就發生了）。

surface
/ˈsɜːfɪs/

After it surfaced that she suffered from mental illness, the public became much more understanding.
她有精神疾病的事情為人所知之後，大眾就變得體諒許多。

transpire
/trænˈspʌɪə/

Many people were shocked when it transpired that Bill had been mentally ill for many years.
Bill 罹患精神疾病多年的事情被揭露時，很多人感到震驚。

radiate
/ˈreɪdɪeɪt/

Public understanding about mental illness radiated from the sympathetic crowd.
大眾對精神疾病的了解，從同情的群眾散播開來了。

USEFUL EXPRESSIONS | 相關實用片語

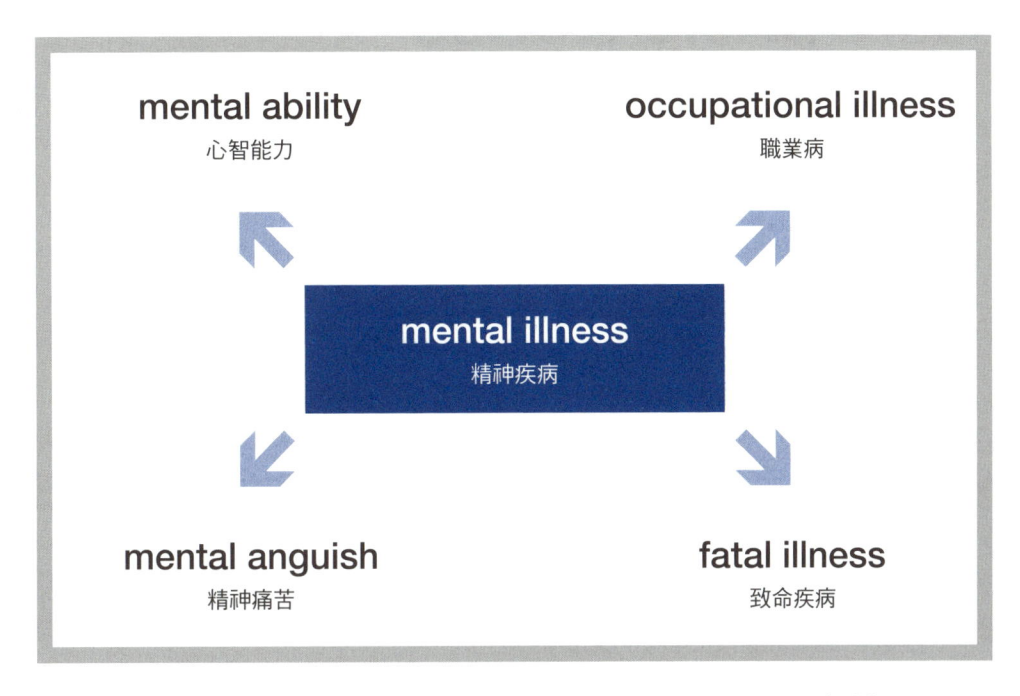

```
         mental ability              occupational illness
           心智能力                          職業病
                    ↖          ↗
                    mental illness
                       精神疾病
                    ↙          ↘
         mental anguish               fatal illness
           精神痛苦                        致命疾病
```

mental illness
/ˈmɛntəl ˈɪlnəs/

Some studies suggest that children breastfed from infancy are less likely to have mental illnesses later in life.　有些研究顯示，從嬰兒時期開始接受哺乳的孩子，在日後的生活中罹患精神疾病的可能性比較低。

mental ability
/ˈmɛntəl əˈbɪlɪti/

A human's mental ability is infinite, and its development depends on one's willingness to absorb knowledge. 人的心智能力是無限的，而它的發展取決於一個人吸收知識的意願。

mental anguish
/ˈmɛntəl ˈæŋgwɪʃ/

The mental anguish that he suffered after the accident hurt his chances of achieving his future dreams.　事故發生後遭受的精神痛苦，傷害（減少）了他達成未來夢想的可能性。

occupational illness
/ˌɑkjʊˈpeɪʃənəl ˈɪlnəs/

Many occupational illnesses, such as skin diseases caused by handling dangerous materials, can be avoided.　許多職業病，例如因為處理危險物質而造成的皮膚疾病，是可以避免的。

fatal illness
/ˈfeɪtəl ˈɪlnəs/

Tuberculosis took many lives in the 1950s and was considered to be a fatal illness.　結核病在 1950 年代奪走了許多人的生命，並且被認為是致命的疾病。

SUN

IELTS **BASIC WORDS**

harvest /ˈhɑːvɪst/ v. 收穫
ENG. to gather
SYS. reap, collect

> If we invest in the right healthcare plan, we will **harvest** bountifully.
> 如果我們投資在對的醫療保健計畫上，我們將收穫豐盛。

同義語 例句
A wider variety of healthcare services will **bring in** more benefits for the public.
更加多樣化的醫療保健服務，將會為大眾帶來更多好處。

同義語 例句
Medical practitioners should pull together to build a healthcare system from which the general public can **obtain** more benefits.
開業醫師應該共同合作，建立一般大眾能夠獲得更多好處的醫療保健體系。

反義語 例句
The lack of medical personnel has caused many rural areas to lose their medical centres.
醫護人員的缺乏，造成許多鄉村地區失去了它們的醫療中心。

halt /hɔːlt/ v. 停止，使停止
ENG. come to a stop
SYS. rest, wait

> When people do not avail themselves of a service, it shall **be halted**.
> 當人們不利用一項服務時，它就應該被停止。

同義語 例句
The healthcare system will **break down** if only a few people make use of the services offered.
如果只有很少人利用醫療保健體系提供的服務，它就會崩解。

同義語 例句
The development of a healthcare system will **come to a standstill** if only a few people use its services.
如果只有很少人使用醫療保健體系的服務，那麼它的發展就會停滯。

反義語 例句
A healthcare system **moves forward** as more and more people utilise its services.
醫療保健系統隨著越來越多人使用它的服務而進步。

WEEK 7 TOPIC **HEALTH**

▶ 基礎單字擴充

prosper /ˈprɒspə/ v. 繁榮，成功
ENG. make steady progress
SYS. flourish, advance

> The healthcare industry will **prosper** if everyone is willing to fully utilise its services.
> 如果每個人都願意徹底運用醫療保健服務，醫療保健產業就會蓬勃發展。

同義語例句 The healthcare industry will **fly high** if given full support by the public.
如果有大眾完全的支持，醫療保健產業就會展翅高飛。

同義語例句 Medical facilities that **do well** are the ones that provide good health services.
（業績）表現得好的醫療設施，是那些提供良好健康服務的設施。

反義語例句 A medical facility will **fail** if there is too much negative feedback from patients.
如果有太多來自患者的負面回饋意見，醫療設施就會失敗。

display /dɪˈspleɪ/ v. 陳列，展現
ENG. to show; make visible or apparent
SYS. exhibit, present

> It is best for medical facilities to **display** posters advertising their services to increase patients' interest.
> 醫療設施最好展示介紹他們服務的海報，以提升患者的興趣。

同義語例句 Printed information should be available in hospitals to **advertise** all available services.
醫院裡應該要提供印刷的資料，宣傳所有可提供的服務。

同義語例句 Information materials should be displayed in areas where they can be **revealed** to patients easily.
告知資訊的資料應該要展示在容易讓患者看到的區域。

反義語例句 The hospital **covered up** information about its medical malpractice to avoid protests from its patients.
這家醫院隱瞞醫療疏失的資訊，避免患者抗議。

SUN

TOPIC: Making healthcare available to everyone

讓每個人都能得到醫療保健服務

Healthcare is an essential service for modern people, yet most countries do not freely provide it to their citizens, even though many of them are unable to afford it. Lack of **adequate** healthcare is one of the top social and economic problems that people around the world face today, and there is a wide **variation** in the services provided even among countries with **comparable** levels of income and health **expenditure**. The rising costs of medical care and health **insurance** are further **impacting** the **livelihood** of many in one way or another. For many poor people, illness is so costly that it may force them into **bankruptcy**. Therefore, modern nations should offer universal health coverage to all, as well as **subsidise** the treatment of poor patients. It is especially important to make sure that as large a percentage as possible of the **destitute** people can get insurance.

TRANS

對現代人而言，醫療保健是不可或缺的服務，但大部分的國家並不免費提供醫療給國民，即使許多人無法負擔。缺乏足夠的醫療保健服務，是今天全世界的人所面對的重大社會與經濟問題之一，而即使是收入水準與健康支出相當的國家，提供的服務也有很大的差異。醫療服務與健康保險逐漸上升的費用更進一步在某些方面影響著許多人的生計。對許多窮人而言，疾病很花錢，而可能迫使他們陷入破產。所以，現代國家應該為所有國民提供全面的健康保障，以及補助貧窮病患的治療。力求盡可能有高比例的窮困者獲得保險尤其重要。

adequate
/ˈædɪkwət/
adj. 足夠的，適當的
She ate an **adequate** amount of food and felt full.
她吃了足夠份量的食物，而且覺得飽了。

variation
/vɛrɪˈeɪʃən/
n. 變化，差異
There was little **variation** between the two collages on the wall.
牆上兩張拼貼畫的差異非常小。

comparable
/ˈkɒmpərəbəl/
adj. 可比較的，相當的
Indian elephants are **comparable** to African elephants in their size.
印度象在體積上與非洲象差不多。

expenditure
/ɪkˈspɛndɪtʃə/
n. 支出
Dan's annual income exceeded his annual **expenditure** last year.
Dan 去年的年收入超過了他的年度支出。

insurance
/ɪnˈʃʊərəns/
n. 保險
Won't you take out **insurance** on your vehicle at our shop?
你不在我們修車廠買你車子的保險嗎？

impact
/ɪmˈpækt/
v. 衝擊，影響
The increased use of plastic in households is **impacting** ocean life.
家庭對塑膠的使用量增加正影響著海洋生物。

livelihood
/ˈlʌɪvlɪhʊd/
n. 生活，生計
Farmers' **livelihood** depends on weather conditions.
農夫的生計取決於天氣狀況。

bankruptcy
/ˈbaŋkrʌptsi/
n. 破產
When she heard that her husband's company filed for **bankruptcy**, she was shocked.
聽到她丈夫的公司聲請破產，她很震驚。

subsidise
/ˈsʌbsɪdʌɪz/
v. 補助
The government **subsidises** the education of the poor in hopes of helping them live a better life in the future.
政府補助窮人的教育，希望幫助他們在未來過更好的生活。

destitute
/ˈdɛstɪtjuːt/
adj. 窮困的
Some people give money to the homeless and other **destitute** citizens.
有些人會給遊民和其他貧窮的市民錢。

WORD TRAINING | 重點單字造句練習

phobia
/ˈfoʊbɪə/

n. 恐懼症

This technology is believed to be ideal for diabetes patients with needle phobia.
這項技術被認為對於有針頭恐懼的糖尿病患者很理想。

Exposure therapy is the most effective and accepted treatment for social phobia today. 暴露療法是今日對於社交畏懼症最有效、最廣為接受的治療方式。

There are still many health insurance companies that do not cover treatment for phobia, so patients who suffer from it usually leave it untreated.
現在還是有很多健康保險公司的保障範圍不包含恐懼症的治療，所以有恐懼症問題的人通常放著它不治療。

In an ideal world, specialists, practitioners and pharmacists would work together to help people who suffer from an intense phobia to manage it.
在理想的世界裡，專家、醫師和藥師會共同合作，幫助有嚴重恐懼症的人控制它。

---

sympathetic
/sɪmpəˈθɛtɪk/

adj. 同情的，有同情心的

We provide a comprehensive range of female healthcare in a sympathetic, caring and interactive manner.
我們以富有同情、關懷與互動的方式，提供範圍全面的女性醫療保健服務。

The physician is sympathetic towards her patients, no matter what kind of disease they suffer from.
那位醫生對患者很有同情心，不管他們遭遇的是什麼疾病。

Ideally, nurses should be caring, sympathetic, responsible and detail-oriented, with every patient's condition and need in their mind.
理想上，護理師應該要能夠關心、有同情心、負責任而且注重細節，心裡要記著每位患者的狀況與需求。

Computer programs can determine the best possible treatment for a medical condition, but patients will still need a sympathetic, responsible and knowledgeable person to guide them through difficult healthcare decisions.
電腦程式可以判定病症最好的可能治療方法，但患者仍然會需要有同情心、負責、有知識的人來引導他們度過困難的醫療決定。

intake
/ˈɪnteɪk/

n. 攝取

💬 Excessive sugar intake may cause serious medical conditions.
攝取過多糖分可能造成嚴重的病症。

Too much cholesterol intake may clog the arteries and cause heart problems.
過多的膽固醇攝取可能會阻塞動脈並且造成心臟問題。

✏️ Adequate intake of dietary fibre, found mainly in fruits, vegetables, grains and nuts, is very effective in relieving constipation and maintaining a normal weight.
攝取足夠的膳食纖維──主要存在於水果、蔬菜、穀物與堅果中──對於緩解便秘與維持正常體重非常有效。

Consumers should be very prudent about their fat intake and must learn how to read and interpret the nutritional facts printed on the package of every food product in supermarkets.
消費者應該對自己的脂肪攝取非常謹慎，並且必須學習如何閱讀並解釋超市中每種食品包裝上所印的營養成分表。

therapy
/ˈθɛrəpi/

n. 治療

💬 It is ideal to make the client relax before a massage therapy session.
在按摩療程開始之前，先讓顧客放鬆是理想的。

An ideal healthcare system would put more emphasis on preventing illness than providing therapy.
相較於提供治療，理想的醫療保健體系會比較著重於預防疾病。

✏️ With an approach that integrates rehabilitation, fitness and nutrition, athletic therapy is the ideal choice for making positive changes in an athlete's health and performance.
因為它的方法整合了復健、體能健康與營養，所以體育治療是為運動員的健康與表現產生正面改變的理想選擇。

I have a vision of ideal healthcare that would address life-threatening diseases for the elderly by providing them with therapy and treatment free of charge.
我有一個理想醫療保健的願景，是藉由提供年長者免費療程與治療，為他們處理威脅生命的疾病。

RELATED WORDS | 相關單字延伸

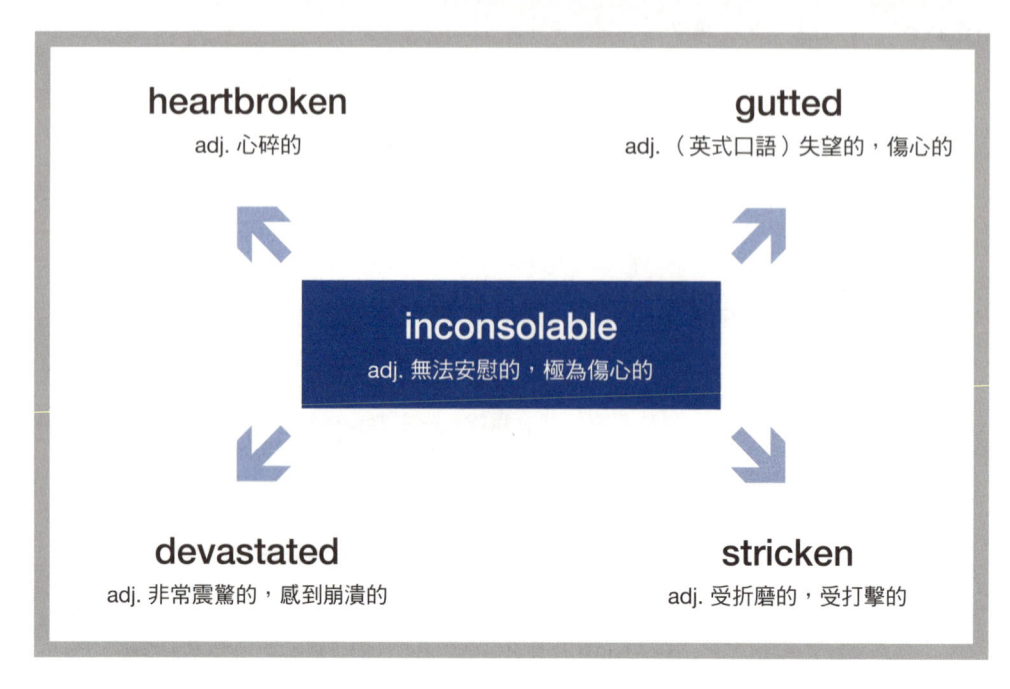

heartbroken
adj. 心碎的

gutted
adj. （英式口語）失望的，傷心的

inconsolable
adj. 無法安慰的，極為傷心的

devastated
adj. 非常震驚的，感到崩潰的

stricken
adj. 受折磨的，受打擊的

inconsolable
/ɪnkənˈsəʊləbəl/
After receiving the news of her father's death, she was inconsolable.
收到她父親過世的消息，她非常傷心。

heartbroken
/ˈhɑːtbrəʊkən/
She was heartbroken when she saw all the poor people on the street suffering from illnesses.
她看到街頭的許多窮人因疾病而受苦，心都碎了。

devastated
/ˈdɛvəsteɪtɪd//
My cousin was devastated after finding out he was deep in debt to the government.
我的表哥發現自己欠政府許多債，感到很震驚。

gutted
/ˈgʌtɪd/
I felt gutted when I realised my disease can't be completely cured.
知道我的疾病無法完全治好，我覺得非常失望。

stricken
/ˈstrɪkən/
Many people stricken with illness cannot work, which in turn leaves them poor and often homeless.
許多罹患疾病的人無法工作，使得他們變得貧窮，也經常使他們流落街頭。

USEFUL EXPRESSIONS | 相關實用片語

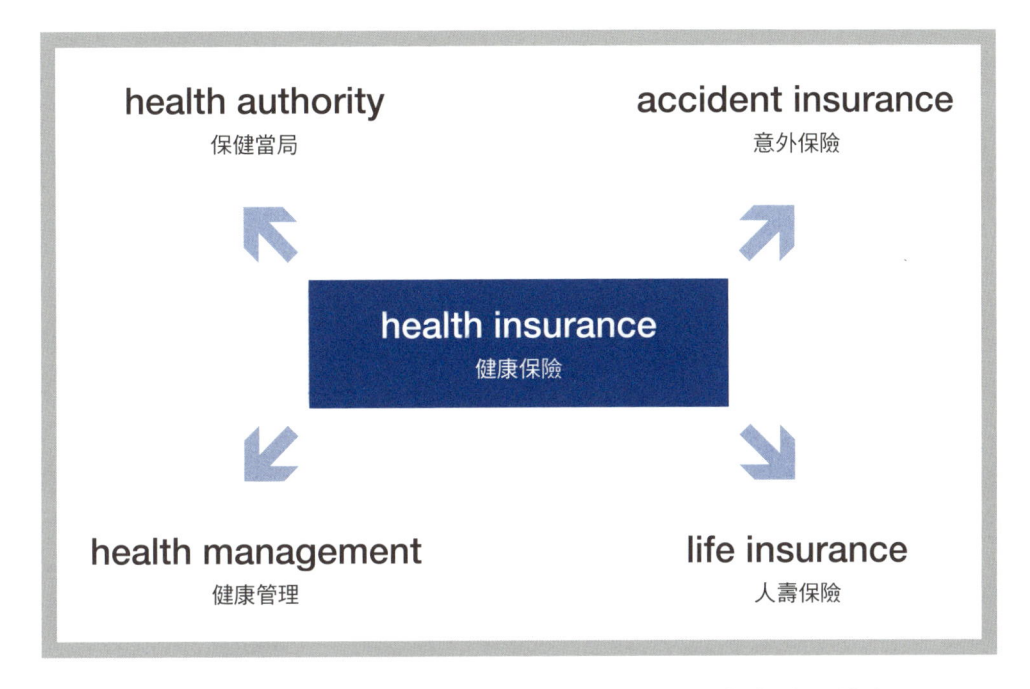

health authority
保健當局

accident insurance
意外保險

health insurance
健康保險

health management
健康管理

life insurance
人壽保險

---

health insurance
/hɛlθ ɪnˈʃʊərəns/

Employees who would like to apply for health insurance may consult the insurance company.
想要申請健康保險的員工，可以諮詢保險公司。

health authority
/hɛlθ ɔːˈθɒrɪti/

According to the health authorities, people tend to incorrectly perceive AIDS as an unmanageable disease.
根據保健當局，人們往往錯誤地認為愛滋病是難以控制的疾病。

health management
/hɛlθ ˈmænɪdʒmənt/

To achieve population health management goals, patients' cooperation with healthcare providers plays a key role.
要達成社群健康管理的目標，患者和醫療保健服務提供者的合作扮演重要角色。

accident insurance
/ˈæksɪdənt ɪnˈʃʊərəns/

Due to his hazardous occupation, the insurance company rejected his accident insurance application.
由於他危險的職業，保險公司拒絕了他意外保險的申請。

life insurance
/lʌɪf ɪnˈʃʊərəns/

Just in case of accidental death, I took out a life insurance policy on my husband.
以防萬一發生意外死亡，我為我老公買了人壽保險。

WEEK 8
MEDIA

名人對年輕人的影響

西方電視節目對兒童的影響

大眾傳播媒體的演變

氣象預報

數位時代中的雜誌

看板廣告

酒類宣傳的負面影響

MON

IELTS BASIC WORDS

reveal /rɪˈviːl/ v. 揭露
ENG. to make previously unknown things known to others
SYS. disclose, divulge

> The actress burst into tears when her secrets were publicly **revealed**.
> 當她的祕密被公諸於世時,那位女演員突然大哭起來。

同義語例句 Many people like to read tabloids which **expose** the private lives of celebrities.
許多人喜歡閱讀揭露名人私生活的小報。

同義語例句 The gossip magazine **brought** the celebrity's affair with several women **to light**.
那份八卦雜誌揭露了那位名人和幾位女性的風流韻事。

反義語例句 Most celebrities prefer their personal life to stay private and undisturbed.
大部分的名人比較希望自己的個人生活保持私人而不被打擾。

intrusion /ɪnˈtruːʒən/ n. 侵入
ENG. any entry into an area not previously occupied
SYS. interruption, encroachment

> The fan's **intrusion** into the movie set annoyed the actress.
> 影迷入侵電影片場,惹惱了女演員。

同義語例句 The fan that appeared unexpectedly was an **unwelcome addition** to the movie staff.
意外出現的影迷,是電影片場的不速之客。

同義語例句 The fan's **invasion** into the movie set alarmed the actors.
影迷入侵電影片場,讓演員們驚慌不安。

反義語例句 Everyone heaved a sigh of relief when the fan made a peaceful **exit**.
當影迷平和地離開時,每個人都鬆了一口氣。

WEEK 8 TOPIC **MEDIA**

▶基礎單字擴充

mistake /mɪˈsteɪk/ n. 錯誤，過失
ENG. An error or fault resulting from defective judgment, deficient knowledge, or carelessness
SYS. blunder, misapprehension

> The athlete made a **mistake** that cost him his sports career.
> 那位運動員犯了讓他賠上運動生涯的錯誤。

同義語例句 **Errors** made by athletes in their sports may damage their reputation.
運動員在運動中犯的錯，可能會損害他們的名聲。

同義語例句 A **mix-up** in a sports team's line-up can cause easy losses.
運動隊伍陣容的混亂，可能會造成容易輸掉比賽。

反義語例句 You must have an **accurate understanding** of the rules to stand a chance to win in a sport.
你必須對規則有準確的了解，才有機會在運動中獲勝。

manifest /ˈmænɪfɛst/ v. 顯示，表明
ENG. to make clearly apparent to the sight or understanding
SYS. display, express

> The celebrity **manifested** her sincere apology during her interview.
> 那位名人在訪談中表現出誠摯的歉意。

同義語例句 The actress **clearly revealed** that she felt regretful for what she had done.
那位女演員清楚地表露，她對自己所做的事感到後悔。

同義語例句 The best way to apologise to the public is to **show plainly** how remorseful one feels.
向大眾道歉最好的方法，是明白表現出自己覺得多麼後悔。

反義語例句 Things will get worse for celebrities if they **cover up** their mistakes with more lies.
如果名人用更多謊言掩蓋自己的錯誤，情況會變得更糟。

419

MON

08-1A

TOPIC   Celebrities' influence on young people
名人對年輕人的影響

Many people believe that our **celebrity-obsessed** culture is the source of the narcissistic behaviour we now see in the younger generation. Viewing celebrities as role models can be a calamitous **trend** for youth, as it influences their clothing styles and moral standards, and confuses them into believing delusions of **glamour**. These superstars in film and music industries are persistently followed by the paparazzi, photographed drinking, wearing **provocative** clothing, doing drugs and acting **amorally**. Are the values they are showing the ones we want our young people to be **absorbing**? That being said, critics tend to **overestimate** the influence celebrities actually have on society. They purport that we are blinded by fame, following in their **footsteps** without considering the **repercussions** of our actions, but this may not be the case for everyone. Even though many young people try to imitate everything celebrities do, they are less likely to do so when they grow older.

TRANS

許多人相信我們對名人迷戀的文化，是我們現在在年輕一代所看到的自戀行為的根源。把名人當成榜樣，對年輕人而言可能是災難性的趨勢，因為這樣會影響他們的穿著風格與道德標準，並且迷惑他們相信名人魅力造成的錯覺。這些電影和音樂界的超級巨星，總是被狗仔隊跟隨、被拍到喝酒、穿著挑逗的服裝、吸毒和行為不道德。他們展現的價值觀是我們希望年輕人吸收的嗎？話雖如此，評論家往往高估名人實際上對社會的影響力。他們聲稱我們被名氣蒙蔽，追隨他們的腳步而不考慮我們行為的後果，但可能不是每個人的情況都這樣。即使許多年輕人試圖模仿名人所做的每件事，但他們長大以後就比較不會這麼做。

celebrity
/sɪˈlɛbrɪti/

n. 名人

A degrading rumour has been spreading around and tarnishing the name of the **celebrity**.
一件不名譽的傳聞已經傳遍，並且玷污了那位名人的名聲。

obsessed
/əbˈsɛst/

adj. 著迷的

Do not become **obsessed** with trying to attain perfection.
不要執迷於試圖達到完美。

trend
/trɛnd/

n. 趨勢，潮流

With her style and sense of fashion, she has again started an irresistible **trend**.
靠著個人風格和時尚感，她再次發起了令人難以抗拒的潮流。

glamour
/ˈɡlæmə/

n. 魅力

Hollywood **glamour** is admired by almost all other countries in the world.
好萊塢的魅力幾乎受到世界上所有其他國家的仰慕。

provocative
/prəˈvɒkətɪv/

adj. 挑逗性的

The way the teenager was dressed was too **provocative** for church.
這個青少年的打扮對教會來說太過挑逗。

amorally
/eɪˈmɒrəlɪ/

adv. 不道德地

When Mike pushed his brother down, he was acting **amorally**.
當 Mike 推倒他的弟弟時，他是在做很不道德的事情。

absorb
/əbˈzɔːb/

v. 吸收

The sponge quickly **absorbed** the smelly spilt milk.
海綿很快地吸收了打翻的臭牛奶。

overestimate
/əʊvərˈɛstɪmeɪt/

v. 高估

Never **overestimate** your ability to work and earn money.
絕對不要高估你工作與賺錢的能力。

footsteps
/ˈfʊtstɛps/

n. 腳步

He lived his life following in the **footsteps** of the greatest man he knew, his father.
他追隨他所認識最偉大的人的腳步過生活，就是他的父親。

repercussion
/riːpəˈkʌʃən/

n. 後果，影響

Watch what you eat because overeating has its **repercussions**.
注意你吃的東西，因為吃得太多可能會有（不好的）後果。

WORD TRAINING | 重點單字造句練習

ethical
/ˈɛθɪkəl/

adj. 道德的

💬 I'm concerned that there is a lack of ethical standards among gossip magazines.
我對於八卦雜誌缺乏道德標準感到擔憂。

The panel discussed the media's obsession with celebrity news and its ethical impact.
討論來賓討論了媒體對於名人消息的執迷與其道德影響。

✎ The audience are easily affected by what they see or hear in the media, so journalists and reporters should be careful when making ethical decisions about how they present the news to the public. 觀眾很容易受到在媒體中看到或聽到的內容影響，所以報章新聞記者和報導記者在做如何向大眾呈現新聞的道德決定時，應該要謹慎。

Paying celebrities to tweet can pose ethical issues because they are so influential that their followers may believe whatever they say without thinking.
付錢給名人在推特上發文，可能會造成道德問題，因為他們很有影響力，他們的追蹤者可能會毫不思考就相信他們所說的任何事情。

tabloid
/ˈtæblɔɪd/

n. 小報

💬 Celebrities' private lives have become products for tabloids to sell to their fans.
名人的私生活已經成為小報賣給粉絲的產品。

The values promoted by tabloids may have negative influence on young people.
小報宣揚的價值觀可能會對青年造成負面影響。

✎ Most of us tend to judge celebrities according to the stories in tabloids, even though the stories often turn out to be untrue. 我們大部分的人傾向於根據小報的報導來評價名人，即使那些報導最後經常不是真的。

It seems that celebrities are constantly exploited and disrespected in tabloids, but many people are not concerned because they believe that celebrities should earn their fame at the cost of personal dignity. 名人似乎在小報中一直受到剝削（被挖掘隱私等等）而且不受尊重，但很多人並不在意，因為他們相信名人應該要犧牲個人尊嚴來賺取名聲。

press
/prɛs/

n. 報刊，新聞媒體

💬 The amount of press coverage of celebrities makes ordinary people envious.
新聞媒體對名人的報導量讓普通人感到羨慕。

Young people are more likely to be influenced by famous people's endorsements in the press.
年輕人比較容易受到名人在媒體中的代言影響。

✒️ Some people claim that the press coverage of celebrities' eccentric behaviour can cause their fans to act radically in public.
有些人主張，新聞媒體對於名人異常行為的報導，可能會造成粉絲在公眾場合做出極端行為。

The press coverage of celebrities' private lives may be detrimental to their health, as the damage of public image can result in psychological conditions.
新聞媒體對於名人私生活的報導可能會對他們的健康有害，因為公眾形象的損害可能會造成心理上的病症。

blogosphere
/ˈblɑgəsfɪə/

n. 部落格圈

💬 There are a larger percentage of people influenced by writers in the blogosphere than by celebrities in traditional media. 受到部落格圈的作者影響的人，比例比受傳統媒體名人影響的人還多。

In the blogosphere, that is the most influential celebrity fashion blog.
在部落格圈中，那是最有影響力的名人時尚部落格。

✒️ In the blogosphere, there are many writers who give beauty advice on how people can look like their favourite television stars.
在部落格圈中，有許多作者提供人們如何看起來像是自己最愛的電視明星的美容建議。

Celebrities today seem to have great influence and power over young people, and this phenomenon is particularly noticeable in the blogosphere.
今日的名人似乎對於年輕人有很大的影響與力量，而這個現象在部落格圈特別顯而易見。

RELATED WORDS | 相關單字延伸

challenging
adj. 有挑戰性的

offensive
adj. 冒犯的，無禮的

provocative
adj. 挑逗的，挑釁的

stimulating
adj. 激動人心的

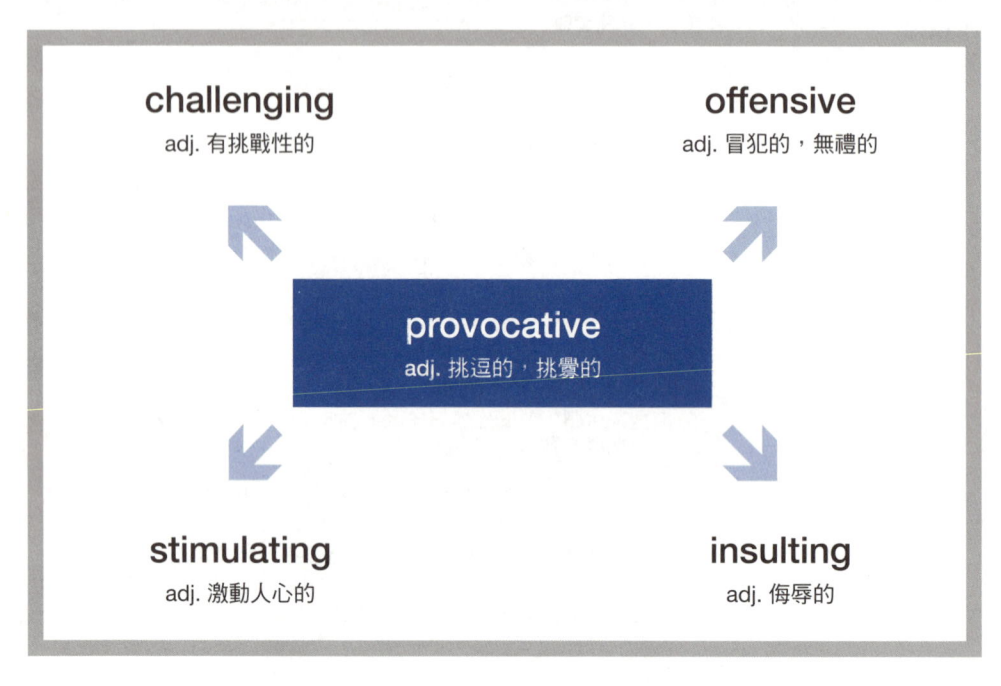

insulting
adj. 侮辱的

provocative
/prəˈvɒkətɪv/

Superstars in film and music industries are persistently followed by the paparazzi, photographed drinking and wearing **provocative** clothing.
電影和音樂界的超級巨星，總是被狗仔隊跟隨、被拍到喝酒、穿著挑逗的服裝。

challenging
/ˈtʃalɪndʒɪŋ/

Many movie stars find it **challenging** to stay calm when they are followed by the paparazzi everywhere they go.
許多電影明星覺得被狗仔隊到處跟隨的時候保持平靜很困難。

stimulating
/ˈstɪmjʊleɪtɪŋ/

Some people find celebrities' success stories quite **stimulating**.
有些人覺得名人的成功故事很激動人心。

offensive
/əˈfɛnsɪv/

The **offensive** T-shirt that the pop singer was wearing made the audience feel uncomfortable.
那個流行歌手穿的有冒犯性的T恤，讓觀眾感覺不舒服。

insulting
/ɪnˈsʌltɪŋ/

What the superstar said to the reporter was quite **insulting**.
那個超級明星對記者說的話很侮辱人。

USEFUL EXPRESSIONS | 相關實用片語

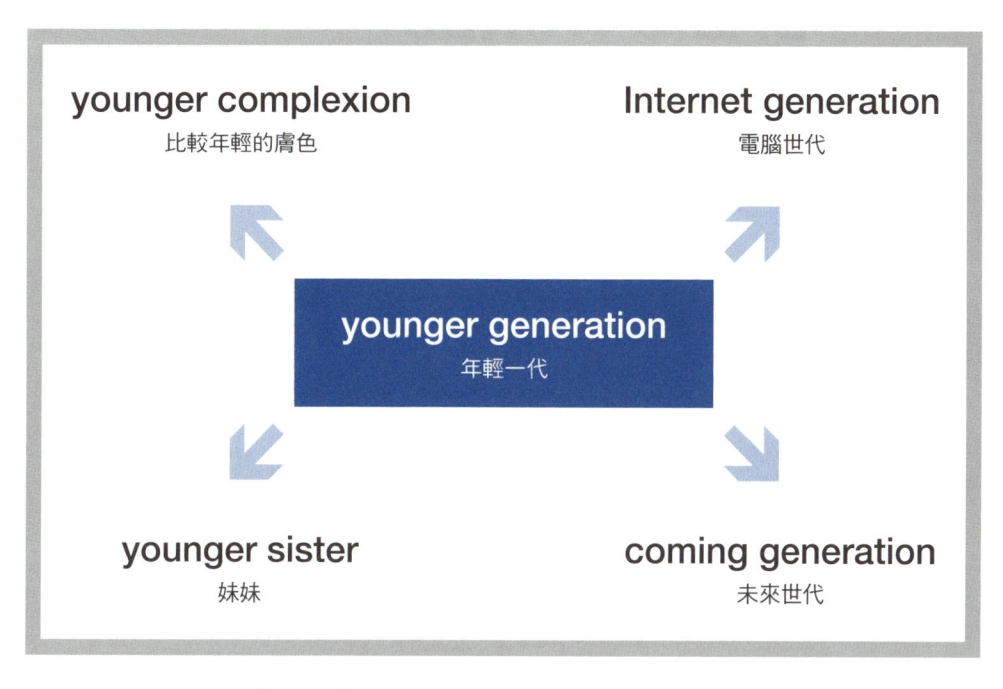

```
younger complexion              Internet generation
比較年輕的膚色                    電腦世代

           ↖        younger generation        ↗
                        年輕一代
           ↙                                  ↘

younger sister                  coming generation
妹妹                             未來世代
```

younger generation
/ˈjʌŋɚ dʒɛnəˈreɪʃən/
The younger generation prefer jobs which enable them to show their creativity.
年輕世代偏好能讓他們展現創意的工作。

younger complexion
/ˈjʌŋɚ kəmˈplɛkʃən/
Many women who desire a younger complexion opt for laser treatments.
許多想要有比較年輕的膚色的女性選擇雷射治療。

younger sister
/ˈjʌŋɚ ˈsɪstɚ/
My younger sister played too rough and scraped her knee.
我妹妹玩得太粗暴而擦傷了她的膝蓋。

Internet generation
/ˈɪntɚnɛt dʒɛnəˈreɪʃən/
The Internet generation are used to searching for information online and tend not to believe traditional media.
網路世代習慣在網路上尋找訊息，而且傾向於不相信傳統媒體。

coming generation
/ˈkʌmɪŋ dʒɛnəˈreɪʃən/
Some say that the coming generation is doomed because of the world's worsening economy.
有些人說未來的世代註定不幸，因為世界的經濟狀況正在變差。

TUE

IELTS BASIC WORDS

eliminate /ɪˈlɪmɪneɪt/ v. 排除，消除
ENG. to get rid of
SYS. eradicate, abolish

> Violence on TV should be **eliminated** for the sake of children.
> 為了兒童們，電視裡的暴力應該被消除。

同義語例句 The media regulatory board should **wipe out** all violent shows on TV.
媒體管制委員會應該徹底消除電視上的暴力節目。

同義語例句 It is time to **get rid of** the shows which are inappropriate for the young audience.
是時候擺脫那些不適合年輕觀眾的節目了。

反義語例句 We should **keep producing** TV shows that teach children right values and good conduct.
我們應該持續製作教導兒童正確價值觀與善良行為的電視節目。

interfere /ˌɪntəˈfɪə/ v. 干涉
ENG. to be or create a hindrance or obstacle
SYS. intervene, intrude

> Some protesters attempt to **interfere** with the government's plan to take full control of TV programmes intended for kids.
> 有些抗議者試圖干預政府全面控制兒童電視節目的計畫。

同義語例句 The protesters **get in the way of** the government's plan to control TV programmes.
抗議者妨礙政府控制電視節目的計畫。

同義語例句 The government must **step in** to ensure that TV shows are suitable for kids.
政府必須加以干預，確保電視節目適合兒童。

反義語例句 Parents must teach their children to **stay clear of** inappropriate TV shows.
父母必須教小孩遠離不適合的電視節目。

WEEK 8 TOPIC **MEDIA**

▶基礎單字擴充

repeat /rɪˈpiːt/ v. 重複
ENG. to say, state or perform again
SYS. reiterate, restate

> It is good to **repeat** a sentence several times for a child to fully understand.
> 重複一個句子幾次讓小孩容易了解，是好的做法。

同義語例句 　If the show does not interest children as expected, the producer must **redo** it.
如果這個節目沒有預期中那麼吸引小孩的興趣，製作人必須重做。

同義語例句 　The speaker **said once more** that TV producers should also consider child viewers when deciding on concepts for their shows.
演講人重申，電視製作人在選定節目的概念時，也應該考慮到兒童觀眾。

反義語例句 　I'm saying **once and for all** that all the shows must be kid-friendly.
這是我最後一次說了：所有節目都必須適合兒童。

concentrate /ˈkɒnsəntreɪt/ v. 專注
ENG. direct one's attention to something
SYS. focus, centre

> Children tend to **concentrate** on whatever they are watching on TV.
> 小孩通常會專心看電視上的任何東西。

同義語例句 　The kids cannot help but **be engrossed in** the TV animation.
那些小孩忍不住專心看電視上的動畫節目。

同義語例句 　The children **are focused on** the show they are watching.
那些小孩專注於他們所看的節目。

反義語例句 　Some parents **pay no attention to** what their children are watching on TV.
有些家長不去注意他們的小孩在看什麼電視節目。

427

TUE

TOPIC: The influence of Western TV programmes on children

西方電視節目對兒童的影響

Television programmes from Western countries have a **profound** influence on children around the world. They usually present Western ideals, **projecting** a seemingly real world which in fact **distorts** the way children view the planet. For example, children in India may be watching English cartoons featuring Caucasian characters that play baseball and celebrate Christmas. The **dominance** of Western TV programmes **leads** children to believe that Western culture is **superior** and does nothing to **pass down** local traditions and customs. The lack of cultural diversity on TV is as **devastating** to society as the lack of biodiversity is to the world of nature. As children are so **impressionable,** and the media is a largely **unexploited** learning tool, TV stations should produce more educational programmes on local culture. The promotion of local culture through TV programmes will benefit not only children but also the whole society.

TRANS

來自西方國家的電視節目，對於全世界的兒童有深遠的影響。它們通常呈現西方的理想，展現出看似真實，但實際上扭曲了兒童對地球的看法的世界。例如，印度的兒童可能會看英語的卡通，有白人角色打棒球、慶祝耶誕節。西方電視節目的優勢地位會導致孩子相信西方文化比較優秀，而且對於傳承本地傳統與習俗沒有任何幫助。電視上缺乏文化多樣性，對於社會的破壞力就像缺乏生物多樣性對自然界的影響一樣大。因為兒童很容易受到影響，而媒體又是很少被利用的學習工具，所以電視台應該製作更多關於本地文化的教育節目。藉由電視節目發揚本地文化，不止對兒童有益，也對整個社會有益。

profound
/prəˈfaʊnd/

adj. 深刻的
She believed what the guest speaker said had **profound** meaning in it.
她相信客座演講者所說的話有很深刻的意義。

project
/prəˈdʒɛkt/

v. 投射，呈現
He tries to **project** a personal image that makes a positive first impression.
他試圖呈現出能給予正面第一印象的個人形象。

distort
/dɪˈstɔːt/

v. 扭曲
Ideally, a good news report would not **distort** the facts.
理想上，好的新聞報導不會扭曲事實。

dominance
/ˈdɒmɪnəns/

n. 支配地位
The **dominance** of white models in the fashion industry has long affected our ideas of beauty.
白人模特兒在時尚界的優勢地位，長久以來一直影響我們對於美的想法。

lead
/liːd/

v. 帶領，誘使，導致
If you keep up this delinquent behaviour, it will eventually **lead** to your incarceration.
如果你繼續這種脫序的行為表現，最終會使你坐牢。

superior
/suːˈpɪərɪə/

adj. 比較好的，比較優秀的
Do you have any valid reason to say that her work is **superior** to the others'?
你有任何令人信服的理由說她的作品比別人的優秀嗎？

pass down
/pɑːs daʊn/

v. 傳下去，傳承
I feel we all have the responsibility to **pass down** our own traditions.
我覺得我們都有責任把自己的傳統傳承下去。

devastating
/ˈdɛvəsteɪtɪŋ/

adj. 破壞性的
The infestations of pine beetles are a **devastating** problem for the forests of British Columbia.
松樹甲蟲的大量孳生，是對不列顛哥倫比亞的森林很有破壞性的問題。

impressionable
/ɪmˈprɛʃənəbəl/

adj. 容易受到影響的
Young, **impressionable** people can be led astray by those who do drugs in front of them.
容易受到影響的年輕人，會被在他們面前吸毒的人帶壞。

unexploited
/ˌʌnɪkˈsplɔɪtɪd/

adj. 未開發的，未利用的
The diamond mine remains **unexploited** by mining companies. 這座鑽石礦還沒有被開礦公司開發。

WORD TRAINING | 重點單字造句練習

violence
/ˈvaɪələns/

n. 暴力

💬 Children are often subject to the influence of violence on television.
孩童經常容易受到電視上的暴力影響。

Parents shouldn't only put the blame on TV shows for their children's inclination to violence.
父母不應該把自己小孩的暴力傾向只怪罪於電視節目。

✏️ As more and more children are influenced by excessive violence shown on the evening news, many parent groups are appealing to news channels to stop sensationalising the stories.
隨著越來越多的孩子受到晚間新聞過多的暴力影響，許多家長團體呼籲新聞頻道停止用聳動的方式處理報導。

With the high demand for action movies including violence and brutality, it might be impossible to keep children from seeing them.
因為對於包含暴力與野蠻行為的動作電影需求很高，所以或許不可能不讓小孩看到這些電影。

---

censorship
/ˈsɛnsəʃɪp/

n. 審查，審查制度

💬 A lot of TV shows are aired without any censorship.
有許多電視節目未經任何審查就播出。

I am opposed to censorship in any form.
我反對任何形式的審查。

✏️ Under the leader's dictatorship, censorship was used to ensure that opposing views and opinions do not reach the public.
在領導者的獨裁統治下，審查被用來確保反對的看法與意見不會接觸到大眾。

Censorship may be easily applied to TV programmes, movies and books, but it is more challenging to impose it online.
對於電視節目、電影和書籍可以輕易進行審查，但要強加在網路上就比較困難。

口說範例 💬　寫作範例 ✏️

explicit
/ɪkˈsplɪsɪt/

adj. 有露骨性愛描寫的

💬 The main reason the series was cancelled was that it has many explicit scenes.
那個影集被取消的主要原因是它有很多露骨的場面。

The fans boycotted their idol's movie because of its explicit theme.
因為有露骨的主題,所以粉絲們抵制他們偶像的電影。

✏️ The sexy actress posed for an explicit magazine after she delivered her first baby and lost her pregnancy weight.
那位性感女演員在生了第一胎並且減去懷孕體重之後,為一本內容露骨的雜誌拍了照片。

Compared to before, there tends to be more explicit scenes in the movies today.
跟以前比起來,今日的電影通常有更多露骨的場面。

integrity
/ɪnˈtɛgrɪti/

n. 正直,誠實,誠懇,(人格的)健全

💬 If the mass media had more integrity, it wouldn't show adult content on TV during daytime hours.
如果大眾媒體能更端正,就不會在白天時段在電視上播成人內容。

The goal of our group is to publish children's magazines and books of the highest integrity.
我們集團的目標是出版內容最端正的兒童雜誌與書籍。

✏️ The entertaining, attention-capturing educational cartoon created for elementary school students teaches them how to become people of integrity through learning and practising basic moral values.
這個為小學生所製作、有趣而能吸引注意力的教育卡通,透過學習與練習基本道德價值觀的方式,教育他們如何成為正直的人。

If we can help teenagers determine whether their actions and choices are moving them closer to or further away from integrity, then a major battle has been won.　如果我們能夠幫助青少年判斷他們的行為與選擇會讓他們接近還是遠離人格的健全,就是贏了重要的一戰。

RELATED WORDS | 相關單字延伸

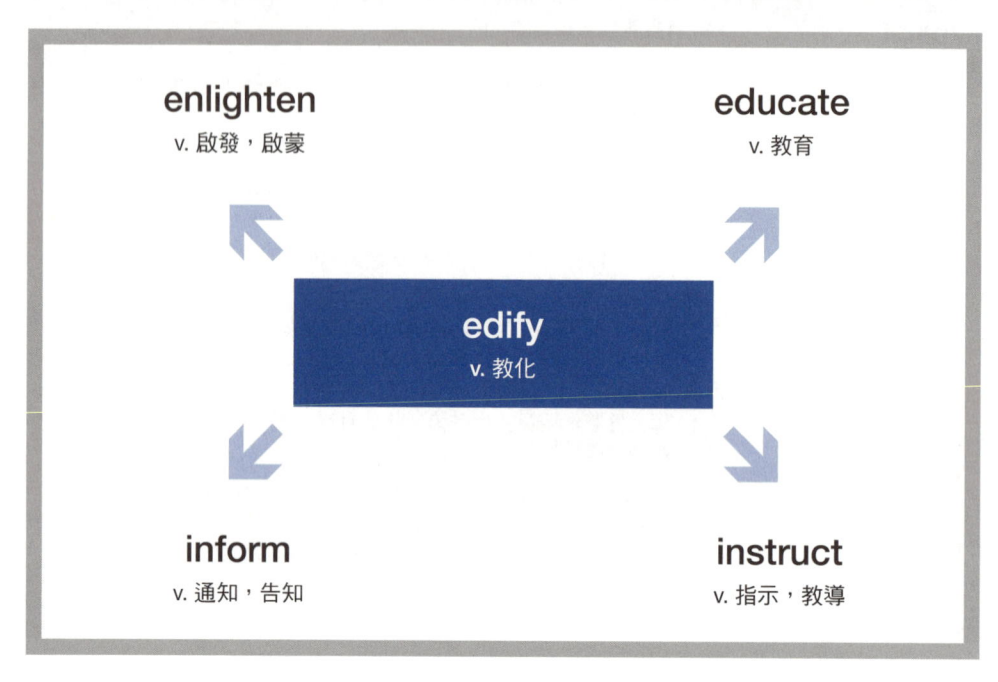

enlighten
v. 啟發，啟蒙

educate
v. 教育

edify
v. 教化

inform
v. 通知，告知

instruct
v. 指示，教導

edify
/ˈɛdɪfʌɪ/

Most TV programmes do nothing to edify the minds of the younger audience.
大部分的電視節目對於教化年輕觀眾的心智沒有任何幫助。

enlighten
/ɪnˈlʌɪtən/

The talk show's discussion enlightened me on the subject of global warming.
談話節目的討論在全球暖化這個主題方面給了我啟發。

inform
/ɪnˈfɔːm/

The news channel's goal is to inform the public about accurate facts regarding current events.
這個新聞頻道的目標是告知大眾關於時事的正確事實。

educate
/ˈɛdjʊkeɪt/

It is about time for us to educate kids about our culture to encourage patriotism.
該是讓我們教育孩童自己的文化，以鼓勵愛國精神的時候了。

instruct
/ɪnˈstrʌkt/

The channel instructs viewers on how to create interesting handicrafts at home.
這個頻道教導觀眾如何在家創造有趣的手工藝品。

USEFUL EXPRESSIONS | 相關實用片語

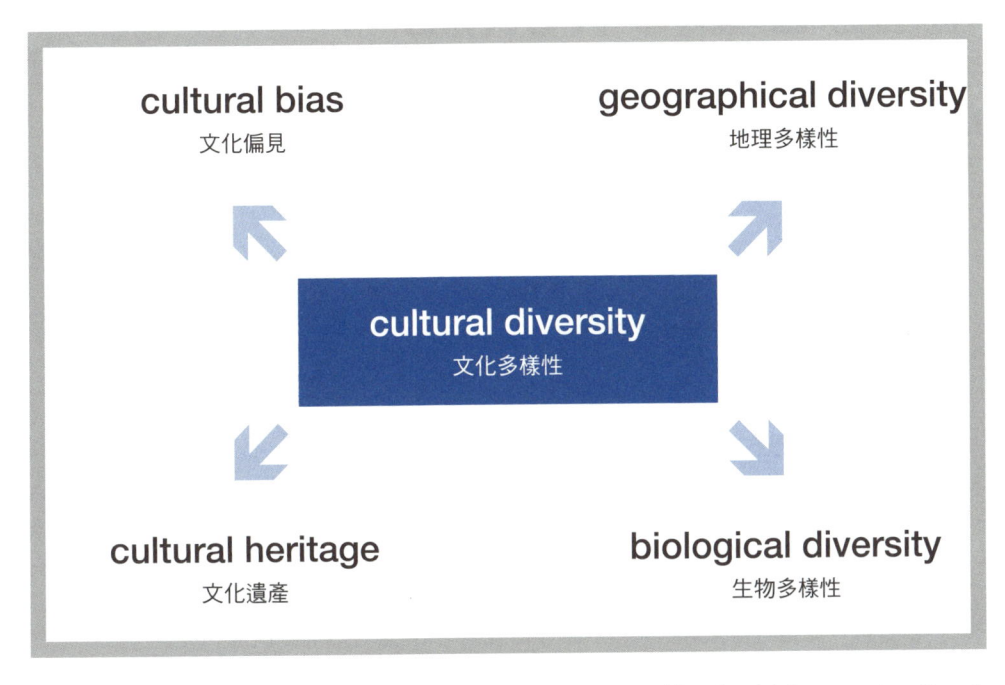

```
                cultural bias              geographical diversity
                 文化偏見                        地理多樣性

                          ↖             ↗
                            cultural diversity
                                文化多樣性
                          ↙             ↘

              cultural heritage           biological diversity
                  文化遺產                       生物多樣性
```

cultural diversity
/ˈkʌltʃərəl daɪˈvɜːsɪti/

Many travellers are attracted by the history and cultural diversity of Europe.
許多旅行者受到歐洲的歷史與文化多樣性吸引。

cultural bias
/ˈkʌltʃərəl ˈbaɪəs/

Some critics believe that it is impossible to judge people from other cultures objectively because of cultural bias.
有些評論家認為，因為文化偏見的關係，要客觀評斷來自其他文化的人是不可能的。

cultural heritage
/ˈkʌltʃərəl ˈhɛrɪtɪdʒ/

There are many important pieces of cultural heritage on display at the museum.
許多重要的文化遺產正在那座博物館展示。

geographical diversity
/dʒiːəˈgræfɪkəl daɪˈvɜːsɪti/

The nation's geographic diversity makes tropical, temperate and Mediterranean types of agriculture possible.
這個國家的地理多樣性使得熱帶、溫帶、地中海型的農業成為可能。

biological diversity
/baɪəʊˈlɒdʒɪkəl daɪˈvɜːsɪti/

An ecosystem which lacks biological diversity can easily become unbalanced.
缺乏生物多樣性的生態系統可能容易變得不平衡。

WED

IELTS **BASIC WORDS**

device /dɪˈvaɪs/ n. 設備，裝置
ENG. an instrumentality invented for a particular purpose
SYS. gadget, apparatus

> More and more innovative **devices** are developed as technology continues to evolve.
> 越來越多創新的設備隨著科技持續進步而被開發出來。

同義語例句 The newest **piece of equipment** will play an important role in our live broadcast.
最新的一件設備將會在我們的現場播出中扮演重要角色。

同義語例句 We need to ensure all the **machines** in the studio work properly for the whole duration of the broadcast.
我們需要確保攝影棚的所有機器在播出全程運作正常。

反義語例句 Older devices became **useless things** as new ones were introduced.
隨著新的設備被採用，舊的就變成沒用的東西。

crucial /ˈkruːʃəl/ adj. 至關重要的
ENG. of extreme importance
SYS. vital, momentous

> It is **crucial** for a news channel to report what is happening in real time.
> 對於新聞頻道來說，即時播報正在發生的事情是很重要的。

同義語例句 Time is **of the essence** when delivering news reports to the public.
在向大眾提供新聞時，時間是非常重要的。

同義語例句 News programmes are **of great importance** as most people watch them every day.
新聞節目很重要，因為大部分的人每天都看。

反義語例句 Reports about Hollywood celebrities are **of little importance** to busy businesspeople.
關於好萊塢名人的報導，對於忙碌的商業人士而言沒有什麼重要性。

WEEK 8 TOPIC **MEDIA**

▶ 基礎單字擴充

equal /ˈiːkwəl/ adj. 相等的，相當的
ENG. be identical or equivalent
SYS. balanced, parallel

> For a broadcasting company to be successful, each of its departments must put in **equal** efforts.
> 廣播電視公司要成功，它的每個部門都必須投入同等的努力。

同義語例句 News anchors must be **evenly matched** to create a good atmosphere.
（兩位）新聞主播必須要平等相稱，以創造好的氣氛。

同義語例句 For a broadcasting company, giving up its own principles is **equivalent** to losing its identity.
對於廣播電視公司而言，放棄它自己的原則就等於失去它的個性。

反義語例句 A celebrity must be **different** from the rest to stand out.
一個名人必須和其他人不同，才能顯得突出。

shape /ʃeɪp/ v. 形塑
ENG. influence or give a form to
SYS. form, influence

> All the media trends today are **shaping** the values of the younger generation.
> 今日所有的媒體趨勢都在形塑著年輕世代的價值觀。

同義語例句 The values represented in TV shows can **mould** young people's views about our society.
電視節目呈現的價值觀會形塑年輕人對於我們社會的看法。

同義語例句 Even after the rise of social media, it is widely considered that traditional media still plays a significant role in **forming** public opinions.
即使在社群媒體興起之後，大眾還是廣泛認為傳統媒體仍然在形塑輿論方面扮演重要角色。

反義語例句 The controversy **has no effect** on the popularity of that TV show.
爭議對於那個電視節目受歡迎的程度沒有影響。

WED

TOPIC: The evolution of mass media
大眾傳播媒體的演變

The mass media has evolved over the years, from print media and radio to television. Today, almost everyone in modern countries has **access** to television, which presents information **visually** and **appeals** to a wide range of audiences. Television's dominance has **rendered** newspapers **archaic**. Furthermore, with the emergence of the Internet and news sites in recent years, people are free to check the news they are interested in everywhere, on their computers or smartphones. They can jump to the subject matters of their choice immediately without turning pages **manually**. Printed newspapers, on the other hand, are more like a relic of the past than a useful source. Despite the newspaper's **demise**, people around the world seem to embrace the real-time distribution of news through **broadcasting** and online transmission. In the end, the development of **electronic** media has **expanded** public awareness of current events worldwide.

TRANS

大眾傳播媒體多年來一直演進，從印刷媒體和廣播到電視。今日，現代國家幾乎每個人都可以接觸到電視，它以視覺的方式呈現資訊，而且能夠迎合廣範圍的觀眾群。電視的優勢地位使得報紙顯得過時。而且，隨著近年來網路與新聞網站的興起，人們可以在任何地方、在電腦或智慧型手機上自由查看有興趣的新聞。他們可以馬上跳到他們選擇的主題，而不用親手翻頁。相對地，印刷的報紙更像是過去的遺跡，而不是有用的來源。儘管報紙式微，全世界的人似乎擁抱了透過電視廣播和線上傳輸進行的即時新聞傳播。結果，電子媒體的發展擴展了大眾對於全世界時事的認識。

access
/ˈæksɛs/
n. 接近，進入，使用
Parents must restrict their children's **access** to certain websites.
父母必須限制他們的小孩拜訪某些網站。

visually
/ˈvɪʒʊəli/
adv. 視覺上
I showed him how to make a **visually** appealing website.
我教他如何做出視覺上吸引人的網站。

appeal
/əˈpiːl/
v. 有吸引力，迎合愛好
This book **appeals** to me because I like science fiction.
這本書合我的胃口，因為我喜歡科幻小說。

render
/ˈrɛndə/
v. 使…成為；提出
The committee was asked to **render** a report on the housing situation.
委員會被要求提出關於住宅情況的報告。

archaic
/ɑːˈkeɪɪk/
v. 古代的
Some readers are confused by the **archaic** words used in this novel.
有些讀者對於這部小說中使用的古字感到困惑。

manually
/ˈmanjuːəli/
adv. 用手
Manually operated machines are gradually replaced by automatic ones.
手動操作的機器逐漸被自動的機器取代。

demise
/dɪˈmʌɪz/
n. 死亡
The end of printed books does not mean the **demise** of the publishing industry.
實體書的結束並不意味著出版業的死亡。

broadcasting
/ˈbrɔːdkɑːstɪŋ/
n. 廣播，廣播業（含電視）
Sam has worked as a news director in **broadcasting** for the last twenty years.
Sam 在過去二十年都是擔任廣播業的新聞主任。

electronic
/ɪlɛkˈtrɒnɪk/
adj. 電子的
Electronic communication saves people's time and conserves their energy for other productive things.
電子通訊省下人們的時間，也把他們的精力留給其他有生產性的事物。

expand
/ɪkˈspand/
v. 擴展
The air inside the bottle **expanded** when it was heated.
瓶子裡的氣體在加熱時膨脹。

WORD TRAINING | 重點單字造句練習

editorial
/ˌɛdɪˈtɔːrɪəl/

adj. 編輯的

- The editorial system provides journalists with tools for fast delivery of gathered and edited news. 這個編輯系統提供記者將收集到與編輯過的新聞快速發送的工具。

- The editorial executive will enter the titles and dates of programmes in a schedule.
編輯主管會把節目名稱與日期輸入時間表。

- This online directory allows you to access information of thousands of journals, with essential contact details including phone and fax numbers, mailing addresses, E-mails, websites and information about editorial scope. 這個網路上的通訊名錄讓你可以查到幾千部期刊的資訊，有基本聯絡資料，包括電話與傳真號碼、郵寄地址、電子郵件、網站，還有關於編輯範圍的資訊。

- All manuscripts prepared must be submitted online, while those submitted to the editorial office will not be processed or reviewed.
所以準備的稿件都必須在網路上提交，而交給編輯室的稿件則不會獲得處理或審查。

publisher
/ˈpʌblɪʃə/

n. 出版人，出版公司

- Electronic publishing makes the publication process faster and cheaper, threatening the future of traditional publishers. 電子出版使得發行的過程更快、更便宜，而威脅到傳統出版公司的未來。

- The publisher will still have to pay royalty fees to the author when the book is published electronically.
當書以電子方式出版時，出版公司還是必須付版稅給作者。

- The web-based framework offers proven solutions to many international publishers in areas such as information analysis, editorial management, and digital fulfilment for both books and journals.
這個以網路為基礎的架構，在資訊分析、編輯管理、書籍及期刊的數位化等領域，提供經證實有用的解決方法給許多國際出版商。

- Publishers are accused of hanging on too firmly to traditional print-on-paper techniques and of being too slow and ineffective in making knowledge available.
出版公司被指責太過於固守傳統的紙張印書技術，以及提供知識的速度太慢而且沒有效率。

telecast
/ˈtɛlɪkɑːst/

n. 電視播放的節目 v. 用電視播出

The special programme was telecast on two channels simultaneously.
那個特別節目同時在兩個電視頻道播出。

The great majority of prime-time telecasts are now available in HDTV.
絕大部分的黃金時段電視節目，現在都提供高畫質了。

In the past, pre-recorded telecasts were far less common than they are today.
在過去，預錄的電視節目還不如今日那麼常見。

Our university strives to maximise the amount of positive exposure it receives in telecasts and on the Internet to gain more public support.
我們的大學努力在電視節目和網路上得到最多的正面曝光，以獲得更多大眾的支持。

feature film
/ˈfiːtʃə fɪlm/

n. 長篇電影

It wasn't until ten years ago that feature films were available over the Internet.
一直到十年前，長篇電影才能在網路上取得。

Several feature films were shown using traditional projectors during the film festival.
在影展期間，有幾部長篇電影以傳統放映機播放。

It has become a convention for a feature film to be released digitally because the revenues online are growing significantly.
現在以數位方式發行長篇電影已經成為慣例，因為網路上的收入正大幅成長。

The first digital delivery and exhibition of the feature film *Star Wars* to paying audiences is widely considered the defining moment for digital cinema's commercial viability.
長篇電影《星際大戰》第一次以數位方式傳送並展示給付費的觀眾，被普遍認為是數位化戲院的商業可行性的決定性時刻。

RELATED WORDS　｜　相關單字延伸

report
v. 報告，播報

advertise
v. 廣告，宣傳

broadcast
v. 廣播，播送

announce
v. 宣布

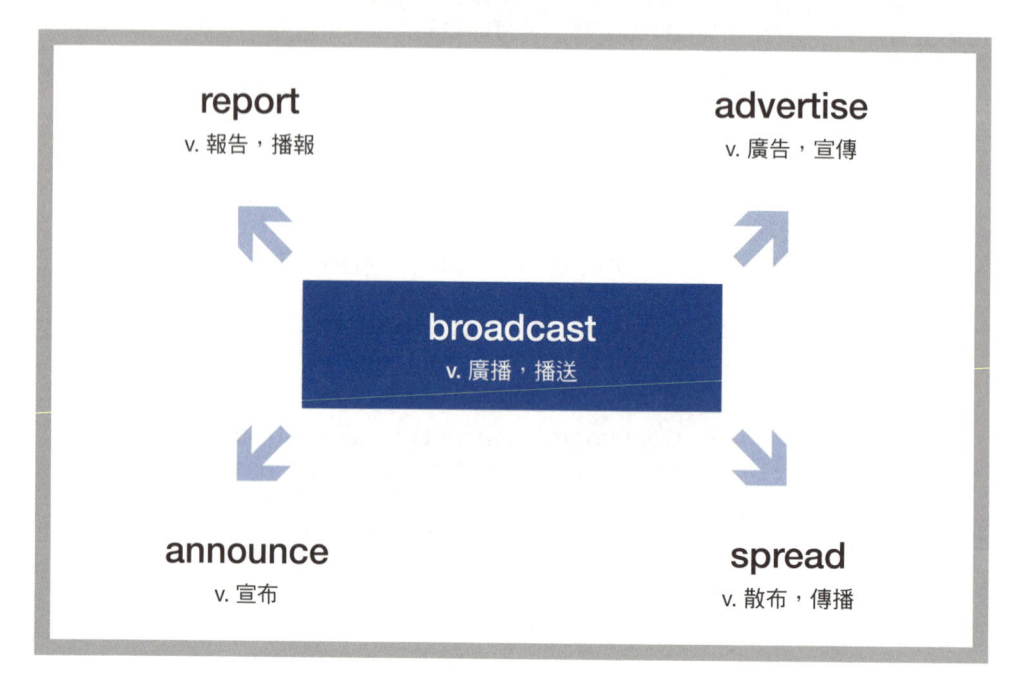

spread
v. 散布，傳播

broadcast
/ˈbrɔːdkɑːst/

The news broadcast on TV twenty-four hours a day expands public awareness of current events.
每天 24 小時播放的電視新聞，擴大了大眾對於時事的認識。

report
/rɪˈpɔːt/

The weatherman happily reported that the coming days will be sunny and rain-free.
氣象播報員愉快的播報接下來幾天的天氣都會是晴朗無雨。

announce
/əˈnaʊns/

The White House speaker announced that the president is out of the country.
白宮發言人宣布總統目前不在國內。

advertise
/ˈædvətʌɪz/

Most celebrities advertise their own businesses on TV to raise their revenues.
大部份的名人在電視上廣告他們的生意來增加營收。

spread
/sprɛd/

The rumour that the actress died due to a heart attack spread quickly online.
女演員死於心臟病的傳聞很快地在網路上散播開來。

USEFUL EXPRESSIONS | 相關實用片語

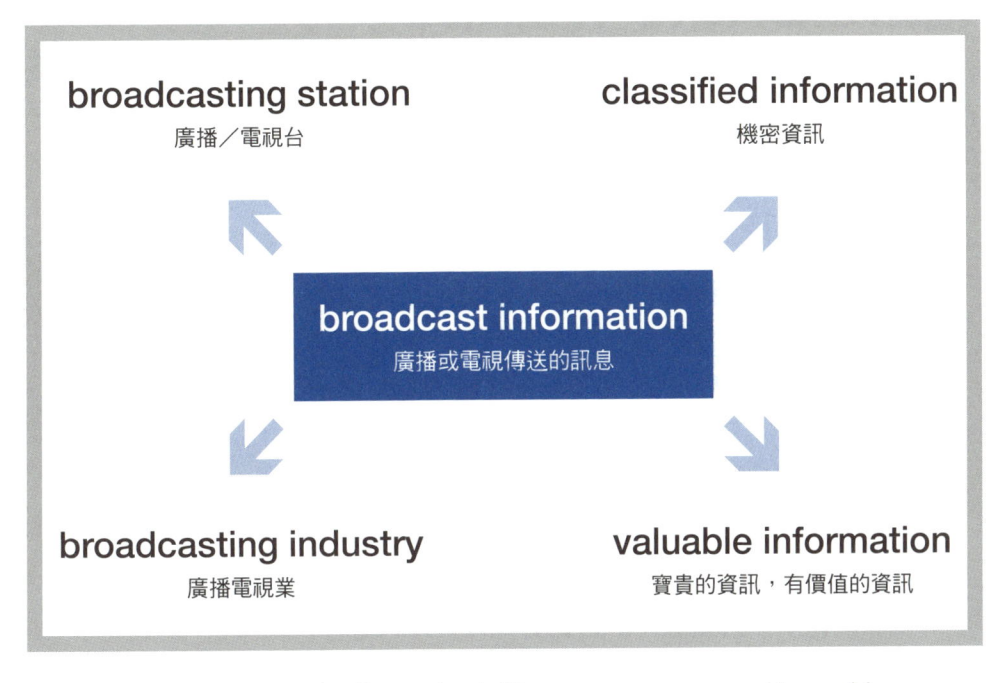

broadcasting station
廣播/電視台

classified information
機密資訊

broadcast information
廣播或電視傳送的訊息

broadcasting industry
廣播電視業

valuable information
寶貴的資訊，有價值的資訊

broadcast information
/ˈbrɔːdkɑːst ɪnfəˈmeɪʃən/

Several satellites were programmed to enable everyone to receive broadcast information at any point in time.
有幾顆衛星經過程式設定，好讓每個人在任何時間都能接收到廣播或電視傳送的訊息。

broadcasting station
/ˈbrɔːdkɑːstɪŋ ˈsteɪʃən/

During the summer vacation, she worked as an intern at the broadcasting station.
暑假的時候，她在廣播電視公司實習。

broadcasting industry
/ˈbrɔːdkɑːstɪŋ ˈɪndəstri/

The development of technology always brings about dramatic changes in the broadcasting industry.
科技的發展總會造成廣播電視業戲劇性的變化。

classified information
/ˈklæsɪfʌɪd ɪnfəˈmeɪʃən/

Only those with security clearance from the President may access the classified information in the archive.
只有得到總統安全許可的人才能存取檔案庫中的機密資訊。

valuable information
/ˈvaljʊbəl ɪnfəˈmeɪʃən/

The valuable information has facilitated those scientists' research into the spread of diseases.
寶貴的資訊讓那些科學家對於疾病傳播的研究變得容易。

THU

IELTS BASIC WORDS

organise /ˈɔːgənʌɪz/ v. 組織,安排
ENG. to put together into an orderly, functional, structured whole
SYS. arrange, coordinate

> A TV producer must **organise** the contents of a programme to convey a clear message.
> 電視製作人必須組織節目的內容,以傳達清楚的訊息。

同義語 例句 A news programme producer must **straighten out** the information to avoid confusion.
新聞節目製作人必須理清資訊以避免造成困惑。

同義語 例句 Producers will **set up** events to promote their TV programmes.
電視製作人會舉辦活動,宣傳他們的電視節目。

反義語 例句 If the information presented in a programme is **mixed-up**, the viewers will be confused.
如果節目中呈現的資訊混亂,觀眾會感到困惑。

accident /ˈaksɪdənt/ n. 意外
ENG. an unexpected and undesirable event resulting in damage or harm
SYS. crash, collision

> The **accident** damaged the cables, messing up the live TV programme.
> 那個意外損毀了電纜,把現場電視節目搞砸了。

同義語 例句 An **unfortunate happening** has forced the organiser to cancel upcoming football games.
不幸發生的事情迫使主辦人取消接下來的足球比賽。

同義語 例句 A **disaster** struck the city **without warning** and caused a power blackout.
災難無預警地襲擊城市,並且造成了停電。

反義語 例句 The unknown actress made a **strategic move** of tripping in front of news cameras to get people to notice her. 那位無名的女演員採取了策略性的行動,就是在新聞攝影機前跌倒,讓人們注意到她。

WEEK 8 TOPIC **MEDIA**

▶基礎單字擴充

coincidental /koʊɪnsɪˈdɛntəl/ adj. 巧合的
ENG. occurring or operating at the same time
SYS. fortuitous, unintentional

> It is purely **coincidental** that Obama and Romney's speeches were on different channels at the same time.
> 歐巴馬與羅姆尼的演說在同一時間不同頻道播放純粹是偶然。

同義語例句　That the two popular shows were aired on the same time slot was **not planned**.
那兩個受歡迎的節目在同一個時段播放，並不是事先計畫好的。

同義語例句　The start of a show on one channel is **synchronous with** that on another.
一個頻道上的某個節目開始時間，和另一個頻道某個節目開始的時間同時。

反義語例句　Sometimes, people think that bad TV programmes are made **on purpose**.
有時候，人們覺得不好的電視節目是被故意製作出來的。

view /vjuː/ v. 觀看，看待，視為
ENG. deem to be
SYS. deem, judge

> Some people **view** TV programmes as tools for relaxation.
> 有些人把電視節目視為放鬆的工具。

同義語例句　People **take** poor production of TV programmes as a sign of dwindling media creativity.
人們把電視節目製作不良視為媒體創意萎縮的徵兆。

同義語例句　If we **consider** TV programmes simply as entertainment, we may be underestimating its educational value.
如果我們只認為電視節目是娛樂，我們可能低估了它的教育價值。

反義語例句　People **refuse to look at** the drawbacks of watching today's TV programmes.
人們不去看觀看今日電視節目的缺點。

THU

TOPIC | Weather forecasts
氣象預報

People often watch the TV news for the latest weather forecasts, safe in their belief in the forecasters' special weather-**divining** gifts. Unfortunately, there are many **bogus** weather forecasts given by **unqualified** meteorologists who are better at exaggerating rather than analysing. It seems as though news channels are more **engrossed** in **airing sensationalised** forecasts aimed at gaining **viewership** rather than forecasting based on evidence and developing **credibility** with the **audience**. Reliable and accurate forecasts are a **critical** element of local news programmes, often being the lone reason why people watch them. Regrettably, the weather information they receive could be meaningless. Despite the over-exaggerated nature of some weather forecasts on TV, however, people will continue to tune in to get a slight inkling of anticipated weather phenomena.

TRANS

人們經常看電視新聞，查看最新的氣象預報，安全地相信預報員特殊的天氣預言天賦。遺憾的是，有許多不合格的氣象專家做著冒牌的天氣預報，比起分析，他們還比較擅長誇大。新聞頻道似乎比較致力於播放聳動、以獲得更多觀眾為目的的預報，而不是依照證據進行預報，並且培養觀眾對自身的信賴。可靠而精確的預報是地方新聞節目的重要元素，而且經常是人們看這些節目的唯一理由。但很可惜，他們接收到的氣象資訊有可能是無意義的。不過，雖然電視上有一些天氣預報太過誇張，人們還是會繼續收看，以獲得關於預期天氣現象的一點線索。

divining
/dɪˈvʌɪnɪŋ/

n. 占卜
Some people use **divining** rods to find underground water.
有些人用占卜杖找地下水。

bogus
/ˈbəʊɡəs/

adj. 假的，假冒的
I thought the used-car salesman had a **bogus** smile.
我覺得那位賣二手車的業務員笑容很虛假。

unqualified
/ʌnˈkwɒlɪfʌɪd/

adj. 不合格的，沒有資格的
Shelley didn't get the job because she was **unqualified** for welding.
Shelley 沒有得到那份工作，因為她的銲接不合格。

engrossed
/ɪnˈɡrəʊst/

adj. 全神貫注的
Lianne was so **engrossed** in the novel that she wept.
Lianne 全神貫注在小說裡看到哭了。

air
/ɛː/

v. 播出
I'm not sure when the local talent show will be **aired**.
我不確定本地的才藝秀什麼時候播出。

sensationalise
/sɛnˈseɪʃənəlʌɪz/

v. 以聳動的方式處理
Disasters are often **sensationalised** in the media.
媒體經常以聳動的方式報導災難。

viewership
/ˈvjuːəʃɪp/

n. 電視觀眾
The TV programme is once again in the top ten in **viewership**.
這個電視節目再一次進入了收視率前十名。

credibility
/krɛdɪˈbɪlɪti/

n. 可信性，可信度
His statements were doubted because he has no **credibility**.
他的陳述被人懷疑，因為他沒有信用。

audience
/ˈɔːdɪəns/

n. 觀眾
The new TV show is aiming for a younger **audience**.
這個新的電視節目是以較年輕的觀眾為目標。

critical
/ˈkrɪtɪkəl/

adj. 至關重要的
His advice on this project is very **critical** in determining its future success.
他對這項計畫的建議對於決定未來的成功非常重要。

WORD TRAINING | 重點單字造句練習

closed-captioned adj. 有隱藏式字幕的
/ˌkloʊzd ˈkæpʃənd/

> Closed-captioned programmes allow people with hearing impairment to enjoy watching TV as normal people do. 有隱藏式字幕的節目讓有聽力障礙的人能夠和一般人一樣享受看電視的樂趣。

> Many children's TV programmes today are closed-captioned, allowing kids to view text when they watch TV.
> 今日許多兒童節目有隱藏式字幕，讓兒童可以在看電視的時候看到文字。

> Closed-captioned TV programmes were created primarily for people who were hearing-impaired, but they are also useful for public spaces such as hotels and airport lounges.
> 有隱藏式字幕的節目主要是為了有聽力障礙的人創造的，但它們對於旅館休息室、機場休息室等公共空間也很有用。

> This country is requiring broadcasting companies to provide more closed-captioned TV programmes for the considerable amount of hearing-impaired citizens.
> 這個國家正要求廣播電視公司為相當多的聽障人民提供更多有隱藏式字幕的電視節目。

---

correspondent n. 通訊記者，特派員
/ˌkɔrɪˈspɒndənt/

> The correspondent was dismissed permanently for the comments he made.
> 那位記者因為他發表的言論而被永久解雇了。

> The correspondent was very poised when she was reporting in front of a lot of protesters.
> 那位記者在許多抗議者前面進行報導時非常鎮定。

> It was announced that he would be named co-anchor of the TV news programme, replacing the long-standing anchor who wanted to work as a correspondent prior to her retirement.
> 他被宣布將成為電視新聞節目的共同主播，取代現任已久、希望在退休前能擔任記者的主播。

> Led by a guide and interpreter who facilitate access, the correspondent conducted interviews with affected people in the regions involved in war.
> 由協助通行的嚮導和翻譯帶領，那位記者在戰爭波及地區採訪受影響的人們。

coverage
/ˈkʌvərɪdʒ/

n. 新聞的報導

🗨 When the barrage of Olympics coverage begins this summer, TV viewers may find there is less local news.
當今年夏天新聞集中火力報導奧運時，電視觀眾可能會發現國內新聞比較少。

The network has already faced criticism from viewers about the level of coverage it is giving to the event.
這個電視網已經因為它給予這件事的報導程度而面臨觀眾的批評。

✍ The extent of news coverage of a scientific research has nothing to do with its quality because news channels pay more attention to whether a finding is interesting or not than its real benefits to the humanity.
科學研究的新聞報導幅度和它的品質無關，因為新聞頻道比較注意研究結果是否有趣，而比較不注意研究結果對於人類真正的助益。

The news programme appeals not only to middle-aged people but also to younger viewers with its coverage on a wide variety of topics such as entertainment, fashion and travel, besides political and social affairs.
這個新聞節目不止符合中年人的胃口，也吸引年輕觀眾，因為它報導範圍很廣的主題，除了政治與社會事件以外，還有像是娛樂、時尚、旅遊等等主題。

interactive
/ˌɪntərˈæktɪv/

adj. 互動的

🗨 An interactive TV programme enables viewers to decide what they see or even change its contents.
互動的電視節目讓觀眾能夠決定看到什麼，甚至改變它的內容。

There is much debate as to how effective and popular interactive TV programmes can be.
關於互動電視節目能夠多有效、多受歡迎，有許多爭論。

✍ We provide an intuitive interactive programme guide that enables cable subscribers to easily find and record the programmes they want to watch.
我們提供一個直覺的互動節目表，讓有線電視用戶能夠輕易找到並錄下他們想要看的節目。

The rise of live TV streaming has given new relevance to the idea of interactive TV, as viewers can now immediately express their opinions online.
電視直播串流的興起，給了互動電視概念新的相關性，因為觀眾現在可以立即在網路上傳達他們的意見。

RELATED WORDS | 相關單字延伸

urgent
adj. 緊急的

indispensable
adj. 必不可少的

critical
adj. 至關重要的

important
adj. 重要的

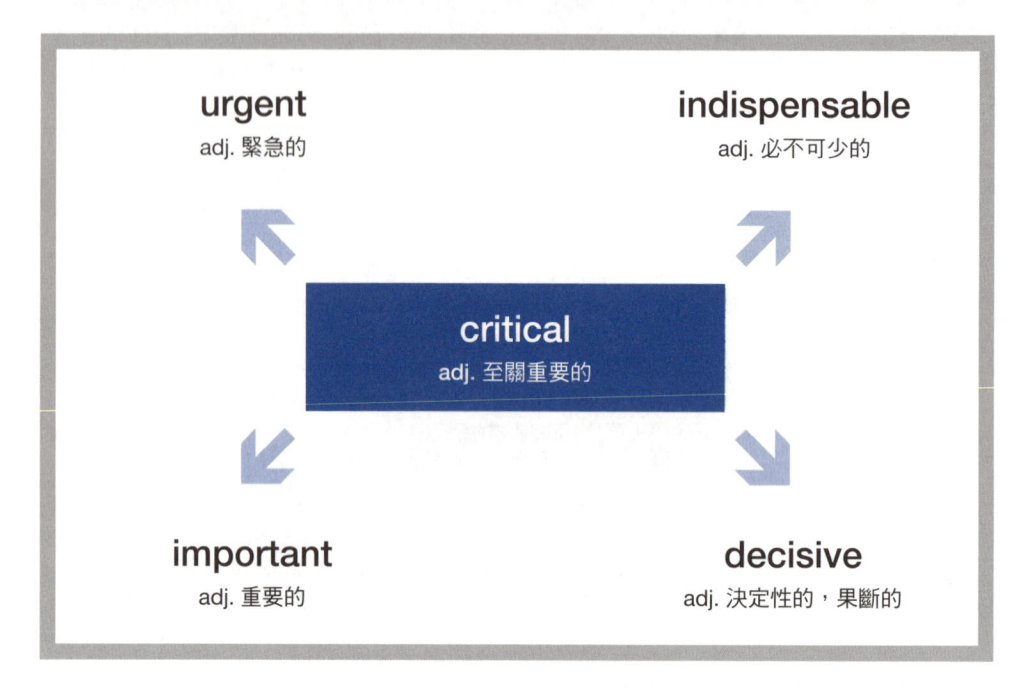

decisive
adj. 決定性的，果斷的

critical
/ˈkrɪtɪkəl/

Reliable and accurate weather forecasts are a critical element of local news programmes, often being the lone reason why people watch them.
可靠而精確的氣象預報是地方新聞節目的重要元素，而且經常是人們看這些節目的唯一理由。

urgent
/ˈɜːdʒənt/

There is an urgent need for a qualified correspondent for the project.
這個計畫目前迫切需要符合資格的通訊記者。

important
/ɪmˈpɔːtənt/

It is important for people to get weather warnings immediately, especially during typhoon season.
即時得到天氣警報對人們來說是很重要的，特別是在颱風季時。

indispensable
/ˌɪndɪˈspɛnsəbəl/

Advertisements are indispensable for every TV show because they are the source of income.
廣告對每個電視節目都是不能捨棄的，因為它們是收入的來源。

decisive
/dɪˈsʌɪsɪv/

Photojournalists strive to capture the decisive moment of an event using their cameras.
攝影記者用他們的相機努力捕捉事件的決定性瞬間。

USEFUL EXPRESSIONS | 相關實用片語

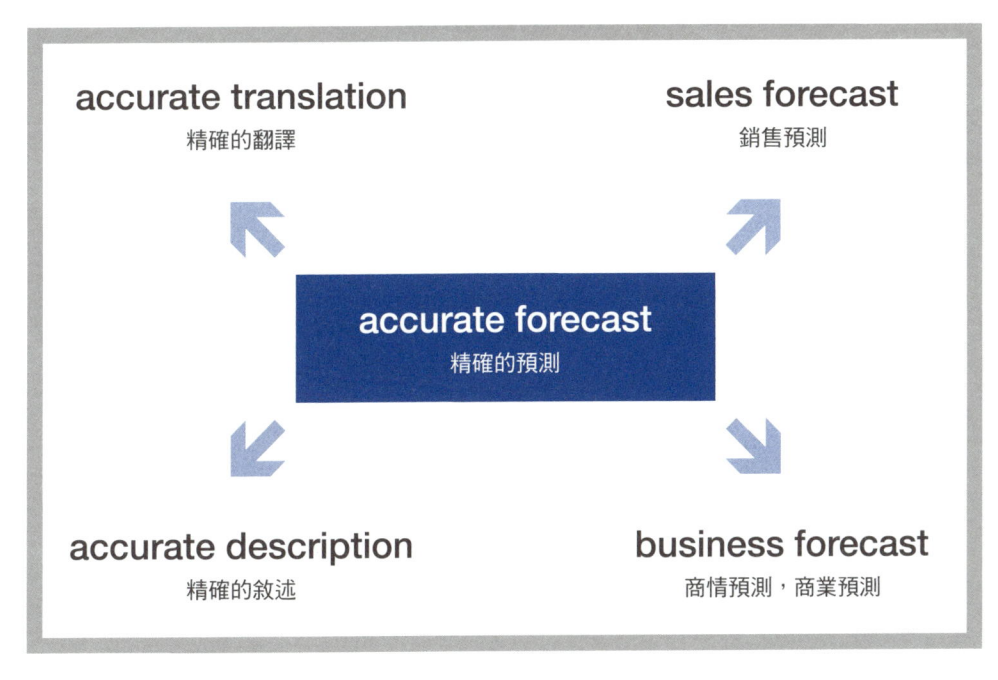

```
accurate translation          sales forecast
   精確的翻譯                    銷售預測

              accurate forecast
                 精確的預測

accurate description         business forecast
   精確的敘述                  商情預測，商業預測
```

accurate forecast
/ˈakjʊrət ˈfɔːkɑːst/

Meteorologists can now give accurate forecasts with the help of advanced weather instruments.
有了先進氣象儀器的幫助，氣象學家現在可以做出精確的預測。

accurate translation
/ˈakjʊrət transˈleɪʃən/

It is impossible to provide an accurate translation between the two languages due to their dissimilarity.
由於這兩個語言的相異性，所以不可能提供兩者之間精確的翻譯。

accurate description
/ˈakjʊrət dɪˈskrɪpʃən/

The most reliable and accurate description of the killer was released by police today.
關於殺人兇手最可靠、最精確的描述，警方今天公布了。

sales forecast
/seɪlz ˈfɔːkɑːst/

If we get together once a month, we can review the sales forecasts and inventories accurately.
如果我們一個月碰一次面，就可以精確地審查銷售預測與庫存。

business forecast
/ˈbɪznəs ˈfɔːkɑːst/

Our sales target need to be reviewed because the business forecast presented yesterday recommended it.
我們的銷售目標需要檢討，因為昨天提出的商情預測建議這麼做。

FRI

IELTS BASIC WORDS

zone /zəʊn/ n. 區域
ENG. a locally circumscribed place characterised by some distinctive features
SYS. sector, district

> In different **zones**, the same newspaper will have different advertisements or even different pages.
> 在不同的區域，同一份報紙會有不同的廣告，甚至不同的頁面。

同義語例句 The newspaper company makes slightly different versions for different **regions**.
報紙公司為不同的區域製作稍微不同的版本。

同義語例句 This is the **area** where people get daily newspapers the earliest.
這是人們能最快買到每日報紙的地區。

反義語例句 Unlike local newspapers, national newspapers are available almost **everywhere**.
和地方報不同，全國性報紙幾乎在任何地方都買得到。

necessitate /nɪˈsɛsɪteɪt/ v. 使成為必需，需要
ENG. require as useful or proper
SYS. compel, oblige

> This class **necessitates** students reading newspapers and magazines and discussing current events.
> 這門課要求學生必須閱讀報紙和雜誌並且討論時事。

同義語例句 Students' ignorance of current events **calls for** the inclusion of newspaper reading as part of their study.
學生對時事的無知，使得將閱讀報紙納入學習的一部分成為必要。

同義語例句 People living in remote areas **ask for** daily newspapers to be delivered for them to stay updated.
住在偏遠地區的人們要求把日報送到那裡，讓他們能得到最新資訊。

反義語例句 We should **rid** ourselves **of** our belief that newspapers bring only bad news.
我們應該讓自己擺脫報紙只會報導壞消息的想法。

WEEK 8 TOPIC **MEDIA**

▶基礎單字擴充

type /tʌɪp/ v. 打字
ENG. write by means of a keyboard
SYS. typewrite, key in

> The magazine editor **typed** her thoughts about the latest issue in her column.
> 雜誌的編輯把她對於最新一期的想法打在專欄裡。

同義語例句 The magazine editor said that the staff should **express** any concerns they have **in writing**.
雜誌編輯說員工應該將他們的任何顧慮用書面表達出來。

同義語例句 As the writer **keyed in** her article in her laptop, she felt excited about the publication of the magazine.
當作者把她的文章輸入筆記型電腦時,她對於雜誌的出版感到很興奮。

反義語例句 These days, it is rarer for writers to **write** their articles **by hand**.
這些日子,作家比較少用手寫自己的文章了。

result /rɪˈzʌlt/ n. 結果
ENG. a phenomenon that follows and is caused by some previous phenomenon
SYS. consequence, outcome

> The **results** of the study show that people who read every day have better analytical skills.
> 研究結果顯示,每天閱讀的人有比較好的分析技能。

同義語例句 The **effect** of his extensive newspaper reading is mastering the history of the past twenty years.
他廣泛閱讀報紙的效果就是精通了過去二十年的歷史。

同義語例句 The **final outcome** of the election turned out to be totally unexpected.
選舉的最後結果完全出乎預料。

反義語例句 The **root of the matter** is that he did not have enough knowledge to have a valid opinion about history and current events.
問題的根源在於,他沒有足夠的知識可以提出關於歷史與時事的合理意見。

451

FRI

08-5A

TOPIC | Magazines in the digital age
數位時代中的雜誌

Digital platforms are becoming a **dominant** way to **distribute publications**, and the growing popularity of **e-magazines** also means the decline of print magazines. It is evident that the method of information **dispersal** has always been changing and is constantly **evolving**. As society moves forward and relies heavily on technology, magazine and newspaper publishers are wondering whether people will read printed materials anymore. Also, with companies increasing their ad dollars spent online, print media is struggling to **survive** with decreasing ad revenues. As magazines are curators of content of a particular **taste** and point of view, they may survive longer than newspapers will in print. Though magazines may have it a little easier than newspapers, this ease is relative. All publications will need to **restructure** their departments by downsizing.

TRANS

數位平台逐漸成為流通刊物的主要方式，而電子雜誌越來越受歡迎，也意味著實體（印刷）雜誌的衰退。顯然，訊息傳播的方式一直在改變，也持續在演進。隨著社會進步並且強烈依賴科技，雜誌和報紙的出版者想要知道，人們是否還會繼續閱讀印出來的東西。而且，在公司逐漸增加網路廣告費用的情況下，印刷媒體正靠著減少中的廣告收入掙扎求生存。因為雜誌是特定品味與觀點內容的「策展人」，所以紙本雜誌可能會比紙本報紙存活得久。雖然雜誌的情況可能比報紙稍微輕鬆一點，但這種輕鬆是相對的。所有刊物都必須裁員以重組部門。

digital
/ˈdɪdʒɪtəl/

adj. 數位的
Today, the image quality of **digital** cameras is comparable to that of traditional cameras.
今日數位相機的畫質比得上傳統相機。

dominant
/ˈdɒmɪnənt/

adj. 佔優勢的，支配的
The automobile is the most **dominant** form of transport.
汽車是最具主導地位的交通工具。

distribute
/dɪˈstrɪbjuːt/

v. 分發，散布，分銷
The influential magazine is **distributed** worldwide.
這份有影響力的雜誌流通全世界。

publication
/ˌpʌblɪˈkeɪʃən/

n. 出版，出版品
There are a few different **publications** dedicated to cocker spaniels.
有一些專門以可卡犬為主題的出版品。

e-magazine
/iː mæɡəˈziːn/

n. 電子雜誌
I prefer reading **e-magazines** because they are cheaper.
我偏好閱讀電子雜誌，因為比較便宜。

dispersal
/dɪˈspɜːsl/

n. 散布，傳播
The **dispersal** of pollen and seeds is important for the reproduction of plants.
花粉和種子的傳播對於植物的繁衍很重要。

evolve
/ɪˈvɒlv/

v. 進化，逐步發展
According to Charles Darwin, species on Earth are constantly **evolving**.
依據查爾斯・達爾文的說法，地球上的物種持續在演化中。

survive
/səˈvaɪv/

v. 倖存，存活
Only a few residents **survived** the massive earthquake.
只有一些居民在大地震中生還。

taste
/teɪst/

n. 品味
The hotel is not decorated to my **taste**.
這間旅館的裝潢不符合我的品味。

restructure
/riːˈstrʌktʃə/

v. 重組，改組
I recommend you to **restructure** your organisation immediately.
我建議你立刻對你的組織進行改組。

WORD TRAINING | 重點單字造句練習

article
/ˈɑːtɪkəl/

n. 文章

💬 Becoming a member of the online news site ensures you always receive the latest articles.
成為那個線上新聞網站的會員，能確保你總是收到最新文章。

E-readers are a popular and easy way to enjoy reading books and magazine articles everywhere. 電子閱讀器是一種流行而且容易隨處享受閱讀書籍及雜誌文章的方式。

✏️ You may read a newspaper or magazine article and disagree or be dissatisfied with it, but there is nowhere you can give your feedback like in the comment section of a blog post.
你可能會閱讀一篇報紙或雜誌文章而不同意或者感到不滿意，但沒有地方可以讓你像在部落格文章的留言欄一樣提出回饋意見。

After the newspaper published a controversial article, companies pulled advertising from it, forcing it to raise its subscription prices.
那份報紙刊出爭議性的文章之後，一些公司抽掉了廣告，迫使報紙提高訂閱費用。

bias
/ˈbaɪəs/

n. 偏見

💬 Readers should be aware of different types of bias in newspapers.
讀者應該察覺報紙中各種不同的偏見。

A media literate reader can sense the political bias in a news article.
有媒體識讀能力的讀者，可以感覺到一篇新聞報導裡的政治偏見。

✏️ Even if every story is written objectively, a newspaper can still show its bias when deciding which stories get published and which stories get shelved.
即使每篇報導都寫得客觀，但一份報紙還是可能在決定刊登哪些報導、擱置哪些報導時展現出它的偏見。

What you read and see in newspapers is not the whole picture of an event, but rather a version of the event that often contains various forms of bias of the publisher.
你在報紙上讀到、看到的並不是事件的全貌，而是事件的一個版本，其中經常包括出版者的各種偏見。

libel
/ˈlaɪbəl/

n. 誹謗，誹謗罪

💬 The newspaper writer is sued for libel for the false accusations he wrote in his article.
這位報紙作家因為他在文章裡寫的不實指控而被控訴誹謗。

If libel laws were stricter, people would be more cautious about what they write.
如果關於誹謗的法律更嚴格的話，人們就會對自己寫的東西更謹慎了。

✏️ To prevent people from committing libel, they should be taught the serious consequences it could have.
要避免人們犯誹謗罪，他們應該被教導誹謗可能造成的嚴重後果。

The celebrity sued the author for libel, claiming that he fabricated stories not given in the information provided to him for the former's biography.
那位名人控告作者誹謗，聲稱他杜撰了提供給他寫傳記的資訊裡沒有的故事。

unscrupulous
/ʌnˈskruːpjʊləs/

adj. 沒有操守的，沒有道德而不擇手段的

💬 It is a news story fabricated by an unscrupulous journalist.
這是一篇無良記者所編造的新聞報導。

The paparazzi's unscrupulous prying on celebrities' lives violates their privacy.
狗仔隊不擇手段地窺探名人的生活，侵犯了他們的隱私。

✏️ The unscrupulous candidate won the election by spreading groundless rumours about his rivals.
那個不擇手段的候選人藉著散播關於對手的不實謠言而贏了選舉。

The unscrupulous ruler does everything to maintain his power, even by violating his own laws.
那個不擇手段的統治者用盡一切方法，甚至違反自己的法律，來維護自己的權力。

RELATED WORDS | 相關單字延伸

develop
v. 發展，開發

advance
v. 前進，進步

evolve
v. 進化，逐步發展

progress
v. 進展，使進展

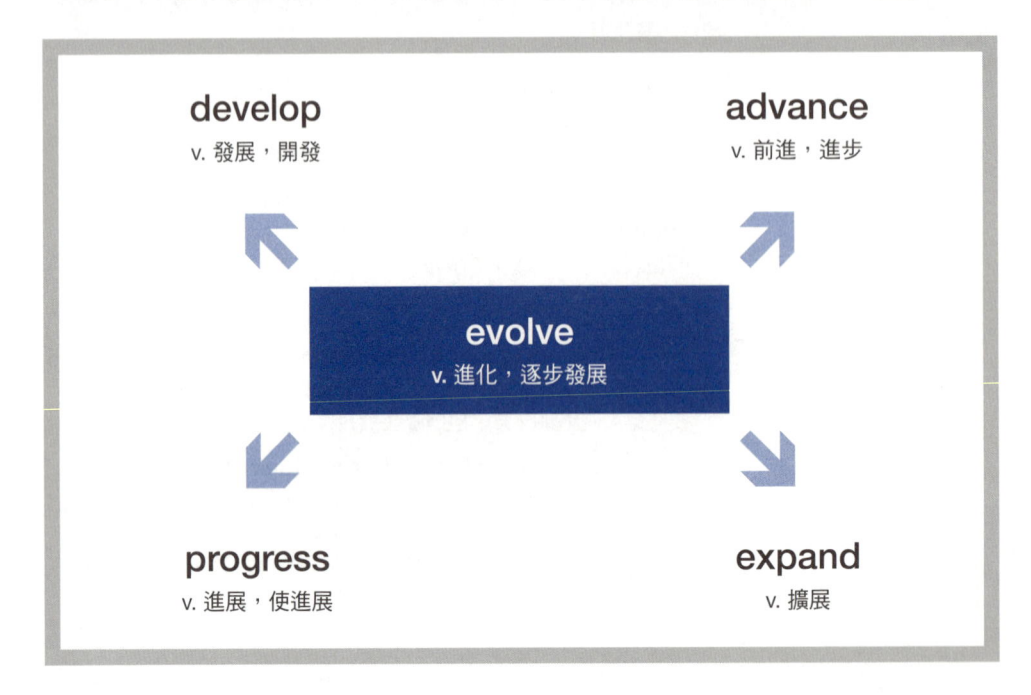

expand
v. 擴展

---

evolve
/ɪˈvɑlv/

The method of information distribution has always been changing and is constantly **evolving**.
訊息流通的方式一直在改變，也持續在演進。

develop
/dɪˈvɛləp/

I am going to **develop** a more effective system for information exchange.
我會開發更有效率的資訊交換系統。

progress
/prəˈgrɛs/

We meet regularly to **progress** the development of our information exchange system.
我們定期開會，讓我們資訊交換系統的開發有所進展。

advance
/ədˈvɑːns/

Their solutions helped their clients' companies **advance** in countless ways.
他們的解決方案幫助客戶的公司在許多方面有所進步。

expand
/ɪkˈspænd/

The company will **expand** its research and development department to diversify its product lines.
這家公司將會擴大研發部門，讓產品線多樣化。

USEFUL EXPRESSIONS | 相關實用片語

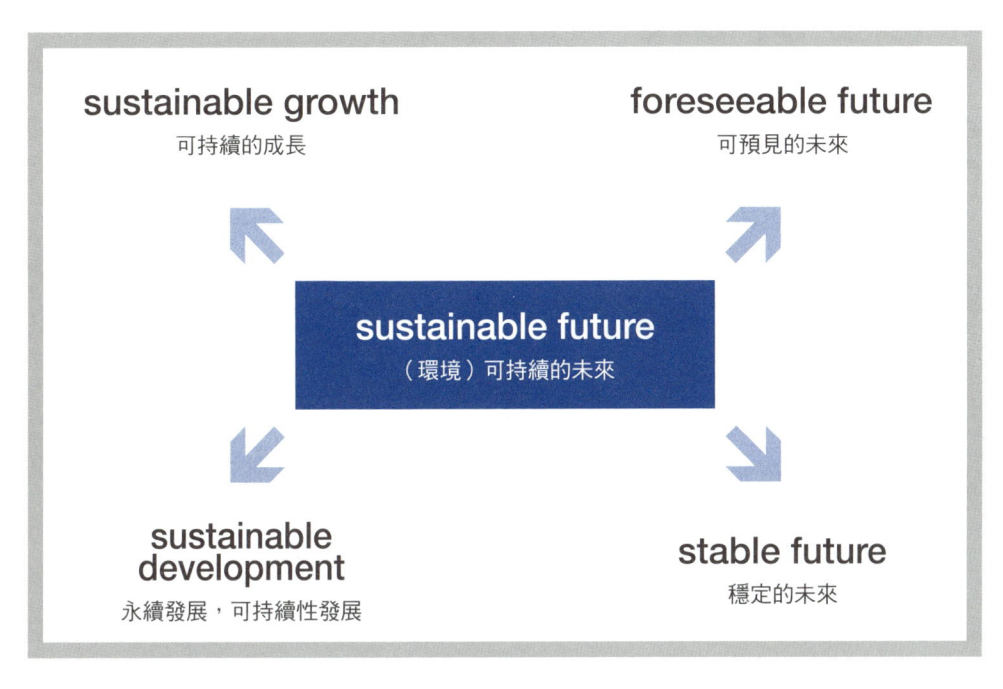

sustainable growth
可持續的成長

foreseeable future
可預見的未來

sustainable future
（環境）可持續的未來

sustainable development
永續發展，可持續性發展

stable future
穩定的未來

---

sustainable future
/səˈsteɪnəbəl ˈfjuːtʃə/

We must be dedicated to finding solutions for a sustainable future through non-profit research and education.
我們必須藉由非營利的研究與教育，致力尋找成就可持續性未來的解決方案。

sustainable growth
/səˈsteɪnəbəl ɡrəʊθ/

The new government grants will improve social services and place emphasis on more sustainable growth.
新的政府補助將改善社會服務，並且著重於更有持續性的成長。

sustainable development
/səˈsteɪnəbəl dɪˈvɛləpmənt/

The environmental issues in developing countries have called for sustainable development initiatives.
發展中國家的環境問題，使得關於永續發展的提案變得有必要。

foreseeable future
/fɔːˈsiːəbl ˈfjuːtʃə/

In the foreseeable future, there may be several hospital closures in the area.
在可預見的未來，這個地區可能會有幾所醫院關閉。

stable future
/ˈsteɪbəl ˈfjuːtʃə/

To build and maintain a stable future for our country, we must take steps in the right direction.
要為我們的國家建立並維持一個穩定的未來，我們必須朝著對的方向循序漸進。

SAT
IELTS **BASIC WORDS**

exist /ɪgˈzɪst/ v. 存在
ENG. be present in the real world
SYS. live, endure

> TV programmes cannot exist without sponsoring companies.
> 電視節目不能在沒有贊助公司的情況下存在。

- 同義語 例句 — People should be able to live without television and print media.
  人應該不看電視和印刷媒體也能活下去。
- 同義語 例句 — It would be difficult for TV shows to stay alive if they have few advertisers.
  如果廣告主很少的話，電視節目就很難生存。
- 反義語 例句 — TV shows would cease to continue if sponsors pull their ads.
  如果贊助商把廣告抽走，電視節目就不會繼續下去。

use /juːz/ v. 使用
ENG. to put into service
SYS. utilise, employ

> We should use social media to our own advantage by targeting our audience.
> 我們應該藉由鎖定目標觀眾，以對我們有利的方式使用社群媒體。

- 同義語 例句 — We must employ social media for the purpose of reaching more customers.
  我們必須利用社群媒體，接觸更多顧客。
- 同義語 例句 — It is wise to avail ourselves of the benefits of social media.
  讓我們利用社群媒體的益處是明智的。
- 反義語 例句 — Some companies refuse to take advantage of social media because they believe it does not bring real profit.
  有些公司拒絕利用社群媒體，因為他們認為它不會帶來真正的收益。

WEEK 8 TOPIC **MEDIA**

▶基礎單字擴充

campaign /kæmˈpeɪn/ n. 運動，活動
ENG. an organised course of action to achieve a goal
SYS. crusade, movement

> The **campaign** aims to increase the awareness of people about false advertising.
> 活動的目的是為了提升人們對不實廣告的意識。

同義語例句　**Coordinated events** were held nationwide to fight deceptive advertising.
全國舉行了串連的活動，對抗欺騙性的廣告。

同義語例句　A **set of activities** were organised to remind the public that some ads are misleading.
為了提醒大眾某些廣告會使人誤解，而安排了一系列的活動。

反義語例句　It turns out that the advertising agency's **random acts** of marketing were not effective at all.
結果證明，那家廣告代理公司隨機的（缺乏原則的）行銷行為完全沒有效。

metropolitan /ˌmɛtrəˈpɒlɪtən/ adj. 大都會的
ENG. relating to or characteristic of a metropolis
SYS. city, urban

> The **metropolitan streets** are filled with visual advertisements that distract the drivers.
> 大都會的街道充斥著讓駕駛分心的視覺廣告。

同義語例句　The **highly developed area** is full of blinding neon lights.
這個高度發展的區域充滿眩目的霓虹燈。

同義語例句　The **central communities** are usually where advertisers put up their billboards.
（城市）中央的社區通常是廣告商樹立看板的地方。

反義語例句　If you want advertisement-free surroundings, go to **rural areas**.
如果你想要沒有廣告的環境，那就去鄉村地區。

459

SAT

TOPIC | Billboard advertising
看板廣告

Amongst all kinds of advertisements, billboards are the most visible in our daily life. This **arresting** form of advertising helps **generate consumer** sales for companies by creating a memorable visual impression in a short instant. Billboard advertisements are often humorous as well as informative, providing commuters stuck in traffic with a message to **ponder**. Unfortunately, the **proliferation** of giant billboards is harming the visual beauty of the cityscape. Clients pay by the square foot, so the billboards get bigger as the ad companies get greedier. Of course, we don't want to **dissuade** companies from **erecting** billboards by charging **exorbitant** land rental fees because their ads **rejuvenate** the economy by stimulating the public's interest about products. The best solution may be to limit the size of the **structures** so that they do not get too distracting.

TRANS

在各種廣告中，看板是在我們的日常生活中最顯而易見的。這種引人注意的廣告形式，藉著在很短的瞬間內留下難忘的視覺印象，幫助公司產生來自消費者的銷售額。看板廣告往往幽默又能提供資訊，提供受困車潮中的通勤者一個可以思考的訊息。遺憾的是，大型看板的激增正在傷害城市風景的視覺美感。客戶依照每平方英尺付費，所以隨著廣告公司越來越貪心，看板也變得越來越大。當然，我們不希望藉著收取過高的土地租賃費用來嚇阻廣告公司豎立看板，因為他們的廣告能夠靠著刺激大眾對於產品的興趣而振興經濟。最好的解決方法可能是限制看板結構的大小，讓它們不會過度分散注意力。

arresting
/əˈrɛstɪŋ/

adj. 引人注意的
His eyes were so blue that they were literally **arresting**.
他的眼睛很藍,簡直令人目不轉睛。

generate
/ˈdʒɛnəreɪt/

v. 產生
One small battery can **generate** enough power to operate the machine.
一顆小電池就可以產生足夠這個機器運作的電力。

consumer
/kənˈsjuːmə/

n. 消費者
The **consumer** report stated that the product was very unsafe.
消費者報告說明這項產品非常不安全。

ponder
/ˈpɒndə/

v. 仔細考慮
James asked Ming to **ponder** moving to the UK.
James 要求小明考慮搬到英國。

proliferation
/prəlɪfəˈreɪʃn/

n. 增殖,激增
The rapid **proliferation** of news websites has made online marketing even more difficult.
新聞網站的迅速暴增,使得網路行銷更加困難了。

dissuade
/dɪˈsweɪd/

v. 勸阻
May wanted to **dissuade** me from joining the club.
May 想勸阻我加入社團。

erect
/ɪˈrɛkt/

v. 豎立
After two hours, the scouts finally finished **erecting** the tent.
兩個小時以後,童子軍終於搭好帳篷。

exorbitant
/ɪgˈzɔːbɪtənt/

adj. 過高的,過分的
Most people cannot afford the **exorbitant** prices at that restaurant.
大部份的人負擔不起那間餐廳過高的價格。

rejuvenate
/rɪˈdʒuːvəneɪt/

v. 使年輕,使更有活力
Spa massage treatments and hot springs can **rejuvenate** your skin.
Spa 按摩療程和溫泉可以讓你的皮膚恢復年輕。

structure
/ˈstrʌktʃə/

n. 結構
I am not sure if the **structures** you built are sound.
我不確定你建造的架構是否穩固。

WORD TRAINING | 重點單字造句練習

publicity
/pʌbˈlɪsɪti/

n. 媒體的關注，宣傳

💬 Magazine advertisements are not as visible as TV commercials, which help gain more publicity.
雜誌廣告不像電視廣告那麼有能見度，可以獲得更多宣傳效應。

The publicity gained through advertising improves a company's sales performance.
透過廣告得到的宣傳效應，能改善公司的銷售表現。

✏️ Most companies still employ the mass media as the main vehicle for gaining publicity and expanding their customer base.
許多公司仍然使用大眾媒體作為獲得宣傳及擴展客群的主要工具。

In recent years, large events and corporate anniversaries have become important publicity platforms for local companies.
最近這些年，大型活動和企業週年紀念已經成為地方性公司重要的宣傳平台。

---

moral
/ˈmɒrəl/

adj. 道德的，道德上的

💬 Advertising can be tasteful and in conformity with high moral standards, and occasionally even uplifting.
廣告宣傳可以有品味、符合高道德標準，有時甚至能振奮人心。

We wish to call attention to the ethical and moral problems that advertising can and does raise.
我們希望呼籲人們關注廣告可能而且的確造成的倫理與道德問題。

✏️ Advertisements aimed at children raise some moral issues significantly different from those raised by advertisements aimed at competent adults.
以兒童為目標的廣告，會有一些和給成熟大人看的廣告相當不同的道德問題。

Advertisements can play an important role in shaping a society's ethical and moral standards by suggesting whether a certain kind of behaviour is acceptable or not.
藉由暗示某種行為是可接受或者不能接受的，廣告可能在形塑社會的倫理與道德標準方面扮演重要角色。

caption
/ˈkapʃən/

n. 伴隨圖片等等的標題或說明文字，字幕　　v. 加說明文字，加字幕

💬 When I read the caption on the advertisement, I was offended.
當我讀到廣告上的文案時，我感覺被激怒了。

The caption on the spine of the cereal box was directly aimed at people watching their weight.
麥片盒側邊的文案是直接針對注意體重的人寫的。

✍ We can make television more accessible to people with hearing impairment by adding captions to TV shows.
我們可以藉由為電視節目加上字幕，讓有聽力障礙的人更能看懂電視。

All political candidates are now required by law to caption their campaign advertisements or otherwise make them accessible to people who are deaf or hard of hearing.
所有政治候選人現在都被法律要求為競選廣告加上字幕，或者用其他方法讓沒有聽力或重聽的人能夠了解。

commercial
/kəˈmɝːʃəl/

v. 商業的　　n. 電視／廣播中的商業廣告

💬 During the commercial break of TV shows, I mute the volume so the ads don't influence me.
在電視節目播廣告的時候，我把音量轉成靜音，讓廣告不會影響到我。

The product advertised during the commercial break became popular in the region.
廣告時間宣傳的產品在那個地區變得受歡迎。

✍ Companies often seek to generate increased sales of their merchandise through TV commercials, which leave a lasting impression on the audience.
公司經常希望藉由能在觀眾心中留下持久印象的電視廣告來產生更高的商品銷售額。

Commercial advertisements should adhere to the codes intended to protect the public from inaccurate and unsubstantiated claims.
商業廣告應該遵守為了保護大眾免於接觸不正確與沒有事實根據的主張所設的法規。

RELATED WORDS | 相關單字延伸

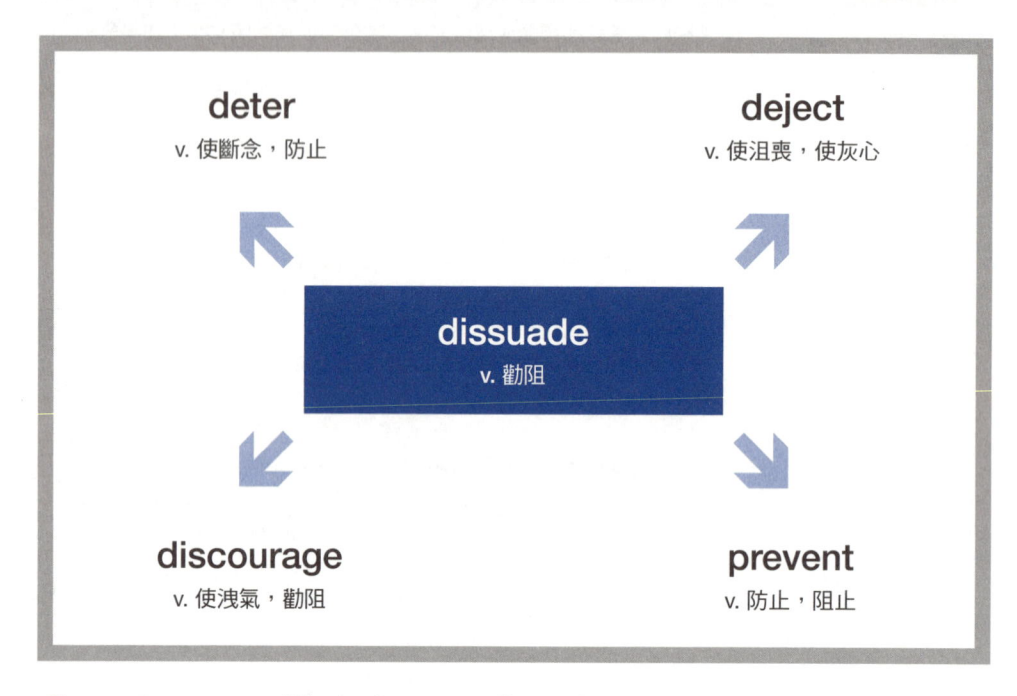

deter
v. 使斷念，防止

deject
v. 使沮喪，使灰心

dissuade
v. 勸阻

discourage
v. 使洩氣，勸阻

prevent
v. 防止，阻止

dissuade
/dɪˈsweɪd/
We don't want to dissuade companies from erecting billboards because their ads stimulate people's interest about products.
我們不希望勸阻廣告公司豎立看板，因為他們的廣告能夠刺激人們對於產品的興趣。

deter
/dɪˈtɚ/
The fear of being penalised deterred some advertising agencies from erecting giant billboards.
被處罰的恐懼讓一些廣告公司打消了豎立大型看板的念頭。

discourage
/dɪsˈkʌrɪdʒ/
The government discourages the practice of advertising via billboards.
政府不鼓勵用看板做廣告宣傳的行為。

deject
/dɪˈdʒɛkt/
The marketing director felt dejected when he found that the billboards on which the ads were put were illegal.
發現廣告刊登的看板不合法，行銷主任覺得很灰心。

prevent
/prɪˈvɛnt/
Local residents staged a protest to prevent a company from erecting billboards in the park.
當地居民發起抗議，阻止一間公司在公園豎立廣告看板。

USEFUL EXPRESSIONS | 相關實用片語

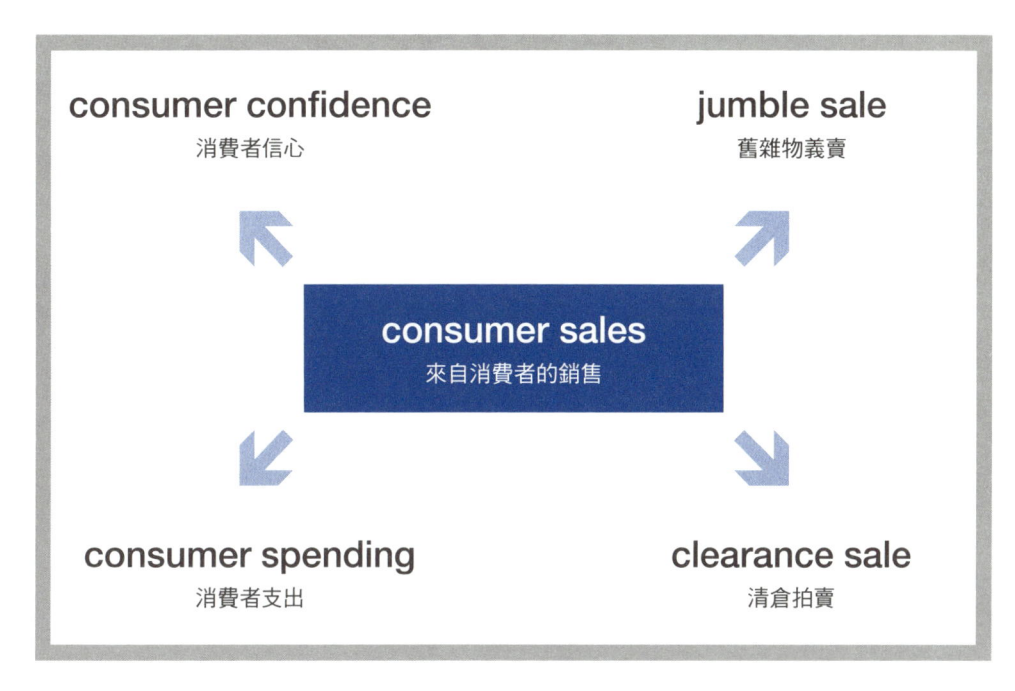

```
consumer confidence                    jumble sale
消費者信心                                舊雜物義賣
            ↖         ↗
         consumer sales
         來自消費者的銷售
            ↙         ↘
consumer spending                     clearance sale
消費者支出                                清倉拍賣
```

consumer sales
/kənˈsjuːmə seɪlz/

According to the report, consumer sales fell by 5% year-on-year in May.
根據報告，來自消費者的銷售在五月份和去年相比下跌 5%。

consumer confidence
/kənˈsjuːmə ˈkɒnfɪdəns/

For the first time in over three years, consumer confidence is at its highest.
這是三年多來第一次消費者信心達到最高點。

consumer spending
/kənˈsjuːmə spɛndɪŋ/

We predict that a fall in consumer spending may threaten the economic recovery of the nation.
我們預測消費者支出的下降可能會威脅到這個國家的經濟復甦。

jumble sale
/ˈdʒʌmbəl seɪl/

The jumble sale raised quite a lot of money for a local charity.
舊雜物義賣為當地的一個慈善團體募集了很多錢。

clearance sale
/ˈklɪərəns seɪl/

Clearance sales caused shoppers to flock to the malls for some last minute Christmas shopping.
清倉拍賣使得購物客湧向賣場，進行最後一刻的聖誕節採購。

SUN

IELTS **BASIC WORDS**

attitude /ˈatɪtjuːd/ n. 態度
ENG. a complex mental state involving beliefs, feelings, values and dispositions to act in certain ways
SYS. perspective, approach

> His **attitude** towards billboard advertisements will affect their yearly budget.　他對看板廣告的態度會影響他們的年度預算。

同義語 例句　His **way of thinking** about advertisements and their effects is one-sided and biased.
他對廣告和廣告效果的想法是單方面而且偏頗的。

同義語 例句　From his **point of view**, advertisements are the root of overspending.
從他的觀點來看，廣告是超支的根源。

反義語 例句　His **disregard** for the effects of advertising makes him keep cutting marketing budgets every year.
他對於廣告效果的漠視，使得他每年持續削減行銷預算。

alter /ˈɔːltə/ v. 修改
ENG. to change or make different
SYS. modify, reform

> Experts say that advertisements **alter** the way we think about certain products.　專家說廣告會改變我們對某些產品的想法。

同義語 例句　Advertisements can **change** the way a person perceives some items in the market.
廣告可以改變一個人看待市場上某些產品的方式。

同義語 例句　We should **adjust** our spending habits when we find ourselves being influenced by advertisements to buy items we don't really need.
當我們發現自己受到廣告影響，而購買不是真的需要的東西時，我們應該調整自己的花費習慣。

反義語 例句　We can **maintain the state** of our finances by remembering to be practical.
我們可以藉著記得保持實際來維持自己的財務狀況。

▶基礎單字擴充

temperature /ˈtɛmpərətʃɚ/ n. 溫度
ENG. degree of hotness or coldness of a body or environment
SYS. hotness, energy

> Leaving too many light bulbs on will increase indoor **temperature**.
> 開著太多燈泡會使室內溫度上升。

同義語例句 The **level of heat** during the summer is aggravated by the overuse of air conditioning.
夏天的熱度因為過度使用空調而更加嚴重。

同義語例句 The **degree of hotness** within cities is affected by the use of air conditioning.
城市的炎熱程度受到空調的使用影響。

反義語例句 The **absence of temperature reading** due to faulty thermometers made it hard to determine how hot it was.
因為溫度計故障而沒有氣溫讀數，所以很難判斷有多熱。

limit /ˈlɪmɪt/ n. 限制，限度，極限
ENG. greatest possible degree of something
SYS. boundary, edge

> Nowadays, despite mandated laws, there seems to be no **limit** to the content of advertisements in the mass media.
> 現在，儘管有明定的法律，但大眾媒體中的廣告內容似乎沒有限度。

同義語例句 There are so many posters on the wall that there seems to be no **restriction** on posting them.
牆上有很多海報，多得像是沒有張貼限制一樣。

同義語例句 Advertising in cyberspace shows the **extent** to which ads can intrude into people's daily activities.
網路空間裡的廣告宣傳，顯示出廣告可以入侵人們的日常活動到什麼程度。

反義語例句 The amount of billboards in a city must be decreased to a **minimum degree**.
城市中廣告看板的數量必須被減少到最小的程度。

SUN

08-7A

TOPIC: The negative effects of alcohol advertising
酒類宣傳的負面影響

Alcohol advertisements affect the way we think about drinking. Online, on television and in magazines, we are surrounded by advertisements suggesting that drinking is fun, desirable and **innocuous**. Such kinds of messages may be easily **identifiable** in advertisements and commercials, but they can also be delivered through films and music videos in a less **obvious** way and thus become more **detrimental** to youth. No matter what form of advertising is taken, alcohol companies aim to **recruit** young drinkers and promote heavy **consumption** of their products. Moreover, as a result of the media's **dependence** on alcohol companies for their **sponsoring**, alcohol use is often **glorified** in the media, and its negative effects are rarely mentioned. Therefore, we must be **conscious** of the intention behind alcohol advertisements and product placements and see the negative side of drinking.

TRANS

酒類廣告影響著我們對於飲酒的想法。在網路、電視和雜誌上，我們被暗示著喝酒很有趣、值得嚮往而且無害的廣告圍繞。這種訊息在平面廣告和廣播電視廣告裡可能很容易辨識，但它也可以透過電影和音樂錄影帶，用比較不明顯的方式傳達，也因此對於青少年更加有害。不管廣告採取的廣告形式是什麼，酒品公司的目標是招攬年輕的飲酒者，並且促進對於產品的大量飲用。而且，由於媒體依賴酒品公司給予贊助，所以酒品的使用在媒體中經常被美化，而它的負面影響很少被提到。所以，我們必須意識到酒類廣告與產品置入背後的意圖，並且看到飲酒的負面影響。

innocuous
/ɪˈnɒkjʊəs/

adj. 無害的
Drugs may seem **innocuous** at first, but they will destroy your health after long-term use.
毒品一開始可能看似無害，但它們會在長期使用後摧毀你的健康。

identifiable
/ˌʌɪdɛntɪˈfʌɪəbəl/

adj. 可辨識的
She is easily **identifiable** by her skin colour.
她的皮膚顏色讓她很容易被認出來。

obvious
/ˈɒbvɪəs/

adj. 明顯的
I think that the reason she got angry is **obvious**.
我想她生氣的理由很明顯。

detrimental
/ˌdɛtrɪˈmɛntəl/

adj. 有害的，不利的
The frost is **detrimental** to the health of tomato plants.
霜不利於番茄株的健康。

recruit
/rɪˈkruːt/

v. 招募
The armed forces are trying to **recruit** young people with advertising campaigns.
軍隊試圖用廣告活動招募年輕人。

consumption
/kənˈsʌmpʃən/

n. 消費，消耗（飲用／食用）
The **consumption** of dairy products can make certain people sick.
食用乳製品可能會造成某些人不舒服。

dependence
/dɪˈpɛndəns/

n. 依賴
Prescription medication should be used as directed to avoid **dependence**.
處方藥應遵照指示使用以避免依賴性。

sponsor
/ˈspɒnsə/

v. 贊助
This research programme is **sponsored** by health authorities.
這個研究計畫是由保健當局贊助的。

glorify
/ˈɡlɔːrɪfʌɪ/

v. 美化
Some publications **glorifying** guns and gangs have been banned for retail sale.
一些美化槍支與幫派的出版品已經被禁止零售販賣。

consciously
/ˈkɒnʃəsli/

adv. 有意識地
I didn't **consciously** lie to the officer—it just happened!
我不是有意對警官說謊的——但就是自然發生了！

WORD TRAINING | 重點單字造句練習

overexposure
/ˌovərɪkˈspoʒə/

n. 過度曝露／接觸，過度曝光

💬 Overexposure to negative news can affect psychological health.
過度接觸負面新聞會影響心理健康。

Overexposure to alcohol advertising is potentially harmful to young people.
過度接觸酒品廣告可能對年輕人有害。

✏️ The overexposure of a news topic, even of an important one such as terrorism, can cause some people to become disinterested in the subject.
新聞主題的過度曝光，即使是恐怖行動這種重要主題的曝光，都可能使某些人變得不感興趣。

Blaming celebrities for their overexposure is moot because it is public attention that calls for the exposure.
責怪名人的過度曝光是沒有實際意義的，因為是大眾的注意要求他們的曝光。

---

propaganda
/ˌprɑpəˈgændə/

n.（經常有偏見的）政治主義、信念的宣傳

💬 Negative propaganda may not have its desired effect because people's reaction to it is not always predictable.
負面宣傳可能不會達到希望的效果，因為人們的反應是不能完全預測到的。

Negative advertising can work in the same way as political propaganda does.
（攻擊對手產品的）負面廣告可以像政治宣傳一樣產生效果。

✏️ Negative propaganda created during elections can stir up a whirlwind of uncertainty by evoking mixed feelings in the audience.
選舉時製造的負面宣傳，會藉由激起觀眾各種不同的感受而引發不確定的旋風。

We must educate young people to think for themselves because most news outlets are now biased, and their analyses of world events often serve as propaganda.
我們必須教育年輕人自己思考，因為現在大部分的新聞媒體都有偏見，而它們對世界事件的分析經常是一種政治信念的宣傳。

criminal
/ˈkrɪmɪnəl/

adj. 犯罪的

💬 I believe that targeting underage people in alcohol advertisements is a criminal offence.
我認為在酒類廣告中以未成年人為廣告目標是一種犯罪。

Parents should be held responsible for their children's criminal behaviour.
父母應該被要求對孩子的犯罪行為負責。

✏️ Some rappers' lyrics glorify criminal activity and degrade women, yet they are allowed to advertise their albums during prime time when impressionable children are watching.
有些饒舌歌手的歌詞美化犯罪行為並且貶低婦女，但他們卻被允許在容易受到影響的孩子收看的電視黃金時段宣傳專輯。

The techniques employed by the aggressive advertiser are nearly criminal in the way they dupe the public, draw in the impressionable and falsely educate the ignorant.　那個激進的廣告主採用的手法近乎犯罪，因為它們欺騙大眾、吸引容易受影響的人，而且錯誤地教育不懂的人。

credible
/ˈkrɛdɪbəl/

adj. 可信的，可靠的

💬 The more credible the source of a message is, the more likely people will believe it.
一個訊息的來源越可靠，人們就越有可能相信它。

When consumers perceive that an ad is credible, they are more likely to have a positive reaction.
當消費者認為廣告是可信的，他們就比較有可能產生正面反應。

✏️ Researchers are now exploring what happens when consumers perceive the advertiser as ill-intentioned, compared to when they believe an ad is credible and not manipulative.
研究者目前正在研究，和相信廣告可信而且沒有人為操縱的情況相比，當顧客認為廣告主有不當的意圖時會發生什麼事情。

As consumers get increasingly market-savvy, advertisers should not attempt to deceive the audience but rather convince them with credible information.
隨著消費者變得越來越熟知市場，廣告主應該不要試圖欺騙觀眾，而是用可信的資訊說服他們。

RELATED WORDS | 相關單字延伸

clear
adj. 清楚的

noticeable
adj. 容易注意到的，明顯的

obvious
adj. 明顯的

palpable
adj. 可以觸摸到的，可以明顯感受到的

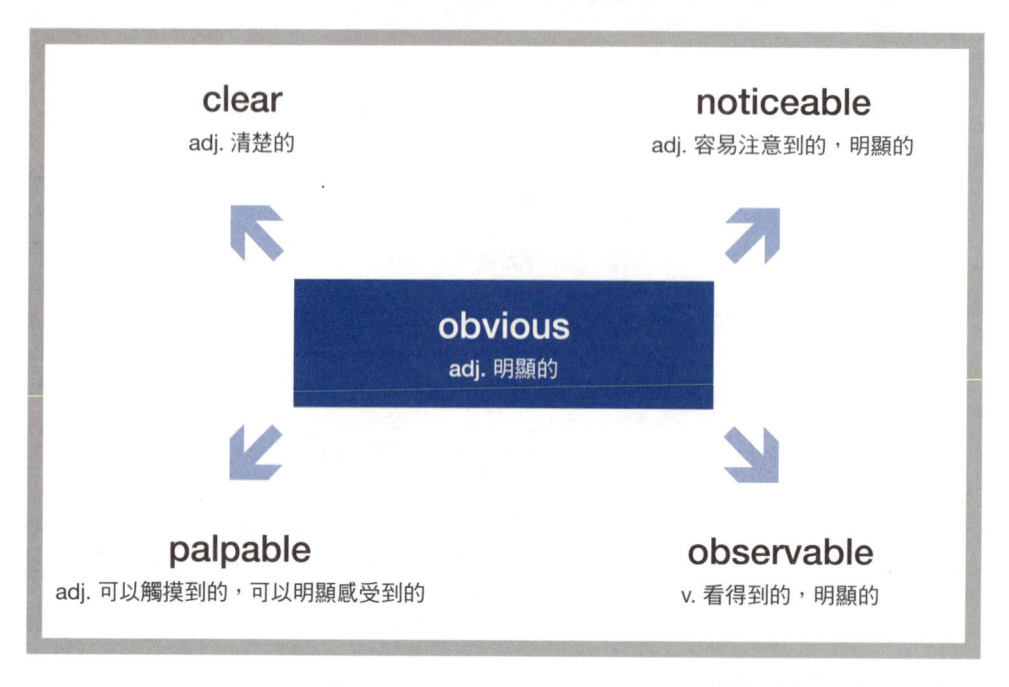

observable
v. 看得到的，明顯的

---

obvious
/ˈɒbvɪəs/

This kind of message may be easily identifiable in advertisements and commercials, but it can be less obvious in films and music videos
這種訊息在平面廣告和廣播電視廣告裡可能很容易辨識，但它在電影和音樂錄影帶裡可能比較不明顯。

clear
/klɪə/

The negative messages shown in the film are so clear that even children can easily notice them.
這部電影裡的負面訊息很清楚，連小孩都能很容易注意到。

palpable
/ˈpalpəbəl/

Many detrimental messages are spread through music videos, with promiscuity being a palpable one.
許多有害的訊息透過音樂錄影帶傳播，其中一個明顯的例子是雜交。

noticeable
/ˈnəʊtɪsəbəl/

I find the detrimental messages in TV programmes aimed at a younger audience are quite noticeable.
我發現以年輕觀眾為目標的電視節目中的有害訊息很容易注意到。

observable
/əbˈzɜːvəbl/

The intention behind the TV commercial is quite observable.
那個電視廣告背後的意圖很明顯。

472

USEFUL EXPRESSIONS | 相關實用片語

negative effect
負面影響，負面效果

seamy side
陰暗面

negative side
負面

negative influence
負面影響

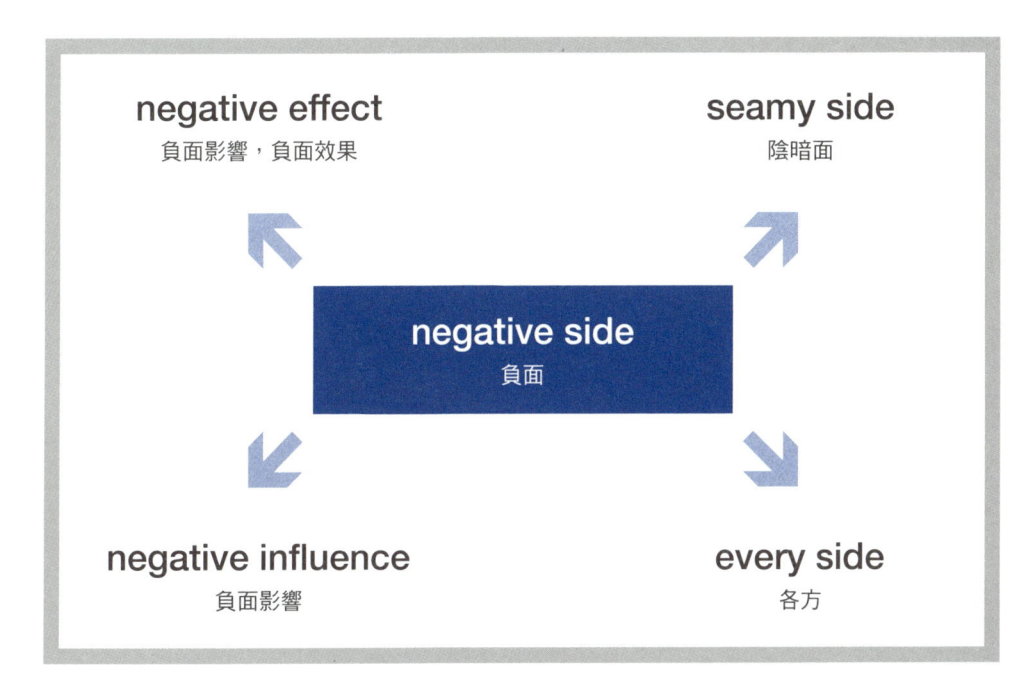

every side
各方

negative side
/ˈnɛɡətɪv sʌɪd/

The negative side of social networking services is revealed in this report.
這份報告揭露出社群網路服務負面的一面。

negative effect
/ˈnɛɡətɪv ɪˈfɛkt/

The beauty culture shaped by cosmetic advertisements featuring airbrushed images is having negative effects on women.
使用修圖過的影像製作的化妝品廣告所塑造出來的美容文化，對女性有負面的影響。

negative influence
/ˈnɛɡətɪv ˈɪnfluəns/

According to traditionalists, Western popular culture has a negative influence on Iranian youth.
根據傳統主義者的說法，西方流行文化對伊朗青少年有負面影響。

seamy side
/ˈsiːmi sʌɪd/

When you see only the seamy side of life, try to spend some quality time with your best friends.
當你只看到生活的陰暗面時，試著和你最好的朋友度過美好的時光。

every side
/ˈɛvri sʌɪd/

Winds were blowing from every side during the typhoon.
在颱風時期，風從四面八方吹來。

WEEK 9
LEISURE

結伴旅行與獨自旅行

海外旅行對年輕人而言是寶貴的經驗

團隊運動對兒童的好處

極限運動

園藝活動

放鬆

在週末工作的優缺點

MON

IELTS **BASIC WORDS**

stay /steɪ/   v. 停留，保持
ENG. remain in a certain state
SYS. remain, rest

> Most people would rather **stay** at home than travel alone during holidays.
> 大部分人放假時寧願待在家裡，也不想自己一個人去旅行。

同義語例句   It is better to **stick around** the house alone than be in a hustle with many travellers during holidays.
放假時比起跟一大堆旅行者擠在一起，還是獨自留在家裡比較好。

同義語例句   Some **continue to be** solo travellers despite the fact that a companion can be helpful when in need.
雖然同伴在需要的時候可以幫得上忙，但有些人還是持續單獨旅行。

反義語例句   Some travellers prefer solo trips because they can **move on** to their next destination without considering many external factors.
有些旅行者偏好單獨旅行，因為他們可以繼續前往下一個目的地，而不用考慮許多外在因素。

allow /əˈlaʊ/   v. 允許
ENG. make it possible for something to happen
SYS. let, permit

> Nowadays, the government **allows** travellers to go to dangerous destinations.
> 現在政府允許旅行者前往危險的目的地。

同義語例句   The travelling group was **granted permission** to enter the war zone.   那個旅行團獲得允許進入戰爭地區。

同義語例句   The government **permits** a limited number of tourists to travel in the area.
政府允許有限的觀光客在那個地區旅行。

反義語例句   The government strictly **forbids** aliens travelling in the country without visas.
這個政府嚴格禁止沒有簽證的外國人在國內旅行。

WEEK 9 TOPIC **LEISURE**

▶ 基礎單字擴充

expensive /ɪkˈspɛnsɪv/ adj. 昂貴的
ENG. high in price
SYS. costly, lavish

> It is more **expensive** to travel in a group than alone.
> 團體旅行比個人旅行貴。

同義語例句 The group trip they won is **worth a lot of money**.
他們贏得的團體旅行價值很多錢。

同義語例句 The package trip he chose for his group was **extravagantly priced**.
他為他的團體選擇的套裝旅行要價不菲。

反義語例句 Air tickets are **cheaper** when bought as a group.
團體購買機票比較便宜。

invest /ɪnˈvɛst/ v. 投資
ENG. to commit one's money to gain financial return
SYS. venture, expend

> It is wise to **invest** early in travelling, whether alone or with a group.
> 不管是單獨還是跟團，早點投資在旅行上是明智的作法。

同義語例句 You should **put in** a little of your money to a travel fund each month.
你應該每個月投入一點錢到旅行基金中。

同義語例句 It is wise to **lay out** some money on travelling once in a while.
偶爾花一點錢旅行是明智的。

反義語例句 He regrets **taking** money **away** from his travel fund.
他後悔把錢從旅行基金裡拿走（用在其他用途）。

477

MON

TOPIC | Travelling with others and alone
結伴旅行與獨自旅行

People often assume that it is easier to travel with others, but there are some **incentives** for one to travel alone. For example, the freedom that unaccompanied **trekking** gives a person outshines the need to take one's companions into account when travelling in a group. Some people believe it is **selfish** to consider only oneself, but what travelling solo really means is to ascertain what **formulates** one's individuality. When forced to fend for oneself, one either adapts to their surroundings and makes **autonomous** decisions, or fails. The self-exploration of strength and character is particularly important in today's frenzied world of work and responsibilities. For many, however, the fear and **trepidation** of **traipsing** around an unfamiliar place all by oneself are enormous. They feel it **reckless** to travel in a **nomadic** way. In reality, though, there are always unplanned surprises in a journey, which is why we want to escape our daily **routine** and go travelling.

TRANS

人們經常假設和其他人一起旅行比較簡單，但也有一些讓人獨自旅行的動機。例如，獨自徒步跋涉旅行能夠帶給一個人的自由，比團體旅行時考慮到別人的需要顯得更出色。有些人認為只考慮自己是很自私的，但單獨旅行真正的意義是確認什麼東西構成了自己的個體性。當被迫照顧自己時，人不是適應環境並且做出自主的決定，就是失敗。在今日充滿工作與責任的瘋狂世界中，對於力量與性格的自我探索特別重要。不過，對很多人來說，獨自在不熟悉的地方遊蕩，讓人非常恐懼、不安。他們覺得用像是遊牧民族的方式旅遊是很魯莽的。但事實上，旅途中總是有計畫之外的驚喜，這也是我們之所以想逃離日常事務去旅行的原因。

incentive
/ɪnˈsɛntɪv/

n. 刺激，鼓勵，動機；作為鼓勵的優待，獎金
A teacher should provide students with opportunities and incentives to learn.
老師應該為學生提供學習的機會與動機。

trekking
/ˈtrɛkɪŋ/

n. 徒步跋涉旅行
It is now popular to go **trekking** from Kathmandu to Everest Base Camp.
現在很流行從加德滿都徒步跋涉到聖母峰登山基地。

selfish
/ˈsɛlfɪʃ/

adj. 自私的
She is too **selfish** to help others in her free time.
她太自私了，所以不會在她有空的時候幫忙別人。

formulate
/ˈfɔːmjʊleɪt/

v. 制定，配製…的配方
While she **formulates** the plan, I'll make the reservations.
當她擬定計畫的時候，我會進行預約。

autonomous
/ɔːˈtɒnəməs/

adj. 自主的
You must be **autonomous** and self-ruling on your job.
你在工作中必須要能自動自發，並且管理自己。

trepidation
/ˌtrɛpɪˈdeɪʃən/

n. 驚恐，不安
The rumour caused **trepidation** among local residents.
那個謠言造成了當地居民的驚慌。

traipse
/treɪps/

v. 長途跋涉；遊蕩
We all went **traipsing** through the snow just for fun.
我們全都在雪中漫步，只是為了好玩。

nomadic
/nəʊˈmadɪk/

adj. 遊牧的
Many indigenous peoples were **nomadic**, following migration patterns of animals.
許多原住民依照動物遷徙的模式過著遊牧生活。

reckless
/ˈrɛkləs/

adj. 魯莽的，不顧危險的
It was **reckless** of him to leave all his tools scattered around the house.
他把所有工具散落在房子裡，是很不顧危險的。

routine
/ruːˈtiːn/

n. 例行事務
Patient care and service are part of nurses' daily **routine**.
患者照顧與服務是護士日常事務的一部分。

WORD TRAINING | 重點單字造句練習

unaccompanied
/ˌʌnəˈkʌmpənɪd/

adj. 沒人陪伴的，獨自一人的

💬 I would rather travel unaccompanied than with someone else.
我寧願沒有人陪我旅行，而不要和別人一起。

It is boring being unaccompanied, so I keep a dog as a pet.
沒有人陪伴很無聊，所以我養狗當寵物。

✏️ The unaccompanied traveller accused the airline of losing her luggage, but the truth is someone stole it when she left it unattended.
那個沒有人陪伴的旅行者指控航空公司弄丟了她的行李，但事實是有人在她沒有看管好行李的時候偷了它。

Children may travel unaccompanied on certain routes depending on their age and provided the child does not require additional care such as toileting or feeding.
取決於年齡，而且如果不需要陪上廁所或餵食等額外照顧的話，小孩可以在沒有人陪伴的情況下搭乘某些航線。

---

timetable
/ˈtaɪmteɪbəl/

n. 時間表

💬 I always download and print out train timetables before I go travelling.
我旅行之前總是下載並且列印火車時間表。

Having bus and train timetables in your pocket allows you to freely explore a place without worrying about time. 口袋裡放著公車和火車的時間表，讓你可以自由探索一個地方，而不用擔心時間。

✏️ One of the downsides of travelling by public transport is that your itinerary will be restricted by train and bus timetables. 用大眾交通工具旅行的缺點之一，就是你的旅程會被火車和公車的時間表限制。

I have learned a lot from the experience of travelling alone, such as how to find public transport timetables, how to ask locals for help and how to adapt to situations. 我從獨自旅行的經驗中學到很多，例如如何找到大眾交通工具的時間表、如何向當地人求助，還有如何適應情況。

encounter
/ɪnˈkaʊntə/

v. 遇到，遭遇

💬 You will encounter more local people and learn more when travelling alone.
獨自旅行的時候，你會遇到更多當地人，而且學到更多。

What makes a trip meaningful is the new experience we encounter during it.
讓旅程有意義的，是我們在其中遇到的新體驗。

✍ When you encounter like-minded people during a group trip, you will feel less pressured.
當你在團體旅行中遇到志同道合的人時，你會感覺比較沒有壓力。

Travelling on your own exposes you to all sorts of new situations that you may never encounter in your ordinary life.
自己一個人旅行，會讓你遇到平常生活中可能永遠遇不到的各種新情況。

island-hop
/ˈʌɪləndhɒp/

v. 跳島旅行

💬 I booked the island-hopping trip in Indonesia for my family.
我為我的家人訂了印尼的跳島旅行。

I want to island-hop in Greece this summer.
我這個夏天想要在希臘跳島旅行。

✍ If you feel you'd rather have some companions to travel with, do a small tour of Fiji and island-hop in the Yasawas, where many young single travellers go.
如果你比較希望有同伴一起旅行，那就在斐濟來趟小旅行，並且在亞薩瓦群島跳島旅行，那裡是許多年輕的單身旅行者會去的地方。

Many young Australians travel to Greece to surf, have parties and island-hop, so it's easy to make friends during your trip there.
許多年輕的澳洲人會去希臘衝浪、開派對和跳島旅行，所以在那裡旅行時交朋友很容易。

RELATED WORDS | 相關單字延伸

egotistical
adj. 自我中心的，自我主義的

narcissistic
adj. 自戀的

selfish
adj. 自私的

egocentric
adj. 自我中心的

arrogant
adj. 傲慢的

selfish
/ˈsɛlfɪʃ/

Some people believe it is selfish to consider only oneself, but what travelling solo really means is to ascertain what formulates one's individuality.
有些人認為只考慮自己是很自私的，但單獨旅行真正的意義是確認什麼東西構成了自己的個體性。

egotistical
/ˌɛɡəˈtɪstɪkəl/

An egotistical football player may be disliked by his teammates but still be popular with the fans.
自我中心的足球員可能不受隊友喜歡，但仍然受到球迷歡迎。

egocentric
/ˌɛɡəʊˈsɛntrɪk/

Improving children's self-esteem doesn't mean making them egocentric.
增進小孩的自尊心，意思並不是把他們變得自我中心。

narcissistic
/ˌnɑːsɪˈsɪstɪk/

Do you think it is narcissistic to praise oneself all the time?
你覺得總是稱讚自己的行為很自戀嗎？

arrogant
/ˈærəɡənt/

Please don't be an arrogant passenger while you're flying just because flight attendants can't be mad at you.
搭飛機時，請不要因為空服員不能對你生氣就當個傲慢的乘客。

USEFUL EXPRESSIONS | 相關實用片語

```
autonomous province          split decision
自治省                        （反映裁判不同意見的）
                             非一致性決定

              autonomous decision
                   自主決定

autonomous vehicle           rash decision
自動駕駛汽車                  草率的決定
```

autonomous decision
/ɔːˈtɒnəməs dɪˈsɪʒən/
The researchers claim that the computer can learn and make autonomous decisions just like human brains do.
研究者宣稱這台電腦能夠像人腦一樣學習並且做出自主的決定。

autonomous province
/ɔːˈtɒnəməs ˈprɒvɪns/
The Vatican City is the world's smallest country and an autonomous province within Italy.
梵蒂岡是世界上最小的國家，也是義大利的一個自治省。

autonomous vehicle
/ɔːˈtɒnəməs ˈviːɪkəl/
An autonomous vehicle should be able to park by itself.
自動駕駛汽車應該要能自己停車。

split decision
/splɪt dɪˈsɪʒən/
The proclaimed victor of the boxing match won the game by a split decision.
拳擊比賽宣布的勝利者，是在裁判決定不一致的情況下獲勝的。

rash decision
/ræʃ dɪˈsɪʒən/
One should avoid making rash decisions by slowing down and thinking carefully.
一個人應該要藉由慢下腳步、仔細思考，避免做出草率的決定。

TUE

IELTS **BASIC WORDS**

instant /ˈɪnstənt/ n. 片刻
ENG. a very short time
SYS. jiffy, wink

> Young adults nowadays can decide to travel abroad in just an **instant**.
> 現在的年輕人可以瞬間決定出國旅行。

同義語 例句 It feels like the trip was over in a **blink of an eye**.
感覺旅行似乎一眨眼就結束了。

同義語 例句 It is now possible to access websites around the world in a **split second**.
現在，用不到一秒的時間連上全世界的網站已經成為可能。

反義語 例句 The **long span of time** it takes to complete a journey discourages some people from travelling.
旅行要花的長時間會打消一些人旅行的念頭。

process /ˈprəʊsɛs/ v. 處理，加工
ENG. subject to a treatment, with the aim of readying for some purpose
SYS. treat, transform

> Before travelling abroad, one must have his travel documents **processed**.
> 在出國旅行之前，旅行文件要先獲得處理。

同義語 例句 Usually, parents will **take care of** the travel papers their children need.
父母通常會處理他們小孩需要的旅行文件。

同義語 例句 Young people must learn to **prepare** the documents they need for a trip overseas.
年輕人必須學習準備海外旅行所需的文件。

反義語 例句 If you **leave** your documents **unfinished**, you will not be able to travel abroad.
如果你把文件放著沒有填好，你就不能出國旅行。

WEEK 9 TOPIC **LEISURE**

▶基礎單字擴充

locate /loʊˈkeɪt/ v. 找出⋯的位置
ENG. determine the place of
SYS. discover, detect

> They first **located** entertainment spots in their travel maps.
> 他們先是在自己的旅行地圖中找出娛樂地點的位置。

同義語例句 It is amazing that young children today can **discover where** foreign cities **are** with their smartphones.
現在的小孩可以用智慧型手機發現國外城市在哪裡,真的很驚人。

同義語例句 With the popularisation of smartphones, most people can **find the location of** a city very easily.
隨著智慧型手機的普及,大部分的人可以非常容易找到一個城市的位置。

反義語例句 When travelling to foreign countries, some people may **lose track of** where they exactly are while enjoying themselves.
出國旅遊的時候,有些人可能會在玩樂時搞不清楚自己到底在什麼地方。

current /ˈkʌrənt/ adj. 現在的,目前的;流行的
ENG. belonging to the present time
SYS. ongoing, happening

> Watching news keeps people informed of **current** international issues.
> 看電視新聞讓人們得知國際時事。

同義語例句 The news they are watching is **up-to-the-minute**.
他們正在看的新聞是消息最新的。

同義語例句 Overseas travelling has been **in fashion** for the past few years.
過去幾年來,很流行海外旅行。

反義語例句 The travel guide books are already **out of date**.
這些旅行指南書已經過時了。

485

TOPIC: Travelling abroad is a valuable experience for young people

海外旅行對年輕人而言是寶貴的經驗

One **ambition** most people have for their **retirement** is travelling around the world. For young people, however, instead of waiting to take a long journey after working for twenty-five years, they should take advantage of their energy and limited **familial** responsibilities to go **backpacking** in their youthful days. Such experience brings them into contact with **inspirational** people, landscapes and cultures. All the stimulation they get in a journey will awaken their inner power and encourage them to make a positive difference to our world. Travel experience will also influence the career paths young people will choose, sometimes prompting them to dedicate themselves to **philanthropic endeavours**. Those who have more travel experience are also more **employable**, as employers are usually impressed by the independence and **erudition** they **exhibit**.

TRANS

大部分人在退休後的野心之一就是環遊世界。不過，對於年輕人而言，與其等到工作二十五年以後再去長途旅行，他們應該趁年輕的時候利用自己的精力和還不多的家庭責任進行背包旅行。這種經驗會讓他們接觸到激發靈感的人、景色和文化。所有在旅程中獲得的刺激，將會喚醒他們的內在力量，並且鼓勵他們對我們的世界做出正面的改變。旅遊經驗也會影響年輕人選擇的職業道路，有時候會促使他們投身慈善事業。旅遊經驗比較多的人，也比較適合雇用，因為雇主通常會對他們展現出來的獨立和學識印象深刻。

ambition
/æmˈbɪʃən/

n. 野心

He is full of **ambition** to become a lawyer.
他充滿野心要成為律師。

retirement
/rɪˈtaɪəmənt/

n. 退休

Some opt for early **retirement** so that they can go travelling when they are still active enough.
有些人選擇提早退休，讓他們可以在自己活動力還夠的時候去旅行。

familial
/fəˈmɪljəl/

adj. 家庭的，家族的

Studies have looked into the **familial** factors in the disease.
研究調查了這種疾病的家族因素。

backpacking
/ˈbækpækɪŋ/

n. 背背包旅行

Would you like to go **backpacking** around Europe with me?
你想跟我一起背包環遊歐洲嗎？

inspirational
/ˌɪnspɪˈreɪʃənəl/

adj. 激發靈感的，鼓舞人心的

Most people think that Gandhi is an **inspirational** man.
大多數人都認為甘地是一個鼓舞人心的人。

philanthropic
/ˌfɪlənˈθrɒpɪk/

adj. 博愛的，慈善的

The organisation regularly holds **philanthropic** activities such as volunteering and fundraising.
那個組織定期舉辦志願服務與募款之類的慈善活動。

endeavour
/ɪnˈdɛvə/

n. 努力

His **endeavour** to improve students' communicative ability has paid off.
他改善學生溝通能力的努力有了成果。

employable
/ɪmˈplɔɪəbəl/

adj. 適合雇用的

I had concealed my past in order to become **employable**.
我隱藏了自己的過去，讓自己能夠被雇用。

erudition
/ˌɛrʊˈdɪʃən/

n. 博學，學識

The young scholar shows great **erudition** in modern medicine.
這位年輕的學者在現代醫學方面顯示出他的博學。

exhibit
/ɪɡˈzɪbɪt/

v. 表現出來

The rider **exhibited** great stress after falling off his horse.
騎士從馬上摔下來之後顯現出很大的壓力。

WORD TRAINING | 重點單字造句練習

journey
/ˈdʒɜːni/

n. 旅程

💬 A journey abroad can change a young person's views on the world.
一趟國外的旅程可能會改變年輕人對世界的看法。

Young backpackers usually expect to meet new friends in hostels during their journey.
年輕的背包客通常希望旅程中在青年旅舍遇見新朋友。

✏️ The students are planning to travel across the country and make the journey the most memorable experience in their college years.
那些學生正在計畫橫跨這個國家旅行，並且讓這趟旅程成為他們大學時期最難忘的經驗。

On a working holiday, young people can get international working experience in their journey and see more opportunities and possibilities for their future.
在打工度假時，年輕人可以在旅行中獲得國際工作經驗，並且看見更多未來的機會和可能性。

challenge
/ˈtʃælɪndʒ/

n. 挑戰，艱鉅的事

💬 Young students who rise to the challenge will gain valuable experience.
勇於迎接挑戰的年輕學生，會得到寶貴的經驗。

Though travelling around Europe by oneself may seem too big of a challenge, it will surely provide invaluable experience. 雖然一個人環遊歐洲似乎是個太大的挑戰，但絕對能帶來非常寶貴的經驗。

✏️ We understand the immense learning opportunities a different culture can provide to young people, so we encourage our son to take the challenge of studying abroad. 我們了解不同的文化能為年輕人帶來的無限學習機會，所以我們鼓勵我們的兒子接受在國外留學的挑戰。

Travelling abroad not only allows young people to escape the pressure in their daily life, but also develops their ability of overcoming challenges in unfamiliar surroundings. 在國外旅行不止能讓年輕人逃離日常生活的壓力，也能培養他們在不熟悉的環境克服挑戰的能力。

destined
/ˈdɛstɪnd/

adj. 註定的；預定往…的

💬 Backpackers are destined to have valuable experiences in their journey.
背包客在旅途中一定會有寶貴的經驗。

The flight destined for Istanbul has been turned back.
預定前往伊斯坦堡的班機被調頭返回了。

✍ Regardless of family background or financial status, every person should be given the opportunity to be educated and become what they are destined to be.
不論家庭背景或財務狀況如何，每個人都應該得到被教育的機會，並且成為他們註定要成為的人。

It may seem that many children in Third World countries are destined to suffer, but their difficult situation is in fact the result of unbalanced global economy.
許多第三世界的兒童似乎註定要受苦，但他們困難的處境其實是不平衡的全球經濟造成的結果。

round-trip
/ˈraʊndtrɪp/

adj. 往返的，來回的

💬 Round-trip flight tickets are sometimes cheaper than one-way tickets.
來回機票有時候比單程機票便宜。

Round-trip airfares are not applicable to those who will stay abroad for several months.
來回機票價格不適用於要在國外待上幾個月的人。

✍ Rather than booking a round-trip ticket, one of my friends usually just flies out and see where his journey takes him.
我有個朋友通常不訂來回機票，而是說飛就飛，看看他的旅程會帶他往哪裡去。

Despite higher airfares, I prefer booking separate one-way tickets rather than a single round-trip ticket, which has some restrictions on date and route changes.
雖然票價比較高，但我偏好分別訂購單程機票，勝過來回機票，因為來回機票對於日期和路線的變更有一些限制。

RELATED WORDS | 相關單字延伸

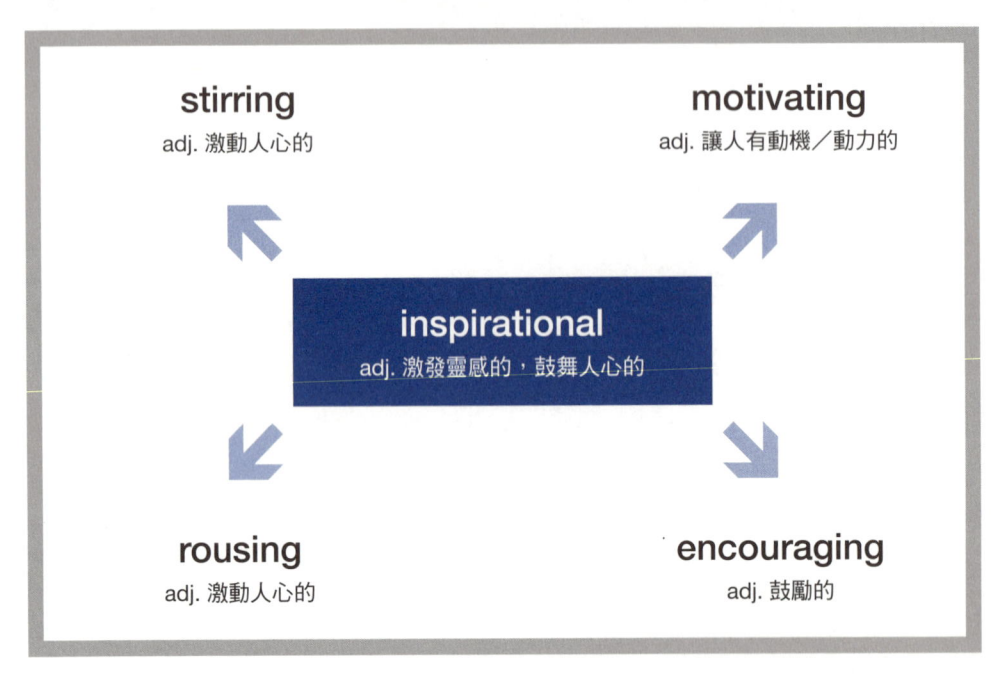

stirring
adj. 激動人心的

motivating
adj. 讓人有動機／動力的

inspirational
adj. 激發靈感的，鼓舞人心的

rousing
adj. 激動人心的

encouraging
adj. 鼓勵的

---

inspirational
/ˌɪnspɪˈreɪʃənəl/

Travelling brings a person into contact with inspirational people, landscapes and cultures.
旅行能夠讓一個人接觸到激發靈感的人、景色和文化。

stirring
/ˈstɜːrɪŋ/

I found the landscape of the place I travelled to quite stirring.
我覺得自己去旅行的地方，景色很激動人心。

rousing
/ˈraʊzɪŋ/

The spectacular ocean view of Mauritius is rousing for many travellers.
模里西斯壯觀的海景讓許多旅行者感到興奮。

motivating
/ˈməʊtɪveɪtɪŋ/

I heard many motivating stories from various strangers I came across during my travel in Europe.
在我的歐洲旅行中，我從我遇到的各種陌生人口中聽到許多激勵人心的故事。

encouraging
/ɛŋˈkʌrɪdʒɪŋ/

Michael travelled to Russia in search of his missing daughter after receiving encouraging news that she could be there.
Michael 聽到令人鼓舞的消息，說他失蹤的女兒可能在俄羅斯，他就旅行到那裡找她。

USEFUL EXPRESSIONS | 相關實用片語

positive outlook
正面的前景

time difference
時差

positive difference
正面的差異（改變）

positive attribute
正面特質

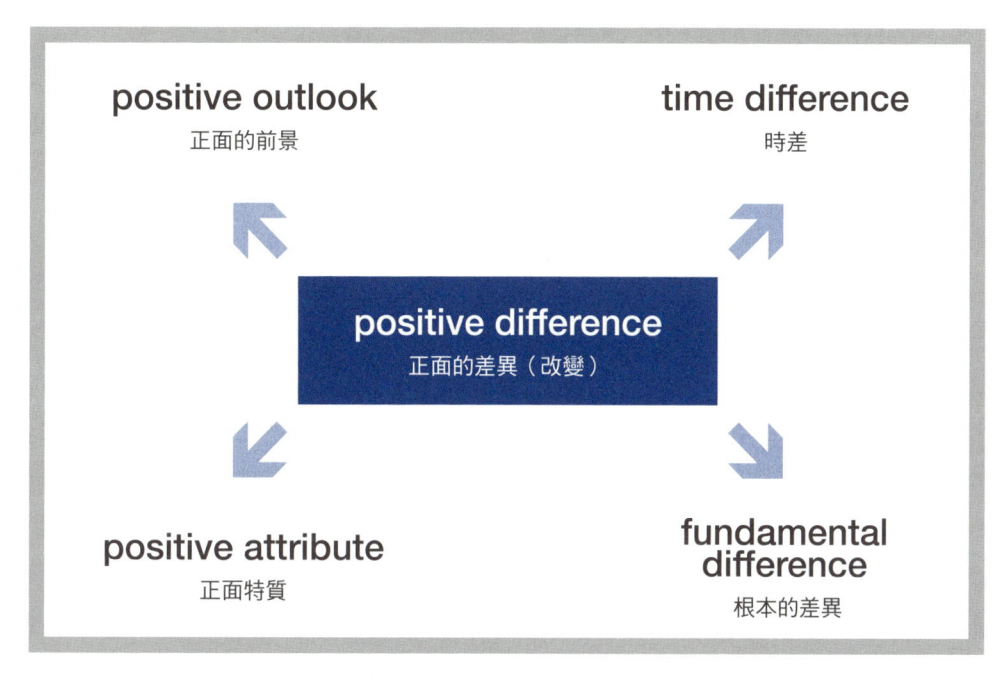

fundamental difference
根本的差異

positive difference
/ˈpɒzɪtɪv ˈdɪfərəns/

Going to college can make positive differences for young people who are committed to becoming professionals. 對於致力於成為專業人士的年輕人而言，上大學會產生很正面的影響。

positive outlook
/ˈpɒzɪtɪv ˈaʊtlʊk/

After the Federal Bank made their comments, the stock markets closed high because of a positive outlook for the economy. 聯邦銀行做出他們的評論後，股市因為正面的經濟前景而收高。

positive attribute
/ˈpɒzɪtɪv ˈatrɪbjuːt/

Inclination for sports will be regarded as a positive attribute by the college admission staff. 愛好運動會被負責辦理大學入學工作的人認為是正面的特質。

time difference
/tʌɪm ˈdɪfərəns/

Travellers experience jet lag due to time differences between countries they travel to and from. 旅行者會因為到達和出發的國家之間的時差而有時差感。

fundamental difference
/fʌndəˈmɛntəl ˈdɪfərəns/

The fundamental difference between his and her points of view is their thoughts on gender stereotypes. 他和她的觀點之間根本的差異，在於他們對於性別刻板印象的想法。

WED

IELTS **BASIC WORDS**

sufficient /səˈfɪʃənt/ adj. 充足的
ENG. enough to meet a need or purpose
SYS. adequate, enough

> Athletes of the national team find it **sufficient** to practise on their own.
> 國家隊的運動員發現自己練習就足夠了。

- 同義語例句 There are **more than enough** candidates to choose from to fill the national team.
  有相當充足的人選可以選擇，以補足國家隊的名額。

- 同義語例句 The government provides **ample supply** of resources in recruiting the sports representatives of our country.
  政府提供豐富的資源來徵召國家的運動代表。

- 反義語例句 Some nations are **short of** funds to send their athletes to the Olympics.
  有些國家缺乏派運動員參加奧運會的資金。

reason /ˈriːzən/ n. 理由，原因
ENG. cause for an action or event
SYS. root, source

> The main **reasons** of the team's victory are teamwork and each player's dedication.
> 這個隊伍勝利的主要原因是團隊合作和每個隊員的奉獻精神。

- 同義語例句 The team's repeated victory **is rooted in** their excellence in communication and admirable dedication during plays.
  這個隊伍的一再勝利，根植於它們優秀的溝通，以及比賽時令人敬佩的投入。

- 同義語例句 The training team is a **producer of** excellent **results** because of its members' team spirit and dedication.
  這個訓練團隊是優秀成果的製造者，因為它的成員有團隊精神和奉獻的精神。

- 反義語例句 The **end result** of their reluctance to practise was revealed in tonight's loss.
  他們不願意練習的最後結果，在今晚的敗戰中顯現出來。

WEEK 9 TOPIC **LEISURE**

▶基礎單字擴充

record /rɪˈkɔːd/ v. 記錄
ENG. set down in permanent form
SYS. enter, note

> At first, the runner **recorded** his finish time by himself until he found an assistant to do the task.
> 一開始,那位跑者自己記錄他跑完的時間,直到他找到助理來做這件事為止。

同義語 例句 The coaches **put down** the finish times of their runners for reference.
教練寫下他們跑者跑完的時間作為參考。

同義語 例句 The coaches **write down** the major errors made by their players for correction.
教練寫下他們的球員犯下的重大失誤以便糾正。

反義語 例句 In his frustration, the sore loser **wiped off** the results board of the competition.
在挫敗感之中,那個輸不起的人把比賽結果的板子擦掉了。

constant /ˈkɒnstənt/ adj. 持續的,不變的
ENG. unvarying in nature
SYS. changeless, invariant

> For an athlete to succeed, **constant** training and practice are necessary to enable him to adapt to changes.
> 運動員要能成功,持續的訓練和練習是必要的,好讓他能夠適應變化。

同義語 例句 Athletes who are **persistent** in their training find it easy to cope with unexpected situations.
堅持訓練的運動員會覺得很容易應付意外的狀況。

同義語 例句 Athletes who have **unwavering** enthusiasm are the ones who will succeed.
有堅定不移的熱情的運動員,就是會成功的運動員。

反義語 例句 Situations are **likely to change** during a game, so athletes must always be ready to adapt.
在比賽中,情況很有可能會改變,所以運動員必須隨時準備適應。

WED

09-3A

TOPIC: The benefits of team sports for children
團隊運動對兒童的好處

Both team and individual sports are beneficial for children in many ways, such as improving physical health, enhancing academic performance, reducing risk of diseases and increasing the ability to **overcome adversity**, but there is an added **dimension** that comes from playing with a team. Children will learn how to take directions from a **superior** in a team, and the combativeness that emerges when a team competes against another is absent when playing as an **individual**. Some parents see sports as a waste of time, but in **actuality**, team sports are a **microcosm** of our lives. They represent an accurate picture of how we live and get ahead with the cooperation of others, teaching children that it takes not only individual **competitiveness** but also teamwork to succeed. By participating in team sports, children will learn the **essence** of teamwork and know that no one is **trivial** in a group.

TRANS

團隊和個人運動都在許多方面對兒童有益，像是改善身體健康、提高學業表現、減少疾病風險與增加克服逆境的能力，但和團隊一起進行運動有一個額外的層面。兒童會在隊伍中學到如何接受上級的指示，而一支隊伍和另一隊對抗時浮現的鬥志，是進行個人運動時缺少的。有些家長認為運動是浪費時間，但事實上，團隊運動是我們生活的縮影。團隊運動表現出我們生活以及靠著與他人合作獲得成功的真實圖景，教導兒童要成功不止要靠個人的競爭力，還要靠團隊合作。藉由參與團隊運動，孩子會學到團隊合作的精髓，並且知道在團體中沒有人是微不足道的。

overcome
/ˌəʊvəˈkʌm/

v. 克服

We must face challenges head on to be able to **overcome** them.
我們必須正面面對挑戰才能克服它們。

adversity
/ədˈvɜːsɪti/

n. 逆境

The wheelchair athlete overcame his **adversity** and became world-famous.
這位輪椅運動員克服了逆境，而且變得舉世聞名。

dimension
/dɪˈmɛnʃən/

n. 尺寸，方面

Dance adds a new **dimension** to your daily aerobic workout.
舞蹈會為你每天的有氧運動增加新的層面。

superior
/suːˈpɪərɪə/

n. 上司，長官

My **superior** is quite intimidating, but he manages the office fairly.
我的上司蠻令人害怕的，但他管理辦公室很公正。

individual
/ˌɪndɪˈvɪdʒuəl/

n. 個人

Every child has to learn how to become an **individual** in society.
每個小孩都必須學習如何成為社會中的個體。

actuality
/ˌaktʃʊˈalɪti/

n. 現實

We have to face the **actuality** that foreign workers have become indispensable for local manufacturers.
我們必須面對外籍勞工已經成為本地製造業者不可缺少的人力的現實。

microcosm
/ˈmʌɪkrəʊkɒzəm/

n. 縮影

The city's mosaic of multiculturalism has created a **microcosm** of the world.
這個城市多樣的多元文化混合創造了世界的縮影。

competitiveness
/kəmˈpɛtɪtɪvnəs/

n. 競爭力

Our success is due to the **competitiveness** of our products.
我們的成功是因為我們產品的競爭力。

essence
/ˈɛsəns/

n. 本質，精髓

The **essence** of democracy is people's participation.
民主的本質在於人民的參與。

trivial
/ˈtrɪvɪəl/

adj. 瑣碎的，不重要的，微不足道的

It's a waste of time to worry about **trivial** problems.
擔心不重要的問題是浪費時間。

WORD TRAINING | 重點單字造句練習

match
/mætʃ/

n. 對戰的比賽

💬 When a match goes on for hours and drains the players' strength, they need to rely on teamwork.
當比賽持續幾個小時並且消耗隊員的體力時,他們需要依靠團隊合作。

I prefer team sports to individual sports because I enjoy the thrill of winning a match through cooperation.
我喜歡團隊運動勝過個人運動,因為我喜歡藉由合作贏得比賽的刺激感。

✏️ In a sports team, every player must be receptive and explicit when communicating with teammates during a match to achieve better cooperation.
在運動隊伍中,每個隊員在比賽中和隊友溝通時都要有接受性而且明確,以達到更好的合作。

The greatest advantages of individual sports are that you can do it whenever you wish, and there is no competition as in a match.
個人運動最大的優點是你可以隨時去做,而且不會有像是在比賽裡一樣的競爭。

sense of accomplishment
/sɛns əv əˈkʌmplɪʃmənt/

n. 成就感

💬 There is much debate about whether one feels a greater sense of accomplishment when playing individual or team sports.　關於在進行個人運動還是團隊運動的時候會有比較大的成就感,有很多的辯論。

Some people claim that it is easier to get a sense of accomplishment when playing individual sports.
有些人宣稱在進行個人運動的時候比較容易有成就感。

✏️ One of the reasons that playing individual sports can lead to a sense of accomplishment is that it requires people to handle all kinds of situations by themselves.　進行個人運動可以帶來成就感的原因之一,在於人們需要獨自處理各種情況。

Individual sports can often bring a sense of accomplishment to beginners because they can usually see their own progress without being judged by others.
個人運動經常可以為新手帶來成就感,因為他們通常可以看到自己的進步,而不用接受別人的評斷。

nerves
/nɜːvz/

n. 緊張的感覺

💬 As the referee blew his whistle, the player's nerves started to kick in.
當裁判吹起哨子，那位選手開始覺得緊張。

No matter how good the player was, his nerves got the best of him.
不論那位選手有多優秀，他的緊張總是會打敗自己。

✏️ The team captain helped his teammates with their nerves by giving them a very inspiring pep talk before their game.
在比賽之前，隊長藉由非常振奮人心的精神喊話來平撫隊友的緊張情緒。

To help calm the nerves before a game, players of the team usually do a couple rounds of practice and warm-up.
為了幫助緩和緊張的情緒，那一隊的隊員通常會做幾回練習和暖身。

willpower
/ˈwɪlpaʊə/

n. 意志力

💬 Despite a height disadvantage, the player still won because of his willpower.
儘管身高居於劣勢，但因為意志力的關係，那名選手還是贏了。

The team's willpower to rise above the others has inspired all the spectators.
那個隊伍要贏過其他人的意志力激勵了全場觀眾。

✏️ In any sport activity, willpower is important for one to keep focused and disciplined.
在任何運動中，意志力對於讓一個人保持專注、有紀律是很重要的。

The underdog basketball team miraculously won in the recent NBA finals not because of luck but because of sheer willpower.
這支弱隊奇蹟似地在最近的 NBA 決賽中獲勝，不是因為運氣，而是因為純粹的意志力。

RELATED WORDS | 相關單字延伸

segregation
n. 隔離

severance
n. 切斷，分離，解雇

individual
n. 個人

solitude
n. 孤獨

partition
n. 分隔，隔板

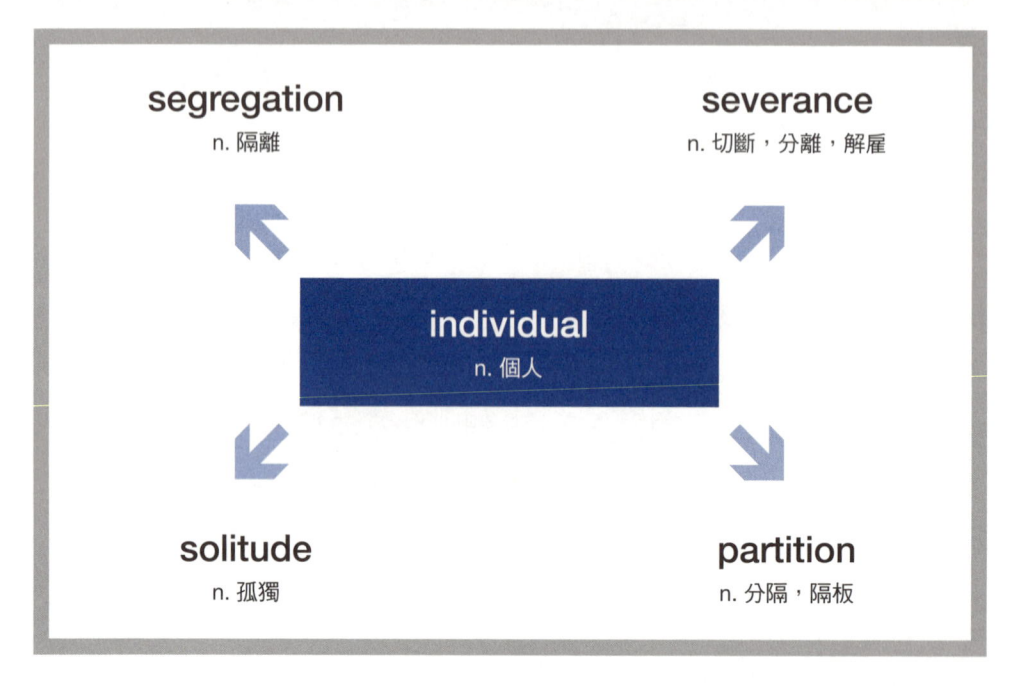

---

individual
/ˌɪndɪˈvɪdʒuəl/

The combativeness that emerges when a team competes against another is absent when playing as an individual.
一支隊伍和另一隊對抗時浮現的鬥志，是進行個人運動時缺少的。

segregation
/ˌsɛgrɪˈgeɪʃən/

The government found it unable to justify its racial segregation policy any more.
那個政府發現它再也無法證明自己的種族隔離政策正當。

solitude
/ˈsɒlɪtjuːd/

When married and with kids, solitude is a luxury you would wish for every once in a while.
當你結婚、有了孩子以後，孤獨就是你偶爾會渴望得到的奢侈。

severance
/ˈsɛvərəns/

When the company decides not to renew the employment contract, it has to offer severance pay according to the worker's working period.
當公司決定不更新雇用契約時，就必須依照員工的工作期間長短提供資遣費。

partition
/pɑːˈtɪʃən/

Light-coloured partitions can create a brighter workspace, in which employees will feel more relaxed.
淡色的隔板可以創造比較明亮的工作空間，員工在其中會感到比較輕鬆。

USEFUL EXPRESSIONS | 相關實用片語

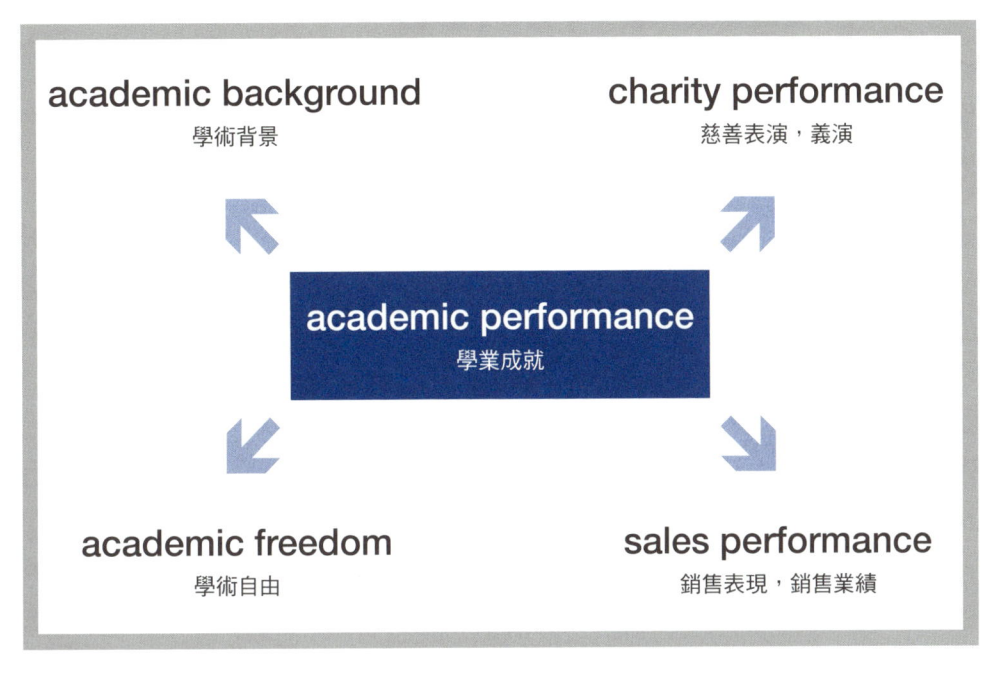

```
academic background          charity performance
     學術背景                    慈善表演，義演
         ↖                         ↗
            academic performance
                  學業成就
         ↙                         ↘
  academic freedom            sales performance
     學術自由                    銷售表現，銷售業績
```

academic performance
/akəˈdɛmɪk pəˈfɔːməns/

His test scores show improved academic performance in the area of science.
他的考試成績顯示出科學領域方面的學業進步。

academic background
/akəˈdɛmɪk ˈbakgraʊnd/

When employing an applicant for a job, a related academic background is the primary requirement.
在雇用應徵者擔任工作時，相關的學術背景是最基本的要求。

academic freedom
/akəˈdɛmɪk friːdəm/

All the researchers must be given the academic freedom to discuss whatever topic they want.
所有研究者都應該得到可以討論任何主題的學術自由。

charity performance
/ˈtʃarɪti pəˈfɔːməns/

He has given numerous charity performances to raise money for homeless people.
為了替遊民募款，他做過很多場慈善表演。

sales performance
/seɪlz pəˈfɔːməns/

They must achieve a twenty-five percent increase in sales performance over the year to meet the goal.
他們必須達成銷售業績年成長率 25% 才能達到目標。

THU

IELTS **BASIC WORDS**

vast /vɑːst/ adj. 巨大的，龐大的
ENG. unusually great in size
SYS. huge, immense

> In the new millennium, there is a **vast** selection of extreme sports.
> 在新的千禧年，極限運動有許多選擇。

同義語 例句 A **large** sum has been invested to promote the newest extreme sport, skyboarding.
有許多錢被投資用來推動最新的極限運動「噴射飛板」。

同義語 例句 There are surprisingly an **enormous** number of extreme sports fans in Asia.
令人驚訝地，亞洲有許多極限運動迷。

反義語 例句 The fan base of extreme sports was **small and negligible** in the beginning, compared to that of mainstream sports.
和主流運動相比，極限運動迷的族群一開始很小而且可以忽略。

explore /ɪkˈsplɔː/ v. 探索
ENG. to investigate systematically
SYS. investigate, consider

> It is exciting to **explore** extreme sports and choose one as a hobby while young.
> 在年輕時探索極限運動，並且選擇一項作為嗜好，是很刺激的。

同義語 例句 Before playing extreme sports, it is worthwhile to **look into** the risks.
在進行極限運動之前，研究風險是值得的。

同義語 例句 For your own safety, **do some research about** safety issues before pursuing an extreme sport.
為了你自己的安全，在從事一項極限運動之前要先研究一下安全問題。

反義語 例句 It would be dangerous to play extreme sports if you remain **ignorant about** its risks.
如果你一直對風險一無所知，那麼進行極限運動會是危險的。

WEEK 9 TOPIC **LEISURE**

▶基礎單字擴充

adapt /əˈdæpt/ v. 適應,使適應
ENG. to make suitable to or fit for
SYS. accommodate, modify

> Extreme sports participants must be able to **adapt** to sudden changes while playing.
> 極限運動玩家必須能夠適應進行途中突然的改變。

同義語例句 It takes some time for beginners to **make themselves comfortable** with the idea of playing extreme sports.
要讓新手對於進行極限運動的想法感到自在,需要一點時間。

同義語例句 The younger generation does a better job **adjusting** to something new like extreme sports.
年輕一代比較擅長適應極限運動之類的新玩意兒。

反義語例句 Many people are concerned about the danger of playing extreme sports, so they choose to **stay irrelevant** and go for milder activities. 很多人擔心進行極限運動的危險性,所以他們選擇不去參與,並且從事比較溫和的活動。

realise /ˈrɪəlaɪz/ v. 了解
ENG. be fully aware of
SYS. understand, recognise

> Not every player **realises** the danger of playing extreme sports.
> 不是每個玩家都了解進行極限運動的危險性。

同義語例句 Some people **are** not **aware** that it is impossible to handle every unexpected situation while playing extreme sports.
有些人不知道在進行極限運動時是不可能應付所有意外情況的。

同義語例句 He retired from extreme sports because he **understands** that it is not without risks to participate in.
他退出極限運動了,因為他了解進行極限運動不是沒有風險的。

反義語例句 If he continues to **be unaware of** the risks in playing extreme sports, injury may strike him soon.
如果他還是不意識到進行極限運動的風險,可能很快就會受傷。

501

THU

TOPIC | Extreme sports
極限運動

People who dare not play extreme sports tend to **imagine** possible accidents, such as the cord breaking while bungee jumping or the parachute not **deploying** when skydiving. For some others, however, it is worth the risk to seek adventure and **conquer** one's fears. Actually, almost all participants in extreme sport can walk away **unscathed** and have nothing but an unforgettable experience, but this fact by no means suggests that one can **embark** without careful preparation. **Thrill seekers** should conduct **precautionary** research ahead of time, analysing safety records, surveying the equipment, asking questions and seeking assurance. If they feel any **qualms** about the sport after the research, they should err on the side of caution and forego participating. That being said, if fear of injury or death is the reason some people **stay away from** extreme sports, they should realise that there are a multitude of daily activities that are statistically much more **perilous**.

TRANS

不敢玩極限運動的人，經常會想像可能發生的意外，例如高空彈跳的時候繩索斷掉，或者高空跳傘時降落傘沒有展開。但對於其他某些人來說，承受風險去追求冒險並征服恐懼是值得的。事實上，幾乎所有參與極限運動的人都可以毫髮無傷，只留下難忘的經驗，但這個事實絕不意味著可以不經過謹慎的準備就開始進行。尋求刺激的人應該事先進行預防性的研究，分析安全紀錄、檢視裝備、問問題並且要求保證。如果研究之後感到任何疑慮，就應該寧可謹慎（也不要冒險），並且放棄參與。話雖如此，如果害怕受傷或死亡是某些人遠離極限運動的理由的話，他們應該了解有許多日常活動在統計上危險得多。

imagine
/ɪˈmadʒɪn/

v. 想像

Bill **imagined** there was a rabbit in the hat.
Bill 想像帽子裡有一隻兔子。

deploy
/dɪˈplɔɪ/

v. 部署，（降落傘）展開

The general began **deploying** the troops after the bomb dropped.
上將在炸彈投下後開始部署部隊。

conquer
/ˈkɒŋkə/

v. 征服，克服

The researchers finally found the way to **conquer** the problem.
研究者最終找到了克服那個問題的方法。

unscathed
/ʌnˈskeɪðd/

adj. 沒有受傷的

Although she fell off the bike, she stood up **unscathed**.
雖然她從腳踏車上摔下來，但是她毫髮無傷地站了起來。

embark
/ɪmˈbɑːk/

v. 開始從事

They **embarked** on their trip in Alaska immediately after their arrival.
他們抵達之後馬上就開始了阿拉斯加之旅。

thrill seeker
/θrɪl ˈsiːkə/

n. 找尋刺激的人

My sister Candace is a **thrill seeker** who likes deep-sea diving.
我姊姊 Candace 是一個找尋刺激的人，喜歡深海潛水。

precautionary
/prɪˈkɔːʃənəri/

adj. 預防性的

Mom made me wear a helmet as a **precautionary** measure.
母親讓我戴上安全帽作為預防措施。

qualm
/kwɑːm/

n. 疑慮

If you have any **qualms**, please speak with our manager.
如果你有任何疑慮，請跟我們的經理談。

stay away from
/steɪ əˈweɪ frɒm/

v. 遠離

The parents told their child to **stay away from** strangers.
那對父母告訴他們的小孩要遠離陌生人。

perilous
/ˈpɛrɪləs/

adj. 危險的

She embarked on her **perilous** journey into the wilderness in search of the endangered animal.
她開始了在荒野中的危險旅程，要尋找那種瀕臨絕種的動物。

WORD TRAINING | 重點單字造句練習

spectator
/spɛkˈteɪtə/

n. 觀眾

Every year, thousands of spectators around the world are injured while watching their favourite sports.
全世界每年有數千名觀眾在觀看他們最愛的運動時受傷。

I admit that I would rather be a spectator than a participant in extreme sports, such as skydiving, bungee jumping and paragliding.
我承認我寧願當一個觀眾，而不是親身參加極限運動，例如高空跳傘、高空彈跳和滑翔傘。

Car racing is among the most dangerous sports on the planet, injuring many drivers and even spectators every year. 賽車是地球上最危險的運動之一，每年造成許多駕駛甚至觀眾受傷。

When an accident happens during a car race, flying car parts may hit some of the spectators and cause them serious injuries.
當賽車中發生事故，飛起來的車輛零件可能會打中某些觀眾，造成他們嚴重受傷。

tension
/ˈtɛnʃən/

n. 緊繃，緊張，緊張的局勢

Tension was building up as the top two motocross racers faced each other head-to-head.
當前兩名的越野摩托車手面對面時，緊張氣氛逐漸升高。

Some teens do parkour in order to ease the tension of modern life.
有些青少年為了緩解現代生活的緊繃而從事跑酷運動。

With an action camera, it is easy to capture the tension of a car race or the excitement of a motorcycle jump.
用運動攝影機，就能很容易捕捉賽車的緊張氣氛或者摩托車跳躍的刺激感。

A bungee-jumping operator must adjust the length and tension of the cord to ensure the safety of a participant.
高空彈跳的操作員必須調整繩索的長度和鬆緊度，以確保參加者的安全。

口說範例 寫作範例

athletic
/æθˈlɛtɪk/

adj. 運動的，運動員的

💬 Having an athletic body to match his daredevil attitude made him this year's best skydiver.
擁有足以匹配他天不怕地不怕態度的運動員體格，使他成為今年最佳的高空跳傘玩家。

His athletic physique helped him excel in the field of free diving.
他的運動員體格讓他在自由潛水領域脫穎而出。

✍ He was already physically and mentally athletic as a kid, which prepared him to be the champion snowboarder he is now.
他還是小孩的時候，體能與心態上就已經是運動員了，這也讓他能夠成為現在的滑雪板冠軍。

The famous skateboarder has kids who are as athletic as he is, and they are trained together with him on the ramps.
那位有名的滑雪板玩家有跟他一樣具有運動能力的小孩，而他們也在斜坡上跟他一起接受訓練。

craze
/kreɪz/

n. 狂熱

💬 There is such a craze for flyboarding because there are many celebrities participating in.
現在噴射飛板引起一陣狂熱，因為有很多名人從事這項運動。

Some people get into the sport just because of the craze.
有些人就只是因為狂熱的風潮而開始從事這項運動。

✍ The latest craze in extreme sports today is flyboarding, but it will probably not last long because of the unreasonable costs it entails.
現在極限運動的最新熱潮是噴射飛板，但因為所需的不合理費用的關係，這陣風潮可能不會持續很久。

Some extreme sports like skateboarding, jet-skiing and BMX biking surpassed the craze stage and remained popular over time.
有些極限運動，像是滑雪板、水上摩托車和特技單車已經超越了一時狂熱的階段，隨著時間過去還保持流行。

505

RELATED WORDS | 相關單字延伸

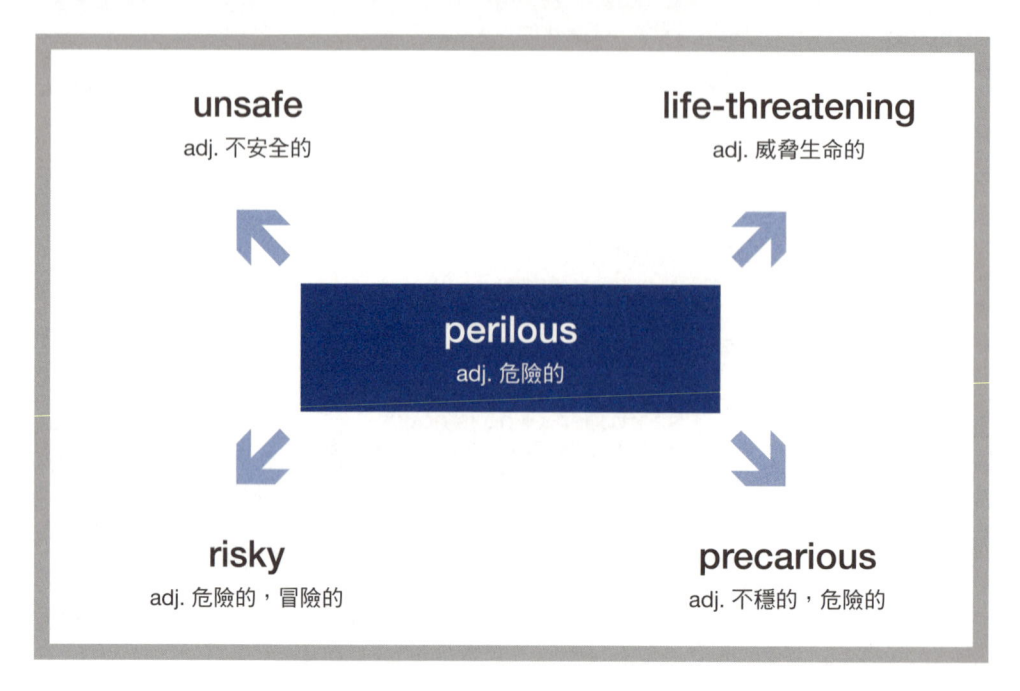

```
        unsafe                          life-threatening
        adj. 不安全的                    adj. 威脅生命的

                    ┌──────────────┐
                    │   perilous   │
                    │   adj. 危險的 │
                    └──────────────┘

        risky                           precarious
        adj. 危險的，冒險的              adj. 不穩的，危險的
```

perilous
/ˈpɛrɪləs/

If fear of injury or death is the reason some people stay away from extreme sports, they should realise that there are a multitude of daily activities that are statistically much more perilous.
如果害怕受傷或死亡是某些人遠離極限運動的理由的話，他們應該了解有許多日常活動在統計上更危險。

unsafe
/ʌnˈseɪf/

Playing extreme sports without necessary safety gear is downright unsafe.
不使用必要的安全裝備進行極限運動，是十分不安全的。

risky
/ˈrɪski/

Playing water sports in a stormy weather is very risky.
在暴風雨的天氣從事水上運動非常危險。

life-threatening
/ˈlʌɪfˌθrɛtənɪŋ/

Most people consider cancer as the most life-threatening disease.
大部分的人認為癌症是最威脅生命的疾病。

precarious
/prɪˈkɛːrɪəs/

The lay-off made his already precarious living conditions even worse.
裁員使他已經很不安穩的生活條件變得更糟了。

USEFUL EXPRESSIONS | 相關實用片語

```
        safety rating              criminal record
         安全評等                       犯罪紀錄
              ↖                   ↗
                  ┌─────────────────┐
                  │  safety record  │
                  │    安全紀錄      │
                  └─────────────────┘
              ↙                   ↘
        safety device            personnel record
         安全裝置                    人事紀錄
```

safety record
/ˈseɪfti ˈrɛkɔːd/

The airline has a perfect safety record in the past five years.
這家航空公司在過去五年有完美的安全紀錄。

safety rating
/ˈseɪfti ˈreɪtɪŋ/

An automobile with a higher safety rating has a better chance of selling well.
安全評等比較高的汽車，比較有機會賣得好。

safety device
/ˈseɪfti dɪˈvʌɪs/

The safety device in the water heater will prevent it from exploding.
熱水器中的安全裝置會防止它爆炸。

criminal record
/ˈkrɪmɪnəl ˈrɛkɔːd/

Before becoming employed, you are required to obtain an updated criminal record check.
在被錄用之前，你必須申請犯罪紀錄更新檢查。

personnel record
/pɜːsəˈnɛl ˈrɛkɔːd/

It is our policy to keep personnel record confidential all the time.
我們的政策是隨時保持人事紀錄的機密性。

FRI

IELTS **BASIC WORDS**

reveal /rɪˈviːl/ v. 揭露
ENG. to make known; make visible
SYS. uncover, unveil

> The newly renovated botanical garden will be **revealed** next week.
> 新近整修的植物園將會在下週揭露面貌。

同義語例句 The plan for future expansion will be **made public** in the public garden's inauguration next Saturday.
公共花園的未來擴展計畫將會在它下週六啟用時公開。

同義語例句 The city will **unveil** the details of the botanical garden in the press conference next week.
市政府將會在下週的記者會揭曉植物園的細節。

反義語例句 The government is trying to **cover up** the extent of the calamity.
政府試圖掩蓋災難的嚴重程度。

lack /læk/ n. 缺乏
ENG. deficiency or absence
SYS. deficiency, want

> The **lack** of funds makes it impossible for the city to carry out the project.
> 資金的缺乏使得市府無法實行計畫。

同義語例句 The city's **deficit** caused funds to be pulled out from the project.
市府的赤字造成那個計畫的資金被抽走。

同義語例句 The **inadequacy** of funds is delaying most of the city's projects.
資金的不足使得市府大部分的計畫被拖延。

反義語例句 The **abundant supply** of natural resources makes it easy for the city to develop industries.
充足的天然資源使得這個城市發展工業很容易。

WEEK 9 TOPIC **LEISURE**

▶ 基礎單字擴充

appropriate /əˈproʊprɪət/ adj. 合適的
ENG. suitable or proper in the circumstances
SYS. suitable, proper

> The mayor's decision to improve the public garden was **appropriate**.
> 市長改善公共花園的決定是適當的。

同義語 例句 The plan for the botanic garden feels **just right** for the city.
植物園的計畫對於城市而言感覺上很恰當。

同義語 例句 The mayor felt the statue was not **suitable** for the family-friendly environment of the public garden.
市長覺得那座雕像不適合公共花園對家庭友善的環境。

反義語 例句 Abandoning the plan to improve the public garden is **not right** for the society.
放棄改善公共花園的計畫，對於社會是不對的。

consider /kənˈsɪdə/ v. 考慮
ENG. to think carefully about
SYS. contemplate, ponder

> We must **consider** if we should plant the garden or build the playground first.
> 我們必須考慮應該先種花園還是先搭建遊戲場。

同義語 例句 The gardeners **talked over** their respective plans to beautify the surroundings.
園丁們討論了他們各自美化環境的計畫。

同義語 例句 We should **think twice** before deciding what to plant in a garden.
我們決定在花園裡種什麼之前應該再三考慮。

反義語 例句 The mayor **ignored** the plan for the botanic garden without considering the potential need for it.
市長不理會植物園的計畫，而沒有考慮對它的潛在需求。

FRI

09-5A

TOPIC | Gardening
園藝活動

Receiving a **bouquet** of flowers can indeed be a **pleasure**, but **sowing** the seeds yourself will bring greater joy. You can feel the life cycle of nature by **engaging** in gardening tasks: planting seeds, caring for the sprouts, **transplanting** young plants, harvesting and **composting** the remains. Besides flowers, you can also grow vegetables at home if you want to. Even with a small vegetable garden, you can enjoy a certain degree of **self-reliance**, and your children can safely eat the vegetables right in the garden without worrying about **pesticides**. With a little bit of initial hard work, a vegetable patch can produce so **prolifically** that many friends and neighbours can enjoy its **bounty**.

TRANS

收到花束的確是一件快樂的事,但自己種下種子會帶來更大的快樂。你可以藉由從事園藝工作,感受自然的生命循環:播種、照顧幼苗、移植年輕的植物、收穫,以及用植物的殘餘物堆肥。如果你想要的話,除了花朵以外,你也可以在家種植蔬菜。即使是小小的蔬菜園,都能讓你享受一定程度的自給自足,而你的孩子可以直接在菜園裡吃蔬菜,不用擔心殺蟲劑。只需要一點初期的努力,一塊菜園可以相當多產,而許多朋友和鄰居都可以享受它的收成。

bouquet
/bʊˈkeɪ/

n. 花束
I received a **bouquet** of flowers from my boyfriend.
我從男朋友那裡收到了一束花。

pleasure
/ˈplɛʒɚ/

n. 愉快，快樂的事
Some people think that getting a pedicure is a sheer **pleasure**.
有些人認為做腳趾美容是很愉快的事。

sow
/soʊ/

v. 播（種）
He **sowed** all of his flower seeds in rows.
他一排排種下花的種子。

engage
/ɪnˈgeɪdʒ/

v. 從事，使從事
The manager wants to ensure that the employees are happily **engaged** at work.
經理想要確定員工樂於從事工作。

transplant
/transˈplɑːnt/

v. 移植，移到別的地方栽種
Please be very careful when **transplanting** the aloe plant.
移植蘆薈時請特別小心。

compost
/ˈkɒmpɒst/

v. 用⋯做堆肥
I'm not sure if you should **compost** those prawn shells.
我不確定你是否應該用那些蝦殼做堆肥。

self-reliance
/ˈsɛlfrɪˈlʌɪəns/

n. 依靠自己，自立
Planting gardens helps develop a sense of **self-reliance**.
種植花園有助於培養自立感。

pesticide
/ˈpɛstɪsʌɪd/

n. 殺蟲劑
The plants got healthier after applying **pesticides**.
在施用殺蟲劑之後，這些植物變得比較健康。

prolifically
/prəˈlɪfɪkəli/

adv. 多產地
Bessie has been writing **prolifically** for the past ten years.
在過去十年，Bessie 在寫作方面相當多產。

bounty
/ˈbaʊnti/

n. 賞金，慷慨的贈與
The garden provides people a space to appreciate Mother Nature's **bounty**.
這座花園提供人們一個欣賞大自然的贈禮的地方。

WORD TRAINING | 重點單字造句練習

dig
/dɪg/

v. 挖掘

We dug a pond in our backyard.
我們在我們的後院挖了一個池塘。

My dog likes to dig holes in my backyard to hide his food inside.
我的狗喜歡在後院挖洞藏食物。

The construction workers were busy digging the foundation.
建設工人忙著挖掘地基部分。

The homeowner dug a huge hole in the middle of his garden to plant an apple tree as the landscape's focal point.
屋主在他的花園中間挖了一個大洞來種植蘋果樹，作為景觀的焦點。

chillax
/tʃɪˈlæks/

v. 靜下心並且放鬆（chill out and relax）

I like my little garden, especially because there's a hammock where I can chillax.
我喜歡我的小花園，尤其是因為有個可以讓我靜下心並且放鬆的吊床。

I love to chillax in the garden by casually planting seeds and pulling weeds.
我喜歡在花園裡隨意種植種子以及拔草，讓我靜下心並且放鬆。

I often chillax with my fellows at the suburban park and enjoy a casual potluck style picnic.
我經常和我的同伴們在那座郊區公園放鬆，並且享受休閒的一人一菜式野餐。

Gardening means patience and planning, and I find pruning and pottering enables me to simply chillax in the environment.
園藝意味著耐心與計畫，而我發現剪枝和從容做事讓我可以純然在環境中放鬆。

unload
/ʌnˈləʊd/

v. 卸下

💬 I helped one of my friends unload geraniums from a cart on Tuesday.
我星期二的時候幫我的朋友把天竺葵從推車上卸下來。

If you need to unload negative feelings in private, you can try pulling weeds in your garden.
如果你需要私底下宣洩負面的情感，你可以試試在花園裡拔雜草。

✏️ The truck model is equipped with a ramp, which makes it easy to unload.
這個卡車款式配備（卸貨用的）坡道，讓卸貨變得容易。

One of our neighbours was unloading the sod they got for free from a local landscaping company.
我的鄰居當時正在把從當地造景公司那邊免費得到的草皮（從車上）卸下來。

disperse
/dɪˈspɜːs/

v. 散播，傳播，驅散

💬 Plants' seeds can be dispersed by water or wind.
植物的種子可以藉由水或風散播。

Every year, I cut back the dry stalks, hold them upside down and shake well to disperse the seed.
我每年都會剪下乾掉的莖，上下顛倒並且揮動以散播種子。

✏️ Flowering plants disperse their embryos by releasing seed pods, which are then distributed by the wind or animals.
開花植物藉由釋放果莢來傳播它們的胚芽，而這些果莢之後會藉由風或動物散播。

One can scatter some parsley leaves throughout the garden to disperse caterpillars.
可以藉由在花園中到處撒歐芹葉來驅散毛毛蟲。

RELATED WORDS | 相關單字延伸

inheritance
n. 繼承，遺產

legacy
n. 遺產，留給後人的東西

heirloom
n. 傳家寶

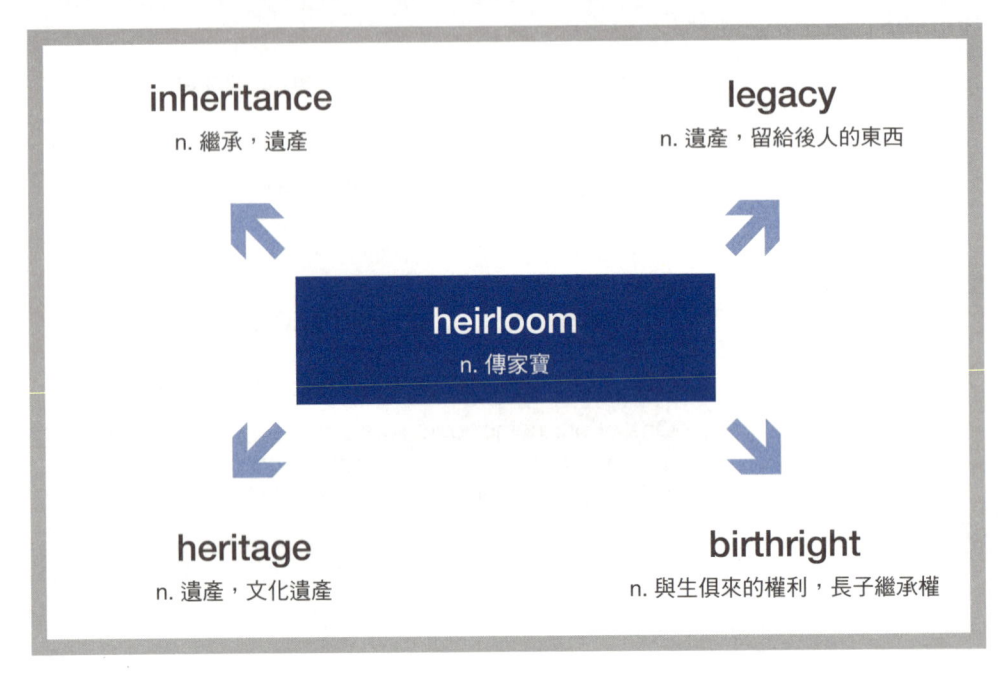

heritage
n. 遺產，文化遺產

birthright
n. 與生俱來的權利，長子繼承權

heirloom
/ˈɛluːm/

The antique vase is a family heirloom.
那個古董花瓶是個傳家寶。

inheritance
/ɪnˈhɛrɪtəns/

It was difficult for me to secure my inheritance, but it was easy for my brother.
我取得我的遺產很困難，但是對我弟弟來說卻很容易。

heritage
/ˈhɛrɪtɪdʒ/

Harvesting vegetables to celebrate Passover is part of the Jewish heritage.
用收獲的蔬菜來慶祝逾越節是猶太文化遺產的一部份。

legacy
/ˈlɛgəsi/

In a Christian society, churches sometimes receive legacies from a former worshipper.
在基督教社會，教堂有時候會收到過世教徒的遺產。

birthright
/ˈbəːθrʌɪt/

He forwent his birthright as the eldest son because he did not want to inherit his family business.
他放棄了自己的長子繼承權，因為他不想繼承家族事業。

USEFUL EXPRESSIONS | 相關實用片語

vegetable oil 蔬菜油

oil patch 油田

vegetable patch 菜圃

vegetable kingdom 植物界

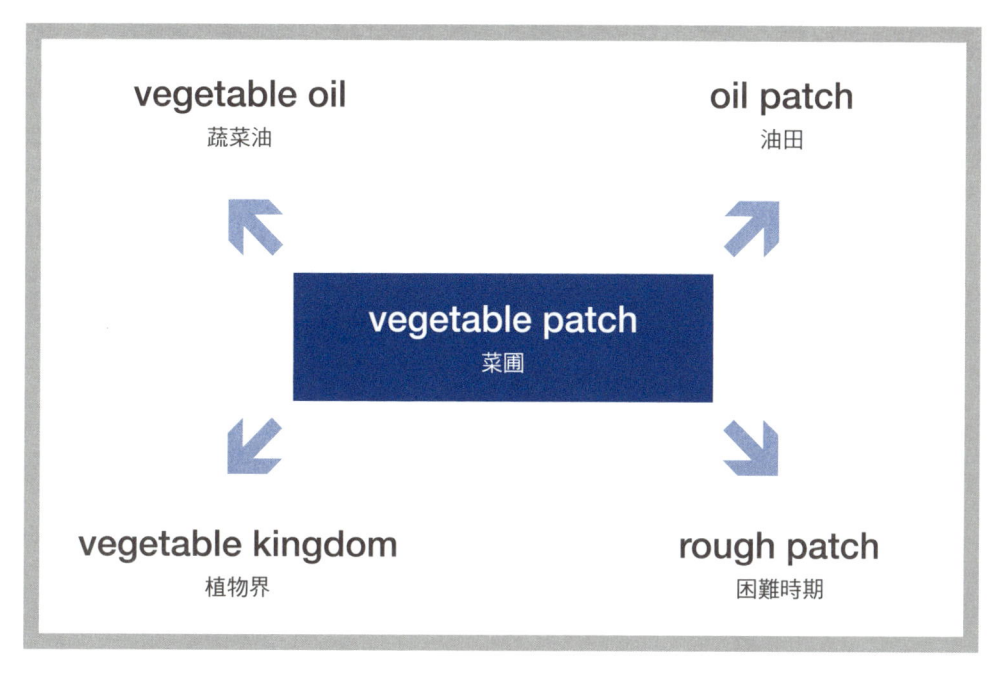

rough patch 困難時期

vegetable patch
/ˈvɛdʒtəbəl pætʃ/

He routinely attends to his vegetable patch next to the flower garden.
他定期照顧花園旁邊的菜圃。

vegetable oil
/ˈvɛdʒtəbəl ɔɪl/

According to most dietitians, vegetable oils are healthier than animal fats.
根據大部分營養學家的說法,植物油比動物油脂來得健康。

vegetable kingdom
/ˈvɛdʒtəbəl ˈkɪŋdəm/

The nature is usually divided into three kingdoms: mineral, animal and vegetable kingdom.
自然通常被分為三個界:礦物界、動物界和植物界。

oil patch
/ɔɪl pætʃ/

An oil patch was discovered during the underwater research.
有一塊油田在進行那個水底研究的時候被發現了。

rough patch
/rʌf pætʃ/

Our friendship has gone through a rough patch lately, but we made it up after all.
我們的友誼最近經歷了一段困難時期,但我們終究和好了。

515

SAT

IELTS **BASIC WORDS**

project /ˈprɒdʒɛkt/ n. 計畫，專案
ENG. any piece of work that is undertaken or attempted
SYS. plan, idea

> He started his first furniture design project when he was young.
> 他在年輕的時候開始了自己的第一個家具設計計畫。

同義語 例句 The initial plan was to make a lounge chair.
一開始的計畫是做一張休閒椅。

同義語 例句 His idea was to make something relaxing out of the broken chair.
他的想法是用壞掉的椅子做出令人放鬆的東西。

反義語 例句 The lack of planning made him forget about what kind of chair he wanted to create at first.
缺乏計畫使得他忘了自己一開始想創造的是哪種椅子。

money /ˈmʌni/ n. 錢
ENG. a current medium of exchange in the form of coins and banknotes
SYS. cash, funds

> The money she kept secret from her husband was for her costly spa treatments.
> 她瞞著她老公留下來的錢，是供她昂貴的 SPA 療程用的。

同義語 例句 Since she has a lot of cash, she will spend it on trips and spa treatments.
因為她有很多現金，所以她會花在旅遊和 SPA 療程上。

同義語 例句 She has so much wealth that she can relax and enjoy hours of luxury in the spa every day.
她的財產很多，所以她可以每天在那家 SPA 放鬆並且享受奢侈的時光。

反義語 例句 Having zero savings discourages her from taking vacations abroad.
沒有存款使得她打消了海外度假的念頭。

WEEK 9 TOPIC **LEISURE**

▶基礎單字擴充

advantage /əd'vɑːntɪdʒ/ n. 優勢，優點
ENG. beneficial factor
SYS. edge, superiority

> It is an **advantage** to know how to minimise stress at work and maintain a relaxed mood.
> 知道如何將工作的壓力減到最少，並且維持放鬆的心情，是有利的。

同義語例句 Knowing how to calm oneself down in times of stress can also be a **competitive edge** over others.
知道如何在壓力大的時期讓自己冷靜下來，也可以是超越別人的競爭優勢。

同義語例句 Knowing how to de-stress after a day of hard work is a **useful quality** for modern people.
知道如何在一天的努力工作之後解除壓力，對於現代人而言是有用的特質。

反義語例句 Panicking in crucial times is a **disadvantage** and must be avoided.
在關鍵時刻驚慌是個缺點，而必須避免。

chief /meɪn/ adj. 主要的
ENG. most important
SYS. main, principal

> A **chief** relaxation technique that most people know is deep breathing.
> 一個大部分的人都知道的主要放鬆技巧是深呼吸。

同義語例句 Among all the relaxation methods, meditation is **of** especially **great significance**.
在所有的放鬆方法之中，靜心（冥想）特別重要。

同義語例句 Deep breathing is generally considered **the most crucial** relaxation technique during sports training.
深呼吸通常被認為是運動訓練時最重要的放鬆技巧。

反義語例句 **It isn't worth trying** to relax with so-called 'shopping therapy'.
用所謂的「購物療法」放鬆並不值得嘗試。

SAT

TOPIC: Relaxation
放鬆

In today's culture of consumption, we enjoy **unprecedented affluence** and virtually unlimited choices, yet many of us still feel **anxious** and **overloaded**. Indeed, we can obtain some satisfaction from material things, but it is more important that we listen to our bodies and combat the excessive stress we feel. **Meditation**, for example, is a **holistic** technique that can help us relax and focus thoughts on one thing for a **sustained** period. It clears the mind and **diverts** it from the problems that are causing stress. It also gives the body some time to rest and **recuperate**. For better results, meditation can also be performed along with other positive **coping** methods, such as exercising, getting enough sleep and reaching out to supportive family and friends.

TRANS

在今日消費的文化中，我們享受前所未有的富足和幾乎無限的選擇，但很多人還是覺得焦慮而且負荷過重。的確，我們可以從物質中獲得一些滿足，但更重要的是傾聽我們的身體，並且對抗我們感受到的過度壓力。舉例來說，靜心（冥想）是一種整體性（醫療）的技巧，可以幫助我們放鬆，並且長時間將思想集中在一件事情上。它能清理心靈，並且將心思帶離造成壓力的問題。它也能給身體一些時間休息並且恢復。要得到更好的效果，靜心也可以和其他處理（壓力等等）的方法一起進行，例如運動、睡眠充足，還有尋求家人和朋友的支持。

unprecedented
/ʌnˈprɛsɪdɛntɪd/

adj. 前所未有的
The mobile game enjoyed **unprecedented** success soon after its release.
這款手機遊戲推出後，很快就獲得前所未有的成功。

affluence
/ˈafluəns/

n. 富裕
The owner of the plantations was reduced from **affluence** to poverty.
農園的主人從富裕落入了貧窮。

anxious
/ˈaŋkʃəs/

adj. 焦慮的
She was so **anxious** before take-off that she vomited.
她在起飛前太焦慮，結果吐了。

overloaded
/əʊvəˈləʊdɪd/

adj. 負荷過重的
You should not stay up late if you already feel **overloaded** at work.
如果你已經覺得在工作方面負荷過重，就不應該熬夜到很晚。

meditation
/mɛdɪˈteɪʃən/

n. 冥想，靜心（讓心靈平靜的方法）
Please do not speak while you are in the **meditation** room.
在靜心室請不要說話。

holistic
/həʊˈlɪstɪk/

adj. 全面的，整體（醫療）的
I will attend the UK's leading school of **holistic** nutrition.
我將會進入英國頂尖的整體營養學校就讀。

sustained
/səˈsteɪnd/

adj. 持久的，持續的
Despite the medical treatments he received, there was a **sustained** decline in his health.
雖然接受了治療，他的健康狀態還是持續變差。

divert
/daɪˈvɜːt/

v. 使改道，轉移
I find it hard to **divert** my attention from those unwanted thoughts.
我發覺很難把注意力從那些不想要的想法轉移開。

recuperate
/rɪˈkuːpəreɪt/

v. 恢復
The doctor says it will take six weeks for my knee to **recuperate**.
醫生說我的膝蓋需要六個星期才能恢復。

cope
/kəʊp/

v. 應付，處理，承受
Arctic plants are adapted to **cope** with extremely cold weather.
北極植物能適應非常冷的天氣。

WORD TRAINING ｜ 重點單字造句練習

strain
/streɪn/

n. 拉緊，緊張，壓力；扭傷

💬 A warm bath can relax me completely and free me from the strain of everyday life.
泡熱水澡可以讓我完全放鬆，並且將我從日常生活的壓力中解放出來。

The doctor prescribed some muscle relaxants to treat my calf strain.
醫生開了一些肌肉鬆弛劑來治療我的小腿拉傷。

✍ Herbal teas are not only relaxing and soothing to the spirit, but they also help ease physical strain.
花草茶不僅能夠放鬆並舒緩精神，還能幫助緩和身體的緊張。

Stresses and strains of everyday life can sometimes get the better of us, making us grouchy, short-tempered and restless, so it is best that we find a way to relax.
日常生活的壓力和緊張，有時候會擊垮我們，讓我們變得愛抱怨、易怒而且焦躁，所以我們最好找到放鬆的方法。

---

voyage
/ˈvɔɪɪdʒ/

n. 航海，旅程

💬 The river cruise took us on a relaxing voyage across the majestic water on a steamboat.
那個遊河之旅帶領我們在蒸氣船上渡過宏偉的水道，進行一段放鬆的旅程。

The movie will take you on a virtual voyage to New Zealand and make you feel the tranquil and relaxing atmosphere there.
那部電影會帶領你進行前往紐西蘭的虛擬旅程，並且讓你感受到那裡寧靜而放鬆的氣氛。

✍ Yoga and meditation music offer a soothing and relaxing voyage to one's inner self.
瑜伽與靜心音樂提供舒緩而放鬆的個人內在旅程。

On the voyage to the Greek isles, you will have the opportunity to explore their rich culture and natural beauty, which have inspired poetry and legends.
在前往希臘群島的航海旅行中，你將有機會探索它們激發了詩歌和傳說的豐富文化與自然之美。

口說範例 💬　　寫作範例 ✍

relaxation
/riːlakˈseɪʃən/

n. 放鬆

💬 I have a particular place for relaxation in my home.
我家裡有個特別用來放鬆的地方。

My sister goes to the park by the lake when she needs some relaxation.
需要放鬆一下的時候，我姊姊就會去湖邊的公園。

✍ When I need some true relaxation, I would get a deep tissue massage at the spa I often go to.
當我需要真正的放鬆時，我會在我常去的 SPA 做深層組織按摩。

One proven relaxation method is meditation, during which one would sit quietly in place for a period of time and tune out the outside world.
一個證明有效的放鬆方法是靜心，在其中一個人會靜靜地坐著一段時間，並且忽略外在的世界。

energise
/ˈɛnədʒʌɪz/

v. 給予活力，使活力充沛

💬 A massage at the spa can energise and rejuvenate a tired body.
在 SPA 的按摩可以讓疲勞的身體有活力而且恢復青春。

When you feel overwhelmed by excessive work, try taking a walk in a park to energise yourself.
當你感覺被過多的工作壓垮的時候，試著在公園散步，讓你感覺有活力。

✍ I could not think of a better relaxation method that will surely energise a person than a full ten-hour sleep.
和睡足十個小時相比，我想不到更好的放鬆方式可以確實讓人活力充沛。

One way to energise the body is to engage in leisure activities such as spending an entire day at the beach.
一個讓身體活力充沛的方法，是進行休閒活動，例如在海邊待一整天。

521

RELATED WORDS | 相關單字延伸

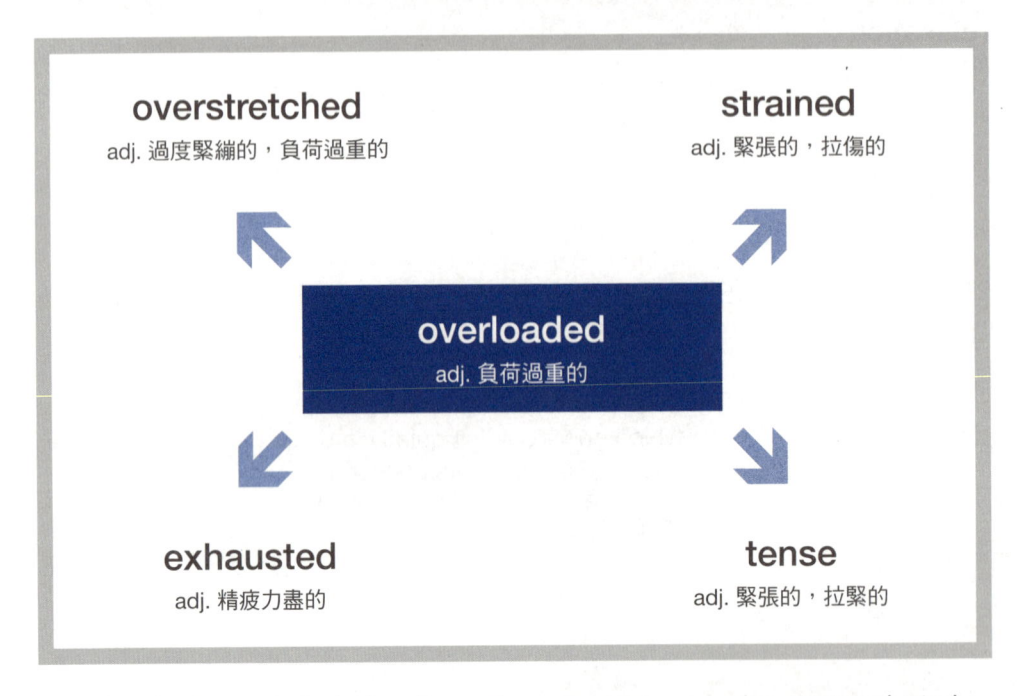

overstretched
adj. 過度緊繃的，負荷過重的

strained
adj. 緊張的，拉傷的

overloaded
adj. 負荷過重的

exhausted
adj. 精疲力盡的

tense
adj. 緊張的，拉緊的

overloaded
/ˌovɚˈlodɪd/

In today's culture of consumption, we enjoy unprecedented affluence and virtually unlimited choices, yet many of us still feel anxious and overloaded.
在今日消費的文化中，我們享受前所未有的富足和幾乎無限的選擇，但很多人還是覺得焦慮而且負荷過重。

overstretched
/ˌovɚˈstrɛtʃt/

When we are overstretched at work, it is important to take some time to relax.
當我們在工作中負荷過重時，花一點時間放鬆是很重要的。

exhausted
/ɪɡˈzɔːstɪd/

When I feel exhausted at work, I usually take a vacation abroad to relax.
當我在工作中感到精疲力盡，我通常會到國外度假放鬆。

strained
/streɪnd/

The best way to heal strained hamstrings is keeping the leg raised up and relaxed.
治療拉傷的腿後腱，最好的方法就是保持腿部抬高並且放鬆。

tense
/tɛns/

Make some time to relax and don't overexert yourself if you feel tense.
如果你覺得緊張的話，留出一些時間放鬆，而且不要讓自己太勞累。

USEFUL EXPRESSIONS | 相關實用片語

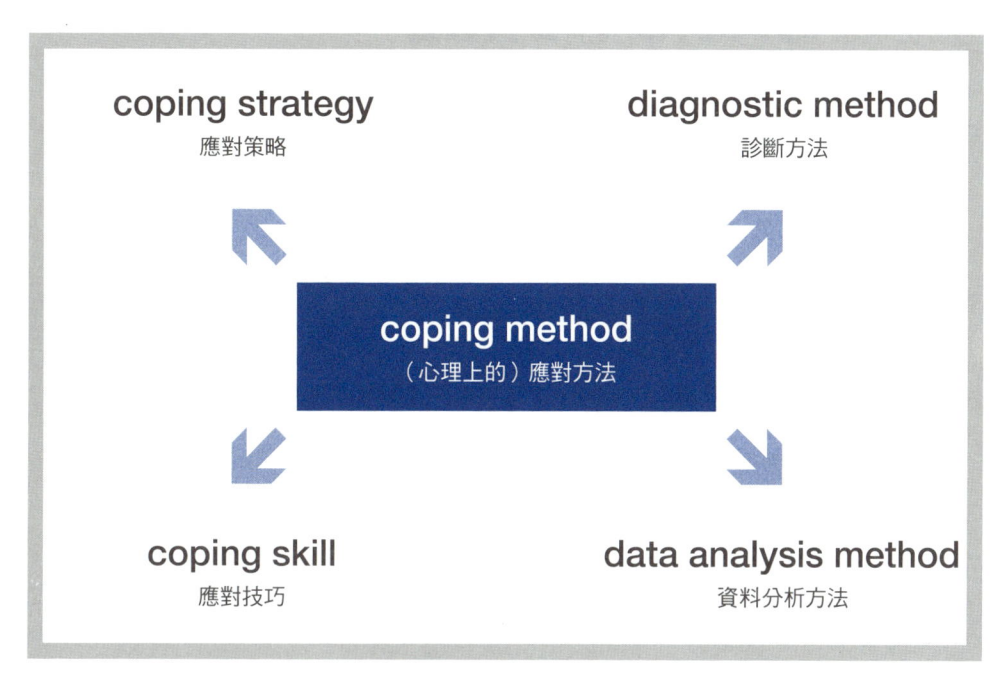

```
     coping strategy              diagnostic method
         應對策略                       診斷方法

                    ↖     ↗
                  coping method
                 （心理上的）應對方法
                    ↙     ↘

       coping skill              data analysis method
         應對技巧                     資料分析方法
```

coping method
/ˈkoʊpɪŋ ˈmɛθəd/

Some coping methods only work when you have a clear mind.
有些應對方法只有在你頭腦清楚的時候有用。

coping strategy
/ˈkoʊpɪŋ ˈstrætɪdʒi/

There are two types of coping strategies: dealing with the situation and taking care of the emotion.
有兩種心理上的應對策略：處理情況，還有照顧情緒。

coping skill
/ˈkoʊpɪŋ skɪl/

Some of his coping skills include drinking and singing out loud.
他應對困難情況的方法包括喝酒和大聲唱歌。

diagnostic method
/ˌdʌɪəɡˈnɒstɪk ˈmɛθəd/

The doctor tried to determine the cause of the disease through various diagnostic methods.
那位醫生試著用各種不同的診斷方式來判斷疾病的原因。

data analysis method
/ˈdeɪtə əˈnalɪsɪs ˈmɛθəd/

Data mining is a popular data analysis method for businesses today.
對今日的業者而言，資料探勘是一種流行的資料分析方法。

523

SUN

IELTS BASIC WORDS

ability /əˈbɪlɪti/   n. 能力
ENG. the quality of being able to perform
SYS. power, potential

> **Ability** is nothing if an employee is unwilling to work.
> 如果不願意工作的話，員工的能力就什麼也不是。

同義語 例句 Her **capability** of analysing complicated situations and offering the best possible solution makes her highly competitive.
她能夠分析複雜情況並且提供最佳解決方案的能力，使得她非常有競爭力。

同義語 例句 Her analytical **skills** are most evident when she is faced with difficult situations.
她的分析技能在面對困難情況的時候最顯著。

反義語 例句 His lack of **competence** is actually the result of reluctance to learn new things.
他的缺乏能力其實是不願意學習新事物的結果。

guide /gʌɪd/   v. 帶領，指導
ENG. to show or indicate the way
SYS. lead, conduct

> The supervisors are always around to **guide** the workers.
> 主管們總是會在場指導員工。

同義語 例句 Usually, the supervisors will **instruct** the workers how to assemble a new product.
通常主管會教員工如何組裝新產品。

同義語 例句 At least one supervisor should be present to **show** the workers **the way** to assemble the product.
至少應該有一位主管在場，向員工示範組裝產品的方法。

反義語 例句 The workers were **left unsupervised** during the manufacturing process.
在生產過程中，員工沒有人監督。

WEEK 9 TOPIC **LEISURE**

▶ 基礎單字擴充

protection /prəˈtɛkʃən/ n. 保護
ENG. the act of protecting or the state of being protected
SYS. shield, refuge

> Banks need extra protection during weekends.
> 銀行在週末的時候需要額外保護。

同義語例句 A defensive strategy that most banks utilise is to install a security camera system.
大部分銀行運用的防禦措施是安裝保全攝影系統。

同義語例句 The bulletproof windows act as a safeguard for bank tellers.
防彈窗的功能是保護銀行出納員。

反義語例句 A big magnet for danger is the absence of security guards in the bank.
一件很容易招惹危險的事情，是銀行裡沒有保全人員。

obtain /əbˈteɪn/ v. 得到，獲得
ENG. to succeed in gaining possession
SYS. acquire, get

> The boss could not obtain office reports because no supervisor was around.
> 老闆沒辦法得到辦公室報告，因為沒有主管在場。

同義語例句 The boss did not receive any office report because all the supervisors were absent.
老闆沒有收到任何辦公室報告，因為所有主管都不在。

同義語例句 The boss collects office reports from the supervisors as long as they are present.
只要主管在場，老闆就會跟他們收辦公室報告。

反義語例句 The supervisor handed over the report to the management after she came back from her vacation.
那位主管在度假回來以後，向經營團隊交出了報告。

SUN

TOPIC: The pros and cons of working at the weekend
在週末工作的優缺點

While most people enjoy their leisure time at the weekend, some do not see Friday as the end of the working week. Working at the weekend has several benefits, which is why some **entrepreneurs**, labourers and professionals choose to forego their weekly rest. First, **disruptions** like telephone calls or emails from clients seldom disturb weekend workers. In addition, working on Saturdays and Sundays allows more time to accomplish normally **postponed** tasks. **Undeniably**, however, there are **obstacles** to working at weekends, such as children and family members **incessantly disturbing** your work. People may also have **gatherings** at weekends that they will be unable to go to if they work. Therefore, for social reasons, some **freelancers** avoid working at weekends even though they are free to decide when to work or rest. No matter a person chooses to work at weekends or not, it is **paramount** to find some time to relax.

TRANS

雖然大部分的人在週末時享受他們的休閒時間，但有些人並不把星期五視為一週工作的結束。在週末工作有幾個好處，那也是為什麼有些企業家、勞工和專業人士選擇放棄他們每週的休息。首先，來自客戶的電話或電子郵件之類的擾亂，很少會打擾到週末工作的人。此外，在週六、週日工作也讓人有更多時間完成平常會被延後的工作。但不可否認，也有些讓人在週末難以工作的阻礙，像是不停打擾工作的小孩和家庭成員。人們在週末可能也有如果工作就不能去的聚會。所以，為了社交上的理由，有些自由工作者會避免在週末工作，即使他們可以自由決定什麼時候工作或休息。不管一個人選擇是否在週末工作，找些時間放鬆是最重要的。

entrepreneur
/ˌɒntrəprəˈnɜː/

n. 企業家
At the bank, the **entrepreneur** asked for a small business loan.
在銀行，那位企業家要求一筆小型企業貸款。

disruption
/dɪsˈrʌpʃn/

n. 中斷，擾亂
I must finish my report without any more **disruptions**.
我必須完成我的報告，不能再受到任何打擾。

postpone
/pəʊstˈpəʊn/

v. 延後，延期
The piano recital has been **postponed** until after the holidays.
鋼琴獨奏會已經被延期到放完假以後。

undeniably
/ˌʌndɪˈnaɪəbli/

adv. 不可否認地
Undeniably, offshore oil drilling can have a significant impact on marine ecosystems.
不可否認地，在海上鑽探石油可能會對海洋生態系統產生重大影響。

obstacle
/ˈɒbstəkəl/

n. 障礙
The main **obstacle** to operating during weekends is the lack of employees who are willing to work.
在週末營業的主要障礙是缺少願意工作的員工。

incessantly
/ɪnˈsɛsntli/

adv. 連續地，不斷地
It has been raining **incessantly** since yesterday morning.
從昨天早上開始，雨就一直不停地下。

disturb
/dɪˈstɜːb/

v. 打擾
The closed door means he doesn't want anyone to **disturb** him.
關上的門表示他不想要有任何人打擾他。

gathering
/ˈɡaðərɪŋ/

n. 聚集，聚會
He usually feels anxious before social **gatherings** because he has difficulty making small talk.
他在社交聚會之前經常覺得焦慮，因為他很難和人閒聊。

freelancer
/ˈfriːlɑːnsə/

n. 自由接案工作者
A **freelancer** can reject a potential client if he or she does not feel right.
自由接案工作者如果感覺不對的話，可以拒絕可能的客戶。

paramount
/ˈparəmaʊnt/

adj. 首要的，最重要的
Securing your oxygen mask is **paramount** when an emergency occurs on a plane.
飛機上發生緊急情況時，戴好氧氣面罩是最重要的。

WORD TRAINING | 重點單字造句練習

flexible
/ˈflɛksɪbəl/

adj. 有彈性的，可變通的，靈活的

💬 Working freelance means one can work a flexible schedule.
當自由工作者意味著工作時間有彈性。

I find flexible working makes it easier to keep work-life balance.
我發現彈性工時讓人比較容易保持工作與生活的平衡。

📝 It may seem that flexible working only benefits employees, but in fact it can also lower absenteeism and result in greater productivity.
彈性工時看似只對員工有益，但事實上它也可以減少缺席，並且創造更高的生產力。

Working as a freelancer may sound ideal for those who wish to have a flexible schedule, but it actually takes responsibility and self-discipline to become one.
當個自由工作者對於想要自由安排時間的人可能聽起來很理想，但事實上要有責任感和自律才能當自由工作者。

schedule
/ˈʃɛdjuːl/

n. 時間表，日程安排

💬 My work schedule does not allow me to take a long vacation.
我的工作日程不允許我休長假。

It is hard to stick to my work schedule when I am constantly interrupted by phone calls.
當我不斷被電話打斷的時候，就很難照我的工作日程做事。

📝 The head office explained that employees will play a more important role in planning the schedules for the production of the new product line.
總公司解釋，員工將會在新產品線的生產日程制定中扮演更重要的角色。

According the manager's schedule for Saturday, he will work in the morning, go for a run in the afternoon and meet a potential client in the evening.
根據經理週六的行程表，他上午會工作、下午會跑步、晚上會和潛在客戶見面。

528

peak
/piːk/

n. 高峰

💬 The job at the fast food restaurant was especially stressful at peak hours.
速食餐廳的那份工作，在尖峰時段壓力特別大。

My favourite tennis player is currently at the peak of his career.
我最愛的網球選手現在正值生涯高峰。

✏️ During last week, the heat wave caused a peak in energy consumption.
上星期，熱浪造成了能源（電力）使用的高峰。

During the peak season for the hotel industry, front desk clerks are asked to work during weekends and holidays.
在旅館業的旺季，櫃台人員被要求在週末和假日工作。

roam
/rəʊm/

v. 漫步，漫遊

💬 I like to go to shopping centres or roam the city during weekends.
我週末的時候喜歡去購物中心，或者在城市漫遊。

My mother doesn't allow my dog to roam freely in the house because he will pee everywhere.
我媽媽不允許我的狗在家裡隨便晃，因為他會到處尿尿。

✏️ Due to the sudden decline in the number of visitors, the theme park workers were roaming around without anything to do.
由於訪客人數突然下降，主題樂園的員工沒事做，到處閒晃。

Supervisors are required to roam around the plant to make sure workers are keeping up with the production schedule.
主管被要求在廠區到處走動，確認員工有跟上生產時程。

RELATED WORDS | 相關單字延伸

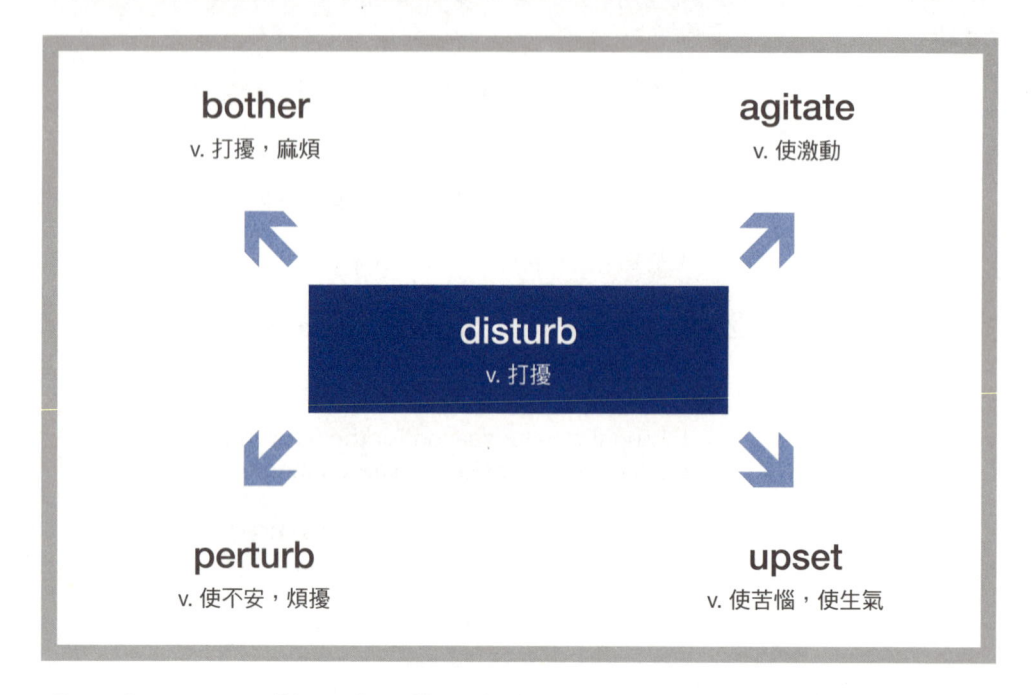

bother
v. 打擾，麻煩

agitate
v. 使激動

disturb
v. 打擾

perturb
v. 使不安，煩擾

upset
v. 使苦惱，使生氣

---

disturb
/dɪˈstɜːb/

Disruptions like telephone calls or emails from clients seldom disturb weekend workers.
來自客戶的電話或電子郵件之類的擾亂，很少會打擾到週末工作的人。

bother
/ˈbɒðə/

When I am working on weekdays, I am often bothered by phone calls from my clients.
當我在上班日工作的時候，我經常被客戶的電話打擾。

perturb
/pəˈtɜːb/

She is perturbed by her supervisor's behaviour, feeling that he is concealing something.
她對上司的行為感到不安，感覺他好像在隱瞞什麼。

agitate
/ˈadʒɪteɪt/

My wife gets agitated if I disrupt her in the middle of a telephone call.
如果我在我太太講電話的時候打斷她，她就會情緒激動。

upset
/ʌpˈsɛt/

It upset my client that no one gave her a phone call before we had the pamphlet printed.
客戶因為我們把摺頁送印之前沒打電話給她而不高興。

USEFUL EXPRESSIONS | 相關實用片語

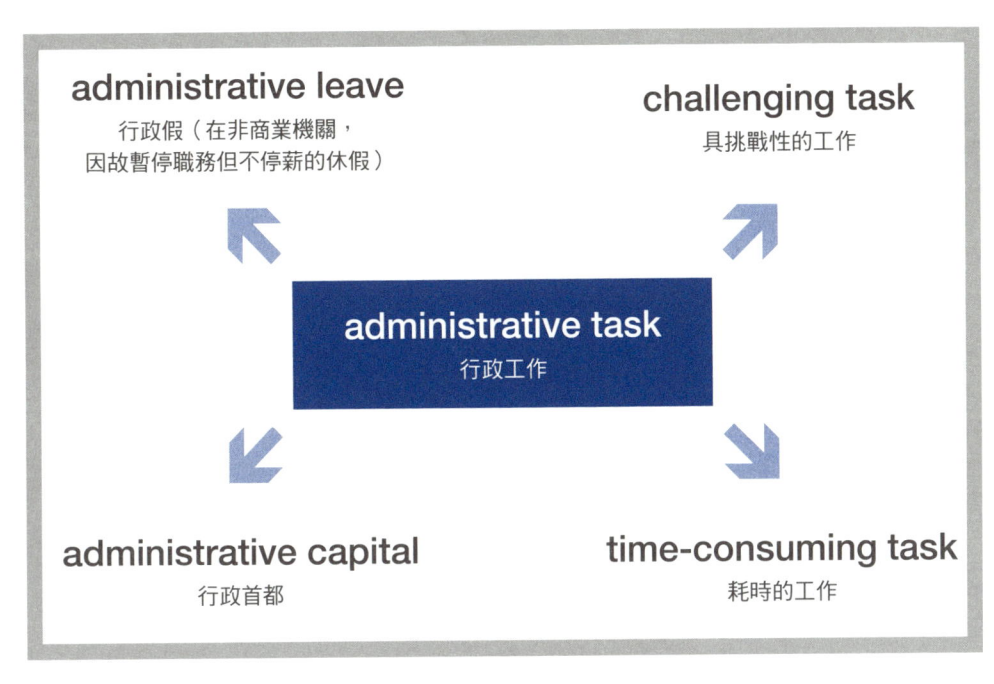

administrative leave
行政假（在非商業機關，因故暫停職務但不停薪的休假）

challenging task
具挑戰性的工作

administrative task
行政工作

administrative capital
行政首都

time-consuming task
耗時的工作

administrative task
/ədˈmɪnɪstrətɪv tɑːsk/

The administrative tasks include managing office equipment and arranging meetings.
行政的工作包括管理辦公設備和安排會議。

administrative leave
/ədˈmɪnɪstrətɪv liːv/

The professor being investigated is placed on administrative leave.
正在接受調查的教授被要求放行政假。

administrative capital
/ədˈmɪnɪstrətɪv ˈkapɪtəl/

The president relocated the administrative capital in order to boost the economic development in the northern region.
總統遷移了行政首都，以促進北部區域的經濟發展。

challenging task
/ˈtʃalɪndʒɪŋ tɑːsk/

Even for the most eloquent speakers, it is a challenging task to present controversial ideas.
即使是最有口才的演講者，要發表爭議性的想法也是很有挑戰性的事情。

time-consuming task
/tʌɪmkənˈsjuːmɪŋ tɑːsk/

Many time-consuming tasks can be finished in an instant with the help of computer programs.
藉由電腦程式的幫忙，很多耗時的工作可以瞬間完成。

WEEK 10
SOCIAL LIFE

從處罰犯罪到預防犯罪

用信用卡取代現金

幸福與財富

持續增加的老年人口比例

投資在年輕人身上的重要性

職場上的性別平等

大型零售業者與小型零售業者

MON

IELTS BASIC WORDS

draw interest /ˈdrɔː ˈɪntərɪst/ v. 引起興趣
ENG. arouse curiosity
SYS. engross, fascinate

> The new laws that will take effect next week seem to **draw** public **interest**.
> 下週將生效的法律似乎引起了大眾的興趣。

- 同義語 例句 The new bill **held the attention of** the conservative politicians.
  新的法案吸引了保守派政治人物的注意。
- 同義語 例句 The process involved in making the new laws **is intriguing to** most people.
  新法律制定牽涉的過程讓大部分的人感到好奇。
- 反義語 例句 The new policy is **neglected** by most citizens who will in fact be affected.
  新的政策被大部分實際上會被影響的民眾忽視了。

burn /bɜːn/ v. 燃燒，燒毀
ENG. be in flames
SYS. blaze, flame

> The new building regulations were passed after the shopping centre **burned** to ashes.
> 那座購物中心燒成灰燼之後，新的建築規定通過了。

- 同義語 例句 The shopping centre **went up in flames** because of its noncompliance with the building regulations.
  因為不遵守建築規定，那座購物中心被火燒毀了。
- 同義語 例句 The government became stricter with the building regulations since the shopping centre **was destroyed in a fire**.
  在那座購物中心被火災摧毀之後，政府對於建築規定變得比較嚴格。
- 反義語 例句 If the shopping centre had complied with the building regulations, **extinguishing the fire** would have been easier.
  要是以前那座購物中心遵守了建築規定，撲滅那場火災就會比較簡單了。

WEEK 10 TOPIC **SOCIAL LIFE**

▶基礎單字擴充

difficulty /ˈdɪfɪkəlti/ n. 困難
ENG. something not easily done
SYS. obstacle, hurdle

> There is **difficulty** enforcing the laws because many people are protesting them.
> 執行這些法律有困難,因為有很多人正在抗議。

同義語例句 It is **an effort beyond our capability** to make sure every citizen follows the laws 24/7.
確定每個人民都隨時守法,是超過我們能力的一件事。

同義語例句 After the laws were passed, protests and criticisms became **obstacles** to enforcing them.
那些法律通過之後,抗議和批評成為執行它們的障礙。

反義語例句 To everyone's surprise, the laws were passed with **no problem**.
出乎每個人的意料,這些法律毫無困難地通過了。

basis /ˈbeɪsɪs/ n. 基礎
ENG. the fundamental assumptions from which something is begun or developed
SYS. premise, groundwork

> It is ideal that the government determines its policies on the **basis** of human rights.
> 政府以人權為基礎制定政策是理想的。

同義語例句 Human rights should be the **foundation** of all the laws being passed.
人權應該要是所有通過的法律的基礎。

同義語例句 The **starting point** of human rights is that all humans should be treated equally.
人權的出發點是所有人都應該獲得平等的對待。

反義語例句 The legislators argued that maintaining morality is a **weak argument** for the passing of the anti-abortion law.
那些立法委員主張,為了維護道德而通過反墮胎法是不充分的論據。

MON

10-1A

TOPIC: From punishing crimes to preventing crimes
從處罰犯罪到預防犯罪

Public opinion on criminal justice has always been varied, though it has undergone a significant **transformation** in recent years. Support for long prison sentences as the primary tool in the fight against crimes is **waning**, as more and more people reject **punitive** approaches to maintaining **justice**. Instead, the public is now beginning to **endorse** an **even-handed**, **multifaceted** solution that focuses on prevention and **rehabilitation**. More than in the past, the public believes we should be addressing the underlying causes of crime rather than the symptoms of crime. Harsh prison sentences for both violent and non-violent **felons** used to be the norm in many countries. Today, most countries strongly favour rehabilitation and re-entry programmes over **incarceration** as the method of ensuring public safety.

TRANS

大眾對於刑事司法一向意見紛歧，但近年來，大眾的看法有了很大的轉變。支持以長期監禁作為對抗犯罪的主要工具的意見正在變少，因為越來越多人拒絕用懲罰的方法來維護正義。取而代之的是，大眾現在開始贊同著重預防犯罪與更生、既公平又多方面的解決方式。和過去相比，大眾現在更認為我們應該處理犯罪的根本原因，而不是犯罪呈現出來的徵象。對暴力和非暴力重刑犯的嚴酷入獄判決，過去一向是許多國家的常態。今日，大部份的國家強烈偏好讓受刑人更生與重返社會的計畫，而不是長期隔離罪犯，作為保障公眾安全的方法。

transformation
/ˌtrænsfəˈmeɪʃən/

v. 轉變

She was impressed with Brandon's speedy weight-loss **transformation**.
她對於 Brandon 快速的減重變身印象深刻。

wane
/weɪn/

v. 變小，減少

The number of honeybees in the world is **waning** quickly.
全世界蜜蜂的數量正在快速減少。

punitive
/ˈpjuːnɪtɪv/

adj. 懲罰的

I'm seeking **punitive** action against the thief who stole my car.
我正在尋求能夠懲罰偷我車子的竊賊的行動。

justice
/ˈdʒʌstɪs/

n. 正義

The courts aim to administer **justice** as defined by the laws.
法院的目的是依照法律的規定主持正義。

endorse
/ɪnˈdɔːs/

v. （為支票）背書，贊同，支持

Could you please **endorse** the cheque before cashing it?
能否請您在兌現之前先在支票後面背書？

even-handed
/ˈiːvənhandɪd/

adj. 公平的，不偏不倚的

The president gave an **even-handed** speech about the conflicting countries.
關於衝突中的國家，總統發表了一段公平的演說。

multifaceted
/mʌltɪˈfasɪtɪd/

adj. 多方面的

There is no quick solution to this complex, **multifaceted** problem.
這個複雜、涉及多個層面的問題沒有快速的解決方式。

rehabilitation
/riːəbɪlɪˈteɪʃən/

n. 復健，（吸毒者）戒毒，（罪犯）更生

The drug addict just started a three-month **rehabilitation** programme.
這名藥物上癮者才剛開始為期三個月的勒戒計畫。

felon
/ˈfɛlən/

n. 重刑犯

Six supervised **felons** were picking up garbage for community service.
六名受監督的重刑犯在撿垃圾作為社會服務。

incarceration
/ɪnˌkɑːsəˈreɪʃən/

n. 監禁

Incarceration through long-term imprisonment is actually a heavy burden for the government.
藉由長期監禁進行罪犯隔離，對於政府其實是很重的負擔。

WORD TRAINING | 重點單字造句練習

prosecution
/ˌprɒsɪˈkjuːʃən/

n. 起訴，檢方

We have a legal system to uphold the law and ensure the prosecution of those who break it.
我們有用來維護法律並且確保犯罪者被起訴的法律體系。

The prosecution grilled the witness to the point of tears, which I found completely unjust.
檢方盤問到目擊者哭了出來，我覺得完全不公正。

The reform of the prosecution function is aimed at eliminating unwarranted disparities and other injustices in our criminal justice system.
對於檢察機關的改革，目標在於消除我們刑事司法體系裡沒有根據的（量刑）差異與其他的不公正。

Prosecutors must cooperate with the police, the courts and the legal profession to ensure the fairness and effectiveness of their prosecution.
檢察官必須和警方、法庭以及法律從業人員合作，以確保起訴的公平性和有效性。

sentence
/ˈsɛntəns/

n. 判決

Those who are found guilty are given sentences to pay for their crimes.
被認為有罪的人，會被判決為犯罪付出代價。

A sentence was ordered by the judge based on the verdict of the jury.
法官根據陪審團的裁決而下了判決。

In every case involving an arrest for possession of narcotics, the prosecutor documents the race and criminal history of the defendant, including sentences given by the courts in the past.
在每個涉及逮捕持有毒品的案件裡，檢察官會記錄被告的種族與犯罪記錄，包括過去的判決結果。

In law, a sentence forms the final explicit act of a judge-ruled process, and also the symbolic principal act connected to his function.
在法律中，判決形成了法官裁決過程最終的明確行動，也是和他的功能相關聯的象徵性主要行動。

illegal
/ɪˈliːɡəl/

adj. 非法的

There are growing concerns that the new law will make the act of protesting illegal.
對於新法律將抗議行為非法化的憂慮逐漸升高。

The functions of the law system include dealing with offences such as drug trafficking and illegal immigration.
法律系統的功能包括處理販毒和非法移民之類的犯罪。

If the amnesty programme for illegal immigrants were to be put in practice, protests by conservative groups would be unavoidable. 如果要實施對於非法移民的特赦計畫，那麼保守團體的抗議是無法避免的。

Cannabis is the most commonly used psychoactive drug in the world and is sometimes prescribed to cancer patients, making its illegal status very controversial in some countries.
大麻是全世界最常被使用的精神藥品，而且有時候被開給癌症患者，使得它的非法地位在某些國家很有爭議性。

incarceration
/ɪnˌkɑːsəˈreɪʃən/

n. 監禁

The incarceration of criminals removes them from the general population and inhibits their ability to commit further crimes. 將罪犯監禁，是將他們從一般大眾中排除，並且約束他們進一步犯罪的能力。

According to his experience with incarceration, he said the only thing that prison teaches him is obedience.
根據他被監禁的經驗，他說監獄教他的就只有服從。

The constitutional amendment that outlawed slavery specifically and intentionally opened a loophole that allowed forced labour in the event of incarceration, which of course is unjust.
禁止奴役的憲法修正案，特別而且故意開了漏洞，允許（犯人）監禁情況下的強迫勞動，這當然是不公正的。

The function of legal enforcement also involves managing the punishment process for people who are convicted of crimes, including the process of incarceration. 執法單位的功能也涉及處理被判有罪的人的處罰過程，包括入獄的過程。

539

RELATED WORDS | 相關單字延伸

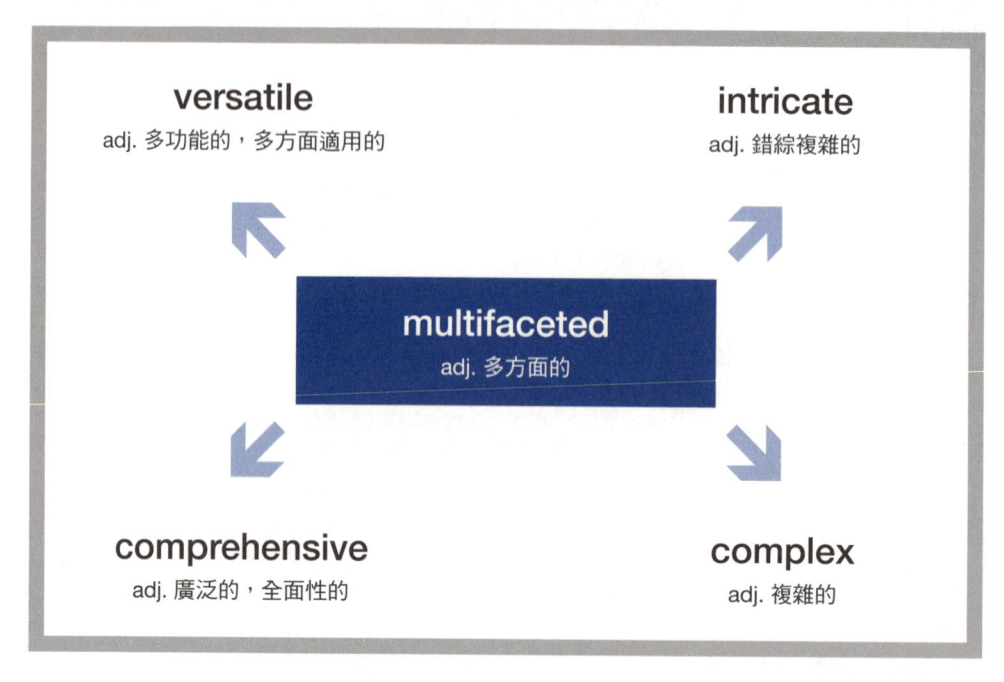

versatile
adj. 多功能的，多方面適用的

intricate
adj. 錯綜複雜的

multifaceted
adj. 多方面的

comprehensive
adj. 廣泛的，全面性的

complex
adj. 複雜的

multifaceted
/mʌltɪˈfæsɪtɪd/
The public is now beginning to endorse an even-handed, **multifaceted** solution that focuses on prevention and rehabilitation.
大眾現在開始贊同著重預防犯罪與更生、既公平又多方面的解決方式。

versatile
/ˈvɜːsətʌɪl/
We need to come up with a more **versatile** solution to deal with the various problems we face.
我們需要想出更有彈性的解決方法，來處理我們面對的多種問題。

comprehensive
/kɒmprɪˈhɛnsɪv/
We endorse a **comprehensive** programme that will focus on prevention and rehabilitation rather than punishment.
我們支持會將重點放在預防和更生，而不是處罰的全面性計畫。

intricate
/ˈɪntrɪkət/
The service they offer is quite **intricate** because it involves the rehabilitation of offenders, who are rejected by most employers.
他們提供的服務很複雜精細，因為它牽涉到犯罪者的更生，而這些人會被大部分的雇主拒絕。

complex
/ˈkɒmplɛks/
Law clauses are often much more **complex** than the public understands.
法律條文經常比大眾了解的還要複雜得多。

USEFUL EXPRESSIONS | 相關實用片語

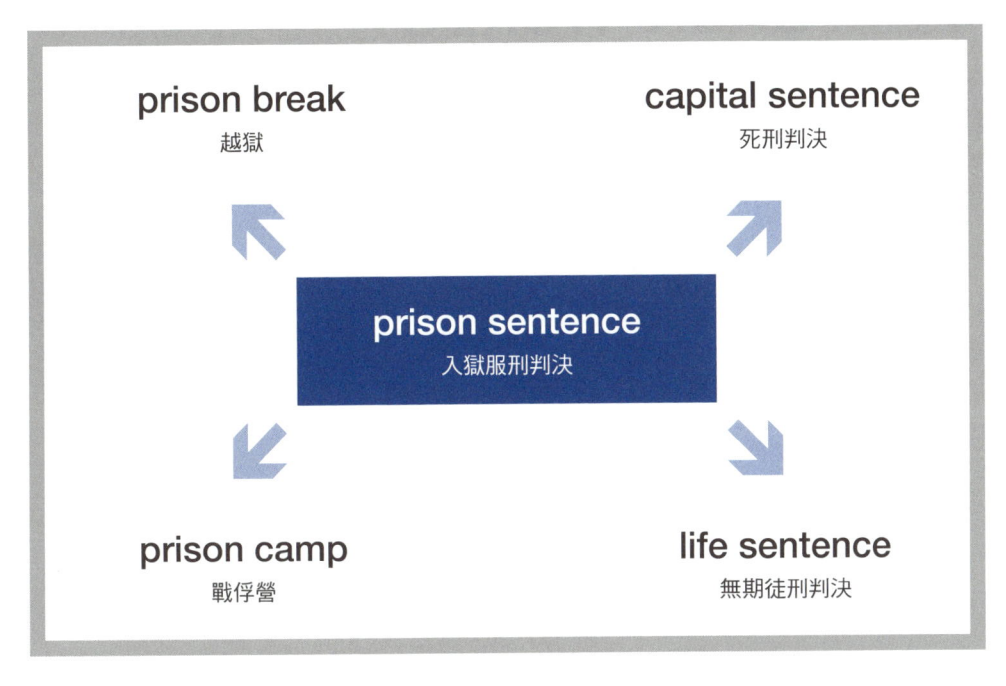

```
         prison break                    capital sentence
            越獄                              死刑判決
                        ↖          ↗
                         prison sentence
                           入獄服刑判決
                        ↙          ↘
         prison camp                     life sentence
            戰俘營                           無期徒刑判決
```

prison sentence
/ˈprɪzən ˈsɛntəns/
Entering a guilty plea on the first court date doesn't really help avoid a prison sentence.
在第一次出庭就作出認罪答辯，並不會真的有助於避免被判入獄。

prison break
/ˈprɪzən breɪk/
The prison break resulted in the escape of five prisoners, and only one of them was found.
這次逃獄造成五名囚犯逃走，而且只有一個人被找到。

prison camp
/ˈprɪzən kæmp/
The owner of the land where the prison camp was located reclaimed his plot after the war.
戰俘營所在地的地主，在戰爭後要回了他的土地。

capital sentence
/ˈkæpɪtəl ˈsɛntəns/
The Iraqi prosecutors pursued capital sentences against ousted President Saddam Hussein and his two co-conspirators.
伊拉克的檢察官要求判流亡的薩達姆·侯賽因總統和他的兩個密謀同夥死刑。

life sentence
/lʌɪf ˈsɛntəns/
The convict received a life sentence for murdering the government official.
那名罪犯因為謀殺政府官員而被判無期徒刑。

TUE

IELTS **BASIC WORDS**

particular /pəˈtɪkjʊlə/ adj. 特別的，特定的
ENG. unique or specific to a person, thing or category
SYS. special, exceptional

> There are **particular** stores that do not accept credit cards.
> 有些特定商店不接受信用卡。

同義語 例句 The 50% discount offered by the new store is **especially for** credit card payers.
這家新商店提供的 50% 折扣是信用卡付款者專屬的。

同義語 例句 Credit card holders of X Bank have benefits **distinct from others**.
X 銀行的信用卡持卡人擁有與眾不同的優惠。

反義語 例句 The exact date that credit cards will be accepted in the new store is still **indefinite**.
這家新商店接受信用卡的確切日期還不確定。

ordinary /ˈɔːdɪnərɪ/ adj. 平常的，普通的
ENG. commonly encountered
SYS. usual, regular

> Nowadays, it is quite **ordinary** to purchase even groceries with your credit card.
> 現在，甚至是用信用卡買食品雜貨都很稀鬆平常。

同義語 例句 In these years, it has become **commonplace** to pay for groceries by card.
這些年來，用信用卡付食品雜貨的錢變得司空見慣。

同義語 例句 Swiping your credit card for grocery shopping is **no big deal** these days.
近來，在購買食品雜貨的時候刷卡沒什麼大不了。

反義語 例句 It was **uncommon** to pay for groceries using a credit card thirty years ago.
三十年前，用信用卡付食品雜貨的錢並不常見。

WEEK 10 TOPIC **SOCIAL LIFE**

▶ 基礎單字擴充

maintain /meɪnˈteɪn/ v. 維持，維護
ENG. keep at the same level
SYS. keep, sustain

> We should **maintain** our credit score by paying our credit card bills on time.
> 我們必須準時付信用卡帳單，以維持信用分數。

同義語例句 We must **keep** our credit score **healthy** to continue enjoying the benefits of credit cards.
我們必須保持信用分數健康，以持續享受信用卡的好處。

同義語例句 It is wise to **care for** our credit scores for fast approval of future loans.
為了日後貸款快速獲准，照顧我們的信用分數是明智的。

反義語例句 Failing to pay your credit card bills will **damage** your credit score.
沒有準時繳信用卡帳單，會傷害你的信用分數。

merit /ˈmɛrɪt/ n. 價值，優點
ENG. the quality of being worthy; a good feature
SYS. value, benefit

> A **merit** of paying by credit card is that you don't have to carry a lot of cash with you.
> 用信用卡付款的一個優點，是你不必帶著很多現金。

同義語例句 An **advantage** of credit card shopping is being able to make a purchase without using cash.
信用卡購物的一個優點是沒有現金也能購買。

同義語例句 The **benefit** of using a credit card is especially obvious when you don't have cash.
使用信用卡的好處在你沒有現金的時候特別明顯。

反義語例句 A **disadvantage** of paying by credit card online is that the card could be charged without authorisation.
在網路上用信用卡付款的一個缺點是卡片可能未經授權被請款（盜刷）。

TUE

10-2A

TOPIC: Using a credit card instead of cash
用信用卡代替現金

One of the best ways you can manage your **finances** is to use credit cards. You can keep track of your expenses by keeping **receipts** and checking your monthly bills. If you pay off the balance each month, most credit cards don't charge you anything. Cash, on the other hand, is not an ideal way to pay for **necessities** because carrying large sums of money around is **risky**. Using a credit card will prevent loss or theft of cash, and even if your credit card number is stolen and **fraudulent** charges appear on your **statement**, you can call the credit card company to **dispute** the charges. What is more, most credit cards have some type of rewards programme, offering cash rewards, airline miles and other **perks** to frequent users. Therefore, those who are **financially conscientious** tend to use plastic money whenever they can.

TRANS

　　管理財務的最佳方式之一是使用信用卡。你可以藉由保留收據和查看每月帳單來掌握你的支出。如果你每個月都繳清餘額，大部分的信用卡不會向你收任何錢。另一方面，現金則不是付款購買必需品的理想方式，因為攜帶大筆金錢出門很危險。使用信用卡可以預防現金遺失或遭竊，而且就算信用卡號被盜用，帳單上出現了盜刷的請款，你可以打電話給信用卡公司向爭議款項提出異議。更好的是，大部分的信用卡公司有回饋方案，提供經常使用者現金回饋、飛行哩程和其他福利。所以，對自己的財務認真的人傾向於只要可以的話就使用塑膠貨幣。

finance
/ˈfaɪnæns/

n. 財務
Credit cards are helpful for monitoring my **finances** and spending.
信用卡對於監控我的財務狀況和支出很有幫助。

receipt
/rɪˈsiːt/

n. 收據
Remember to verify the card number and amount charged on the **receipt**.
記得要確認收據上的卡號和請款金額。

necessity
/nɪˈsɛsɪtɪ/

n. 必需品
Bruce packed the **necessities** for his camping trip.
Bruce 打包了他露營旅行要用的必需品。

risky
/ˈrɪski/

adj. 有風險的，危險的
It is very **risky** to invest in volatile stocks.
投資波動很大的股票是很有風險的。

fraudulent
/ˈfrɔːdjʊlənt/

adj. 詐欺的，假冒的
Mike was charged for his **fraudulent** business practices.
Mike 因為他詐欺的商業行為而被控告。

statement
/ˈsteɪtmənt/

n. 結算單，對帳單
You should check your credit card **statement** carefully to spot any unauthorised charge.
你應該仔細檢查你的信用卡對帳單，找出任何盜刷的款項。

dispute
/dɪˈspjuːt/

v. 爭論，對⋯表示質疑
You cannot **dispute** the fact that global warming is happening.
你無法質疑全球暖化正在發生的事實。

perks
/pɜːks/

n. 好處，福利
Most credit card holders will try to make the most of the **perks** offered.
大部分的信用卡持卡人會努力善用卡片所提供的福利。

financially
/faɪˈnænʃəli/

adv. 財務上
A **financially** smart way to commute is by bus.
一個財務上聰明的通勤方式是搭公車。

conscientious
/ˌkɒnʃɪˈɛnʃəs/

adj. 勤勉認真的，勤懇的
He is known as a very **conscientious** man at work.
大家都知道他在工作上是個很勤勉的人。

WORD TRAINING | 重點單字造句練習

fraud
/frɔːd/

n. 欺騙,詐騙

Many credit card scammers take fraud as a way to make easy money.
許多信用卡詐騙者把詐騙當成輕鬆賺錢的方法。

Banks now take measures to protect us from credit card fraud.
銀行現在會採取措施來保護我們免於信用卡盜刷。

Using cash could reduce your risk of credit card fraud because cashiers, waiters and attendants could steal your credit card information when you are paying.
使用現金可以減少信用卡盜刷的風險,因為收銀員、服務生和服務員有可能在你付款的時候偷走你的信用卡資訊。

There is a rise in online banking fraud these days, in particular the phishing sites that replicate bank websites perfectly and record your username and password when you enter them.
近來網路銀行的盜用行為變多,尤其是釣魚網站,它們完全模仿了銀行的網站,而且在你輸入用戶名稱和密碼時把這些資訊記錄下來。

investigate
/ɪnˈvɛstɪɡeɪt/

v. 調查

The issuer temporarily suspended my credit card when they were investigating the transaction.
信用卡發卡行在調查那筆交易的時候,暫時停止了我的信用卡。

The police were investigating a credit card cloning scam at a restaurant in my neighbour.
警方當時正在調查我家附近一間餐廳發生的信用卡複製盜用案件。

When you dispute a transaction, the credit card company will investigate it and recover funds on your behalf.
當你對爭議交易提出異議時,信用卡公司會代替你調查,並且追回款項。

Before your credit card is issued, you must agree with the rules which enable the issuer to investigate any transaction you dispute.
在信用卡發行之前,你必須同意讓發卡行可以調查爭議交易的規定。

unaffordable
/ˌʌnəˈfɔːdəbəl/

adj. 負擔不起的

💬 The rapid inflation has made food unaffordable to many.
快速的通貨膨脹使得食物對很多人來說變得負擔不起。

Using a credit card to finance an unaffordable lifestyle can make you bankrupt.
用信用卡支持負擔不起的生活型態，會讓你破產。

✏️ If you always make a partial credit card payment rather than pay in full, the accumulation of interests and unpaid balances could eventually make your debt unaffordable.
如果你總是付一部分的信用卡款項，而不是付清全額，那麼利息和未付餘額的累積最終可能使你的債變得負擔不起。

Financial experts recommend that we keep track of our spending when using credit cards so that our monthly bills do not become unaffordable.
財務專家建議我們使用信用卡時掌握自己的消費，讓我們的每月帳單不會變得無法負擔。

debt
/dɛt/

n. 債

💬 I don't use credit cards because I feel uncomfortable about owing a debt.
我不用信用卡，因為我對於欠債覺得不舒服。

Buying unaffordable things by credit card can get you into a debt trap.
用信用卡買你買不起的東西，可能會讓你掉進債務陷阱。

✏️ Credit card holders should pay their monthly bills before the due date to avoid late payment fees and keep credit card debt under control.
信用卡持卡人應該在到期日之前付每月帳單，以避免產生滯納金，並且保持卡債在控制之中。

Taking out a cash advance on your credit card is expensive and carries the potential for debt, so it is advisable to avoid doing so.
用信用卡預支現金很貴（利息、費用很高），而且有可能讓你負債，所以避免這樣做是明智的。

547

RELATED WORDS | 相關單字延伸

misappropriate
v. 盜用，挪用

cheat
v. 欺騙

compromise
v. 危及，損害，洩露

steal
v. 偷竊

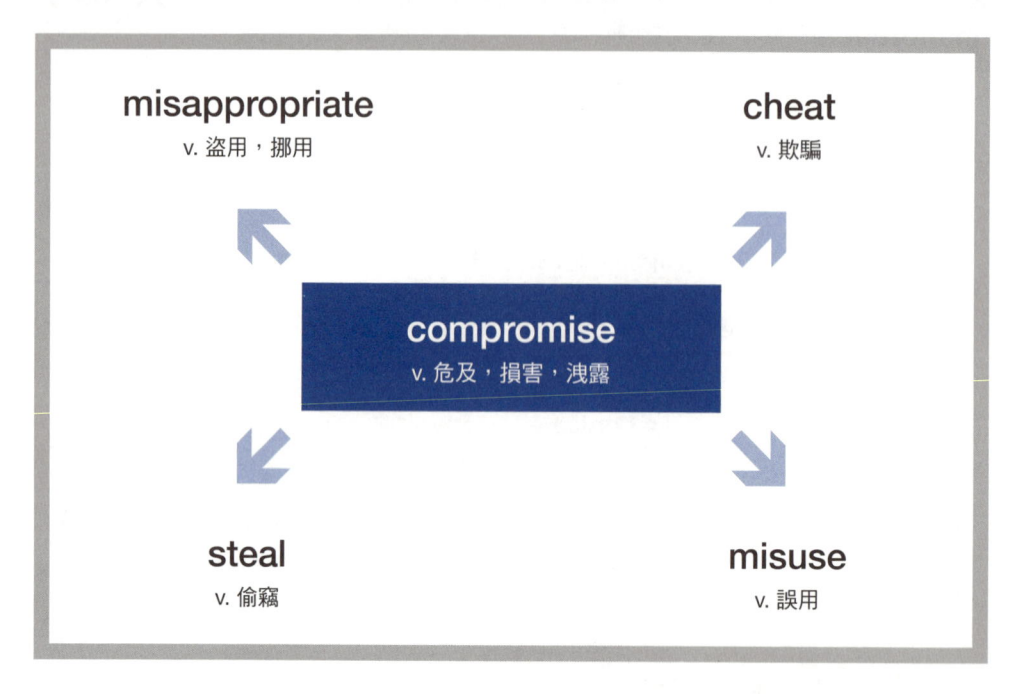

misuse
v. 誤用

compromise
/ˈkɒmprəmaɪz/

Even if your credit card number is **compromised** and fraudulent charges appear on your statement, you can call the credit card company to dispute the charges.
就算信用卡號洩露，而帳單上出現了盜刷的請款，你可以打電話給信用卡公司向爭議款項提出異議。

misappropriate
/ˌmɪsəˈprəʊprieɪt/

I knew the company credit card was **misappropriated** because fraudulent charges were on the statement.
因為對帳單上有盜刷款項，所以我知道公司的信用卡被盜用了。

steal
/stiːl/

I immediately alerted my credit card company after I realised my credit card had been **stolen**.
當我發現信用卡被偷之後，我馬上就提醒了我的信用卡公司。

cheat
/tʃiːt/

People who steal credit card numbers and **cheat** credit card companies should be charged.
偷信用卡號碼並且欺騙信用卡公司的人應該被起訴。

misuse
/mɪsˈjuːz/

Although credit cards can in theory help people manage their finances, some people **misuse** them and become deeply in debt.
雖然信用卡理論上可以幫助人們管理財務，但有些人誤用它們，而且深陷負債之中。

USEFUL EXPRESSIONS | 相關實用片語

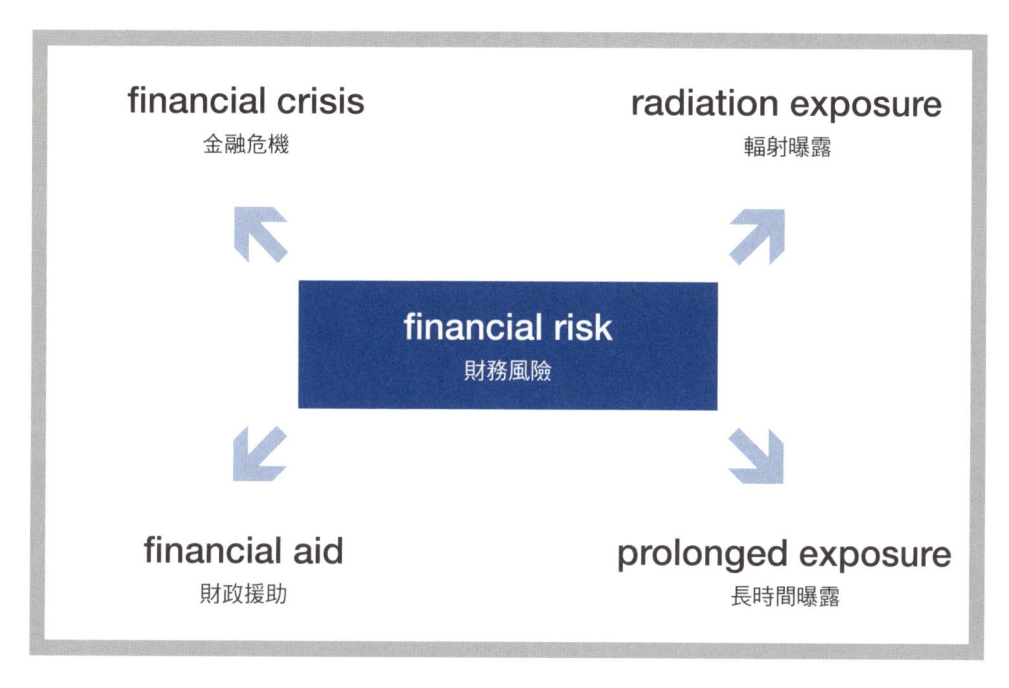

```
financial crisis              radiation exposure
  金融危機                         輻射曝露

              ↖         ↗

              financial risk
                財務風險

              ↙         ↘

financial aid                 prolonged exposure
  財政援助                         長時間曝露
```

financial risk
/fʌɪˈnanʃəl rɪsk/

In order to minimise your financial risk, you should take appropriate action immediately.
為了把你的財務風險降到最低，你應該立即採取適合的行動。

financial crisis
/fʌɪˈnanʃəl ˈkrʌɪsɪs/

Even though the financial crisis was over, the future of the car company looked bleak.
雖然金融危機已經結束，但這間汽車公司的未來看起來還是很黯淡。

financial aid
/fʌɪˈnanʃəl eɪd/

Students who cannot afford tuition may apply for financial aid.
無法負擔學費的學生可以申請財務援助。

radiation exposure
/reɪdɪˈeɪʃən ɪkˈspəʊʒə/

Childhood radiation exposure is risky according to the latest study published in the medical journal.
根據發表在那本醫學期刊的最新研究，兒童時期的輻射暴露很危險。

prolonged exposure
/prəˈlɒŋd ɪkˈspəʊʒə/

After prolonged exposure to the elements, the mountainside showed signs of erosion.
經過長期風吹雨打，山坡呈現出侵蝕的跡象。

WED

IELTS BASIC WORDS

advantageous /ˌædvənˈteɪdʒəs/ adj. 有利的
ENG. creating favourable circumstances that increase the chances of success
SYS. beneficial, helpful

> In today's world, it seems more **advantageous** to be rich than wise.
> 在今日的世界，有錢似乎比有智慧更有利。

同義語 例句 It is sad that only wealth is considered **valuable** these days.
最近只有財富被認為有價值，是很悲哀的事情。

同義語 例句 Being rich **creates favourable circumstances** for people's lives and the realisation of their dreams.
有錢能為人們的生活和夢想的實現創造有利的情況。

反義語 例句 Just being wealthy **does not help** to build a good reputation.
只是有錢，對於建立好的名聲並沒有幫助。

stable /ˈsteɪbəl/ adj. 穩定的
ENG. resistant to change of position or condition
SYS. secure, lasting

> For me, a successful life means physical and emotional well-being based on a **stable** financial situation.
> 對我來說，成功的人生意味著建立於穩定財務狀況之上的身體與情緒健康、幸福感。

同義語 例句 Truly successful people are those who feel financially **secure** enough to enjoy their life.
真正成功的人，是覺得自己財務夠穩定而能夠享受人生的人。

同義語 例句 Happiness won't **last long** without a certain level of financial independence.
沒有一定程度的財務獨立，幸福不會持久。

反義語 例句 Many people feel emotionally **insecure** even though they are financially stable.
很多人即使財務穩定，情緒上還是覺得不安。

WEEK 10 TOPIC **SOCIAL LIFE**

▶ 基礎單字擴充

extend /ɪkˈstɛnd/ v. 延長;伸出,提供
ENG. stretch out over a distance, time, space or scope
SYS. broaden, continue

> Some rich people feel happy when they extend a helping hand to the poor.
> 有些富人在對窮人伸出援手時感到快樂。

同義語例句 By stretching out a helping hand to poor people, the billionaire feels the joy of sharing.
藉著向窮人伸出援手,那位億萬富翁感受到分享的快樂。

同義語例句 Wealthy people must give away their fortune wisely to help those really in need.
富人必須聰明地送出他們的財富,幫助真正需要的人。

反義語例句 Some rich people just keep their wealth to themselves and live in luxury as long as they can.
有些富人就只是盡可能把財富留在身邊,並且過奢華的生活。

serious /ˈsɪərɪəs/ adj. 嚴肅的,嚴重的
ENG. grave in quality or manner
SYS. critical, crucial

> The wealth concentration induced by globalisation is a serious issue.
> 全球化引起的財富集中是個嚴肅的問題。

同義語例句 It is worrying that the rich are earning more and more while most people's incomes stagnate.
富人越賺越多,而大部分的人收入停滯不前的現象令人擔憂。

同義語例句 The fact that most of the wealth is possessed by only a few people is no laughing matter.
大部分的財富為少數人擁有的事實不是件好笑的事。

反義語例句 The minister of finance takes wealth inequality as a minor problem, stressing that most economic indicators look favourable.
財政部長把財富不均當成小問題,強調大部分的經濟指標看起來很好。

WED

TOPIC: Happiness and wealth
幸福與財富

To many age-old tales that involve the **pursuit** of **treasure**, the **axiom** that money cannot buy happiness applies. While this **proverb** is **indubitably** true, it doesn't mean poverty can bring **contentment**. For most people, **prosperity** and happiness are equally important and both worth pursuing, but sometimes we become obsessed with material things and forget about our feelings and relations. Seeking satisfaction through buying things usually ends up in **futility** because it is love and friendship that can really fulfil our emotional needs. Unfortunately, such intangible assets are often **disregarded**. Even though material wealth is **alluring**, especially for those who have had a taste of it, its power seems feeble compared to intimate relationship, which can bring us lasting joy.

TRANS

「金錢買不到幸福」這句格言適用於許多古老的尋寶故事。不過，雖然這句諺語無疑是正確的，但它的意思並不是貧窮可以帶來滿足。對於大部分的人而言，富足和幸福同等重要，而且都是值得追求的，但有時候我們著迷於物質，而忘了自己的感情和人際關係。透過買東西來尋求滿足，結果通常是徒勞的，因為愛和友誼才能真正滿足我們情緒上的需要。遺憾的是，這種無形的資產經常被忽視。即使物質財富很誘人，對於嘗過它的滋味的人尤其如此，但和能為我們帶來持久喜悅的親密關係相比，它的力量就顯得薄弱。

pursuit
/pəˈsjuːt/

n. 追逐，追求
The police car was in **pursuit** of the fleeing suspect.
警車在追捕正在逃跑的嫌疑犯。

treasure
/ˈtrɛʒə/

n. 寶藏
Do you know where the buried **treasure** is located?
你知道被埋藏的寶藏在哪裡嗎？

axiom
/ˈaksɪəm/

n. 不言自明的道理，格言，箴言
It is a famous **axiom** that history repeats itself.
「歷史會重演」是有名的格言。

proverb
/ˈprɒvəːb/

n. 諺語，俗語
As the **proverb** goes, 'a penny saved is a penny earned.'
俗話說：「省一塊錢就是賺一塊錢。」

indubitably
/ɪnˈdjuːbɪtəbli/

adv. 不容置疑地
2 plus 2 **indubitably** equals 4 in the decimal number system.
在十進數系統裡，2 加 2 當然等於 4。

contentment
/kənˈtɛntmənt/

n. 滿足
James felt great **contentment** when he graduated from university.
James 從大學畢業時感到很大的滿足。

prosperity
/prɒˈspɛrɪti/

n. 繁榮，富足
I wish you health, happiness and **prosperity** in your marriage.
我希望你在婚姻中健康、幸福而富足。

futility
/fjʊˈtɪlɪti/

n. 無用，徒勞
I finally realised the **futility** of trying to find an answer to everything.
我終於了解到試圖為每件事尋找答案的徒勞。

disregard
/dɪsrɪˈɡɑːd/

v. 不理會，忽視
Please **disregard** the previous mail.
請忽略上一封郵件。

alluring
/əˈljʊərɪŋ/

adj. 誘人的
She wore a rather **alluring** shade of lipstick tonight.
她今晚擦了相當誘人的唇色。

WORD TRAINING | 重點單字造句練習

exhilaration
/ɪɡzɪləˈreɪʃən/

n. 興奮、高興、愉快的感覺

💬 After winning a lottery, it is likely that one will buy unnecessary things out of exhilaration.
贏了樂透之後，一個人很有可能因為興奮而買不必要的東西。

If I become rich, I think I will feel great exhilaration at first, but I don't think wealth will give me long-lasting happiness. 如果我變有錢，我覺得我一開始會欣喜若狂，但我覺得財富不能給我持久的快樂。

✏️ This consumer society has made us feel that happiness lies in being wealthy, but true exhilaration comes from personal accomplishments and love in intimate relations. 消費社會使我們覺得幸福存在於富有之中，但真正的愉快來自於個人成就，還有親密關係中的愛。

Their happiness is not shallow exhilaration that depends on material indulgence, but rather a deep sense of inner peace stemming from a life of purpose.
他們的幸福不是取決於物質享受的膚淺快樂，而是從有目的的人生而來的深層內在平靜。

gratification
/ɡrætɪfɪˈkeɪʃn/

n. 滿足，喜悅，令人滿足的事物

💬 The book *Don't Eat the Marshmallow Yet* argues that we can be more successful by delaying instant gratifications. 《先別急著吃棉花糖》這本書主張，我們可以藉著延後立即的滿足而變得更成功。

Working is not merely for making money, but also for our own gratification.
工作不只是為了賺錢，也是為了我們自己的滿足感。

✏️ What keeps most people from becoming rich is the habit of wanting instant gratification rather than setting long-term goals and working hard to achieve them.
大部分的人無法變有錢的原因，在於想要得到立即滿足的習慣，而不是設定長期目標並且努力達成。

You may feel a deep sense of gratification as a result of your hard work, but in order to feel true happiness, you should find inner peace within yourself.
你可能會因為努力工作而感受到深刻的滿足，但要感覺到真正的快樂，你應該從自己的內心找到內在的平靜。

vandal
/ˈvandəl/

n. 破壞他人財物者

The **vandal** took advantage of my forgetfulness and entered my house when I forgot to close the door.
那個破壞者利用我的健忘，在我忘記關門的時候進了我的房子。

The **vandal** admitted to targeting mansions because their owners are too wealthy.
那個破壞者承認，因為豪宅主人太有錢而鎖定他們的房子。

My wealthy neighbour complained that a **vandal** painted graffiti on the side of his brand-new Ferrari.
我的有錢鄰居抱怨有破壞者在他全新的法拉利車側噴漆塗鴉。

The rich person hired several security guards to prevent **vandals** from approaching her house.
那個有錢人雇用了幾位保全人員，防止破壞者接近她家。

anonymity
/ˌanəˈnɪmɪti/

n. 匿名，無名

Poor people may not have mansions full of luxuries, but they do have the benefit of **anonymity**.
窮人可能沒有充滿奢侈物品的豪宅，但他們有沒沒無聞的好處。

Modern people who live in **anonymity** have more freedom to do what they want than those in a village where everybody knows one another.
過著沒沒無聞的生活的現代人，跟每個人都認識彼此的村莊居民比起來，有更多自由可以做自己想做的事。

The benefactor insisted on **anonymity** when she donated millions of dollars to several orphanages.
那位捐助者捐出數百萬美元給幾家孤兒院時堅持匿名。

The lottery winner opted for **anonymity** and asked that his win not be published in newspapers or celebrated by the retailer.
那位樂透得主選擇匿名，而且要求他的得獎不要刊登在報紙上或者被彩券行拿來慶祝。

RELATED WORDS | 相關單字延伸

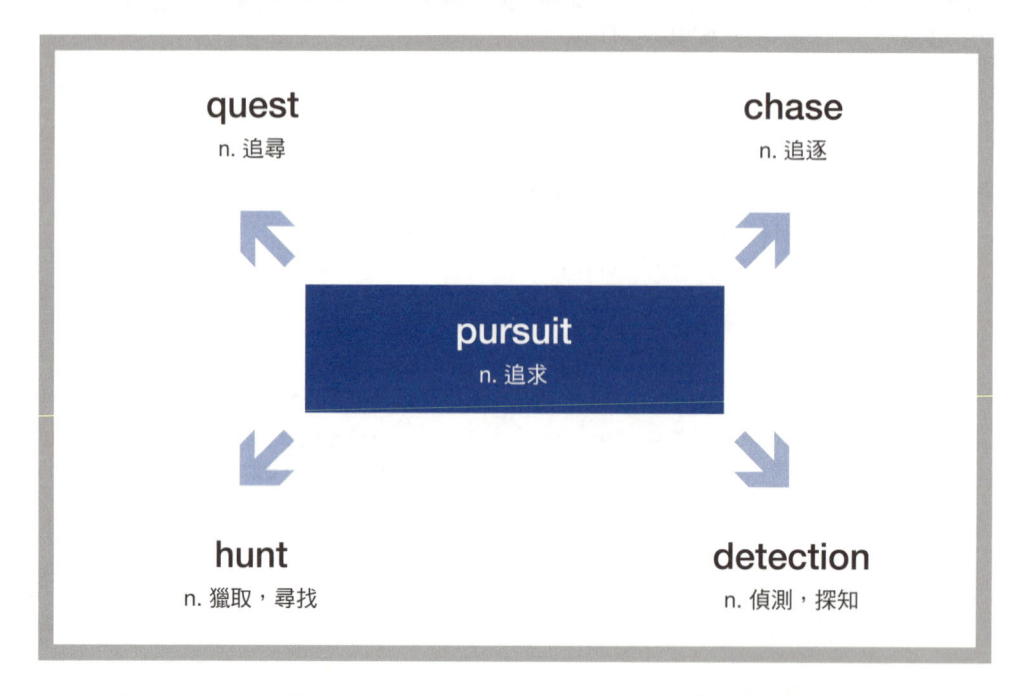

quest
n. 追尋

chase
n. 追逐

pursuit
n. 追求

hunt
n. 獵取，尋找

detection
n. 偵測，探知

pursuit
/pəˈsjuːt/

To many age-old tales that involve the pursuit of treasure, the axiom that money cannot buy happiness applies.
「金錢買不到幸福」這句格言適用於許多古老的尋寶故事。

quest
/kwɛst/

I visited many furniture stores in my quest to find the perfect sofas for my living room.
在尋找適合我客廳的完美沙發的過程中，我去了許多家具店。

hunt
/hʌnt/

He spent his whole life travelling everywhere in a hunt for treasure.
他花了一輩子到處旅行尋找寶藏。

chase
/tʃeɪs/

The chase for money itself is devoid of meaning and not necessarily brings happiness.
對於金錢本身的追求是缺乏意義的，而且不必然會帶來幸福。

detection
/dɪˈtɛkʃən/

This machine's purpose is the detection of metal objects buried deep in the sand.
這台機器的目的是探測埋在沙子深處的金屬物品。

USEFUL EXPRESSIONS | 相關實用片語

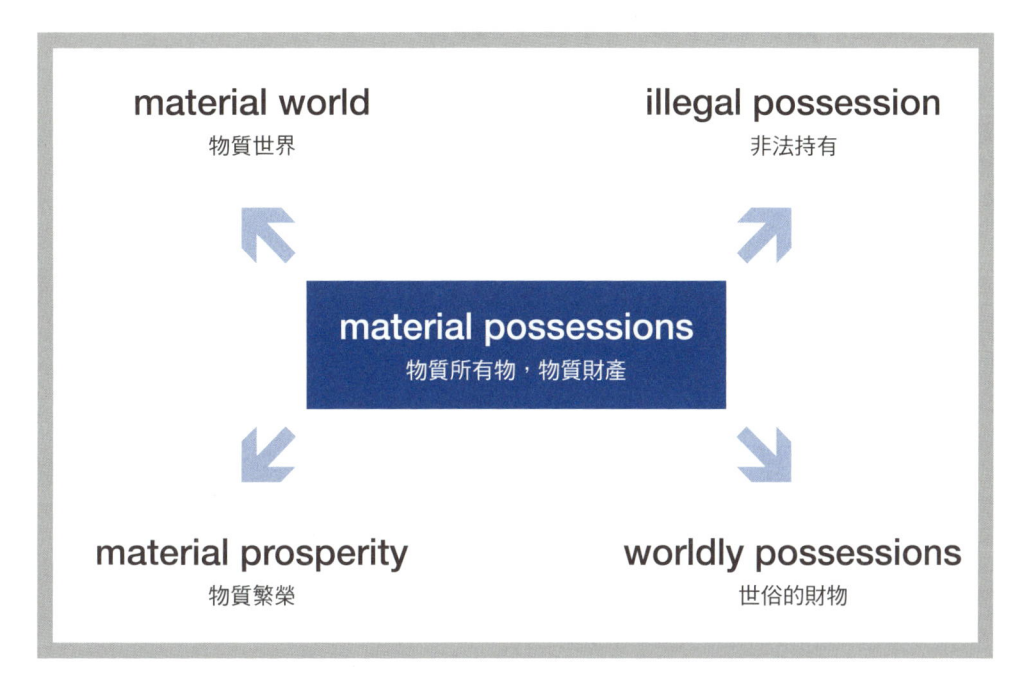

```
material world          illegal possession
  物質世界                    非法持有
         ↖            ↗
          material possessions
           物質所有物，物質財產
         ↙            ↘
material prosperity      worldly possessions
   物質繁榮                   世俗的財物
```

material possessions
/məˈtɪrɪəl pəˈzɛʃənz/

The world that we live in is entirely obsessed with the acquisition of material possessions.
我們生活的這個世界已經完全沈迷於對物質財產的獲取。

material world
/məˈtɪrɪəl wɝld/

Even though you live an abundant life in the material world, you may still feel empty inside.
即使你在物質世界中過著富足的生活，你內心可能還是會覺得空虛。

material prosperity
/məˈtɪrɪəl prɑˈspɛrɪti/

America's 1920s sports heroes and national icons came out of the country's celebration of material prosperity.
美國 1920 年代的運動英雄與國家代表人物是國家慶祝物質繁榮下的產物。

illegal possession
/ɪˈliːɡəl pəˈzɛʃən/

He was sentenced to five years in prison for illegal possession of weapons.
他因為非法持有武器而被判坐牢五年。

worldly possessions
/ˈwɝldli pəˈzɛʃənz/

To live a truly austere life, one must give up all of their worldly possessions.
要過真正的苦行生活，必須放棄世俗的所有。

THU

IELTS **BASIC WORDS**

influence /ˈɪnfluəns/ v. 影響
ENG. have and exert effect
SYS. persuade, control

> The growing number of elders in the society **influenced** the government's policy choices.
> 社會中老年人逐漸成長的人數，影響了政府的政策選擇。

同義語 例句 The high proportion of elders in the community **played a part in** the approval of the laws.
社會中老年人的高比例，對於那些法律的通過扮演了重要角色。

同義語 例句 The issues caused by population ageing **affected** the legislators' decisions. 人口老化造成的問題，影響了立法委員的決定。

反義語 例句 The increasing number of seniors **has no effect on** the employment rate of the city.
逐漸增加的老年人口數，對於這個城市的就業率沒有影響。

key /kiː/ adj. 關鍵的，重要的
ENG. serving as an essential component
SYS. major, fundamental

> Population ageing is a **key** factor in the expansion of social welfare spending. 人口老化是社會福利支出擴大的一項關鍵因素。

同義語 例句 The growing number of elders is the **main cause** of increasing government spending on healthcare.
逐漸增加的老年人口數，是政府對醫療保健支出增加的主要原因。

同義語 例句 The rise in the proportion of the elderly population is a **fundamental reason** why the government spends more and more on public health.
老年人口的比例上升，是政府之所以花越來越多錢在公共健康上的一項基本原因。

反義語 例句 The growth of the senior population is **not the primary cause** of the increase in government expenditure.
老年人口的成長，並不是政府支出增加的主因。

WEEK 10 TOPIC **SOCIAL LIFE**

▶基礎單字擴充

range /reɪndʒ/ n. 範圍
ENG. the limits within which something can be effective
SYS. limit, extent

> The age range of living senior citizens in our city is from 60 to 102.
> 本市現有的年長市民年齡範圍是從 60 到 102 歲。

同義語例句 The **minimum and maximum** age **limits** must be determined so that the benefits will not be abused.
必須制定最低和最高年齡限制，以免補助金被濫用。

同義語例句 The **limitation** to the age of an applicant is necessary for the benefits to be used correctly.
申請者的年齡限制，對於讓補助金被正確使用是必要的。

反義語例句 The **lack of** exact age **limits** resulted in the abuse of the benefits.
缺少確切的年齡限制，導致了補助金的濫用。

discuss /dɪˈskʌs/ v. 討論
ENG. speak with others about something
SYS. debate, review

> The issue on the growing number of senior citizens was discussed in the senate meeting.
> 參議院的會議中討論了老年人口數逐漸成長的議題。

同義語例句 The senator **exchanged views** with the rest about the plans he has to deal with the issue of population ageing.
關於他處理人口老化議題的計畫，那位參議員和其他人交換了看法。

同義語例句 The problems on the growing senior population were **talked over** many times but remain unsolved.
老年人口持續成長的問題，被討論了很多次，但還是沒有解決。

反義語例句 Some people **keep mum** when the issue of senior population comes up.
當老年人口的議題出現時，有些人就會保持沉默。

559

TOPIC: The increasing proportion of older people

持續增加的老年人口比例

Population ageing has become a worldwide trend since the twentieth century. As the proportion of older people steadily increases in many countries, concerns are **amassing** about the long-term **viability** of **intergenerational** social support systems. This is not the only **quandary** associated with having a **maturing** population. With more people living longer, retirement **pensions** and other social benefits tend to extend over greater lengths of time. This means that social security systems must change substantially in order to remain effective. **Longevity** can also result in rising medical costs and increasing demands for health services, since older people are typically more **vulnerable** to chronic diseases and **epidemics**. Rather than treating these **phenomena** separately, we should recognise that they all result from a fundamental change in the population structure and require us to see the whole society in a different way.

TRANS

　　從二十世紀開始，人口老化成為了全世界的趨勢。隨著許多國家的老年人口比例持續增加，有越來越多人擔心跨世代社會支援體系的長期可行性。關於社會人口老化，這並不是唯一的窘境。隨著更多人活得更久，退休金和其他社會福利也傾向於延長更久。這意味著社會安全體系必須大幅改變以維持效果。增長的壽命也會導致醫療費用上升，以及對於保健服務的需求增加，因為老年人通常比較容易受到慢性疾病和傳染病流行的傷害。與其分別處理這些現象，我們應該認清它們都是人口結構根本上的改變造成的結果，而且需要我們用不同的方式去看整個社會。

amass /əˈmæs/
v. 累積
James spent twenty years **amassing** his collection of stamps.
James 花了二十年時間累積他的郵票收藏。

viability /vʌɪəˈbɪlɪti/
n. 可行性
The **viability** of the project was studied before its implementation.
計畫的可行性在實施之前研究過。

intergenerational /ˌɪntədʒɛnəˈreɪʃənəl/
adj. 不同世代之間的
The young students urged the president to take action to improve **intergenerational** equity.
那些年輕學生要求總統採取行動促進世代間的平等。

quandary /ˈkwɒndəri/
n. 為難，困窘
These findings clearly pose a **quandary** for council members.
這些研究結果顯然讓議會的成員很為難。

mature /məˈtʃʊə/
v. 成熟
He is **maturing** much faster than his sister did.
他發育得比他的姊姊快得多。

pension /ˈpɛnʃən/
n. 養老金，退休金
My grandfather receives basic state **pensions** of £105 a week.
我祖父每個星期接受國家的基本年金 105 英鎊。

longevity /lɒnˈdʒɛvɪti/
n. 長壽
Quitting smoking is important for your **longevity**.
戒菸對於長壽很重要。

vulnerable /ˈvʌlnərəbəl/
adj. 易受傷害的，易受影響的
The elderly are **vulnerable** to the side effects of these drugs.
老人家很容易受到這些藥物的副作用影響。

epidemic /ˌɛpɪˈdɛmɪk/
n. 傳染病的流行
The first case of the foot-and-mouth **epidemic** was reported in England.
第一個口蹄疫大規模流行的案例發生在英格蘭。

phenomenon /fəˈnɒmɪnən/
n. 現象
An unexplainable **phenomenon** happened when some people claimed they saw a UFO.
一些人聲稱他們看到不明飛行物體的時候，發生了無法解釋的現象。

WORD TRAINING | 重點單字造句練習

alarming
/əˈlɑːmɪŋ/

adj. 令人擔憂的

💬 It is **alarming** that many elderly people disregard their symptoms of dementia and refuse to see a doctor.
許多年長者不理會自己的痴呆症狀,而且不去看醫生,令人擔憂。

The fact that many companies haven't installed smoke detectors in their facilities is **alarming**.
許多公司沒有在設施中安裝煙霧偵測器的事實令人擔憂。

✏️ The rapid growth of older population is **alarming**, as it could intensify spending pressures in areas such as healthcare and elderly benefits.
老年人口的快速成長令人擔憂,因為它可能增強醫療保健與年長者福利等領域的支出壓力。

The **alarming** pension shortfall has caused concern among older people, making them worry about possible changes to the government pension scheme.
令人擔憂的年金赤字造成了老年人的不安,讓他們擔心政府年金計畫可能產生的改變。

demographic
/ˌdɛməˈɡræfɪk/

adj. 人口統計的

💬 The **demographic** structure of this city is changing as elderly people increase.
隨著老年人增加,這個城市的人口結構正在改變。

Population ageing is a **demographic** phenomenon resulted from increasing longevity and declining fertility.
人口老化是壽命增長和生育率下降造成的人口統計現象。

✏️ Many countries are faced with the consequences of the **demographic** shift towards an older population and need to reform their social security systems. 許多國家面臨了人口結構老化的結果,並且需要改革他們的社會安全體系。

Besides paying attention to the obvious effects caused by an ageing population in the fields of healthcare, housing and employment, policymakers also need to understand the **demographic** shift as a long-term transition.
除了注意人口老化在醫療保健、居住與就業等領域造成的明顯影響,政策制定者也需要將人口結構改變理解為長期的轉變。

compassion
/kəmˈpaʃən/

n. 同情

💬 We must have more compassion for elderly people and take the issue of population ageing seriously.
我們必須對老年人有更多的同情，並且認真看待人口老化的議題。

The government promises to improve the healthcare system with compassion for elder people.
政府承諾帶著對老年人的同情來改善醫療保健體系。

✍ As more and more women are diagnosed with breast cancer, we should encourage women to routinely perform breast self-exams for early detection and show more compassion for the patients.
因為有越來越多女性被診斷出乳癌，我們應該鼓勵女性定期進行乳房自我檢查以利早期發現，並且對病患展現更多同情。

While many people blame the ageing population for the financial burden on younger generations and the high youth unemployment rate, we should still have compassion for the elderly.
雖然很多人責怪人口老化造成年輕世代的財務負擔和年輕人失業率高，但我們還是應該對老年人有同情心。

welfare
/ˈwɛlfɛː/

n. 福祉，福利

💬 Older people have more health problems and require more care to ensure their welfare.
老年人有比較多的健康問題，需要更多照顧來確保他們的福祉。

Since medical advances help us live longer, we now pay more attention to elderly welfare.
因為醫藥進步幫助我們活得更久，我們現在更注意老年人的福祉。

✍ As the population ages, young people must work longer and harder to support an increasing number of retirees, and the social welfare system will collapse if it remains unchanged.
隨著人口老化，年輕人必須工作更久、更辛苦以支持越來越多的退休者，而社會福利體系如果保持不變就會崩潰。

To ensure the welfare of our nation during the demographic shift toward an older population, we must adjust immigration policies to attract young and skilled workers. 為了確保我們的國家在人口結構老化中的福祉，我們必須調整移民政策以吸引年輕而且有技術的工作者。

RELATED WORDS | 相關單字延伸

permanence
n. 永久性，持久性

endurance
n. 忍耐，耐久

longevity
n. 長壽

durability
n. 耐用，持久

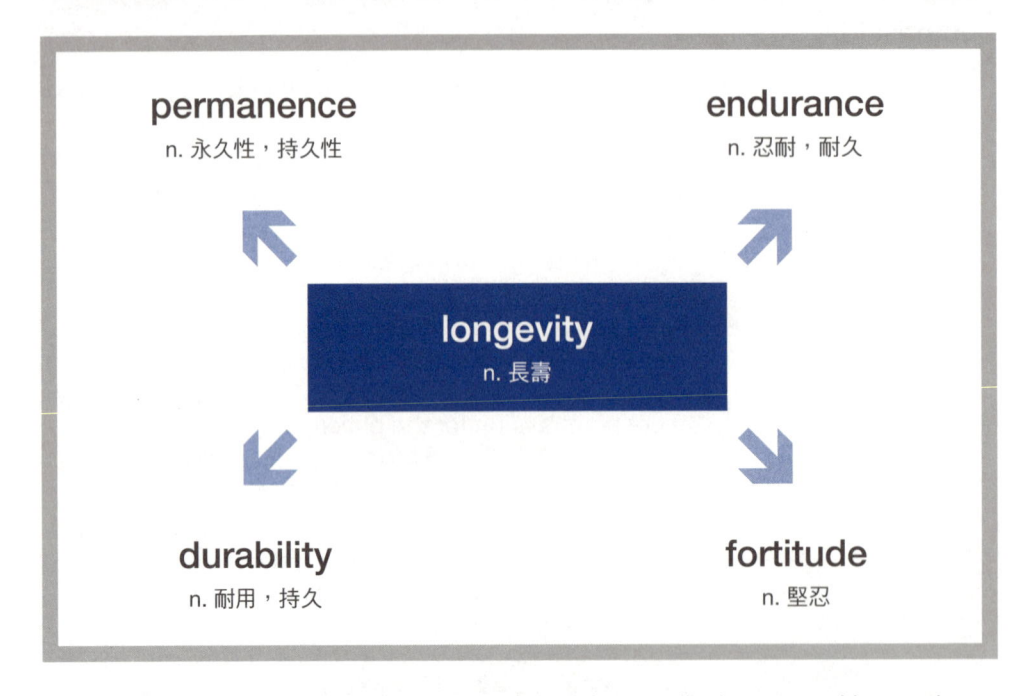

fortitude
n. 堅忍

longevity
/lɒnˈdʒɛvɪti/

Longevity can result in rising medical costs and increasing demands for health services.
增長的壽命會導致醫療費用上升，以及對於保健服務的需求增加。

permanence
/ˈpɜːmənəns/

As can be seen in the ever-increasing divorce rates, modern people no longer believe in the permanence of marriage.
就像可以從持續升高的離婚率看到的一樣，現代人已經不相信婚姻的永久性了。

durability
/dʒɔːrəˈbɪlɪti/

When getting dental implants, it is important to know about the durability of the materials.
在接受植牙的時候，了解材質的耐久性很重要。

endurance
/ɪnˈdjʊərəns/

Pursuing medical technology development requires extraordinary patience and endurance.
追求醫學科技的發展，需要過人的耐心與毅力。

fortitude
/ˈfɔːtɪtjuːd/

It takes fortitude to work in medical and health services industries.
在醫藥保健服務產業工作，需要堅忍的精神。

USEFUL EXPRESSIONS | 相關實用片語

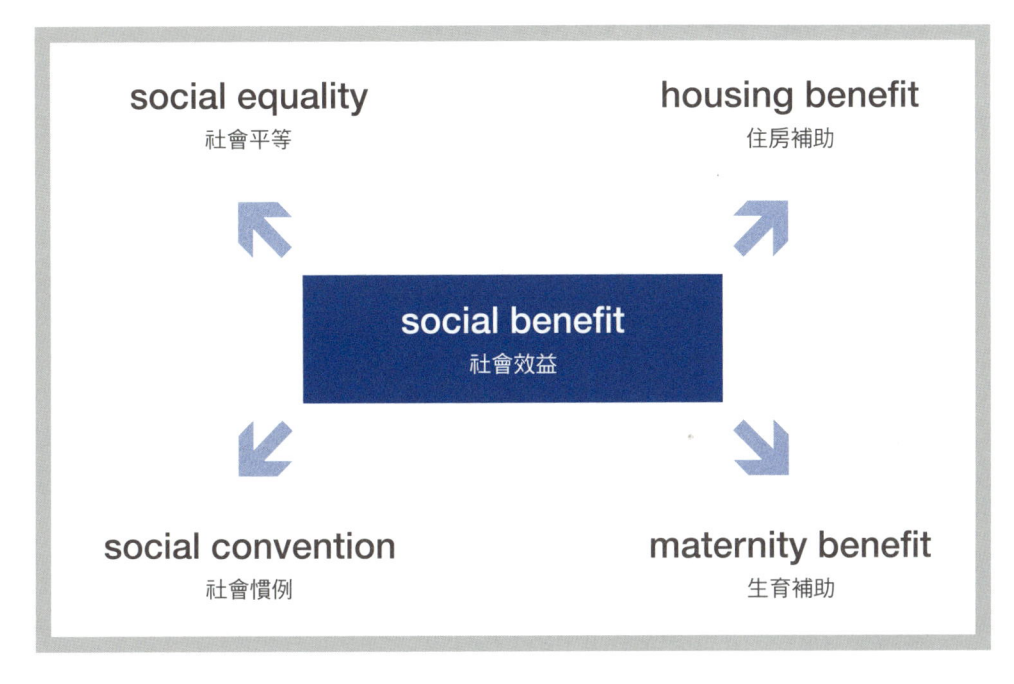

```
     social equality              housing benefit
        社會平等                      住房補助
             ↖                    ↗
                  social benefit
                     社會效益
             ↙                    ↘
    social convention           maternity benefit
        社會慣例                      生育補助
```

social benefit
/ˈsəʊʃəl ˈbɛnɪfɪt/
Some scholars argue that the nationalisation of enterprises will result in more social benefits than social costs.
有些學者主張，企業國有化產生的社會效益比社會成本多。

social equality
/ˈsəʊʃəl ɪˈkwɒlɪti/
Generally speaking, the members of the young generation care about economic freedom and social equality.
大致上來說，年輕世代的人關心經濟自由和社會平等。

social convention
/ˈsəʊʃəl kənˈvɛnʃən/
Freedom of expression has always been restricted by established social conventions.
表達的自由一直受限於已經確立的社會慣例。

housing benefit
/ˈhaʊzɪŋ ˈbɛnɪfɪt/
If people apply for housing benefits, they can expect that they will be subsidised for their rent.
如果人們申請住房補助，他們可以預期租金會得到補貼。

maternity benefit
/məˈtɜːnɪti ˈbɛnɪfɪt/
The maternity benefits were eliminated for women having a third child.
生第三胎的婦女的生育補助被刪掉了。

FRI

IELTS **BASIC WORDS**

respond /rɪˈspɒnd/　v. 反應，回答
ENG. show reaction to something
SYS. react, answer

> The best thing about working with young people is that they always **respond** positively to projects.
> 和年輕人共事最棒的一點，就是他們總是會對計畫有正面的反應。

同義語例句　The younger employees **reacted** positively to the management's decision to reform the company's systems.
年輕員工對於經營團隊改革公司制度的決定反應正面。

同義語例句　The president **replied** to the young people's complaints with a promise to invest more in them.
總統回應年輕人的不滿，承諾會投資更多在他們身上。

反義語例句　If we **remain silent**, the government will cut spending on education, which is important for young people to thrive in the future.　如果我們保持沈默，政府就會削減教育支出，而教育對於年輕人未來的成功是很重要的。

innate /ɪˈneɪt/　adj. 與生俱來的
ENG. possessed at birth
SYS. inborn, natural

> It is every child's **innate** ability to acquire a mother tongue.
> 習得母語是每個小孩與生俱來的能力。

同義語例句　It seems that baseball is **in** his family's **blood**, since most of them are baseball players.
打棒球似乎是他的家族與生俱來的能力，因為他們大部分都是棒球員。

同義語例句　Eye colour is an **inherited** trait determined by several different genes.
眼睛顏色是一種由幾個不同基因決定的遺傳特徵。

反義語例句　Riding a bicycle is a skill that must be **learned through experience**.
騎腳踏車是一種必須藉由經驗學習的技能。

WEEK 10 TOPIC **SOCIAL LIFE**

▶ 基礎單字擴充

natural /ˈnætʃərəl/ adj. 天然的
ENG. existing in or formed by nature
SYS. pure, raw

> Many parents nowadays choose only **natural** products for their young children.
> 現在許多父母只為他們的小孩選擇天然的產品。

同義語例句 Parents now prefer to feed their young children with foods **free from artificial additives**.
現在的父母偏好用沒有人工添加物的食品餵自己的小孩。

同義語例句 There are more **chemical-free** products for children today.
今日有更多無化學物質的兒童產品。

反義語例句 It is a surprise to many parents that most powdered milk contains **artificial** ingredients.
大部分的奶粉都含有人工成分，是一件讓許多父母感到意外的事情。

safe /seɪf/ adj. 安全的
ENG. secure from evil, harm or danger
SYS. protected, secure

> Some parents take every possible measure to keep their children **safe** at home.
> 有些父母用盡任何方法讓小孩在家中保持安全。

同義語例句 Some parents are willing to invest in anything that can keep their children **unharmed**.
有些父母願意投資任何可以保持小孩不受傷的東西。

同義語例句 Some parents install security systems in their homes to keep their children **safe from harm**.
有些父母在家裡安裝保全系統，保護小孩免於傷害。

反義語例句 Neglecting safety precautions at home will make children **exposed to danger**.
忽視家中的安全預防措施，會使小孩暴露於危險之中。

FRI

TOPIC | The importance of investing in young people
投資在年輕人身上的重要性

In the world today, while some young people receive a **superior** education and can look forward to **decent** jobs and rewarding lives, those in **developing** countries usually lack the education and opportunities they deserve. When the youth are not given a chance to develop their talents and contribute to the society, they are prone to violent crimes and drug addiction, and can easily fall to the bottom of the social scale. This is why it is **imperative** to invest in the younger **generation**. Besides providing especially talented adolescents with **gratis** university education, we should also **revolutionise** the education system to make **vocational** education an equally favourable option. Despite the global economic **downturn** we are now faced with, investing in young people will help our society **progress** to higher levels of achievement in all areas.

TRANS

在今日的世界，雖然有些年輕人得到比較好的教育，而能夠期待體面的工作和報酬多的生活，但開發中國家的年輕人通常欠缺他們應得的教育與機會。當年輕人沒有機會開發自己的天分並且貢獻社會時，他們就很有可能參與暴力犯罪、染上毒癮，而容易掉到社會階級的底層。這就是必須投資在年輕世代身上的理由。除了提供免費的大學教育給特別有天分的青少年，我們也應該徹底改革教育體系，讓職業教育成為同樣有利的選擇。雖然我們現在面臨全球性的經濟衰退，但投資在年輕人身上，可以幫助我們的社會在所有領域進步而達到更高的成就。

superior
/suˈpɪərɪə/

adj. 比較高等的，比較優秀的
The purse I just bought is **superior** to the one I have been using.
我剛買的包包比我一直在用的高級。

decent
/ˈdiːsənt/

adj. 體面的，還不錯的
I won't dream of living like a celebrity, but I hope to lead a **decent** and purposeful life at least.
我不會夢想活得像名人一樣，但我希望至少可以過還不錯又有目的的生活。

developing
/dɪˈvɛləpɪŋ/

adj. 開發中的，發展中的
Some **developing** countries are suffering because of the economic crisis.
一些開發中國家正因為經濟危機而受苦。

imperative
/ɪmˈpɛrətɪv/

adj. 必須服從的，必要的
It is **imperative** that you listen to your father's advice.
你必須聽你父親的建議。

generation
/ˌdʒɛnəˈreɪʃən/

n. 世代
The older **generation** tend to think that many young people today are spoiled.
老一輩的人通常認為許多年輕人被寵壞了。

gratis
/ˈɡrætɪs/

adj. 免費的　adv. 免費地
Scrambled eggs are served **gratis** at this restaurant.
炒蛋在這家餐廳免費供應。

revolutionise
/ˌrɛvəˈluːʃənaɪz/

v. 徹底改革，徹底革新
E-commerce **revolutionised** the way we shop for goods.
電子商務徹底改變了我們購買產品的方式。

vocational
/voʊˈkeɪʃənəl/

adj. 職業的
Vocational training can make a student well-prepared for a certain trade.
職業訓練可以讓學生對特定行業作好準備。

downturn
/ˈdaʊntɜːn/

n. 衰退，下降
The company paid high dividends even in a time of economic **downturn**.
即使在經濟衰退的情況下，那家公司還是給了很高的股利。

progress
/prəˈɡrɛs/

v. 進步
She used her knowledge to help her company **progress**.
她運用她的知識幫助公司進步。

WORD TRAINING | 重點單字造句練習

luxury
/ˈlʌkʃəri/

n. 奢侈，奢侈品 adj. 奢侈的

💬 Buying a home is a luxury for most young people today.
對於今天大部分的年輕人來說，買房子是件奢侈的事。

Rich people should invest in the education of their children rather than shower them with luxury.
有錢人應該投資孩子的教育，而不是給他們很多奢侈品。

✍ The company's advertising department is faced with budget cuts because advertising is now considered a luxury rather than a necessity under a difficult financial situation. 那間公司的宣傳部門面臨了預算刪減，因為在困難的財務情況下，現在廣告宣傳被認為是一件奢侈而非必要的事情。

Luxury brands secure their place in the market by targeting the wealthiest people and inviting celebrities to their events, which in turn create an impression that branded goods symbolise high social status and are thus worth owning. 奢侈品牌藉由鎖定最有錢的人以及邀請名人參加活動來鞏固市場地位，而這樣又能進一步創造出名牌商品象徵高社會地位而值得擁有的印象。

altruism
/ˈæltruːɪzəm/

n. 利他主義

💬 Those doctors work in developing countries out of altruism.
那些醫生出於利他的精神而在開發中國家工作。

We can teach our children about altruism by donating to charities in their names.
我們可以藉由以孩子的名義捐款給慈善機構來教導他們利他的精神。

✍ Volunteering is a form of altruism because a volunteer will not ask for any material reward.
志願服務是一種利他的形式，因為志工不會要求任何物質的回報。

Motivated by altruism, the successful entrepreneur is devoted not only to the arrangement of charity events, but also to the development of new technologies that will benefit developing countries.
出於利他的精神，這位成功的企業家不僅投身於安排慈善活動，也開發能幫助開發中國家的新科技。

budget
/ˈbʌdʒɪt/

n. 預算

💬 It seems that the education of the youth is not a priority in the current government budget.
青年教育似乎不是現在政府預算的優先事項。

My family's budget only allows us to dine out at a fine restaurant once a month.
我家的預算只能讓我們一個月去一次高級餐廳。

✎ The research in higher education institutions is paramount in the government's budget, while students who need financial aid seem to be neglected.
高等教育機構的研究在政府的預算裡很重要,但需要金錢支援的學生似乎被忽略了。

The budget shows a commitment to giving young people the opportunities they deserve in its large proportion going to student grants.
這個預算展現出給年輕人應得的機會的承諾,因為它有很大一部分是用在助學金上。

satisfaction
/ˌsætɪsˈfækʃən/

n. 滿足,滿意

💬 Some parents find satisfaction in teaching their children what they know.
有些父母在教導孩子自己所知道的事情時感到滿足。

Material things may bring you satisfaction, but real happiness comes from love and friendship.
物質的東西可能會帶來滿足,但真正的幸福來自愛和友誼。

✎ The volunteers feel deep satisfaction in what they do because they believe they are making a difference for the lives of children in the area.
這些義工在自己所做的事情中感受到很深的滿足,因為他們相信自己正在為那個地區的兒童的生活創造改變。

By encouraging creative expression through writing and painting, the summer camp provides a great deal of satisfaction and a sense of achievement for its participants.
藉由鼓勵透過寫作與繪畫進行創意表達,這個夏令營為參加者提供許多滿足與成就感。

RELATED WORDS ｜ 相關單字延伸

advance
v. 前進，進步

evolve
v. 演進，逐步發展

progress
v. 進步

proceed
v. 繼續進行，接著進行

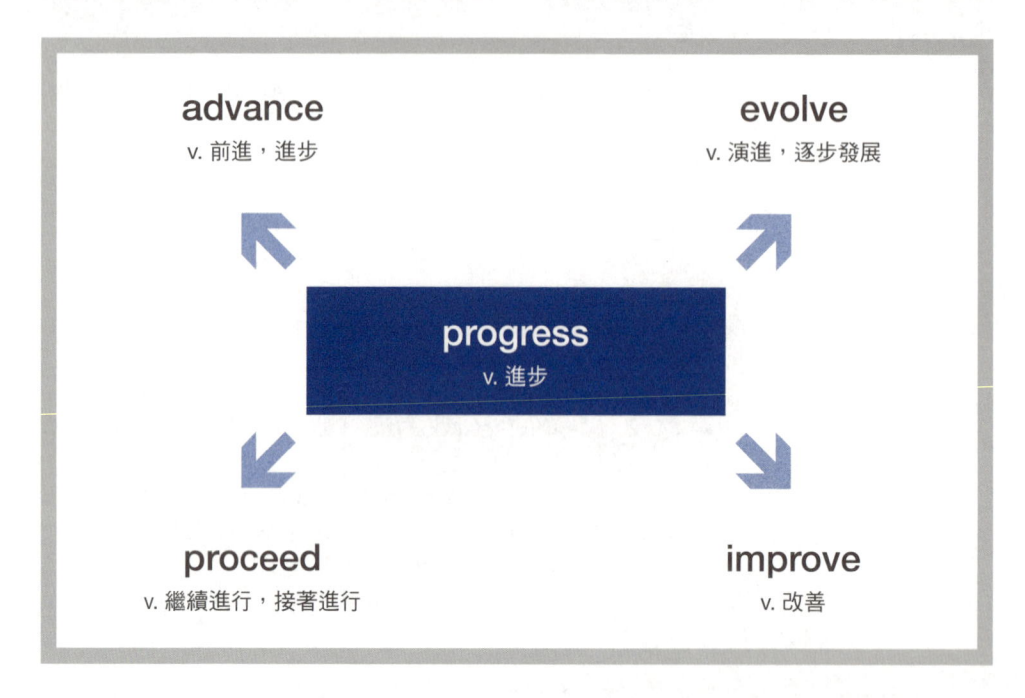

improve
v. 改善

progress
/prəˈgrɛs/

Investing in young people will help our society progress to higher levels of achievement in all areas.
投資在年輕人身上，可以幫助我們的社會在所有領域進步而達到更高的成就。

advance
/ədˈvɑːns/

The government provides student grants to enable those in need to advance in their education.
政府提供助學金，讓有需要的人能夠接受更高的教育（在教育方面前進）。

proceed
/prəˈsiːd/

Will the government proceed with its plan to reduce university tuition fees?
政府會繼續進行減少大學學費的計畫嗎？

evolve
/ɪˈvɒlv/

The plan is still evolving, so feel free to express your opinions to improve it.
這個計畫還在發展中，所以請隨意表達你的意見來改善它。

improve
/ɪmˈpruːv/

If we want to improve our current education system, we should allow teachers to experiment with different teaching methods.
如果我們想要改善我們現在的教育體系，我們應該允許教師實驗不同的教學方法。

USEFUL EXPRESSIONS | 相關實用片語

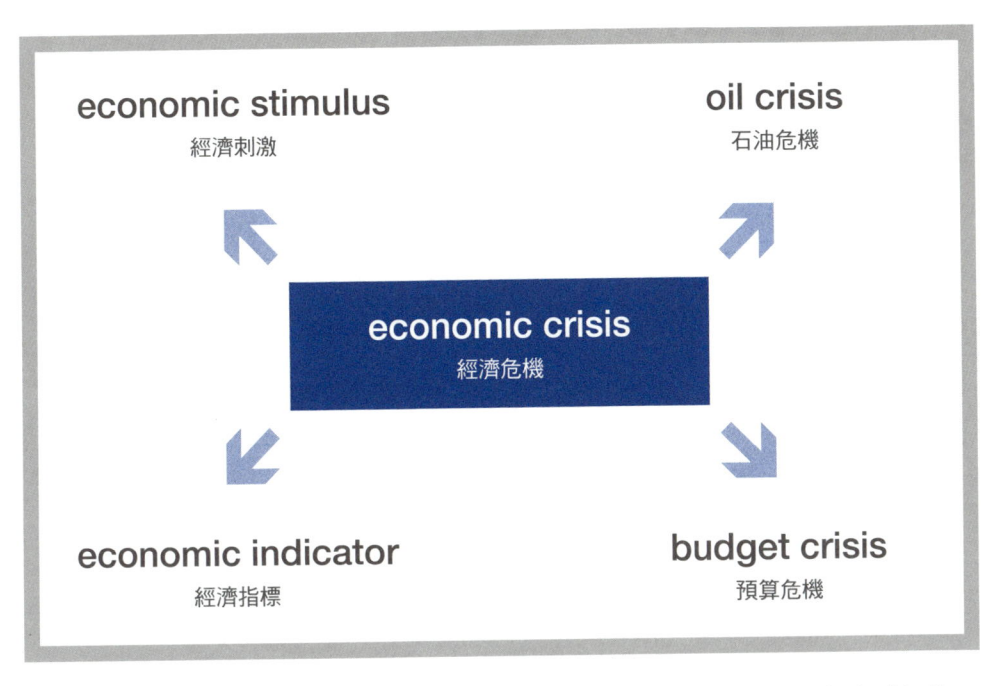

```
economic stimulus        oil crisis
   經濟刺激                石油危機

            ↖         ↗
            economic crisis
                經濟危機
            ↙         ↘

economic indicator       budget crisis
    經濟指標                預算危機
```

economic crisis
/ˌiːkəˈnɒmɪk ˈkraɪsɪs/
The government revised the laws in an attempt to tackle the economic crisis.
政府修訂法律，試圖處理經濟危機。

economic stimulus
/ˌiːkəˈnɒmɪk ˈstɪmjʊləs/
The economic stimulus package includes funding for infrastructure and public education.
經濟刺激方案的內容包括對基礎建設和公共教育提供資金。

economic indicator
/ˌiːkəˈnɒmɪk ˈɪndɪkeɪtə/
Accountants across the nation are tracking economic indicators to predict the country's economic health.
全國各地的會計師正在追蹤經濟指標，以預測國家的經濟健康。

oil crisis
/ɔɪl ˈkraɪsɪs/
With another oil crisis looming, the government is funding clean, renewable fuel research.
隨著另一個石油危機逼近，政府正在資助乾淨、可再生燃料的研究。

budget crisis
/ˈbʌdʒɪt ˈkraɪsɪs/
The ageing warships were scrapped for metal as the budget crisis continued.
由於預算危機持續，所以老化的戰艦被廢棄以取得金屬。

SAT

IELTS **BASIC WORDS**

outnumber /aʊtˈnʌmbə/ v. 數目超過…
ENG. be more numerous than
SYS. exceed, surpass

> Women have greatly **outnumbered** men in this company.
> 在這間公司，女性的人數已經大幅超過男性。

同義語 例句 The number of women working at this company has **exceeded** that of men.
在這間公司工作的女性人數已經超過男性。

同義語 例句 Women **occupy the majority** of the company's workforce.
女性佔這間公司員工的多數。

反義語 例句 Women occupy fewer positions of power compared to men in general.
整體來說，女性佔有權力的職位人數比男性少。

species /ˈspiːʃiːz/ n. 物種
ENG. a specific kind of living thing
SYS. sort, kind

> People who disapprove same work, same pay for two genders assert that women and men are like two different **species** and should be treated differently. 不贊成兩性同工同酬的人，聲稱女人和男人就像兩種不同的物種，應該以不同方式對待。

同義語 例句 A workplace is like a habitat of different **life forms** characterised by various workers.
職場就像是如同不同生物的各種員工棲息的地方。

同義語 例句 Certain **kinds** of women have less difficulty getting promoted in companies.
某些類型的女性在公司裡獲得升遷比較沒有困難。

反義語 例句 In the past, women in the workplace are sometimes treated like **objects** by men.
在過去，職場上的女性有時候被男性當成物品對待。

purpose /ˈpɜːpəs/ n. 目的
ENG. an anticipated outcome
SYS. aim, intent

> The **purpose** of having equal numbers of men and women at work is to promote gender equality.
> 讓職場男女人數相等的目的是促進性別平等。

同義語例句 A **goal** of gender equality is to make women and men feel equally valued.
性別平等的一個目標是讓女性和男性感覺同樣受到重視。

同義語例句 The **objective** of hiring an equal number of men and women is to let women participate in the decision-making process.
雇用人數相等的男性和女性,目的是讓女性參與決策過程。

反義語例句 At the company's board meeting, the members had **no intention** of discussing the issue of equal pay for men and women.
在公司的董事會上,董事們沒有要討論男女同酬議題的意思。

efficient /ɪˈfɪʃənt/ adj. 效率高的
ENG. working in a well-organised and competent way
SYS. effective, productive

> Workers are more **efficient** when they know they are treated equally in the workplace.
> 當員工知道自己在職場上受到平等對待時,會比較有效率。

同義語例句 Workers are observed to accomplish their tasks **with ease** when their supervisors are impartial.
員工被觀察到,當他們的主管很公正的時候,他們就很容易完成工作。

同義語例句 Workers are more **productive** in a fair workplace.
在公平的職場中,員工比較有生產力。

反義語例句 The seminar about gender equality in the workplace did **not produce** its intended effect.
關於職場性別平等的研討會沒有產生期望的效果。

SAT

TOPIC | Gender equality in the workplace
職場上的性別平等

Women have the legal right to equal participation in the workplace in most countries of the world; however, they are still vastly **under-represented** in many professions that are historically **dominated** by men. The **preferential** selection of men over women in such professions has **generated** intense **controversy** in recent years. Therefore, some countries have introduced **affirmative action** policies for women to have equal opportunities to pursue law enforcement, firefighting and higher education careers, just to name a few. All **debate** aside, it cannot be **disputed** that having a certain **proportion** of women in the most male-dominated professions is actually beneficial. For example, female police officers are important for undercover work and can be particularly useful in cases of domestic violence. In fact, many female victims feel more comfortable talking to another woman when reporting their cases. Although not without **dissent**, the general opinion is that women can play far more different roles than people could imagine in the past.

TRANS

在世界上大部分的國家，女性都有平等參與工作的法定權利，然而在歷史上由男性主導的許多行業裡，女性的任職人數還是很少。這些職業偏好男性勝過女性的選擇，在最近這些年引起了熱烈的爭論。所以，有些國家採用了平權政策，讓女性有同樣的機會可以追求例如執法（警察）、消防和高等教育等職業。把所有爭辯撇開不談，毋庸置疑的是，在男性主導性最強的職業裡，擁有一定比例的女性其實是有益的。例如，女性警察對於臥底工作很重要，而且在家暴案件中特別有用。事實上，許多女性受害者在報警時，和另一個女人談話會感覺比較自在。雖然並不是沒有異議，但一般的意見是，女性能扮演的不同角色，比以前的人所能想像的還要多得多。

under-represented
/ˌʌndərɪpriˈzɛntɪd/

adj. 未被充分代表的，代表名額不足的

She said that teachers of Asian descent were **under-represented** in schools.
她說亞裔教師在學校的任職數不足。

dominate
/ˈdɒmɪneɪt/

v. 主宰，佔主要地位

The professor **dominated** the conversation at the science seminar yesterday.
那位教授在昨天的科學研討會上主導了對話。

preferential
/ˌprɛfəˈrɛnʃəl/

adj. 優先的，優惠的

The councillor argues that military families and veterans should not be given **preferential** treatment.
那位議員主張軍眷和退休官兵不應該得到優惠待遇。

generate
/ˈdʒɛnəreɪt/

v. 產生

There is a decline in the revenue **generated** in wool sales.
羊毛銷售產生的收入有下降的現象。

controversy
/ˈkɒntrəvɜːsi/

n. 爭議

There was **controversy** over the appointment of the new chairman.
新任主席的任命有爭議。

affirmative action
/əˈfɜːmətɪv ˈakʃən/

n.（肯定、支持弱勢族群的）平權措施（英國稱為 positive discrimination = 正向的差別待遇）

The **affirmative action** in university admissions is meant to encourage more minorities into higher education.
大學入學的平權措施，用意是鼓勵更多弱勢族群接受高等教育。

debate
/dɪˈbeɪt/

n. 辯論，討論

She could not stop the **debate** between the two lawyers.
她無法停止那兩位律師的爭辯。

dispute
/dɪˈspjuːt/

v. 爭議，對⋯表示懷疑

I **disputed** my speeding ticket because I was innocent.
我對我的超速罰單提出異議，因為我是無辜的。

proportion
/prəˈpɔːʃən/

n. 比例

The doll's head is in **proportion** to its body.
這個娃娃的頭和身體成比例。

dissent
/dɪˈsɛnt/

n. 異議

There is no room for **dissent** in that political party.
那個政黨沒有容許異議的空間。

WORD TRAINING | 重點單字造句練習

inclusion
/ɪnˈkluːʒən/

n. 包含

💬 Female inclusion is important to our company's hiring practices.
包含女性對於我們公司的員工雇用是重要的。

The inclusion of women in firefighting has sparked much debate surrounding gender in the workforce.
在消防人力中包含女性，引發了許多關於職場中性別的爭論。

✍ Gender equality in the workplace does not imply that women and men are the same; it simply means that the inclusion of both men and women is important.
職場上的性別平等並不意味著女人和男人是一樣的；它的意義只是同時包含男人和女人很重要。

Even though the inclusion of women is no longer a problem in most workplaces, gender equality still has a long way to go since women are often paid less than men for doing the same work.
雖然在許多職場上，包含女性已經不再是個問題，但性別平等還有很長的路要走，因為女人的薪酬經常比做同樣工作的男人少。

consultancy
/kənˈsʌltənsi/

n. 諮詢，顧問工作，顧問公司

💬 The consultancy company suggested we hire more female workers.
顧問公司建議我們雇用更多女性工作者。

Many people use their previous experience in businesses to set up consultancies in specific areas.
有很多人用他們以前的事業經驗，成立特定領域的顧問公司。

✍ There are more and more organisations that provide consultancy and advice to government agencies and non-governmental enterprises on women's rights and gender equality issues.　現在有越來越多組織提供政府機關與非政府企業關於女權與性別平等議題的諮詢與建議。

As modern companies face growing challenges in an increasingly global market, consultancy services have become indispensable for them to gain a competitive advantage in their specialised fields.
隨著現代公司在越來越全球化的市場中面臨增長中的挑戰，顧問服務對於他們在專業領域中獲得競爭優勢已經變得不可或缺。

representative
/ˌrɛprɪˈzɛntətɪv/

n. 代表人

💬 There are still many companies that have no female representatives at board level.
還是有很多公司在董事會階級沒有女性的代表。

The representative claimed the company strives to provide equal opportunities for men and women in the workplace.
代表人聲稱公司努力在職場上為男性和女性提供平等的機會。

✏️ Even though there are now more women who work as company representatives, many people still focus more on their gender than on what they say.
即使現在有更多女性擔任公司的代表，很多人還是比較注意她們的性別，而不是她們所說的話。

The executive believes that every employee is a representative of the company, and this awareness must be reflected in their behaviour and communication with clients.　主管認為，每位員工都是公司的代表，而這樣的意識應該反映在他們的行為以及和客戶之間的溝通上。

precedent
/ˈprɛsɪdənt/

n. 先例

💬 My company set a precedent by promoting a female employee to vice president in early 90s.
我的公司在 90 年代的時候開了將女性員工升為副總裁的先例。

The decision to pay men and women equally set a precedent in my company.
付男性和女性相同酬勞的決定，在我的公司裡開了先例。

✏️ Fear of setting a precedent is no justification for not considering a female employee for promotion to an executive position.
害怕開先例並不能作為不考慮將女性員工升為管理職的正當理由。

The judgement set a precedent by describing pregnancy discrimination as illegal and contributed to the legislation for paid maternity leave.
那個判決開了先例，把懷孕歧視描述為不合法，也促成了有薪產假的立法。

579

RELATED WORDS ｜ 相關單字延伸

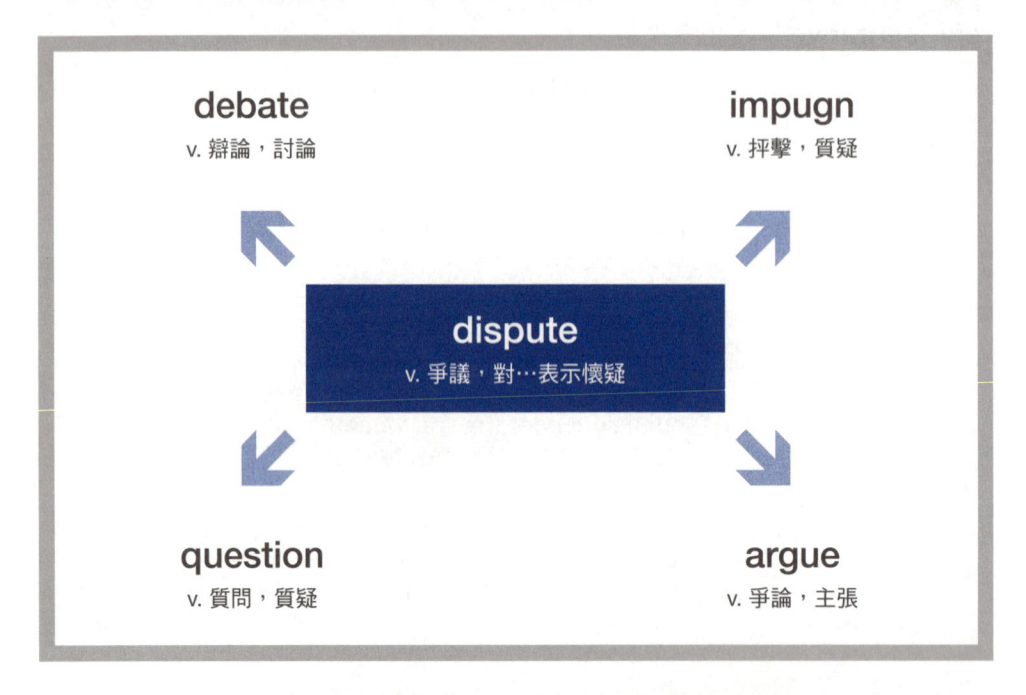

debate
v. 辯論，討論

impugn
v. 抨擊，質疑

dispute
v. 爭議，對⋯表示懷疑

question
v. 質問，質疑

argue
v. 爭論，主張

dispute
/dɪˈspjuːt/

It cannot be disputed that having a certain proportion of women in the most male-dominant professions is actually beneficial. 毋庸置疑的是，在男性主導性最強的職業裡，擁有一定比例的女性其實是有益的。

debate
/dɪˈbeɪt/

I don't think we need to debate on the fact that women are necessary to complement men in every workplace.
我覺得我們不需要討論每個職場上都需要女性來補足男性的事實。

question
/ˈkwɛstʃən/

I won't question the importance of gender equality in the workplace, but I want to stress that not every task is equally suitable for both sexes. 我不會質疑職場性別平等的重要性，但我想要強調，不是每件工作都同樣適合男性和女性。

impugn
/ɪmˈpjuːn/

Far be it from me to impugn his motives, but I don't think his decision to hire more women than men is beneficial for us.
我絕對不會質疑他的動機，但我覺得他要雇用女性多於男性的決定對我們無益。

argue
/ˈɑːgjuː/

I'm not at the position to argue against his decision to prefer men over women when hiring.
以我的地位，沒辦法反對他在雇用員工的時候偏好男性勝過女性的決定。

USEFUL EXPRESSIONS | 相關實用片語

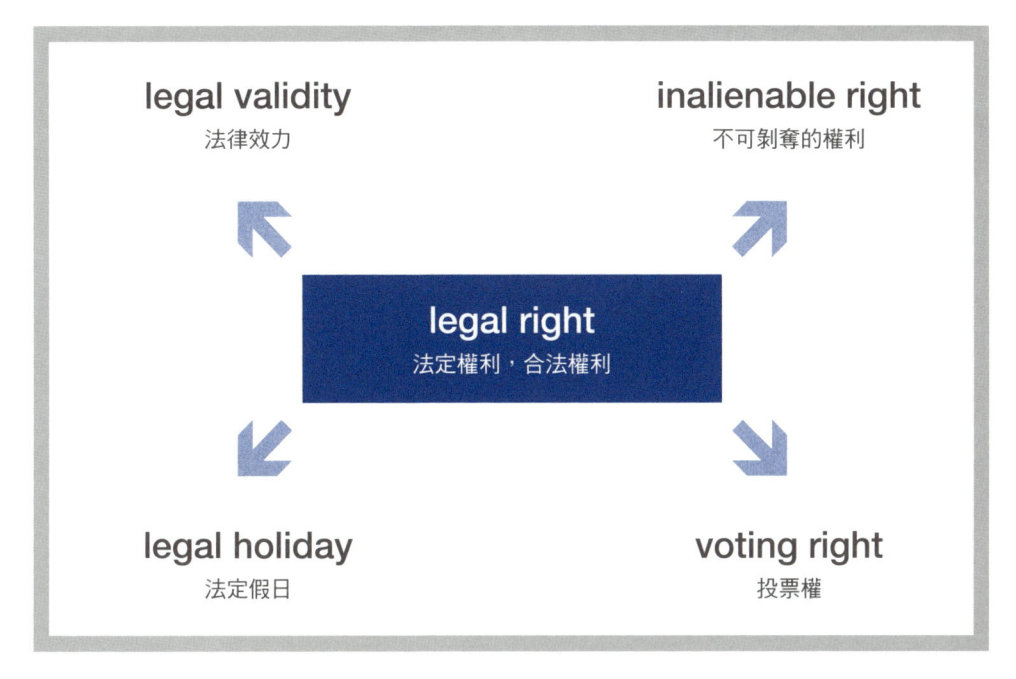

```
legal validity                    inalienable right
法律效力                           不可剝奪的權利

              legal right
              法定權利，合法權利

legal holiday                     voting right
法定假日                           投票權
```

legal right
/ˈliːɡəl raɪt/

Respect is not something that prisoners feel often, but technically, it is their legal right to be respected.
尊重不是囚犯經常可以感受到的，但嚴格來說，被尊重是他們的合法權利。

legal validity
/ˈliːɡəl vəˈlɪdɪti/

Millions of gay couples felt encouraged when the Supreme Court recognised the legal validity of same-sex marriage.
當最高法院認可同性婚姻的法律效力時，數百萬對同性伴侶感覺受到了鼓勵。

legal holiday
/ˈliːɡəl ˈhɒlɪdeɪ/

Christmas Day is recognised as a legal holiday by the United States government.
聖誕節被美國政府認為是法定的假日。

inalienable right
/ɪnˈeɪliənəbəl raɪt/

Inalienable rights, such as freedom of religion and freedom of speech, are not to be infringed upon by anyone.
不可剝奪的權利，例如宗教自由與言論自由，是不能被任何人侵犯的。

voting right
/ˈvəʊtɪŋ raɪt/

The proposal to grant voting rights for all elections to legal foreign residents is still under debate.
賦予合法外國居民所有選舉投票權的提案還在討論中。

SUN

IELTS **BASIC WORDS**

attract /əˈtrakt/ v. 吸引
ENG. direct toward itself or oneself by means of some psychological power or physical attribute
SYS. appeal, allure

> Large malls **attract** the public with oversized billboards, which are unaffordable for smaller stores.
> 大型購物中心用超大型廣告看板吸引大眾，而這些看板是較小的商店無法負擔的。

- 同義語例句 — Unlike small stores, large department stores **draw in** customers with advertising campaigns featuring celebrities.
  不像小型商店，大型的百貨公司用名人演出的廣告宣傳活動來吸引顧客。

- 同義語例句 — The wide space and relaxing atmosphere of large malls **appeal to** family customers.
  大型購物中心的寬敞空間和放鬆的氣氛對家庭顧客來說有吸引力。

- 反義語例句 — The old mall now **seems unattractive** to fashion-conscious customers with many small yet trendy stores emerging.
  隨著許多小而時髦的商店興起，這間舊的購物中心現在看起來對有流行意識的顧客而言不具吸引力。

minimal /ˈmɪnɪməl/ adj. 最小的
ENG. smallest in amount or degree
SYS. smallest, slightest

> He tried to keep the operation costs of his store **minimal** at the beginning.
> 他一開始努力將自己商店的營運成本保持在最小。

- 同義語例句 — The owner spends **the least possible** amount of money to run his store.
  店主花盡可能最少量的錢來經營他的店。

- 同義語例句 — He only has **barely enough** money to rent a stall in the mall.
  他只有勉強足夠的錢可以租購物中心的攤位。

- 反義語例句 — Shop owners always try their best to earn as much as possible.
  店主們總是盡可能賺最多的錢。

WEEK 10 TOPIC **SOCIAL LIFE**

▶ 基礎單字擴充

unite /juːˈnaɪt/ v. 團結，聯合
ENG. come or bring together for a common purpose or action
SYS. gather, unify

> If local stores **unite** to fight against retail chains, there is a good chance they will survive and thrive.
> 如果地方商家聯合起來對抗連鎖零售業者，他們就很有機會存活並且生意興旺。

同義語例句 If small stores **put together** their resources, they can compete with large retail chains.
如果小商店整合他們的資源，就能和大型連鎖零售業者競爭。

同義語例句 The small store owners often **gather together** to discuss how to compete with chain stores.
那些小型商店店主經常聚在一起討論如何和連鎖店競爭。

反義語例句 If every small store **goes its own way**, they stand no chance of winning against large chains.
如果每家小店各行其是，他們就沒有機會贏過大型連鎖業者。

bottom /ˈbɒtəm/ n. 底部
ENG. the deepest part
SYS. base, foot

> At the **bottom** of the hierarchy of shops are the smallest ones, while large malls are at the top.
> 在商店的等級體系中，最小的店在最下層，而大型購物中心在頂端。

同義語例句 As to market share, small shops are in **the last place**, while malls come in first.
至於市占率，小型商店店在最後一名，而購物中心是第一名。

同義語例句 When you look at the market share, this brand is on **the lowest position**.
當你看市占率的時候，這個品牌是最後一名。

反義語例句 The luxury brand uses all kinds of resources to remain at the **pinnacle** in the industry.
那個奢侈品牌用各種資源讓自己保持在業界的頂端。

TOPIC: Large retailers and small retailers
大型零售業者與小型零售業者

Large retail **establishments** have become familiar to people living in large cities. Big-box **retailers** like Wal-Mart and Costco are well-known and **frequented** by millions of families daily. Even though some citizens claim they hate large retailers, there are many more consumers who are attracted by such retailers' product availability and low prices. With more and more consumers preferring big-box stores, they are able to **monopolise** the market, while independent stores will likely go **bankrupt** if they try to compete with large retailers' predatory price-cutting. Not every small business, however, will be defeated in the competition. Stores selling something different in the vicinity of a **supercentre** can experience **mounting** sales as customers **overflow**. Although many people **lament** the loss of **mom-and-pop** grocery stores, big-box stores can benefit a community by making it a regional centre.

TRANS

大型零售業設施對於居住在大城市的人已經變得熟悉。Wal-Mart 和 Costco 之類的大型商場很有名，而且每天有數百萬的家庭經常光顧。雖然有些市民宣稱他們討厭大型零售業者，但有更多的消費者被這些零售業者的產品可得性和低價格吸引。隨著越來越多消費者偏好大型商場，這些商場可以壟斷市場，而獨立商店如果試圖和大型零售業者的掠奪性大減價競爭，很有可能會破產。不過，也不是每個小型業者都會在競爭中被打敗。在大型商場附近賣不太一樣的東西的店，可以隨著顧客滿溢而出而使業績上升。雖然許多人哀嘆家庭經營的雜貨店消失，但大型商場能夠使社區成為地區的中心而受益。

establishment
/ɪˈstablɪʃmənt/

n. 機構

The existing hotel **establishments** are no longer enough to accommodate the ever-increasing tourists.
現有的旅館設施已經不夠容納持續增加中的遊客。

retailer
/ˈriːteɪlə/

n. 零售商

Many local **retailers** were forced to close in the intense competition.
許多地方零售業者在激烈的競爭中被迫關門。

frequent
/frɪˈkwɛnt/

v. 常去…

The hotel was **frequented** by businesspeople in the late 1980s.
這間旅館在 1980 年代晚期是商務人士經常光顧的地方。

monopolise
/məˈnɒpəlʌɪz/

v. 壟斷

The hot dog company tries to **monopolise** the market.
這間熱狗公司試圖壟斷市場。

bankrupt
/ˈbaŋkrʌpt/

adj. 破產的

The business owner sold his own house before he went **bankrupt**.
那位事業主在他破產之前賣掉了自己的房子。

supercentre
/ˈsuːpəˌsɛntə/

n. 大型商場

My small business went under when the **supercentre** opened in the neighbourhood.
我的小生意在大型商場開在附近以後失敗了。

mount
/maʊnt/

v. 上升，增長

Under **mounting** pressure from local residents, the owner reluctantly closed his pub.
由於當地居民的壓力逐漸增加，店主很不情願地關了他的酒吧。

overflow
/əʊvəˈfləʊ/

v. 滿溢，流出

People who want to visit the newly-opened museum **overflowed** into the streets.
想參觀新開幕的博物館的人滿到了街上。

lament
/ləˈmɛnt/

v. 哀悼，悲嘆

Elder people often **lament** the loss of the good old days when life was simple.
年長的人經常哀嘆過去生活簡單的美好時光已經失去了。

mom-and-pop
/ˈmɒməndpɒp/

adj.（北美）〔店鋪〕小型的，典型上由夫妻經營的

Nothing compares to the warm atmosphere in **mom-and-pop** stores. 沒有什麼比得上家庭式店鋪的溫暖氣氛。

WORD TRAINING | 重點單字造句練習

numerous
/ˈnjuːmərəs/

adj. 許多的

💬 Nowadays, there are usually numerous big-box stores in large cities.
今天，大城市通常有許多大型商場。

There used to be numerous independent shops and boutiques in my neighbourhood.
以前我家附近有很多獨立的商店和精品店。

✏️ Big-box stores have killed numerous competing mom-and-pop stores in the city, undermining the vitality of local communities.
大型商場消滅了市內許多與其競爭的家庭式商店，逐漸傷害地方社群的活力。

There are numerous drunk-driving accidents reported each year, and many of them are caused by teenagers who have easy access to alcohol.
每年報告的酒駕事故都很多，而其中有許多是能輕易取得酒類的青少年造成的。

prominent
/ˈprɒmɪnənt/

adj. 顯著的，突出的

💬 A megastore is often a prominent landmark in a city block.
大型商店經常是城市街區中顯眼的地標。

The owner of the local retail chain is very prominent in business circles there.
那個地方連鎖店的業主，在那裡的商業圈很著名。

✏️ Hypermarkets stand as one of the most prominent symbols of mass production and mass consumption in the modern world.
大型超市是現代世界大量生產、大量消費最顯著的象徵符號之一。

One of the most prominent characteristics of modern consumer culture is that people are encouraged to buy whatever they want rather than buy what they really need.
現代消費文化最顯著的特色是，人們被鼓勵去買任何想要的東西，而不是買真正需要的東西。

irresistible
/ɪrɪˈzɪstɪbəl/

adj. 無法抗拒的

💬 The dominance of large retailers is an irresistible trend in modern times.
大型零售商佔主導地位是現代無法抗拒的趨勢。

The low prices provided by large retailers are so irresistible that many customers no longer shop at smaller stores. 大型零售商提供的低價格令人很難抗拒，所以許多顧客不再到比較小的店購物了。

✏️ Large retailers' practice of selling household products like toothpaste and toilet paper at discounted prices proves to be irresistible for consumers.
大型零售商以折扣價販賣如牙膏、衛生紙等日用品的行為，證實對消費者而言是無法抗拒的。

Even though shopping centres have attracted many customers with their wide variety of shops, independent boutiques still have an irresistible charm.
雖然購物中心用種類廣泛的店面吸引了許多顧客，但獨立的精品店還是有無法抗拒的魅力。

displace
/dɪsˈpleɪs/

v. 取代⋯（的地位），迫使⋯離開

💬 Some believe that large shops will displace small ones when the former appear in a neighbourhood.
有些人認為，當大型商店出現在街坊時，就會取代小型商店。

I don't think e-books will displace physical books in the foreseeable future.
我認為，在可預見的未來，電子書不會取代實體書。

✏️ The competition watchdog warns that providing tax incentives to multinational conglomerates will cause most local manufacturers to be displaced in the near future.
監督市場競爭的機構警告，提供租稅優惠給跨國企業集團，將會造成大部分的本地製造業者在不久的將來被取代。

Factory workers doing repetitive tasks were gradually displaced by machines, which can work in a much more consistent and precise way.
做重複性工作的工廠工人逐漸被機器取代，而機器工作起來穩定而且準確得多。

RELATED WORDS | 相關單字延伸

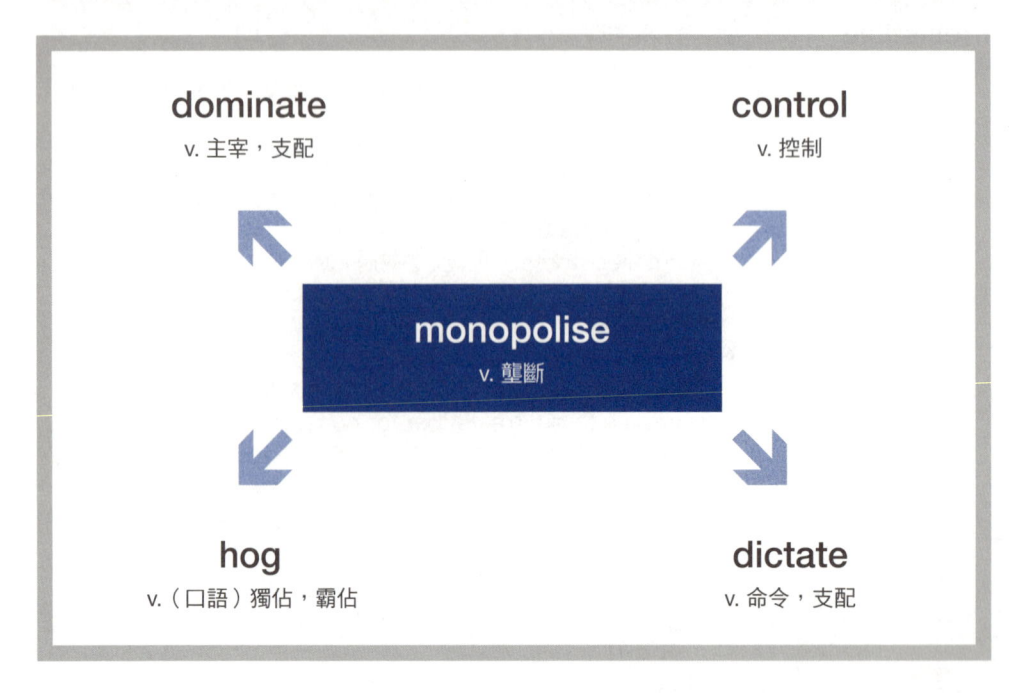

dominate
v. 主宰，支配

control
v. 控制

monopolise
v. 壟斷

hog
v.（口語）獨佔，霸佔

dictate
v. 命令，支配

monopolise
/məˈnɒpəlʌɪz/

Big-box stores are able to monopolise the market with their predatory price-cutting.
大型商場可以用掠奪性的大減價壟斷市場。

dominate
/ˈdɒmɪneɪt/

The market for household detergents and cleaning products has been dominated by multinationals.
家用清潔劑與清潔產品的市場已經被跨國企業主宰。

hog
/hɒɡ/

She hogged all the attention in her extravagantly glamorous dress.
她穿著奢華而富有魅力的服裝，獨佔了所有人的注意力。

control
/kənˈtrəʊl/

Large retailers can control the market with their abundant resources.
大型零售商可以用豐富的資源控制市場。

dictate
/dɪkˈteɪt/

No one has the right to dictate how we live our lives.
沒有人有權命令我們怎麼過生活。

USEFUL EXPRESSIONS | 相關實用片語

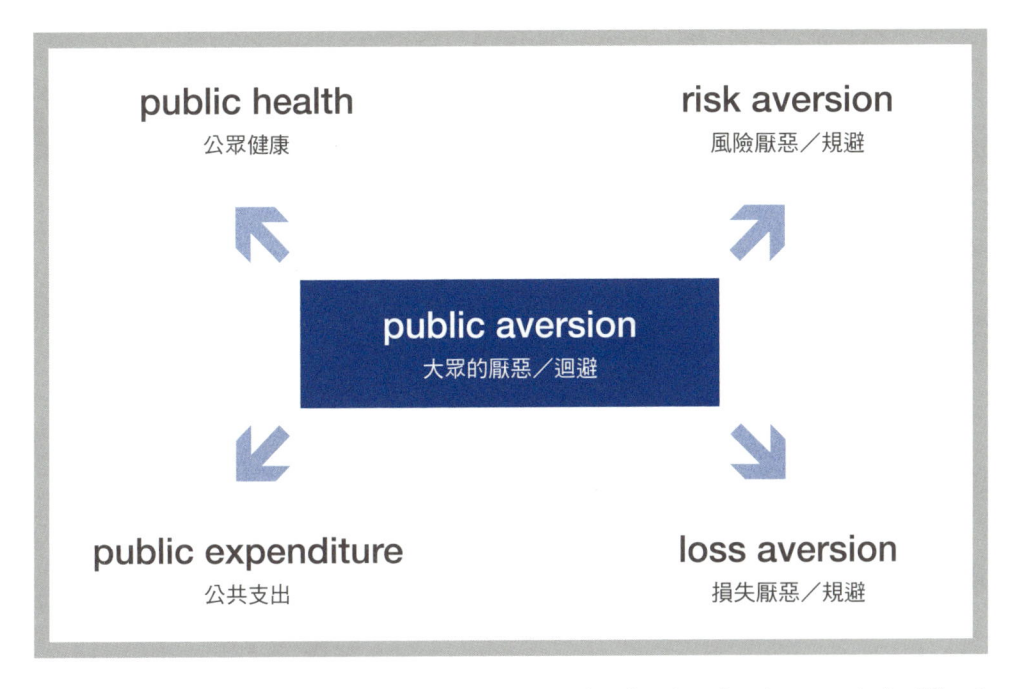

```
        public health                    risk aversion
        公眾健康                          風險厭惡／規避

                    ↖            ↗
                   ┌─────────────────┐
                   │  public aversion │
                   │   大眾的厭惡／迴避 │
                   └─────────────────┘
                    ↙            ↘

     public expenditure              loss aversion
         公共支出                      損失厭惡／規避
```

public aversion
/ˈpʌblɪk əˈvɜːʃən/

India's public aversion to family planning has made it difficult to slow down its population growth.
印度大眾對於家庭計畫的厭惡，使得將人口成長減緩很困難。

public health
/ˈpʌblɪk hɛlθ/

It is impossible for public health programmes to cover all citizens.
公眾健康計畫不可能包含所有公民在內。

public expenditure
/ˈpʌblɪk ɪkˈspɛndɪtʃə/

The government has cut public expenditures due to serious financial problems.
由於嚴重的財政問題，政府已經削減了公共支出。

risk aversion
/rɪsk əˈvɜːʃən/

Risk aversion has caused stock prices to stagnate.
對風險的規避造成了股價停滯。

loss aversion
/lɒs əˈvɜːʃən/

Loss aversion means an inclination to avoid losses rather than acquire gains.
損失厭惡的意思是想要避免損失而不是得到獲利的傾向。

備考全民英檢、多益測驗、雅思
無論是單字、文法、聽力、閱讀、解題策略、

語言檢定

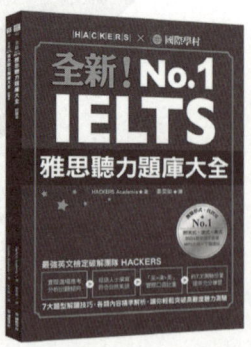

托福、新日檢JLPT、韓檢TOPIK題庫，你需要的都在國際學村！

唯一選擇！

台灣廣廈 國際出版集團
Taiwan Mansion International Group

國家圖書館出版品預行編目（CIP）資料

雅思單字大全 / William Jang著. -- 修訂一版. -- 新北市：國際學村，2024.10
　　面；　　公分
QR碼行動學習版
ISBN 978-986-454-388-5（平裝）
1.CST: 國際英語語文測試系統 2.CST: 詞彙

805.189　　　　　　　　　　　　　　113013306

國際學村

雅思單字大全

作　　　者／張大錫 William Jang	編輯中心編輯長／伍峻宏・編輯／賴敬宗
翻　　　譯／亞理莎・關	封面設計／何偉凱・內頁排版／菩薩蠻數位文化有限公司
	製版・印刷・裝訂／皇甫・秉成

行企研發中心總監／陳冠蒨　　　　線上學習中心總監／陳冠蒨
媒體公關組／陳柔彣　　　　　　　數位營運組／顏佑婷
綜合業務組／何欣穎　　　　　　　企製開發組／江季珊、張哲剛

發　行　人／江媛珍
法 律 顧 問／第一國際法律事務所 余淑杏律師・北辰著作權事務所 蕭雄淋律師
出　　　版／國際學村
發　　　行／台灣廣廈有聲圖書有限公司
　　　　　　　地址：新北市235中和區中山路二段359巷7號2樓
　　　　　　　電話：(886) 2-2225-5777・傳真：(886) 2-2225-8052
讀者服務信箱／cs@booknews.com.tw

代理印務・全球總經銷／知遠文化事業有限公司
　　　　　　　地址：新北市222深坑區北深路三段155巷25號5樓
　　　　　　　電話：(886) 2-2664-8800・傳真：(886) 2-2664-8801
郵 政 劃 撥／劃撥帳號：18836722
　　　　　　　劃撥戶名：知遠文化事業有限公司（※單次購書金額未達1000元，請另付70元郵資）

■出版日期：2024年10月修訂一版　　ISBN：978-986-454-388-5
　　　　　　2025年09月4刷　　　　版權所有，未經同意不得重製、轉載、翻印。

Perfect IELTS Vocabulary
Copyright ©2014 William Jang
All rights reserved.
Original Korean edition published by Wisdom Garden.
Chinese (complex) Translation rights arranged with Wisdom Garden.
Chinese (complex) Translation Copyright ©2024 by Taiwan Mansion Publishing Co., Ltd.
through M.J. Agency, in Taipei.